FOUR
FRONTIERS

Books by Robert A. Heinlein

Novels

Beyond This Horizon (1948)
Sixth Column (1949)
The Puppet Masters (1951)
Double Star (1956)
The Door Into Summer (1957)
Methuselah's Children (1958)
Starship Troopers (1959)
Stranger in a Strange Land (1961)
Glory Road (1963)
Orphans of the Sky (1963)
Farnham's Freehold (1964)
The Moon Is a Harsh Mistress (1966)
I Will Fear No Evil (1970)
Time Enough for Love (1973)
The Number of the Beast (1980)
Friday (1982)
Job: A Comedy of Justice (1984)
The Cat Who Walks Through Walls (1985)
To Sail Beyond the Sunset (1987)
For Us, The Living (2003)

Juvenile Novels

Rocket Ship Galileo (1947)
Space Cadet (1948)
Red Planet (1949)
Farmer in the Sky (1950)
Between Planets (1951)
The Rolling Stones (1952)
Starman Jones (1953)
The Star Beast (1954)
Tunnel in the Sky (1955)
Time for the Stars (1956)
Citizen of the Galaxy (1957)
Have Space Suit—Will Travel (1958)
Podkayne of Mars (1963)

Short Fiction & Miscellaneous

The Man Who Sold the Moon (1950)
Waldo and Magic, Inc. (1950)
The Green Hills of Earth (1951)
Revolt in 2100 (1953)
Assignment in Eternity (1953)
The Menace From Earth (1959)
The Unpleasant Profession of
  Jonathan Hoag (1959)
The Worlds of Robert A. Heinlein
  (1966)
The Past Through Tomorrow (1967)
Expanded Universe (1980)
Grumbles from the Grave (1989)
Requiem: New Collected Works
  (1992)
Tramp Royale (1992)
The Fantasies of Robert A. Heinlein
  (1999)

FOUR FRONTIERS

ROCKET SHIP GALILEO
SPACE CADET
RED PLANET
FARMER IN THE SKY

ROBERT A. HEINLEIN

SCIENCE
FICTION

ROCKET SHIP GALILEO   Copyright © 1947 by Robert A. Heinlein. Copyright renewed 1974 by Robert A. Heinlein. Copyright © 1988 by the Robert A. & Virginia Heinlein Library Foundation

SPACE CADET   Copyright © 1948 by Robert A. Heinlein. Copyright renewed 1975 by Robert A. Heinlein. Copyright © 1988 by the Robert A. & Virginia Heinlein Library Foundation

RED PLANET   Copyright © 1949 by Robert A. Heinlein. Copyright renewed 1976 by Robert A. Heinlein. Copyright © 2003 by The Robert A. & Virginia Heinlein Prize Trust.

FARMER IN THE SKY   Copyright © 1950 by Robert A. Heinlein. Copyright renewed 1977 by Robert A. Heinlein. Copyright © 2003 by The Robert A. & Virginia Heinlein Prize Trust.

First SFBC Science Fiction Printing: June 2005

Published by arrangement with
The Robert A. & Virginia Heinlein Prize Trust and The Robert A. & Virginia Heinlein Library Foundation,
c/o Spectrum Literary Agency
320 Central Park West, Suite 1D
New York, NY 10025
and
Tor Books
Tom Doherty Associates, LLC
175 Fifth Avenue
New York, NY 10010
and
The Berkley Publishing Group
a division of Penguin Group (USA) Inc.
375 Hudson Street
New York, NY 10014

Visit The SFBC online at *http://www.sfbc.com*
Visit the Heinlein Society at *http://www.heinleinsociety.org*

ISBN 0-7394-5345-9

Printed in the United States of America.

CONTENTS

ROCKET SHIP GALILEO

For Colin, Matt, and Buddy

1.
"LET THE ROCKET ROAR"

"Everybody all set?" Young Ross Jenkins glanced nervously at his two chums. "How about your camera, Art? You sure you got the lens cover off this time?"

The three boys were huddled against a thick concrete wall, higher than their heads and about ten feet long. It separated them from a steel stand, anchored to the ground, to which was bolted a black metal shape, a pointed projectile, venomous in appearance and ugly—a rocket. There were fittings on each side to which stub wings might be attached, but the fittings were empty; the creature was chained down for scientific examination.

"How about it, Art?" Ross repeated. The boy addressed straightened up to his full five feet three and faced him.

"Look," Art Mueller answered, "of course I took the cover off—it's on my check-off list. You worry about your rocket—last time it didn't fire at all and I wasted twenty feet of film."

"But you forgot it once—okay, okay, how about your lights?"

For answer Art switched on his spotlights; the beams shot straight up, bounced against highly polished stainless-steel mirrors and brilliantly illuminated the model rocket and the framework which would keep it from taking off during the test. A third boy, Maurice Abrams, peered at the scene through a periscope which allowed them to look over the reinforced concrete wall which shielded them from the rocket test stand.

"Pretty as a picture," he announced, excitement in his voice. "Ross—do you really think this fuel mix is what we're looking for?"

Ross shrugged. "I don't know. The lab tests looked good—we'll soon know. All right—places, everybody! Check-off lists—Art?"

"Complete."

"Morrie?"

"Complete."

"And mine's complete. Stand by! I'm going to start the clock. Here goes!" He started checking off the seconds until the rocket was fired. "Minus ten . . . minus nine . . . minus eight . . . minus seven . . . minus six . . . minus five . . . minus four . . ." Art wet his lips and started his camera. "Minus three! Minus two! Minus one!—*Contact!*"

"*Let it roar!*" Morrie yelled, his voice already drowned by the ear-splitting noise of the escaping rocket gas.

A great plume of black smoke surged out the orifice of the thundering rocket when it was first fired, billowed against an earth ramp set twenty feet behind the rocket test stand and filled the little clearing with choking fumes. Ross shook his head in dissatisfaction at this and made an adjustment in the controls under his hand. The smoke cleared away; through the periscope in front of him he could see the rocket exhaust on the other side of the concrete barricade. The flame had cleared of the wasteful smoke and was almost transparent, save for occasional sparks. He could actually see trees and ground through the jet of flame. The images shimmered and shook but the exhaust gases were smoke-free.

"What does the dynamometer read?" he shouted to Morrie without taking his eyes away from the periscope.

Morrie studied that instrument, rigged to the test stand itself, by means of a pair of opera glasses and his own periscope. "I can't read it!" he shouted. "Yes, I can—wait a minute. Fifty-two—no, make it a hundred and fifty-two; it's second time around. Hunderfiftytwo, fif'three, -four. Ross, you've done it! You've done it! That's more than twice as much thrust as the best we've ever had."

Art looked up from where he was nursing his motion picture camera. It was a commercial 8-millimeter job, modified by him to permit the use of more film so that every second of the test could be recorded. The modification worked, but was cantankerous and had to be nursed along. "How much more time?" he demanded.

"Seventeen seconds," Ross yelled at him. "Stand by—I'm going to give her the works." He twisted his throttle-monitor valve to the right, wide open.

The rocket responded by raising its voice from a deep-throated roar to a higher pitch with an angry overtone almost out of the audible range. It spoke with snarling menace.

Ross looked up to see Morrie back away from his periscope

and climb on a box, opera glasses in hand. "Morrie—get your head down!" The boy did not hear him against the scream of the jet, intent as he was on getting a better view of the rocket.

Ross jumped away from the controls and dived at him, tackling him around the waist and dragging him down behind the safety of the barricade. They hit the ground together rather heavily and struggled there. It was not a real fight; Ross was angry, though not fighting mad, while Morrie was merely surprised. "What's the idea?" he protested, when he caught his breath.

"You crazy idiot!" Ross grunted in his ear. "What were you trying to do? Get your head blown off?"

"But I wasn't—" But Ross was already clambering to his feet and returning to his place at the controls; Morrie's explanation, if any, was lost in the roar of the rocket.

"What goes on?" Art yelled. He had not left his place by his beloved camera, not only from a sense of duty but at least partly from indecision as to which side of the battle he should join.

Ross heard his shout and turned to speak. "This goon," he yelled bitterly, jerking a thumb at Morrie, "tried to—"

Ross's version of the incident was lost; the snarling voice of the rocket suddenly changed pitch, then lost itself in a bone-shaking explosion. At the same time there was a dazzling flash which would have blinded the boys had they not been protected by the barricade, but which nevertheless picked out every detail of the clearing in the trees with brilliance that numbed the eyes.

They were still blinking at the memory of the ghastly light when billowing clouds of smoke welled up from beyond the barricade, surrounded them, and made them cough.

"Well," Ross said bitterly and looked directly at Morrie, "that's the last of the *Starstruck V*."

"Look, Ross," Morrie protested, his voice sounding shrill in the strange new stillness, "I didn't do it. I was only trying to—"

"I didn't say you did," Ross cut him short. "I know you didn't do it. I had already made my last adjustment. She was on her own and she couldn't take it. Forget it. But keep your head down after this—you darn near lost it. That's what the barricade is *for*."

"But I wasn't going to stick my head up. I was just going to try—"

"Both of you forget it," Art butted in. "So we blew up another one. So what? We'll build another one. Whatever happened, I got it right here in the can." He patted his camera. "Let's take a look at the wreck." He started to head around the end of the barricade.

"Wait a minute," Ross commanded. He took a careful look through his periscope, then announced: "Seems okay. Both fuel chambers are split. There can't be any real danger now. Don't burn yourselves. Come on." They followed him around to the test stand.

The rocket itself was a complete wreck but the test stand was undamaged; it was built to take such punishment. Art turned his attention to the dynamometer which measured the thrust generated by the rocket. "I'll have to recalibrate this," he announced. "The loop isn't hurt, but the dial and the rack-and-pinion are shot."

The other two boys did not answer him; they were busy with the rocket itself. The combustion chamber was split wide open and it was evident that pieces were missing. "How about it, Ross?" Morrie inquired. "Do you figure it was the metering pump going haywire, or was the soup just too hot for it?"

"Hard to tell," Ross mused absently. "I don't think it was the pump. The pump might jam and refuse to deliver fuel at all, but I don't see how it could deliver too much fuel—unless it reared back and passed a miracle."

"Then it must have been the combustion chamber. The throat is all right. It isn't even pitted—much," he added as he peered at it in the gathering twilight.

"Maybe. Well, let's throw a tarp over it and look it over to-morrow morning. Can't see anything now. Come on, Art."

"Okay. Just a sec while I get my camera." He detached his camera from its bracket and placed it in its carrying case, then helped the other two drag canvas tarpaulins over all the test gear—one for the test stand, one for the barricade with its controls, instruments, and periscopes. Then the three turned away and headed out of the clearing.

The clearing was surrounded by a barbed wire fence, placed there at the insistence of Ross's parents, to whom the land belonged, in order to keep creatures, both four-legged and two-legged, from wandering into the line of fire while the boys were experimenting. The gate in this fence was directly behind the barricade and about fifty feet from it.

They had had no occasion to glance in the direction of the gate since the beginning of the test run—indeed, their attentions had been so heavily on the rocket that anything less than an earthquake would hardly have disturbed them.

Ross and Morrie were a little in front with Art close at their heels, so close that, when they stopped suddenly, he stumbled over them and almost dropped his camera. "Hey, watch where you're going, can't you?" he protested. "Pick up your big feet!"

They did not answer but stood still, staring ahead and at the ground. "What gives?" he went on. "Why the trance? Why do— *oh!*" He had seen it too. "It" was the body of a large man, crumpled on the ground, half in and half out the gate. There was a bloody wound on his head and blood on the ground.

They all rushed forward together, but it was Morrie who shoved them back and kept them from touching the prone figure. "Take it easy!" he ordered. "Don't touch him. Remember your first aid. That's a head wound. If you touch him, you may kill him."

"But we've got to find out if he's alive," Ross objected.

"I'll find out. Here—give me those." He reached out and appropriated the data sheets of the rocket test run from where they stuck out of Ross's pocket. These he rolled into a tube about an inch in diameter, then cautiously placed it against the back of the still figure, on the left side over the heart. Placing his ear to the other end of the improvised stethoscope he listened. Ross waited breathlessly.

Presently his tense face relaxed into a grin. "His motor is turning over," he announced. "Good and strong. At least we didn't kill him."

" 'We'?"

"Who do you think? How do you think he got this way? Take a look around and you'll probably find the piece of the rocket that konkcd him." He straightened up. "But never mind that now. Ross, you shag up to your house and call an ambulance. Make it fast! Art and I will wait here with . . . with, uh, *him.* He may come to and we'll have to keep him quiet."

"Okay." Ross was gone as he spoke.

Art was staring at the unconscious man. Morrie touched him on the arm. "Sit down, kid. No use getting in a sweat. We'll have trouble enough later. Even if this guy isn't hurt much I suppose you realize this about winds up the activities of the Galileo Marching-and-Chowder Society—at least the rocketry-and-loud-noises branch of it."

Art looked unhappy. "I suppose so."

" 'Suppose' nothing. It's certain. Ross's father took a very dim view of the matter the time we blew all the windows out of his basement—not that I blame him. Now we hand him this. Loss of the use of the land is the least we can expect. We'll be lucky not to have handed him a suit for damages too."

Art agreed miserably. "I guess it's back to stamp collecting for us," he assented, but his mind was elsewhere. Law suit. The use of the land did not matter. To be sure the use of the Old Ross Place on the edge of town had been swell for all three of them, what with him and his mother living in back of the store, and Morrie's folks living in a flat, but—*law suit!* Maybe Ross's parents could afford it; but the little store just about kept Art and his mother going, even with the after-school jobs he had had ever since junior high—a law suit would take the store away from them.

His first feeling of frightened sympathy for the wounded man was beginning to be replaced by a feeling of injustice done him. What was the guy doing there anyhow? It wasn't just trespass; the whole area was posted with warning signs.

"Let me have a look at this guy," he said.

"Don't touch him," Morrie warned.

"I won't. Got your pocket flash?" It was becoming quite dark in the clearing.

"Sure. Here . . . catch."

Art took the little flashlight and tried to examine the face of their victim—hard to do, as he was almost face down and the side of his face that was visible was smeared with blood.

Presently Art said in an odd tone of voice, "Morrie—would it hurt anything to wipe some of this blood away?"

"You're dern tootin' it would! You let him be till the doctor comes."

"All right, all right. Anyhow I don't need to—I'm sure anyhow. Morrie, I know who he is."

"You do? Who?"

"He's my uncle."

"Your *uncle!*"

"Yes, my uncle. You know—the one I've told you about. He's my Uncle Don. Doctor Donald Cargraves, my 'Atomic Bomb' uncle."

2.
A MAN-SIZED CHALLENGE

"*At least I'm* pretty sure it's my uncle," Art went on. "I could tell for certain if I could see his whole face."

"Don't you know whether or not he's your uncle? After all, a member of your own family—"

"Nope. I haven't seen him since he came through here to see Mother, just after the war. That's been a long time. I was just a kid then. But it looks like him."

"But he doesn't look old enough," Morrie said judiciously. "I should think—Here comes the ambulance!"

It was indeed, with Ross riding with the driver to show him the road and the driver cussing the fact that the road existed mostly in Ross's imagination. They were all too busy for a few minutes, worrying over the stranger as a patient, to be much concerned with his identity as an individual. "Doesn't look too bad," the interne who rode with the ambulance announced. "Nasty scalp wound. Maybe concussion, maybe not. Now over with him—easy!—while I hold his head." When turned face up and lifted into the stretcher, the patient's eyes flickered; he moaned and seemed to try to say something. The doctor leaned over him.

Art caught Morrie's eye and pressed a thumb and forefinger together. There was no longer any doubt as to the man's identity, now that Art had seen his face.

Ross started to climb back in the ambulance but the interne waved him away. "But all of you boys show up in the hospital. We'll have to make out an accident report on this."

As soon as the ambulance lumbered away Art told Ross about

his discovery. Ross looked startled. "Your uncle, eh? Your own uncle. What was he doing here?"

"I don't know. I didn't know he was in town."

"Say, look—I hope he's not hurt bad, especially seeing as how he's your uncle—but is this *the* uncle, the one you were telling us about who has been mentioned for the Nobel Prize?"

"That's what I've been trying to tell you. He's my Uncle Donald Cargraves."

"Doctor Donald Cargraves!" Ross whistled. "Jeepers! When we start slugging people we certainly go after big game, don't we?"

"It's no laughing matter. Suppose he dies? What'll I tell my mother?"

"I wasn't laughing. Let's get over to the hospital and find out how bad he's hurt before you tell her anything. No use in worrying her unnecessarily." Ross sighed. "I guess we might as well break the news to my folks. Then I'll drive us over to the hospital."

"Didn't you tell them when you telephoned?" Morrie asked.

"No. They were out in the garden, so I just phoned and then lammed out to the curb to wait for the ambulance. They may have seen it come in the drive but I didn't wait to find out."

"I'll bet you didn't."

Ross's father was waiting for them at the house. He answered their greetings, then said, "Ross—"

"Yes, sir?"

"I heard an explosion down toward your private stamping ground. Then I saw an ambulance drive in and drive away. What happened?"

"Well, Dad, it was like this: We were making a full-power captive run on the new rocket and—" He sketched out the events.

Mr. Jenkins nodded and said, "I see. Come along, boys." He started toward the converted stable which housed the family car. "Ross, run tell your mother where we are going. Tell her I said not to worry." He went on, leaning on his cane a bit as he walked. Mr. Jenkins was a retired electrical engineer, even-tempered and taciturn.

Art could not remember his own father; Morrie's father was still living but a very different personality. Mr. Abrams ruled a large and noisy, children-cluttered household by combining a loud voice with lavish affection.

When Ross returned, puffing, his father waved away his offer to drive. "No, thank you. I want us to get there." The trip was made in silence. Mr. Jenkins left them in the foyer of the hospital with an injunction to wait.

"What do you think he will do?" Morrie asked nervously.

"I don't know. Dad'll be fair about it."

"That's what I'm afraid of," Morrie admitted. "Right now I don't want justice; I want charity."

"I hope Uncle Don is all right," Art put in.

"Huh? Oh, yes, indeed! Sorry, Art, I'm afraid we've kind of forgotten your feelings. The principal thing is for him to get well, of course."

"To tell the truth, before I knew it was Uncle Don, I was more worried over the chance that I might have gotten Mother into a law suit than I was over what we might have done to a stranger."

"Forget it," Ross advised. "A person can't help worrying over his own troubles. Dad says the test is in what you do, not in what you think. We all did what we could for him."

"Which was mostly not to touch him before the doctor came," Morrie pointed out.

"Which was what he needed."

"Yes," agreed Art, "but I don't check you, Ross, on it not mattering what you think as long as you act all right. It seems to me that wrong ideas can be just as bad as wrong ways to do things."

"Easy, now. If a guy does something brave when he's scared to death is he braver than the guy who does the same thing but isn't scared?"

"He's less . . . no, he's more. . . . You've got me all mixed up. It's not the same thing."

"Not quite, maybe. Skip it."

They sat in silence for a long time. Then Morrie said, "Anyhow, I hope he's all right."

Mr. Jenkins came out with news. "Well, boys, this is your lucky day. Skull uninjured according to the X-ray. The patient woke when they sewed up his scalp. I talked with him and he has decided not to scalp any of you in return." He smiled.

"May I see him?" asked Art.

"Not tonight. They've given him a hypo and he is asleep. I telephoned your mother, Art."

"You did? Thank you, sir."

"She's expecting you. I'll drop you by."

* * *

Art's interview with his mother was not too difficult; Mr. Jenkins had laid a good foundation. In fact, Mrs. Mueller was incapable of believing that Art could be "bad." But she did worry about him and Mr. Jenkins had soothed her, not only about Art but also as to the welfare of her brother.

Morrie had still less trouble with Mr. Abrams. After being assured that the innocent bystander was not badly hurt, he had shrugged. "So what? So we have lawyers in the family for such things. At fifty cents a week it'll take you about five hundred years to pay it off. Go to bed."

"Yes, Poppa."

The boys gathered at the rocket testing grounds the next morning, after being assured by a telephone call to the hospital that Doctor Cargraves had spent a good night. They planned to call on him that afternoon; at the moment they wanted to hold a postmortem on the ill-starred *Starstruck V*.

The first job was to gather up the pieces, try to reassemble them, and then try to figure out what had happened. Art's film of the event would be necessary to complete the story, but it was not yet ready.

They were well along with the reassembling when they heard a whistle and a shout from the direction of the gate. "Hello there! Anybody home?"

"Coming!" Ross answered. They skirted the barricade to where they could see the gate. A tall, husky figure waited there—a man so young, strong, and dynamic in appearance that the bandage around his head seemed out of place, and still more so in contrast with his friendly grin.

"Uncle Don!" Art yelled as he ran up to meet him.

"Hi," said the newcomer. "You're Art. Well, you've grown a lot but you haven't changed much." He shook hands.

"What are you doing out of bed? You're sick."

"Not me," his uncle asserted. "I've got a release from the hospital to prove it. But introduce me—are these the rest of the assassins?"

"Oh—excuse me. Uncle Don, this is Maurice Abrams and this is Ross Jenkins. . . . Doctor Cargraves."

"How do you do, sir?"

"Glad to know you, Doctor."

"Glad to know you, too." Cargraves started through the gate, then hesitated. "Sure this place isn't booby-trapped?"

Ross looked worried. "Say, Doctor—we're all sorry as can

be. I still can't see how it happened. The gate is covered by the barricade."

"Ricochet shot probably. Forget it. I'm not hurt. A little skin and a little blood—that's all. If I had turned back at your first warning sign, it wouldn't have happened."

"How did you happen to be coming here?"

"A fair question. I hadn't been invited, had I?"

"Oh, I didn't mean that."

"But I owe you an explanation. When I breezed into town yesterday, I already knew of the Galileo Club; Art's mother had mentioned it in letters. When my sister told me where Art was and what he was up to, I decided to slide over in hope of getting here in time to watch your test run. Your hired girl told me how to find my way out here."

"You mean you hurried out here just to see this stuff we play around with?"

"Sure. Why not? I'm interested in rockets."

"Yes, but—we really haven't got anything to show you. These are just little models."

"A new model," Doctor Cargraves answered seriously, "of anything can be important, no matter who makes it nor how small it is. I wanted to see how you work. May I?"

"Oh, certainly sir—we'd be honored."

Ross showed their guest around, with Morrie helping out and Art chipping in. Art was pink-faced and happy—this was *his* uncle, one of the world's great, a pioneer of the Atomic Age. They inspected the test stand and the control panel. Cargraves looked properly impressed and tut-tutted over the loss of *Starstruck V*.

As a matter of fact he was impressed. It is common enough in the United States for boys to build and take apart almost anything mechanical, from alarm clocks to hiked-up jaloppies. It is not so common for them to understand the sort of controlled and recorded experimentation on which science is based. Their equipment was crude and their facilities limited, but the approach was correct and the scientist recognized it.

The stainless steel mirrors used to bounce the spotlight beams over the barricade puzzled Doctor Cargraves. "Why take so much trouble to protect light bulbs?" he asked. "Bulbs are cheaper than stainless steel."

"We were able to get the mirror steel free," Ross explained. "The spotlight bulbs take cash money."

The scientist chuckled. "That reason appeals to me. Well, you fellows have certainly thrown together quite a set-up. I wish I had seen your rocket before it blew up."

"Of course the stuff we build," Ross said diffidently, "can't compare with a commercial unmanned rocket, say like a mail-carrier. But we would like to dope out something good enough to go after the junior prizes."

"Ever competed?"

"Not yet. Our physics class in high school entered one last year in the novice classification. It wasn't much—just a powder job, but that's what got us started, though we've all been crazy about rockets ever since I can remember."

"You've got some fancy control equipment. Where do you do your machine-shop work? Or do you have it done?"

"Oh, no. We do it in the high-school shop. If the shop instructor okays you, you can work after school on your own."

"It must be quite a high school," the physicist commented. "The one I went to didn't have a machine shop."

"I guess it is a pretty progressive school," Ross agreed. "It's a mechanical-arts-and-science high school and it has more courses in math and science and shop work than most. It's nice to be able to use the shops. That's where we built our telescope."

"Astronomers too, eh?"

"Well—Morrie is the astronomer of the three of us."

"Is that so?" Cargraves inquired, turning to Morrie.

Morrie shrugged. "Oh, not exactly. We all have our hobbies. Ross goes in for chemistry and rocket fuels. Art is a radio ham and a camera nut. You can study astronomy sitting down."

"I see," the physicist replied gravely. "A matter of efficient self-protection. I knew about Art's hobbies. By the way, Art, I owe you an apology; yesterday afternoon I took a look in your basement. But don't worry—I didn't touch anything."

"Oh, I'm not worried about your touching stuff, Uncle Don," Art protested, turning pinker, "but the place must have looked a mess."

"It didn't look like a drawing room but it did look like a working laboratory. I see you keep notebooks—no, I didn't touch them, either!"

"We all keep notebooks," Morrie volunteered. "That's the influence of Ross's old man."

"So?"

"Dad told me he did not care," Ross explained, "how much I messed around as long as I kept it above the tinkertoy level. He used to make me submit notes to him on everything I tried and he would grade them on clearness and completeness. After a while I got the idea and he quit."

"Does he help you with your projects?"

"Not a bit. He says they're our babies and we'll have to nurse them."

They prepared to adjourn to their clubhouse, an outbuilding left over from the days when the Old Ross Place was worked as a farm. They gathered up the forlorn pieces of *Starstruck V*, while Ross checked each item. "I guess that's all," he announced and started to pick up the remains.

"Wait a minute," Morrie suggested. "We never did search for the piece that clipped Doctor Cargraves."

"That's right," the scientist agreed. "I have a personal interest in that item, blunt instrument, missile, shrapnel, or whatever. I want to know how close I came to playing a harp."

Ross looked puzzled. "Come here, Art," he said in a low voice.

"I *am* here. What do you want?"

"Tell me what piece is still missing—"

"What difference does it make?" But he bent over the box containing the broken rocket and checked the items. Presently he too looked puzzled. "Ross—"

"Yeah?"

"There isn't anything missing."

"That's what *I* thought. But there has to be."

"Wouldn't it be more to the point," suggested Cargraves, "to look around near where I was hit?"

"I suppose so."

They all searched, they found nothing. Presently they organized a system which covered the ground with such thoroughness that anything larger than a medium-small ant should have come to light. They found a penny and a broken Indian arrowhead, but nothing resembling a piece of the exploded rocket.

"This is getting us nowhere," the doctor admitted. "Just where was I when you found me?"

"Right in the gateway," Morrie told him. "You were collapsed on your face and—"

"Just a minute. On my *face?*"

"Yes. You were—"

"But how did I get knocked on my face? I was facing toward your testing ground when the lights went out. I'm sure of that. I should have fallen backwards."

"Well . . . I'm sure you didn't, sir. Maybe it was a ricochet, as you said."

"Hmm . . . maybe." The doctor looked around. There was nothing near the gate which would make a ricochet probable. He looked at the spot where he had lain and spoke to himself.

"What did you say, Doctor?"

"Uh? Oh, nothing, nothing at all. Forget it. It was just a silly idea I had. It couldn't be." He straightened up as if dismissing the whole thing. "Let's not waste any more time on my vanishing 'blunt instrument.' It was just curiosity. Let's get on back."

The clubhouse was a one-story frame building about twenty feet square. One wall was filled with Ross's chemistry workbench with the usual clutter of test-tube racks, bunsen burners, awkward-looking, pretzel-like arrangements of glass tubing, and a double sink which looked as if it had been salvaged from a junk dealer. A home-made hood with a hinged glass front occupied one end of the bench. Parallel to the adjacent wall, in a little glass case, a precision balance of a good make but of very early vintage stood mounted on its own concrete pillar.

"We ought to have air-conditioning," Ross told the doctor, "to do really good work."

"You haven't done so badly," Cargraves commented. The boys had covered the rough walls with ply board; the cracks had been filled and the interior painted with washable enamel. The floor they had covered with linoleum, salvaged like the sink, but serviceable. The windows and door were tight. The place was clean.

"Humidity changes could play hob with some of your experiments, however," he went on. "Do you plan to put in air-conditioning sometime?"

"I doubt it. I guess the Galileo Club is about to fold up."

"What? Oh, that seems a shame."

"It is and it isn't. This fall we all expect to go away to Tech."

"I see. But aren't there any other members?"

"There used to be, but they've moved, gone away to school, gone in the army. I suppose we could have gotten new members but we didn't try. Well . . . we work together well and . . . you know how it is."

Cargraves nodded. He felt that he knew more explicitly than did the boy. These three were doing serious work; most of their schoolmates, even though mechanically minded, would be more interested in needling a stripped-down car up to a hundred miles an hour than in keeping careful notes. "Well, you are certainly comfortable here. It's a shame you can't take it with you."

A low, wide, padded seat stretched from wall to wall opposite the chemistry layout. The other two boys were sprawled on it, listening. Behind them, bookshelves had been built into the wall. Jules Verne crowded against Mark's *Handbook of Mechanical Engineering*. Cargraves noted other old friends: H. G. Wells' *Seven Famous Novels, The Handbook of Chemistry and Physics*, and Smyth's *Atomic Energy for Military Purposes*. Jammed in with them, side by side with Ley's *Rockets* and Eddington's *Nature of the Physical World*, were dozens of pulp magazines of the sort with robot men or space ships on their covers.

He pulled down a dog-eared copy of Haggard's *When the Earth Trembled* and settled his long body between the boys. He was beginning to feel at home. These boys he knew; he had only to gaze back through the corridors of his mind to recognize himself.

Ross said, "If you'll excuse me, I want to run up to the house."

Cargraves grunted, "Sure thing," with his nose still in the book.

Ross came back to announce, "My mother would like all of you to stay for lunch."

Morrie grinned, Art looked troubled. "My mother thinks I eat too many meals over here as it is," he protested feebly, his eyes on his uncle.

Cargraves took him by the arm. "I'll go your bail on this one, Art," he assured him; then to Ross, "Please tell your mother that we are very happy to accept."

At lunch the adults talked, the boys listened. The scientist, his turban bandage looking stranger than ever, hit it off well with his elders. Any one would hit it off well with Mrs. Jenkins, who could have been friendly and gracious at a cannibal feast, but the boys were not used to seeing Mr. Jenkins in a chatty mood.

The boys were surprised to find out how much Mr. Jenkins knew about atomics. They had the usual low opinion of the mental processes of adults; Mr. Jenkins they respected but had subconsciously considered him the anachronism which most of his generation in fact was, a generation as a whole incapable of realizing that the world had changed completely a few years before, at Alamogordo, New Mexico, on July 16, 1945.

Yet Mr. Jenkins seemed to know who Doctor Cargraves was

and seemed to know that he had been retained until recently by North American Atomics. The boys listened carefully to find out what Doctor Cargraves planned to do next, but Mr. Jenkins did not ask and Cargraves did not volunteer the information.

After lunch the three and their guest went back to the clubhouse. Cargraves spent most of the afternoon spread over the bunk, telling stories of the early days at Oak Ridge when the prospect of drowning in the inescapable, adhesive mud was more dismaying than the ever-present danger of radioactive poisoning, and the story, old but ever new and eternally exciting, of the black rainy morning in the New Mexico desert when a great purple-and-golden mushroom had climbed to the stratosphere, proclaiming that man had at last unloosed the power of the suns.

Then he shut up, claiming that he wanted to reread the old H. Rider Haggard novel he had found. Ross and Maurice got busy at the bench; Art took a magazine. His eyes kept returning to his fabulous uncle. He noticed that the man did not seem to be turning the pages very often.

Quite a while later Doctor Cargraves put down his book. "What do you fellows know about atomics?"

The boys exchanged glances before Morrie ventured to answer. "Not much I guess. High-school physics can't touch it, really, and you can't mess with it in a home laboratory."

"That's right. But you are interested?"

"Oh, my, yes! We've read what we could—Pollard and Davidson, and Gamov's new book. But we don't have the math for atomics."

"How much math do you have?"

"Through differential equations."

"*Huh?*" Cargraves looked amazed. "Wait a minute. You guys are still in high school?"

"Just graduated."

"What kind of high school teaches differential equations? Or am I an old fuddy-duddy?"

Morrie seemed almost defensive in his explanation. "It's a new approach. You have to pass a test, then they give you algebra through quadratics, plane and spherical trigonometry, plane and solid geometry, and plane and solid analytical geometry all in one course, stirred in together. When you finish that course—and you take it as slow or as fast as you like—you go on."

Cargraves shook his head. "There've been some changes

made while I was busy with the neutrons. Okay, Quiz Kids, at that rate you'll be ready for quantum theory and wave mechanics before long. But I wonder how they go about cramming you this way? Do you savvy the postulational notion in math?"

"Why, I think so."

"Tell me."

Morrie took a deep breath. "No mathematics has any reality of its own, not even common arithmetic. All mathematics is purely an invention of the mind, with no connection with the world around us, except that we find some mathematics convenient in describing things."

"Go on. You're doing fine!"

"Even then it isn't real—or isn't 'true'—the way the ancients thought of it. Any system of mathematics is derived from purely arbitrary assumptions, called 'postulates,' the sort of thing the ancients called 'axioms.' "

"Your jets are driving, kid! How about the operational notion in scientific theory? No . . . Art—you tell me."

Art looked embarrassed; Morrie looked pleased but relieved. "Well, uh . . . the operational idea is, uh, it's building up your theory in terms of the operations you perform, like measuring, or timing, so that you don't go reading into the experiments things that aren't there."

Cargraves nodded. "That's good enough—it shows you know what you're talking about." He kept quiet for a long time, then he added, "You fellows really interested in rockets?"

Ross answered this time, "Why, er, yes, we are. Rockets among other things. We would certainly like to have a go at those junior prizes."

"That's all?"

"Well, no, not exactly. I guess we all think, well, maybe some day . . ." His voice trailed off.

"I think I see." Cargraves sat up. "But why bother with the competition? After all, as you pointed out, model rockets can't touch the full-sized commercial jobs. The prizes are offered just to keep up interest in rocketry—it's like the model airplane meets they used to have when I was a kid. But you guys can do better than that—why don't you go in for the *senior prizes?*"

Three sets of eyes were fixed on him. "What do you mean?"

Cargraves shrugged. "Why don't you go to the moon—with me?"

3.
CUT-RATE COLUMBUS

The silence that filled the clubhouse had a solid quality, as if one could slice it and make sandwiches. Ross recovered his voice first. "You don't mean it," he said in a hushed tone.

"But I do," Doctor Cargraves answered evenly. "I mean it quite seriously. I propose to try to make a trip to the moon. I'd like to have you fellows with me. Art," he added, "close your mouth. You'll make a draft."

Art gulped, did as he was told, then promptly opened it again. "But look," he said, his words racing, "Uncle Don . . . if you take us—I mean, how could we—or if we did, what would we use for—how do you propose—"

"Easy, easy!" Cargraves protested. "All of you keep quiet and I'll tell you what I have in mind. Then you can think it over and tell me whether or not you want to go for it."

Morrie slapped the bench beside him. "I don't care," he said, "I don't care if you're going to try to fly there on your worn broom—I'm in. I'm going along."

"So am I," Ross added quickly, moistening his lips.

Art looked wildly at the other two. "But I didn't mean that I wasn't—I was just asking—Oh, shucks! Me, too! You know that."

The young scientist gave the impression of bowing without getting up. "Gentlemen, I appreciate the confidence you place in me. But you are not committed to anything just yet."

"But—"

"So kindly pipe down," he went on, "and I'll lay out my cards, face up. Then we'll talk. Have you guys ever taken an oath?"

"Oh, sure—Scout Oath, anyhow."

"I was a witness in court once."

"Fine. I want you all to promise, on your honor, not to spill anything I tell you without my specific permission, whether we do business or not. It is understood that you are not bound thereby to remain silent if you are morally obligated to speak up—you are free to tell on me if there are moral or legal reasons why you should. Otherwise, you keep mum—on your honor. How about it?"

"Yes, sir!" "Right!" "Check."

"Okay," agreed Cargraves, settling back on his spine. "That was mostly a matter of form, to impress you with the necessity of keeping your lips buttoned. You'll understand why, later. Now here is the idea: all my life I've wanted to see the day when men would conquer space and explore the planets—and I wanted to take part in it. I don't have to tell you how that feels." He waved a hand at the book shelves. "Those books show me you understand it; you've got the madness yourselves. Besides that, what I saw out on your rocket grounds, what I see here, what I saw yesterday when I sneaked a look in Art's lab, shows me that you aren't satisfied just to dream about it and read about it—you want to *do* something. Right?"

"Right!" It was a chorus.

Cargraves nodded. "I felt the same way. I took my first degree in mechanical engineering with the notion that rockets were mechanical engineering and that I would need the training. I worked as an engineer after graduation until I had saved up enough to go back to school. I took my doctor's degree in atomic physics, because I had a hunch—oh, I wasn't the only one!—I had a hunch that atomic power was needed for practical space ships. Then came the war and the Manhattan Project.

"When the Atomic Age opened up a lot of people predicted that space flight was just around the corner. But it didn't work out that way—nobody knew how to harness the atom to a rocket. Do you know why?"

Somewhat hesitantly Ross spoke up. "Yes, I think I do."

"Go ahead."

"Well, for a rocket you need mass times velocity, quite a bit of mass in what the jet throws out and plenty of velocity. But in an atomic reaction there isn't very much mass and the energy comes out in radiations in all directions instead of a nice, lined-up jet. Just the same—"

" 'Just the same' what?"

"Well, there *ought* to be a way to harness all that power. Darn it—with so much power from so little weight, there ought to be *some* way."

"Just what I've always thought," Cargraves said with a grin. "We've built atomic plants that turn out more power than Boulder Dam. We've made atomic bombs that make the two used in the war seem like firecrackers. Power to burn, power to throw away. Yet we haven't been able to hook it to a rocket. Of course there are other problems. An atomic power plant takes a lot of shielding to protect the operators—you know that. And that means weight. Weight is everything in a rocket. If you add another hundred pounds in dead load, you have to pay for it in fuel. Suppose your shield weighed only a ton—how much fuel would that cost you, Ross?"

Ross scratched his head. "I don't know what kind of fuel you mean nor what kind of a rocket you are talking about—what you want it to do."

"Fair enough," the scientist admitted. "I asked you an impossible question. Suppose we make it a chemical fuel and a moon rocket and assume a mass-ratio of twenty to one. Then for a shield weighing a ton we have to carry twenty tons of fuel."

Art sat up suddenly. "Wait a minute, Uncle Don."

"Yes?"

"If you use a *chemical* fuel, like alcohol and liquid oxygen say, then you won't need a radiation shield."

"You got me, kid. But that was just for illustration. If you had a decent way to use atomic power, you might be able to hold your mass-ratio down to, let's say, one-to-one. Then a one-ton shield would only require one ton of fuel to carry it. That suit you better?"

Art wriggled in excitement. "I'll say it does. That means a *real* space ship. We could go anywhere in it!"

"But we're still on earth," his uncle pointed out dryly. "I said *'if.'* Don't burn out your jets before you take off. And there is still a third hurdle: atomic power plants are fussy to control—hard to turn on, hard to turn off. But we can let that one alone till we come to it. I still think we'll get to the moon."

He paused. They waited expectantly.

"I think I've got a way to apply atomic power to rockets."

Nobody stood up. Nobody cheered. No one made a speech starting, "On this historic occasion—" Instead they held their breaths, waiting for him to go on.

"Oh, I'm not going into details now. You'll find out all about it, if we work together."

"We will!" "Sure thing!"

"I hope so. I tried to interest the company I was with in the scheme, but they wouldn't hold still."

"Gee whillickers! Why not?"

"Corporations are in business to make money; they owe that to their stockholders. Do you see any obvious way to make money out of a flight to the moon?"

"Shucks." Art tossed it off. "They ought to be willing to risk going broke to back a thing like this."

"Nope. You're off the beam, kid. Remember they are handling other people's money. Have you any idea how much it would cost to do the research and engineering development, using the ordinary commercial methods, for anything as big as a trip to the moon?"

"No," Art admitted. "A good many thousands, I suppose."

Morrie spoke up. "More like a hundred thousand."

"That's closer. The technical director of our company made up a tentative budget of a million and a quarter."

"Whew!"

"Oh, he was just showing that it was not commercially practical. He wanted to adapt my idea to power plants for ships and trains. So I handed in my resignation."

"Good for you!"

Morrie looked thoughtful. "I guess I see," he said slowly, "why you swore us to secrecy. They own your idea."

Cargraves shook his head emphatically, "No, not at all. You certainly would be entitled to squawk if I tried to get you into a scheme to jump somebody else's patent rights—even if they held them by a yellow-dog, brain-picking contract." Cargraves spoke with vehemence. "My contract wasn't that sort. The company owns the idea for the purposes for which the research was carried out—power. And I own anything else I see in it. We parted on good terms. I don't blame them. When the queen staked Columbus, nobody dreamed that he would come back with the Empire State Building in his pocket."

"Hey," said Ross, "these senior prizes—they aren't big enough. That's why nobody has made a real bid for the top ones. The prize wouldn't pay the expenses, not for the kind of budget you mentioned. It's a sort of a swindle, isn't it?"

"Not a swindle, but that's about the size of it," Cargraves conceded. "With the top prize only $250,000 it won't tempt General Electric, or du Pont, or North American Atomic, or any other big research corporation. They can't afford it, unless some other profit can be seen. As a matter of fact, a lot of the prize money comes from those corporations." He sat up again. "But we can compete for it!"

"How?"

"I don't give a darn about the prize money. I just want to go!" "Me too!" Ross made the statement; Art chimed in.

"My sentiments exactly. As to how, that's where you come in. I can't spend a million dollars, but I think there is a way to tackle this on a shoestring. We need a ship. We need the fuel. We need a lot of engineering and mechanical work. We need overhead expenses and supplies for the trip. I've got a ship."

"You have? Now? A *space ship?*" Art was wide-eyed.

"I've got an option to buy an Atlantic freighter-rocket at scrap prices. I can swing that. It's a good rocket, but they are replacing the manned freighters with the more economical robot-controlled jobs. It's a V-17 and it isn't fit to convert to passenger service, so we get it as scrap. But if I buy it, it leaves me almost broke. Under the UN trusteeship for atomics, a senior member of the Global Association of Atomic Scientists—that's me!" he stuck in, grinning, "can get fissionable material for experimental purposes, if the directors of the Association approve. I can swing that. I've picked thorium, rather than uranium-235, or plutonium—never mind why. But the project itself had me stumped, just too expensive. I was about ready to try to promote it by endorsements and lecture contracts and all the other claptrap it sometimes takes to put over scientific work—when I met you fellows."

He got up and faced them. "I don't need much to convert that old V-17 into a space ship. But I do need skilled hands and brains and the imagination to know what is needed and why. You'd be my mechanics and junior engineers and machine-shop workers and instrument men and presently my crew. You'll do hard, dirty work for long hours and cook your own meals in the bargain. You'll get nothing but coffee-and-cakes and a chance to break your necks. The ship may never leave the ground. If it does, chances are you'll never live to tell about it. It won't be one big adventure. I'll work you till you're sick of me and probably nothing will come of it. But that's the proposition. Think it over and let me know."

There was the nerve-tingling pause which precedes an earthquake. Then the boys were on their feet, shouting all at once. It was difficult to make out words, but the motion had been passed by acclamation; the Galileo Club intended to go to the moon.

When the buzzing had died down, Cargraves noticed that Ross's face was suddenly grave. "What's the matter, Ross? Cold feet already?"

"No." Ross shook his head. "I'm afraid it's too good to be true."

"Could be, could be. I think I know what's worrying you. Your parents?"

"Uh, huh. I doubt if our folks will ever let us do it."

4.
THE BLOOD OF PIONEERS

Cargraves looked at their woebegone faces. He knew what they were faced with; a boy can't just step up to his father and say, "By the way, old man, count me out on those plans we made for me to go to college. I've got a date to meet Santa Claus at the North Pole." It was the real reason he had hesitated before speaking of his plans. Finally he said, "I'm afraid it's up to each of you. Your promise to me does not apply to your parents, but ask them to respect your confidence. I don't want our plans to get into the news."

"But look, Doctor Cargraves," Morrie put in, "why be so secret about it? It might make our folks feel that it was just a wild-eyed kid's dream. Why can't you just go to them and explain where we would fit into it?"

"No," Cargraves answered, "they are *your* parents. When and if they want to see me, I'll go to them and try to give satisfactory answers. But you will have to convince them that you mean business. As to secrecy, the reasons are these: there is only one aspect of my idea that can be patented and, under the rules of the UN Atomics Convention, it can be licensed by any one who wants to use it. The company is obtaining the patent, but not as a rocket device. The idea that I can apply it to a cheap, shoestring venture into space travel is mine and I don't want any one else to beat me to it with more money and stronger backing. Just before we are ready to leave we will call in the reporters—probably to run a story about how we busted our necks on the takeoff.

"But I see your point," he went on. "We don't want this to look like a mad-scientist-and-secret-laboratory set-up. Well, I'll try to convince them."

* * *

Doctor Cargraves made an exception in the case of Art's mother, because she was his own sister. He cautioned Art to retire to his basement laboratory as soon as dinner was over and then, after helping with the dishes, spoke to her. She listened quietly while he explained. "Well, what do you think of it?"

She sat very still, her eyes everywhere but on his face, her hands busy twisting and untwisting her handkerchief. "Don, you can't do this to me."

He waited for her to go on.

"I can't let him go, Don. He's all I've got. With Hans gone . . ."

"I know that," the doctor answered gently. "But Hans has been gone since Art was a baby. You can't limit the boy on that account."

"Do you think that makes it any easier?" She was close to tears.

"No, I don't. But it is on Hans' account that you must not keep his son in cotton batting. Hans had courage to burn. If he had been willing to knuckle under to the Nazis he would have stayed at Kaiser Wilhelm Institute. But Hans was a scientist. He wouldn't trim his notion of truth to fit political gangsters. He—"

"And it killed him!"

"I know, I know. But remember, Grace, it was only the fact that you were an American girl that enabled you to pull enough strings to get him out of the concentration camp."

"I don't see what that's got to do with it. Oh, you should have seen him when they let him out!" She was crying now.

"I did see him when you brought him to this country," he said gently, "and that was bad enough. But the fact that you are American has a lot to do with it. We have a tradition of freedom, personal freedom, scientific freedom. That freedom isn't kept alive by caution and unwillingness to take risks. If Hans were alive he would be going with me—you know that, Sis. You owe it to his son not to keep him caged. You can't keep him tied to your apron strings forever, anyhow. A few more years and you will have to let him follow his own bent."

Her head was bowed. She did not answer. He patted her shoulder. "You think it over, Sis. I'll try to bring him back in one piece."

When Art came upstairs, much later, his mother was still sitting, waiting for him. "Arthur?"

"Yes, Mother."

"You want to go to the moon?"

"Yes, Mother."

She took a deep breath, then replied steadily. "You be a good boy on the moon, Arthur. You do what your uncle tells you to."

"I will, Mother."

Morrie managed to separate his father from the rest of the swarming brood shortly after dinner. "Poppa, I want to talk to you man to man."

"And how else?"

"Well, this is different. I know you wanted me to come into the business, but you agreed to help me go to Tech."

His father nodded. "The business will get along. Scientists we are proud to have in the family. Your Uncle Bernard is a fine surgeon. Do we ask him to help with the business?"

"Yes, Poppa, but that's just it—I don't want to go to Tech."

"So? Another school?"

"No, I don't want to go to school." He explained Doctor Cargraves' scheme, blurting it out as fast as possible in an attempt to give his father the whole picture before he set his mind. Finished, he waited.

His father rocked back and forth. "So it's the moon now, is it? And maybe next week the sun. A man should settle down if he expects to accomplish anything, Maurice."

"But, Poppa, *this* is what I want to accomplish!"

"When do you expect to start?"

"You mean you'll let me? I *can?*"

"Not so fast, Maurice. I did not say yes; I did not say no. It has been quite a while since you stood up before the congregation and made your speech, 'Today I am a man—' That meant you were a man, Maurice, right that moment. It's not for me to let you; it's for me to advise you. I advise you not to. I think it's foolishness."

Morrie stood silent, stubborn but respectful.

"Wait a week, then come back and tell me what you are going to do. There's a pretty good chance that you will break your neck on this scheme, isn't there?"

"Well . . . yes, I suppose so."

"A week isn't too long to make up your mind to kill yourself. In the meantime, don't talk to Momma about this."

"Oh, I won't!"

"If you decide to go ahead anyway, I'll break the news to her. Momma isn't going to like this, Maurice."

* * *

Doctor Donald Cargraves received a telephone call the next morning which requested him, if convenient, to come to the Jenkins' home. He did so, feeling, unreasonably he thought, as if he were being called in on the carpet. He found Mr. and Mrs. Jenkins in the drawing room; Ross was not in sight.

Mr. Jenkins shook hands with him and offered him a chair. "Cigarette, Doctor? Cigar?"

"Neither, thank you."

"If you smoke a pipe," Mrs. Jenkins added, "please do so."

Cargraves thanked her and gratefully stoked up his old stinker.

"Ross tells me a strange story," Mr. Jenkins started in. "If he were not pretty reliable I'd think his imagination was working overtime. Perhaps you can explain it."

"I'll try, sir."

"Thanks. Is it true, Doctor, that you intend to try to make a trip to the moon?"

"Quite true."

"Well! Is it also true that you have invited Ross and his chums to go with you on this fantastic adventure?"

"Yes, it is." Doctor Cargraves found that he was biting hard on the stem of his pipe.

Mr. Jenkins stared at him. "I'm amazed. Even if it were something safe and sane, your choice of boys as partners strikes me as outlandish."

Cargraves explained why he believed the boys could be competent junior partners in the enterprise. "In any case," he concluded, "being young is not necessarily a handicap. The great majority of the scientists in the Manhattan Project were very young men."

"But not boys, Doctor."

"Perhaps not. Still, Sir Isaac Newton was a boy when he invented the calculus. Professor Einstein himself was only twenty-six when he published his first paper on relativity—and the work had been done when he was still younger. In mechanics and in the physical sciences, calendar age has nothing to do with the case; it's solely a matter of training and ability."

"Even if what you say is true, Doctor, training takes time and these boys have not had time for the training you need for such a job. It takes years to make an engineer, still more years to make a toolmaker or an instrument man. Tarnation, I'm an engineer myself. I know what I'm talking about."

"Ordinarily I would agree with you. But these boys have what I need. Have you looked at their work?"

"Some of it."

"How good is it?"

"It's good work—within the limits of what they know."

"But what they know is just what I need for this job. They are rocket fans now. They've learned in their hobbies the specialties I need."

Mr. Jenkins considered this, then shook his head. "I suppose there is something in what you say. But the scheme is fantastic. I don't say that space flight is fantastic; I expect that the engineering problems involved will some day be solved. But space flight is not a back-yard enterprise. When it comes it will be done by the air forces, or as a project of one of the big corporations, not by half-grown boys."

Cargraves shook his head. "The government won't do it. It would be laughed off the floor of Congress. As for corporations, I have reason to be almost certain they won't do it, either."

Mr. Jenkins looked at him quizzically. "Then it seems to me that we're not likely to see space flight in our lifetimes."

"I wouldn't say so," the scientist countered. "The United States isn't the only country on the globe. It wouldn't surprise me to hear some morning that the Russians had done it. They've got the technical ability and they seem to be willing to spend money on science. They might do it."

"Well, what if they do?"

Cargraves took a deep breath. "I have nothing against the Russians; if they beat me to the moon, I'll take off my hat to them. But I prefer our system to theirs; it would be a sour day for us if it turned out that they could do something as big and as wonderful as this when we weren't even prepared to tackle it, under our set-up. Anyhow," he continued, "I have enough pride in my own land to want it to be *us*, rather than some other country."

Mr. Jenkins nodded and changed his tack. "Even if these three boys have the special skills you need, I still don't see why you picked boys. Frankly, that's why the scheme looks rattlebrained to me. You should have experienced engineers and mechanics and your crew should be qualified rocket pilots."

Doctor Cargraves laid the whole thing before them, and explained how he hoped to carry out his plans on a slim budget. When he had finished Mr. Jenkins said, "Then as a matter of fact you braced these three boys because you were hard up for cash?"

"If you care to put it that way."

"I didn't put it that way; you did. Candidly, I don't altogether approve of your actions. I don't think you meant any harm, but you didn't stop to think. I don't thank you for getting Ross and his friends stirred up over a matter unsuited to their ages without consulting their parents first."

Donald Cargraves felt his mouth grow tense but said nothing; he felt that he could not explain that he had lain awake much of the night over misgivings of just that sort.

"However," Mr. Jenkins went on, "I understand your disappointment and sympathize with your enthusiasm." He smiled briefly. "I'll make you a deal. I'll hire three mechanics—you pick them—and one junior engineer or physicist, to help you in converting your ship. When the time comes, I'll arrange for a crew. Hiring will not be needed there, in my opinion—we will be able to pick from a long list of volunteers. Wait a minute," he said, as Cargraves started to speak, "you'll be under no obligation to me. We will make it a business proposition of a speculative sort. We'll draw up a contract under which, if you make it, you assign to me a proper percentage of the prize money and of the profits from exclusive news stories, books, lectures, and so forth. Does that look like a way out?"

Cargraves took a deep breath. "Mr. Jenkins," he said slowly, "if I had had that proposition last week, I would have jumped at it. But I can't take it."

"Why not?"

"I can't let the boys down. I'm already committed."

"Would it make a difference if I told you there was absolutely no chance of Ross being allowed to go?"

"No. I will have to go looking for just such a backer as yourself, but it can't be you. It would smack too much of allowing myself to be bought off—No offense intended, Mr. Jenkins!—to welch on the proposition I made Ross."

Mr. Jenkins nodded. "I was afraid you would feel that way. I respect your attitude, Doctor. Let me call Ross in and tell him the outcome." He started for the door.

"Just a moment, Mr. Jenkins—"

"Yes?"

"I want to tell you that I respect your attitude, too. As I told you, the project is dangerous, quite dangerous. I think it is a proper danger but I don't deny your right to forbid your son to risk his neck with me."

"I am afraid you don't understand me, Doctor Cargraves. It's dangerous, certainly, and naturally that worries me and Mrs. Jenkins, but that is not my objection. I would not try to keep Ross out of danger. I let him take flying lessons; I even had something to do with getting two surplus army trainers for the high school. I haven't tried to keep him from playing around with explosives. That's not the reason."

"May I ask what it is?"

"Of course. Ross is scheduled to start in at the Technical Institute this fall. I think it's more important for him to get a sound basic education than for him to be first man on the moon." He turned away again.

"Wait a minute! If it's his education you are worried about, would you consider me a competent teacher?"

"Eh? Well . . . yes."

"I will undertake to tutor the boys in technical and engineering subjects. I will see to it that they do not fall behind."

Mr. Jenkins hesitated momentarily. "No, Doctor, the matter is settled. An engineer without a degree has two strikes against him to start with. Ross is going to get his degree." He stepped quickly to the door and called out, "Ross!"

"Coming, Dad." The center of the argument ran downstairs and into the room. He looked around, first at Cargraves, then anxiously at his father, and finally at his mother, who looked up from her knitting and smiled at him but did not speak. "What's the verdict?" he inquired.

His father put it bluntly. "Ross, you start in school in the fall. I cannot okay this scheme."

Ross's jaw muscles twitched but he did not answer directly. Instead he said to Cargraves, "How about Art and Morrie?"

"Art's going. Morrie phoned me and said his father didn't think much of it but would not forbid it."

"Does that make any difference, Dad?"

"I'm afraid not. I don't like to oppose you, son, but when it comes right down to cases, I am responsible for you until you are twenty-one. You've got to get your degree."

"But . . . but . . . look, Dad. A degree isn't everything. If the trip is successful, I'll be so famous that I won't need a tag on my name to get a job. And if I don't come back, I won't need a degree!"

Mr. Jenkins shook his head. "Ross, my mind is made up."

Cargraves could see that Ross was fighting to keep the tears back. Somehow it made him seem older, not younger. When he spoke again his voice was unsteady. "Dad?"

"Yes, Ross?"

"If I can't go, may I at least go along to help with the rebuilding job? They'll need help."

Cargraves looked at him with new interest. He had some comprehension of what the proposal would cost the boy in heartache and frustration.

Mr. Jenkins looked surprised but answered quickly. "You may do that—up till the time school opens."

"Suppose they aren't through by then? I wouldn't want to walk out on them."

"Very well. If necessary you can start school the second semester. That is my last concession." He turned to Doctor Cargraves. "I shall count on you for some tutoring." Then to his son, "But that is the end of the matter, Ross. When you are twenty-one you can risk your neck in a space ship if you like. Frankly, I expect that there will still be plenty of chance for you to attempt the first flight to the moon if you are determined to try it." He stood up.

"Albert."

"Eh? Yes, Martha?" He turned deferentially to his wife.

She laid her knitting in her lap and spoke emphatically. "Let him go, Albert!"

"Eh? What do you mean, my dear?"

"I mean, let the boy go to the moon, if he can.

"I know what I said, and you've put up a good argument for me. But I've listened and learned. Doctor Cargraves is right; I was wrong. We can't expect to keep them in the nest.

"Oh, I know what I said," she went on, "but a mother is bound to cry a little. Just the same, this country was not built by people who were afraid to go. Ross's great-great-grandfather crossed the mountains in a Conestoga wagon and homesteaded this place. He was nineteen, his bride was seventeen. It's a matter of family record that their parents opposed the move." She stirred suddenly and one of her knitting needles broke. "I would hate to think that I had let the blood run thin." She got up and went quickly from the room.

Mr. Jenkins' shoulders sagged. "You have my permission, Ross," he said presently. "Doctor, I wish you good luck. And now, if you will excuse me . . ." He followed his wife.

5.
GROWING PAINS

"*How much farther?*" The noise of the stripped-down car combined with desert wind caused Art to shout.

"Look at the map," Ross said, his hands busy at the wheel in trying to avoid a jack rabbit. "It's fifty-three miles from Route 66 to the turn-off, then seven miles on the turn-off."

"We left Highway 66 about thirty-nine, forty miles back," Art replied. "We ought to be in sight of the turn-off before long." He squinted out across bare, colorful New Mexico countryside. "Did you ever see so much wide-open, useless country? Cactus and coyotes—what's it good for?"

"I like it," Ross answered. "Hang on to your hat." There was a flat, straight stretch ahead, miles along; Ross peeled off and made the little car dig . . . seventy . . . eighty . . . ninety . . . ninety-five. The needle quivered up toward three figures.

"Hey, Ross?"

"Yeah?"

"This rig ain't young any more. Why crack us up?"

"Sissy," said Ross, but he eased up on the gas.

"Not at all," Art protested. "If we kill ourselves trying to get to the moon, fine—we're heroes. But if we bust our fool necks before we start, we'll just look silly."

"Okay, okay—is that the turn-off?"

A dirt road swung off to the right and took out over the desert. They followed it about a quarter of a mile, then pulled up at a steel gate barring the road. A strong fence, topped by barbed wire, stretched out in both directions. There was a sign on the gate:

DANGER

Unexploded Shells

Enter this area at your own risk.
Disturb nothing—report all suspicious objects
to the District Forester.

"This is it," Ross stated. "Got the keys?" The area beyond was an abandoned training ground of the war, part of more than 8,000,000 acres in the United States which had been rendered useless until decontaminated by the hazardous efforts of army engineer specialists. This desert area was not worth the expense and risk of decontamination, but it was ideal for Cargraves; it assured plenty of room and no innocent bystanders—and it was rent free, loaned to the Association of Atomic Scientists, on Cargraves' behalf.

Art chucked Ross some keys. Ross tried them, then said, "You've given me the wrong keys."

"I don't think so. Nope," he continued, "those are the keys Doc sent."

"What do we do?"

"Bust the lock, maybe."

"Not this lock. Do we climb it?"

"With the rig under one arm? Be your age."

A car crawled toward them, its speed lost in the vastness of the desert. It stopped near them and a man in a military Stetson stuck his head out. "Hey, there!"

Art muttered, "Hey, yourself," then said, "Good morning."

"What are you trying to do?"

"Get inside."

"Don't you see the sign? Wait a minute—either one of you named Jenkins?"

"He's Ross Jenkins. I'm Art Mueller."

"Pleased to know you. I'm the ranger hereabouts. Name o' Buchanan. I'll let you in, but I don't rightly know as I should."

"Why not?" Ross's tone was edgy. He felt that they were being sized up as youngsters.

"Well . . . we had a little accident in there the other day. That's why the lock was changed."

"Accident?"

"Man got in somehow—no break in the fence. He tangled with a land mine about a quarter of a mile this side of your cabin."

"Did it . . . kill him?"

"Deader 'n a door nail. I spotted it by the buzzards. See here—I'll let you in; I've got a copy of your permit. But don't go exploring. You stay in the marked area around the cabin, and stay on the road that follows the power line."

Ross nodded. "We'll be careful."

"Mind you are. What are you young fellows going to do in there, anyway? Raise jack rabbits?"

"That's right. Giant jack rabbits, eight feet tall."

"So? Well, keep 'em inside the marked area, or you'll have jack rabbit hamburger."

"We'll be careful," Ross repeated. "Any idea who the man was that had the accident? Or what he was doing here?"

"None, on both counts. The buzzards didn't leave enough to identify. Doesn't make sense. There was nothing to steal in there; it was before your stuff came."

"Oh, it's here!"

"Yep. You'll find the crates stacked out in the open. He wasn't a desert man," the Ranger went on. "You could tell by his shoes. Must 'a' come by car, but there was no car around. Doesn't make sense."

"No, it doesn't seem to," Ross agreed, "but he's dead, so that ends it."

"Correct. Here are your keys. Oh, yes—" He put his hand back in his pocket. "Almost forgot. Telegram for you."

"For us? Oh, thanks!"

"Better put up a mail box out at the highway," Buchanan suggested. "This reached you by happenstance."

"We'll do that," Ross agreed absently, as he tore open the envelope.

"So long." Buchanan kicked his motor into life.

"So long, and thanks again."

"For Heaven's sake, what does it say?" Art demanded.

"Read it:"

PASSED FINAL TESTS TODAY. LEAVING SATURDAY. PLEASE PROVIDE BRASS BAND, DANCING GIRLS, AND TWO FATTED CALVES—ONE RARE, ONE MEDIUM. (signed) DOC AND MORRIE.

Ross grinned. "Imagine that! Old Morrie a rocket pilot! I'll bet his hat doesn't fit him now."

"I'll bet it doesn't. Darn! We all should have taken the course."

"Relax, relax. Don't be small about it—we'd have wasted half the summer." Ross dismissed the matter.

Art himself did not understand his own jealousy. Deep inside, it was jealousy of the fact that Morrie had been able to go to Spaatz Field in the company of Art's idolized uncle rather than the purpose of the trip. All the boys had had dual-control airplane instruction; Morrie had gone on and gotten a private license. Under the rules—out of date, in Art's opinion—an airplane pilot could take a shortened course for rocket pilot. Doctor Cargraves held a slightly dusty aircraft license some fifteen years old. He had been planning to qualify for rocket operation; when he found that Morrie was eligible it was natural to include him.

This had left Ross and Art to carry out numerous chores for the enterprise, then to make their own way to New Mexico to open up the camp.

The warning to follow the power line had been necessary; the boys found the desert inside pock-marked by high explosive and criss-crossed with tracks, one as good as another, carved years before by truck and tank and mobile carrier. The cabin itself they found to be inside a one-strand corral a quarter of a mile wide and over a mile long. Several hundred yards beyond the corral and stretching away for miles toward the horizon was an expanse which looked like a green, rippling lake—the glassy crater of the atom bomb test of 1951, the UN's Doomsday Bomb.

Neither the cabin nor the piled-up freight could hold their attention until they had looked at it. Ross drove the car to the far side of the enclosure and they stared.

Art gave a low respectful whistle. "How would you like to have been under that?" Ross inquired in a hushed voice.

"Not any place in the same county—or the next county. How would you like to be in a city when one of those things goes off?"

Ross shook his head. "I want to zig when it zags. Art, they better never have to drop another one, except in practice. If they ever start lobbing those things around, it 'ud be the end of civilization."

"They won't," Art assured him. "What d'you think the UN police is for? Wars are out. Everybody knows that."

"You know it and I know it. But I wonder if everybody knows it?"

"It'll be just too bad if they don't."

"Yeah—too bad for *us*."

Art climbed out of the car. "I wonder if we can get down to it?"

"Well, don't try. We'll find out later."

"There can't be any duds in the crater or anywhere in the area—not after that."

"Don't forget our friend that the buzzards ate. Duds that weren't exposed to the direct blast might not go off. This bomb was set off about five miles up."

"Huh? I thought—"

"You were thinking about the test down in Chihuahua. That was a ground job. Come on. We got work to do." He trod on the starter.

The cabin was pre-fab, moved in after the atom bomb test to house the radioactivity observers. It had not been used since and looked it. "Whew! What a mess," Art remarked. "We should have brought a tent."

"It'll be all right when we get it fixed up. Did you see keroscne in that stuff outside?"

"Two drums of it."

"Okay. I'll see if I can make this stove work. I could use some lunch." The cabin was suitable, although dirty. It had a drilled well; the water was good, although it had a strange taste. There were six rough bunks needing only bedding rolls. The kitchen was the end of the room, the dining room a large pine table, but there were shelves, hooks on the walls, windows, a tight roof overhead. The stove worked well, even though it was smelly; Ross produced scrambled eggs, coffee, bread and butter, German-fried potatoes, and a bakery apple pie with only minor burns and mishaps.

It took all day to clean the cabin, unload the car, and uncrate what they needed at once. By the time they finished supper, prepared this time by Art, they were glad to crawl into their sacks. Ross was snoring gently before Art closed his eyes. Between Ross's snores and the mournful howls of distant coyotes Art was considering putting plugs in his ears, when the morning sun woke him up.

"Get up, Ross!"

"Huh? What? Wassamatter?"

"Show a leg. We're burning daylight."

"I'm tired," Ross answered as he snuggled back into the bedding. "I think I'll have breakfast in bed."

"You and your six brothers. Up you come—today we pour the foundation for the shop."

"That's right." Ross crawled regretfully out of bed. "Wonderful weather—I think I'll take a sun bath."

"I think you'll get breakfast, while I mark out the job."

"Okay, Simon Legree."

The machine shop was a sheet metal and stringer affair, to be assembled. They mixed the cement with the sandy soil of the desert, which gave them a concrete good enough for a temporary building. It was necessary to uncrate the power tools and measure them before the fastening bolts could be imbedded in the concrete. Ross watched as Art placed the last bolt. "You sure we got 'em all?"

"Sure. Grinder, mill, lathe—" He ticked them off. "Drill press, both saws—" They had the basic tools needed for almost any work. Then they placed bolts for the structure itself, matching the holes in the metal sills to the bolts as they set them in the wet concrete. By nightfall they had sections of the building laid out, each opposite its place, ready for assembly.

"Do you think the power line will carry the load?" Art said anxiously, as they knocked off.

Ross shrugged. "We won't be running all the tools at once. Quit worrying, or we'll never get to the moon. We've got to wash dishes before we can get supper."

By Saturday the tools had been hooked up and tested, and Art had rewound one of the motors. The small mountain of gear had been stowed and the cabin was clean and reasonably orderly. They discovered in unpacking cases that several had been broken open, but nothing seemed to have been hurt. Ross was inclined to dismiss the matter, but Art was worried. His precious radio and electronic equipment had been gotten at.

"Quit fretting," Ross advised him. "Tell Doc about it when he comes. The stuff was insured."

"It was insured *in transit*," Art pointed out. "By the way, when do you think they will get here?"

"I can't say," Ross answered. "If they come by train, it might be Tuesday or later. If they fly to Albuquerque and take the bus, it might be tomorrow—what was that?" He glanced up.

"Where?" asked Art.

"There. Over there, to your left. Rocket."

"So it is! It must be a military job; we're off the commercial routes. Hey, he's turned on his nose jets!"

"He's going to land. He's going to land *here!*"

"You don't suppose?"

"I don't know. I thought—there he comes! It can't—" His words were smothered when the thunderous, express-train roar reached them, as the rocket decelerated. Before the braking jets had been applied, it was traveling ahead of its own din, and had been, for them, as silent as thought. The pilot put it down smoothly not more than five hundred yards from them, with a last blast of the nose and belly jets which killed it neatly.

They began to run.

As they panted up to the sleek, gray sides of the craft, the door forward of the stub wings opened and a tall figure jumped down, followed at once by a smaller man.

"Doc! Doc! Morrie!"

"Hi, sports!" Cargraves yelled. "Well, we made it. Is lunch ready?"

Morrie was holding himself straight, almost popping with repressed emotion. "*I* made the landing," he announced.

"You did?" Art seemed incredulous.

"Sure. Why not? I got my license. Want to see it?"

" 'Hot Pilot Abrams,' it says here," Ross alleged, as they examined the document. "But why didn't you put some glide on it? You practically set her down on her jets."

"Oh, I was practicing for the moon landing."

"You were, huh? Well, Doc makes the moon landing or I guarantee I don't go."

Cargraves interrupted the kidding. "Take it easy. Neither one of us will try an airless landing."

Morrie looked startled. Ross said, "Then who—"

"Art will make the moon landing."

Art gulped and said, "Who? Me?"

"In a way. It will have to be a radar landing; we can't risk a crack-up on anything as hard as an all-jet landing when there is no way to walk home. Art will have to modify the circuits to let the robot-pilot do it. But Morrie will be the stand-by," he went on, seeing the look on Morrie's face. "Morrie's reaction time is better than mine. I'm getting old. Now how about lunch? I want to change clothes and get to work."

Morrie was dressed in a pilot's coverall, but Cargraves was wearing his best business suit. Art looked him over. "How come the zoot suit, Uncle? You don't look like you expected to come by rocket. For that matter, I thought the ship was going to be ferried out?"

"Change in plans. I came straight from Washington to the field and Morrie took off as soon as I arrived. The ship was ready, so we brought it out ourselves, and saved about five hundred bucks in ferry pilot charges."

"Everything on the beam in Washington?" Ross asked anxiously.

"Yes, with the help of the association's legal department. Got some papers for each of you to sign. Let's not stand here beating our gums. Ross, you and I start on the shield right away. After we eat."

"Good enough."

Ross and the doctor spent three days on the hard, dirty task of tearing out the fuel system to the tail jets. The nose and belly jets, used only in maneuvering and landing, were left unchanged. These operated on aniline-and-nitric fuel; Cargraves wanted them left as they were, to get around one disadvantage of atomic propulsion— the relative difficulty in turning the power off and on when needed.

As they worked, they brought each other up to date. Ross told him about the man who had tangled with a dud land mine. Cargraves paid little attention until Ross told him about the crates that had been opened. Cargraves laid down his tools and wiped sweat from his face. "I want the details on that," he stated.

"What's the matter, Doc? Nothing was hurt."

"You figure the dead man had been breaking into the stuff?"

"Well, I thought so until I remembered that the Ranger had said flatly that this bozo was already buzzard meat before our stuff arrived."

Cargraves looked worried and stood up. "Where to, Doc?"

"You go ahead with the job," the scientist answered absently. "I've got to see Art." Ross started to speak, thought better of it, and went back to work.

"Art," Cargraves started in, "what are you and Morrie doing now?"

"Why, we're going over his astrogation instruments. I'm tracing out the circuits on the acceleration integrator. The gyro on it seems to be off center, by the way."

"It has to be. Take a look in the operation manual. But never mind that. Could you rig an electric-eye circuit around this place?"

"I could if I had the gear."

"Never mind what you might do 'if'—what can you do with the stuff you've got?"

"Wait a minute, Uncle Don," the younger partner protested. "Tell me what you want to *do*—I'll tell you if I can wangle it."

"Sorry. I want a prowler circuit around the ship and cabin. Can you do it?"

Art scratched his ear. "Let me see. I'd need photoelectric cells and an ultraviolet light. The rest I can piece together. I've got two light meters in my photo kit; I could rig them for the cells, but I don't know about UV light. If we had a sun lamp, I could filter it. How about an arc? I could jimmy up an arc."

Cargraves shook his head. "Too uncertain. You'd have to stay up all night nursing it. What else can you do?"

"Mmmm . . . Well, we could use thermocouples maybe. Then I could use an ordinary floodlight and filter it down to infra-red."

"How long would it take? Whatever you do, it's got to be finished by dark, even if it's only charging the top wire of the fence."

"Then I'd better do just that," Art agreed, "if that—Say!"

"Say what?"

"Instead of giving the fence a real charge and depending on shocking anybody that touches it, I'll just push a volt or two through it and hook it back in through an audio circuit with plenty of gain. I can rig it so that if anybody touches the fence it will howl like a dog. How's that?"

"That's better. I want an alarm right now. Get hold of Morrie and both of you work on it." Cargraves went back to his work, but his mind was not on it. The misgivings which he had felt at the time of the mystery of the missing 'blunt instrument' were returning. Now more mysteries—his orderly mind disliked mysteries.

He started to leave the rocket about an hour later to see how Art was making out. His route led him through the hold into the pilot compartment. There he found Morrie. His eyebrows went up. "Hi, sport," he said. "I thought you were helping Art."

Morrie looked sheepish. "Oh, that!" he said. "Well, he did say something about it. But I was busy." He indicated the computer, its cover off.

"Did he tell you I wanted you to help him?"

"Well, yes—but he didn't need my help. He can do that sort of work just as well alone."

Cargraves sat down. "Morrie," he said slowly, "I think we had better have a talk. Have you stopped to think who is going to be second-in-comand of this expedition?"

Morrie did not answer. Cargraves went on. "It has to be you, of course. You're the other pilot. If anything happens to me the other two will have to obey you. You realize that?"

"Art won't like that." Morrie's voice was a mutter.

"Not as things stand now. Art's got his nose out of joint. You can't blame him—he was disappointed that he didn't get to take pilot training, too."

"But that wasn't my fault."

"No, but you've got to fix it. You've got to behave so that, if the time comes, they'll *want* to take your orders. This trip is no picnic. There will be times when our lives may depend on instant obedience. I put it to you bluntly, Morrie—if I had had a choice I would have picked Ross for my second-in-command—he's less flighty than you are. But you're it, and you've got to live up to it. Otherwise we don't take off."

"Oh, we've got to take off! We can't give up now!"

"We'll make it. The trouble is, Morrie," he went on, "American boys are brought up loose and easy. That's fine. I like it that way. But there comes a time when loose and easy isn't enough, when you have to be willing to obey, and do it wholeheartedly and without argument. See what I'm driving at?"

"You mean you want me to get on back to the shop and help Art."

"Correct." He swung the boy around and faced him toward the door, slapped him on the back and said, "Now git!"

Morrie "got." He paused at the door and flung back over his shoulder, "Don't worry about me, Doc. I can straighten out and fly right."

"Roger!" Cargraves decided to have a talk with Art later.

6.
DANGER IN THE DESERT

The space suits were delivered the next day, causing another break in the work, to Cargraves' annoyance. However, the boys were so excited over this evidence that they were actually preparing to walk on the face of the moon that he decided to let them get used to the suits.

The suits were modified pressurized stratosphere suits, as developed for the air forces. They looked like diving suits, but were less clumsy. The helmets were "goldfish bowls" of Plexiglas, laminated with soft polyvinyl-butyral plastic to make them more nearly shatter-proof. There were no heating arrangements. Contrary to popular belief, vacuum of outer space has no temperature; it is neither hot nor cold. Man standing on the airless moon would gain or lose heat only by radiation, or by direct contact with the surface of the moon. As the moon was believed to vary from extreme subzero to temperatures hotter than boiling water, Cargraves had ordered thick soles of asbestos for the shoes of the suits and similar pads for the seats of the pants of each suit, so that they could sit down occasionally without burning or freezing. Overgloves of the same material completed the insulation against contact. The suits were so well insulated, as well as air-tight, that body heat more than replaced losses through radiation. Cargraves would have preferred thermostatic control, but such refinements could be left to the pioneers and colonists who would follow after.

Each suit had a connection for an oxygen bottle much larger and heavier than the jump bottle of an aviator, a bottle much too heavy to carry on earth but not too heavy for the surface of the moon, where weight is only one-sixth that found on earth.

The early stratosphere suits tended to starfish and become rigid, which made the simplest movements an effort. In trying on his own suit, Cargraves was pleased to find that these suits were easy to move around in, even when he had Ross blow him up until the suit was carrying a pressure of three atmospheres, or about forty-five pounds to the square inch. The constant-volume feature, alleged for the de-Camp joints, appeared to be a reality.

Cargraves let them experiment, while seeing to it that as many field tests as possible were made to supplement the manufacturer's laboratory tests. Then the suits were turned over to Art for installation of walky-talky equipment.

The following day the doctor turned all the boys to work on the conversion of the drive mechanism. He was expecting delivery of the atomic fission element, thorium; the antiradiation shield had to be ready. This shield was constructed of lead, steel, and organic plastic, in an arrangement which his calculations indicated would be most effective in screening the alpha, beta, and gamma radiations and the slippery neutrons, from the forward part of the rocket.

Of these radiations, the gamma are the most penetrating and are much like X-rays. Alpha particles are identical with the nuclei of helium atoms; beta particles are simply electrons moving at extremely high speeds. Neutrons are the electrically uncharged particles which make up much of the mass of most atomic nuclei and are the particles which set off or trigger the mighty explosions of atomic bombs.

All of these radiations are dangerous to health and life.

The thorium drive unit was to be shielded only on the forward side, as radiations escaping to outer space could be ignored. Morrie had landed the rocket with one side facing the cabin, inside the corral. It was now necessary to jack the rocket around until the tubes pointed away from the cabin, so that radiations, after the thorium was in place, would go harmlessly out across the crater of the Doomsday Bomb and, also, so that the rocket would be in position for a captive test run with the exhaust directed away from the cabin.

The jacking-around process was done with hydraulic jacks, muscle, and sweat, in sharp contrast to the easy appearing, powered manipulation of rockets by dolly and cradle and mobile sling, so familiar a sight on any rocket field. It took all of them until late afternoon. When it was over Cargraves declared a holiday and took them on a long-promised trip into the Doomsday Crater.

This bomb site had been pictured and described so much and the boys were so used to seeing it in the distance that the thrill of being in it was limited. Nevertheless the desolation, the utter deadness, of those miles and miles of frozen, glassy waste made their flesh creep. Cargraves marched ahead, carrying a Geiger radiation counter, of the sort used to prospect for uranium in Canada during the war. This was largely to impress the boys with the necessity for unsleeping watchfulness in dealing with radioactive elements. He did not really expect to hear the warning rattle of danger in the ear phones; the test had been made so long before that the grim lake was almost certainly as harmless as the dead streets of Hiroshima.

But it put them in the mood for the lecture he had in mind. "Now, listen, sports," he started in when they got back, "day after tomorrow the thorium arrives. From then on the holiday is over. This stuff is poison. You've got to remember that all the time."

"Sure," agreed Morrie. "We all know that."

"You know it at the tops of your minds. I want you to know it every minute, way down in your guts. We'll stake out the unshielded area between the ship and the fence. If your hat blows into that stretch, let it stay there, let it rot—but don't go after it!"

Ross looked perturbed. "Wait a second, Doc. Would it really hurt anything to expose yourself for just a few seconds?"

"Probably not," Cargraves agreed, "provided that were all the dosage you ever got. But we will all get some dosage all the time, even through the shield. Radioactivity accumulates its poisonous effect. Any exposure you can possibly avoid, you *must* avoid. It makes your chances better when you get a dose of it accidentally. Art!"

"Uh? Yes, sir!"

"From now on you are the medical officer. You must see to it that everybody wears his X-ray film all the time—and I mean *all* the time—and his electroscope. I want you to change the films and develop them and check the electroscopes according to the dope in the manual. Complete charts on everything, and report to me each Friday morning—oftener if you find anything outside the limits. Got me?"

"Got you, Doc."

"Besides that, you arrange for blood counts once a week for everybody, over in town."

"I think I could learn to do a blood count myself," Art offered.

"You let the regular medico do it. You've got enough to worry about to keep all the electronic equipment purring along properly. One more thing." He looked around him, waiting to get their full attention.

"If any one shows the possibility of overdosage of radiation, by film or by blood count or whatever, I will have to send him home for treatment. It won't be a case of 'just one more chance.' You are dealing with hard facts here—not me, but natural laws. If you make a mistake, out you go and we'll have to find somebody to take your place."

They all nodded solemnly. Art said, "Doc?"

"Yes?"

"Suppose it's your film that shows the overdosage?"

"Me? Not likely! If it does you can kick me all the way to the gate—I'm afraid of that stuff!

"Just the same," he went on more seriously, "you run the same checks on me as on everybody else. Now let's have supper. I want you and Morrie to do the KP tonight, so that Ross can start his study period right after supper. Ross, you and I are getting up at five, so let's hit the sack early."

"Okay. What's cookin'?"

"Trip into Albuquerque—shopping." He was reluctant to explain. The place had no firearms. They had seemed a useless expense—many a man has spent years in the desert without shooting off anything but his mouth, he had reasoned. As for the dreamed-of trip—what could one shoot on the moon?

But signs of prowlers, even in this fenced and forbidding area, had him nervous. Art's watch-dog fence was tested each night and Art slept with the low power-hum of the hot circuit in his ears; thus far there had been no new alarm. Still he was nervous.

Cargraves was awakened about three A.M. to find Art shaking his shoulder and light pouring in his eyes. "Doc! Doc! Wake up!"

"Huh? Wassamatter?"

"I got a squawk over the loudspeaker."

Cargraves was out of bed at once. They bent over the speaker. "I don't hear anything."

"I've got the volume low, but you'd hear it. There it is again— get it?" There had been an unmistakable squawk from the box. "Shall I wake the others?"

"Mmmm . . . no. Not now. Why did you turn on the light?"

"I guess I wanted it," Art admitted.

"I see." Cargraves hauled on trousers and fumbled with his shoes. "I want you to turn out the lights for ten seconds. I'm going out that window. If I'm not back in twenty minutes, or if you hear anything that sounds bad, wake the boys and come get me. But stay together. Don't separate for any reason." He slipped a torch in his pocket. "Okay."

"You ought not to go by yourself."

"Now, Art. I thought we had settled such matters."

"Yes, but—oh, well!" Art posted himself at the switch.

Cargraves was out the window and had cat-footed it around behind the machine shop before the light came on again. He lurked in the shadow and let his eyes get used to the darkness.

It was a moonless night, clear and desert sharp. Orion blazed in the eastern sky. Cargraves soon was able to pick out the sage bushes, the fence posts, the gloomy bulk of the ship a hundred yards away.

The padlock on the machine shop was undisturbed and the shop's windows were locked. Doing his best to take advantage of the scanty cover, he worked his way down to the ship.

The door was ajar. He could not remember whether he or Ross had been last man out. Even if it had been Ross, it was not like Ross to fail to lock the door.

He found that he was reluctant to enter the craft. He wished that he had not put off buying guns; a forty-five in his hand would have comforted him.

He swung the door open and scrambled in fast, ducking quickly away from the door, where his silhouette would make a target. He crouched in the darkness, listening and trying to slow his pounding heart. When he was sure he could hear nothing, he took the flashlight, held it at arm's length away from him and switched it on.

The piloting compartment was empty. Somewhat relieved, he sneaked back through the hold, empty also, and into the drive compartment. Empty. Nothing seemed disturbed.

He left the ship cautiously, this time making sure that the door was locked. He made a wide sweep around the cabin and machine shop and tried to assure himself that no one was inside the corral. But in the starlight, fifty men might have hidden in the sage, simply by crouching down and holding still.

He returned to the cabin, whistling to Art as he approached.

"About time you got back," Art complained. "I was just about to roust out the others and come and get you. Find anything?"

"No. Anything more out of the squawk box?"

"Not a peep."

"Could it have been a coyote brushing against the wire?"

"How would a coyote get through the outer fence?" Art wanted to know.

"Dig under it. There *are* coyotes in here. We've heard them."

"You can't tell how far a coyote is from you by its howl."

"Listen to the old desert rat! Well, leave the light on, but go back to bed. I'll be awake. I've got to be up in another hour in any case. Crawl in the sack." Cargraves settled down to a pipe and some thought.

Cargraves was too busy on the trip to Albuquerque to worry about the preceding night. Ross's style of herding his hot rod left little time to think about anything but the shortness of life and the difficulty of hanging on to his hat. But Ross poured them into the city with plenty of time for shopping.

Cargraves selected two Garand rifles, Army surplus stock at a cheap price, and added a police thirty-eight special, on a forty-five frame. His mouth watered at a fancy sporting rifle with telescopic sights, but money was getting short; a few more emergency purchases or any great delay in starting would bankrupt the firm.

He ordered a supply of army-style C-rations and K-rations for the trip. Ross remarked privately, while the clerk wrote up the order, "In most stories about space travel, they just eat pills of concentrated food. Do you think it will ever come to that?"

"Not with my money," the physicist answered. "You guys can eat pills if you want to. I want food I can get my teeth in."

"Check," said Ross.

They stopped at a nursery where Cargraves ordered three dozen young rhubarb plants. He planned to use a balanced oxygen-carbon-dioxide air-refreshing system during the stay on the moon, if possible, and the plants were to supply the plant-life half of the cycle. Enough liquid oxygen would be carted along for breathing throughout the round trip, but a "balanced aquarium" arrangement for renewing their air supply would enable them to stay on the moon as long as their food lasted.

The chemical fertilizers needed for hydroponic farming of the rhubarb were ordered also. This done, they grabbed a chocolate malt and a hamburger apiece and high-tailed it for the camp.

Morrie and Art swarmed out of the machine shop as they arrived. "Hi, Doc! Hi, Ross! What's the good word?"

Ross showed them the guns. Art was eager to try them and Cargraves okayed it. Morrie hung back and said, "By the way, Doc, the CAB inspector was here today."

"The what?"

"The Civil Aeronautics inspector. He had a letter from you."

"From me? What did it say?"

"Why, it requested them to send an inspector to go over the re-built parts of the rocket and approve it for flight. I told him it wasn't ready."

"What else did you say? Did you tell him it was atomic-powered?"

"No, but he seemed to know it. He knew that we planned a space flight, too. What's the pitch, Doc? I thought you were going to keep it quiet a while longer?"

"So did I," Cargraves said bitterly. "What *did* you tell him?"

"Nothing—so help me. I decided you ought to handle it, so I played stupid. I tipped Art and he did the same. Did we do wrong?" he went on anxiously. "I know he was CAB, but it seemed to me he ought to talk to you. Do you suppose we offended him?"

"I hope you gave him apoplexy," Cargraves said savagely. "He was no CAB inspector, Morrie. He was a phony."

"Huh? Why . . . But he had your letter."

"Faked. I'll bet he's been holed up somewhere outside the gate, waiting for me to be away. Did you leave him alone at any time?"

"No. Wait a minute—only once, for about five minutes. We were down at the ship and he sent me back for a flashlight. I'm sorry." The boy looked miserable.

"Forget it. It was the natural, polite thing to do. You didn't know he was phony. I wonder how he got through the gate? Did he come in a car?"

"Yes. I . . . Was the gate locked?"

"Yes, but he might have bulldozed the forester into letting him in." They had been moving down toward the ship as they talked. Cargraves made a quick examination of the ship, but found nothing amiss. It seemed likely that the intruder had not found what he was looking for, probably because the drive was not yet installed.

He still worried about the matter of the locked gate. "I'm going to run down to the gate," he announced, heading for the car. "Tell the boys."

"I'll drive you." None of the boys approved the way Cargraves drove a car; it was one respect in which they did not look up to him. Privately, they considered his style stuffy.

"Okay. Snap it up." Morrie ran down toward where the other two were wasting ammunition on innocent tin cans and bellowed at them. Seconds later he had the engine revved up and was ready to gun the rig when Cargraves slid into the seat beside him.

The padlock was intact, but one link of the bullchain had been hack-sawed away and replaced with wire. "So that's that." Cargraves dismissed the matter.

"Hadn't we better put on a new chain?" inquired Morrie.

"Why bother? He's still got the hacksaw."

The trip back was gloomy. Cargraves was worried. Morrie felt responsible for not having unmasked and made prisoner the impostor. In retrospect he could think of a dozen dramatic ways to have done it.

Cargraves told him to keep his lip buttoned until after supper. When the dishes were out of the way, he brought the others up to date on the ominous happenings. Art and Ross took it with grave faces but without apparent excitement. "So that's how it is," Ross said. "Seems like somebody doesn't like us."

"Why that dirty so-and-so," Art said softly. "I thought he was too smooth. I'd like to have him on the other end of one of those Garands."

"Maybe you will," Cargraves answered him soberly. "I might as well admit, fellows, that I've been worried. . . ."

"Shucks, we knew that when you ordered that watchdog hook-up."

"I suppose so. I can't figure out *why* anybody would do this. Simple curiosity I can understand, once the fact leaked out—as it seems to have done—that we are after space flight. But whoever it is has more than curiosity eating him, considering the lengths he is willing to go to."

"I'll bet he wants to steal your space drive, Uncle Don."

"That would make a swell adventure yarn, Art, but it doesn't make sense. If he knows I've got a rocket drive, all he has to do is apply for a license to the commission and use it."

"Maybe he thinks you are holding out some secrets on the commission?"

"If he thinks so, he can post a bond for the costs and demand an examination. He wouldn't have to fake letters, or bust open gates. If he proves it on me, I go to jail."

"The point is," Morrie asserted, "not why he's snooping but what we can do to stop him. I think we ought to stand watches at night." He glanced at the two rifles.

"No," Cargraves disagreed. "Art's squawk circuit is better than a guard. You can't see enough at night. I found that out."

"Say," put in Art. "Look—I could take the pilot radar and mount it on the roof of the cabin. With it set to scan for a landing it'll pick up anything in the neighborhood."

"No," Cargraves answered. "I wouldn't want to risk jimmying up the equipment. It's more important to have it just right for the moon landing than it is to use it for prowlers."

"Oh, I won't hurt it!"

"I still think," insisted Morrie, "that getting a shot at him is the best medicine."

"So much the better," Art pointed out. "I'll spot him in the 'scope. You wear phones with about a thousand feet of cord and I'll coach you right up to him, in the dark. Then you got 'im."

"Sounds good," Morrie agreed.

"Take it easy," Cargraves cautioned. "You fellows may think this is the Wild West but you will find that a judge will take a very sour attitude if you plug a man engaged in simple trespass. You boys've read too many comic books."

"I never touch the things," Art denied fiercely. "Anyhow, not often," he amended.

"If we can't shoot, then why did you buy the guns?" Ross wanted to know.

"Fair enough. You *can* shoot—but you have to be certain it's self-defense; I'll take those guns back to the shop before I'll have a bunch of wild men running around with blood in their eyes and an itch in their trigger fingers. The other use for the guns is to throw a scare into any more prowlers. You can shoot, but shoot where he *isn't*—unless he shoots first."

"Okay." "Suits." "I hope he shoots first!"

"Any other ideas?"

"Just one," Art answered. "Suppose our pal cut our power line. We've got everything on it—light, radio, even the squawk box. He could cut the line after we went to sleep and loot the whole place without us knowing it."

Cargraves nodded. "I should have thought of that." He considered it. "You and I will string a temporary line right now from the ship's batteries to your squawk box. Tomorrow we'll hook up an emergency lighting circuit." He stood up. "Come on, Art. And you guys get busy. Study hour."

"Study hour?" Ross protested. "Tonight? We can't keep our minds on books—not tonight."

"You can make a stab at it," the doctor said firmly. "Guys have been known to write books while waiting to be hanged."

The night passed quietly. Ross and Doc were down at the ship early the next morning, leaving Art and Morrie to work out an emergency lighting circuit from the battery of the car. Doc planned to have everything ready for the thorium when it arrived. He and Ross climbed into the rocket and got cheerfully to work. Cargraves started laying out tools, while Ross, whistling merrily off key, squeezed himself around the edge of the shield.

Cargraves looked up just in time to see a bright, bright flash, then to be hit in the face by a thunderous pressure which threw him back against the side of the ship.

7.

"WE'LL GO IF WE HAVE TO WALK"

Art was shaking his shoulder. "Doc!" he was pleading. "Doc! Wake up—are you hurt bad?"

"Ross . . ." Cargraves said vaguely.

"It's not Ross; it's Art."

"But Ross—how's Ross? Did it, did it kill him?"

"I don't know. Morrie's with him."

"Go find out."

"But you're—"

"Go find out, I said!" Whereupon he passed out again.

When he came to a second time, Art was bending over him. "Uncle," he said, "the thorium has come. What do we do?"

Thorium. Thorium? His head ached, the word seemed to have no meaning. "Uh, I'll be out in a . . . what about Ross? Is he dead?"

"No, he's not dead."

"How bad is he hurt?"

"It seems to be his eyes, mostly. He isn't cut up any, but he can't see. What'll I tell them about the thorium, Uncle?"

"Oh, hang the thorium! Tell them to take it back."

"What?"

He tried to get up, but he was too dizzy, too weak. He let his head fall back and tried to collect his spinning thoughts. "Don't be a dope, Art," he muttered peevishly. "We don't need thorium. The trip is off, the whole thing was a mistake. Send it back—it's poison." His eyes were swimming; he closed them. "Ross . . ." he said.

He was again brought back to awareness by the touch of hands on his body. Morrie and Art were gently but firmly going over him. "Take it easy, Doc," Morrie warned him.

"Well . . ." Morrie wrinkled his brow. "Ross seems all right, except for his eyes. He says he's all right."

"But he's blind?"

"Well, he can't see."

"We've got to get him to a hospital." Cargraves sat up and tried to stand up. "Ow!" He sat down suddenly.

"It's his foot," said Art.

"Let's have a look at it. Hold still, Doc." They took his left shoe off gently and peeled back the sock. Morrie felt it over. "What do you think, Art?"

Art examined it. "It's either a sprain or a break. We'll have to have an X-ray."

"Where's Ross?" Cargraves persisted. "We've got to get him to a hospital."

"Sure, sure," Morrie agreed. "We've got to get you to one, too. We moved Ross up to the cabin."

"I want to see him."

"Comin' up! Half a sec, while I get the car."

With Art's help Cargraves managed to get up on his good foot and hobble to the door. Getting down from the ship's door was painful, but he made it, and fell thankfully into the seat of the car.

"Who's there?" Ross called out, as they came in with Cargraves leaning on the two boys.

"All of us," Art told him.

Cargraves saw that Ross was lying in his bunk with his eyes covered with a handkerchief. Cargraves hobbled over to him. "How is it, kid?" he said huskily.

"Oh, it's you, Doc. I'll get by. It'll take more than that to do me in. How are you?"

"I'm all right. How about your eyes?"

"Well," Ross admitted, "to tell the truth, they don't work too well. All I see is purple and green lights." He kept his voice steady, almost cheerful, but the pulse in his neck was throbbing visibly. Cargraves started to remove the bandage. Morrie stopped him.

"Let the bandage alone, Doc," he said firmly. "There's nothing to see. Wait till we get him to a hospital."

"But . . . Okay, okay. Let's get on with it."

"We were just waiting for you. Art will drive you."

"What are you going to do?"

"I," said Morrie, "am going to climb up on the roof of this

shack with a load of sandwiches and a gun. I'll still be there when you get back."

"But—" Cargraves shrugged and let the matter pass.

Morrie scrambled down when they got back and helped Cargraves hobble into the cabin. Ross was led in by Art; his eyes were bandaged professionally and a pair of dark glasses stuck out of his shirt pocket. "What's the score?" Morrie demanded of all of them, but his eyes were fastened on Ross.

"It's too early to tell," Cargraves said heavily, as he eased into a chair. "No apparent damage, but the optic nerve seems paralyzed."

Morrie clucked and said nothing. Ross groped at a chair and sat down. "Relax," he advised Morrie. "I'll be all right. The flash produced a shock in the eyes. The doctor told me all about it. Sometimes a case like this goes on for three months or so, then it's all right."

Cargraves bit his lip. The doctor had told him more than he had told Ross; sometimes it was not all right; sometimes it was permanent.

"How about you, Doc?"

"Sprain, and a wrenched back. They strapped me up."

"Nothing else?"

"No. Anti-tetanus shots for both of us, but that was just to be on the safe side."

"Well," Morrie announced cheerfully, "it looks to me as if the firm will be back in production in short order."

"No," Cargraves denied. "No, it won't be. I've been trying to tell these goons something ever since we left the hospital, but they wouldn't listen. We're through. The firm is busted."

None of the boys said anything. He went on, raising his voice. "There won't be any trip to the moon. Can't you see that?"

Morrie looked at him impassively. "You said, 'The firm is busted.' You mean you're out of money?"

"Well, not quite, but that's a factor. What I meant—"

"I've got some E-bonds," Ross announced, turning his bandaged head.

"That's not the point," Cargraves answered, with great gentleness. "I appreciate the offer; don't think I don't. And don't think I want to give up. But I've had my eyes opened. It was foolish, foolish from the start, sheer folly. But I let my desires outweigh my judgment. I had no business getting you kids into this. Your father was right, Ross. Now I've got to do what I can to make amends."

Ross shook his head. Morrie glanced at Art and said, "How about it, medical officer?"

Art looked embarrassed, started to speak, and changed his mind. Instead he went to the medicine cabinet, and took out a fever thermometer. He came back to Cargraves. "Open your mouth, Uncle."

Cargraves started to speak. Art popped the tube in his mouth. "Don't talk while I'm taking your temperature," he warned, and glanced at his wrist watch.

"Why, what the—"

"Keep your mouth closed!"

Cargraves subsided, fuming. Nobody said anything until Art reached again for the thermometer. "What does it say?" Morrie demanded.

"A tenth over a hundred."

"Let me see that," Cargraves demanded. Art held it away from him. The doctor stood up, absent-mindedly putting his weight on his injured foot. He then sat down quite suddenly. Art shook down the thermometer, cleaned it and put it away.

"It's like this," Morrie said firmly. "You aren't boss; I'm boss."

"Huh? What in the world has got into you, Morrie?"

Morrie said, "How about it, Art?"

Art looked embarrassed but said stubbornly, "That's how it is, Uncle."

"Ross?"

"I'm not sure of the pitch," Ross said slowly, "but I see what they are driving at. I'm stringing along with Art and Morrie."

Cargraves' head was beginning to ache again. "I think you've all gone crazy. But it doesn't make any difference; we're washed up anyhow."

"No," Morrie said, "we're not crazy, and it remains to be seen whether or not we're washed up. The point is: you are on the sick list. That puts me in charge; you set it up that way yourself. You can't give any orders or make any decisions for us until you are off the sick list."

"But—" He stopped and then laughed, his first laugh in hours. "This is nuts. You're hijacking me, with a technicality. You can't put me on the sick list for a little over a degree of temperature."

"You weren't put on the sick list for that; you are being kept on the sick list for it. Art put you on the sick list while you were unconscious. You stay there until he takes you off—you made him medical officer."

"Yes, but—Look here, Art—you put me on the sick list earlier? This isn't just a gag you thought up to get around me?"

"No, Uncle," Art assured him, "when I told Morrie that you said not to accept the thorium, he tried to check with you. But you were out like a light. We didn't know what to do, until Morrie pointed out that I was medical officer and that I had to decide whether or not you were in shape to carry out your job. So—"

"But you don't have . . . Anyway, all this is beside the point. I sent the thorium back; there isn't going to be any trip; there isn't any medical officer; there isn't any second-in-command. The organization is done with."

"But that's what I've been trying to tell you, Uncle. We didn't send the thorium back."

"Huh?"

"I've signed for it," Morrie explained, "as your agent."

Cargraves rubbed his forehead. "You kids—you beat me! However, it doesn't make any difference. I have made up my mind that the whole idea was a mistake. *I* am not going to the moon and that puts the kibosh on it. Wait a minute, Morrie! I'm not disputing that you are in charge, temporarily—but I can talk, can't I?"

"Sure. You can talk. But nothing gets settled until your temperature is down and you've had a night's sleep."

"Okay. But you'll see that things settle themselves. You have to have me to build the space drive. Right?"

"Mmmm . . . yes."

"No maybes about it. You kids are learning a lot about atomics, fast. But you don't know enough. I haven't even told you, yet, how the drive is supposed to work."

"We could get a license on your patent, even without your permission," Ross put in. "We're going to the moon."

"Maybe you could—if you could get another nuclear physicist to throw in with you. But it wouldn't be this enterprise. Listen to me, kids. Never mind any touch of fever I've got. I'm right in the head for the first time since I got banged on the head at your rocket test. And I want to explain some things. We've got to bust up, but I don't want you sore at me."

"What do you mean: 'since you got banged on the head'?"

Cargraves spoke very soberly. "I knew at that time, after we looked over the grounds, that that 'accident' was no accident. Somebody put a slug on me, probably with a blackjack. I couldn't see why then and I still don't see why. I should have seen the light when we started having prowlers. But I couldn't believe that it was really serious. Yesterday I knew it was. Nobody impersonates a federal inspector unless he's playing for high stakes and willing to do almost anything. It had me worried sick. But I still didn't see why anybody would want anything we've got and I certainly didn't think they would try to kill us."

"You think they meant to kill us?" asked Ross.

"Obviously. The phony inspector booby-trapped us. He planted some sort of a bomb."

"Maybe he meant to wreck the ship rather than to kill us."

"What for?"

"Well," said Art, "maybe they're after the senior prizes."

"Wrecking our ship won't win him any prize money."

"No, but it could keep us from beating him."

"Maybe. It's far-fetched but it's as good an answer as any. But the reason doesn't matter. Somebody is out to get us and he's willing to go to any lengths. This desert is a lonely place. If I could afford a squadron of guards around the place we might bull it through. But I can't. And I can't let you kids get shot or bombed. It's not fair to you, nor to your parents."

Art looked stubborn and unhappy. Morrie's face was an impassive mask. Finally he said, "If that's all you've got to say, Doc, I suggest we eat and adjourn until tomorrow."

"All right."

"Not just yet." Ross had stood up. He groped for the back of his chair and tried to orient himself. "Where are you, Doc?"

"I'm here—to your left."

"All right. Now I've got some things to say. I'm going to the moon. I'm going to the moon, somehow, whether you want to go or not. I'm going to the moon even if I never get back the use of my eyes. I'm going to the moon even if Morrie or Art has to lead me around. You can do as you please.

"But I'm surprised at you, Doc," he went on. "You're afraid to take the responsibility for us, aren't you? That's the size of it?"

"Yes, Ross, that's the size of it."

"Yet you were willing to take the responsibility of leading us on a trip to the moon. That's more dangerous than anything that could happen here, isn't it? Isn't it?"

Cargraves bit his lip. "It's different."

"I'll tell you how it's different. If we get killed trying to make the jump, ninety-nine chances out of a hundred we all get killed together. You don't have to go back and explain anything to our parents. That's how it's different!"

"Now, Ross!"

"Don't 'Now, Ross' me. What the deuce, Doc?" he went on bitterly. "Suppose it had happened on the moon: would you be twittering around, your morale all shot? Doc, I'm surprised at you. If you are going to have an attack of nerves every time the going gets a little tough, I vote for Morrie for permanent captain."

"That's about enough, Ross," Morrie put in quietly.

"Okay. I was through, anyway." Ross sat down.

There was an uncomfortable silence. Morrie broke it by saying, "Art, let's you and me throw together some food. Study hour will be late as it is." Cargraves looked surprised. Morrie saw his expression and continued. "Sure. Why not? Art and I can take turns reading aloud."

Cargraves pretended to be asleep that night long before he was. Thus he was able to note that Morrie and Art stood alternate watches all night, armed and ready. He refrained from offering any advice.

The boys both went to bed at sunrise. Cargraves got painfully but quietly out of bed and dressed. Leaning on a stick he hobbled down to the ship. He wanted to inspect the damage done by the bomb, but he noticed first the case containing the thorium, bulking large because of its antiradiation shipping shield. He saw with relief that the seal of the atomics commission was intact. Then he hunched himself inside the ship and made his way slowly to the drive compartment.

The damage was remarkably light. A little welding, he thought, some swaging, and some work at the forge would fix it. Puzzled, he cautiously investigated further.

He found six small putty-like pieces of a plastic material concealed under the back part of the shield. Although there were no primers and no wiring attached to these innocent-appearing little objects, he needed no blueprint to tell him what they were. It was evident that the saboteur had not had time to wire more than one of his deadly little toys in the few minutes he had been alone. His intentions had certainly been to wreck the drive compartment— and kill whoever was unlucky enough to set off the trap.

With great care, sweating as he did so, he removed the chunks of explosive, then searched carefully for more. Satisfied, he slipped them into his shirt pocket and went outside. The scramble, hampered by his game leg, out of the door of the rocket, made him shaky; he felt like a human bomb. Then he limped to the corral

fence and threw them as far as he could out into the already con-
taminated fields. He took the precaution of removing them all
from his person before throwing the first one, as he wanted to be
ready to fall flat. But there was no explosion; apparently the stuff
was relatively insensitive to shock. Finished, he turned away, content to let sun and rain disintegrate the stuff.

He found Ross outside the cabin, turning his bandaged face to
the morning sun. "That you, Doc?" the young man called out.

"Yes. Good morning, Ross."

"Good morning, Doc." Ross moved toward the scientist, feeling the ground with his feet. "Say, Doc—I said some harsh things
last night. I'm sorry. I was upset, I guess."

"Forget it. We are all upset." He found the boy's groping hand
and pressed it. "How are your eyes?"

Ross's face brightened. "Coming along fine. I slipped a peek
under the bandage when I got up. I can see—"

"Good!"

"I can see, but everything's fuzzy and I see double, or maybe
triple. But the light hurt my eyes so I put the bandage back."

"It sounds as if you are going to be all right," Cargraves ventured. "But take it easy."

"Oh, I will. Say, Doc . . ."

"Yes, Ross?"

"Nnnn . . . oh, nothing. Never mind."

"I think I know, Ross. I've changed my mind. I changed my
mind last night before I got to sleep. We're going through with it."

"Good!"

"Maybe it's good, maybe it's bad. I don't know. But if that's
the way you fellows feel about it, I'm with you. We'll go if we
have to walk."

8.
SKYWARD!

"*That sounds more like you*, Doc!"

"Thanks. Are the others up yet?"

"Not yet. They didn't get much sleep."

"I know. Let's let them sleep. We'll sit out in the car. Take my arm."

When they had settled themselves Ross asked, "Doc, how much longer will it take to get ready?"

"Not long. Why?"

"Well, I think the key to our problems lies in how fast we can get away. If these attempts to stop us keep up, one of them is going to work. I wish we would leave today."

"We can't do that," Cargraves answered, "but it shouldn't be long. First I've got to install the drive, but it's really just a matter of fitting the parts together. I had almost everything prepared before I ever laid eyes on you guys."

"I wish my blinkers weren't on the fritz."

"It's one job I'll have to do myself. Not that I am trying to keep you out of it, Ross," he added hastily, seeing the boy's expression. "I've never explained it because I thought it would be easier when we had all the gear in front of us."

"Well, how does it work?"

"You remember Heron's turbine in elementary physics? Little boiler on the bottom and a whirligig like a lawn sprinkler on top? You heat the boiler, steam comes up through the whirligig, and makes it whirl around. Well, my drive works like that. Instead of fire, I use a thorium atomic power pile; instead of water, I use zinc.

We boil the zinc, vaporize it, get zinc 'steam.' We let the 'steam' exhaust through the jet. That's the works."

Ross whistled. "Simple—and neat. But will it work?"

"I know it'll work. I was trying for a zinc 'steam' power plant when I hit on it. I got the hard, hot jet I wanted, but I couldn't get the turbine to stand up under it. Broke all the blades. Then I realized I had a rocket drive."

"It's slick, Doc! But say—why don't you use lead? You'd get more mass with less bulk."

"A good point. Concentrated mass means a smaller rocket motor, smaller tanks, smaller ship, less dead weight all around. But mass isn't our main trouble; what we've got to have is a high-velocity jet. I used zinc because it has a lower boiling point than lead. I want to superheat the vapor so as to get a good, fast jet, but I can't go above the stable limit of the moderator I'm using."

"Carbon?"

"Yes, carbon—graphite. We use carbon to moderate the neutron flow and cadmium inserts to control the rate of operation. The radiations get soaked up in a bath of liquid zinc. The zinc boils and the zinc 'steam' goes whizzing out the jet as merry as can be."

"I see. But why don't you use mercury instead of zinc? It's heavier than lead and has a lower boiling point than either one of them."

"I'd like to, but it's too expensive. This is strictly a cut-rate show." Doc broke off as Morrie stuck his head out the cabin door.

"Hi, there! Come to breakfast, or we'll throw it out!"

"Don't do that!" Cargraves slipped a leg over the side of the car—the wrong leg—touched the ground and said, "Ouch!"

"Wait a minute, and lean on me," Ross suggested.

They crept back, helping each other. "Aside from the pile," Cargraves went on, "there isn't much left. The thorium is already imbedded in the graphite according to my calculations. That leaves just two major jobs: the air lock and a teststand run."

The rocket, although it had operated on the trans-Atlantic run above the atmosphere, had no air lock, since its designers had never intended it to be opened up save on the ground. If they were to walk the face of the moon, an air lock, a small compartment with two doors, was necessary. Cargraves planned to weld a steel box around the inside of the present door frame, with a second airtight door, opening inward.

"I can weld the lock," Ross offered, "while you rig the pile. That is, if my eyes clear up in time."

"Even if they do, I don't think it would be smart to stare at a welding arc. Can't the others weld?"

"Well, yes, but just between us chickens, I run a smoother seam."

"We'll see."

At breakfast Cargraves told the other two of his decision to go ahead. Art turned pink and got his words twisted. Morrie said gravely, "I thought your temperature would go down over night. What are the plans?"

"Just the same, only more so. How's your department?"

"Shucks, I could leave this afternoon. The gyros are purring like kittens; I've calculated Hohmann orbits and S-trajectories till I'm sick of 'em; the computer and me are like that." He held out two fingers.

"Fine. You concentrate on getting the supplies in, then. How about you, Art?"

"Who, me? Why, I've got everything lined up, I guess. Both radars are right on the beam. I've got a couple wrinkles I'd like to try with the FM circuit."

"Is it all right the way it is?"

"Good enough, I guess."

"Then don't monkey with the radios. I can keep you busy."

"Oh, sure."

"How about the radar screen Art was going to rig?" Morrie inquired.

"Eh? Oh, you mean the one for our friend the prowler. Hm . . ." Cargraves studied the matter. "Ross thinks and I agree that the best way to beat the prowler is to get out of here as fast as we can. I don't want that radar out of the ship. It would waste time and always with the chance of busting a piece of equipment we can't afford to replace and can't get along without."

Morrie nodded. "Suits. I still think that a man with a gun in his hands is worth more than a gadget anyhow. See here—there are four of us. That's two hours a night. Let's stand guard."

Cargraves agreed to this. Various plans were offered to supplement the human guard and the charged fence, but all were voted down as too time-consuming, too expensive or impractical. It was decided to let the matter stand, except that lights would be left burning at night, including a string to be rigged around the ship. All of these lines were to be wired to cut over automatically to the ship's batteries.

Cargraves sat down to lunch on Wednesday of the following week with a feeling of satisfaction. The thorium power pile was in place, behind the repaired shield. This in itself was good; he disliked the finicky, ever-dangerous work of handling the radioactive element, even though he used body shields and fished at it with tongs.

But the pile was built; the air lock had been welded in place and tested for air-tightness; almost all the supplies were aboard. Acceleration hammocks had been built for Art and Ross (Cargraves and Morrie would ride out the surges of power in the two pilot seats). The power pile had been operated at a low level; all was well, he felt, and the lights on the board were green.

The phony inspector had not showed up again, nor were the night watches disturbed. Best of all, Ross's eyesight had continued to improve; the eye specialist had pronounced him a cure on Monday, subject to wearing dark glasses for a couple of weeks.

Cargraves' sprain still made him limp, but he had discarded his stick. Nothing bothered him. He tackled *Aggregate à la Galileo* (hash to ordinary mortals) with enthusiasm, while thinking about a paper he would write for the *Physical Review. Some Verified Experimental Factors in Space Flight* seemed like a good title—by Doctor Donald Morris Cargraves, B.S., Sc.D., LL.D., Nobel Prize, Nat. Adad., Fr. Acad., etc. The honors were not yet his—he was merely trying them on for size.

The car ground to a stop outside and Art came in with the mail. "Santa Claus is here!" he greeted them. "One from your folks, Ross, and one from that synthetic blonde you're sweet on."

"I'm not sweet on her and she's a natural blonde," Ross answered emphatically.

"Have it your own way—you'll find out. Three for you, Morrie—all business. The rest are yours, Doc," he finished, holding back the one from his mother. "Hash again," he added.

"It's to soften you up for what you're going to eat on the moon," said the cook. "Say, Doc—"

"Yes, Morrie?"

"The canned rations are at the express office in town, it says here. I'll pick 'em up this afternoon. The other two are bills. That finishes my check-off list."

"Good," he answered absently, as he tore open a letter. "You can help Ross and me on the test stand. That's the only big job left." He unfolded the letter and read it.

Then he reread it. Presently Ross noticed that he had stopped eating and said, "What's the matter, Doc?"

"Well, nothing much, but it's awkward. The Denver outfit can't supply the dynamometers for the test stand run." He tossed the letter to Ross.

"How bad off does that leave us?" asked Morrie.

"I don't know, yet. I'll go with you into town. Let's make it right after lunch; I have to call the East Coast and I don't want to get boxed in by the time difference."

"Can do."

Ross handed the letter back. "Aren't there plenty of other places to buy them?"

"Hardly 'plenty.' Half-a-million-pound dynamometers aren't stock items. We'll try Baldwin Locomotives."

"Why don't we make them?" asked Art. "We made our own for the *Starstruck* series."

Cargraves shook his head. "High as my opinion is of you lugs as good, all-around jack-leg mechanics and pretzel benders, some jobs require special equipment. But speaking of the *Starstruck* series," he went on, intentionally changing the subject, "do you guys realize we've never named the ship? How does *Starstruck VI* appeal to you?"

Art liked it. Morrie objected that it should be *Moonstruck*. But Ross had another idea. "*Starstruck* was a good enough name for our model rockets, but we want something with a little more—oh, I don't know; dignity, I guess—for the moon ship."

"The *Pioneer*?" "Corny." "The *Thor*—for the way she's powered." "Good, but not enough." "Let's call it the *Einstein*."

"I see why you want to name it for Doctor Einstein," Cargraves put in, "but maybe I've got another name that will symbolize the same thing to you. How about the *Galileo*?"

There was no dissension; the members of the Galileo Club again were unanimous. The man who had first seen and described the mountains of the moon, the man whose very name had come to stand for steadfast insistence on scientific freedom and the freely inquiring mind—his name was music to them.

Cargraves wondered whether or not their own names would be remembered after more than three centuries. With luck, with lots of luck—Columbus had not been forgotten. If the luck ran out, well, a rocket crash was a fast clean death.

The luck appeared to be running out, and with nothing as gallant and spectacular as a doomed and flaming rocket. Cargraves sweated in a phone booth until after five o'clock, East Coast time, and then another hour until it was past five in Chicago as well before he admitted that dynamometers of the size he needed were not to be had on short notice.

He blamed himself for having slipped up, while neglecting to credit himself with having planned to obtain the instruments from the Denver firm for reasons of economy; he had expected to get them second-hand. But blaming himself comforted him.

Morrie noted his long face as he climbed into the heavily loaded little car. "No soap, eh?"

"No soap. Let's get back to camp."

They sped along the desert road in worried silence for several minutes. Finally Morrie spoke up. "How about this, Doc? Make a captive run on the ground with the same yoke and frame you planned to use, but without dynamometers."

"What good would that do? I have to know what the thrust is."

"I'm getting to that. We put a man inside. He watches the accelerometer—the pendulum accelerometer of course; not the distance-integrating one. It read in g's. Figure the number of gravities against the gross weight of the ship at the time and you come out with your thrust in pounds."

Cargraves hesitated. The boy's mistake was so obvious and yet so easy to make that he wished to point it out without hurting his pride. "It's a clever plan, except that I would want to use remote control—there's always the chance that a new type of atomic-fission power plant will blow up. But that's not the hitch; if the ship is anchored to the ground, it won't be accelerating no matter how much thrust is developed."

"Oh!" said Morrie. "Hmm. I sure laid an egg on that one, Doc."

"Natural mistake."

After another five miles Morrie spoke again. "I've got it, Doc. The *Galileo* has to be free to move to show thrust on the accelerometer. Right? Okay, I'll test-fly it. Hold it, hold it," he went on quickly. "I know exactly what you are going to say: you won't let any one take a risk if you can help it. The ship might blow up, or it might crash. Okay, so it might. But it's my job. I'm not essential to the trip; you are. You have to have Ross as flight engineer; you have to have Art for the radar and radio; you don't have to have a second pilot. I'm elected."

Cargraves tried to make his voice sound offhand. "Morrie, your analysis does your heart credit, but not your head. Even if what you said is true, the last part doesn't quite add up. I may be essential, *if* the trip is made. But if the test flight goes wrong, if the power pile blows, or if the ship won't handle and crashes, then there won't be any trip and I'm *not* essential."

Morrie grinned. "You're sharp as a tack, Doc."

"Tried to frame me, eh? Well, I may be old and feeble but I'm not senile. Howsomever, you've given me the answer. We skip the captive run and test-fly it. I test-fly it."

Morrie whistled, "When?"

"Just as soon as we get back."

Morrie pushed the accelerator down to the floor boards; Cargraves wished that he had kept quiet until they reached the camp.

Forty minutes later he was handing out his final instructions. "Drive outside the reservation and find some place at least ten miles away where you can see the camp and where you can huddle down behind a road cut or something. If you see a Hiroshima mushroom, *don't try to come back.* Drive on into town and report to the authorities." He handed Ross a briefcase. "In case I stub my toe, give this stuff to your father. He'll know what to do with it. Now get going. I'll give you twenty minutes. My watch says seven minutes past five."

"Just a minute, Doc."

"What is it, Morrie?" His tones showed nervous irritability.

"I've polled the boys and they agree with me. The *Galileo* is expendable but you aren't. They want you left around to try it again."

"That's enough on that subject, Morrie."

"Well, I'll match you for it."

"You're on thin ice, Morrie!"

"Yes, sir." He climbed in the car. The other two squeezed in beside him. "So long!" "Good luck!"

He waved back at them as they drove away, then turned toward the open door of the *Galileo.* He was feeling suddenly very lonely.

The boys found such a spot and crouched down behind a bank, like soldiers in a trench. Morrie had a small telescope; Art and Ross were armed with the same opera glasses they had used in their model rocket tests. "He's closed the door," announced Morrie.

"What time is it?"

"I've got five twenty-five."

"Any time now. Keep your eyes peeled." The rocket was tiny even through the opera glasses; Morrie's view was slightly better. Suddenly he yelled. "That's it! Geronimo!"

The tail jet, bright silver even in the sun light, had flared out. The ship did not move. "There go his nose jets!" Red and angry, the aniline-and-nitric reached out in front. The *Galileo*, being equipped with nose and belly maneuvering jets, could take off without a launching platform or catapult. He brought his belly jets into play now; the bow of the *Galileo* reared up, but the opposing nose and tail jets kept her nailed to one spot.

"He's off!" The red plumes from the nose were suddenly cut and the ship shot away from the ground. It was over their heads almost before they could catch their breaths. Then it was beyond them and shooting toward the horizon. As it passed over the mountains, out of sight, the three exhaled simultaneously. "Gosh!" said Art, very softly.

Ross started to run. "Hey, where y' going?"

"Back to the camp! We want to be there before he is!"

"Oh!" They tore after him.

Ross set a new high in herding the rig back to the camp site, but his speed did not match their urgency. Nor were they ahead of time. The *Galileo* came pouring back over the horizon and was already braking on her nose jets when the car slammed to a stop.

She came in at a steep dive, with the drive jet already dead. The nose jets splashed the ground on the very spot where she had taken off. He kicked her up with the belly jets and she pancaked in place. Morrie shook his head. "What a landing!" he said reverently.

Cargraves fell out of the door into a small mob. The boys yelled and pounded him on the back.

"How did she behave? How did she handle?"

"Right on the button! The control of the drive jet is logy but we expected that. Once she's hot she doesn't want to cool off. You have to get rid of your head of 'steam.' I was half way to Oklahoma City before I could slow down enough to turn and come back."

"Boy, oh boy! What a ship!"

"When do we start?"

Cargraves' face sobered. "Does staying up all night to pack suit you?"

"Does it! Just try us!"

"It's a deal. Art, get in the ship and get going with the radio. Get the Associated Press station at Salt Lake. Get the United Press. Call up the radio news services. Tell them to get some television pick-ups out here. The lid is off now. Make them realize there is a story here."

"On my way!" He scrambled up into the ship, then paused in the door. "Say—what if they don't believe me?"

"Make them believe you. Tell them to call Doctor Larksbee at the commission for confirmation. Tell them that if they miss they'll be scooped on the biggest story since the war. And say—call up Mr. Buchanan on the forestry frequency. He's kept his mouth shut for us; he ought to be in on it."

By midnight the job was practically complete and Cargraves insisted that they take turns lying down, two at a time, not to sleep, but just to keep from starting the trip completely tired out. The fuel tanks for the belly and nose jets were topped off and the specially installed reserve tanks were filled. The tons of zinc which served the main drive were already aboard as well as an equal weight of powdered reserve. The food was aboard; the carefully rationed water was aboard. (Water was no problem; the air-conditioner would scavenge the vapor of their own exhalations.) The liquid oxygen tanks were full. Cargraves himself had carried aboard the two Garands, excusing it to himself on the pretext that they might land in some wild spot on the return trip . . . that, despite the fact they had ripped the bindings from their few books in order to save space and weight.

He was tired. Only the carefully prepared lists enabled him to be sure that the ship was in all respects ready—or would be soon.

The boys were tired, confused, and excited. Morrie had worked the problem of their departure trajectory three times and then had gotten nerves over it, although it had checked to the last decimal each time. He was gnawed by fear that he had made some silly and fatal mistake and was not satisfied until Cargraves had gotten the same answer, starting with a clear board.

Mr. Buchanan, the Ranger, showed up about one o'clock. "Is this the Central New Mexico Insane Asylum?" he inquired pleasantly.

Cargraves admitted it. "I've wondered what you folks were up to," the Ranger went on. "Of course I saw your ship, but your message surely surprised me. I hope you don't mind me thinking you're crazy; I wish you luck just the same."

"Thanks." Cargraves showed him the ship, and explained their plans. The moon was full and an hour past its greatest elevation. They planned to take off shortly after daybreak, as it was sinking in the west. This would lose them the earth's spin, but, after the trial run, Cargraves did not care; he had power to throw away. Waiting twelve hours to save a difference of about 1,600 miles per hour was more than his nerves could stand.

He had landed the rocket faced west; it would save jacking her around as well.

Buchanan looked the layout over and asked where the jets would splash. Cargraves showed him. Whereupon Buchanan asked, "Have you arranged for any guards?"

In truth, Cargraves had forgotten it. "Never mind," said Buchanan, "I'll call Captain Taylor and get some state police over."

"Never mind calling; we'll radio. Art!"

The press started showing up at four; by the time the state police arrived, Cargraves knew that he had been saved real grief. The place was crowded. Escorts were necessary from the outer gate to the corral to make sure that no one drove on the danger-studded mock-battle fields. Once in the corral it took the firm hand of the state police to keep them there—and to keep them from swarming over the ship.

At five they ate their last breakfast in the camp, with a guard at the door to give them some peace. Cargraves refused to be interviewed; he had prepared a typed handout and given copies to Buchanan to distribute. But the boys were button-holed whenever his back was turned. Finally Captain Taylor assigned a bodyguard to each.

They marched in a hollow square of guards to the ship. Flash guns dazzled their eyes and television scanners followed their movements. It seemed impossible that this was the same lonely spot where, only hours before, they had worried about silent prowlers in the dark.

Cargraves had the boys climb in, then turned to Buchanan and Captain Taylor. "Ten minutes, gentlemen. Are you sure you can keep everybody clear? Once I get in the seat I can't see the ground near me."

"Don't worry, Captain Cargraves," Taylor assured him. "Ten minutes it is."

Buchanan stuck out his hand. "Good luck, Doctor. Bring me back some green cheese."

A man came puffing up, dodged past a guard, and thrust a folded paper in Cargraves' hand. "Here, what's this?" demanded Taylor. "Get back where you belong."

The man shrugged. "It's a court order."

"Eh? What sort?"

"Temporary injunction against flying this ship. Order to appear and show cause why a permanent injunction should not be issued to restrain him from willfully endangering the lives of minors."

Cargraves stared. It felt to him as if the world were collapsing around him. Ross and Art appeared at the door behind him. "Doc, what's up?"

"Hey, there! You boys—come down out of there," yelled the stranger, and then said to Captain Taylor, "I've got another paper directing me to take them in charge on behalf of the court."

"Get back in the ship," Cargraves ordered firmly, and opened the paper. It seemed in order. State of New Mexico and so forth. The stranger began to expostulate. Taylor took him by the arm.

"Take it easy," he said.

"Thanks," said Cargraves. "Mr. Buchanan, can I have a word with you? Captain, will you hang on to this character?"

"Now, I don't want any beef," protested the stranger. "I'm just carrying out my duty."

"I wonder," Cargraves said thoughtfully. He led Buchanan around the nose of the craft and showed him the paper.

"It seems to be in order," Buchanan admitted.

"Maybe. This says it's the order of a *state* court. This is federal territory, isn't it? As a matter of fact, Captain Taylor and his men are here only by your invitation and consent. Isn't that right?"

"Hmmm . . . yes. That's so." Buchanan suddenly jammed the paper in his pocket. "I'll fix his clock!"

"Just a minute." Cargraves told him rapidly about the phony inspector, and the prowlers, matters which he had kept to himself, save for a letter to the Washington CAB office. "This guy may be a phony, or a stooge of a phony. Don't let him get away until you check with the court that supposedly issued this order."

"I won't!"

They went back, and Buchanan called Taylor aside. Cargraves

took the stranger by the arm, not gently. The man protested. "How would you like a poke in the eye?" Cargraves inquired.

Cargraves was six inches taller, and solid. The man shut up. Taylor and Buchanan came back in a moment or two. The state policeman said, "You are due to take off in three minutes, Captain. I had better be sure the crowd is clear." He turned and called out, "Hey! Sergeant Swanson!"

"Yes, sir!"

"Take charge of this guy." It was the stranger, not Cargraves, whom he indicated.

Cargraves climbed in the ship. As he turned to close the door a cheer, ragged at first but growing to a solid roar, hit him. He clamped the door and locked it, then turned. "Places, men."

Art and Ross trotted to their hammocks, directly behind the pilots' seats. These hammocks were vertical, more like stretchers braced upright than garden hammocks. They snapped safety belts across their knees and chests.

Morrie was already in his chair, legs braced, safety belts buckled, head back against the shock pad. Cargraves slipped into the seat beside him, favoring his bad foot as he did so. "All set, Morrie." His eyes glanced over the instrument board, particularly noticing the temperature of the zinc and the telltale for position of the cadmium damping plates.

He buckled himself in and glanced out the quartz glass screen ahead of him. The field was clear as far as he could see. Staring straight at him, round and beautiful, was their destination. Under his right hand, mounted on the arm rest, was a large knurled knob. He grasped it.

"Art?"

"Ready, sir."

"Ross?"

"Ready, Captain."

"Co-pilot?"

"Ready, Captain. Time, six-oh-one."

He twisted the knob slowly to the right. Back behind him, actuated by remote control, cadmium shields slowly withdrew from between lattices of graphite and thorium; uncountable millions of neutrons found it easier to seek atoms of thorium to destroy. The tortured nuclei, giving up the ghost, spent their energy in boiling the molten zinc.

The ship began to tremble.

With his left hand he cut in the nose rockets, balancing them against the increasing surge from the rear. He slapped in the belly jets; the ship reared. He let the nose jets die.

The *Galileo* leaped forward, pressing them back into their pads.

They were headed skyward, out and far.

9.
INTO THE LONELY DEPTHS

To Ross and Art the world seemed to rotate dizzily through ninety degrees. They had been standing up, strapped to their up-right hammocks, and staring straight forward past Cargraves and Morrie out through the conning port at the moon and the western horizon.

When the rocket took off it was as if they had been suddenly forced backwards, flat on their backs and pushed heavily into the cushions and springs. Which, in a way, was exactly what had happened to them. It was the powerful thrust of the jet which had forced them back against the springs and held them there. The force of the drive made the direction they were traveling "up."

But the moon still stared back at them, dead ahead through the port; "up" was also "west." From where the lay, flat on their backs, Cargraves and Morrie were above them and were kept from falling on them by the heavy steel thrust members which supported the piloting chairs.

The moon shimmered and boiled under the compression waves of air. The scream of the frantic molecules of air against the skin of the craft was louder and even more nerve-racking than steady thunder of the jet below them. The horizon dropped steadily away from the disk of the moon as they shot west and gained altitude. The sky, early morning gray as they took off, turned noonday blue as their flat climb took them higher and higher into the sunlight.

The sky started to turn purple and the stars came out. The scream of the air was less troublesome. Cargraves cut in his gyros and let Joe the Robot correct his initial course; the moon swung gently to the right about half its width and steadied. "Everybody all right?" he called out, his attention free of the controls for a moment.

"Swell!" Art called back.

"Somebody's sitting on my chest," Ross added.

"What's that?"

"I say, somebody's sitting on my chest!" Ross shouted.

"Well, wait a bit. His brother will be along in a minute."

"What did you say?"

"Never mind!" Cargraves shouted. "It wasn't important. Copilot!"

"Yes, Captain!"

"I'm going into full automatic. Get ready to check our course."

"Aye, aye, sir." Morrie clamped his octant near his face and shifted his head a little so that he could see the scope of the belly radar easily. He dug his head into the pads and braced his arms and hands; he knew what was coming. "Astrogator ready!"

The sky was black now and the stars were sharp. The image of the moon had ceased to shake and the unearthly scream of the air had died away, leaving only the tireless thunder of the jet. They were above the atmosphere, high and free.

Cargraves yelled, "Hang on to your hats, boys! *Here we go!*" He turned full control over to Joe, the robot pilot. That mindless, mechanical-and-electronic worthy figuratively shook his nonexistent head and decided he did not like the course. The image of the moon swung "down" and toward the bow, in terms of the ordinary directions in the ship, until the rocket was headed in a direction nearly forty degrees further east than was the image of the moon.

Having turned the ship to head for the point where the moon would be when the *Galileo* met it, rather than headed for where it now was, Joe turned his attention to the jet. The cadmium plates were withdrawn a little farther; the rocket really bit in and began to dig.

Ross found that there was indeed a whole family on his chest. Breathing was hard work and his eyes seemed foggy.

If Joe had had feelings he need have felt no pride in what he had just done, for his decisions had all been made for him before the ship left the ground. Morrie had selected, with Cargraves' approval, one of several three-dimensional cams and had installed it in Joe's innards. The cam "told" Joe what sort of a course to follow to the moon, what course to head first, how fast to gun the rocket and how long to keep it up. Joe could not see the moon—Joe had never heard of the moon—but his electronic senses could perceive how the ship was headed in relation to the steady, unswerving spin of the gyroes and then head the ship in the direction called for by the cam in his tummy.

The cam itself had been designed by a remote cousin of Joe's, the great "Eniac" computer at the University of Pennsylvania. By means of the small astrogation computer in the ship either Morrie or Cargraves could work out any necessary problem and control the *Galileo* by hand, but Joe, with the aid of his cousin, could do the same thing better, faster, more accurately and with unsleeping care—provided the human pilot knew what to ask of him and how to ask it.

Joe had not been invented by Cargraves; thousands of scientists, engineers, and mathematicians had contributed to his existence. His grandfathers had guided the Nazi V-2 rockets in the horror-haunted last days of World War II. His fathers had been developed for the deadly, ocean-spanning guided-missiles of the UN world police force. His brothers and sisters were found in every rocket ship, private and commercial, passenger-carrying or unmanned, that cleft the skies of earth.

Trans-Atlantic hop or trip to the moon, it was all one to Joe. He did what his cam told him to do. He did not care, he did not even know.

Cargraves called out, "How you making out down there?"

"All right, I guess," Ross answered, his voice laboring painfully.

"I feel sick," Art admitted with a groan.

"Breathe through your mouth. Take deep breaths."

"I can't."

"Well, hang on. It won't be long."

In fact it was only fifty-five seconds at full drive until Joe, still advised by his cam, decided that they had had enough of full drive. The cadmium plates slid farther back into the power pile, thwarting the neutrons; the roar of the rocket drive lessened.

The ship did not slow down; it simply ceased to accelerate so rapidly. It maintained all the speed it had gained and the frictionless vacuum of space did nothing to slow its headlong plunge. But the acceleration was reduced to one earth-surface gravity, one *g*, enough to overcome the powerful tug of the earth's mighty weight and thereby permit the ship to speed ahead unchecked—a little less than one *g*, in fact, as the grasp of the earth was already loosening and would continue to drop off to the change-over, more than 200,000 miles out in space, where the attraction of the moon and that of the earth are equal.

For the four in the ship the reduction in the force of the jet had returned them to a trifle less than normal weight, under an artificial gravity produced by the drive of the jet. This false "gravity" had nothing to do with the pull of the earth; the attraction of the earth can be felt only when one is anchored to it and supported by it, its oceans, or its air.

The attraction of the earth exists out in space, but the human body has no senses which can perceive it. If a man were to fall from a tremendous height, say fifty thousand miles, it would not seem to him that he was falling but rather that the earth was rushing up to meet him.

After the tremendous initial drive had eased off, Cargraves called out again to Art. "Feeling any better, kid?"

"I'm all right now," Art replied.

"Fine. Want to come up here where you can see better?"

"Sure!" responded both Art and Ross, with one voice.

"Okay. Watch your step."

"We will." The two unstrapped themselves and climbed up to the control station by means of hand and toe holds welded to the sides of the ship. Once there they squatted on the supporting beams for the pilots' chairs, one on each side. They looked out.

The moon had not been visible to them from their hammock positions after the change in course. From their new positions they could see it, near the "lower" edge of the conning port. It was full, silver white and so dazzling bright that it hurt their eyes, although not sufficiently nearer to produce any apparent increase in size. The stars around it in the coal-black sky were hard bright diamonds, untwinkling.

"Look at that," breathed Ross. "Look at old Tycho shining out like a searchlight. Boy!"

"I wish we could see the earth," said Art. "This bucket ought to have more than one view port."

"What do you expect for a dollar-six-bits?" asked Ross. "Chimes? The *Galileo* was a freighter."

"I can show it to you in the scope," Morrie offered, and switched on the piloting radar in the belly. The screen lit up after a few seconds but the picture was disappointing. Art could read it well enough—it was his baby—but aesthetically it was unsatisfying. It was no more than a circular plot reading in bearing and distance; the earth was simply a vague mass of light on that edge of the circle which represented the astern direction.

"That's not what I want," Art objected. "I want to *see* it. I want to see it shape up like a globe and see the continents and the oceans."

"You'll have to wait until tomorrow, then, when we cut the drive and swing ship. Then you can see the earth and the sun, too."

"Okay. How fast are we going? Never mind—I see," he went on, peering at the instrument board. "Thirty-three hundred miles per hour."

"You're looking at it wrong," Ross corrected him. "It says 14,400 miles per hour."

"You're crazy."

"Like fun. Your eyes have gone bad."

"Easy, boys, easy," Cargraves counseled. "You are looking at different instruments. What kind of speed do you want?"

"I want to know how fast we're going," Art persisted.

"Now, Art, I'm surprised at you. After all, you've had every one of these instruments apart. Think what you're saying."

Art stared at the instrument board again, then looked sheepish. "Sure, I forgot. Let's see now—we've gained 14,000 and some, close to 15,000 now, miles per hour in free fall—but we're not falling."

"We're always falling," Morrie put in, smug for the moment in his status as pilot. "You fall all the time from the second you take off, but you drive to beat the fall."

"Yes, yes, I know," Art cut him off. "I was just mixed up for a moment. Thirty-three hundred is the speed I want— 3310 now."

"Speed" in space is a curiously slippery term, as it is relative to whatever point you select as "fixed"—but the points in space are never fixed. The speed Art settled for was the speed of the *Galileo* along a line from the earth to their meeting place with the moon. This speed was arrived at deep inside Joe the Robot by combining by automatic vector addition three very complicated figures: first was the accumulated acceleration put on the ship by its jet drive, second the motions imposed on the ship by its closeness to the earth—its "free fall" speed of which Art had spoken. And lastly, there was the spin of the earth itself, considered both in amount and direction for the time of day of the take-off and the latitude of the camp site in New Mexico. The last was subtracted, rather than added, insofar as the terms of ordinary arithmetic apply to this sort of figuring.

The problem could be made vastly more complicated. The *Galileo* was riding with the earth and the moon in their yearly journey around the sun—at a speed of about 19 miles per second or approximately 70,000 miles per hour as seen from outer space. In addition, the earth-moon line was sweeping around the earth once each month as it followed the moon—but Joe the Robot had compensated for that when he set them on a course to where the moon *would be* rather than where it *was*.

There were also the complicated motions of the sun and its planets with reference to the giddily whirling "fixed" stars, speeds which could be nearly anything you wanted, depending on which types of stars you selected for your reference points, but all of which speeds are measured in many miles per second.

But Joe cared nothing for these matters. His cam and his many circuits told him how to get them from the earth to the moon; he knew how to do that and Doctor Einstein's notions of relativity worried him not. The mass of machinery and wiring which made up his being did not have worry built into it. It was, however, capable of combining the data that came to it to show that the *Galileo* was now moving somewhat more than 3,300 miles per hour along an imaginary line which joined earth to the point where the moon would be when they arrived.

Morrie could check this figure by radar observations for distance, plus a little arithmetic. If the positions as observed did not match what Joe computed them to be, Morrie could feed Joe the corrections and Joe would accept them and work them into his future calculations as placidly and as automatically as a well-behaved stomach changes starch into sugar.

"Thirty-three hundred miles per hour," said Art. "That's not so much. The V-2 rockets in the war made more than that. Let's open her up wide and see what she'll do. How about it, Doc?"

"Sure," agreed Ross, "we've got a clear road and plenty of room. Let's bust some space."

Cargraves sighed. "See here," he answered, "I did not try to keep you darned young speed demons from risking your necks in that pile of bailing wire you call an automobile, even when I jeopardized my own life by keeping quiet. But I'm going to run this rocket my way. I'm in no hurry."

"Okay, okay, just a suggestion," Ross assured him. He was quiet for a moment, then added, "But there's one thing that bothers me—"

"What?"

"Well, if I've read it once I've read it a thousand times, that you have to go seven miles per second to get away from the earth. Yet here we are going only 3,300 miles per hour."

"We're moving, aren't we?"

"Yeah, but—"

"As a matter of fact we are going to build up a lot more speed before we start to coast. We'll make the first part of the trip much faster than the last part. But suppose we just held our present speed—how long would it take to get to the moon?"

Ross did a little fast mental arithmetic concerning the distance of the moon from the earth, rounding the figure off to 240,000 miles. "About three days."

"What's wrong with that? Never mind," Cargraves went on. "I'm not trying to be a smart Aleck. The misconception is one of the oldest in the book, and it keeps showing up again, every time some non-technical man decides to do a feature story on the future of space travel. It comes from mixing up *shooting* with *rocketry*. If you wanted to fire a shot at the moon, the way Jules Verne proposed, it would have to go seven miles per second when it left the gun or it would fall back. But with a rocket you could make the crossing at a slow walk if you had enough power and enough fuel to keep on driving just hard enough to keep from falling back. Of course it would raise Cain with your mass-ratio. But we're doing something of that sort right now. We've got power to spare; I don't see why we should knock ourselves out with higher acceleration than we have to just to get there a little sooner. The moon will wait. It's waited a long time.

"Anyhow," he added, "no matter what you say and no matter how many physics textbooks are written and studied, people still keep mixing up gunnery and rocketry. It reminds me of that other old chestnut—about how a rocket can't work out in empty space, because it wouldn't have anything to *push* on.

"Go ahead and laugh!" Cargraves continued, seeing their expressions. "It strikes you as funny as a The-World-Is-Flat theory. But I heard an aeronautical engineer, as late as 1943, say just that."

"No! Not really!"

"I certainly did. He was a man with twenty-five years of professional experience and he had worked for both Wright Field and the Navy. But he said that in *1943*. Next year the Nazis were bombing London with V-2s. Yet according to him it couldn't be done!"

"I'd think any man who had ever felt the kick of a shotgun would understand how a rocket works," Ross commented.

"It doesn't work out that way. Mostly it has no effect on his brain cells; it just gives him a sore shoulder." He started to lift himself out of his semi-reclining position in his pilot's chair. "Come on. Let's eat. Wow! My foot's gone to sleep. I want to stoke up and then get some sleep. Breakfast wasn't much good for me—too many people staring down our necks."

"Sleep?" said Art. "Did you say 'sleep'? I can't sleep; I'm too excited. I don't suppose I'll sleep the whole trip."

"Suit yourself. Me, I'm going to soak up shut-eye just as soon as we've eaten. There's nothing to see now, and won't be until we go into free fall. You've had better views of the moon through the telescope."

"It's not the same thing," Art pointed out.

"No, it's not," Cargraves conceded. "Just the same, I intend to reach the moon rested up instead of worn out. Morrie, where did you stow the can openers?"

"I—" Morrie stopped and a look of utter consternation came over his face. "I think I left them behind. I put them down on the sink shelf and then some female reporter started asking me some fool question and—"

"Yeah, I saw," Ross interrupted him. "You were practically rolling over and playing dead for her. It was cute."

Cargraves whistled tunelessly. "I hope that we find out that we haven't left behind anything really indispensable. Never mind the can openers, Morrie. The way I feel I could open a can with my bare teeth."

"Oh, you won't have to do that, Doc," Morrie said eagerly. "I've got a knife with a gadget for—" He was feeling in his pocket as he talked. His expression changed abruptly and he withdrew his hand. "Here are the can openers, Doc."

Ross looked at him innocently. "Did you get her address, Morrie?"

Supper, or late breakfast, as the case may be, was a simple meal, eaten from ration cans. Thereafter Cargraves got out his bedding roll and spread it on the bulkhead—now a deck—which separated the pilot compartment from the hold. Morrie decided to sleep in his co-pilot's chair. It, with its arm rests, head support, and foot rest, was not unlike an extremely well-padded barber's chair for the purpose, one which had been opened to a semi-reclining position. Cargraves let him try it, cautioning him only to lock his controls before going to sleep.

About an hour later Morrie climbed down and spread his roll beside Cargraves. Art and Ross slept on their acceleration hammocks, which were very well adapted to the purpose, as long as the occupant was not strapped down.

Despite the muted roar of the jet, despite the excitement of being in space, they all were asleep in a few minutes. They were dead tired and needed it.

During the "night" Joe the Robot slowly reduced the drive of the jet as the pull of the earth grew less.

Art was first to awaken. He had trouble finding himself for a moment or two and almost fell from his hammock on to the two sleepers below before he recollected his surroundings. When he did it brought him wide awake with a start. Space! He was out in space!—headed for the moon!

Moving with unnecessary quiet, since he could hardly have been heard above the noise of the jet in any case and since both Ross and Cargraves were giving very fair imitations of rocket motors themselves, he climbed out of the hammock and monkeyfooted up to the pilots' seats. He dropped into Morrie's chair, feeling curiously but pleasantly light under the much reduced acceleration.

The moon, now visibly larger and almost painfully beautiful, hung in the same position in the sky, such that he had to let his gaze drop as he lay in the chair in order to return its stare. This bothered him for a moment—how were they ever to reach the moon if the moon did not draw toward the point where they were aiming?

It would not have bothered Morrie, trained as he was in a pilot's knowledge of collision bearings, interception courses, and the like. But, since it appeared to run contrary to common sense, Art worried about it until he managed to visualize the situation somewhat thus: if a car is speeding for a railroad crossing and a train is approaching from the left, so that their combined speeds will bring about a wreck, then the bearing of the locomotive from the automobile will not change, right up to the moment of the collision.

It was a simple matter of similar triangles, easy to see with a diagram but hard to keep straight in the head. The moon was speeding to their meeting place at about 2,000 miles an hour, yet she would never change direction; she would simply grow and grow and grow until she filled the whole sky.

He let his eyes rove over her, naming the lovely names in his mind, Mare Tranquilitatis, Oceanus Procellarum, the lunar Apennines, LaGrange, Ptolemaeus, Mare Imbrium, Catharina. Beautiful words, they rolled on the tongue.

He was not too sure of the capitals of all the fifty-one United States and even naming the United Nations might throw him, but the geography—or was it lunography?—of the moon was as familiar to him as the streets of his home town.

This face of the moon, anyway—he wondered what the other face was like, the face the earth had never seen.

The dazzle of the moon was beginning to hurt his eyes; he looked up and rested them on the deep, black velvet of space, blacker by contrast with the sprinkle of stars.

There were few of the really bright stars in the region toward which the *Galileo* was heading. Aldebaran blazed forth, high and aft, across the port from the moon. The right-hand frame of the port slashed through the Milky Way and a small portion of that incredible river of stars was thereby left visible to him. He picked out the modest lights of Aries, and near mighty Aldebaran hung the ghostly, fairy Pleiades, but dead ahead, straight up, were only faint stars and a black and lonely waste.

He lay back, staring into this remote and solitary depth, vast and remote beyond human comprehension, until he was fascinated by it, drawn into it. He seemed to have left the warmth and safety of the ship and to be plunging deep into the silent blackness ahead.

He blinked his eyes and shivered, and for the first time felt himself wishing that he had never left the safe and customary and friendly scenes of home. He wanted his basement lab, his mother's little shop, and the humdrum talk of ordinary people, people who stayed home and did not worry about the outer universe.

Still the black depths fascinated him. He fingered the drive control under his right hand. He had only to unlock it, twist it all the way to the right, and they would plunge ahead, nailed down by unthinkable acceleration, and speed on past the moon, too early for their date in space with her. On past the moon, away from the sun and the earth behind them, on and on and out and out, until the thorium burned itself cold or until the zinc had boiled away, but not to stop even then, but to continue forever into the weary years and the bottomless depths.

He blinked his eyes and then closed them tight, and gripped both arms of the chair.

10.
THE METHOD OF SCIENCE

"Are you asleep?" The voice in his ear made Art jump; he had still had his eyes closed—it startled him. But it was only Doc, climbing up behind him.

"Oh! Good morning, Doc. Gee, I'm glad to see you. This place was beginning to give me the jim-jams."

"Good morning to you, if it is morning. I suppose it is morning, somewhere." He glanced at his watch. "I'm not surprised that you got the willies, up here by yourself. How would you like to make this trip by yourself?"

"Not me."

"Not me, either. The moon will be just about as lonely but it will feel better to have some solid ground underfoot. But I don't suppose this trip will be really popular until the moon has some nice, noisy night clubs and a bowling alley or two." He settled himself down in his chair.

"That's not very likely, is it?"

"Why not? The moon is bound to be a tourists' stop some day—and have you ever noticed how, when tourists get somewhere new, the first thing they do is to look up the same kind of entertainments they could find just as easily at home?"

Art nodded wisely, while tucking the notion away in his mind. His own experience with tourists and travel was slight—until now! "Say, Uncle, do you suppose I could get a decent picture of the moon through the port?"

Cargraves squinted up at it. "Might. But why waste film? They get better pictures of it from the earth. Wait until we go into a free

orbit and swing ship. Then you can get some really unique pics—
the earth from space. Or wait until we swing around the moon."

"That's what I really want! Pictures of the other side of the
moon."

"That's what I thought." Cargraves paused a moment and then
added, "But how do you know you can get any?"

"But . . . Oh, I see what you mean. It'll be dark on that side."

"That's not exactly what I meant, although that figures in, too,
since the moon will be only about three days past 'new moon,'
'new moon,' that is, for the other side. We'll try to time it to get all
the pics you want on the trip back. But that isn't what I mean: how
do you know there is any back side to the moon? You've never
seen it. Neither has any one else, for that matter."

"But—there has to—I mean, you can see . . ."

"Did I hear you say there wasn't any other side to the moon,
Doc?" It was Ross, whose head had suddenly appeared beside
Cargraves.

"Good morning, Ross. No, I did not say there was no other
side to the moon. I had asked Art to tell me what leads him to
think there *is* one."

Ross smiled. "Don't let him pull your leg, Art. He's just trying
to rib you."

Cargraves grinned wickedly. "Okay, Aristotle, you picked it.
Suppose you try to prove to me that there is a far side to the
moon."

"It stands to reason."

"What sort of reason? Have you ever been there? Ever seen it?"

"No, but—"

"Ever met anybody who's ever seen it? Ever read any accounts by anybody who claimed to have seen it?"

"No, I haven't, but I'm sure there is one."

"Why?"

"Because I can see the front of it."

"What does that prove? Isn't your experience, up to now, limited to things you've seen on earth? For that matter I can name a
thing you've seen on earth that hasn't any back side."

"Huh? What sort of a thing? What are you guys talking
about?" It was Morrie this time, climbing up on the other side.

Art said, "Hi, Morrie. Want your seat?"

"No, thanks. I'll just squat here for the time being." He settled
himself, feet dangling. "What's the argument?"

"Doc," Ross answered, "is trying to prove there isn't any other side to the moon."

"No, no, no," Cargraves hastily denied. "And repeat 'no.' I was trying to get you to prove your assertion that there was one. I was saying that there was a phenomenon even on earth which hasn't any back side, to nail down Ross's argument from experience with other matters—even allowing that earth experience necessarily applies to the moon, which I don't."

"Woops! Slow up! Take the last one first. Don't natural laws apply anywhere in the universe?"

"Pure assumption, unproved."

"But astronomers make predictions, eclipses and such, based on that assumption—and they work out."

"You've got it backwards. The Chinese were predicting eclipses long before the theory of the invariability of natural law was popular. Anyhow, at the best, we notice certain limited similarities between events in the sky and events on earth. Which has nothing to do with the question of a back side of the moon which we've never seen and may not be there."

"But we've seen a lot of it," Morrie pointed out.

"I get you," Cargraves agreed. "Between librations and such—the eccentricity of the moon's orbit and its tilt, we get to peek a little way around the edges from time to time and see about 60 per cent of its surface—*if* the surface is globular. But I'm talking about that missing 40 per cent that we've never seen."

"Oh," said Ross, "you mean the side we can't see might just be sliced off, like an apple with a piece out of it. Well, you may be right, but I'll bet you six chocolate malts, payable when we get back, that you're all wet."

"Nope," Cargraves answered. "This is a scientific discussion and betting is inappropriate. Besides, I might lose. But I did not mean anything of the slice-out-of-an-apple sort. I meant just what I said: no back side at all. The possibility that when we swing around the moon to look at the other side, we won't find anything at all, nothing, just empty space—that when we try to look at the moon from behind it, there won't be any moon to be seen—not from that position. I'm not asserting that that is what we will find; I'm asking you to *prove* that we will find anything."

"Wait a minute," Morrie put in, as Art glanced wildly at the moon as if to assure himself that it was still there—it was! "You mentioned something of that sort on earth—a thing with no back. What was it? I'm from Missouri."

"A rainbow. You can see it from just one side, the side that faces the sun. The other side does not exist."

"But you can't get behind it."

"Then try it with a garden spray some sunny day. Walk around it. When you get behind it, it ain't there."

"Yes, but Doc," Ross objected, "you're just quibbling. The cases aren't parallel. A rainbow is just light waves; the moon is something substantial."

"That's what I'm trying to get you to prove, and you haven't proved it yet. How do you know the moon is substantial? All you have ever seen of it is just light waves, as with the rainbow."

Ross thought about this. "Okay, I guess I see what you're getting at. But we *do* know that the moon is substantial; they bounced radar off it, as far back as '46."

"Just light waves again, Ross. Infra-red light, or ultrashort-wave radio, but the same spectrum. Come again."

"Yes, but they *bounced*."

"You are drawing an analogy from earth conditions again. I repeat, we know nothing of moon conditions except through the insubstantial waves of the electromagnetic spectrum."

"How about tides?"

"Tides exist, certainly. We have seen them, wet our feet in them. But that proves nothing about the moon. The theory that the moon causes the tides is a sheer convenience, pure theory. We change theories as often as we change our underwear. Next year it may be simpler to assume that the tides cause the moon. Got any other ideas?"

Ross took a deep breath. "You're trying to beat me down with words. All right, so I haven't seen the other side of the moon. So I've never felt the moon, or taken a bite out of it. By the way, you can hang on to the theory that the moon is made of green cheese with that line of argument."

"Not quite," said Cargraves. "There is some data on that, for what it's worth. An astronomer fellow made a spectrograph of green cheese and compared it with a spectrograph of the moon. No resemblance."

Art chortled. "He didn't, really?"

"Fact. You can look it up."

Ross shrugged. "That's no better than the radar data," he said correctly. "But to get on with my proof. Granted that there is a front side to the moon, whatever its nature, just as long as it isn't so insubstantial that it won't even reflect radar, then there has to be some sort of a back, flat, round, square, or wiggly. That's a matter of certain mathematical deduction."

Morrie snorted.

Cargraves limited himself to a slight smile. "Now, Ross. Think it over. What is the content of mathematics?"

"The content of mathe—" He collapsed suddenly. "Oh . . . I guess I finally get it. Mathematics doesn't have any content. If we found there wasn't any other side, then we would just have to invent a new mathematics."

"That's the idea. Fact of the matter is, we won't *know* that there is another side to the moon until we get there. I was just trying to show you," he went on, "just how insubstantial a 'common sense' idea can be when you pin it down. Neither 'common sense' nor 'logic' can *prove* anything. Proof comes from experiment, or to put it another way, from experience, and from nothing else. Short lecture on the scientific method—you can count it as thirty minutes on today's study time. Anybody else want breakfast but me? Or has the low weight made you queasy?" He started to climb out of his chair.

Ross was very thoughtful while they made preparations for breakfast. This was to be a proper meal, prepared from their limited supply of non-canned foods. The *Galileo* had been fitted with a galley of sorts, principally a hot plate and a small refrigerator. Dishes and knives, forks, and spoons could be washed, sparingly, with the water which accumulated in the sump of the air-conditioner, and then sterilized on the hot plate. The ship had everything necessary to life, even a cramped but indispensable washroom. But every auxiliary article, such as dishes, was made of zinc—reserve mass for the hungry jet.

They sat, or rather squatted, down to a meal of real milk, cereal, boiled eggs, rolls, jam, and coffee. Cargraves sighed contentedly when it had been tucked away. "We won't get many like that," he commented, as he filled his pipe. "Space travel isn't all it's cracked up to be, not yet."

"Mind the pipe, Skipper!" Morrie warned.

Cargraves looked startled. "I forgot," he admitted guiltily. He stared longingly at the pipe. "Say, Ross," he inquired, "do you think the air-conditioner would clean it out fast enough?"

"Go ahead. Try it," Ross urged him. "One pipeful won't kill us. But say, Doc—"

"Yes?"

"Well, uh, look—don't you really *believe* there is another side to the moon?"

"Huh? Still on that, eh? Of course I do."

"But—"

"But it's just my opinion. I believe it because all my assumptions, beliefs, prejudices, theories, superstitions, and so forth, tend that way. It's part of the pattern of fictions I live by, but that doesn't prove it's right. So if it turns out to be wrong I hope I am sufficiently emotionally braced not to blow my top.

"Which brings us right back to study time," he went on. "You've all got thirty minutes' credit, which gives you an hour and a half to go. Better get busy."

Art looked dumfounded. "I thought you were kidding, Uncle. You don't mean to run such a schedule *on the moon*, do you?"

"Unless circumstances prevent. Now is a good time to work up a little reserve, for that matter, while there is nothing to see and no work to do."

Art continued to look astonished, then his face cleared. "I'm afraid we can't, Uncle. The books are all packed down so far that we can't get at them till we land."

"So? Well, we won't let that stop us. A school," he quoted. "is a log with a pupil on one end and a teacher on the other. We'll have lectures and quizzes—starting with a review quiz. Gather round, victims."

They did so, sitting cross-legged in a circle on the hold bulkhead. Cargraves produced a pencil and a reasonably clean piece of paper from his always bulging pockets. "You first, Art. Sketch and describe a cyclotron. Basic review—let's see how much you've forgotten."

Art commenced outlining painfully the essential parts of a cyclotron. He sketched two hollow half-cylinders, with their open sides facing each other, close together. "These are made of copper," he stated, "and each one is an electrode for a very high frequency, high voltage power source. It's actually a sort of short-wave radio transmitter—I'll leave it out of the sketch. Then you have an enormously powerful electromagnet with its field running through the opening between the dees, the half-cylinders, and vertical to them. The whole thing is inside a big vacuum chamber. You get a source of ions—"

"What sort of ions?"

"Well, maybe you put a little hydrogen in the vacuum chamber and kick it up with a hot filament at the center point of the two dees. Then you get hydrogen nuclei-protons."

"Go ahead."

"The protons have a positive charge, of course. The alternating current would keep them kicking back and forth between the two electrodes—the dees. But the magnetic field, since the protons are charged particles, tends to make them whirl around in circles. Between the two of them, the protons go whirling around in a spiral, gaining speed each revolution until they finally fly out a little thin, metal window in the vacuum chamber, going to beat the band."

"But why bother?"

"Well, if you aim this stream of high-speed protons at some material, say a piece of metal, things begin to happen. It can knock electrons off the atoms, or it can even get inside and stir up the nuclei and cause transmutations or make the target radioactive—things like that."

"Good enough," Cargraves agreed, and went on to ask him several more questions to bring out details. "Just one thing," he said afterwards. "You know the answers, but just between ourselves, that sketch smells a bit. It's sloppy."

"I never did have any artistic talent," Art said defensively. "I'd rather take a photograph any day."

"You've taken too many photographs, maybe. As for artistic talent, I haven't any either, but I learned to sketch. Look, Art—the rest of you guys get this, too—if you can't sketch, you can't see. If you really see what you're looking at, you can put it down on paper, accurately. If you really remember what you have looked at, you can sketch it accurately from memory."

"But the lines don't go where I intend them to."

"A pencil will go where you push it. It hasn't any life of its own. The answer is practice and more practice and thinking about what you are looking at. All of you lugs want to be scientists. Well, the ability to sketch accurately is as necessary to a scientist as his slipstick. More necessary, you can get along without a slide rule. Okay, Art. You're next, Ross. Gimme a quick tell on the protactinium radioactive series."

Ross took a deep breath. "There are three families of radioactive isotopes: the uranium family, the thorium family, and the protoactinium family. The last one starts with isotope U-235 and—"

They kept at it for considerably longer than an hour and a half, for Cargraves had the intention of letting them be as free as possible later, while still keeping to the letter and spirit of his contract with Ross's father.

At last he said, "I think we had better eat again. The drive will cut out before long. It's been cutting down all the time—notice how light you feel?"

"How about a K-ration?" inquired Morrie, in his second capacity as commissary steward.

"No, I don't think so," Cargraves answered slowly. "I think maybe we had better limit this meal to some amino acids and some gelatine." He raised his eyebrows.

"Umm—I see," Morrie agreed, glancing at the other two. "Maybe you are right." Morrie and Cargraves, being pilots, had experienced free fall in school. The stomachs of Ross and Art were still to be tried.

"What's the idea?" Art demanded.

Ross looked disgusted. "Oh, he thinks we'll toss our cookies. Why, we hardly weigh anything now. What do you take us for, Doc? Babies?"

"No," said Cargraves, "but I still think you might get dropsick. I did. I think predigested foods are a good idea."

"Oh, shucks. My stomach is strong. I've never been air sick."

"Ever been seasick?"

"I've never been to sea."

"Well, suit yourself," Cargraves told him. "But one thing I insist on. Wear a sack over your face. I don't want what you lose in the air-conditioner." He turned away and started preparing some gelatine for himself by simply pouring the powder into water, stirring, and drinking.

Ross made a face but he did not dig out a K-ration. Instead he switched on the hot plate, preparatory to heating milk for amino-acid concentrates.

A little later Joe the Robot awoke from his nap and switched off the jet completely.

They did not bounce up to the ceiling. The rocket did not spin wildly. None of the comic-strip things happened to them. They simply gradually ceased to weigh anything as the thrust died away. Almost as much they noticed the deafening new silence. Cargraves had previously made a personal inspection of the entire ship to be sure that everything was tied, clamped, or stored firmly so that the ship would not become cluttered up with loosely floating bric-a-brac.

Cargraves lifted himself away from his seat with one hand,

turned in the air like a swimmer, and floated gently down, or rather across—up and down had ceased to exist—to where Ross and Art floated, loosely attached to their hammocks by a single belt as an added precaution. Cargraves checked his progress with one hand and steadied himself by grasping Art's hammock. "How's everybody?"

"All right, I guess," Art answered, gulping. "It feels like a falling elevator." He was slightly green.

"You, Ross?"

"I'll get by," Ross declared, and suddenly gagged. His color was gray rather than green.

Space sickness is not a joke, as every cadet rocket pilot knows. It is something like seasickness, like the terrible, wild retching that results from heavy pitching of a ship at sea—except that the sensation of everything dropping out from under one does not stop!

But the longest free-flight portions of a commercial rocket flight from point to point on earth last only a few minutes, with the balance of the trip on thrust or in glide, whereas the course Cargraves had decided on called for many hours of free fall. He could have chosen, with the power at his disposal, to make the whole trip on the jet, but that would have prevented them from turning ship, which he proposed to do now, until the time came to invert and drive the jet toward the moon to break their fall.

Only by turning the ship would they be able to see the earth from space; Cargraves wanted to do so before the earth was too far away.

"Just stay where you are for a while," he cautioned them. "I'm about to turn ship."

"I want to see it," Ross said stoutly. "I've been looking forward to it." He unbuckled his safety belt, then suddenly he was retching again. Saliva overflowed and drooled out curiously, not down his chin but in large droplets that seemed undecided where to go.

"Use your handkerchief," Cargraves advised him, feeling none too well himself. "Then come along if you feel like it." He turned to Art.

Art was already using his handkerchief.

Cargraves turned away and floated back to the pilot's chair. He was aware that there was nothing that he could do for them, and his own stomach was doing flip-flops and slow, banked turns. He wanted to strap his safety belt across it. Back in his seat, he noticed that Morrie was doubled up and holding his stomach, but he said nothing and gave his attention to turning the ship. Morrie would be all right.

Swinging the ship around was a very simple matter. Located at the center of gravity of the ship was a small, heavy, metal wheel. He had controls on the panel in front of him whereby he could turn this wheel to any axis, as it was mounted freely on gymbals, and then lock the gymbals. An electric motor enabled him to spin it rapidly in either direction and to stop it afterwards.

This wheel by itself could turn the ship when it was in free fall and then hold it in the new position. (It must be clearly understood that this turning had no effect at all on the course or speed of the *Galileo*, but simply on its attitude, the direction it faced, just as a fancy diver may turn and twist in falling from a great height, without thereby disturbing his fall.)

The little wheel was able to turn the huge vessel by a very simple law of physics, but in an application not often seen on the earth. The principle was the conservation of momentum, in this case angular momentum or spin. Ice skaters understand the application of this law; some of their fanciest tricks depend on it.

As the little wheel spun rapidly in one direction the big ship spun slowly in the other direction. When the wheel stopped, the ship stopped and just as abruptly.

"Dark glasses, boys!" Cargraves called out belatedly as the ship started to nose over and the stars wheeled past the port. In spite of their wretched nausea they managed to find their goggles, carried on their persons for this event, and get them on.

They needed them very soon. The moon slid away out of sight. The sun and the earth came into view. The earth was a great shining crescent like a moon two days past new. At this distance— one-fourth the way to the moon—it appeared sixteen times as wide as the moon does from the earth and many times more magnificent. The horns of the crescent were blue-white from the polar ice caps. Along its length showed the greenish blue of sea and the deep greens and sandy browns of ocean and forest and field . . . for the line of light and dark ran through the heart of Asia and down as if it had been a globe standing across a school room from them. The Indian Ocean was partly obscured by a great cloud bank, stormy to those underneath it perhaps, but blazing white as the polar caps to those who watched from space.

In the arms of the crescent was the nightside of earth, lighted dimly but plainly by the almost full moon behind them. But—and this is never seen on the moon when "the new moon holds the old moon in her arms"—the faintly lighted dark face was picked out here and there with little jewels of light, the cities of earth, warm and friendly and beckoning!

Halfway from equator to northern horn were three bright ones, not far apart—London, and Paris, and reborn Berlin. Across the dark Atlantic, at the very edge of the disk, was one especially bright and rosy light, the lights of Broadway and all of Greater New York.

All three of the boys were seeing New York for the first time, not to mention most of the rest of the great globe!

But, although it was their home, although they were seeing it from a glorious vantage point new to mankind, their attention was torn away from the earth almost at once. There was a still more breath-taking object in the sky—the sun.

Its apparent width was only one-sixteenth that of the mighty crescent earth, but it brooked no competition. It hung below the earth—below when referred to the attitude of the *Galileo*, not in the sense of "up" or "down"—and about four times the width of the earth away. It was neither larger nor smaller than it appears from the earth and not appreciably brighter than it is on a clear, dry desert noon. But the sky was black around it in the airless space; its royal corona shone out; its prominences could be seen; its great infernal storms showed on its face.

"Don't look too directly at it," Cargraves warned, "even when you have the polarizer turned to maximum interference." He referred to the double lenses the boys wore, polaroid glass with the outer lens rotatable.

"I gotta have a picture of this!" Art declared, and turned and swam away. He had forgotten that he was space sick.

He was back shortly with his Contax and was busy fitting his longest lens into it. The camera was quite old, being one of the few things his mother had managed to bring out of Germany, and was his proudest possession. The lens in place, he started to take his Weston from its case. Cargraves stopped him.

"Why burn out your light meter?" he cautioned.

Art stopped suddenly. "Yes, I guess I would," he admitted. "But how am I going to get a picture?"

"Maybe you won't. Better use your slowest film, your strongest filter, your smallest stop, and your shortest exposure. Then pray."

Seeing that the boy looked disappointed, he went on, "I

wouldn't worry too much about pictures of the sun. We can leave
that to the astronomers who will follow us after we've blazed the
trail. But you ought to be able to get a swell picture of the earth.
Waste a little film on the sun first, then we will try it. I'll shade
your lens from the sunlight with my hand."

Art did so, then prepared to photograph the earth. "I can't get
a decent light reading on it, either," he complained. "Too much interference from the sun."

"Well, you *know* how much light it is getting—the works.
Why not assume it's about like desert sunlight, then shoot a few
both above and below what that calls for?"

When Art had finished Cargraves said, "Mind the sunburn,
boys." He touched the plastic inner layer of the quartz port. "This
stuff is supposed to filter out the worst of it—but take it easy."

"Shucks, we're tanned." And *so* they were; New Mexico sun
had left its mark.

"I know, but that's the brightest sunshine you ever saw. Take it
easy."

"How much chance is there," asked Morrie, "that this pure
stuff is dangerous? I mean aside from bad sunburn."

"You read the same papers I did. We're getting more cosmic
radiation, too. Maybe it'll knock us down dead. Maybe it'll cause
your children to have long green tendrils. That's one of the
chances we take."

"Well, Columbus took a chance."

"And look how far he got!" put in Art.

"Yeah, thrown in the hoosegow for his trouble."

"Be that as it may," said Cargraves, "I'm going to turn the ship
again so that the sun doesn't shine in so directly. This tub is getting too hot." It was no trouble to keep the *Galileo* warm enough,
but how to get rid of unwanted heat was another matter. Her polished sides reflected most of the heat that struck them, but sunshine pouring directly in the view port produced a most
uncomfortable greenhouse effect. Refrigeration, in the ordinary
sense, was no answer; the ship was a closed system and could lose
heat only by radiation to outer space. At the moment she was ab-
sorbing radiant heat from the sun much faster than she was radiat-
ing it.

"I want to take some more pictures," Art protested.

"I'll keep the earth in sight," Cargraves promised, and set the
controls of the spinning wheel to suit his purpose. Then he floated

back to the view port and joined the others, who were swimming in front of it like goldfish in a bowl.

Ross touched the transparent wall with a finger tip; the light contact pushed him back from the port. "Doc, what do you think would happen if a meteor hit this port?"

"I don't like to think about it. However, I wouldn't worry too much about it. Ley has calculated that the chance of being hit by a meteor on a trip out to the moon and back is about one in a half a million. I figure I was in much graver danger every time I climbed into that alleged automobile you guys drive."

"That's a good car."

"I'll admit it performs well." He turned away with a motion much like that of a sprint swimmer turning on the side of a pool. "Art, when you are through snapping that Brownie, I've got something better for you to do. How about trying to raise earth?"

"Just one more of—Huh? What did you say ?"

"How about heating up your tubes and seeing if there is anybody on the air—or lack-of-air, as the case may be?"

No attempt had been made to use the radios since blasting off. Not only did the jet interfere seriously, but also the antennae were completely retracted, even spike antennae, during the passage through the atmosphere. But now that the jet was silent an attempt at communication seemed in order.

True, the piloting radar had kept them in touch by radio, in a manner of speaking, during the early part of the journey, but they were now beyond the range of the type of equipment used for piloting. It bore little resemblance to the giant radars used to bounce signals against the moon. The quartz windows through which it operated would have been quite inadequate for the large antenna used to fling power from the earth to the moon.

Art got busy at once, while stating that he thought the chances of picking up anything were slim. "It would have to be beamed tight as a, as a, well—tight. And why would anybody be beaming stuff out this way?"

"At us, of course," Ross offered.

"They can't find us. Radar won't pick up anything as small as this ship at this distance—too little mirror cross section." Art spoke authoritatively. "Not the radars they've got so far. Maybe some day, if—hey!"

"What have you got?"

"Keep quiet!" Art stared ahead with that look of painful, unseeing concentration found only under a pair of earphones. He twiddled his dials carefully, then fumbled for pencil and paper. Writing, he found, was difficult without gravity to steady himself and his hand. But he scribbled.

"Get a load of this," he whispered a few minutes later. He read:

"RADIO PARIS CALLING ROCKET SHIP *GALILEO* RADIO PARIS CALLING ROCKET SHIP *GALILEO* RADIO PARIS CALLING ROCKET SHIP *GALILEO* DOCTOR DONALD CARGRAVES ARTHUR MUELLER MAURICE ABRAMS ROSS JENKINS GREETINGS YOUR FLIGHT FOLLOWED UNTIL OH ONE ONE THREE GREENWICH TIME SEPTEMBER TWENTY-FIFTH CONTACT LOST WILL CONTINUE TO CALL YOU ON THIS BEAM AND FREQUENCY FOLLOWING PROBABLE TRAJECTORY GOOD LUCK TO YOU RADIO PARIS CALLING ROCKET SHIP *GALILEO* RADIO PARIS—

"And then they repeat. It's a recording." His voice was shaky.

"Gosh!" Ross had no other comment.

"Well, boys, it looks like we're celebrities." Cargraves tried to make his words sound casual. Then he found that he was holding a piece of his pipe in each hand; he had broken it in two without knowing it. Shrugging, he let the pieces float away from him.

"But how did they find us?" persisted Art.

"The message shows it," Morrie pointed out. "See that time? That's the time we went into free fall. They followed the jet."

"How? By telescope?"

"More likely," Cargraves put in, "by anti-rocket radiation tracer."

"Huh? But the UN patrol are the only ones with that sort of gear."

Cargraves permitted himself a grin. "And why shouldn't the UN be interested in us? See here, kid—can you squirt anything back at them?"

"I'll sure try!"

11.
ONE ATOM WAR TOO MANY?

Art got busy at his task, but nothing came back which would tell him whether or not his attempts had been successful. The recording continued to come in whenever he listened for it, between attempts to send, for the next three and a half hours. Then it faded out—they were off the beam.

Nevertheless, it was the longest direct communication of record in human history.

The Galileo continued her climb up from earth, toward that invisible boundary where the earth ceased to claim title and the lesser mass of the moon took charge. Up and up, out and farther out, rising in free flight, slowing from the still effective tug of the earth but still carried on by the speed she had attained under the drive of the jet, until at last the *Galileo* slipped quietly over the border and was in the moon's back yard. From there on she accelerated slowly as she fell toward the silvery satellite.

They ate and slept and ate again. They stared at the receding earth. And they slept again.

While they slept, Joe the Robot stirred, consulted his cam, decided that he had had enough of this weightlessness, and started the jet. But first he straightened out the ship so that the jet faced toward the moon, breaking their fall, while the port stared back at earth.

The noise of the jet woke them up. Cargraves had had them strap themselves down in anticipation of weight. They unstrapped and climbed up to the control station. "Where's the moon?" demanded Art.

"Under us, of course," Morrie informed him.

"Better try for it with radar, Morrie," Cargraves directed.

"Check!" Morrie switched on the juice, waited for it to warm, then adjusted it. The moon showed as a large vague mass on one side of the scope. "About fifteen thousand miles," he declared. "We'd better do some checking, Skipper."

They were busy for more than an hour, taking sights, taking readings, and computing. The bearing and distance of the moon, in relation to the ship, were available by radar. Direct star sights out the port established the direction of drive of the ship. Successive radar readings established the course and speed of the ship for comparison with the courses and speeds as given by the automatic instruments showing on the board. All these factors had to be taken into consideration in computing a check on the management of Joe the Robot.

Minor errors were found and the corrections were fed to the automatic pilot. Joe accepted the changes in his orders without comment.

While Morrie and Cargraves did this, Art and Ross were preparing the best meal they could throw together. It was a relief to have weight under their feet and it was a decided relief to their stomachs. Those organs had become adjusted to free fall, but hardly reconciled. Back on firm footing they hollered for solid food.

The meal was over and Cargraves was thinking sadly of his ruined pipe, when the control alarm sounded. Joe the Robot had completed his orders, his cam had run out, he called for relief.

They all scrambled up to the control station. The moon, blindingly white and incredibly huge was shouldering its way into one side of the port. They were so close to it now that their progress was visible, if one looked closely, by sighting across the frame of the port at some fixed object, a crater or a mountain range.

"Whee!" Art yelled.

"Kinda knocks your eyes out, doesn't it?" Ross said, gazing in open wonder.

"It does," agreed Cargraves. "But we've got work to do. Get back and strap yourself down and stand by for maneuvering."

While he complied, he strapped himself into his chair and then flipped a switch which ordered Joe to go to sleep; he was in direct, manual command of the rocket. With Morrie to coach him by instrument, he put the ship through a jockeying series of changes, gentle on the whole and involving only minor changes in course at any one time, but all intended to bring the ship from the flat conoid trajectory it had been following into a circular orbit around the moon.

"How'm I doin'?" he demanded a long time later.

"Right in the groove," Morrie assured him, after a short delay.

"Sure enough of it for me to go automatic and swing ship?"

"Let me track her a few more minutes." Presently Morrie assured him as requested. They had already gone into free flight just before Cargraves asked for a check. He now called out to Art and Ross that they could unstrap. He then started the ship to swinging so that the port faced toward the moon and switched on a combination which told Joe that he must get back to work; it was now his business to watch the altitude by radar and to see to it that altitude and speed remained constant.

Art was up at the port, with his camera, by the time he and Morrie had unstrapped.

"Goshawmighty," exclaimed Art, "this is something!" He unlimbered his equipment and began snapping frantically, until Ross pointed out that his lens cover was still on. Then he steadied down.

Ross floated face down and stared out at the desolation. They were speeding silently along, only two hundred miles above the ground, and they were approaching the sunrise line of light and darkness. The shadows were long on the barren wastes below them, the mountain peaks and the great gaping craters more horrendous on that account. "It's scary," Ross decided. "I'm not sure I like it."

"Want off at the next corner?" Cargraves inquired.

"No, but I'm not dead certain I'm glad I came."

Morrie grasped his arm, to steady himself apparently, but quite as much for the comfort of solid human companionship. "You know what I think, Ross," he began, as he stared out at the endless miles of craters. "I think I know how it got that way. Those aren't volcanic craters, that's certain—and it wasn't done by meteors. *They did it themselves!*"

"Huh? Who?"

"The moon people. They did it. They wrecked themselves. They ruined themselves. *They had one atomic war too many.*"

"Huh? What the—" Ross stared, then looked back at the surface as if to read the grim mystery there. Art stopped taking pictures.

"How about it, Doc?"

Cargraves wrinkled his brow. "Could be," he admitted. "None of the other theories for natural causes hold water for one reason or another. It would account for the relatively smooth parts we call 'seas.' They really were seas; that's why they weren't hit very hard."

"And that's why they aren't seas any more," Morrie went on. "They blew their atmosphere off and the seas boiled away. Look at Tycho. That's where they set off the biggest ammunition dump on the planet. It cracked the whole planet. I'll bet somebody worked out a counter-weapon that worked too well. It set off every atom bomb on the moon all at once and it ruined them! I'm sure of it."

"Well," said Cargraves, "I'm not sure of it, but I admit the theory is attractive. Perhaps we'll find out when we land. The notion of setting off all the bombs at once—there are strong theoretical objections to that. Nobody has any idea how to do it."

"Nobody knew how to make an atom bomb a few years ago," Morrie pointed out.

"That's true." Cargraves wanted to change the subject; it was unpleasantly close to horrors that had haunted his dreams since the beginning of World War II. "Ross, how do you feel about the other side of the moon now?"

"We'll know pretty soon," Ross chuckled. "Say—this *is* the Other Side!"

And so it was. They had leveled off in their circular orbit near the left limb of the moon as seen from the earth and were coasting over the mysterious other face. Ross scanned it closely. "Looks about the same."

"Did you expect anything different?"

"No, I guess not. But I had hoped." Even as he spoke they crossed the sunrise line and the ground below them was dark, not invisible, for it was still illuminated by faint starlight—starlight only, for the earthshine never reached this face. The suncapped peaks receded rapidly in the distance. At the rate they were traveling, a speed of nearly 4,000 miles per hour necessary to maintain them in a low-level circular orbit, the complete circuit of the planet would take a little over an hour and a half.

"No more pictures, I guess," Art said sadly. "I wish it was a different time of the month."

"Yes," agreed Ross, still peering out, "it's a dirty shame to be this close and not see anything."

"Don't be impatient," Cargraves told him; "when we start back in eight or nine days, we swing around again and you can stare and take pictures till you're cross-eyed."

"Why only eight or nine days? We've got more food than that."

"Two reasons. The first is, if we take off at new moon we won't have to stare into the sun on the way back. The second is, I'm homesick and I haven't even landed yet." He grinned. In utter seriousness he felt that it was not wise to stretch their luck by sticking around too long.

The trip across the lighted and familiar face of the moon was delightful, but so short that it was like window shopping in a speeding car. The craters and the "seas" were old familiar friends, yet strange and new. It reminded them of the always strange experience of seeing a famous television star on a personal appearance tour—recognition with an odd feeling of unreality.

Art shifted over to the motion-picture camera once used to record the progress of the *Starstruck* series, and got a complete sequence from *Mare Fecunditatis* to the crater Kepler, at which point Cargraves ordered him emphatically to stop at once and strap himself down.

They were coming into their landing trajectory. Cargraves and Morrie had selected a flat, unnamed area beyond *Oceanus Procellarum* for the landing because it was just on the border between the earth side and the unknown side, and thereby fitted two plans: to attempt to establish radio contact with earth, for which direct line-of-sight would be necessary, and to permit them to explore at least a portion of the unknown side.

Joe the Robot was called again and told to consult a second cam concealed in his dark insides, a cam which provided for the necessary braking drive and the final ticklish contact on maneuvering jets and radar. Cargraves carefully leveled the ship at the exact altitude and speed Joe would need for the approach and slipped over to automatic when Morrie signaled that they were at the exact, precalculated distance necessary for the landing.

Joe took over. He flipped the ship over, using the maneuvering rockets, then started backing in to a landing, using the jet in the tail to kill their still tremendous speed. The moon was below them now and Cargraves could see nothing but the stars, the stars and the crescent of the earth—a quarter of a million miles away and no help to him now.

He wondered if he would ever set foot on it again.

Morrie was studying the approach in the radar scope. "Checking out to nine zeros, Captain," he announced proudly and with considerable exaggeration. "It's in the bag."

The ground came up rapidly in the scope. When they were close and no longer, for the moment, dropping at all, Joe cut the main jet and flipped them over.

When he had collected himself from the wild gyration of the somersault, Cargraves saw the nose jets reach out and splash in front of them and realized that the belly jets were in play, too, as the surge of power pushed the seat of the chair up against him. He felt almost as if he could land it himself, it seemed so much like his first wild landing on the New Mexico desert.

Then for one frantic second he saw the smooth, flat ground ahead of the splash of the plowing nose jets give way to a desolation of rocky ridges, sharp crevasses, loose and dangerous cosmic rubble . . . soil from which, if they landed without crashing, they could not hope to take off.

The sunlight had fooled them. With the sun behind them the badlands had cast no shadows they could see; the flat plain had appeared to stretch to the mountains ahead. These were no mountains, but they were quite sufficient to wreck the *Galileo*.

The horrible second it took him to size up the situation was followed by frantic action. With one hand he cut the automatic pilot; with the other he twisted violently on the knob controlling the tail jet. He slapped the belly jets on full.

Her nose lifted.

She hung there, ready to fall, kept steady on her jets only by her gyros. Then slowly, slowly, slowly, the mighty tail jet reached out—so slowly that he knew at that moment that the logy response of the atomic pile would never serve him for what he had to do next, which was to land her himself.

The *Galileo* pulled away from the surface of the moon.

"That was close," Morrie said mildly.

Cargraves wiped the sweat from his eyes and shivered.

He knew what was called for now, in all reason. He knew that he should turn the ship away from the moon, head her in the general direction of the earth and work out a return path, a path to a planet with an atmosphere to help a pilot put down his savage ship. He knew right then that he was not the stuff of heroes, that he was getting old and knew it.

But he hated to tell Morrie.

"Going to put her down on manual?" the boy inquired.

"Huh?"

"That's the only way we'll get her down on a strange field. I can see that now—you've got to be able to see your spot at the last half minute—nose jets and no radar."

"I can't do it, Morrie."

The younger man said nothing. He simply sat and stared ahead without expression.

"I'm going to head her back to earth, Morrie."

The boy gave absolutely no sign of having heard him. There was neither approval nor disapproval on his face, nor any faint suggestion.

Cargraves thought of the scene when Ross, blind and bandaged, had told him off. Of Art, quelling his space sickness to get his pictures. He thought, too, of the hot and tiring days when he and Morrie had qualified for piloting together.

The boy said nothing, neither did he look at him.

These kids, these damn kids! How had he gotten up here, with a rocket under his hand and a cargo of minors to be responsible for? He was a laboratory scientist, not a superman. If it had been Ross, if Ross were a pilot—even where he now was, he shivered at the recollection of Ross's hair-raising driving. Art was about as bad. Morrie was worse.

He knew he would never be a hot pilot—not by twenty years. These kids, with their casual ignorance, with their hot rod rigs, it was for them; piloting was their kind of a job. They were too young and too ignorant to care and their reflexes were not hobbled by second thoughts. He remembered Ross's words: "I'll go to the moon if I have to walk!"

"Land her, Morrie."

"Aye, aye, sir!"

The boy never looked at him. He flipped her up on her tail, then let her drop slowly by easing off on the tail jet. Purely by the seat of his pants, by some inner calculation—for Cargraves could see nothing through the port but stars, and neither could the boy— he flipped her over again, cutting the tail jet as he did so.

The ground was close to them and coming up fast.

He kicked her once with the belly jets, placing them thereby over a smooth stretch of land, and started taking her down with quick blasts of the nose jets, while sneaking a look between blasts.

When he had her down so close that Cargraves was sure that he was going to land her on her nose, crushing in the port and killing them, he gave her one more blast which made her rise a trifle, kicked her level and brought her down on the belly jets, almost horizontal, and so close to the ground that Cargraves could see it ahead of them, out the port.

Glancing casually out the port, Morrie gave one last squirt with the belly jets and let her settle. They grated heavily and were stopped. The *Galileo* sat on the face of the moon.

"Landed, sir. Time: Oh-eight-three-four."

Cargraves drew in a breath. "A beautiful, beautiful landing, Morrie."

"Thanks, Captain."

12.
"THE BARE BONES—"

Ross and Art were already out of their straps and talking loudly about getting out the space suits when Cargraves climbed shakily out of his chair—and then nearly fell. The lowered gravitation, one-sixth earth-normal, fooled him. He was used to weightlessness by now, and to the chest-binding pressure of high acceleration; the pseudo-normal weight of a one-*g* drive was no trouble, and maneuvering while strapped down was no worse than stunting in an airplane.

This was different and required a little getting used to, he decided. It reminded him a little of walking on rubber, or the curiously light-footed feeling one got after removing snow shoes or heavy boots.

Morrie remained at his post for a few moments longer to complete and sign his log. He hesitated over the space in the log sheet marked "position." They had taught him in school to enter here the latitude and longitude of the port of arrival—but what were the latitude and longitude of this spot?

The moon had its north and south poles just as definitely as the earth, which gave any spot a definite latitude, nor was longitude uncertain once a zero meridian was selected. That had been done; Tycho was to be the Greenwich of the moon.

But his navigation tables were tables for the *earth*.

The problem could be solved; he knew that. By spherical trigonometry the solutions of celestial triangles on which all navigation was based could be converted to the special conditions of Luna, but it would require tedious calculation, not at all like the precalculated short cuts used by all pilots in the age of aircraft and rockets. He would have to go back to the Marc St. Hilaire method, obsolete for twenty years, after converting laboriously each piece of data from earth reference terms to moon reference terms.

Well, he could do it later, he decided, and get Cargraves to check him. The face of the moon called him.

He joined the little group huddled around the port. In front of them stretched a dun and lifeless floor, breaking into jagged hills a few miles beyond them. It was hot, glaring hot, under the oblique rays of the sun, and utterly still. The earth was not in sight; they had dropped over the rim into the unknown side in the last minutes of the impromptu landing.

Instead of the brassy sky one might expect over such a scene of blistering desert desolation, a black dome of night, studded brilliantly with stars, hung over it. At least, thought Morrie, his mind returning to his problem in navigation, it would be hard to get lost here. A man could set a course by the stars with no trouble.

"When are we going out?" demanded Art.

"Keep your shirt on," Ross told him and turned to Cargraves. "Say, Doc, that was sure a slick landing. Tell me—was that first approach just a look around on manual, or did you feed that into the automatic pilot, too?"

"Neither one, exactly." He hesitated. It had been evident from their first remarks that neither Ross nor Art had been aware of the danger, nor of his own agonizing indecision. Was it necessary to worry them with it now? He was aware that, if he did not speak, Morrie would never mention it.

That decided him. The man—*man* was the word, he now knew, not "boy"—was entitled to public credit. "Morrie made that landing," he informed them. "We had to cut out the robot and Morrie put her down."

Ross whistled.

Art said, "Huh? What did you say? Don't tell me that radar cut out—I checked it six ways."

"Your gadgets all stood up," Cargraves assured him, "but there are some things a man can do that a gadget can't. This was one of them." He elaborated what had happened.

Ross looked Morrie up and down until Morrie blushed. "Hot Pilot I said, and Hot Pilot it is," Ross told him. "But I'm glad I didn't know." He walked aft, whistling *Danse Macabre*, off key again, and began to fiddle with his space suit.

"When do we go outside?" Art persisted.

"Practically at once, I suppose."

"Whoopee!"

"Don't get in a hurry. You might be the man with the short straw and have to stay with the ship."

"But . . . Look, Uncle, why does anybody have to stay with the ship? Nobody's going to steal it."

Cargraves hesitated. With automatic caution, he had intended always to keep at least one man in the ship, as a safety measure. On second thought there seemed no reason for it. A man inside the ship could do nothing for a man outside the ship without first donning a pressure suit and coming outside. "We'll compromise," he said. "Morrie and I—no, you and I." He realized that he could not risk both pilots at once. "You and I will go first. If it's okay, the others can follow us. All right, troops," he said, turning. "Into your space suits!"

They helped each other into them, after first applying white sunburn ointment liberally over the skin outside their goggles. It gave them an appropriate out-of-this-world appearance. Then Cargraves had them check their suits at twice normal pressure while he personally inspected their oxygen-bottle back packs.

All the while they were checking their walkie-talkies; ordinary conversation could be heard, but only faintly, through the helmets as long as they were in the air of the ship; the radios were louder.

"Okay, sports," he said at last. "Art and I will go into the lock together, then proceed around to the front, where you can see us. When I give you the high sign, come on out. One last word: stay together. Don't get more than ten yards or so away from me. And remember this. When you get out there, every last one of you is going to want to see how high you can jump; I've heard you talking about it. Well, you can probably jump twenty-five or thirty feet high if you try. But don't do it!"

"Why not?" Ross's voice was strange, through the radio.

"Because if you land on your head and crack your helmet open, we'll bury you right where you fall! Come on, Morrie. No, sorry—I mean 'Art.' "

They crowded into the tiny lock, almost filling it. The motor which drove the impeller to scavenge the air from the lock whirred briefly, so little was the space left unoccupied by their bodies, then sighed and stopped. The scavenger valve clicked into place and Cargraves unclamped the outer door.

He found that he floated, rather than jumped, to the ground. Art came after him, landing on his hands and knees and springing lightly up.

"Okay, kid?"

"Swell!"

They moved around to the front, boots scuffing silently in the loose soil. He looked at it and picked up a handful to see if it looked like stuff that had been hit by radioactive blast. He was thinking of Morrie's theory. They were on the floor of a crater; that was evident, for the wall of hills extended all around them. Was it an atomic bomb crater?

He could not tell. The moon soil did have the boiled and bubbly look of atom-scorched earth, but that might have been volcanic action, or, even, the tremendous heat of the impact of a giant meteor. Well, the problem could wait.

Art stopped suddenly. "Say! Uncle, I've got to go back."

"What's the matter?"

"I forgot my camera!"

Cargraves chuckled. "Make it next time. Your subjects won't move." Art's excitement had set a new high, he decided; there was a small school of thought which believed he bathed with his camera.

Speaking of baths, Cargraves mused, I could stand one. Space travel had its drawbacks. He was beginning to dislike his own smell, particularly when it was confined in a space suit!

Ross and Morrie were waiting for them, not patiently, at the port. Their radio voices, blanked until now by the ship's sides, came clearly through the quartz. "How about it, Doc?" Ross sang out, pressing his nose to the port.

"Seems all right," they heard him say.

"Then here we come!"

"Wait a few minutes yet. I want to be sure."

"Well—okay." Ross showed his impatience, but discipline was no longer a problem. Art made faces at them, then essayed a little dance, staying close to the ground but letting each step carry him a few feet into the air—or, rather, vacuum. He floated slowly and with some grace. It was like a dance in slow motion, or a ballet under water.

When he started rising a little higher and clicking his boot heels together as he sailed, Cargraves motioned for him to stop. "Put down your flaps, chum," he cautioned, "and land. You aren't Nijinsky."

"Who's Nijinsky?"

"Never mind. Just stay planted. Keep at least one foot on the ground. Okay, Morrie," he called out, "come on out. You and Ross."

The port was suddenly deserted.

When Morrie set foot on the moon and looked around him at the flat and unchanging plain and at the broken crags beyond he felt a sudden overwhelming emotion of tragedy and of foreboding welling up inside him. "It's the bare bones," he muttered, half to himself, "the bare bones of a dead world."

"Huh?" said Ross. "Are you coming, Morrie?"

"Right behind you."

Cargraves and Art had joined them. "Where to?" asked Ross, as the captain came up.

"Well, I don't want to get too far from the ship this first time," Cargraves declared. "This place might have some dirty tricks up its sleeve that we hadn't figured on. How much pressure you guys carrying?"

"Ship pressure."

"You can cut it down to about half that without the lower pressure bothering you. It's oxygen, you know."

"Let's walk over to those hills," Morrie suggested. He pointed astern where the rim of the crater was less than half a mile from the ship. It was the sunward side and the shadows stretched from the rim to within a hundred yards or so of the ship.

"Well, part way, anyhow. That shade might feel good. I'm beginning to sweat."

"I think," said Morrie, "if I remember correctly, we ought to be able to see earth from the top of the rim. I caught a flash of it, just as we inverted. We aren't very far over on the back side."

"Just where are we?"

"I'll have to take some sights before I can report," Morrie admitted. "Some place west of *Oceanus Procellarum* and near the equator."

"I know that."

"Well, if you're in a hurry, Skipper, you had better call up the Automobile Club."

"I'm in no hurry. Injun not lost—wigwam lost. But I hope the earth is visible from there. It would be a good spot, in that case, to set up Art's antenna, not too far from the ship. Frankly, I'm opposed to moving the ship until we head back, even if we miss a chance to try to contact earth."

They were in the shadows now, to Cargraves' relief. Contrary to popular fancy, the shadows were not black, despite the lack of air-dispersed sunlight. The dazzle of the floor behind them and the glare of the hills beyond all contrived to throw quite a lot of reflected light into the shadows.

When they had proceeded some distance farther toward the hills, Cargraves realized that he was not keeping his party together too well. He had paused to examine a place, discovered by Ross, where the base rock pushed up through the waste of the desert floor, and was trying in the dim light to make out its nature, when he noticed that Morrie was not with them.

He restrained his vexation; it was entirely possible that Morrie, who was in the lead, had not seen them stop. But he looked around anxiously.

Morrie was about a hundred yards ahead, where the first folds of the hills broke through. "Morrie!"

The figure stood up, but no answer came over the radio. He noticed then that Morrie was veering, weaving around. "Morrie! Come back here! Are you all right?"

"All right? Sure, I'm all right." He giggled.

"Well, come back here."

"Can't come back. 'M busy—I've found it!" Morrie took a careless step, bounded high in the air, came down, and staggered.

"Morrie! Stand still." Cargraves was hurrying toward him.

But he did not stand still. He began bounding around, leaping higher and higher. "I've found it!" he shrieked. "I've found it!" He gave one last bound and while he floated lazily down, he shouted, "I've found . . . the bare bones—" His voice trailed off. He lit feet first, bounced through a complete forward flip and collapsed.

Cargraves was beside him almost as he fell, having himself approached in great flying leaps.

First the helmet—no, it was not cracked. But the boy's eyes stared out sightlessly. His head lolled, his face was gray.

Cargraves gathered him up in his arms and began to run toward the *Galileo*. He knew the signs though he had seen it only in the low-pressure chamber used for pilot training—anoxia! Something had gone wrong; Morrie was starved for oxygen. He might die before he could be helped, or, still worse, he might live with his brain permanently damaged, his fine clear intellect gone.

It had happened before that way, more than once during the brave and dangerous days when man was conquering high-altitude flying.

The double burden did not slow him down. The two together,

with their space suits, weighed less than seventy pounds. It was just enough to give him stability.

He squeezed them into the lock, holding Morrie close to his chest, and waited in agonizing impatience as the air hissed through the valve. All his strength would not suffice to force that door open until the pressure equalized.

Then he was in and had laid him on the deck. Morrie was still out. He tried to remove the suit with trembling, glove-hampered fingers, then hastily got out of his own suit and unclamped Morrie's helmet. No sign of life showed as the fresh air hit the patient.

Cursing bitterly he tried to give the boy oxygen directly from his suit but found that the valve on Morrie's suit, for some reason, refused to respond. He turned then to his own suit, disconnected the oxygen line and fed the raw oxygen directly to the boy's face while pushing rhythmically on his chest.

Morrie's eyes flickered and he gasped.

"What happened? Is he all right?" The other two had come through the lock while he worked.

"Maybe he is going to be all right. I don't know."

In fact he came around quickly, sat up and blinked his eyes. "Whassa matter?" he wanted to know.

"Lie down," Cargraves urged and put a hand on his shoulder.

"All right . . . hey! I'm inside."

Cargraves explained to him what had happened. Morrie blinked. "Now that's funny. I was all right, except that I was feeling exceptionally fine—"

"That's a symptom."

"Yes, I remember. But it didn't occur to me then. I had just picked up a piece of metal with a hole in it, when—"

"A *what?* You mean worked metal? Metal that some one had—"

"Yes, that's why I was so ex—" He stopped and looked puzzled. "But it couldn't have been."

"Possible. This planet might have been inhabited . . . or visited."

"Oh, I don't mean that." Morrie shrugged it off, as if it were of no importance. "I was looking at it, realizing what it meant, when a little bald-headed short guy came up and . . . but it couldn't have been."

"No," agreed Cargraves, after a short pause, "it couldn't have been. I am afraid you were beginning to have anoxia dreams by then. But how about this piece of metal?"

Morrie shook his head. "I don't know," he admitted. "I remember holding it and looking at it, just as clearly as I remember anything, ever. But I remember the little guy just as well. He was standing there and there were others behind him and I knew that they were the moon people. There were buildings and trees." He stopped. "I guess that settles it."

Cargraves nodded, and turned his attention to Morrie's oxygen pack. The valve worked properly now. There was no way to tell what had been wrong, whether it had frosted inside when Morrie walked on into the deeper shadows, whether a bit of elusive dirt had clogged it, or whether Morrie himself had shut it down too far when he had reduced pressure at Cargraves' suggestion and thereby slowly suffocated himself. But it must not happen again. He turned to Art.

"See here, Art. I want to rig these gimmicks so that you can't shut them off below a certain limit. Mmmm . . . no, that isn't enough. We need a warning signal, too—something to warn the wearer if his supply stops. See what you can dream up."

Art got the troubled look on his face that was habitual with him whenever his gadget-conscious mind was working at his top capacity. "I've got some peanut bulbs among the instrument spares," he mused. "Maybe I could mount one on the neck ring and jimmy it up so that when the flow stopped it would—" Cargraves stopped listening; he knew that it was only a matter of time until some unlikely but perfectly practical new circuit would be born.

13.
"SOMEBODY IS NUTS!"

The top of the ring of hills showed them the earth, as Morrie had thought. Cargraves, Art, and Ross did the exploring, leaving Morrie back to recuperate and to work on his celestial navigation problem. Cargraves made a point of going along because he did not want the two passengers to play mountain goat on the steep crags—a great temptation under the low gravity conditions.

Also, he wanted to search over the spot where Morrie had had his mishap. Little bald men, no; a piece of metal with a hole in it—possible. If it existed it might be the first clue to the greatest discovery since man crawled up out of the darkness and became aware of himself.

But no luck—the spot was easy to find; footprints were new to this loose soil! But search as they might, they found nothing. Their failure was not quite certain, since the gloom of the crater's rim still hung over the spot. In a few days it would be daylight here; he planned to search again.

But it seemed possible that Morrie might have flung it away in his anoxia delirium, if it ever existed. It might have carried two hundred yards before it fell, and then buried itself in the loose soil.

The hill top was more rewarding. Cargraves told Art that they would go ahead with the attempt to try to beam a message back to earth . . . and then had to restrain him from running back to the ship to get started. Instead they searched for a place to install the "Dog House."

The Dog House was a small pre-fab building, now resting in sections fitting snugly to the curving walls of the *Galileo*. Art had worked on it during the summer while Cargraves and Morrie were training. It was listed as a sheet-metal garage, with a curved roof, not unlike a Quonset hut, but it had the special virtue that each panel could be taken through the door of the *Galileo*.

It was not their notion simply to set it up on the face of the moon; such an arrangement would have been alternately too hot and then too cold. Instead it was to be the frame for a sort of tailor-made cave.

They found a place near the crest, between two pinnacles of rock with a fairly level floor between and of about the right size. The top of one of the crags was easily accessible and had a clear view of earth for line-of-sight, beamed transmission. There being no atmosphere, Art did not have to worry about horizon effects; the waves would go where he headed them. Having settled on the location, they returned for tools and supplies.

Cargraves and Ross did most of the building of the Dog House. It would not have been fair to Art to require him to help; he was already suffering agonies of indecision through a desire to spend all his time taking pictures and an equally strong desire to get his set assembled with which he hoped to raise earth. Morrie, at Cargraves' request, stayed on light duty for a few days, cooking, working on his navigation, and refraining from the strain of space-suit work.

The low gravitational pull made light work of moving the building sections, other materials, and tools to the spot. Each could carry over five hundred pounds, earth-weight, of the total each trip, except on the steeper portions of the trail where sheer bulk and clumsiness required them to split the loads.

First they shoveled the sandy soil about in the space between the two rocks until the ground was level enough to receive the metal floor, then they assembled the little building in place. The work went fast; wrenches alone were needed for this and the metal seemed light as cardboard. When that was done, they installed the "door," a steel drum, barrel-sized, with an air-tight gasketed head on each end.

Once the door was in place they proceeded to shovel many earth-tons of lunar soil down on top of the roof, until the space between the rock walls was filled, some three feet higher than the roof of the structure. When they were finished, nothing showed of the Dog House but the igloo-style door, sticking out between the rocky spires. The loose soil of Luna, itself a poor conductor of heat, and the vacuum spaces in it, would be their insulation.

But it was not yet air-tight. They installed portable, temporary lights, then dragged in sealed canisters and flat bales. From the canisters came sticky, tacky sheets of a rubbery plastic. This they hung like wallpaper, working as rapidly as possible in order to finish before the volatiles boiled out of the plastic. They covered ceiling, walls and floor, then from the bales they removed aluminum foil, shiny as mirrors, and slapped it on top of the plastic, all except the floor, which was covered with heavier duraluminum sheets.

It was ready for a pressure test. There were a few leaks to patch and they were ready to move in. The whole job had taken less than two "days."

The Dog House was to be Art's radio shack, but that was not all. It was to be also a storeroom for everything they could possibly spare from the ship, everything not necessary to the brief trip back. The cargo space would then be made available for specimens to take back to earth, even if the specimens were no more than country rock, lunar style.

But to Cargraves and to the three it was more than a storeroom, more than a radio shack. They were moving their personal gear into it, installing the hydroponic tank for the rhubarb plants to make the atmosphere self-refreshing, fitting it out as completely as possible for permanent residence.

To them it was a symbol of man's colonization of this planet, his intention to remain permanently, to fit it to his needs, and wrest a living from it.

Even though circumstances required them to leave it behind them in a few days, they were declaring it to be their new home; they were hanging up their hats.

They celebrated the completion of it with a ceremony which Cargraves had deliberately delayed until the Dog House was complete. Standing in a semicircle in front of the little door, they were addressed by Cargraves:

"As commander of this expedition, duly authorized by a commission of the United Nations and proceeding in a vessel of United States registry, I take possession of this planet as a colony, on behalf of the United Nations of earth in accordance with the laws thereof and the laws of the United States. Run 'em up, Ross!"

On a short and slender staff the banner of the United Nations and the flag of the United States whipped to the top. No breeze disturbed them in that airless waste—but Ross had taken the forethought to stiffen the upper edges of each with wire; they showed their colors.

Cargraves found himself gulping as he watched the flag and banner hoisted. Privately he thought of this little hole in the ground as the first building of Luna City. He imagined that in a year or so there would be dozens of such cave dwellings, larger and better equipped, clustered around this spot. In them would live prospectors, scientists, and tough construction workers— workers who would be busy building the permanent Luna City down under the floor of the crater, while other workers installed a great rocket port up on the surface.

Nearby would be the beginning of the Cargraves Physical Laboratory, the Galileo Lunar Observatory.

He found that tears were trickling down his cheeks; he tried futilely to wipe them away—through his helmet. He caught Ross's eye and was embarrassed. "Well, sports," he said with forced heartiness, "let's get to work. Funny," he added, looking at Ross, "what effect a few little symbols can have on a man."

Ross looked from Cargraves to the bits of gay bunting. "I don't know," he said slowly. "A man isn't a collection of chemical reactions; he is a collection of ideas."

Cargraves stared. His "boys" were growing up!

"When do we start exploring?" Morrie wanted to know. "Any reason why we shouldn't get going, now that the Dog House is finished?"

"Before long, I think," Cargraves answered uncomfortably. He had been stalling Morrie's impatience for the last couple of days; Morrie was definitely disappointed that the rocket ship was not to be used, as originally planned, for point to point exploration. He felt confident that he could repeat his remarkable performance in making the first landing.

Cargraves, on the other hand, was convinced that a series of such landings would eventually result in a crash, leaving them marooned to starve or suffocate even if they were not killed in the crash. Consequently he had not budged from his decision to limit exploration to trips on foot, trips which could not be more than a few hours in duration.

"Let's see how Art is getting on," he suggested. "I don't want to leave him behind—he'll want to take pictures. On the other hand, he needs to get on with his radio work. Maybe we can rally around and furnish him with some extra hands."

"Okay." They crawled through the air lock and entered the Dog House. Art and Ross had already gone inside.

"Art," Cargraves inquired when he had taken off his clumsy suit, "how long will it be until you are ready to try out your earth sender?"

"Well, I don't know, Uncle. I never did think we could get through with the equipment we've got. If we had been able to carry the stuff I wanted—"

"You mean if we had been able to afford it," put in Ross.

"Well . . . anyhow, I've got another idea. This place is an electronics man's dream—all that vacuum! I'm going to try to gimmick up some really *big* power tubes—only they won't be tubes. I can just mount the elements out in the open without having to bother with glass. It's the easiest way to do experimental tube design anybody ever heard of."

"But even so," Morrie pointed out, "that could go on indefinitely. Doc, you've got us scheduled to leave in less than ten earthdays. Feel like stretching the stay?" he added hopefully.

"No, I don't," Cargraves stated. "Hmmm . . . Art, let's skip the transmitter problem for a moment. After all, there isn't any law that says we've got to establish radio contact with the earth. But how long would it take to get ready to receive from the earth?"

"Oh, that!" said Art. "*They* have to do all the hard work for that. Now that I've got everything up here I can finish that hookup in a couple of hours."

"Fine! We'll whip up some lunch."

It was nearer three hours when Art announced he was ready to try. "Here goes," he said. "Stand by."

They crowded around. "What do you expect to get?" Ross asked eagerly.

Art shrugged. "Maybe nothing. NAA, or Berlin Sender, if they are beamed on us. I guess Radio Paris is the best bet, if they are still trying for us." He adjusted his controls with the vacant stare that always came over him.

They all kept very quiet. If it worked, it would be a big moment in history, and they all knew it.

He looked suddenly startled.

"Got something?"

He did not answer for a moment. Then he pushed a phone off one ear and said bitterly, "One of you guys left the power on your walkie-talkie."

Cargraves checked the suits himself. "No, Art, they are all dead."

Art looked around the little room. "But . . . but . . . there's nothing else it could be. Somebody is nuts!"

"What's the matter?"

" 'What's the matter?' I'm getting a power hum from somewhere and it's from somewhere around here . . . *close!*"

14.
"NO CHANCE AT ALL!"

"Are you sure?" Cargraves demanded.

"Of course I'm sure!"

"It's probably Radio Paris," Ross suggested. "You don't know how far away it is."

Art looked indignant. "Suppose you sit down here and try your luck, Mr. de Forrest. It was *close*. It couldn't have been an earth station."

"Feed back?"

"Don't be silly!" He tried fiddling with his dials a bit more. "It's gone now."

"Just a minute," said Cargraves. "We've got to be sure about this. Art, can you get any sort of a transmitter rigged?"

"Not very eas—yes, I can, too. The homing set is all set to go." The homing set was a low-power transmitter intended simply for communication between the Dog House and any member of the party outside in a suit.

"Gimme half a second to hook it up." It took more than half a second but shortly he was leaning toward the microphone, shouting, "Hello! Hello! Is there anybody there! Hello!"

"He must have been dreaming," Morrie said quietly to Cargraves. "There couldn't be anybody out there."

"Shut up," Art said over his shoulder and went back to calling, "Hello! Hello, hello."

His expression suddenly went blank, then he said sharply, "Speak English! Repeat!"

"What was it?" demanded Cargraves, Ross, and Morrie.

"Quiet . . . please!" Then, to the mike, "Yes, I hear you. Who is this? What? Say that again? . . . This is the Space Ship *Galileo*, Arthur Mueller transmitting. Hold on a minute." Art flipped a switch on the front of the panel. "Now go ahead. Repeat who you are."

A heavy, bass voice came out of the transmitter:

"This is Lunar Expedition Number One," the voice said. "Will you be pleased to wait one minute while I summon our leader?"

"Wait a minute," yelled Art. "Don't go away!" But the speaker did not answer.

Ross started whistling to himself. "Stop that whistling," Art demanded.

"Sorry." Ross paused, then added, "I suppose you know what this means?"

"Huh? I don't know what anything means!"

"It means that we are too late for the senior prizes. Somebody has beaten us to it."

"Huh? How do you figure that?"

"Well, it's not certain, but it's likely."

"I'll bet we landed first."

"We'll see. Listen!" It was the speaker again, this time a different voice, lighter in timbre, with a trace of Oxford accent. "Are you there? This is Captain James Brown of the First Lunar Expedition. Is this the Rocket Ship *Galileo?*"

Cargraves leaned over to the mike. "Rocket Ship *Galileo*, Captain Cargraves speaking. Where are you?"

"Some distance away, old chap. But don't worry. We are locating you. Keep sending, please."

"Let us know where we are in reference to you."

"Do not worry about that. We will come to you. Just remain where you are and keep sending."

"What is your lunar latitude and longitude?"

The voice seemed to hesitate, then went on, "We have you located now. We can exchange details later. Good-by."

Thereafter Art shouted "hello" until he was hoarse, but there was no answer. "Better stay on the air, Art," Cargraves decided. "Ross and I will go back to the ship. That's what they will see. I don't know, though. They might not show up for a week." He mused. "This presents a lot of new problems."

"*Somebody* ought to go to the ship," Morrie pointed out, "without waiting. They may be just coming in for a landing. They may show up any time."

"I don't think it was ship transmission," said Art, then turned back to his microphone.

Nevertheless it was decided that Cargraves and Ross would go back to the ship. They donned their suits and crawled through the air lock, and had no more than started down the steep and rocky slope when Ross saw the rocket.

He did not hear it, naturally, but he had glanced back to see if Cargraves was behind him. "Look!" he called into his helmet mike, and pointed.

The ship approached them from the west, flying low and rather slowly. The pilot was riding her on her jet, for the blast shot more downward than to the stern. "We had better hurry!" Ross shouted, and went bounding ahead.

But the rocket did not come in for a landing. It nosed down, forward jets driving hard against the fall, directly toward the *Galileo*. At an altitude of not more than five hundred feet the pilot kicked her around, belly first, and drove away on his tail jet.

Where the *Galileo* lay, there was a flash, an utterly silent explosion, and a cloud of dust which cleared rapidly away in the vacuum. The sound reached them through their feet, after a long time—it seemed to them.

The *Galileo* lay on her side, a great gaping hole in her plates. The wound stretched from shattered view port to midships.

Cargraves stood perfectly still, staring at the unbelievable. Ross found his voice first. "They gave us no chance," he said, shaking both fists at the sky. "No chance at all!"

15.
WHAT POSSIBLE REASON?

He turned and stumbled back up the slope to where Cargraves still stood forlorn and motionless. "Did you see that, Doc?" he demanded. "Did you see that? The dirty rats bombed us—they bombed us. Why? Why, Doc? Why would they do such a thing?"

Tears were streaming down his face. Cargraves patted him clumsily. "I don't know," he said slowly. "I don't know," he repeated, still trying to readjust himself to the shock.

"Oh, I want to kill somebody!"

"So do I." Cargraves turned away suddenly. "Maybe we will. Come on—we've got to tell the others." He started up the slope.

But Art and Morrie were already crawling out of the lock when they reached it. "What happened?" Morrie demanded. "We felt a quake."

Cargraves did not answer directly. "Art, did you turn off your transmitter?"

"Yes, but what happened?"

"Don't turn it on again. It will lead them to us here." He waved a hand out at the floor of the crater. "Look!"

It took a minute or two for what they saw to sink in. Then Art turned helplessly to Cargraves. "But, Uncle," he pleaded, "what happened? Why did the ship blow up?"

"They blitzed us," Cargraves said savagely. "They bombed us out. If we had been aboard they would have killed us. That's what they meant to do."

"But why?"

"No possible reason. They didn't want us here." He refrained from saying what he felt to be true: that their unknown enemy had failed only temporarily in his intent to kill. A quick death by high explosive would probably be a blessing compared with what he felt was in store for them . . . marooned . . . on a dead and airless planet.

How long would they last? A month? Two months? Better by far if the bomb had hit them.

Morrie turned suddenly back toward the lock. "What are you doing, Morrie?"

"Going to get the guns!"

"Guns are no good to us."

But Morrie had not heard him. His antenna was already shielded by the metal drum.

Ross said, "I'm not sure that guns are no good, Doc."

"Huh? How do you figure?"

"Well, what are they going to do next? Won't they want to see what they've done? They didn't even see the bomb hit; they were jetting away."

"Yes?"

"If they land we'll hijack their ship!"

Art came up closer. "Huh? Hey, Ross, that's tellin' 'em! We'll get them! We'll show them! Murderers!" His words tumbled over one another, squeaking and squawking in their radios.

"We'll try!" Cargraves decided suddenly. "We'll try. If they land we won't go down without a fight. We can't be any worse off than we are." He was suddenly unworried; the prospect of a gun fight, something new to his experience, did not upset him further. It cheered him. "Where do you think we ought to hide, Ross? In the *Galileo?*"

"If we have—*There they come!*" The rocket had suddenly appeared over the far rim.

"Where's Morrie?"

"Here." He came up from behind them, burdened with the two rifles and the revolver. "Here, Ross, you take . . . *hey!*" He had caught sight of the strangers' rocket. "We've got to hurry," he said.

But the rocket did not land. It came down low, dipping below the level of the crater's rim, then scooted on its tail across near the wreckage of the *Galileo*, up, out, and away.

"And we didn't even get a crack at them," Morrie said bitterly.

"Not yet," Ross answered, "but I think they'll be back. This was a second bombing run, sure as anything, in case they missed the first time. They'll still come back to see what they've done. How about it, Doc?"

"I think they will," Cargraves decided. "They will want to look over our ship and to kill us off if they missed any of us. But we don't go to the *Galileo*."

"Why not?"

"We haven't time. They will probably turn as fast as they can check themselves, come back and land. We might be caught out in the open."

"That's a chance we'll have to take."

It was decided for them. The rocket appeared again from the direction it had gone. This time it was plainly a landing trajectory. "Come on!" shouted Cargraves, and went careening madly down the slope.

The rocket landed about halfway between the *Galileo* and the shadows, now close to the foot of the hills, for the sun had climbed four "days" higher in the sky. The ship was noticeably smaller than the *Galileo* even at that distance.

Cargraves did not notice such details. His immediate intent was to reach the door of the craft before it opened, to be ready to grapple with them as they came out.

But his good sense came to his aid before he was out in the sunlight. He realized he had no gun. Morrie had kept one, Ross had the other, and Art was waving the revolver around. He paused just short of the dazzling, sunlighted area. "Hold it," he ordered. "I don't think they have seen us. I don't think they will—yet."

"What are your plans?" Morrie demanded.

"Wait for them to get out, then rush the ship—after they get well away from it. Wait for my signal."

"Can't they hear us?"

"Maybe. If they are on this frequency, we're goners. Switch off your talkies, everybody." He did so himself; the sudden silence was chilling.

The rocket was almost tail towards them. He now saw three suit-clad figures pile out from a door that swung out from the side. The first looked around briefly, but he appeared not to see them. Since it was almost certain that he was wearing sun goggles, it was doubtful if he could see much inside the shadows.

He motioned to the other two and moved toward the *Galileo*, using a long, loping gallop that the *Galileo*'s crew had learned was the proper way to walk on the moon. That alone was enough to tell Cargraves that these men, their enemies, were not grounding on the moon for the first time.

Cargraves let them get all the way to the *Galileo*, and, in fact, to disappear behind it, before he got up from where he had been crouching. "Come on!" he yelled into a dead microphone, and slammed ahead in great leaps that took him fifty feet at a stride.

The outer door of the lock stood open. He swarmed into it and closed it after him. It clamped by means of a wheel mounted in its center; the operation was obvious. That done he looked around. The tiny lock was dimly illuminated by a pane of glass set in the inner door. In this feeble light he looked and felt for what he needed next—the spill valve for air.

He found it and heard the air hissing into the compartment. He leaned his weight against the inner door and waited.

Suddenly it gave way; he was in the rocket and blinking his eyes.

There was a man still seated in the pilot's chair. He turned his head, and appeared to say comething. Cargraves could not hear it through his helmet and was not interested. Taking all advantage of the low gravity he dived at the man and grappled him about the head and shoulders.

The man was too surprised to put up much of a fight—not that it would have mattered; Cargraves felt ready to fight anything up to and including tigers.

He found himself banging the man's head against the soft padding of the acceleration chair. That, he realized, was no good. He drew back a gauntleted fist and buried it in the pit of the man's stomach.

The man grunted and seemed to lose interest. Cargraves threw a short jab straight to the unguarded chin. No further treatment was needed. Cargraves pushed him down to the floor, noticing without interest that the belt of his victim carried a holster with what appeared to be a heavy-caliber Mauser, and then stood on him. He looked out the conning port.

There was a figure collapsed on the ground near the broken bow of the *Galileo*, whether friend or foe it was impossible to say. But another was standing over him and concerning him there was no doubt. It was not alone the unfamiliar cut of his space suit, it was the pistol in his hand. He was firing in the direction of the rocket in which Cargraves stood.

He saw the blaze of a shot, but no answering report. Another shot followed it—and this one almost deafened him; it struck the ship containing him, making it ring like a giant bell.

He was in a dilemma. He wanted very urgently to join the fight; the weapon on the person of his disabled opponent offered a way. Yet he could not leave his prisoner inside the ship while he went out, nor did he, even in the heat of fighting, have any stomach for killing an unconscious man.

He had already decided, in the space of a breath, to slug his man heavily and get outside, when the fast drama beyond the port left him no time. The space-suited stranger at the bow of the *Galileo* was suddenly without a helmet. Around his neck was only a jagged collar.

He dropped his pistol and clutched at his face. He stood there for a moment, as if puzzled by his predicament, took two hesitant steps forward, and sank gently to the ground.

He thrashed around a bit but did not get up. He was still convulsing when a third man appeared around the end of the ship. He did not last long. He appeared confused, unable to comprehend the turn of events, which was quite likely, in view of the ghostly stillness of the gun fight. It was entirely possible that he never knew what hit him, nor why. He was still reaching for his iron when he was struck twice, first in the chest and the second shot lower down.

He bowed forward, until his helmet touched the ground, then collapsed.

Cargraves heard a noise behind him. Snatching the gun he had taken to the ready, and turning, he watched the door of the air lock open.

It was Art, wild-eyed and red. "Any more in here?" the boy called out to him, while swinging his revolver in a wide arc. His voice reached Cargraves faintly, muffled by their two helmets.

"No. Turn on your radio," he shouted back, then realized his own was still off. Switching it on, he repeated his statement.

"Mine *is* on," Art replied. "I turned it on while the lock filled. How are they doing outside?"

"All right, it looks like. Here, you guard this guy." He pointed down at his feet. "I'm going outside."

But it was unnecessary. The lock opened again and both Ross and Morrie bulged out of it. Cargraves wondered absently how the two had managed to squeeze into that coffin-like space.

"Need any help?" demanded Morrie.

"No. It doesn't look like you guys did, either."

"We ambushed 'em," Ross said jubilantly. "Hid in the shadow of the ship and picked 'em off as they showed up. All but the second one. He darn near got us before we got him. Do you know," he went on conversationally, as if he had spent a lifetime shooting it out, "it's almost impossible to sight a gun when you're wearing one of these fish bowls over your head?"

"Hmm . . . You made out all right."

"Pure luck. Morrie was shooting from the hip."

"I was not," Morrie denied. "I aimed and squeezed off every shot."

Cargraves cautioned them to keep an eye on the prisoner, as he wanted to take a look around outside. "Why," demanded Art, "bother to guard him? Shoot him and chuck him out, I say."

"Cool down," Cargraves told him. "Shooting prisoners isn't civilized."

Art snorted. "Is *he* civilized?"

"Shut up, Art. Morrie—take charge." He shut himself in the air lock.

The examination took little time. Two of the strangers had received wounds which would have been fatal in any case, it seemed to him, but their suits were deflated in any event. The third, whose helmet had been struck, was equally beyond help. His eyes bulged sightlessly at the velvet sky. Blood from his nose still foamed. He was gone—drowned in vacuum.

He went back to the little ship, without even a glance at the dismal pile of junk that had been the sleekly beautiful *Galileo*.

Back in the ship, he threw himself in one of the acceleration chairs and sighed. "Not so bad," he said. "We've got a ship."

"That's what you think," Art said darkly. "Take a look at that instrument board."

16.
THE SECRET BEHIND THE MOON

"What!" said Cargraves and looked where he was pointing.

"This is no space ship," Art said bitterly. "This thing is a jeep. Look at that." He indicated two gauges. One was marked *SAUER-STOFF*, the other *ALKOHOL*. "Oxygen and alcohol. This thing is just a kiddy wagon."

"Maybe those are just for the maneuvering jets," Cargraves answered, not very hopefully.

"Not a chance, Doc," Ross put in. "I've already given her the once-over, with Art translating the Jerry talk for me. Besides, did you notice that this boat hasn't any wings of any sort? It's purely a station wagon for the moon. Look—we've got company."

The prisoner had opened his eyes and was trying to sit up.

Cargraves grabbed him by a shoulder, yanked him to his feet, and shoved him into the chair he had just vacated. "Now, you," he snapped. "Talk!"

The man looked dazed and did not answer. "Better try German on him, Uncle," Art suggested. "The labels are all in German."

Cargraves reached far back into his technical education and shifted painfully to German. "What is your name?"

"My name is Friedrich Lenz, sergeant-technician of the second class. To whom am I speaking?"

"Answer the questions you are asked. Why did you bomb our ship?"

"In line of duty. I was ordered."

"That is not a reason. Why did you bomb a peaceful ship?"

The man simply looked sullen. "Very well," Cargraves went

on, still speaking in German. "Get the air lock open, Art. We'll throw this trash out on the face of the moon."

The self-styled sergeant-technician suddenly began talking very rapidly. Cargraves wrinkled his forehead. "Art," he said, returning to English, "you'll have to help me out. He's slinging it too fast for me."

"And translate!" protested Ross. "What does he say?"

"I'll try," Art agreed, then shifted to German. "Answer the question over again. Speak slowly."

"*Ja—*" the man agreed, addressing his words to Cargraves.

" '*Herr Kapitän!*' " Art thundered at him.

" '*Ja, Herr Kapitän,*' " the man complied respectfully, "I was trying to explain to you—" He went on at length.

Art translated when he paused. "He says that he is part of the crew of this rocket. He says that it was commanded by Lieutenant—I didn't catch the name; it's one of the guys we shot—and that they were ordered by their leader to seek out and bomb a ship at this location. He says that it was not a . . . uh, a *wanton* attack because it was an act of war."

"War?" demanded Ross. "What in thunder does he mean, 'war'? There's no war. It was sheer attempted murder."

Art spoke with the prisoner again.

"He says that there is a war, that there always has been a war. He says that there will always be war until the National Socialist Reich is victorious." He listened for a moment. "He says that the Reich will live a thousand years."

Morrie used some words that Cargraves had never heard him use before. "Ask him how he figures that one."

"Never mind," put in Cargraves. "I'm beginning to get the picture." He addressed the Nazi directly. "How many are there in your party, how long has it been on the moon, and where is your base?"

Presently Art said, "He claims he doesn't have to answer questions of that sort, under international law."

"Hummph! You might tell him that the laws of warfare went out when war was abolished. But never mind—tell him that, if he wants to claim prisoner-of-war privileges, we'll give him his freedom, right now!" He jerked a thumb at the air lock.

He had spoken in English, but the prisoner understood the gesture. After that he supplied details readily.

He and his comrades had been on the moon for nearly three

months. They had an underground base about thirteen miles west of the crater in which the shattered *Galileo* lay. There was one rocket at the base, much larger than the *Galileo*, and it, too, was atom-powered. He regarded himself as a member of the army of the Nazi Reich. He did not know why the order had been given to blast the *Galileo*, but he supposed that it was an act of military security to protect their plans.

"What plans?"

He became stubborn again. Cargraves actually opened the inner door of the lock, not knowing himself how far he was prepared to go to force information out of the man, when the Nazi cracked.

The plans were simple—the conquest of the entire earth. The Nazis were few in number, but they represented some of the top military, scientific, and technical brains from Hitler's crumbled empire. They had escaped from Germany, established a remote mountain base, and had been working there ever since for the redemption of the Reich. The sergeant appeared not to know where the base was; Cargraves questioned him closely. Africa? South America? An island? But all that he could get out of him was that it was a long submarine trip from Germany.

But it was the objective, *der Tag*, which left them too stunned to worry about their own danger. The Nazis had atom bombs, but, as long as they were still holed up in their secret base on earth, they dared not act, for the UN had them, too, and in much greater quantity.

But when they achieved space flight, they had an answer. They would sit safely out of reach on the moon and destroy the cities of earth one after another by guided missiles launched from the moon, until the completely helpless nations of earth surrendered and pleaded for mercy.

The announcement of the final plan brought another flash of arrogance back into their prisoner. "And you cannot stop it," he concluded. "You may kill me, but you cannot stop it! *Heil dem Führer!*"

"Mind if I spit in his eye, Doc?" Morrie said conversationally.

"Don't waste it," Cargraves counseled. "Let's see if we can think ourselves out of this mess. Any suggestions?" He hauled the prisoner out of the chair and made him lie face down on the deck. Then he sat down on him. "Go right ahead," he urged. "I don't think he understands two words of English. How about it, Ross?"

"Well," Ross answered, "it's more than just saving our necks now. We've *got* to stop them. But the notion of tackling fifty men with two rifles and two pistols sounds like a job for Tarzan or Superman. Frankly, I don't know how to start."

"Maybe we can start by scouting them out. Thirteen miles isn't much. Not on the moon."

"Look," said Art, "in a day or two I might have a transmitter rigged that would raise earth. What we need is reinforcements."

"How are they going to get here?" Ross wanted to know. "We had the only space ship—except for the Nazis."

"Yes, but listen—Doc's plans are still available. You left full notes with Ross's father—didn't you, Doc? They can get busy and rebuild some more and come up here and blast those skunks out."

"That might be best," Cargraves answered. "We can't afford to miss, that's sure. They could raid the earth base of the Nazis first thing and then probably bust this up in a few weeks, knowing that our ship did work and having our plans."

Morrie shook his head. "It's all wrong. We've got to get at them *right now*. No delay at all, just the way they smashed us. Suppose it takes the UN six weeks to get there. Six weeks might be too long. Three weeks might be too long. A week might be too long. An atom war could be all over in a day."

"Well, let's ask our pal if he knows when they expect to strike, then," Ross offered.

Morrie shook his head and stopped Art from doing so. "Useless. We'll never get a chance to build a transmitter. They'll be swarming over this crater like reporters around a murder trial. Look—they'll be here any minute. *Don't you think they'll miss this rocket?*"

"Oh, my gosh!" It was Art. Ross added, "What time is it, Doc?"

To their complete amazement it was only forty minutes from the time the *Galileo* had been bombed. It had seemed like a full day.

It cheered them up a little but not much. The prisoner had admitted that the rocket they were in was the only utility, short-jump job. And the Nazi space ship—the *Wotan*, he termed it—would hardly be used for search. Perhaps they had a few relatively free hours.

"But I still don't see it," Cargraves admitted. "Two guns and two pistols—four of us. The odds are too long—and we can't afford to lose. I know you sports aren't afraid to die, but we've got to *win*."

"Why," inquired Ross, "does it have to be rifles?"

"What else?"

"This crate bombed us. I'll bet it carries more than one bomb."

Cargraves looked startled, then turning to the prisoner, spoke rapidly in German. The prisoner gave a short reply. Cargraves nodded and said, "Morrie, do you think you could fly this clunker?"

"I could sure make a stab at it."

"Okay. You are it. We'll make Joe Masterrace here take it off, with a gun in his ribs, and you'll have to feel her out. You won't get but one chance and no practice. Now let's take a look at the bomb controls."

The bomb controls were simple. There was no bombsight, as such. The pilot drove the ship on a straight diving course and kicked it out just before his blast upwards. There was a gadget to expel the bomb free of the ship; it continued on the ship's previous trajectory. Having doped it out, they checked with the Nazi pilot who gave them the same answers they had read in the mechanism.

There were two pilot seats and two passenger seats, directly behind the pilot seats. Morrie took one pilot seat; the Nazi the other. Ross sat behind Morrie, while Cargraves sat with Art in his lap, one belt around both. This squeezed Art up close to the back of the Nazi's chair, which was good, for Art reached around and held a gun in the Nazi's side.

"All set, Morrie?"

"All set. I make one pass to get my bearings and locate the mouth of their hideaway. Then I come back and give 'em the works."

"Right. Try not to hit their rocket ship, if you can. It would be nice to go home. Blast off! *Achtung! Aufstieg!*"

The avengers raised ground.

"How is it going?" Cargraves shouted a few moments later. "Okay!" Morrie answered, raising his voice to cut through the roar. "I could fly her down a chimney. There's the hill ahead, I think—there!"

The silvery shape of the *Wotan* near the hill they were shooting towards put a stop to any doubts. It appeared to be a natural upthrust of rock, quite different from the craters, and lay by itself a few miles out in one of the "seas."

They were past it and Morrie was turning, blasting heavily to kill his momentum, and pressing them hard into their seats. Art fought to steady the revolver without firing it.

Morrie was headed back on his bombing run, coming in high

for his dive. Cargraves wondered if Morrie had actually seen the air lock of the underground base; he himself had had no glimpse of it.

There was no time left to wonder. Morrie was diving; they were crushed against the pads as he fought a moment later to recover from the dive, kicking her up and blasting. They hung for a second and Cargraves thought that Morrie had played it too fine in his anxiety to get in a perfect shot; he braced himself for the crash.

Then they were up. When he had altitude, Morrie kicked her over again, letting his jet die. They dropped, view port down, with the ground staring at them.

They could see the splash of dust and sand still rising. Suddenly there was a *whoosh* from the middle of it, a mighty blast of air, bits of debris, and more sand. It cleared at once in the vacuum of that plain, and they saw the open wound, a black hole leading downward.

He had blown out the air lock with a bull's-eye.

Morrie put her down to Cargraves' plan, behind the *Wotan* and well away from the hole. "Okay, Doc!"

"Good. Now let's run over the plan—I don't want any slipup. Ross comes with me. You and Art stay with the jeep. We will look over the *Wotan* first, then scout out the base. If we are gone longer than thirty minutes, you must assume that we are dead or captured. No matter what happens, under no circumstances whatever are you to leave this rocket. If any one comes toward you, blast off. Don't even let us come near you unless we are by ourselves. Blast off. You've got one more bomb—you know what to do with it."

Morrie nodded. "Bomb the *Wotan*. I hate to do that." He stared wistfully at the big ship, their one chain to the earth.

"But you've got to. You and Art have got to run for it, then, and get back to the Dog House and hole up. It'll be your business, Art, to manage somehow or other to throw together a set that can get a message back to earth. That's your only business, both of you. Under no circumstances are you to come back here looking for Ross and me. If you stay holed up, they may not find you for weeks—and that will give you your chance, the *earth's* chance. Agreed?"

Morrie hesitated. "Suppose we get a message through to earth. How about it then?"

Cargraves thought for a moment, then replied, "We can't stand here jawing—there's work to be done. If you get a message through with a reply that makes quite clear that they believe you and are getting busy, then you are on your own. But I advise you not to take any long chances. If we aren't back here in thirty minutes, you probably can't help us." He paused for a moment and decided to add one more thing—the boy's personal loyalty had made him doubtful about one point. "You know, don't you, that when it comes to dropping that bomb, if you do, you must drop it where it has to go, even if Ross and I are standing on your target?"

"I suppose so."

"Those are orders, Morrie."

"I understand them."

"Morrie!"

"Aye aye, Captain!"

"Very well, sir—that's better. Art, Morrie is in charge. Come on, Ross."

Nothing moved on the rocket field. The dust of the bombing, with no air to hold it up, had dissipated completely. The broken air lock showed dark and still across the field; near them the sleek and mighty *Wotan* crouched silent and untended.

Cargraves made a circuit of the craft, pistol ready in his gloved fist, while Ross tailed him, armed with one of the Garands. Ross kept well back, according to plan.

Like the *Galileo*, the *Wotan* had but one door, on the port side just abaft the conning compartment. He motioned Ross to stay back, then climbed a little metal ladder or staircase and tried the latch. To his surprise the ship was not locked—then he wondered why he was surprised. Locks were for cities.

While the pressure in the air chamber equalized, he unsnapped from his belt a flashlight he had confiscated from the Nazi jeep rocket and prepared to face whatever lay beyond the door. When the door sighed open, he dropped low and to one side, then shot his light around the compartment. Nothing . . . nobody.

The ship was empty of men from stem to stern. It was almost too much luck. Even if it had been a rest period, or even if there had been no work to do in the ship, he had expected at least a guard on watch.

However a guard on watch would mean one less pair of hands for work . . . and this was the moon, where every pair of hands counted for a hundred or a thousand on earth. Men were at a premium here; it was more likely, he concluded, that their watch was a radar, automatic and unsleeping. Probably with a broad-band radio alarm as well, he thought, remembering how promptly their own call had been answered the very first time they had ever sent anything over the rim of their crater.

He went through a passenger compartment equipped with dozens of acceleration bunks, through a hold, and farther aft. He was looking for the power plant.

He did not find it. Instead he found a welded steel bulkhead with no door of any sort. Puzzled, he went back to the control station. What he found there puzzled him still more. The acceleration chairs were conventional enough; some of the navigational instruments were common types and all of them not too difficult to figure out; but the controls simply did not make sense.

Although this bewildered him, one point was very clear. The Nazis had not performed the nearly impossible task of building a giant space ship in a secret hide-out, any more than he and the boys had built the *Galileo* singlehandedly. In each case it had been a job of conversion plus the installation of minor equipment.

For the *Wotan* was one of the finest, newest, biggest ships ever to come out of Detroit!

The time was getting away from him. He had used up seven minutes in his prowl through the ship. He hurried out and rejoined Ross. "Empty," he reported, saving the details for later. "Let's try their rat hole." He started loping across the plain.

They had to pick their way carefully through the rubble at the mouth of the hole. Since the bomb had not been an atom bomb but simply ordinary high explosive, they were in no danger of contamination, but they were in danger of slipping, sliding, falling, into the darkness.

Presently the rubble gave way to an excellent flight of stairs leading deep into the moon. Ross flashed his torch around. The walls, steps, and ceiling were covered with some tough lacquer, sprayed on to seal the place. The material was transparent, or nearly so, and they could see that it covered carefully fitted stonework.

"Went to a lot of trouble, didn't they?" Ross remarked.

"Keep quiet!" answered Cargraves.

More than two hundred feet down the steep passageway ended, and they came to another door, not an air lock, but intended apparently as an air-tight safety door. It had not kept the owners safe; the blast followed by a sudden letting up of normal pressure had been too much for it. It was jammed in place but so bulged and distorted that there was room for them to squeeze through.

There was some light in the room beyond. The blast had broken most of the old-fashioned bulbs the Nazis had used, but here and there a light shone out, letting them see that they were in a large hall. Cargraves went cautiously ahead.

A room lay to the right from the hall, through an ordinary non-air-tight door, now hanging by one hinge. In it they found the reason why the field had been deserted when they had attacked.

The room was a barrack room; the Nazis had died in their bunks. "Night" and "day" were arbitrary terms on the moon, insofar as the working times and eating times and sleeping times of men are concerned. The Nazis were on another schedule; they had had the bad luck to be sleeping when Morrie's bomb had robbed them of their air.

Cargraves stayed just long enough in the room to assure himself that all were dead. He did not let Ross come in at all. There was some blood, but not much, being mostly bleeding from mouths and bulging eyes. It was not this that caused his squeamish consideration; it was the expressions which were frozen on their dead faces.

He got out before he got sick.

Ross had found something. "Look here!" he demanded.

Cargraves looked. A portion of the wall had torn away under the sudden drop in pressure and had leaned crazily into the room. It was a metal panel, instead of the rock masonry which made up the rest of the walls. Ross had pulled and pried at it to see what lay behind, and was now playing his light into the darkness behind it.

It was another corridor, lined with carefully dressed and fitted stones. But here the stone had not been covered with the sealing lacquer.

"I wonder why they sealed it off after they built it?" Ross wanted to know. "Do you suppose they have stuff stored down there? Their A-bombs maybe?"

Cargraves studied the patiently fitted stones stretching away into the unfathomed darkness. After a long time he answered softly, "Ross, you haven't discovered a Nazi storeroom. You have discovered the homes of the people of the moon."

17.
"—UNTIL WE ROT—"

For once Ross was almost as speech-bound as Art. When he was able to make his words behave he demanded, "Are you sure? Are you sure, Doc?"

Cargraves nodded. "As sure as I can be at this time. I wondered why the Nazis had built such a deep and extensive a base and why they had chosen to use fitted stone masonry. It would be hard to do, working in a space suit. But I assigned it to their reputation for doing things the hard way, what they call 'efficiency.' I should have known better." He peered down the mysterious, gloomy corridor. "Certainly this was not built in the last few months."

"How long ago, do you think?"

"How long? How long is a million years? How long is ten million years? I don't know—I have trouble imagining a thousand years. Maybe we'll never know."

Ross wanted to explore. Cargraves shook his head. "We can't go chasing rabbits. This is wonderful, the biggest thing in ages. But it will wait. Right now," he said, glancing at his watch, "we've got eleven minutes to finish the job and get back up to the surface—or things will start happening up there!"

He covered the rest of the layout at a fast trot, with Ross guarding his rear from the central hall. He found the radio "shack," with a man dead in his phones, and noted that the equipment did not appear to have suffered much damage when the whirlwind of escaping air had slammed out of the place. Farther on, an arsenal contained bombs for the jeep, and rifles, but no men.

He found the storeroom for the guided missiles, more than two hundred of them, although the cradles were only half used up. The sight of them should have inspired terror, knowing as he did that each represented a potentially dead and blasted city, but he had no time for it. He rushed on.

There was a smaller room, well furnished, which seemed to be sort of a wardroom and common room for the officers. It was there that he found a Nazi who was not as the others.

He was sprawled face down and dressed in a space suit. Although he did not move Cargraves approached him very cautiously.

The man was either dead or unconscious. However, he did not have the grimace of death on his face and his suit was still under pressure. Wondering what to do, Cargraves knelt over him. There was a pistol in his belt; Cargraves took it and stuck it in his own.

He could feel no heart-beat through the heavy suit and his own gauntlet, nor could he listen for it, while wearing a helmet himself.

His watch showed five minutes of the agreed time left; whatever he did must be done fast. He grappled the limp form by the belt and dragged it along.

"What have you got there?" Ross demanded.

"Souvenir. Let's get going. No time." He saved his breath for the climb. The sixty-pound weight that he and his burden made, taken together, flew up the stairs six at a time. At the top his watch still showed two minutes to go. "Leg it out to the jeep," he commanded Ross. "I can't take this item there, or Morrie may decide it's a trap. Meet me in the *Wotan*. Get going!" Heaving his light burden over one shoulder, he set out for the big ship at a gallop.

Once inside he put his load down and took the man out of his space suit. The body was warm but seemed dead. However, he found he could detect a faint heart-beat. He was starting an artificial respiration when the boys piled out of the lock.

"Hi," he said, "who wants to relieve me here? I don't know much about it."

"Why bother?" asked Morrie.

Cargraves paused momentarily and looked at him quizzically. "Well, aside from the customary reasons you have been brought up to believe in, he might be more use to us alive than dead."

Morrie shrugged. "Okay, I'll take over." He dropped to his knees, took Cargraves' place, and started working.

"Did you bring them up to date?" Cargraves asked Ross.

"I gave them a quick sketch. Told them the place seemed to be ours and I told them what we found—the ruins."

"Not very ruined," Cargraves remarked.

"Look, Uncle," demanded Art. "Can I go down there? I've got to get some pictures."

"Pictures can wait," Cargraves pointed out. "Right now we've got to find out how this ship works. As soon as we get the hang of it, we head back. That comes first."

"Well, sure," Art conceded, "but . . . after all—I mean. No pictures at all?"

"Well . . . Let's put it this way. It may take Ross and Morrie and me, not to mention yourself, quite some time to figure out how they handle this craft. There might be twenty minutes when we could spare you. In the meantime, table the motion. Come on, Ross. By the way, what did you do with the prisoner?"

"Oh, him," Morrie answered, "we tied him up and left him."

"Huh? Suppose he gets loose? He might steal the rocket."

"He won't get loose. I tied him myself and I took a personal interest in it. Anyhow he won't try to get away—no space suit, no food. That baby knows his chance of living to a ripe old age depends on us and he doesn't want to spoil it."

"That's right, Uncle," Art agreed. "You should have heard what he promised me."

"Good enough, I guess," Cargraves conceded. "Come on, Ross." Morrie went on with his job, with Art to spell him.

Cargraves returned, with Ross, to the central compartment a few minutes later. "Isn't that pile of meat showing signs of life yet?" he asked.

"No. Shall I stop?"

"I'll relieve you. Sometimes they come to after an hour or more. Two of you go over to the jeep with an additional space suit and bring back Sergeant What's-his-name. Ross and I are as much in the dark as ever," he explained. "The sergeant bloke is a pilot. We'll sweat it out of him."

He had no more than gotten firmly to work when the man under him groaned. Morrie turned back at the lock. "Go ahead," Cargraves confirmed. "Ross and I can handle this guy."

The Nazi stirred and moaned. Cargraves turned him over. The man's eyelids flickered, showing bright blue eyes. He stared up at Cargraves. "How do you do?" he said in a voice like a stage Englishman. "May I get up from here?"

Cargraves backed away and let him up. He did not help him.

The man looked around. Ross stood silently, covering him with a Garand. "That isn't necessary, really," the Nazi protested. Ross glanced at Cargraves but continued to cover the prisoner.

The man turned to Cargraves. "Whom have I the honor of addressing?" he asked. "Is it Captain Cargraves of the *Galileo?*"

"That's right. Who are you?"

"I am Helmut von Hartwick, Lieutenant Colonel, Elite Guard." He pronounced lieutenant "leftenant."

"Okay, Helmut, suppose you start explaining yourself. Just what is the big idea?"

The self-styled colonel laughed. "Really, old man, there isn't much to explain, is there? You seem to have eluded us somehow and placed me at a disadvantage. I can see that."

"You had better see that, but that is not what I mean, and that is not enough." Cargraves hesitated. The Nazi had him somewhat baffled; he did not act at all like a man who has just come out of a daze. Perhaps he had been playing 'possum—if so, for how long?

Well, it did not matter, he decided. The Nazi was still his prisoner. "Why did you order my ship bombed?"

"Me? My dear chap, why do you think *I* ordered it?"

"Because you sound just like the phony English accent we heard over our radio. You called yourself 'Captain James Brown.' I don't suppose there is more than one fake Englishman in this crowd of gangsters."

Von Hartwick raised his eyebrows. "'Gangsters' is a harsh term, old boy. Hardly good manners. But you are correct on one point; I was the only one of my colleagues who had enjoyed the questionable advantage of attending a good English school. I'll ask you not to call my accent 'phony.' But, even if I did borrow the name 'Captain James Brown,' that does not prove that I ordered your ship bombed. That was done under the standing orders of our Leader—a necessary exigency of war. I was not personally responsible."

"I think you are a liar on both counts. I don't think you ever attended an English school; you probably picked up that fake accent from Lord Haw-Haw, or from listening to the talkies. And your Leader did not order us bombed, because he did not know we were there. You ordered it, just as soon as you could take a bearing on us, as soon as you found out we were here."

The Nazi spread his hands, palms down, and looked pained. "Really, you Americans are so ready to jump to conclusions. Do you truly think that I could fuel a rocket, call its crew, and equip it for bombing, all in ten minutes? My only function was to report your location."

"You expected us, then?"

"Naturally. If a stupid radarman had not lost you when you swung into your landing orbit, we would have greeted you much sooner. Surely you don't think that we would have established a military base without preparing to defend it? We plan, we plan for everything. That is why we will win."

Cargraves permitted himself a thin smile. "You don't seem to have planned this."

The Nazi tossed it off. "In war there are setbacks. One expects them."

"Do you call it 'war' to bomb an unarmed, civilian craft without even a warning?"

Hartwick looked pained. "Please, my dear fellow! It ill befits you to split hairs. You seemed to have bombed *us* without warning. I myself would not be alive this minute had I not had the good fortune to be just removing my suit when you struck. I assure you *I* had no warning. As for your claim to being a civilian, unarmed craft, I think it very strange that the *Galileo* was able to blast our base if you carried nothing more deadly than a fly swatter. You Americans amaze me. You are always so ready to condemn others for the very things you do yourselves."

Cargraves was at a loss for words at the blind illogic of the speech. Ross looked disgusted; he seemed about to say something. Cargraves shook his head at him.

"That speech," he announced, "had more lies, half-truths, and twisted statements per square inch than anything you've said yet. But I'll put you straight on one point: the *Galileo* didn't bomb your base; she's wrecked. But your men were careless. We seized your rocket and turned your own bombs on you—"

"*Idioten!*"

"They *were* stupid, weren't they? The Master Race usually is stupid when it comes to a showdown. But you claimed we bombed you without warning. That is not true; you had all the warning you were entitled to and more. You struck the first blow. It's merely your own cocksureness that led you to think we couldn't, or wouldn't strike back."

Von Hartwick started to speak. "Shut up!" Cargraves said sharply. "I'm tired of your nonsense. Tell me how you happen to have this American ship. Make it good."

"Oh, that! We bought it."

"Don't be silly."

"I am not being silly. Naturally we did not walk in and place an order for one military space ship, wrapped and delivered. The transaction passed through several hands and eventually our friends delivered to us what we needed."

Cargraves thought rapidly. It was possible; something of the sort had to be true. He remembered vaguely an order for twelve such ships as the *Wotan* had originally been designed to be, remembered it because the newspapers had hailed the order as a proof of post-war recovery, expansion, and prosperity.

He wondered if all twelve of those rockets were actually operating on the run for which they had supposedly been purchased.

"That is the trouble with you stupid Americans," von Hartwick went on. "You assume that every one shares your silly belief in such rotten things as democracy. But it is not true. We have friends everywhere. Even in Washington, in London, yes, even in Moscow. Our friends are everywhere. That is another reason why we will win."

"Even in New Mexico, maybe?"

Von Hartwick laughed. "That was a droll comedy, my friend. I enjoyed the daily reports. It would not have suited us to frighten you too much, until it began to appear that you might be successful. You were very lucky, my friend, that you took off as soon as you did."

"Don't call me 'my friend,'" Cargraves said testily. "I'm sick of it."

"Very well, my dear Captain." Cargraves let the remark pass. He was getting worried by the extended absence of Art and Morrie. Was it possible that some other of the Nazis were still around, alive and capable of making trouble?

He was beginning to think about tying up the prisoner here present and going to look for them when the lock sighed open. Morrie and Art stepped out, prodding the other prisoner before them. "He didn't want to come, Uncle," Art informed him. "We had to convince him a little." He chuckled. "I don't think he trusts us."

"Okay. Get your suits off."

The other prisoner seemed completely dumfounded by the sight of von Hartwick. Hastily he unclamped his helmet, threw it back, and said in German, "*Herr Oberst*—it was not my fault. I was—"

"Silence!" shouted the Nazi officer, also in German. "Have you told these pig-dogs anything about the operation of this ship?"

"*Nein, nein, Herr Oberst*—I swear it!"

"Then play stupid or I'll cut your heart out!"

Cargraves listened to this interesting little exchange with an expressionless face, but it was too much for Art. "Uncle," he demanded, "did you hear that? Did you hear what he said he'd do?"

Von Hartwick looked from nephew to uncle. "So you understand German?" he said quietly. "I was afraid that you might."

Ross had let the muzzle of his gun wander away from von Hartwick when the boys came in with their prisoner. Cargraves had long since shoved the pistol he had appropriated into his belt.

Von Hartwick glanced from one to another. Morrie and Art were both armed, one with a Garand, the other with a revolver, but they had them trained on the Nazi pilot. Von Hartwick lunged suddenly at Cargraves and snatched the pistol from his belt.

Without appearing to stop to take aim he fired once. Then Cargraves was at him, clawing at his hands.

Von Hartwick brought the pistol down on his head, club fashion, and moved in to grapple him about the waist.

The Nazi pilot clasped his hands to his chest, gave a single bubbly moan, and sank to the floor. No one paid him any attention. After a split second of startled inaction, the three boys were milling around, trying to get in a shot at von Hartwick without hitting Cargraves. Cargraves himself had jerked and gone limp when the barrel of the pistol struck his head. Von Hartwick held the doctor's thirty pounds of moon weight up with one arm. He shouted, "Silence!"

His order would have had no effect had not the boys seen something else: Von Hartwick was holding the pistol to Cargraves' head. "Careful, gentlemen," he said, speaking very rapidly. "I have no wish to harm your leader and will not do so unless you force me. I am sorry I was forced to strike him; I was forced to do so when he attacked me."

"Watch out!" commanded Morrie. "Art! Ross! Don't try to shoot."

"That is sensible," von Hartwick commended him. "I have no wish to try to shoot it out with you. My only purpose was to dispose of *him*." He indicated the body of the Nazi pilot.

Morrie glanced at it. "Why?"

"He was a soft and foolish pig. I could not afford to risk his courage. He would have told you what you want to know." He paused, and then said suddenly, "And now—I am your prisoner again!" The pistol sailed out of his hand and clanged against the floor.

"Get Doc out of my way," Ross snapped. "I can't get a shot in."

"No!" Morrie thundered. "Art, pick up the pistol. Ross, you take care of Doc."

"What are you talking about?" Ross objected. "He's a killer. I'll finish him off."

"No!"

"Why not?"

"Well—Doc wouldn't like it. That's reason enough. Don't shoot. That's an order, Ross. You take care of Doc. Art, you tie up the mug. Make it good."

"It'll be good!" promised Art.

The Nazi did not resist and Morrie found himself able to give some attention to what Ross was doing. "How bad is it?" he inquired, bending over Cargraves.

"Not too bad, I think. I'll know better when I get some of this blood wiped away."

"You will find dressings and such things," von Hartwick put in casually, as if he were not in the stages of being tied up, "in a kit under the instrument board in the control room."

"Go look for them, Ross," Morrie directed. "I'll keep guard. Not," he said to von Hartwick, "that it will do you any good if he dies. If he does, out you go, outside, without a suit. Shooting's too good for you."

"He won't die. I hit him very carefully."

"You had better hope he doesn't. You won't outlive him more than a couple of minutes."

Von Hartwick shrugged. "It is hardly possible to threaten me. We are all dead men. You realize that, don't you?"

Morrie looked at him speculatively. "Finished with him, Art? Sure he's tied up tight?"

"He'll choke himself to death if he tries to wiggle out of that one."

"Good. Now you," he went on to von Hartwick, "you may be a dead man. I wouldn't know. But we're not. We are going to fly this ship back to earth. You start behaving yourself and we might take you with us."

Von Hartwick laughed. "Sorry to disillusion you, dear boy, but none of us is going back to earth. That is why I had to dispose of that precious pilot of mine."

Morrie turned away, suddenly aware that no one had bothered to find out how badly the sergeant-pilot was wounded. He was soon certain; the man was dead, shot through the heart. "I can't see that it matters," he told von Hartwick. "We've still got you. You'll talk, or I'll cut your ears off and feed them to you."

"What a distressing thought," he was answered, "but it won't help you. You see, I am unable to tell you anything; I am not a pilot."

Art stared at him. "He's kidding you, Morrie."

"No," von Hartwick denied. "I am not. Try cutting my ears off and you will see. No, my poor boys, we are all going to stay here a long time, until we rot, in fact. *Heil dem Führer!*"

"Don't touch him, Art," Morrie warned. "Doc wouldn't like it."

18.
TOO LITTLE TIME

Cargraves was wide enough awake to swear by the time Ross swabbed germicide on the cut in his hair line. "Hold still, Doc!"

"I am holding still. Take it easy."

They brought him up to date as they bandaged him. "The stinker thinks he's put one over on us," Ross finished. "He thinks we can't run this boat without somebody to show us."

"He may be perfectly right," Cargraves admitted. "So far it's got us stumped. We'll see. Throw him in the hold, and we'll have another look. Morrie, you did right not to let him be shot."

"I didn't think you would want him killed until you had squeezed him dry."

Cargraves gave him an odd smile. "That wasn't your only reason, was it?"

"Well—shucks!" Morrie seemed almost embarrassed. "I didn't want to just shoot him down after he dropped the gat. That's a Nazi trick."

Cargraves nodded approvingly. "That's right. That's one of the reasons they think we are soft. But we'll have a little surprise for him." He got up, went over, and stirred von Hartwick with his toe. "Listen to me, you. If possible, I am going to take you back to earth to stand trial. If not, we'll try you here."

Von Hartwick lifted his eyebrows. "For making war on you? How delightfully American!"

"No, not for making war. There isn't any war, and there hasn't been any war. The Third Reich disappeared forever in the spring of 1945 and today there is peace between Germany and the United States, no matter how many pip-squeak gangsters may still be hiding out. No, you phony superman, you are going to be tried for the murder of your accomplice—that poor dupe lying over there." He turned away. "Chuck him in the hold, boys. Come on, Ross."

Three hours later Cargraves was quite willing to admit that von Hartwick was correct when he said that the operation of the *Wotan* could not be figured out by a stranger. There were strange controls on the arms of the piloting seats which certainly had to be the flight controls, but no matter what they twisted, turned or moved, nothing happened. And the drive itself was sealed away behind a bulkhead which, from the sound it gave off when pounded, was inches thick.

Cargraves doubted whether he could cut through even with a steel-cutting flame. He was very reluctant to attempt to do so in any case; an effort to solve the mysteries of the ship by such surgery might, as likely as not, result in disabling the ship beyond any hope of repairing it.

There should be an operation manual somewhere. They all searched for it. They opened anything that would open, crawled under anything that could be crawled under, lifted everything that would move. There was no control manual in the ship.

The search disclosed something else. There was no food in the ship. This latter point was becoming important.

"That's enough, sports," he announced when he was certain that further search would be useless. "We'll try their barracks next. We'll find it. Not to mention food. You come with me, Morrie, and pick out some groceries."

"Me, too!" Art shouted. "I'll get some pictures. The moon people! Oh, boy!"

Cargraves wished regretfully that he were still young enough for it to be impossible to stay worried. "Well, all right," he agreed, "but where is your camera?"

Art's face fell. "It's in the Dog House," he admitted.

"I guess the pictures will have to wait. But come along; there is more electronic equipment down there than you can run and jump over. Maybe raising earth by radio will turn out to be easy."

"Why don't we all go?" Ross wanted to know. "*I* found the ruins, but I haven't had a chance to look at them."

"Sorry, Ross, but you've got to stay behind and stand guard over Stinky. He might know more about this ship than he admits. I would hate to come up that staircase and find the ship missing. Stand guard over him. Tell him that if he moves a muscle you'll slug him. And mean it."

"Okay. I hope he does move. How long will you be gone?"

"If we can't find it in two hours we'll come back."

Cargraves searched the officers' room first, as it seemed the most likely place. He did not find it, but he did find that some of the Nazis appeared to have some peculiar and unpleasant tastes in books and pictures. The barrack room he took next. It was as depressing a place as it had been earlier, but he was prepared for it. Art he had assigned to the radio-and-radar room and Morrie to the other spaces; there seemed to be no reason for any one but himself to have to touch the bloating corpses.

He drew a blank in the barrack room. Coming out, he heard Art's voice in his phones. "Hey, Uncle, look what I've found!"

"What is it?" he said, and Morrie's voice cut in at once, "Found the manual, Art?"

"No, but look!" They converged in the central hall. "It" was a Graflex camera, complete with flash gun. "There is a complete darkroom off the radio room. I found it there. How about it, Uncle? Pictures?"

"Well, all right. Morrie, you go along—it may be your only chance to see the ruins. Thirty minutes. Don't go very far, don't bust your necks, don't take any chances, and be back on time, or I'll be after you with a Flit gun." He watched them go regretfully, more than a little tempted to play hookey himself. If he had not been consumed with the urgency of his present responsibilities—

But he was. He forced himself to resume the dreary search.

It was all to no good. If there was an instructional manual in existence he had to admit that he did not know how to find it. But he was still searching when the boys returned.

He glanced at his watch. "Forty minutes," he said. "That's more prompt than I thought you would be; I expected to have to go look for you. What did you find? Get any good pictures?"

"Pictures? Did we get pictures! Wait till you see!"

"I never saw anything like it, Doc," Morrie stated impressively. "The place is a city. It goes down and down. Great big arched halls, hundreds of feet across, corridors running every which way, rooms, balconies—I can't begin to describe it."

"Then don't try. Write up full notes on what you saw as soon as we get back."

"Doc, this thing's tremendous!"

"I realize it. But it's so big I'm not even going to try to comprehend it, not yet. We've got our work cut out for us just to get out of here alive. Art, what did you find in the radio room? Anything you can use to raise earth?"

"Well, Uncle, that's hard to say, but the stuff doesn't look promising."

"Are you sure? We know that they were in communication—at least according to our nasty-nice boy friend."

Art shook his head. "I thought you said they *received* from earth. I found their equipment for that but I couldn't test it out because I couldn't get the earphones inside my suit. But I don't see how they could *send* to earth."

"Why not? They need two-way transmission."

"Maybe they need it but they can't afford to use it. Look, Uncle, they can beam towards the moon from their base on earth—that's all right; nobody gets it but them. But if the Nazis on this end try to beam back, they can't select some exact spot on earth. At that distance the beam would fan out until it covered too much territory—it would be like a broadcast."

"Oh!" said Cargraves, "I begin to see. Chalk up one for yourself, Art; I should have thought of that. No matter what sort of a code they used, if people started picking up radio from the direction of the moon, the cat would be out of the bag."

"That's what I thought, anyhow."

"I think you're dead right. I'm disappointed; I was beginning to pin my hopes on getting a message across." He shrugged. "Well, one thing at a time. Morrie, have you picked out the supplies you want to take up?"

"All lined up." They followed him into the kitchen space and found he had stacked three piles of tin cans in quantities to make three good-sized loads. As they were filling their arms Morrie said. "How many men were here, Doc?"

"I counted forty-seven bodies, not counting the one von Hartwick shot. Why?"

"Well, I noticed something funny. I've sort of acquired an eye for estimating rations since I've been running the mess. There isn't food enough here to keep that many men running two weeks. Does that mean what I think it means?"

"Hunnh . . . Look, Morrie, I think you've hit on something important. That's why von Hartwick is so cocky. It isn't just whistling in the dark. He actually expects to be rescued."

"What do you mean, Uncle?" Art wanted to know.

"He is expecting a supply ship, almost any time."

Art whistled. "He thinks we'll be caught by surprise!"

"And we would have been. But we won't be now." He put down his load of groceries. "Come along."

"Where?"

"I just remembered something." In digging through the officers' quarters he had come across many documents, books, manuals, records, and papers of many sorts. He had scanned them very briefly, making certain only that no one of them contained anything which would give a clue to the operation of the *Wotan*.

One of them was the day book or journal of the task-force commander. Among other things it had given the location of the Nazi base on earth; Cargraves had marked it as something he wanted to study later. Now he decided to do it at once.

It was long. It covered a period of nearly three months with Teutonic thoroughness. He read rapidly, with Art reading over his shoulder. Morrie stood around impatiently and finally pointed out that the time was approaching when they had promised Ross to return.

"Go ahead," Cargraves said absently. "Take a load of food. Get a meal started." He read on.

There was a roster of the party. He found von Hartwick listed as executive officer. He noted that as an indication that the Nazi was lying when he claimed not to understand the piloting of the *Wotan*. Not proof, but a strong indication. But falsehood was all that he expected of the creature.

He was beginning to find what he was looking for. Supply trips had been made each month. If the schedule was maintained—and the state of supplies certainly indicated it—the next ship should be along in six or seven days.

But the most important fact he was not sure of until he had finished the journal: there was more than one big rocket in their possession; the *Wotan* was not about to leave to get supplies; she would not leave, if the schedule had been followed, until the supply ship landed. Then she would be taken back empty and the other ship would be unloaded. By such an arrangement the party on the moon was never left without a means of escape—or, at least, that was the reason he read into the account.

There were just two and only two Nazi moon rockets—the *Wotan* and the *Thor*. The *Thor* was due in a week, as nearly as he could make out, which meant that she would leave her home base in about five days. The transit times for each trip had been logged in; forty-six hours plus for the earth-moon jump was the way the record read.

Fast time! he thought.

If the *Thor* ever took off, it might be too late for good intentions, too late for warnings. The Nazis were certainly aware that the techniques of space flight were now an open secret; there was reference after reference to the *Galileo* including a last entry noting that she had been located. They would certainly strike at the earliest possible moment.

He could see in his mind's eye the row upon row of A-bomb guided-missiles in a near-by cavern. He could see them striking the defenseless cities of earth.

No time to rig a powerful transmitter. No time for anything but drastic measures.

Not time enough, he was afraid!

19.
SQUEEZE PLAY

"*Soup's on!*" *Morrie* greeted him as he came hurrying into the *Wotan*. Cargraves started shucking off his suit as he answered.

"No time for that—no, gimme a couple of those sandwiches."

Morrie complied. Ross inquired, "What's the rush?"

"Got to see the prisoner." He turned away, then stopped. "No—wait. Come here, guys." He motioned them into a football huddle. "I'm going to try something." He whispered urgently for a few minutes. "Now play up. I'll leave the door open."

He went into the hold and prodded von Hartwick with his boot. "Wake up, you." He took a bite of sandwich.

"I am awake." Von Hartwick turned his head with some difficulty as he was trussed up with his ankles pulled up toward his wrists, which were tied behind him. "Ah, food," he said cheerfully. "I was wondering when you would remember the amenities in dealing with prisoners."

"It's not for you," Cargraves informed him. "The other sandwich is for me. You won't need one."

Von Hartwick looked interested but not frightened. "So?"

"Nope," said Cargraves, wiping his mouth with his sleeve, "you won't. I had intended to take you to earth for trial, but I find I won't have time for that. I'll try you myself—now."

Von Hartwick shrugged under his bonds. "You are able to do as you like. I've no doubt you intend to kill me, but don't dignify it with the name of a trial. Call it a lynching. Be honest with yourself. In the first place my conduct has been entirely correct. True, I was forced to shoot one of my own men, but it was a necessary emergency military measure—"

"Murder," put in Cargraves.

"—in defense of the security of the Reich," von Hartwick went on unhurriedly, "and no concern of yours in any case. It was my own ship, entirely out of jurisdiction of any silly laws of the corrupt democracies. As for the bombing of your ship, I have explained to you—"

"Shut up," Cargraves said. "You'll get a chance to say a few words later. Court's in session. Just to get it straight in your head, this entire planet is subject to the laws of the United Nations. We took formal possession and have established a permanent base. Therefore—"

"Too late, Judge Lynch. The New Reich claimed this planet three months ago."

"I told you to keep quiet. You're in contempt of court. One more peep and we'll think up a way to keep you quiet. Therefore, as the master of a vessel registered under the laws of the United Nations it is my duty to see that those laws are obeyed. Your so-called claim doesn't hold water. There isn't any New Reich, so it can't claim anything. You and your fellow thugs aren't a nation; you are merely gangsters. We aren't bound to recognize any fictions you have thought up and we don't. Morrie! Bring me another sandwich."

"Coming up, Captain!"

"Now as master of the *Galileo*," Cargraves went on, "I have to act for the government when I'm off by myself, as I am now. Since I haven't time to take you back to earth for trial, I'm trying you now. Two charges: murder in the first degree and piracy."

"Piracy? My dear fellow!"

"Piracy. You attacked a vessel of UN register. On your own admission you took part in it, whether you gave the orders or not. All members of a pirate crew are equally guilty, and it's a capital offense. Murder in the first degree is another one. Thanks for the sandwich, Morrie. Where did you find fresh bread?"

"It was canned."

"Clever, these Nazis. There was some doubt in my mind as to whether to charge you with first or second degree. But you had to grab the gun away from me first, before you could shoot your pal. That's premeditation. So you're charged—piracy and first-degree murder. How do you plead? Guilty or not guilty?"

Von Hartwick hesitated a bit before replying. "Since I do not admit the jurisdiction of this so-called court, I refuse to enter a plea. Even if I concede—which I don't—that you honestly believe this to be United Nations territory, you still are not a court."

"A ship's master has very broad powers in an emergency. Look it up some time. Get a ouija board and look it up."

Von Hartwick raised his eyebrows. "From the nature of that supposedly humorous remark I can see that I am convicted before the trial starts."

Cargraves chewed reflectively. "In a manner of speaking, yes," he conceded. "I'd like to give you a jury, but we don't really need one. You see, there aren't any facts to be established because there aren't any facts in doubt. We were all there. The only question is: what do those facts constitute under the law? This is your chance to speak your piece if you intend to."

"Why should I bother? You mongrel nations prate of justice and equality under the law. But you don't practice it. You stand there with your hands dripping with the blood of my comrades, whom you killed in cold blood, without giving them a chance— yet you speak to me of piracy and murder!"

"We discussed that once before," Cargraves answered carefully. "There is a world of difference, under the laws of free men, between an unprovoked attack and striking back in your own defense. If a footpad assaults you in a dark alley, you don't have to get a court order to fight back. Next. Got any more phony excuses?"

The Nazi was silent. "Go ahead," Cargraves persisted. "You could still plead not guilty by reason of insanity and you might even convince me. I always have thought a man with a Master-Race complex was crazy as a hoot owl. You might convince me that you were crazy in a legal sense as well."

For the first time, von Hartwick's air of aloof superiority seemed to crack. His face got red and he appeared about to explode. Finally he regained a measure of control and said, "Let's have no more of this farce. Do whatever it is you intend to do and quit playing with me."

"I assure you that I am not playing. Have you anything more to say in your own defense?"

"No!"

"I find you guilty on both charges. Have you anything to say before sentence is passed?"

The accused did not deign to answer.

"Very well. I sentence you to death."

Art took a quick, gasping breath and backed out of the doorway where he had been huddled, wide-eyed, with Ross and Morrie. There was no other sound.

"Have you anything to say before the sentence is executed?"

Von Hartwick turned his face away. "I am not sorry. At least I will have a quick and merciful death. The best you four swine can hope for is a slow and lingering death."

"Oh," said Cargraves, "I intended to explain to you about that. We aren't going to die."

"You think not?" There was undisguised triumph in von Hartwick's voice.

"I'm sure of it. You see, the *Thor* arrives in six or seven days—"

"*What?* How did you find that out?" The Nazi seemed stunned for a moment, then muttered, "Not that it matters . . . four of you—but I see why you decided to kill me. You were afraid I would escape you."

"Not at all," returned Cargraves. "You don't understand. If it were practical to do so, I would take you back to earth to let you appeal your case before a higher court. Not for your sake—you're guilty as sin!—but for my own. However, I do not find it possible. We will be very busy until the *Thor* gets here and I have no means of making sure that you are securely imprisoned except by standing guard over you every minute. I can't do that; we haven't time enough. But I don't intend to let you escape punishment. I don't have a cell to put you in. I had intended to drain the fuel from your little rocket and put you in there, without a suit. That way, you would have been safe to leave alone while we worked. But, now that the *Thor* is coming, we will need the little rocket."

Von Hartwick smiled grimly. "Think you can run away, eh? That ship will never take you home. Or haven't you found that out yet?"

"You still don't understand. Keep quiet and let me explain. We are going to take several of the bombs such as you used on the *Galileo* and blow up the room containing your guided missiles. It's a shame, for I see it's one of the rooms built by the original inhabitants. Then we are going to blow up the *Wotan*."

"The *Wotan?* Why?" Von Hartwick was suddenly very alert.

"To make sure it never flies back to earth. We can't operate it; I must make sure that no one else does. For then we intend to blow up the *Thor*."

"The *Thor?* You can't blow up the *Thor!*"

"Oh, yes, we can—the same way you blew up the *Galileo*. But I can't chance the possibility of survivors grabbing the *Wotan*—so she must go first. And that has a strong bearing on why you must die at once. After we blast the *Wotan* we are going back to our own base—you didn't know about that, did you?—but it is only one room. No place for prisoners. I had intended, as I said, to keep you in the jeep rocket, but the need to blast the *Thor* changes that. We'll have to keep a pilot in it at all times, until the *Thor* lands. And that leaves no place for you. Sorry," he finished, and smiled.

"Anything wrong with it?" he added.

Von Hartwick was beginning to show the strain. "You may succeed—"

"Oh, we will!"

"But if you do, you are still dead men. A quick death for me, but a long and slow and lingering death for you. If you blast the *Thor*, you lose your own last chance. Think of it," he went on, "starving or suffocating or dying with cold. I'll make a pact with you. Turn me loose now and I'll give you my parole. When the *Thor* arrives, I'll intercede with the captain on your behalf. I'll—"

Cargraves cut him off with a gesture. "The word of a Nazi! You wouldn't intercede for your own grandmother! You haven't gotten it through your thick head yet that we hold all the aces. After we kill you and take care of your friends, we shall sit tidy and cozy and warm, with plenty of food and air, until we are picked up. We won't even be lonesome; we were just finishing our earth sender when you picked up one of our local signals. We'll—"

"You lie!" shouted von Hartwick. "No one will pick you up. Yours was the only ship. I know, I know. We had full reports."

"*Was* the only ship." Cargraves smiled sweetly. "But under a quaint old democratic law which you wouldn't understand, the plans and drawings and notes for my ship were being studied eagerly the minute we took off. We'll be able to take our pick of ships before long. I hate to disappoint you on another score. Your death will not be as clean and pleasant as you had hoped."

"What do you mean?"

"I mean I am not going to get this ship all bloodied up again by shooting you. I'm going to—"

"Wait. A dying man is entitled to a last request. Leave me in the *Wotan*. Let me die with my ship!"

Cargraves laughed full in his face. "Lovely, von Nitwit. Perfectly lovely. And have you take off in her. Not likely!"

"I am no pilot—believe me!"

"Oh, I do believe. I would not think of doubting a dying man's last words. But I won't risk a mistake. Ross!"

"Yes, sir!"

"Take this thing and throw it out on the face of the moon."

"Dee-lighted!"

"And that's all." Cargraves had been squatting down; he got up and brushed the crumbs from his hands. "I shan't even have you untied so that you can die in a comfortable position. You are too handy at grabbing guns. You'll just have to flop around as you are. It probably won't take long," he went on conversationally. "They say it's about like drowning. In seven or eight minutes you won't know a thing. Unless your heart ruptures through your lungs and finishes you a little sooner."

"Swine!"

"*Captain* Swine, to you."

Ross was busily zipping his suit into place. "Okay, Doc?"

"Go ahead. No, on second thought," he added, "I'll do this job myself. I might be criticized for letting a boy touch it. My suit, Morrie."

He whistled as they helped him dress. He was still whistling as he picked up von Hartwick like a satchel, by the line which bound his ankles to his wrists, and walked briskly to the lock. He chucked his bundle in ahead of him, stepped in, waved to the boys, said, "Back soon!" and clamped the door.

As the air started whistling out von Hartwick began to gasp. Cargraves smiled at him, and said, "Drafty, isn't it?" He shouted to make himself heard through the helmet.

Von Hartwick's mouth worked.

"Did you say something?"

The Nazi opened his mouth again, gasped, choked, and sprayed foam out on his chest. "You'll have to talk louder," Cargraves shouted. "I can't hear you." The air whistled away.

"I'm a pilot!"

"What?"

"I'm a pilot! I'll teach you—"

Cargraves reached up and closed the exhaust valve. "I can't hear with all that racket. What were you saying?"

"I'm a pilot!" gasped von Hartwick.

"Yes? Well, what about it?"

"Air. Give me air—"

"Shucks," said Cargraves. "You've got plenty of air. I can still hear you talking. Must be four or five pounds in here."

"Give me air. I'll tell you how it works."

"You'll tell me *first*," Cargraves stated. He reached for the exhaust valve again.

"Wait! There is a little plug, in the back of the instrument—"

He paused and gasped heavily. "The instrument panel. Star-board side. It's a safety switch. You wouldn't notice it; it looks just like a mounting stud. You push it in." He stopped to wheeze again.

"I think you'd better come show me," Cargraves said judicially. "If you aren't lying again, you've given me an out to take you back to earth for your appeal. Not that you deserve it."

He reached over and yanked on the spill valve; the air rushed back into the lock.

Ten minutes later Cargraves was seated in the left-hand pilot's chair, with his safety belt in place. Von Hartwick was in the right-hand chair. Cargraves held a pistol in his left hand and cradled it over the crook of his right arm, so that it would remain pointed at von Hartwick, even under drive.

"Morrie! Everybody ready?"

"Ready, Captain," came faintly from the rear of the ship. The boys had been forced to use the acceleration bunks in the passenger compartment. They resented it, especially Morrie, but there was no help for it. The control room could carry just two people under acceleration.

"Okay! Here we go!" He turned again to von Hartwick. "Twist her tail, Swine—Colonel Swine, I mean."

Von Hartwick glared at him. "I don't believe," he said slowly, "that you ever intended to go through with it."

Cargraves grinned and rubbed the chair arm. "Want to go back and see?" he inquired.

Von Hartwick swiveled his head around to the front. *"Achtung!"* he shouted. "Prepare for acceleration! Ready—" Without waiting for a reply he blasted off.

The ship had power to spare with the light load; Cargraves had him hold it at two *g*'s for five minutes and then go free. By that time, having accelerated at nearly 64 feet per second for each second of the five minutes, even with due allowance for loss of one-sixth *g* to the pull of the moon at the start, they were making approximately 12,000 miles per hour.

They would have breezed past earth in twenty hours had it not been necessary to slow down in order to land. Cargraves planned to do it in a little less than twenty-four hours.

Once in free fall, the boys came forward and Cargraves required of von Hartwick a detailed lecture on the operation of the craft. When he was satisfied, he said, "Okay. Ross, you and Art take the prisoner aft and lash him to one of the bunks. Then strap yourselves down. Morrie and I are going to practice."

Von Hartwick started to protest. Cargraves cut him short. "Stow it! You haven't been granted any pardon; we've simply been picking your brains. You are a common criminal, going back to appeal your case."

They felt out the ship for the next several hours, with time only to eat. The result of the practice on the course and speed were null; careful check was kept by instrument to see that a drive in one direction was offset by the same amount of drive in the opposite direction. Then they slept.

They needed sleep. By the time they got it they had been awake and active at an unrelenting pace for one full earthday.

When they woke Cargraves called Art. "Think you could raise earth on this Nazi gear, kid?"

"I'll try. What do you want me to say and who do you want to talk to?"

Cargraves considered. Earth shone gibbous, more than half full, ahead. The Nazi base was not in line-of-sight. That suited him. "Better make it Melbourne, Australia," he decided, "and tell them this—"

Art nodded. A few minutes later, having gotten the hang of the strange set, he was saying endlessly: "Space Ship *City of Detroit* calling UN police patrol, Melbourne; Space Ship *City of Detroit* calling UN police patrol, Melbourne—"

He had been doing this for twenty-five minutes when a querulous voice answered: "Pax, Melbourne; Pax, Melbourne—calling Space Ship *City of Detroit*. Come in, *City of Detroit*."

Art pushed up one phone and looked helpless. "You better talk to 'em, Uncle."

"Go ahead. You tell them what I told you. It's your show."

Art shut up and did so.

Morrie let her down carefully and eased her over into a tight circular orbit just outside the atmosphere. Their speed was still nearly five miles per second; they circled the globe in ninety minutes. From that orbit he killed her speed slowly and dipped down cautiously until the stub wings of the *City of Detroit* né *Wotan* began to bite the tenuous stratosphere in a blood-chilling thin scream.

Out into space again they went and then back in, each time

deeper and each time slower. On the second of the braking orbits they heard the broadcast report of the UN patrol raid on the Nazi nest and of the capture of the *Thor*. On the next lap two chains bid competitively for an exclusive broadcast from space. On the third there was dickering for television rights at the field. On the fourth they received official instructions to attempt to land at the District-of-Columbia Rocket Port.

"Want me to take her down?" Morrie yelled above the scream of the skin friction.

"Go right ahead," Cargraves assured him. "I'm an old man. I want a chauffeur."

Morrie nodded and began his approach. They were somewhere over Kansas.

The ground of the rocket port felt strange and solid under the ship. Eleven days—only eleven days?—away from the earth's massive pull had given them new habits. Cargraves found that he staggered a little in trying to walk. He opened the inner door of the lock and waited for the boys to get beside him. Latching the inner door open, he stepped to the outer door and broke the seal.

As he swung it open, a solid wall of sound beat him in the face, an endless mass of eager eyes looked up at him. Flash guns flickered like heat lightning. He turned back to Ross. "Oh, my gosh!" he said. "This is awful! Say—don't you guys want to take the bows?"

SPACE
CADET

For William Ivar Bacchus

1.
TERRA BASE

"*To Matthew Brooks* Dodson," the paper in his hand read, "greetings:

"Having successfully completed the field elimination tests for appointment to the position of cadet in the Interplanetary Patrol you are authorized to report to the Commandant, Terra Base, Santa Barbara Field, Colorado, North American Union, Terra, on or before One July 2075, for further examination.

"You are cautioned to remember that the majority of candidates taking these final tests usually fail and you should provide—"

Matt folded the paper and stuck it back in his belt pouch. He did not care to think about the chance of failure. The passenger across from him, a boy about his own age, caught his eye. "That paper looks familiar, you a candidate too?"

"That's right."

"Well, shake! M' name's Jarman—I'm from Texas."

"Glad to know you, Tex. I'm Matt Dodson, from Des Moines."

"Howdy, Matt. We ought to be about there—" The car sighed softly and slowed; their chairs rocked to meet the rapid deceleration. The car stopped and their chairs swung back to normal position. "We *are* there," Jarman finished.

The telescreen at the end of the car, busy a moment before with a blonde beauty demonstrating Sorkin's Super-Stellar Soap, now read: TERRA BASE STATION. The two boys grabbed their bags, and hurried out. A moment later, they were on the escalator, mounting to the surface.

Facing the station a half mile away in the cool, thin air stood

Hayworth Hall, Earth headquarters of the fabulous Patrol. Matt stared at it, trying to realize that he was at last seeing it.

Jarman nudged him. "Come on."

"Huh? Oh—sure." A pair of slidewalks stretched from the station to the hall; they stepped onto the one running toward the building. The slidewalk was crowded; more boys streamed out of the station behind them. Matt noticed two boys with swarthy, thin features who were wearing high, tight turbans, although dressed otherwise much like himself. Further down the walk he glimpsed a tall, handsome youth whose impassive face was shiny black.

The Texas boy hooked his thumbs in his belt and looked around. "Granny, kill another chicken!" he said. "There's company for dinner. Speaking of that," he went on, "I hope they don't wait lunch too long. I'm hungry."

Matt dug a candy bar out of his pouch, split it and gave half to Jarman, who accepted it gratefully. "You're a pal, Matt, I've been living on my own fat ever since breakfast—and that's risky. Say, your telephone is sounding."

"Oh!" Matt fumbled in his pouch and got out his phone. "Hello?"

"That you, son?" came his father's voice.

"Yes, Dad."

"Did you get there all right?"

"Sure, I'm about to report in."

"How's your leg?"

"Leg's all right, Dad." His answer was not frank; his right leg, fresh from a corrective operation for a short Achilles' tendon, was aching as he spoke.

"That's good. Now see here, Matt—if it should work out that you aren't selected, don't let it get you down. You call me at once and—"

"Sure, sure, Dad," Matt broke in. "I'll have to sign off—I'm in a crowd. Good-by. Thanks for calling."

"Good-by, son. Good luck."

Tex Jarman looked at him understandingly. "Your folks always worry, don't they? I fooled mine—packed my phone in my bag." The slidewalk swung in a wide curve preparatory to heading back; they stepped off with the crowd, in front of Hayworth Hall. Tex paused to read the inscription over the great doorway. "*Quis custodi*— What does it say, Matt?"

"*Quis custodiet ipsos custodes*. That's Latin for: Who will watch the guardians?"

"You read Latin, Matt?"

"No, I just remember that bit from a book about the Patrol."

The rotunda of Hayworth Hall was enormous and seemed even larger, for, despite brilliant lighting at the floor level, the domed ceiling gave back no reflection at all; it was midnight black—black and studded with stars. Familiar stars—blazing Orion faced the tossing head of Taurus; the homely shape of the Dipper balanced on its battered handle at north-northeast horizon; just south of overhead the Seven Sisters shone.

The illusion of being outdoors at night was most persuasive. The lighted walls and floor at the level at which people walked and talked and hurried seemed no more than a little band of light, a circle of warmth and comfort, against the awful depth of space, like prairie schooners drawn up for the night under a sharp desert sky.

The boys caught their breaths, as did everyone who saw it for the first time. But they could not stop to wonder as something else demanded their attention. The floor of the rotunda was sunk many feet below the level at which they entered; they stood on a balcony which extended around the great room to enclose a huge, shallow, circular pit. In this pit a battered spaceship lurched on a bed of rock and sand as if it had crash-landed from the mimic sky above.

"It's the *Kilroy*—" Tex said, almost as if he doubted it.

"It *must* be," Matt agreed in a whisper.

They moved to the balcony railing and read a plaque posted there:

USSF Rocket Ship *Kilroy Was Here*
FIRST INTERPLANETARY SHIP

From Terra to Mars and return—Lieut. Colonel Robert deFries Sims, Commanding; Captain Saul S. Abrams; Master Sergeant Malcolm MacGregor. None survived the return landing. Rest in Peace.

They crowded next to two other boys and stared at the *Kilroy*. Tex nudged Matt. "See the gash in the dirt, where she skidded? Say, do you suppose they just built right over her, where she lay?"

One of the other two—a big-boned six-footer with tawny hair—answered, "No, the *Kilroy* landed in North Africa."

"Then they must have fixed it to look like where she crashed. You a candidate too?"

"That's right."

"I'm Bill Jarman—from Texas. And this is Matt Dodson."

"I'm Oscar Jensen—and this is Pierre Armand."

"Howdy, Oscar. Glad to know you, Pierre."

"Call me Pete," Armand acknowledged. Matt noticed that he spoke Basic English with an accent, but Matt was unable to place it. Oscar's speech was strange, too—a suggestion of a lisp. He turned back to the ship.

"Imagine having the guts to go out into space in a cracker box like that," he said. "It scares me to think about it."

"Me, too," agreed Oscar Jensen.

"It's a dirty shame," Pierre said, softly.

"What is, Pete?" Jarman demanded.

"That their luck didn't hold. You can see it was an almost perfect landing—they didn't just crash in, or there would have been nothing left but a hole in the ground."

"Yeah, I guess you're right. Say, there's a stairway down, over on the far side—see it, Matt? Do you suppose we could look through her?"

"Maybe," Matt told him, "but I think we had better put it off. We've got to report in, you know."

"We had all better check in," agreed Jensen. "Coming, Pete?"

Armand reached for his bag. Oscar Jensen pushed him aside and picked it up with his own. "That's not necessary!" Armand protested, but Oscar ignored him.

Jarman looked at Pierre. "You sick, Pete?" he asked. "I noticed you looked kind of peaked. What's the trouble?"

"If you are," put in Matt, "ask for a delay."

Armand looked embarrassed. "He's not sick and he'll pass the exams," Jensen said firmly. "Forget it."

"Sho', sho'," Tex agreed. They followed the crowd and found a notice which told all candidates to report to room 3108, third corridor. They located corridor three, stepped on the slideway, and put down their baggage.

"Say, Matt," said Tex, "tell me—who was Kilroy?"

"Let me see," Matt answered. "He was somebody in the Second Global War, an admiral, I think. Yeah, Admiral 'Bull' Kilroy, that sounds right."

"Funny they'd name it after an admiral."

"He was a flying admiral."

"You're a savvy cuss," Tex said admiringly. "I think I'll stick close to you during the tests."

Matt brushed it off. "Just a fact I happened to pick up."

In room 3108 a decorative young lady waved aside their credentials but demanded their thumb prints. She fed these into a machine at her elbow. The machine quickly spit out instruction sheets headed by the name, serial number, thumb print, and photograph of each candidate, together with temporary messing and rooming assignments.

The girl handed out the sheets and told them to wait next door. She abruptly turned away.

"I wish she hadn't been so brisk," complained Tex, as they went out. "I wanted to get her telephone code. Say," he went on, studying his sheet, "there's no time left on here for a siesta."

"Did you expect it?" asked Matt.

"Nope—but I can hope, can't I?"

The room next door was filled with benches but the benches were filled with boys. Jarman stopped at a bench which was crowded by three large cases, an ornate portable refresher kit, and a banjo case. A pink-faced youth sat next to this. "Your stuff?" Tex asked him.

The young man grudgingly admitted it. "You won't mind if we move it and sit down," Tex went on. He started putting the items on the floor. The owner looked sulky but said nothing.

There was room for three. Tex insisted that the others sit down, then sat down on his bag and leaned against Matt's knees, with his legs stretched out. His footwear, thus displayed, were seen to be fine western boots, high-heeled and fancy.

A candidate across from them stared at the boots, then spoke to the boy next to him. "Pipe the cowboy!"

Tex snorted and started to get up. Matt put a hand on his shoulder, shoving him back. "It's not worth it, Tex. We've got a busy day ahead."

Oscar nodded agreement. "Take it easy, fellow."

Tex subsided. "Well—all right. Just the same," he added, "my Uncle Bodie would stuff a man's feet in his mouth for less than that." He glared at the boy across from him.

Pierre Armand leaned over and spoke to Tex. "Excuse me— but are those really shoes for riding on horses?"

"Huh? What do you think they are? Skis?"

"Oh, I'm sorry! But you see, I've never seen a horse."

"What?"

"*I* have," announced Oscar, "in the zoo, that is."

"In a *zoo?*" repeated Tex.

"In the zoo at New Auckland."

"Oh—" said Tex. "I get it. You're a Venus colonial." Matt then recalled where he had heard Oscar's vaguely familiar lisp before—in the speech of a visiting lecturer. Tex turned to Pierre. "Pete, are you from Venus, too?"

"No, I'm—" Pete's voice was drowned out.

"Attention, please! Quiet!" The speaker was dressed in the severely plain, oyster-white uniform of a space cadet. "All of you," he went on, speaking into a hand amplifier, "who have odd serial numbers come with me. Bring your baggage. Even numbers wait where you are."

"Odd numbers?" said Tex. "That's me!" He jumped up.

Matt looked at his instructions. "Me, too!"

The cadet came down the aisle in front of them. Matt and Tex waited for him to pass. The cadet did not hold himself erectly; he crouched the merest trifle, knees relaxed and springy, hands ready to grasp. His feet glided softly over the floor. The effect was cat-like, easy grace; Matt felt that if the room were suddenly to turn topsy-turvy the cadet would land on his feet on the ceiling— which was perfectly true.

Matt wanted very much to look like him.

As the cadet was passing, the boy with the plentiful baggage plucked at his sleeve. "Hey, mister!"

The cadet turned suddenly and crouched, then checked himself as quickly. "Yes?"

"I've got an odd number, but I can't carry all this stuff. Who can I get to help me?"

"You can't." The cadet prodded the pile with his toe. "*All* of this is yours?"

"Yes. What do I do? I can't leave it here. Somebody'd steal it."

"I can't see why anyone would." The cadet eyed the pile with distaste. "Lug it back to the station and ship it home. Or throw it away."

The youngster looked blank. "You'll have to, eventually," the cadet went on. "When you make the lift to the school ship, twenty pounds is your total allowance."

"But—Well, suppose I do, who's to help me get it to the station?"

"That's your problem. If you want to be in the Patrol, you'll have to learn to cope with problems."

"But—"

"Shut up." The cadet turned away. Matt and Tex trailed along.

Five minutes later Matt, naked as an egg, was stuffing his bag and clothes into a sack marked with his serial number. As ordered, he filed through a door, clutching his orders and a remnant of dignity. He found himself in a gang refresher which showered him, scrubbed him, rinsed him, and blew him dry again, assembly-line style. His instruction sheet was waterproof; he shook from it a few clinging drops.

For two hours he was prodded, poked, thumped, photographed, weighed, X-rayed, injected, sampled, and examined until he was bewildered. He saw Tex once, in another queue. Tex waved, slapped his own bare ribs, and shivered. Matt started to speak but his own line started up.

The medicos examined his repaired leg, making him exercise it, inquired the date of the operation, and asked if it hurt him. He found himself admitting that it did. More pictures were taken; more tests were made. Presently he was told, "That's all. Get back into line."

"Is it all right, sir?" Matt blurted out.

"Probably. You'll be given some exercises. Get along."

After a long time he came into a room in which several boys were dressing. His path took him across a weighing platform; his body interrupted electric-eye beams. Relays closed, an automatic sequence took place based on his weight, height, and body dimensions. Presently a package slid down a chute and plunked down in front of him.

It contained an undergarment, a blue coverall, a pair of soft boots, all in his size.

The blue uniform he viewed as a makeshift, since he was anxious to swap it for the equally plain, but oyster white, uniform of a cadet. The shoes delighted him. He zipped them on, relishing their softness and glovelike fit. It seemed as if he could stand on a coin and call it, heads or tails. "Cat feet"—his first space boots! He took a few steps, trying to walk like the cadet he had seen earlier.

"Dodson!"

"Coming." He hurried out and shortly found himself thrust into a room with an older man in civilian clothes.

"Sit down. I'm Joseph Kelly." He took Matt's instruction sheet. "Matthew Dodson . . . nice to know you, Matt."

"How do you do, Mr. Kelly."

"Not too badly. Why do you want to join the Patrol, Matt?"

"Why, uh, because—" Matt hesitated. "Well, to tell the truth, sir, I'm so confused right now that I'm darned if I know!"

Kelly chuckled. "That's the best answer I've heard today. Do you have any brothers or sisters, Matt?" The talk wandered along, with Kelly encouraging Matt to talk. The questions were quite personal, but Matt was sophisticated enough to realize that "Mr. Kelly" was probably a psychiatrist; he stammered once or twice but he tried to answer honestly.

"Can you tell me now why you want to be in the Patrol?"

Matt thought about it. "I've wanted to go out into space ever since I can remember."

"Travel around, see strange planets and strange people—that's understandable, Matt. But why not the merchant service? The Academy is a long, hard grind, and it's three to one you won't finish, even if you are sworn in as a cadet—and not more than a quarter of the candidates will pass muster. But you could enter the merchant school—I could have you transferred today—and with your qualifications you'd be a cinch to win your pilot's ticket before you are twenty. How about it?"

Matt looked stubborn.

"Why not, Matt? Why insist on trying to be an officer of the Patrol? They'll turn you inside out and break your heart and no one will thank you for your greatest efforts. They'll make you over into a man your own mother wouldn't recognize—and you won't be any happier for it. Believe me, fellow—I know."

Matt did not say anything.

"You still want to try it, knowing chances are against you?"

"Yes. Yes, I think I do."

"Why, Matt?"

Matt still hesitated. Finally he answered in a low voice. "Well, people look up to an officer in the Patrol."

Mr. Kelly looked at him. "That's enough reason for now, Matt. You'll find others—or quit." A clock on the wall suddenly spoke up:

"Thirteen o'clock! Thirteen o'clock!" Then it added thoughtfully, "I'm hungry."

"Mercy me!" said Kelly. "So am I. Let's go to lunch, Matt."

2.
ELIMINATION PROCESS

Matt's instructions told him to mess at table 147, East Refectory. A map on the back of the sheet showed where East Refectory was; unfortunately he did not know where Matt was—he had gotten turned around in the course of the morning's rat race. He ran into no one at first but august personages in the midnight black of officers of the Patrol and he could not bring himself to stop one of them.

Eventually he got oriented by working back to the rotunda and starting over, but it made him about ten minutes late. He walked down an endless line of tables, searching for number 147 and feeling very conspicuous. He was quite pink by the time he located it.

There was a cadet at the head of the table; the others wore the coveralls of candidates. The cadet looked up and said, "Sit down, mister—over there on the right. Why are you late?"

Matt gulped. "I got lost, sir."

Someone tittered. The cadet sent a cold glance down the table. "You. You with the silly horse laugh—what's your name?"

"Uh, Schultz, sir."

"Mister Schultz, there is nothing funny about an honest answer. Have you never been lost?"

"Why—Well, uh, once or twice, maybe."

"Hm . . . I shall be interested in seeing your work in astrogation, *if* you get that far." The cadet turned back to Matt. "Aren't you hungry? What's your name?"

"Yes, sir. Matthew Dodson, sir." Matt looked hurriedly at the controls in front of him, decided against soup, and punched the "entrée," "dessert," and "milk" buttons. The cadet was still watching him as the table served him.

"I am Cadet Sabbatello. Don't you like soup, Mr. Dodson?"

"Yes, sir, but I was in a hurry."

"There's no hurry. Soup is good for you." Cadet Sabbatello stretched an arm and punched Matt's "soup" button. "Besides, it gives the chef a chance to clean up the galley." The cadet turned away, to Matt's relief. He ate heartily. The soup was excellent, but the rest of the meal seemed dull compared with what he had been used to at home.

He kept his ears open. One remark of the cadet stuck in his memory. "Mr. van Zook, in the Patrol we never ask a man where he is from. It is all right for Mr. Romolus to volunteer that he comes from Manila; it is incorrect for you to ask him."

The afternoon was jammed with tests; intelligence, muscular control, reflex, reaction time, sensory response. Others required him to do two or more things at once. Some seemed downright silly. Matt did the best he could.

He found himself at one point entering a room containing nothing but a large, fixed chair. A loudspeaker addressed him: "Strap yourself into the chair. The grips on the arms of the chair control a spot of light on the wall. When the lights go out, you will see a lighted circle. Center your spot of light in the circle and keep it centered."

Matt strapped himself down. A bright spot of light appeared on the wall in front of him. He found that the control in his right hand moved the spot up and down, while the one in his left hand moved it from side to side. "Easy!" Matt told himself. "I wish they would start."

The lights in the room went out; the lighted target circle bobbed slowly up and down. He found it not too difficult to bring his spot of light into the circle and match the bobbing motion.

Then his chair turned upside down.

When he recovered from his surprise at finding himself hanging head down in the dark, he saw that the spot of light had drifted away from the circle. Frantically he brought them together, swung past and had to correct.

The chair swung one way, the circle another, and a loud explosion took place at his left ear. The chair bucked and teetered; a jolt of electricity convulsed his hands and he lost the circle entirely.

Matt began to get sore. He forced his spot back to the circle and nailed it. "Gotcha!"

Smoke poured through the room, making him cough, watering his eyes, and veiling the target. He squinted and hung on grimly, intent only on hanging onto that pesky circle of light—through more explosions, screaming painful noise, flashing lights, wind in his eyes, and endless, crazy motions of his chair.

Suddenly the room lights flared up, and the mechanical voice said: "Test completed. Carry out your next assignment."

Once he was given a handful of beans and a small bottle, and was told to sit down and place the bottle at a mark on the floor and locate in his mind the exact position of the bottle. Then he was to close his eyes and drop the beans one at a time into the bottle—if possible.

He could tell from the sound that he was not making many hits, but he was mortified to find, when he opened his eyes, that only one bean rested in the bottle.

He hid the bottom of his bottle in his fist and queued up at the examiner's desk. Several of those lined up had a goodly number of beans in their bottles, although he noted two with no beans at all. Presently he handed his bottle to the examiner. "Dodson, Matthew, sir. One bean."

The examiner noted it without comment. Matt blurted out, "Excuse me, sir—but what's to keep a person from cheating by peeking?"

The examiner smiled. "Nothing at all. Go on to your next test."

Matt left, grumbling. It did not occur to him that he might not know what was being tested.

Late in the day he was ushered into a cubbyhole containing a chair, a gadget mounted on a desk, pencil and paper, and framed directions.

"If any score from a previous test," Matt read, "appears in the window marked SCORE, return the starting lever to the position marked NEUTRAL to clear the board for your test."

Matt found the window labeled "SCORE"; it had a score showing in it—"37." Well, he thought, that gives me a mark to shoot at. He decided not to clear the board until he had read the instructions.

"After the test starts," he read, "a score of '1' will result each time you press the lefthand button except as otherwise provided here below. Press the lefthand button whenever the red light appears provided the green light is not lighted as well except that no button should be pressed when the righthand gate is open unless all lights are out. If the righthand gate is open and the lefthand gate is closed, no score will result from pressing any button, but the lefthand button must nevertheless be pressed under these circumstances if all other conditions permit a button to be pressed before any score may be made in succeeding phases of the test. To put out the green light, press the righthand button. If the lefthand gate is not closed, no button may be pressed. If the lefthand gate is closed while the red light is lighted, do not press the lefthand button if the green light is out unless the righthand gate is open. To start the test move the starting lever from neutral all the way to the right. The test runs for two minutes from the time you move the starting lever to the right. Study these instructions, then select your own time for commencing the test. You are not permitted to ask questions of the examiner, so be sure that you understand the instructions. Make as high a score as possible."

"Whew!" said Matt.

Still, the test looked simple—one lever, two pushbuttons, two colored lights, two little gates. Once he mastered the instructions, it would be as easy as flying a kite, and a durn sight simpler than flying a copter!—Matt had had his copter license since he was twelve. He got to work.

First, he told himself, there seems to be just two ways to make a score, one with the red light on and one with both lights out and one gate open.

Now for the other instructions—Let's see, if the lefthand gate is not closed—no, if the lefthand gate *is* closed—he stopped and read them over again.

Some minutes later he had sixteen possible positions of gates and conditions of lights listed. He checked them against the instructions, seeking scoring combinations. When he was through he stared at the result, then checked everything over again.

After rechecking he stared at the paper, whistled tunelessly, and scratched his head. Then he picked up the paper, left the booth, and went to the examiner.

That official looked up. "No questions, please."

"I don't have a question," Matt said. "I want to report something. There's something wrong with that test. Maybe the wrong instructions sheet was put in there. In any case, there is no possible way to make a score under the instructions that are in there."

"Oh, come, now!" the examiner answered. "Are you sure of that?"

Matt hesitated, then answered firmly, "I'm sure of it. Want to see my proof?"

"No. Your name is Dodson?" The examiner glanced at a timer, then wrote on a chart. "That's all."

"But—Don't I get a chance to make a score?"

"No questions, please! I've recorded your score. Get along—it's dinner time."

There were a large number of vacant places at dinner. Cadet Sabbatello looked down the long table. "I see there have been some casualties," he remarked. "Congratulations, gentlemen, for having survived thus far."

"Sir—does that mean we've passed all the tests we took to-day?" one of the candidates asked.

"Or at least won a retest. You haven't flunked." Matt sighed with relief. "Don't get your hopes up. There will be still fewer of you here tomorrow."

"Does it get worse?" the candidate went on.

Sabbatello grinned wickedly. "Much worse. I advise you all to eat little at breakfast. However," he went on, "I have good news, too. It is rumored that the Commandant himself is coming down to Terra to honor you with his presence when you are sworn in—if you are sworn in."

Most of those present looked blank. The cadet glanced around. "Come, come, gentlemen!" he said sharply. "Surely not all of you are that ignorant. You!" He addressed Matt. "Mister, uh—Dodson. You seem to have some glimmering of what I am talking about. Why should you feel honored at the presence of the Commandant?"

Matt gulped. "Do you mean the Commandant of the Academy, sir?"

"Naturally. What do you know about him?"

"Well, sir, he's Commodore Arkwright." Matt stopped, as if the name were explanation.

"And what distinguishes Commodore Arkwright?"

"Uh, he's blind, sir."

"Not blind, Mr. Dodson, not blind! It simply happens that he had his eyes burned out. How did he lose his eyesight?" The cadet stopped him. "No—don't tell them. Let them find out for themselves."

The cadet resumed eating and Matt did likewise, while thinking about Commodore Arkwright. He himself had been too young to pay attention to the news, but his father had read an account of the event to him—a spectacular, singlehanded rescue of a private yacht in distress, inside the orbit of Mercury. He had forgotten just how the Patrol officer had exposed his eyes to the Sun— something to do with transferring the yacht's personnel—but he could still hear his father reading the end of the report: "—these actions are deemed to be in accordance with the tradition of the Patrol."

He wondered if any action of his would ever receive that superlative distinction. Unlikely, he decided; "duty satisfactorily performed" was about the best an ordinary man could hope for.

Matt ran into Tex Jarman as he left the mess hall. Tex pounded him on the back. "Glad to see you, kid. Where are you rooming?"

"I haven't had time to look up my room yet."

"Let's see your sheet." Jarman took it. "We're in the same corridor—swell. Let's go up."

They found the room and walked in. Sprawled on the lower of two bunks, reading and smoking a cigarette, was another candidate. He looked up.

"Enter, comrades," he said. "Don't bother to knock."

"We didn't," said Tex.

"So I see." The boy sat up. Matt recognized the boy who had made the crack about Tex's boots. He decided to say nothing— perhaps they would not recognize each other. The lad continued, "Looking for someone?"

"No," Matt answered, "this is the room I'm assigned to."

"My roommate, eh? Welcome to the palace. Don't trip over the dancing girls. I put your stuff on your bed."

The sack containing Matt's bag and civilian clothes rested on the upper bunk. He dragged it down.

"What do you mean, his bed?" demanded Tex. "You ought to match for the lower bunk."

Matt's roommate shrugged. "First come, first served."

Tex clouded up. "Forget it, Tex," Matt told him. "I prefer the upper. By the way," he went on, to the other boy, "I'm Matt Dodson."

"Girard Burke, at your service."

The room was adequate but austere. Matt slept in a hydraulic bed at home, but he had used mattress beds in summer camp. The adjoining refresher was severely functional but very modern— Matt noted with pleasure that the shower was installed with robot massage. There was no shave mask, but shaving was not yet much of a chore.

In his wardrobe he found a package, marked with his serial number, containing two sets of clothing and a second pair of space boots. He stowed them and his other belongings; then turned to Tex. "Well, what'll we do now?"

"Let's look around the joint."

"Fine. Maybe we can go through the *Kilroy*."

Burke chucked his cigarette toward the oubliette. "Wait a sec. I'll go with you." He disappeared into the 'fresher.

Tex said in a low voice. "Tell him to go fly a kite, Matt."

"It'ud be a pleasure. But I'd rather get along with him, Tex."

"Well, maybe they'll eliminate him tomorrow."

"Or me." Matt smiled wryly.

"Or me. Shucks, no, Matt—we'll get by. Have you thought about a permanent roomie? Want to team up?"

"It's a deal." They shook hands.

"I'm glad that's settled," Tex went on. "My cellmate is a nice little guy, but he's got a blood brother, or some such, he wants to room with. Came to see him before dinner. They chattered away in Hindustani, I guess it was. Made me nervous. Then they shifted to Basic out of politeness, and that made me more nervous."

"You don't look like the nervous type."

"Oh, all us Jarmans are high strung. Take my Uncle Bodie. Got so excited at the county fair he jumped between the shafts of a sulky and won two heats before they could catch him and throw him."

"Is that so?"

"My solemn word. Didn't pay off, though. They disqualified him because he wasn't a two-year-old."

Burke joined them and they sauntered down to the rotunda. Several hundred other candidates had had the same idea but the administration had anticipated the rush. A cadet stationed at the stairway into the pit was permitting visitors in parties of ten only, each party supervised by a cadet. Burke eyed the queue. "Simple arithmetic tells me there's no point in waiting."

Matt hesitated. Tex said, "Come on, Matt. Some will get tired and drop out."

Burke shrugged, said, "So long, suckers," and wandered away.

Matt said doubtfully, "I think he's right, Tex."

"Sure—but I got rid of him, didn't I?"

The entire rotunda was a museum and memorial hall of the Patrol. The boys found display after display arranged around the walls—the original log of the first ship to visit Mars, a photo of the take-off of the disastrous first Venus expedition, a model of the German rockets used in the Second Global War, a hand-sketched map of the far side of the Moon, found in the wrecked *Kilroy*.

They came to an alcove the back wall of which was filled by a stereo picture of an outdoor scene. They entered and found themselves gazing, in convincing illusion, out across a hot and dazzling lunar plain, with black sky, stars, and Mother Terra herself in the background.

In the foreground, life size, was a young man dressed in an old-fashioned pressure suit. His features could be seen clearly through his helmet, big mouth, merry eyes, and thick sandy hair cut in the style of the previous century.

Under the picture was a line of lettering: *Lieutenant Ezra Dahlquist, Who Helped Create the Tradition of the Patrol—1969–1996.*

Matt whispered, "There ought to be a notice posted somewhere to tell us what he did."

"I don't see any," Tex whispered back. "Why are you whispering?"

"I'm not—yes, I guess I was. After all, *he* can't hear us, can he? Oh—there's a vocal!"

"Well, punch it."

Matt pressed the button; the alcove filled with the first bars of Beethoven's Fifth. The music gave way to a voice: "The Patrol was originally made up of officers sent to it by each of the nations then in the Western Federation. Some were trustworthy, some were not. In 1996 came a day shameful and glorious in the history of the Patrol, an attempted *coup d'état*, the so-called Revolt of the Colonels. A cabal of high-ranking officers, acting from Moon Base, tried to seize power over the entire world. The plot would have been successful had not Lieutenant Dahlquist disabled every atom-bomb rocket at Moon Base by removing the fissionable material from each and wrecking the triggering mechanisms. In so doing he received so much radiation that he died of his burns." The voice stopped and was followed by the Valhalla theme from *Götterdämmerung*.

Tex let out a long sigh; Matt realized that he had been holding his own breath. He let it go, then took another; it seemed to relieve the ache in his chest.

They heard a chuckle behind them. Girard Burke was leaning against the frame of the alcove. "They go to a lot of trouble to sell it around here," he remarked. "Better watch it, me lads, or you will find yourselves buying it."

"What do you mean by that? Sell what?"

Burke gestured toward the picture. "That. And the plug that goes with it. If you care for that sort of thing, there are three more, one at each cardinal point of the compass."

Matt stared at him. "What's the matter with you, Burke? Don't you want to be in the Patrol?"

Burke laughed. "Sure I do. But I'm a practical man; I don't have to bamboozled into it by a lot of emotional propaganda." He pointed to the picture of Ezra Dahlquist. "Take him. They don't tell you he disobeyed orders of his superior officer—if things had fallen the other way, he'd be called a traitor. Besides that, they don't mention that it was sheer clumsiness that got him burned. Do you expect me to think he was a superman?"

Matt turned red. "No, I wouldn't expect it." He took a step forward. "But, since you are a practical man, how would you like a nice, practical punch in the snoot?"

Burke was no larger than Matt and a shade shorter, but he leaned forward, balanced on the balls of his feet, and said softly, "I'd love it. You and who else?"

Tex stepped forward. "I'm the 'who else.' "

"Stay out of this, Tex!" Matt snapped.

"I will not! I don't believe in wasting fair fighting on my social inferiors."

"Stay out, I tell you!"

"Nope, I want a piece of this. You slug him and I'll kick him in the stomach as he goes down."

Burke looked at Jarman, and relaxed, as if he knew that the fighting moment was past. "Tut, tut, gentlemen! You're squabbling among yourselves." He turned away. "Goodnight, Dodson. Don't wake me coming in."

Tex was still fuming. "We should have let him have it. He'll make your life miserable until you slap him down. My Uncle Bodie says the way to deal with that sort of pimple is to belt him around until he apologizes."

"And get kicked out of the Patrol before we're in it? I let him get me mad, so that puts him one up. Come on—let's see what else there is to see."

But Call-to-Quarters sounded before they worked around to the next of the four alcoves. Matt said good night to Tex at his door and went inside. Burke was asleep or shamming. Matt peeled off his clothes, shinnied up into his bunk, looked for the light switch, spotted it, and ordered it to switch off.

The unfriendly presence under him made him restless, but he was almost asleep when he recalled that he had not called his father back. The thought awakened him. Presently he became aware of a vague ache somewhere inside him. Was he coming down with something?

Could it be that he was homesick? At his age? The longer he considered it the more likely it seemed, much as he hated to admit it. He was still pondering it when he fell asleep.

3.
OVER THE BUMPS

The next morning Burke ignored the trouble they had had; he made no mention of it. He was even moderately cooperative about sharing the 'fresher. But Matt was glad to hear the call to breakfast.

Table 147 was not where it should be. Puzzled, Matt moved down the line until he found a table marked "147–149," with Cadet Sabbatello in charge. He found a place and sat down, to find himself sitting next to Pierre Armand. "Well! Pete!" he greeted him. "How are things going?"

"Glad to see you, Matt. Well enough, I guess." His tone seemed doubtful.

Matt looked him over. Pete seemed—"dragged through a knothole" was the phrase Matt settled on. He was about to ask what was wrong when Cadet Sabbatello rapped on the table. "Apparently," said the cadet, "some of you gentlemen have forgotten my advice last night, to eat sparingly this morning. You are about to go over the bumps today—and ground-hogs have been known to lose their breakfasts as well as their dignity."

Matt looked startled. He had intended to order his usual lavish breakfast; he settled for milk toast and tea. He noticed that Pete had ignored the cadet's advice; he was working on a steak, potatoes, and fried eggs—whatever ailed Pete, Matt decided, it had not affected his appetite.

Cadet Sabbatello had also noticed it. He leaned toward Pete. "Mister, uh—"

"Armand, sir," Pete answered between bites.

"Mr. Armand, either you have the digestion of a Martian

sandworm, or you thought I was joking. Don't you expect to be dropsick?"

"No, sir."

"No?"

"You see, sir, I was born on Ganymede."

"Oh! I beg your pardon. Have another steak. How are you doing?"

"Pretty well, on the whole, sir."

"Don't be afraid to ask for dispensations. You'll find that everyone around here understands your situation."

"Thank you, sir."

"I mean it. Don't play 'iron man.' There's no sense in it."

After breakfast, Matt fell in step with Armand. "Say, Pete, I see why Oscar carried your bag yesterday. Excuse me for being a stupe."

Pete looked self-conscious. "Not at all. Oscar has been looking out for me—I met him on the trip down from Terra Station."

Matt nodded. "I see." He had no expert knowledge of interplanetary schedules, but he realized that Oscar, coming from Venus, and Pete, coming from one of Jupiter's moons, would have to change ships at the artificial satellite of Earth called Terra Station, before taking the shuttle rocket down. It accounted for the two boys being well acquainted despite cosmically different backgrounds. "How do you feel?" he went on.

Pete hesitated. "As a matter of fact, I feel as if I were wading in quicksand up to my neck. Every move is an effort."

"Gee, that's too bad! Just what is the surface gravity on Ganymede? About one-third 'g' isn't it?"

"Thirty-two per cent. Or from my point of view, everything here weighs three times as much as it ought to. Including me."

Matt nodded. "As if two other guys were riding on you, one on your shoulders, and one on your back."

"That's about it. The worst of it is, my feet hurt all the time. I'll get over it—"

"Sure you will!"

"—since I'm of Earth ancestry and potentially just as strong as my grandfather was. Back home, I'd been working out in the centrifuge the last couple of earth-years. I'm a lot stronger than I used to be. There's Oscar." Matt greeted Oscar, then hurried to his room to phone his father in private.

A copter transport hopped Matt and some fifty other candidates to the site of the variable acceleration test—in cadet slang, the "Bumps." It was west of the base, in the mountains, in order to have a sheer cliff for free fall. They landed on a loading platform at the edge of this cliff and joined a throng of other candidates. It was a crisp Colorado morning. They were near the timberline; gaunt evergreens, twisted by the winds, surrounded the clearing.

From a building just beyond the platform two steel skeletons ran vertically down the face of the two-thousand-foot cliff. They looked like open frames for elevators, which one of them was. The other was a guide for the testing car during the drop down the cliff.

Matt crowded up to the rail and leaned over. The lower ends of the skeleton frameworks disappeared, a dizzy distance below, in the roof of a building notched into the sloping floor of the canyon. He was telling himself that he hoped the engineer who had designed the thing knew what he was doing when he felt a dig in the ribs. It was Tex. "Some roller coaster, eh, Matt?"

"Hi, Tex. That's an understatement if I ever heard one."

The candidate on Matt's left spoke up. "Do you mean to say we ride down that thing?"

"No less," Tex answered. "Then they gather the pieces up in a basket and haul 'em up the other one."

"How fast does it go?"

"You'll see in a mom—Hey! *Thar she blows!*"

A silvery, windowless car appeared inside one guide frame, at its top. It poised for a split second, then dropped. It dropped and dropped and dropped, gathering speed, until it disappeared with what seemed incredible velocity—actually about two hundred and fifty miles per hour—into the building below. Matt braced himself for the crash. None came, and he caught his breath.

Seconds later the car reappeared at the foot of the other framework. It seemed to crawl; actually it was accelerating rapidly during the first half of the climb. It passed from view into the building at the top of the cliff.

"Squad nine!" a loudspeaker bawled behind them.

Tex let out a sigh "Here I go, Matt," he said. "Tell mother my last words were of her. You can have my stamp collection." He shook hands and walked away.

The candidate who had spoken before gulped; Matt saw that he was quite pale. Suddenly he took off in the same direction but did not line up with the squad; instead he went up to the cadet mustering the squad and spoke to him, briefly and urgently. The cadet shrugged and motioned him away from the group.

Matt found himself feeling sympathetic rather than contemptuous.

His own test group was mustered next. He and his fellows were conducted into the upper building, where a cadet explained the test: "This test examines your tolerance for high acceleration, for free fall or weightlessness, and for violent changes in acceleration. You start with centrifugal force of three gravities, then all weight is removed from you as the car goes over the cliff. At the bottom the car enters a spiraling track which reduces its speed at deceleration of three gravities. When the car comes to rest, it enters the ascending tower; you make the climb at two gravities, dropping to one gravity, and momentarily to no weight, as the car reaches the top. Then the cycle is repeated, at higher accelerations, until each of you has reacted. Any questions?"

Matt asked, "How long is the free fall, sir?"

"About eleven seconds. We would increase it, but to double it would take four times as high a cliff. However, you will find this one high enough." He smiled grimly.

A timid voice asked, "Sir, what do you mean by 'react'?"

"Any of several things—hemorrhage, loss of consciousness."

"It's dangerous?"

The cadet shrugged. "What isn't? There has never been any mechanical failures. Your pulse, respiration, blood pressure, and other data are telemetered to the control room. We'll try not to let you die under test."

Presently he led them out of the room, down a passage and through a door into the test car. It had pendulum seats, not unlike any high-speed vehicle, but semi-reclining and heavily padded. They strapped down and medical technicians wired them for telemetering their responses. The cadet inspected, stepped out and returned with an officer, who repeated the inspection. The cadet then distributed "sick kits"—cloth bags of double thickness to be tied and taped to the mouth, so that a person might retch without inundating his companions. This done, he asked, "Are you all ready?" Getting no response, he went out and closed the door.

Matt wished that he had stopped him before it was too late.

For a long moment nothing happened. Then the car seemed to incline; actually, the seats inclined as the car started to move and picked up speed.

The seats swung back to the at-rest position but Matt felt himself getting steadily heavier and knew thereby that they were being centrifuged. He pressed against the pads, arms leaden, legs too heavy to move.

The feeling of extra weight left him, he felt his normal weight again, when suddenly that, too, was taken from him. He surged against the safety belts.

His stomach seemed to drop out of him. He gulped and swallowed; his breakfast stayed down. Somebody yelled, "We're falling!" It seemed to Matt the most unnecessary statement he had ever heard.

He set his jaw and braced himself for the bump. It did not come—and still his stomach seemed trying to squirm its way out of his body. Eleven seconds? Why, he had been falling more than eleven seconds already! What had gone wrong?

And still they fell, endlessly.

And fell.

Then he was forced back against the pads. The pressure increased smoothly until he was as heavy as he had been just before the drop. His abused stomach tried to retch but the pressure was too much for it.

The pressure eased off to normal weight. A short while later the car seemed to bounce and momentarily he was weightless, while his insides grabbed frantically for anchorage. The feeling of no weight lasted only an instant; he sagged into the cushions.

The door was flung open; the cadet strode in, followed by two medical technicians. Someone yelled, "Let me out of here! Let me out of here!" The cadet paid no attention but went to the seat in front of Matt. He unstrapped the occupant and the two medical assistants carried him out. His head lolled loosely as they did so. The cadet then went to the candidate who was kicking up the fuss, unstrapped him, and stepped back. The boy got up, staggered, and shuffled out.

"Anyone need a fresh sick kit?" There were muffled responses. Working swiftly, the cadet helped those who needed it. Matt felt weakly triumphant that his own kit was still clean.

"Stand by for five gravities," commanded the cadet. He made them answer to their names, one by one. While he was doing so another boy started clawing at his straps. Still calling the roll, the cadet helped him free and let him leave. He followed the lad out the door and shut it.

Matt felt himself tensing unbearably. He was relieved when the pressure took hold—but only momentarily, for he found that five gravities were much worse than three. His chest seemed para-lyzed, he fought for air.

The giant pressure lifted—they were over the edge again, falling. His mistreated stomach revenged itself at once; he was sorry that he had eaten any breakfast at all.

They were still falling. The lights went out—and someone screamed. Falling and still retching, Matt was sure that the black-ness meant some sort of accident; this time they would crash—but it did not seem to matter.

He was well into the black whirlpool of force that marked the deceleration at the bottom before he realized that he had come through without being killed. The thought brought no particular emotion; breathing at five gravities fully occupied him. The ride up the cliff, at double weight dropping off to normal weight, seemed like a vacation—except that his stomach protested when they bounced to a stop.

The lights came on and the cadet re-entered the room. His gaze stopped at the boy on Matt's right. The lad was bleeding at his nose and ears. The candidate waved him away feebly. "I can take it," he protested. "Go on with the test."

"Maybe you can," the cadet answered, "but you are through for today." He added, "Don't feel bad about it. It's not necessarily a down check."

He inspected the others, then called in the officer. The two held a whispered consultation over one boy, who was then half led, half carried from the test chamber. "Fresh sick kits?" asked the cadet.

"Here," Matt answered feebly. The change was made, while Matt vowed to himself never to touch milk toast again.

"Seven gravities," announced the cadet. "Speak up, or stand by." He called the roll again. Matt was ready to give up, but he heard himself answer "ready" and the cadet was gone before he could make up his mind. There were only six of them left now.

It seemed to him that the lights were going out again, gradu-ally, as the weight of his body built up to nearly a thousand pounds. But the lights "came on" again as the car dropped over the cliff; he realized dully that he had blacked out.

He had intended to count seconds on this fall to escape the feeling of endless time, but he was too dazed. Even the disquiet in his middle section seemed remote. Falling—falling—

Again the giant squeezed his chest, drained the blood from his brain, and shut the light from his eyes. The part that was Matt squeezed out entirely. . . .

"How do you feel?" He opened his eyes, saw a double image, and realized dimly that the cadet was leaning over him. He tried to answer. The cadet passed from view; he felt someone grasping him; he was being lifted and carried.

Someone wiped his face with a wet, cold towel. He sat up and found himself facing a nurse. "You're all right now," she said cheerfully. "Keep this until your nose stops bleeding." She handed him the towel. "Want to get up?"

"Yes, I think so."

"Take my arm. We'll go out into the air."

Out on the loading platform Matt sat in the sunshine, dabbling at his nose and regaining his strength. He could hear sounds of excitement from the rail behind each time the car dropped. He sat there, soaking in the sun and wondering whether or not he really wanted to be a spaceman.

"Hey, Matt." It was Tex, looking pale and not too sure of himself. There was a blood stain down the front of his coverall.

"Hello, Tex. I see you've had it."

"Yeah."

"How many g's?"

"Seven."

"Same here. What do you think of it?"

"Well—" Tex seemed at a loss. "I wish my Uncle Bodie could have tried it. He wouldn't talk so much about the time he rassled the grizzly."

There were many vacant seats at lunch. Matt thought about those who had gone—did they mind being "bumped out," or were they relieved?

He was hungry but ate little, for he knew what was ahead that afternoon—rocket indoctrination. He had looked forward to this part of the schedule most eagerly. Space flight! Just a test jump, but the real thing nevertheless. He had been telling himself that, even if he failed, it would be worth it to get this first flight.

Now he was not sure; the "bumps" had changed his viewpoint. He had a new, grim respect for acceleration and he no longer thought drop-sickness funny; instead he was wondering whether or not he would ever get adjusted to free fall. Some never did, he knew.

His test group was due in Santa Barbara Field at fourteen-thirty. He had a long hour to kill with nothing to do but fret. Finally it was time to go underground, muster, and slidewalk out to the field.

The cadet in charge led them up to the surface into a concrete trench about four feet deep. Matt blinked at the sunlight. His depression was gone; he was anxious to start. On each side and about two hundred yards away were training rockets, lined up like giant birthday candles, poised on their fins with sharp snouts thrusting against the sky.

"If anything goes wrong," the cadet said, "throw yourself flat in the trench. Don't let that get your goat—I'm required to warn you.

"The jump lasts nine minutes, with the first minute and a half under power. You'll feel three gravities, but the acceleration is only two gravities, because you are still close to the Earth.

"After ninety seconds you'll be travelling a little faster than a mile a second and you will coast on up for the next three minutes for another hundred miles to an altitude of about one hundred fifty miles. You fall back toward the earth another three minutes, brake your fall with the jet and ground at the end of the ninth minute.

"A wingless landing on an atmosphere planet with gravity as strong as that of Earth is rather tricky. The landing will be radar-robot controlled, but a human pilot will stand by and check the approach against the flight plan. He can take over if necessary. Any questions?"

Someone asked, "Are these atomic-powered ships?"

The cadet snorted. "These jeeps? These are chemically powered, as you can see from the design. Monatomic hydrogen. They are much like the first big rockets ever built, except that they have variable thrust, so that the pilot and the passengers won't be squashed into strawberry jam as the mass-ratio drops off."

A green signal flare arched up from the control tower. "Keep your eyes on the second rocket from the end, on the north," advised the cadet.

There was a splash of orange flame, sun bright, at the base of the ship. *There she goes!*

The ship lifted majestically, and poised for an instant, motionless as a hovering helicopter. The noise reached Matt, seemed to press against his chest. It was the roar of an impossibly huge blowtorch. A searchlight in the tower blinked, and the ship mounted, up and up, higher and faster, its speed increasing with such smoothness that it was hard to realize how fast it was going—except that the roar was gone. Matt found himself staring straight at the zenith, watching a dwindling artificial sun, almost as dazzling as Sol himself.

Then it was gone. Matt closed his mouth and started to look away when his attention was seized by the ice trail left as the rocket sliced its way through the outer atmosphere. White and strange, it writhed like a snake with a broken back. Under the driving force of the many-hundred-miles-an-hour winds of that far altitude it twisted visibly as he watched.

"That's all!" the cadet shouted. "We can't wait for the landing."

They went underground, down a corridor, and entered an elevator. It went up right out of the ground and into the air, supported by a hydraulic piston. It mounted close by the side of a rocket ship; Matt was amazed to see how large it was close up.

The elevator stopped and its door let down drawbridge fashion into the open hatch in the rocket's side. They trooped across; the cadet raised the bridge and went down again.

They were in a conical room. Above them the pilot lay in his acceleration rest. Beside them, feet in and head out, were acceleration couches for passengers. "Get in the bunks!" shouted the pilot. "Strap down."

Ten boys jostled one another to reach the couches. One hesitated. "Uh, oh, Mister!" he called out.

"Yes? Get in your couch."

"I've changed my mind. I'm not going."

The pilot used language decidedly not officerlike and turned to his control board. "Tower! Remove passenger from number nineteen." He listened, then said, "Too late to change the flight plan. Send up mass." He shouted to the waiting boy, "What do you weigh?"

"Uh, a hundred thirty-two pounds, sir."

"One hundred and thirty-two pounds and make it fast!" He turned back to the youngster. "You better get off this base fast, for if I have to skip my take-off I'll wring your neck."

The elevator climbed into place presently and three cadets poured across. Two were carrying sandbags, one had five lead weights. They strapped the sandbags to the vacant couch, and clamped the weights to its sides. "One thirty-two mass," announced one of the cadets.

"Get going," snapped the pilot and turned back to the board.

"Don't blow your tubes, Harry," advised the cadet addressed.

Matt was amazed, then decided the pilot must be a cadet, too. The three left, taking with them the boy; the hatch door shut with a *whish*.

"Stand by to raise!" the pilot called out, then looked down to check his passengers. "Passengers secure, nineteen," he called to the tower. "Is that confounded elevator clear?"

There was silence as the seconds trickled away.

The ship shivered. A low roar, muffled almost below audibility, throbbed in Matt's head. For a moment he felt slightly heavy, the feeling passed, then he was pressed strongly against the pads.

Matt was delighted to find that three gravities were not bad, flat on his back as he was. The minute and a half under power stretched out; there was nothing to hear but the muted blast of the reactor, nothing to see but the sky through the pilot's port above.

But the sky was growing darker. Already it was purple; as he watched it turned black. Fascinated, he watched the stars come out.

"Stand by for free fall!" the pilot called out, using an amplifier. "You'll find sick kits under each pillow. If you need 'em, put 'em on. I don't want to have to scrape it off the port."

Matt fumbled with heavy fingers under his head, found the kit. The sound of the jet died away, and with it the thrust that had kept them pinned down. The pilot swung out of his rest and floated, facing them. "Now look, sports—we've got six minutes. You can unstrap, two at a time and come up for a look-see. But get this: Hang on tight. Any man who starts floating free, or skylarking, gets a down check." He pointed to a boy. "You—and the next guy."

The "next guy" was Matt. His stomach was complaining and he felt so wretched that he did not really want the privilege offered—but his face was at stake; he clamped his jaws, swallowed the saliva pouring into his mouth, and unstrapped.

Free, he clung to one strap, floating loosely, and tried to get his bearings. It was curiously upsetting to have no up-and-down; it made everything swim—he had trouble focusing his eyes. "Hurry up there!" he heard the pilot shout, "or you'll miss your turn."

"Coming, sir."

"Hang on—I'm going to turn the ship." The pilot unclutched his gyros and cut in his precessing flywheels. The ship turned end over end. By the time Matt worked his way to the control station, moving like a cautious and elderly monkey, the rocket was pointed toward Earth.

Matt stared out at the surface, nearly a hundred miles below and still receding. The greens and browns seemed dark by contrast with the white dazzle of clouds. Off to the left and right he could see the inky sky, stabbed with stars. "That's the Base, just below," the pilot was saying. "Look sharp and you can make out Hayworth Hall, maybe, by its shadow."

It did not seem "just below" to Matt; it seemed "out"—or no direction at all. It was disquieting. "Over there—see?—is the crater where Denver used to be. Now look south—that brown stretch is Texas; you can see the Gulf beyond it."

"Sir," asked Matt, "can we see Des Moines from here?"

"Hard to pick out. Over that way—let your eye slide down the Kaw River till it strikes the Missouri, then up river. That dark patch—that's Omaha and Council Bluffs. Des Moines is between there and the horizon." Matt strained his eyes, trying to pick out his home. He could not be sure—but he did see that he was staring over the bulge of the Earth at a curved horizon; he was *seeing* the Earth as round. "That's all," ordered the pilot. "Back to your bunks. Next pair!"

He was glad to strap a belt across his middle. The remaining four minutes or so stretched endlessly; he resigned himself to never getting over space sickness. Finally the pilot chased the last pair back, swung ship jet toward Earth, and shouted, "Stand by for thrust—we're about to ride 'er down on her tail!"

Blessed weight pressed down on him and his stomach stopped complaining. The ninety seconds of deceleration seemed longer; it made him jumpy to know that the Earth was rushing up at them and not be able to see it. But at last there came a slight bump and his weight dropped suddenly to normal. "Grounded," announced the pilot, "and all in one piece. You can unstrap, sports."

Presently a truck arrived, swung a telescoping ladder up to the hatch, and they climbed down. On the way back they passed a great unwieldy tractor, crawling out to retrieve the rocket. Some- one stuck his head out of the tractor. "Hey! Harry—why didn't you land it in Kansas?"

Their pilot waved at the speaker. "Be grateful I didn't!"

Matt was free until mess; he decided to return to the observa- tion trench; he still wanted to see a ship land on its jet. He had seen winged landings of commercial stratosphere rockets, but never a jet landing.

Matt had just found a vacant spot in the trench when a shout went up—a ship was coming in. It was a ball of flame, growing in the sky, and then a pillar of flame, streaking down in front of him. The streamer of fire brushed the ground, poised like a ballet dancer, and died out. The ship was down.

He turned to a candidate near him. "How long till the next one?"

"They've come in about every five minutes. Stick around."

Presently a green flare went up from the control tower and he looked around, trying to spot the ship about to take off, when another shout caused him to turn back. There again was a ball of fire in the sky, growing.

Unbelievably, it went out. He stood there, stupefied—to hear a cry of "Down! Down, everybody! Flat on your faces!" Before he could shake off his stupor, someone tackled him and threw him.

He was rocked by a sharp shock, on top of it came the roar of an explosion. Something snatched at his breath.

He sat up and looked around. A cadet near him was peering cautiously over the parapet. "Allah the Merciful," he heard him say softly.

"What happened?"

"Crashed in. Dead, all dead." The cadet seemed to see him for the first time. "Get back to your quarters," he said sharply.

"But how did it happen?"

"Never mind—this is no time for sightseeing." The cadet moved down the line, clearing out spectators.

4.
FIRST MUSTER

Matt's room was empty, which was a relief. He did not want to see Burke, nor anyone. He sat down and thought about it.

Eleven people—just like that. All happy and excited and then—*crrump!*—not enough left to cremate. Suddenly he himself was back up in the sky— He broke off the thought, trembling.

At the end of an hour he had made up his mind that the Patrol was not for him. He had thought of it, he realized, through a kid's bright illusions—*Captain Jenks of the Space Patrol, The Young Rocketeers*, stuff like that. Well, those books were all right—for kids—but he wasn't hero material, he had to admit.

Anyhow, his stomach would never get used to free fall. Right now it tightened up when he thought about it.

By the time Burke returned he was calm and, if not happy, at least he was not unhappy, for his mind was at rest.

Burke came in whistling. He stopped when he saw Matt. "Well, junior, still here? I thought the bumps would send you home."

"No."

"Didn't you get dropsick?"

"Yes." Matt waited and tried to control his temper. "Didn't you?"

Burke chuckled. "Not likely. I'm no groundhog, junior. I—"

"Call me 'Matt.'"

"Okay, Matthew. I was going out into space before I could walk. My old man builds 'em, you know."

"I didn't know."

"Sure. 'Reactors, Limited'—he's chairman of the board. Say, did you see the fireworks out at the field?"

"You mean the ship that crashed?"

"What else? Quite a show, wasn't it?"

Matt could feel himself coming to a slow boil. "Do you mean to stand there and tell me," he said quietly, "that you regard the deaths of eleven human beings as 'quite a show'?"

Burke stared at him. Then he laughed. "I'm sorry, old fellow. I apologize. But it actually didn't occur to me that you didn't know."

"Didn't know what?"

"But you weren't supposed to know, of course. Relax, son—no one was killed. You were framed."

"Huh? What are you talking about?"

Burke sat down and laughed until he had tears. Matt grabbed him by the shoulder. "Cut that out and talk."

The other candidate stopped and looked up. "Honest, I rather like you, Dodson—you're such a perfect country cousin. How do you feel about Santa Claus and the Stork?"

"Talk!"

"Haven't you caught on to what they've been doing to you ever since you checked in?"

"Doing what?"

"War of nerves, man. Haven't you noticed some tests were too easy—too easy to cheat in, that is? When you went over the bumps, didn't you notice that they let you take a good look at the drop before you made it? When they could just as easily have kept you inside where it wouldn't worry you?"

Matt thought about it. It was an enticing notion—he could see how some of the things he had not understood would fit in to such a theory. "Go on."

"Oh, it's a good gag—it cleans out the weak sisters and it cleans out the stupes, too—the guys so dumb that they can't resist an invitation to cheat, never dreaming that it might be booby-trapped. It's efficient—a Patrol officer has to be smart and fast on his feet and cool-headed. It keeps from wasting money on second-raters."

"You just called me dumb and yet I got by."

"Of course you did, junior, because your heart is pure." He laughed again. "And I got by. But you'll never make a Patrolman, Matt. They've got other ways to get rid of the good, dumb boys. You'll see."

"Okay, so I'm dumb. But don't call me junior again. What's this got to do with the ship that crashed?"

"Why, it's simple. They want to eliminate all the deadwood before swearing us in. There are candidates with cast-iron stomachs who don't get upset by the bumps, or anything. So they send up a ship under robot control—no pilot, no passengers—and crash it, just to scare off those who can be scared. It's a darn sight cheaper than training just one cadet, if he doesn't pay off in the long run."

"How do you know? Have you got inside information on it?"

"In a way, yes. It's a logical necessity—those ships *can't* crash, unless you crash 'em on purpose. I *know*—my old man makes them."

"Well—maybe you're right." Matt dropped the matter, unsatisfied but lacking basis for further argument. It did convince him of one thing, however—spacesickness or not, come what may, he resolved to hang on as long as Girard Burke did, and at least twenty-four hours longer!

His table at dinner that night was numbered "147, 149, 151 & 153." There was room enough to seat the survivors.

Cadet Sabbatello looked them over pleasantly. "Congratulations, gentlemen, on having lasted it out. Since you will be sworn in tonight, when next we meet it will be in a different status." He grinned. "So relax and enjoy your last meal of freedom."

In spite of no effective breakfast and little lunch, Matt found himself unable to eat much. Girard Burke's interpretation of the tests and what they meant troubled him. He still intended to take the oath, but he had an uneasy feeling that he was about to take it without knowing what it signified—what the Patrol really was.

When the meal broke up, on sudden impulse he followed the cadet in charge of the table out. "Excuse me—Mr. Sabbatello, could I speak to you privately, sir?"

"Eh? I suppose so—come along." He led Matt to his own room; it was exactly like Matt's. "Now what is it?"

"Uh—Mr. Sabbatello, that crash today: was anybody hurt?"

"Hurt? It killed eleven people. Don't you call that 'hurt'?"

"Are you sure? Is it possible that it was a drone and nobody was inside?"

"It's possible, but it's not the case. I wish it were—the pilot was a friend of mine."

"Oh—I'm sorry. But I had to know, for sure. You see, it's very important to me."

"Why?"

Matt sketched out Burke's version of what had happened, without giving Burke's name. As he talked, Sabbatello showed more and more annoyance. "I see," he said, when Matt was done. "It is true that some of the tests are psychological rather than overt. But this matter of the crash—who fed you that nonsense?"

Matt did not say anything.

"Never mind. You can protect your informant—it won't matter in the least in the long run. But about the crash—" He considered. "I'd give my word of honor to you—in fact I do—but if you accept the hypothesis your friend holds, then you won't pay any attention to my sworn word." He thought a moment. "Are you a Catholic?"

"Uh, nossir." Matt was startled.

"It doesn't matter. Do you know who Saint Barbara is?"

"Not exactly, sir. The field—"

"Yes, the field. She was a third-century martyr. The point is that she is the patron saint of all who deal with high explosives, rocket men among others." He paused.

"If you go over to the chapel, you will find that a mass is scheduled during which Saint Barbara will be asked to intercede for the souls of the men who were lost this afternoon. I think you realize that no priest would lend his office to any such chicanery as your friend suggests?"

Matt nodded solemnly. "I see your point, sir. I don't need to go to the chapel—I've found out what I needed to know."

"Fine. You had better hightail it and get ready. It would be embarrassing to be late to your own swearing in."

First Muster was scheduled for twenty-one o'clock in the auditorium. Matt was one of the first to arrive, scrubbed and neat and wearing a fresh coverall. A cadet took his name and told him to wait inside. The floor of the hall had been cleared of seats. Above the stage at the far end were the three closed circles of the Federation—Freedom, Peace, and Law, so intertwined that, if any one were removed, the other two would fall apart. Under them was the Patrol's own sign, a star blazing in the night.

Tex was one of the last to show up. He was greeting Matt, breathlessly, when a cadet, speaking from the rostrum, called out, "Attention!

"Gather on the left side of the hall," he went on. The candidates milled and shuffled into a compact group. "Remain where you are until muster. When your name is called, answer 'Here!', then walk across to the other side. You will find white guide lines on the deck there. Toe the lines to form ranks."

Another cadet came down from the rostrum and moved toward the mass of boys. He stopped, picked a slip of paper from four such slips he held, and fixed Tex with his eye. "You, mister," he said. "Take this."

Jarman took it, but looked puzzled. "What for?"

"As well as answering to your own name, when you hear this name, speak up. Step out in front and sing out, 'I answer for him!' "

Tex looked at the slip. Matt saw that it read: "John Martin."

"But why?" demanded Tex.

The cadet looked at him. "You really don't know?"

"Nary a notion."

"Hmmph! Well, since the name doesn't ring a bell, just take it that he is a classmate of yours who can't be here tonight, in person. So you answer for him to make the muster complete. Get it?"

"Yes, sir. Can do."

The cadet moved on down the line. Tex turned to Matt. "What gives, d'you s'pose?"

"It beats me."

"Me, too. Well, we'll probably find out."

The cadet on the rostrum moved to stage left. "Silence!" he commanded. "The Commandant!"

From the rear entered two men dressed in the midnight black. The younger of them walked so that his sleeve brushed the elbow of his senior. They moved to the center of the platform; the younger man stopped. The elder halted immediately, whereupon the aide withdrew. The Commandant of the Academy stood facing the new class.

Or, rather, facing down the center of the hall. He stood still for a long moment; someone coughed and shuffled, at which he turned toward the group and faced them thereafter. "Good evening, gentlemen."

Seeing him, Matt was reminded strongly of Cadet Sabbatello's protest: "Not *blind*, Mr. Dodson!" Commodore Arkwright's eyes looked strange—the sockets were deep set and the eyelids drooped like a man in thought. Yet, as that sightless gaze rested on him, it seemed to Matt that the Commandant could not only see him but could peer inside his head.

"I welcome you to our fellowship. You come from many lands, some from other planets. You are of various colors and creeds. Yet you must and shall become a band of brothers.

"Some of you are homesick. You need not be. From this day on every part of this family of planets is your home, each place equally. Each living, thinking creature in this system is your neighbor—and your responsibility.

"You are about to take an oath, by your own choice, as a member of the Patrol of this our System. In time, you expect to become an officer of that Patrol. It is necessary that you understand the burden you assume. You expect to spend long hours studying your new profession, acquiring the skills of the spaceman and the arts of the professional soldier. These skills and arts you must have, but they will not make you an officer of the Patrol."

He paused, then went on, "An officer in command of a ship of the Patrol, away from base, is the last of the absolute monarchs, for there is none but himself to restrain him. Many places where he must go no other authority reaches. He himself must embody law, and the rule of reason, justice and mercy.

"More than that, to the members of the Patrol singly and together is entrusted such awful force as may compel or destroy, all other force we know of—and with this trust is laid on them the charge to keep the peace of the System and to protect the liberties of its peoples. They are soldiers of freedom.

"It is not enough that you be skillful, clever, brave— The trustees of this awful power must each possess a meticulous sense of honor, self-discipline beyond all ambition, conceit, or avarice, respect for the liberties and dignity of all creatures, and an unyielding will to do justice and give mercy. He must be a true and gentle knight."

He stopped and there was no sound at all in the huge room. Then he said, "Let those who are prepared to take the oath be mustered."

The cadet who had been acting as adjutant stepped forward briskly. "Adams!"

"Uh—here, sir!" A candidate trotted across the room.

"Akbar."

"Here!"

"Alvarado—"

"Anderson, Peter—"

"Anderson, John—"

"Angelico—"

Then, presently, it was, "Dana—Delacroix—DeWitt—Diaz—Dobbs," and "Dodson!"

"Here!" shouted Matt. His voice squeaked but no one laughed.

He hurried over to the other side, found a place and waited, panting. The muster went on:

"Eddy—Eisenhower—Ericsson—" Boys trickled across the room until few were left. "Sforza, Stanley, Suliman," and then, finally: "Zahm!" The last candidate joined his fellows.

But the cadet did not stop. "Dahlquist!" he called out.

There was no answer.

"Dahlquist!" he repeated. "Ezra Dahlquist!"

Matt felt cold prickles around his scalp. He recognized the name now—but Dahlquist would not be here, not Ezra Dahlquist. Matt was sure of that, for he remembered an alcove in the rotunda, a young man in a picture, and the hot, bright sand of the Moon.

There was a stir in the rank behind him. A candidate pushed his way through and stepped forward. "I answer for Ezra Dahlquist!"

"Martin!"

This time there was no hesitation. He heard Tex's voice, his tone shrill: "I answer for him."

"Rivera."

A strong baritone: "Answering for Rivera!"

"Wheeler!"

"I answer for Wheeler."

The cadet turned toward the Commandant and saluted:

"All present, sir. Class of 2075, First Muster complete."

The man in black returned the salute. "Very well, sir. We will proceed with the oath." He stepped forward to the very edge of the platform, the cadet at his elbow. "Raise your right hands."

The Commandant raised his own hand. "Repeat after me: Of my own free will, without reservation—"

" 'Of my own free will, without reservation—' "

"I swear to uphold the peace of the Solar System—"

In chorus they followed him.

"—to protect the lawful liberties of its inhabitants—

"—to defend the constitution of the Solar Federation—

"—to carry out the duties of the position to which I am now appointed—

"—and to obey the lawful orders of my superior officers.

"To these ends I subordinate all other loyalties and renounce utterly any that may conflict with them.

"This I solemnly affirm in the Name I hold most sacred."

"So help me, God," concluded the Commandant. Matt repeated his words, but the response around him took a dozen different forms, in nearly as many languages.

The Commandant turned his head to the cadet by his side. "Dismiss them, sir."

"Aye aye, sir." The cadet raised his voice. "On being dismissed, face to the right and file out. Maintain your formation until clear of the door. Dismissed!"

At the cue of his command, music swelled out and filled the hall; the newly created cadets marched away to the strains of the Patrol's own air, *The Long Watch.* It persisted until the last of them were gone, then faded out.

The Commandant waited until the youngster cadets had left, then faced around. His aide joined him at once, whereupon the acting cadet adjutant moved quickly from his side. Commodore Arkwright turned toward the departing cadet. "Mr. Barnes."

"Yes, sir?"

"Are you ready to be commissioned?"

"Er—I don't think so, sir. Not quite."

"So? Well, come see me soon."

"Yes, sir. Thank you."

The Commodore turned away and headed rapidly for the stage exit, with his aide's sleeve brushing his. "Well, John," asked the senior, "What did you think of them?"

"A fine bunch of boys, sir."

"That was my impression. All youth and eagerness and young expectation. But how many of them will we have to eliminate? It's a sorry thing, John, to take a boy and change him so that he is no longer a civilian, then kick him out. It's the cruelest duty we have to perform."

"I don't see a way to avoid it."

"There is no way. If we had some magic touchstone—Tell the field that I want to raise ship in thirty minutes."

"Aye aye, sir."

5.
INTO SPACE

The Patrol Academy may lack ivy-covered buildings and tree-shaded walks; it does not lack room. There are cadets in every reach of the Federation, from ships circling Venus, or mapping the scorched earth of Mercury, to ships patrolling the Jovian moons.

Even on years-long exploration flights to the frozen fringes of the Solar System cadets go along—and are brevetted as officers when their captains think them ready, without waiting to return.

The public thinks of the Academy as the school ship P.R.S. *James Randolph*, but every cadet mess in every ship of the Patrol is part of the Academy. A youngster cadet is ordered to the *Randolph* as soon as he is sworn in and he remains attached to that ship until he is ready to go to a regular Patrol vessel as a passed cadet. His schooling continues; in time he is ordered back to where he started, Hayworth Hall, to receive his final polish.

An oldster, attached to Hayworth Hall, will not necessarily be there. He may be at the radiation laboratories of Oxford University, or studying interplanetary law at the Sorbonne, or he may even be as far away as Venus, at the Institute for System Studies. Whatever his route—and no two cadets pursue exactly the same course of training—the Academy is still in charge of him, until, and *if*, he is commissioned.

How long it takes depends on the cadet. Brilliant young Hartstone, who died on the first expedition to Pluto, was brevetted less than a year after he reported to Hayworth Hall as a groundhog candidate. But it is not unusual to find oldsters at Terra Base who have been cadets for five years or more.

* * *

Cadet Matthew Dodson admired himself in the mirror of the 'fresher. The oyster-white uniform he had found waiting when he returned from First Muster the evening before, and with it a small book of regulations embossed with his name and clipped to a new assignment schedule. The schedule had started out: "1. Your first duty as a cadet is to read the regulation book herewith, at once. Hereafter you are responsible for the contents."

He had read it before taps, until his mind was a jumble of undigested rules: "A cadet is an officer in a limited sense—" "—behave with decorum and sobriety appropriate to the occasion—" "—in accordance with local custom rather than Patrol custom unless in conflict with an invariant law of the Federation or regulation of the Patrol." "—but the responsibility of determining the legality of the order rests on the person ordered as well as on the person giving the order." "—circumstances not covered by law or regulation must be decided by the individual in the light of the living tradition of the Patrol." "Cadets will at all times be smooth-shaven and will not wear their hair longer than two inches."

He felt that he understood the last mentioned.

He got up before reveille the next morning and dived into the 'fresher, shaved hastily and rather unnecessarily and got into uniform.

It fit him well enough, but to his eye the fit was perfect, the styling superb. As a matter of fact, the uniform lacked style, decoration, trim, insignia, or flattering cut.

But Matt thought he looked wonderful.

Burke pounded on the 'fresher door. "Have you died in there?" He stuck his head in. "Oh—all right, so you look sweet. Now how about getting out?"

"Coming." Matt stalled around the room for a few minutes, then overcome by impatience, tucked his regulation book in his tunic (regulation #383), and went to the refectory. He walked in feeling self-conscious, proud, and about seven feet tall. He sat down at his table, one of the first to arrive. Cadets trickled in; Cadet Sabbatello was one of the last.

The oldster looked grimly down the table. "Attention," he snapped. "All of you—stand up."

Matt jumped to his feet with the rest. Sabbatello sat down. "From now on, gentlemen, make it a rule to wait until your seniors are seated. Be seated." The oldster studied the studs in front of him, punched his order, and looked up. The youngsters had resumed eating. He rapped the table sharply. "Quiet, please. Gentlemen, you have many readjustments to make. The sooner you make them, the happier you will be. Mr. Dodson—stop dunking your toast; you are dripping it on your uniform. Which brings me," he went on, "to the subject of table manners—"

Matt returned to his quarters considerably subdued.

He stopped by Tex's room and found him thumbing through the book of regulations. "Hello, Matt. Say, tell me something—is there anything in this bible that says Mr. Dynkowski has the right to tell me not to blow on my coffee?"

"I see you've had it, too. What happened?"

Jarman's friendly face wrinkled. "Well, I'd begun to think of Ski as an all-right guy, helpful and considerate. But this morning at breakfast he starts out by asking me how I manage to carry around all that penalty-weight." Tex glanced at his waist line; Matt noted with surprise that Tex looked quite chubby in cadet uniform.

"All us Jarmans are portly," Tex went on defensively. "He should see my Uncle Bodie. Then he—"

"Skip it," said Matt. "I know the rest of it—now."

"Well, I guess I shouldn't have lost my temper."

"Probably not." Matt looked through the book. "Maybe this will help. It says here that, in case of doubt, you may insist that the officer giving the order put it in writing and stamp his thumb print, or use other means to provide a permanent record."

"Does it, really?" Tex grabbed the book. "That's for me!—'cause I sure am in doubt. Boy! Just wait and see his face when I pull this one."

"I'd like to," agreed Matt. "Which way do you take the lift, Tex?" The Patrol Rocket Ship *Simon Bolivar*, transport, was at Santa Barbara Field, having discharged a battalion of Space Marines, but P.R.S. *Bolivar* could take but about half the new class. The rest were to take the public shuttle rocket from Pike's Peak launching catapult to Terra Space Station, there to be transferred to the *Randolph*.

"Transport," Tex answered. "How about you?"

"Me, too. I'd like to see Terra Station, but I'm glad we're going in a Patrol ship. What are you taking with you?"

Tex hauled out his luggage and hefted it. "It's a problem. I've got about fifty pounds here. Do you suppose if I rolled it up real small I could get it down to twenty pounds?"

"An interesting theory," Matt said. "Let's have a look at it— you've got to eliminate thirty pounds of penalty-weight."

Jarman spread his stuff out on the floor. "Well," Matt said at once, "you don't need all those photographs." He pointed to a dozen large stereos, each weighing a pound or more.

Tex looked horrified. "Leave my harem behind?" He picked up one. "There is the sweetest redhead in the entire Rio Grande Valley." He picked up another. "And Smitty—I couldn't get along without Smitty. She thinks I'm wonderful."

"Wouldn't she still think so if you left her pic behind?"

"Oh, of course. But it wouldn't be gallant." He considered. "I'll compromise—I'll leave behind my club."

"Your club?" Matt asked, failing to see anything of that description.

"The one I use to beat off the little darlings when they get too persistent."

"Oh. Maybe someday you'll teach me your secret. Yes, leave your club behind; there aren't any girls in the *Randolph*."

"Is that good?" demanded Tex.

"I refuse to commit myself." Matt studied the pile. "You know what I'd suggest? Keep that harmonica—I like harmonica music. Have those photos copied in micro. Feed the rest to the cat."

"That's easy for you to say."

"I've got the same problem." He went to his room. The class had the day free, for the purpose of getting ready to leave Earth. Matt spread his possessions out to look them over. His civilian clothes he would ship home, of course, and his telephone as well, since it was limited by its short range to the neighborhood of an earth-side relay office.

He made a note to telephone home before he packed the instrument. Might as well make one other call, too, he decided; even though he was resolved not to waste time on girls in his new life, it would be polite to phone and say good-by. He did so.

He put the instrument down a few minutes later, baffled to find that he had apparently promised to write regularly.

He called home, spoke with his parents and kid brother, and then put the telephone with things to be shipped. He was scratching his head over what remained when Burke came in. He grinned. "Trying to swallow your penalty-weight?"

"I'll figure it out."

"You don't have to leave that junk behind, you know."

"Huh?"

"Ship it up to Terra Station, rent a locker, and store it. Then, when you go on liberty to the Station, you can bring back what you want. Sneak it aboard, if it's that sort of thing." Matt made no comment; Burke went on, "What's the matter, Galahad? Shocked at the notion of running contraband?"

"No. But I don't have a locker at Terra Station."

"Well, if you're too cheap to rent one, you can ship the stuff to mine. You scratch me and I'll scratch you."

"No, thanks." He thought about expressing some things to the Terra Station post office, then discarded the idea—the rates were too high. He went on sorting. He would keep his camera, but his micro kit would have to go, and his chessmen. Presently he had cut the list to what he hoped was twenty pounds; he took the stuff away to weigh it.

Reveille and breakfast were an hour early the next day. Shortly after breakfast the call-to-muster ran through Hayworth Hall, to be followed by heart-quickening strains of "Raise Ship!" Matt slung his jump bag over his shoulder and hurried down to the lower corridors. He pushed his way through a throng of excited youngster cadets and found his assigned area.

Muster was by squads and Matt was a temporary squad leader, as his name came first, alphabetically, in his squad. He had been given a list; he reached into his pouch and had an agonizing moment of thinking he had left it up in his room before his fingers closed on it. "Dodsworth!"

"Here."

"Dunstan."

"Here."

He was still working through Frankel, Freund, and Funston when the oldster mustering the entire corridor shouted for him to report. He hurried to a conclusion, faced around, and saluted. "Squad nineteen—all present!"

Someone tittered and Matt realized suddenly that he had used the scout salute, rather than the relaxed, open-palmed gesture of the Patrol. His cheeks burned.

A brassy amplified voice called out, "All deck parties report." In turn, the oldster in Matt's corridor called out, "Third deck party, all present." When all reports were in there was a momentary silence, long enough for Matt to have a spine-tingling anticipation of what was to come. Would they? But they were doing so; the voice over the speaker called out: "Dahlquist?"

Another voice—heard only through the speaker—replied, "I answer for him."

It went on, until the Four were mustered, whereupon the first voice stated, "All present, sir."

"Man the ship."

They mounted a slidewalk, to step off in a large underground room, far out under Santa Barbara Field. There were eight large elevators arranged in a wide circle around the room. Matt and his squad were crowded into one of them and mounted to the surface. Up it went, much higher than had been necessary to enter the test-flight rocket, up and up, close by the huge bulk of the *Bolivar*.

It stopped and they trotted across the drawbridge into the ship. Inside the airlock stood a space-marines sergeant, gaudy and splendid who kept repeating, "Seventh deck! Down the hatch to your own deck—step lively!" He pointed to the hatch, down which disappeared a narrow, vertical steel ladder.

Matt hitched his jump bag out of his way and lowered himself into the hatch, moving fast to avoid getting his fingers stepped on by the cadet who followed him. He lost track of the decks, but there was a sergeant master-at-arms on each. He got off when he heard, "Third deck!"

He was in a wide, low cylindrical compartment, the deck of which was covered with plastic-foam padding. It was marked off in sections, each about seven feet by three and fitted with safety belts.

Matt found an unoccupied section, sat down, and waited. Presently cadets stopped dribbling in, the room was crowded. The master-at-arms called out, "Down, everybody—one to a section." He then counted them by noting that all sections were filled.

A loudspeaker warned, "All hands, prepare for acceleration!" The sergeant told them to strap down and remained standing until all had done so. He then lay down, grasped two handholds, and reported the third deck ready.

"All hands, stand by to raise!" called out the speaker.

There was a long and breathless wait.

"Up ship!" shouted the speaker.

Matt felt himself pressed into the padding.

Terra Space Station and the school ship *Randolph* lie in a circular orbit 22,300 miles above the surface of the Earth, where they circle the Earth in exactly twenty-four hours, the natural period of a body at that distance.

Since the Earth's rotation exactly matches their period, they face always one side of the Earth—the ninetieth western meridian, to be exact. Their orbit lies in the ecliptic, the plane of the Earth's orbit around the Sun, rather than in the plane of the Earth's equator. This results in them swinging north and south each day as seen from the earth. When it is noon in the Middle West, Terra Station and the *Randolph* lie over the Gulf of Mexico; at midnight they lie over the South Pacific.

The state of Colorado moves eastward about 830 miles per hour. Terra Station and the *Randolph* also move eastward nearly 7000 miles per hour—1.93 miles per second, to be finicky. The pilot of the *Bolivar* had to arrive at the *Randolph* precisely matched in course and speed. To do this he must break his ship away from our heavy planet, throw her into an elliptical orbit just tangent to the circular orbit of the *Randolph* and with that tangency so exactly placed that, when he matched speeds, the two ships would lie relatively motionless although plunging ahead at two miles per second. This last maneuver was no easy matter like jockeying a copter over a landing platform, as the two speeds, unadjusted, would differ by 3000 miles an hour.

Getting the *Bolivar* from Colorado to the *Randolph*, and all other problems of journeying between the planets, are subject to precise and elegant mathematical solution under four laws formulated by the saintly, absent-minded Sir Isaac Newton nearly four centuries earlier than this flight of the *Bolivar*—the three Laws of Motion and the Law of Gravitation. These laws are simple; their application in space to get from where you are to where you want to be, at the correct time with the correct course and speed, is a nightmare of complicated, fussy computation.

The "weight" pressing Matt into the padding was four gravities—Matt weighed nearly six hundred pounds. He lay there, breathing with difficulty, while the ship punched its way through the thick soup of air and out into free space. The heavy weight bound down the cadets while the *Bolivar* attained a speed of some six miles per second and climbed to an altitude of 900 miles.

At the end of five minutes and a few odd seconds the drive stopped.

Matt raised his head, while the sudden silence rang in his ears. The master-at-arms detected Matt's movement and others. He shouted, "Stay where you are—don't move."

Matt relaxed. They were in free fall, weightless, even though the *Bolivar* was speeding away from the Earth at more than 20,000 miles an hour. Each body—ship, planet, meteor, atom—in space falls continually. It moves also with whatever other motion it has inherited from its past experience.

Matt was acutely aware of his weightlessness, for his stomach told him about it, complainingly. To be on the safe side, he removed a sick kit from his jump bag, but he did not put it on. He was feeling queasy; it was not as bad as it had been on his test flight, not half as bad as the "bumps." He hoped to get by without losing his breakfast.

The loudspeaker sang out, "End of acceleration. Four hours of free fall." The master-at-arms sat up. "You can unstrap now," he said.

In a matter of seconds the compartment took on the look of a particularly crowded aquarium. One hundred boys were floating, swimming, squirming in every attitude and position between the deck and the overhead. These two barriers no longer seemed like floor and ceiling since up-and-down was gone; they were simply walls which rotated slowly and erratically for each observer as his own body turned past them.

"Hey, you guys!" yelled the sergeant. "Grab on to something and listen to me." Matt looked around, found himself near the overhead, spotted a handhold, and grasped it. "It's time you kids learned some traffic rules for free flight. You got to learn to zig when the other guy zags. If you happen to meet the Captain and you zig when you should 'a' zagged and bump him, he ain't going to like it. See?"

He stuck out a scarred thumb. "Rule one: all groundhogs—that's you and don't try to tell me anything different—are required to hold on with at least one hand at all times. That applies until you pass your free-fall acrobatics test. Rule two: give way to officers and don't make them have to shout 'Gangway!' Besides that, give way to anybody on duty, or busy, or with his hands full.

"If you're moving aft, pass inboard of the man you meet, and contrariwise if you're moving forward. If you're moving clockwise, figuring 'clockwise' from the bow end of the ship, you pass the man you meet outboard and let him pass inboard—contrariwise for counterclockwise. No matter what direction you're going, if you overtake a man you pass inboard of him. Is that all clear?"

Matt thought it was, though he doubted if he could remember it. But a remaining possibility occurred to him. "Sergeant," he asked innocently, "suppose you're moving directly in or out from the center of the ship—what do you do?"

The sergeant looked disgusted, which gave his face an odd appearance to Matt, as their two faces were upside down with respect to each other. "You get what usually happens to jaywalkers—okay, so you're moving across the traffic: just stay out of everybody's way. It's your lookout. Any more questions?"

No one answered; he went on: "All right, go out and look around the ship—but try to behave yourselves and not bump into anybody so you'll be a credit to deck three."

The third deck had no ports of any sort, but the *Bolivar* was a long-jump transport; she possessed recreation rooms and viewports. Matt started forward, seeking a place from which to get a glimpse of the Earth.

He remembered to pass outboard as he pulled himself along, but apparently some passengers had not been indoctrinated. Each hatchway was a traffic jam of youngsters, each trying to leave his own deck to sight-see in some other deck, any deck.

The sixth deck, he found, was a recreation room. It contained the ship's library—locked—and games equipment, also locked. But it did have six large viewports.

The recreation deck had carried a full load of passengers. Now, in free fall, cadets from all other decks gradually found their way to the recreation deck, just as Matt had, seeking a view of outside; at the same time the original roster of that deck showed no tendency to want to leave their favored billet.

It was crowded.

Crowded as a basket full of kittens—Matt removed someone's space boot from his left eye and tried to worm his way toward one of the ports. Judicious work with his knees and elbows and a total disregard of the rules of the road got him to the second or third layer near one port. He placed a hand on a shoulder in front of him. The cadet twisted around. "Hey! Who do you think you're shoving? Oh—hello, Matt."

"Hi, Tex. How's it going?"

"All right. Say, you should have been here a few minutes ago. We passed one of the television relay stations, close by. Boy, oh, boy, are we traveling!"

"We did, huh? What did it look like?"

"Couldn't see much of it, must have been ten miles away, maybe. But, with the time we're making it was just there she comes and there she goes."

"Can you see the Earth?" Matt squirmed toward the port.

"Natch." Tex gave way and let Matt slide into his place. The frame of the port cut across the eastern Atlantic. Matt could see an arc extending almost from the North Pole to the Equator.

It was high noon over the Atlantic. Beyond it, bright in the afternoon sunlight, he could make out the British Isles, Spain, and the brassy Sahara. The browns and greens of land were in sharp contrast to the deep purple of the ocean. In still greater contrast stood the white dazzle of cloud. As his eye approached the distant, rounded horizon the details softened, giving a strong effect of stereo, of depth, of three-dimensional globularness—the world indeed was round!

Round and green and beautiful! He discovered presently that he had been holding his breath. His nausea was quite gone.

Someone tugged at his leg. "Don't stay there all day. Do you want to hog it?"

Regretfully Matt gave way to another cadet. He turned and shoved himself away from the port and in so doing became disoriented. He could not find Tex in the helter-skelter mass of floating bodies.

He felt a grip on his right ankle. "Let's get out of here, Matt."

"Right." They worked their way to the hatch and moved to the next deck. Being without ports it was not heavily populated. They propelled themselves toward the center of the room, away from the traffic, and steadied themselves on handholds. "Well," said Matt, "so this is it—space, I mean. How do you like it?"

"Makes me feel like a goldfish. And I'm getting cross-eyed trying to figure out which side is up. How's your gizzard? Been dropsick?"

"No." Matt swallowed cautiously. "Let's not talk about it. Where were you last night, Tex? I looked for you a couple of times, but your rommate said he hadn't seen you since dinner."

"Oh, that—" Tex looked pained. "I was in Mr. Dynkowski's room. Say, Matt, that was a bum steer you gave me."

"Huh? What steer?"

"You know—when you advised me to ask Mr. Dynkowski to put an order in writing if I was in doubt about it. Man, oh man, did you get me in a jam!"

"Wait a minute—I didn't advise you to do that; I just pointed out that the regs let you do it if you wanted to."

"Just the same, you were egging me on."

"The deuce I was! My interest was purely theoretical. You were a free agent."

"Oh, well—skip it. Skip it."

"What happened?"

"Well, last night at dinner I ordered pie for dessert. I picked it up, just like I always have ever since I got too big for Ma to slap my hands for it, and started shoveling it in my face, happy as a pup in a pansy bed. Ski ordered me to cease and desist—told me to use my fork."

"Yeah? Go on."

"I said to put it in writing, please, sir, polite as a preacher."

"It stopped him?"

"Like fun it did! He said, 'Very well, Mr. Jarman,' cool as could be, took out his notebook, wrote it out, stamped his thumb print on it, tore out the page and handed it to me."

"So you used your fork. Or didn't you?"

"I sure did. But that's only the beginning. Immediately he wrote out another order and handed it to me. He told me to read it aloud. Which I did."

"What did it say?"

"Wait a minute . . . I've got it here somewhere." Tex poked around in his pouch. "Here—read it."

Matt read, " 'Cadet Jarman—immediately after this meal you will report to the officer-of-the-watch, taking with you the first written order I gave you. Explain to him the events leading up to the first order and get an opinion from him as to the legality of orders of this type—S. Dynkowski, psd. cdt.' "

Matt whistled. "Oh, oh. . . . What did you do?"

"I finished my pie, the way he told me to, though I didn't want it very much by then. Ski was nice about it. He grinned at me and said, 'No hard feelings, Mr. Jarman. All according to protocol and all that sort of thing.' Then he wanted to know where in the world I had gotten the idea."

Matt felt his neck grow warm. "You told him it was my idea?"

"Do I look stupid? I just told him somebody had pointed out regulation number nine-oh-seven to me."

Matt relaxed. "Thanks, Tex. I'll remember that."

"Forget it. But he sent you a message."

"Me?"

"It was just one word: 'Don't.' "

"Don't what?"

"Just 'Don't.' He added that amateur space lawyers frequently talked themselves out of the Patrol."

"Oh." Matt tucked this away and started trying to digest it. "What happened afterwards? When you saw the duty officer?"

"I reported to the duty office and the cadet on watch sent me on in. I saluted and announced my name, like a good little boy, and showed him the two orders." Tex paused and stared into the distance.

"Yes? Go on, man—don't stop like that."

"Then he most scientifically ate my ears off. My Uncle Bodie couldn't have done a better job." Tex paused again, as if the memory were too painfully sharp. "Then he quieted down a little bit and explained to me in words of one syllable that reg nine-oh-seven was for emergencies only and that youngster cadets were under the orders of oldster cadets at all times and in all matters, unless the regulations specifically say otherwise."

"He did? Say, that covers an awful lot of ground. Why, that means a senior cadet can order us to do almost anything. You mean it's covered by law that an oldster can tell me how to part my hair?"

"Just precisely that—you happened to pick the very words Lieutenant von Ritter used. An oldster can't tell you to violate a regulation—he can't tell you to take a poke at the captain and he can't order you to hold still while he takes a poke at you. But that's about all that limits him. Mr. von Ritter says that it's left up to the good judgment and discretion of the senior, and table manners were very definitely Mr. Dynowski's business and not to forget it! Then he told me to report back to Ski."

"Did he crow over you?"

"Not a bit." Tex's brow wrinkled. "That's the funny part about it. Ski treated the whole affair just as if he had been giving me a lesson in geometry. He said that now that I was assured that his orders were according to regulation he wanted me to know why he had told me how to eat my pie. He even said he could see that I would regard it as improper interference with my private life. I said I guessed I didn't have any private life any more. He said no, I had one all right, but it would feel pretty microscopic for a while.

"Then he explained the matter. A patrol officer is supposed to be able to move in all society—if your hostess eats with her knife, then you eat with your knife."

"Everybody knows that."

"Okay. He pointed out that candidates come from everywhere. Some of them even come from families and societies where it's good manners for everybody to eat out of one dish, with their fingers . . . some of the Moslem boys. But there is an over-all way to behave that is acceptable anywhere among the top crust."

"Nuts," said Matt. "I've seen the Governor of Iowa with a hot dog in one hand and a piece of pie in the other."

"I'll bet it wasn't at a state dinner," Tex countered. "No, Matt, it made sense the way he told it. He said pie wasn't important, but it was part of a larger pattern—for instance that you must never mention death on Mars or to a Martian."

"Is that a fact?"

"I guess so. He said that in time I would learn how to 'eat pie with a fork' as he put it, under any possible circumstances on any planet. He let it go at that."

"I should think he would. I take it he lectured you all evening?"

"Oh, my, no. Ten minutes, maybe."

"Then where were you? You still hadn't come back to your room, just before taps."

"Oh, I was still in Ski's room, but I was busy."

"Doing what? Stroking his brow?"

"No." Tex looked mildly embarrassed. "I was writing—'I will always eat my pie with my fork,' two thousand times."

Tex and Matt attempted to explore the ship and did in fact visit every deck that was open to them. But the power-room door was locked and a space-marine guard kept them from entering the passageway leading to the pilot room. They tried to get another view from the ports in the recreation room but found that a degree of order had been instituted; the master-at-arms of that deck was requiring each cadet that entered to state that he had not yet had a chance to look out before the cadet was allowed to tarry.

As for the other passenger decks, they found that when they had seen one, they had seen all. Shipboard refreshers interested them for a while, as the curious and clever modifications necessary to make a refresher function properly in space were new to both of them. But four hours is too long to spend inspecting showers and fixtures; after a while they found another fairly quiet spot to loaf and experienced for the first time the outstanding characteristic of all space travel—its monotony.

Much later the ship's speaker blared, "Prepare for acceleration. Ten minute warning."

Strapped down again, each in his place, the boys felt short blasts of power at rather long intervals, then a very considerable wait, after which there was the softest and gentlest of bumps. "That's the drag line," remarked the sergeant in Matt's compartment. "They'll warp us in. It won't be long now."

Ten minutes later the speaker announced, "By decks, in succession—discharge passengers."

"Unstrap," said the sergeant. He left his midships position and posted himself at the hatch ladder. Transferring passengers was a lengthy process, as the two ships were linked by only one air lock each. Matt's party waited while four decks forward of them were emptied, then they pulled themselves along the ladder to the seventh deck. There a passenger port was open but beyond it, instead of empty space, was the inside of a corrugated tube, six feet in diameter. A line ran down the center of it and was made fast to a padeye in the ship. Along this line swarmed a steady stream of cadets, monkey fashion.

In his turn, Matt grabbed the line and pulled himself along. Fifty feet beyond the air lock, the tube suddenly opened out into another compartment, and Matt found himself inside his new home, the P.R.S. *Randolph*.

6.
"READING, AND 'RITING, AND 'RITHMETIC—"

The *P.R.S. Randolph* had been a powerful and modern cruiser of her day. Her length was 900 feet, her diameter 200, making her of moderate size, but her mass, as a school ship, was only 60,000 tons, more or less.

She was kept ten miles astern of Terra Station in their common orbit. Left to the influence of their mutual gravitations, she would have pursued a most leisurely orbit around the ten-times-more-massive Terra Station, but, for the safety of traffic at Terra Station, it was better to keep in a fixed position.

This was easy to accomplish. The mass of Earth is six billion trillion tons; the mass of Terra Station is one hundred-million-billionth of that, a mere 600,000 tons. At ten miles the "weight" of the *Randolph* with respect to Terra Station was roughly one thirtieth of an ounce, about the weight on Earth of enough butter for one half slice of bread.

On entering the *Randolph* Matt found himself in a large, well-lighted compartment of odd shape, somewhat like a wedge of cake. Clumps of youngster cadets were being herded out exits by other cadets who wore black armbands. One such cadet headed toward him, moving through the air with the easy grace of a pollywog. "Squad nineteen—where's the squad leader of squad nineteen?"

Matt held out his arm. "Here, sir! I'm squad leader of nineteen."

The upperclassman checked himself with one hand on the guide line to which Matt still clung. "I relieve you, sir. But stick close to me and help me round up these yahoos. I suppose you know them by sight?"

"Uh, I think so, sir."

"You should—you've had time." Matt was chagrined to find, in the next few moments that the new squad leader—Cadet Lopez—knew the squad muster roll by heart, whereas Matt had to refer to his copy to assist him in locating the members. He was not really aware of the implications of order and efficient preparation; it did impress him as "style." With Matt to spot and Lopez to dive, hawklike, all the way across the compartment if necessary, to round up stragglers, squad nineteen was soon assembled near one exit, where they clung like a colony of bats.

"Follow me," Lopez told them, "and hang on. No free maneuvers. Dodson—bring up the rear."

"Aye aye, sir."

They snaked their way through endless passages, by guide line across compartment after compartment, through hatches, around corners. Matt was quite lost. Presently the man just head of him stopped. Matt closed in and found the squad gathered just inside another compartment. "Soup's on," announced Lopez. "This is your messroom. Lunch in a few minutes."

Behind Lopez, secured firmly to the far wall, were mess tables and benches. The table tops faced Matt—under him, over him, or across from him—what you will. It seemed an impractical arrangement. "I'm not very hungry," one youngster said faintly.

"You ought to be," Lopez answered reasonably. "It's been five hours or more since you had breakfast. We're on the same time schedule here as Hayworth Hall, zone plus eight, Terra. Why aren't you hungry?"

"Uh, I don't know, sir. I'm just not."

Lopez grinned and suddenly looked as young as his charges. "I was just pulling your leg, kiddo. The chief engineer will have some spin on us in no time, as soon as we break loose from the *Bolivar*. Then you can sit down on your soft, round fanny and console your tender stomach in peace. You'll have an appetite. In the meantime, take it easy."

Two more squads filtered in. While they waited Matt said to Lopez, "How fast will the ship spin, sir?"

"We'll build up to one gravity at the outer skin. Takes about two hours to do it, but we'll eat as soon as we're heavy enough for you groundhogs to swallow your soup without choking."

"But how fast is that, sir?"

"Can you do simple arithmetic?"

"Why, yes, sir."

"Then do it. The *Randolph* is two hundred feet through and we spin on her main axis. The square of the rim speed divided by her radius—what's the rpm?"

Matt got a faraway look on his face. Lopez said, "Come, now, Mr. Dodson—pretend you're heading for the surface and about to crash. *What's the answer?*"

"Uh—I'm afraid I can't do it in my head, sir."

Lopez looked around. "All right—who's got the answer?" No one spoke up. Lopez shook his head mournfully. "And you laddies expect to learn to astrogate! Better by far you should have gone to cow colleges. Never mind—it works out to about five and four-tenths revolutions per minute. That gives one full gravity for the benefit of the women and children. Then it's cut down day by day, until a month from now we're in free fall again. That gives you time to get used to it—or else."

Someone said, "Gee, it must take a lot of power."

Lopez answered, "Are you kidding? It's done by electric-braking the main axis flywheels. The shaft has field coils wound on it; you cut it in as a generator and let the reaction between the wheel and the ship put a spin on the ship. You store the juice. Then when you want to take the spin off, you use the juice to drive it as a motor and you are back where you started, free for nothing, except for minor losses. Savvy?"

"Er, I guess so, sir."

"Look it up in the ship's library, sketch the hook-up, and show it to me after supper." The junior cadet said nothing; Lopez snapped. "What's the matter, Mister? Didn't you hear me?"

"Yes, sir—aye aye, sir."

"That's better."

Very slowly they drifted against a side wall, bumped against it, and started sliding slowly toward the outboard wall, the one to which the mess tables were fastened. By the time they reached it there was enough spin on the ship to enable them to stand up and the mess tables now assumed their proper relationship, upright on the floor, while the hatch through which they had lately floated was a hole in the ceiling above.

Matt found that there was no sensation of dizziness; the effect was purely one of increasing weight. He still felt light, but he weighed enough to sit down at a mess table and stay in contact with his seat; minute by minute, imperceptibly, he grew heavier.

He looked over his place at the table, seeking controls that would permit him to order his meal. There were clips and locking holes which he guessed were intended for use in free flight, but nothing else. He looked up as Lopez banged on the table.

"And now, gentlemen, this is not a resort hotel. Count off, around the table." He waited until the youngsters had done so, then said, "Remember your order. Numbers one and two will rustle up the calories today, and all of you in rotation thereafter."

"Where, sir?"

"Use your eyes. Over there."

"Over there" was a door which concealed a delivery conveyor. Cadets from other tables were gathering around it. The two cadets designated as waiters went over and returned shortly with a large metal rack containing twenty rations, each packed in its service platter and still steaming hot. Clipped to each were knife, fork, and spoons—and sipping tubes.

Matt found that the solid foods were covered by lids that snapped back over the food unless clipped up out of the way, while the liquids were in covered containers fitted with valves through which sipping tubes might be slipped. He had never before seen table utensils adapted for free-fall conditions in space. They delighted him, even though Earthside equipment would have served as long as the ship was under spin.

Lunch was hot roast beef sandwiches with potatoes, green salad, lime sherbert, and tea. Lopez kept up a steady fire of questions throughout the meal, but Matt did not come into his range. Twenty minutes later the metal tray in front of Matt was polished almost as well as the sterilizer would achieve. He sat back, feeling that the Patrol was a good outfit and the *Randolph* a fine place to be.

Before turning his charges loose Lopez gave them each their schedule of assignments. Matt's room number was A-5197. All living quarters were on A-deck which was the insulated outer skin of the ship. Lopez gave them a brief, condescending lecture on the system of numbering the spaces in the ship and dismissed them. His manner gave no hint that he himself had been lost for one full day shortly after his own arrival a year earlier.

Matt got lost, of course.

He attempted to take a short cut straight through the ship on the advice of a passing marine and got completely twisted when he found himself at the no-weight center of the *Randolph*. When he had worked his way back down levels of increasing weight until he found himself at one gravity and could go no further he stopped the first cadet with a black arm band whom he could find and threw himself on his mercy. A few minutes later he was led to corridor five and found his own room.

Tex was already there. "Hello, Matt," he greeted him. "What do you think of our little cabin in the sky?"

Matt put down his jump bag. "Looks all right, but the first time I have to leave it I'm going to unroll a ball of string. Is there a viewport?"

"Not likely! What did you expect? A balcony?"

"I don't know. I sort of hoped that we'd be able to look out and see Earth." He started poking around, opening doors. "Where's the 'fresher?"

"Better start unrolling your ball of string. It's way down the passage."

"Oh. Kind of primitive. Well, I guess we can stand it." He went on exploring. There was a common room about fifteen feet square. It had doors, two on each side, leading into smaller cubicles. "Say, Tex," he announced when he had opened them all, "this place is fitted up for four people."

"Go to the head of the class."

"I wonder who we'll draw."

"So do I." Tex took out his assignment sheet. "It says here that we can reshuffle roommates until supper time tomorrow. Got any ideas, Matt?"

"No, I can't say I really know anybody but you. It doesn't matter as long as they don't snore—and as long as it isn't Burke."

They were interrupted by a rap on the door. Tex called out, "Come in!" and Oscar Jensen stuck his blond head inside.

"Busy?"

"Not at all."

"I've got a problem. Pete and I found ourselves assigned to one of these four-way rooms and the two roommates we landed with want us to make room for two other fellows. Are you guys tied down as yet?"

Tex looked at Matt, who nodded. Tex turned back to Oscar. "You can kiss me, Oscar—we're practically married."

An hour later the four had settled down to domesticity. Pete was in high spirits. "The *Randolph* is just what the doctor ordered," he announced. "I'm going to like it here. Any time my legs start to ache all I have to do is go up to G-deck and it's just like being back home—I weigh my proper weight again."

"Yep," agreed Tex, "if the joint were co-educational it would be perfect."

Oscar shook his head. "Not for me. I'm a woman-hater."

Tex clucked sorrowfully. "You poor, poor boy. Now take my Uncle Bodie—he thought he was a woman-hater, too. . . ."

Matt never found out how Uncle Bodie got over his disability. An announcer, mounted in the common room, summoned him to report to compartment B-121. He got there, after a few wrong turns, and found another youngster cadet just coming out. "What's it for?" he asked.

"Go on in," the other told him. "Orientation."

Matt went in and found an officer seated at a desk. "Cadet Dodson, sir, reporting as ordered."

The officer looked up and smiled. "Sit down, Dodson. Lieutenant Wong is my name. I'm your coach."

"My coach, sir?"

"Your tutor, your supervisor, anything you care to call it. It's my business to see that you and a dozen more like you study what you need to study. Think of me as standing behind you with a black snake whip." He grinned.

Matt grinned back. He began to like Mr. Wong.

Wong picked up a sheaf of papers. "I've got your record here—let's lay out a course of study. I see you type, use a slide rule and differential calculator, and can take short-hand—those are all good. Do you know any outer languages? By the way, don't bother to talk Basic; I speak North American English fairly well. How long have you spoken Basic?"

"Er, I don't know any outer languages, sir. I had Basic in high school, but I don't really *think* in it. I have to watch what I'm saying."

"I'll put you down for Venerian, Martian, and Venus trade talk. Your voicewriter—you've looked over the equipment in your room?"

"Just glanced at it, sir. I saw there was a study desk and a projector."

"You'll find a spool of instructions in the upper righthand drawer of the desk. Play them over when you go back. The voicewriter built into your desk is a good model. It can hear and transcribe not only the Basic vocabulary, but the Patrol's special vocabulary of technical words. If you will stick to its vocabulary, you can even write love letters on it—" Dodson glanced sharply at

Lieutenant Wong, but Wong's face was impassive; Matt decided not to laugh.

"—so it's worth your while to perfect your knowledge of Basic even for social purposes. However, if you speak a word the machine can't find on its list, it will just 'beep' complainingly until you come to its rescue. Now about math—I see you have a condition in tensor calculus."

"Yes, sir," Matt admitted. "My high school didn't offer it."

Wong shook his head sadly. "I sometimes think that modern education is deliberately designed to handicap a boy. If cadets arrived here having already been taught the sort of things the young human animal can learn, and *should* learn, there would be fewer casualties in the Patrol. Never mind—we'll start you on tensors at once. You can't study nuclear engineering until you've learned the language of it. Your school was the usual sort, Dodson? Classroom recitations, daily assignments, and so forth?"

"More or less. We were split into three groups."

"Which group were you in?"

"I was in the fast one, sir, in most subjects."

"That's some help, but not much. You're in for a shock, son. We don't have classrooms and fixed courses. Except for laboratory work and group drills, you study alone. It's pleasant to sit in a class daydreaming while the teacher questions somebody else, but we haven't got time for that. There is too much ground to cover. Take the outer languages alone—have you ever studied under hypnosis?"

"Why, no, sir."

"We'll start you on it at once. When you leave here, go to the Psycho Instruction Department and ask for a first hypno in Beginning Venerian. What's the matter?"

"Well. . . . Sir, is it absolutely necessary to study under hypnosis?"

"Definitely. Everything that can possibly be studied under hypno you will have to learn that way in order to leave time for the really important subjects."

Matt nodded. "I see. Like astrogation."

"No, no, no! Not astrogation. A ten-year-old child could learn to pilot a spaceship if he had the talent for mathematics. That is kindergarten stuff, Dodson. The arts of space and warfare are the least part of your education. I know, from your tests, that you can soak up the math and physical sciences and technologies. Much more important is the world around you, the planets and their inhabitants—extraterrestrial biology, history, cultures, psychology, law and institutions, treaties and conventions, planetary ecologies, system ecology, interplanetary economics, applications of extraterritorialism, comparative religious customs, law of space, to mention a few."

Matt was looking bug-eyed. "My gosh! How long does it take to learn all those things?"

"You'll still be studying the day you retire. But even those subjects are not your education; they are simply raw materials. Your real job is to learn how to think—and that means you must study several other subjects: epistemology, scientific methodology, semantics, structures of languages, patterns of ethics and morals, varieties of logics, motivational psychology, and so on. This school is based on the idea that a man who can think correctly will automatically behave morally—or what we call 'morally.' What is moral behavior for a Patrolman, Matt? You are called Matt, aren't you? By your friends?"

"Yes, sir. Moral behavior for a Patrolman . . ."

"Yes, yes. Go on."

"Well, I guess it means to do your duty, live up to your oath, that sort of thing."

"Why should you?"

Matt kept quiet and looked stubborn.

"Why should you, when it may get you some messy way of dying? Never mind. Our prime purpose here is to see to it that you learn how your own mind works. If the result is a man who fits into the purposes of the Patrol because his own mind, when he knows how to use it, works that way—then fine! He is commissioned. If not, then we have to let him go."

Matt remained silent until Wong finally said, "What's eating on you, kid? Spill it."

"Well—look here, sir. I'm perfectly willing to work hard to get my commission. But you make it sound like something beyond my control. First I have to study a lot of things I've never heard of. Then, when it's all over, somebody decides my mind doesn't work right. It seems to me that what this job calls for is a superman."

"Like me." Wong chuckled and flexed his arms. "Maybe so, Matt, but there aren't any supermen, so we'll have to do the best we can with young squirts like you. Come, now, let's make up the list of spools you'll need."

It was a long list. Matt was surprised and pleased to find that some story spools had been included. He pointed to an item that puzzled him—*An Introduction to Lunar Archeology.* "I don't see why I should study that—the Patrol doesn't deal with Selenites; they've been dead for millions of years."

"Keeps your mind loosened up. I might just as well have stuck in modern French music. A Patrol officer shouldn't limit his horizons to just the things he is sure to need. I'm marking the items I want you to study first, then you beat it around to the library and draw out those spools, then over to Psycho for your first hypno. In about a week, when you've absorbed this first group, come back and see me."

"You mean you expect me to study all the spools I'm taking out today in *one week?*" Matt looked at the list in amazement.

"That's right. In your off hours, that is—you'll be busy with drills and lab a lot. Come back next week and we'll boost the dose. Now get going."

"But—Aye aye, sir!"

Matt located the Psycho Instruction Department and was presently ushered into a small room by a bored hypno technician wearing the uniform of the staff services of the Space Marines. "Stretch out in that chair," he was told. "Rest your head back. This is your first treatment?" Matt admitted that it was.

"You'll like it. Some guys come in here just for the rest—they already know more than they ought to. What course was it you said you wanted?"

"Beginning Venerian."

The technician spoke briefly to a pick-up located on his desk. "Funny thing—about a month ago an oldster was in here for a brush up in electronics. The library thought I said 'colonics' and now he's loaded up with a lot of medical knowledge he'll never use. Lemme have your left arm." The technician irradiated a patch on his forearm and injected the drug. "Now just lay back and follow the bouncing light. Take it easy . . . relax . . . relax . . . and . . . close . . . your . . . eyes . . . and . . . relax . . . you're . . . getting—"

Someone was standing in front of him, holding a hypodermic pressure injector "That's all. You've had the antidote."

"Huh?" said Matt. "Wazzat?"

"Sit still a couple of minutes and then you can go."

"Didn't it take?"

"Didn't what take? I don't know what you were being exposed to; I just came on duty."

Matt went back to his room feeling rather depressed. He had

been a little afraid of hypnosis, but to find that he apparently did not react to the method was worse yet. He wondered whether or not he could ever keep up with his studies if he were forced to study everything, outer languages as well, by conventional methods.

Nothing to do but to go back and see Lieutenant Wong about it—tomorrow, he decided.

Oscar was alone in the suite and was busy trying to place a hook in the wall of a common room. A framed picture was leaning against the chair on which he stood. "Hello, Oscar."

"Howdy, Matt." Oscar turned his head as he spoke; the drill he was using slipped and he skinned a knuckle. He started to curse in strange, lisping speech. *"May maledictions pursue this nameless thing to the uttermost depths of world slime!"*

Matt clucked disapprovingly. *"Curb thy voice, thou impious fish."*

Oscar looked up in amazement. "Matt—I didn't know you knew any Venerian."

Matt's mouth sagged open. He closed it, then opened it to speak. "Well, I'll be a—Neither did I!"

7.
TO MAKE A SPACEMAN

The sergeant crouched in the air, his feet drawn up. "At the count of one," he was saying, "take the ready position, with your feet about six inches from the steel. At the count of two, place your feet firmly against the steel and push off." He shoved against the steel wall and shot into the air, still talking, "Hold the count of four, turn on the count of five—" His body drew up into a ball and turned over a half turn. "—check your rotation—" His body extended again. "—and make contact on the count of seven—" His toes touched the far wall. "—letting your legs collapse softly so that your momentum will be soaked up without rebound." He collapsed loosely, like an empty sack, and remained floating near the spot where he had landed.

The room was a cylinder fifty feet in diameter in the center of the ship. The entire room was mounted in rollers and was turned steadily in the direction opposite to the spin of the ship and with the same angular speed: thus it had no net spin. It could be entered only from the end, at the center of rotation.

It was a little island of "free fall"—the free-fall gymnasium. A dozen youngster cadets clung to a grab line running fore-and-aft along the wall of the gym and watched the sergeant. Matt was one of the group.

"And now, gentlemen, let's try it again. By the numbers— One! Two! Three!" by the count of five, at which time they all should have turned in the air, neatly and together, all semblance of order was gone. There were collisions, one cadet had even failed to get away from the grab line, and two cadets, refugees from a midair skirmish, were floating aimlessly toward the far end of the room. Their faces had the bewildered look of a dog trying to get traction on smooth ice as they threshed their arms and legs in an effort to stay their progress.

"No! No! No!" said the sergeant and covered his face with his hands. "I can't bear to look. Gentlemen—*please!* A little coordination. Don't throw yourself at the far wall like an Airedale heading into a fight. A steady, firm shove—like this."

He took off sideways, using the traction given him by his space boots, and intercepted the two deserters, gathering one in each arm and letting his momentum carry the three bodies slowly toward the far end of the grab line. "Grab on," he told them, "and back to your places. Now, gentlemen—once more. Places! By the numbers—normal push off, with arrested contact—one!"

A few moments later he was assuring them that he would much rather teach a cat to swim.

Matt did not mind. He had managed to reach the far wall and stay there. Without grace, proper timing, nor at the spot he had aimed for, but he had managed it, after a dozen failures. For the moment he classed himself as a spaceman.

When the class was dismissed he hurried to his room and into his own cubicle, selected a spool on Martian history, inserted it in his projector, and began to study. He had been tempted to remain in the free-fall gymnasium to practice; he wanted very badly to pass the "space legs" test—free-fall acrobatics—as those who had passed it and qualified in the use of basic space suits as well were allowed one liberty a month at Terra Station.

But he had had an extra interview with Lieutenant Wong a few days before. It had been brief, biting, and had been concerned with the efficient use of his time.

Matt did not want another such—nor the five demerits that went with it. He settled his head in the neck rest of his study chair and concentrated on the recorded words of the lecturer while scenes in color-stereo passed in front of him, portraying in chill beauty the rich past of the ancient planet.

The projector was much like the study box he had used at home, except that it was more gadgeted, could project in three dimensions, and was hooked in with the voicewriter. Matt found this a great time-saver. He could stop the lecture, dictate a summary, then cause the projector to throw his printed notes on the screen.

Stereo-projection was a time-saver for manual subjects as well. "You are now entering the control room of a type A-6 utility rocket," the unseen lecturer would say, "and will practice an airless landing on Luna"—while the camera moved through the door of the rocket's pilot room and panned down to a position corresponding to the pilot's head. From there on a pictured flight could be made very realistic.

Or it might be a spool on space suits. "This is a four-hour suit," the voice would say, "type M, and may be worn anywhere outside the orbit of Venus. It has a low-capacity rocket unit capable of producing a total change of speed in a 300-lb. mass of fifty foot-seconds. The built-in radio has a suit-to-suit range of fifty miles. Internal heating and cooling is—" By the time Matt's turn came for space-suit drill he knew as much about it as could be learned without practice.

His turn came when he passed the basic free-fall test. He was not finished with free-fall drill—there remained group precision drill, hand-to-hand combat, use of personal weapons, and other refinements—but he was judged able to handle himself well enough. He was free, too, to go out for free-fall sports, wrestling, bank tennis, jai alai, and several others—up to now he had been eligible only for the chess club. He picked space polo, a game combining water polo and assault with intent to maim, and joined the local league, in the lowest or "bloodynose" group.

He missed his first chance at space-suit drill because a battered nose had turned him into a mouth breather—the respirator for a type-M suit calls for inhaling through the nose and exhaling through the mouth. But he was ready and anxious the following week. The instructor ordered his group to "Suit up!" without preliminary, as it was assumed that they had studied the instruction spool.

The last of the ship's spin had been removed some days before. Matt curled himself into a ball, floating free, and spread open the front of his suit. It was an unhandy process; he found shortly that he was trying to get both legs down one leg of the suit. He backed out and tried again. This time the big fishbowl flopped forward into the opening.

Most of the section were already in their suits. The instructor swam over to Matt and looked at him sharply. "You've passed your free-fall basic?"

"Yes," Matt answered miserably.

"It's hard to believe. You handle yourself like a turtle on its back. Here." The instructor helped Matt to tuck in, much as if he were dressing a baby in a snow suit. Matt blushed.

The instructor ran through the check-off list—tank pressure, suit pressure, rocket fuel charge, suit oxygen, blood oxygen (measured by a photoelectric gadget clipped to the earlobe) and finally each suit's walky-talky unit. Then he herded them into the airlock.

Matt felt his suit swell up as the pressure died away in the lock. It was becoming slightly harder to move his arms and legs. "Hook up your static lines," called out the instructor. Matt uncoiled his from his belt and waited. Reports came in: "Number one hooked." "Number two hooked."

"Number three hooked," Matt sang out into the mike in his helmet as he snapped his line to the belt of cadet number four. When they were all linked like mountain climbers the instructor hooked himself to the chain and opened the outer door of the lock. They looked out into the star-flecked void.

"Click on," directed the instructor, and placed his boots gently against the side of the lock. Matt did likewise and felt the magnetic soles of his boots click against the steel. "Follow me and stay closed up." Their teacher walked along the wall to the open door and performed an awkward little squatting spread-eagle step. One boot was still inside the door, flat to the wall, with the toe pointing inboard; with the other he reached around the corner, bent his knees, and felt for the outer surface of the ship. He withdrew the foot still in the lock and straightened his body—with which he almost disappeared, for he now stuck straight out from the ship, his feet flat to her side.

Following in order, Matt went out through the door. The ninety degree turn to get outside the lock and "standing" on the outer skin of the ship he found to be tricky; he was forced to use his hands to steady himself on the door frame. But he got outside and "standing up." There was no true up-and-down; they were still weightless, but the steel side was a floor "under" them; they stuck to it as a fly sticks to a ceiling.

Matt took a couple of trial steps. It was like walking in mud; his feet would cling stickily to the ship, then pull away suddenly. It took getting used to.

They had gone out on the dark side of the ship. Sun, Moon and Earth lay behind its bulk, underfoot. Not even Terra Station could be seen.

"We'll take a walk," announced the instructor, his voice hollow in their helmets. "Stick together." He started around the curving side of the ship. A cadet near the end of the chain tried to break both magnetized boots free from the ship at the same time. He accomplished it, by jumping—and then had no way to get back. He moved out until his static line tugged at the two boys on each side of him.

One of them, caught with one foot free of the ship in walking, was broken loose also, though he reached wildly for the steel and missed. The cadet next to him, last in line, came loose in turn.

No more separated, as the successive tugs on the line had used up the energy of the first cadet's not-so-violent jump. But three cadets now dangled on the line, floating and twisting grotesquely.

The instructor caught the movement out of the corner of his eye, and squatted down. He found what he sought, a steel ring recessed in the ship's side, and snapped his static line to it. When he was certain that the entire party was not going to be dragged loose, he ordered, "Number nine—haul them in, gently—very gently. Don't pull yourself loose doing it."

A few moments later the vagrants were back and sticking to the ship. "Now," said the instructor, "who was responsible for that piece of groundhog stupidity?"

No one answered. "Speak up," he said sharply. "It wasn't an accident; it's impossible to get both feet off unless you hop. Speak up, confound it, or I'll haul every last one of you up in front of the Commandant."

At the mention of that awful word a small, meek voice answered, "I did it, sergeant."

"Hold out your hand, so I'll know who's talking. I'm not a mind reader."

"Vargas—number ten." The cadet held out his arm.

"Okay. Back to the airlock, everybody. Stick together." When they were there, the instructor said, "Inside, Mr. Vargas. Unhook your line, snap to the lock and wait for us. You'll take this drill over—about a month from now."

"But sergeant—"

"Don't give me any lip, or swelp me, I'll report you for AWOL—jumping ship."

Silently the cadet did as ordered. The instructor leaned inside to see that Vargas actually anchored himself, then straightened out. "Come, gentlemen—we'll start again—and no monkeyshines. This is a drill, not a tea party."

Presently Matt said, "Sergeant Hanako—"

"Yes? Who is it?"

"Dodson. Number three. Suppose we had all pulled loose?"

"We'd 'ave had to work our way back on our rocket units."

Matt thought about it. "Suppose we didn't have reaction units?"

"Nothing much—under these circumstances. The officer of the watch knows we're outside; the radio watch is guarding our frequency. They would just have tracked us by radar until they could man a scooter and come get us. Just the same—listen, all of you—just because they've got you wrapped in cotton batting is no reason to behave like a bunch of school girls. I don't know of any nastier, or lonelier, way to die than all by yourself in a space suit, with your oxygen running out." He paused. "I saw one once, after they found him and fetched him back."

They were rounding the side of the ship, and the bulging sphere of the Earth had been rising over their metal horizon.

Suddenly the Sun burst into view.

"Mind the glare!" Sergeant Hanako called out. Hastily Matt set his visor for maximum interference and adjusted it to shade his face and eyes. He did not attempt to look at the Sun; he had dazzled his eyes often enough from the viewports of the ship's recreation rooms, trying to blank out the disc of the Sun exactly, with a coin, so that he might see the prominences and the ghostly aurora. It was an unsatisfactory business; the usual result was a headache and spots before his eyes.

But he never grew tired of looking at Earth.

She hung before him, great and fat and beautiful, and seeming more real than when seen through a port. She swelled across Aquarius, so huge that had she been in Orion she would have concealed the giant hunter from Betelgeuse to Rigel.

Facing them was the Gulf of Mexico. Above it sprawled North America wearing the polar cap like a chef's hat. The pole was still bright under the failing light of late northern summer. The sunrise line had cleared North America except for the tip of Alaska; only the central Pacific was dark.

Someone said, "What's that bright dot in the Pacific, over near the edge? Honolulu?"

Honolulu did not interest Matt; he searched, as usual, for Des Moines—but the Mississippi Valley was cloudy; he could not find it. Sometimes he could pick it out with his naked eyes, when the day was clear in Iowa. When it was night in North America he could always tell which jewel of light was home—or thought he could.

They were facing Earth so that the north pole seemed "up" to them. Far off to the right, almost a ship's width from the Earth, nearly occulting Regulus in Leo, was the Sun, and about half way between the Sun and Earth, in Virgo, was a crescent Moon. Like

the Sun, the Moon appeared no larger than she did from Earth surface. The gleaming metal sides of Terra Station, in the sky between Sun and Moon and ninety degrees from Earth, outshone the
Moon. The Station, a mere ten miles away, appeared half a dozen
times as wide as the Moon.

"That's enough rubbernecking," announced Hanako. "Let's
move around." They walked forward, looking the ship over and
getting the feel of her size, until the sergeant stopped them. "Any
further and we'd be slapping our feet over the Commandant's
head. He might be asleep." They sauntered aft and Hanako let
them work around the edge of the stern until they looked across
the openings of her mighty tubes. He called them back promptly.
"Even though she ain't blasted in years, this area is a little bit
hot—and you're not shielded from the pile abaft frame ninety-
three anyhow. Forward, now!"

By hot he did not mean warm to the touch, but radioactive.

He led them amidships, unhooked himself from the cadet next
to him and hooked the lad's line to the ship. "Number twelve—
hook to steel," he added.

"The trick to jetting yourself in space," he went on, "lies in
balancing your body on the jet—the thrust has to pass through
your center of gravity. If you miss and don't correct it quickly, you
start to spin, waste your fuel, and have the devil's own time stopping your spin.

"It's no harder than balancing a walking stick on your finger—
but the first time you try it, it seems hard.

"Rig out your sight." He touched a stud at his belt; a light
metal gadget snapped up in front of his helmet so that a small
metal ring was about a yard in front of his face. "Pick out a bright
star, or a target of any sort, lined up in the direction you want to
go. Then take the ready position—no, no! Not yet—I'll take it."

He squatted down, lifted himself on his hands, and very cautiously broke his boots loose from the side, then steadied himself
on a cadet within reach. He turned and stretched out, so that he
floated with his back to the ship, arms and legs extended. His
rocket jet stuck straight back at the ship from the small of his
back; his sight stuck out from his helmet in the opposite direction.

He went on, "Have the firing switch ready in your right hand.
Now, have you fellows ever seen a pair of adagio dancers? You
know what I mean—a man wears a piece of leopard skin and a girl
wearing less than that and they go leaping around the stage, with
him catching her?"

Several voices answered yes. Hanako continued, "Then you know what I'm talking about. There's one stunt they always do—the girl jumps and the man pushes her up and balances her overhead on one hand. He has his hand at the small of her back and she lays there, artistic-like.

"That's exactly the way you got to ride a jet. The push comes at the small of your back and you balance on it. Only *you* have to do the balancing—if the push doesn't pass exactly through your center of gravity, you'll start to turn. You can see yourself starting to turn by watching through your sight.

"You have to correct it before it gets away from you. You do this by shifting your center of gravity. Drag in the arm or leg on the side toward which you've started to turn. The trick is—"

"Just a second, Sarge," someone cut in, "you said that just backwards. You mean; haul in the arm or leg on the *other* side, don't you?"

"Who's talking?"

"Lathrop, number six. Sorry."

"I meant what I said, Mr. Lathrop."

"But—"

"Go ahead, do it your way. The rest of the class will do it my way. Let's not waste time. Any questions? Okay, stand clear of my jet."

The half circle backed away until stopped by the anchored static lines. A bright orange flame burst from the sergeant's back and he moved straight out or "up," slowly at first, then with increasing speed. His microphone was open; Matt could hear, by radio only, the muted rush of his jet—and could hear the sergeant counting seconds: "And . . . *one!* . . . and . . . *two!* . . . and . . . *three!*" With the count of ten, the jet and the counting stopped.

Their instructor was fifty feet "above" them and moving away, back toward them. He continued to lecture. "No matter how perfectly you've balanced you'll end up with a small amount of spin. When you want to change direction, double up in a ball—" He did so. "—to spin faster—and snap out of it when you've turned as far as you want." He suddenly flattened out and was facing them. "Cut in your jet and balance on it to straighten out on your new course—before you drift past the direction you want."

He did not cut in his jet, but continued to talk, while moving away from them and slowly turning. "There is always some way to squirm around on your axis of rotation so that you can face the way you need to face for a split second at least. For example, if I wanted to head toward the Station—" Terra Station was almost a right angle away from his course; he went through contortions appropriate to a monkey dying in convulsions and again snapped out in starfish spread, facing the Station—but turning slow cartwheels now, his axis of rotation unchanged.

"But I don't want to go to the Station; I want to come back to the ship." The monkey died again; when the convulsions ceased, the sergeant was facing them. He cut in his jet and again counted ten seconds. He hung in space, motionless with respect to the ship and his class and about a quarter mile away. "I'm coming in on a jet landing, to save time." The jet blasted for twenty seconds and died; he moved toward them rapidly.

When he was still a couple of hundred feet away, he flipped over and blasted *away* from the ship for ten seconds. The sum of his maneuvers was to leave him fifty feet away and approaching at ten feet per second. He curled up in a ball again and came out of it feet toward the ship.

Five seconds later his boots clicked to steel and he let himself collapse without rebound. "But that is not the way you'll do it," he went on. "My tanks hold more juice than yours do—you've got fifty seconds of power, with each second good for a change of speed on one foot-second—that's for three hundred pounds of mass; some of you skinny guys will go a little faster.

"Here's your flight plan: ten seconds out, counted. Turn as quick as you can and blast fifteen seconds back. That means you'll click on with five foot-seconds. Even your crippled grandmother ought to be able to do that without bouncing off. Lathrop! Unhook—you're first."

As the cadet came up, Hanako anchored himself to the ship with two short lines and took from his belt a very long line. He snapped one end to a hook in the front of the cadet's belt and the other to his own suit. The student looked at it with distaste. "Is the sky hook necessary?"

Sergeant Hanako stared at him. "Sorry, Commodore— regulations. And shut up. Take the ready position."

Silently the cadet crouched, then he was moving away, a fiery brush growing out of his back. He moved fairly straight at first, then started to turn.

He pulled in a leg—and turned completely over.

"Lathrop—cut off your jet!" snapped Hanako. The flame died out, but the figure in the suit continued to turn and to recede. Hanako paid out his safety line. "Got a big fish here, boys," he said cheerfully. "What do you think he'll weigh?" He tugged on the line, which caused Lathrop to spin the other way, as the line had wound itself around him. When the line was free he hauled the cadet in.

Lathrop clicked on. "You were right, sergeant. I want to try it again—your way."

"Sorry. The book says a hundred per cent reserve fuel for this drill; you'd have to recharge." Hanako hesitated. "Sign up for to-morrow morning—I'll take you as an extra."

"Oh—thanks, Sarge!"

"Don't mention it. Number one!"

The next cadet moved out smoothly, but returned on an angle and had to be snubbed with the safety line before he could click on. The next cadet had trouble orienting himself at all. He receded, his back to the ship, and seemed to be about to continue in the direction of Draco till the end of time. Hanako tugged gently on the safety line while letting it run through his gloves and turned him around toward the ship. "Ten seconds on the jet, while I keep a strain on the line," he ordered. The safety line kept the cadet straightened out until he got back. "Number three!" called out Hanako.

Matt stepped forward with a feeling of tight excitement. The instructor hooked the safety line and said, "Any questions? Go ahead when ready."

"Okay." Matt crouched, broke his boots free, and stretched out. He steadied himself against the sergeant's knee. In front of him lay the northern constellations. He picked out the Pole Star as a target, then loosened the safety catch of the firing switch in his glove.

"And . . . one!" He felt a soft, steady pressure across his saddle, a shove of not quite ten pounds. Polaris seemed to vibrate to the blasting of the tiny jet. Then the star swung to the left, beyond the ring of the sight.

He pulled in his right arm and right leg. The star swung faster, checked and started back. Cautiously he extended his right-side limbs again—and almost forgot to cut the jet on the count of ten.

He could not see the ship. Earth swam in the velvety darkness off to the right. The silence and aloneness were more intense, more complete, than he had ever experienced.

"Time to turn," said Hanako in his ear.

"Oh—" said Matt, and grabbed his knees.

The heavens wheeled around him. He saw the ship swinging

into sight, too late. He checked by starfishing, but it had moved on past. "Take it easy," advised the sergeant. "Don't curl up quite so tight, and catch it on the next time around. There's no hurry."

He drew himself in again, but not so much. The ship came around again, though twice as far away as it had been before. This time he checked before it swung past. The figures crawling on her side were about three hundred feet away and still backing away from him. He got someone's helmet centered in his sight, pressed the switch and began to count.

For a few worried seconds he thought that something had gone wrong. The figures on the ship did not seem to be getting nearer and now they were swinging slowly past him. He was tempted to blast again—but Hanako's orders had been specific; he decided not to.

The ship swung out of sight; he doubled up in a ball to bring it around more quickly. When it showed up it was distinctly nearer and he felt relieved. Actually the two bodies, ship and man, had been closing at five feet per second—but five feet per second is a slow walk.

A little more than a minute after cutting his jet, he jackknifed to bring his boots in front of him and clicked on, about ten feet from the instructor.

Hanako came over and placed his helmet against Matt's so he could speak to him privately, with the radio shut off. "A good job, kid, the way you kept your nerve when you swung past. Okay— I'll post you for advanced training."

Matt remembered to cut out his walky-talky. "Gee, thanks!"

"You did it, not me." Hanako cut back in the voice circuit. "Okay, there—number four."

Matt wanted to chase back to his room, find Tex, and do some boasting. But there were seven more to go. Some did well, some had to be fished out of difficulty.

The last man outdid himself. He failed to cut off his power in spite of Hanako's shouts for him to do so. He moved away from the ship in a wide curve and commenced to spin, while the sergeant whipped at the safety line to try to stop the spin and head him back. At the end of a long fifty seconds his power gave out; he was nearly a thousand feet away and still receding rapidly.

The sergeant played him like a fisherman fighting a barracuda, then brought him in very, very slowly, for there was no way to check whatever speed the tension on the line placed on him.

When at last he was in, clicked down, and anchored by static line, Hanako sighed. "Whew!" he said. "I thought I was going to have to go get him." He went to the cadet and touched helmets, radio off.

The cadet did not shut off his instrument. "I don't know," they heard him reply. "The switch didn't go bad—I just couldn't seem to move a muscle. I could hear you shouting but I couldn't move."

Matt went back to the airlock with the group, feeling considerably sobered. He suspected that there would be a vacant place at supper. It was the Commandant's policy to get a cadet who was to be dropped away from the ship without delay. Matt did not question the practice, but it jarred him when he saw it happening—it brought the cold breath of disaster on his own neck.

But he cheered up as soon as he was dismissed. Once he was out of his suit and had inspected it and stowed it as the rules required, he zipped to his room, bouncing his turns in a fashion not approved for in-ship progress.

He banged on the door of Tex's cubicle. "Hey, Tex! Wake up! I've got news for you."

No answer—he opened the door, but Tex was not there. Nor, as it happened, were Pete nor Oscar. Disconsolately he went into his own sanctum and picked out a study spool.

Nearly two hours later Tex came bouncing in as Matt was getting ready for lunch and shouted, "Hey! Matt! Mitt me, big boy—shake hands with a spaceman!"

"Huh?"

"I just passed 'basic space suit'—sergeant said it was the best first test he had ever seen."

"He did? Oh—"

"He sure did. Oh boy—Terra Station, here I come!"

8.
TERRA STATION

"Liberty party—man the scooter!"

Matt zipped up the front of his space suit and hurriedly ran through the routine check. Oscar and Tex urged him along, as the liberty party was already filing through the door of the lock. The cadet officer-of-the-watch checked Matt in and sealed the door of the lock behind him.

The lock was a long corridor, sealed at each end, leading to a hangar pocket in the side of the *Randolph* in which the scooter rockets were stowed. The pressure died away and the far end of the lock opened; Matt pulled himself along, last in line, and found the scooter loaded. He could not find a place; the passenger racks were filled with space-suited cadets, busy strapping down.

The cadet pilot beckoned to him. Matt picked his way forward and touched helmets. "Mister," said the oldster, "can you read instruments?"

Guessing that he referred only to the simple instrument panel of a scooter, Matt answered, "Yes, sir."

"Then get in the co-pilot's chair. What's your mass?"

"Two eighty-seven, sir," Matt answered, giving the combined mass, in pounds, of himself and his suit with all its equipment. Matt strapped down, then looked around, trying to locate Tex and Oscar. He was feeling very important, even though a scooter requires a co-pilot about as much as a hog needs a spare tail.

The oldster entered Matt's mass on his center-of-gravity and moment-of-inertia chart, stared at it thoughtfully and said to Matt, "Tell Gee-three to swap places with Bee-two." Matt switched on his walky-talky and gave the order. There was a scramble while a heavy-set youngster changed seats with a smaller cadet. The pilot gave a high sign to the cadet manning the hangar pocket; the scooter and its launching cradle swung out of the pocket, pushed by power-driven lazy tongs.

A scooter is a passenger rocket reduced to its simplest terms and has been described as a hat rack with an outboard motor. It operates only in empty space and does not have to be streamlined.

The rocket motor is unenclosed. Around it is a tier of light metal supports, the passenger rack. There is no "ship" in the sense of a hull, airtight compartments, etc. The passengers just belt themselves to the rack and let the rocket motor scoot them along.

When the scooter was clear of the ship the cadet in the hangar pocket turned the launching cradle, by power, until the scooter pointed at Terra Station. The pilot slapped the keys in front of him; the scooter took off.

The cadet pilot watched his radarscope. When the distance to the Station was closing at eighty-eight feet per second he cut his jet. "Latch on to the Station," he told Matt.

Matt plugged in and called the station. "Scooter number three, *Randolph*—scheduled trip. Arriving nine minutes, plus or minus," Matt sent, and congratulated himself on having studied the spool on small-craft procedures.

"Roger," a feminine voice answered, then added, "Use out-orbit contact platform Bee-for-Busy."

"Bee-for-Busy," acknowledged Matt. "Traffic?"

"None out-orbit. *Winged Victory* in-orbit, warping in."

Matt reported to his pilot. "No traffic," repeated the oldster. "Mister, I'm going to catch forty winks. Wake me when we've closed to a mile and a half."

"Aye aye, sir."

"Think you could bring her in?"

Matt gulped. "I'll try, sir."

"Figure it out while I'm asleep." The cadet promptly closed his eyes, floating as comfortably in free fall as if he had been in his own cubicle. Matt concentrated on the instrument dials.

Seven minutes later he shook the oldster, who opened his eyes and said, "What's your flight plan, Mister?"

"Well, uh—if we keep going as is, we'll just slide past on the out-orbit side. I don't think I'd change it at all. When we close to four thousand feet I'd blast until our relative speed is down to about ten foot-seconds, then forget the radar and brake by eye as we pass along the side."

"You've been studying too hard."

"Is that wrong?" Matt asked anxiously.

"Nope. Go ahead. Do it." The oldster bent over the tracking 'scope to assure himself that the scooter would miss the Station. Matt watched the closing range, while excitement built up inside him. Once he glanced ahead at the shining cylindrical bulk of the Station, but looked back quickly. A few seconds later he punched his firing key and a plume of flame shot out in front of them.

A scooter has jets at both ends, served by the same interconnected tanks, fuel pumps and piping. Scooters are conned "by the seat of your pants" rather than by complex mathematics. As such they are invaluable in letting student pilots get the feel of rocket ships.

As the distance decreased Matt felt for the first time the old nightmare of rocket pilots: is the calculated maneuver enough to avoid a crash? He felt this, even though he knew his course would slide him past the corner of the mammoth structure. It was a relief to release the firing key.

The oldster said, "Can you spot Bee-for-Busy when you see it?"

Matt shook his head. "No, sir. This is my first trip to Terra Station."

"It is? And I let you pilot! Well, there it is, ahead—third platform down. Better start braking."

"Aye aye, sir." The scooter was passing along the side of the Station and about a hundred yards out, at the speed of a brisk walk. Matt let Bee-for-Busy approach for a few moments more, then gave a short, experimental blast. It did not seem to slow them much; he gave a somewhat longer blast.

A few minutes later he had the scooter almost dead in space and practically abreast their contact point. He looked inquiringly at the pilot. "I've seen worse," the oldster grunted. "Tell them to bring us in."

"*Randolph* number three—ready for contact," Matt reported, via radio.

"We see you," the girl's voice answered. "Stand by for a line."

A line, shot by a gun, came sailing out in perfectly flat trajectory and passed through a metal loop sticking out from the scooter. "I relieve you, sir," the pilot told Matt. "Shinny out there and make that line fast."

A few minutes later the scooter was secured to platform Bee-for-Busy and the cadets were filing into the platform's airlock. Matt located Oscar and Tex in the suiting room and they undressed together. "What did you think of that contact?" Matt said to them, with studied casualness.

"All right, I guess," answered Tex. "What about it?"

"*I* made it."

Oscar raised his eyebrows. "You did? Nice going, kid."

Tex looked amazed. "The pilot let you jockey it? On your first trip?"

"Well, why not? You think I'm kidding?"

"No, I'm just impressed. May I touch you? How about an autograph?"

"Oh, come off it!"

They were, of course, in the free-fall part of the Station. As soon as they had stowed their suits, they hurried to the centrifuged belt frequented by the traveling public. Oscar knew his way around somewhat, having changed ships at the Station when he was a candidate, and led them to the door at the axis of rotation—the only possible place to pass from the free-fall zone to the weight zone.

From the axis they went down several levels, past offices and private quarters to the first of the public levels. It was, in effect, a wide, brightly lighted street, with a high ceiling and with slideways down the middle. Shops and restaurants lined it. The slideways curved up and away in the distance, for the corridor curved completely around the Station. "This," Oscar told them, "is Paradise Walk."

"I see why," agreed Tex, and gave a low whistle. The others followed his gaze. A tall, willowy blonde, dressed in some blue wisps of nothing much, was looking in the display window of a jewelry shop.

"Take it easy, Tex," advised Oscar. "She's taller than you are."

"I like them tall," Tex answered. "Watch me."

He sauntered over to the young woman. Matt and Oscar could not hear his opening remark, but it did not offend her, for she laughed. Then she looked him up and down with cool amusement and spoke. Her voice carried quite clearly. "I am married and at least ten years older than you are. I never pick up cadets."

Tex appeared to tuck his tail between his legs and slunk back toward his friends. He started to say, fiercely, "Well, you can't rule a guy out for try—," when the woman called out:

"Wait a moment! All three of you." She came up to them and looked from Matt to Oscar, "You are youngsters, aren't you?"

"Younster cadets, yes, ma'am," answered Oscar.

She fumbled in her jewelled pouch. "If you want to have some fun and meet some younger girls, you might try this address." She handed Oscar a card.

He looked startled and said, "Thank you, ma'am."

"Not at all." She moved away and managed to lose herself in the crowd at once.

"What does it say?" demanded Matt.

Oscar looked at it, then held it out. "Read it."

Terra Station First Baptist Church
Ralph Smiley, D.D., Pastor

SOCIAL HALL

#2437, Level "C"

Tex grinned. "Well, you can't say I scored a clean miss."

There ensued an argument. Matt and Tex wanted to go at once to the social hall; Oscar insisted that he was hungry and wanted some civilized food. The longer they argued the more reasonable seemed. Oscar's case. Finally Tex switched sides and Matt gave in to the majority.

He regretted it a few minutes later, when he saw the prices on the menu. The restaurant they selected was a tourist trap, a fancy dining room with an adjoining bar. It had human waiters instead of automatic tables and items were priced accordingly.

Tex saw the expression on his face. "Relax, Matt," he told him. "This is on me—Pop sent me a check."

"Oh, I wouldn't want to do that."

"Want to fight?"

Matt grinned. "Okay, thanks."

Oscar said, "How hard shall we punish you, Tex? Tea and toast?"

"Anything you want. Let's really celebrate. Which reminds me—I think we ought to have a drink."

"Huh?" said Oscar. "And have an M.P. catch us? No, thank you."

Matt started to protest but Tex stood up. "Just leave this to Father Jarman. It's high time you two poor, underprivileged outlanders tasted a real old Southern mint julep." He started for the bar. Oscar shrugged.

Tex scouted out the bar before entering. There were no cadets, of course; more important there were no officers and no marine M.P.'s. The hour was early and the bar almost deserted. He went up to the bartender. "Can you make a mint julep?" he asked.

The bartender looked up and answered, "Beat it. I'm not supposed to serve you liquor. This is off limits to cadets."

"I didn't ask you if this was off limits—I asked you if you could make a mint julep." Tex slid a bill across the counter. "Three mint juleps, in fact."

The barman eyed the bill. Finally he caused it to disappear. "Go on back into the dining room."

"Right!" said Tex.

A few minutes later a waiter placed a complete tea service in front of them, but the teapot did not contain tea. Tex poured out the drink, splitting it carefully three ways, in tea cups. "Here's to you, chums—drink up."

Matt took a sip. "It tastes like medicine," he announced.

"Like medicine?" Tex protested. "This noble potion? I'll meet you at dawn, suh—coffee and pistols for two."

"I still say it tastes like medicine. What do you think of it, Oscar?"

"It's not bad."

Matt pushed his aside. "Aren't you going to drink it?" asked Tex.

"No. Thanks, Tex, really—but I think it would make me sick. I guess I'm a sissy."

"Well, we won't waste it." He picked up Matt's cup and poured some into his own. "Split it with me, Oscar?"

"No. You go ahead."

"Okay, if you say so." He poured the rest into his cup.

When the food they ordered was served, Tex was no longer interested. While Matt and Oscar were busily chewing he kept urging them to sing. "Come on, Oscar! You can learn it."

"I can't sing."

"Sure you can. I've heard you sing, with the Hog Alley band. I'll sing the verse, we'll all clap, then hit the chorus together: 'Deep in . . . the heart of . . . Texas!' Like that."

"Shut up," said Oscar, "or you'll be deep in the heart of trouble."

"Kill-joy! Come on, Matt."

"I can't sing with my mouth full."

"Look," said Oscar to Matt, in a tense, low voice. "Do you see what I see?"

Matt looked and saw Lieutenant Wong entering the far end of

the dining room. He went to a table, sat down, looked around, spotted the table of cadets, nodded, and started studying a menu. "Oh, mother!" Matt breathed softly.

"Then we'll sing 'Ioway,'" announced Tex. "I'm broadminded."

"We won't sing anything. For the love of Mike, Tex—shut up! An officer just came into the joint."

"Where?" demanded Tex. "Invite him over. I don't hold any grudges. They're good boys, all of 'em, the stinkers." Matt shot a quick glance at Lieutenant Wong and was dismayed to see the officer crooking a finger at him, beckoning. He got up and walked stiffly toward the officer.

"Dodson—"

"Yes, sir."

"Go back and tell Jarman to quiet down before I have to come over there and ask him what his name is."

"Uh—aye aye, sir!"

When he got back to the table, Tex was already quiet and appeared sobered but very much puzzled. Oscar's usually pleasant face was dark with anger. "What's the verdict?"

Matt reported. "I see. Wong's all right. Well, we got to get him out of here." Oscar flagged the waiter, then opened Tex's pouch and paid the bill.

He stood up. "Let's go. Pull yourself together, Tex, or I'll break your neck."

"Where to?" asked Matt.

"Into the 'fresher."

Fortunately it turned out that they had that room to themselves. Oscar marched Tex to a washbasin and told him to stick his finger down his throat. "Why?" objected Tex.

"Because if you don't, I'll do it for you. Look, Matt—can you take care of him? I'll be back in a few minutes."

It was nearly twenty minutes before Oscar returned, bearing a carton of hot, black coffee and a tube of pills. He forced the coffee and half a dozen of the pills on the patient. "What are the pills?" Matt wanted to know.

"Thiamin chloride."

"You seem to know your way around?"

"Well . . ." Oscar wrinkled his brow. "Venus isn't like Earth, you know. Still sort of wild and woolly. You see a lot of things go on. Drink the rest of the coffee, Tex."

"Yessir."

"The front of his uniform is all messed up," said Matt.

"So I see. I guess we should have undressed him."

"What'll we do? If he goes back like that, there will be questions asked—bad ones."

"Let me think." Presently he said to Tex, "Go in there—" Oscar indicated one of a row of 'fresher booths. "—and take off your uniform. Hand it out and lock yourself in. We'll be back after a while." Tex seemed to feel that he was being consigned to the salt mines, but there was no real opposition left in him. He went. Shortly thereafter Matt and Oscar left, Oscar with a tightly rolled bundle of a cadet uniform under one arm.

They took the slideway half around the Station, through crowds of gorgeously dressed and hurrying people, past rich and beckoning shops. Matt enjoyed it thoroughly.

"They say," said Oscar, "that this is what the big cities used to be like, back before the Disorders."

"It certainly doesn't look like Des Moines."

"Nor like Venus." Oscar found what he was looking for, an automatic laundry service, in a passageway off the waiting room of the emigrant zone. After a considerable wait the uniform came back to them, clean, pressed, and neatly packaged. It being Terra Station, the cost was sky high. Matt looked at what remained of his funds.

"Might as well be broke," he said and invested the remainder in a pound of chocolate-coated cherries. They hurried back. Tex looked so woe-begone and so glad to see them that Matt had a sudden burst of generosity and handed the box to Tex. "Present to you, you poor, miserable, worthless critter."

Tex seemed touched by the gesture—it was no more than a gesture, since candy and such are, by ancient right, community property among roommates.

"Hurry up and get dressed, Tex. The scooter shoves off in just thirty-two minutes." Twenty-five minutes later, suited up, they were filing into the airlock, Tex with the chocolates under his arm.

The trip back was without incident, except for one thing: Matt had not thought to specify a pressure container for the candy. Before Tex could strap down the box had bulged. By the time they reached the *Randolph* the front and left side of his space suit was covered with a bubbly, sticky mess compounded of cherry juice, sugar syrup, and brown stains of chocolate as the semi-liquid confection boiled and expanded in the vacuum. He would have thrown the package away had not the oldster, strapped next to him in the rack, reminded him of the severe penalties for jettisoning anything in a traffic lane.

The cadet in charge of the hangar pocket in the *Randolph* looked Tex over in disgust. "Why didn't you pack it inside your suit?"

"Uh, I just didn't think of it, sir."

"Hummph! Next time you will, no doubt. Go on inside and place yourself on the report for 'gross untidiness in uniform.' And clean up that suit."

"Aye aye, sir."

Pete was in their suite when they got back. He came out of his cubicle. "Have fun? Gee, I wish I hadn't had the duty."

"You didn't miss much," said Oscar.

Tex looked from one to the other. "Gee, fellows, I'm sorry I ruined your liberty."

"Forget it," said Oscar. "Terra Station will still be there next month."

"That's right," agreed Matt, "but see here, Tex—tell us the truth. That was the first drink you ever had—wasn't it?"

Tex looked shame-faced. "Yes . . . my folks are all temperance—except my Uncle Bodie."

"Never mind your Uncle Bodie. If I catch you taking another, I'll beat you to death with the bottle."

"Aw, shucks, Matt!"

Oscar looked at Matt quizzically. "Easy on that holier-than-thou stuff, kid. Maybe it could happen to you."

"Maybe it could. Maybe some day I'll get you to chaperone me and find out what happens. But not in public."

"It's a date."

"Say," demanded Pete, "what goes on here? What's it all about?"

9.
LONG HAUL

Life in the Randolph had a curious aspect of timelessness—or, rather, datelessness. There was no weather, there were no seasons. The very divisions into "night" and "day" were arbitrary and were continually being upset by night watches and by laboratory periods at any hour, in order to make maximum use of limited facilities. Meals were served every six hours around the clock and the meal at one in the "morning" was almost as well attended as breakfast at seven hundred.

Matt got used to sleeping when he could find time—and the "days" tumbled past. It seemed to him that there was never time enough for all that he was expected to do. Mathematics and the mathematical subjects, astrogation and atomic physics in particular, began to be a bugaboo; he was finding himself being rushed into practical applications of mathematics before he was solidly grounded.

He had fancied himself, before becoming a cadet, as rather bright in mathematics, and so he was—by ordinary standards. He had not anticipated what it would be like to be part of a group of which every member was unusually talented in the language of science. He signed up for personal coaching in mathematics and studied harder than ever. The additional effort kept him from failing, but that was all.

It is not possible to work all the time without cracking up, but the environment would have kept Matt from overworking even if he had been so disposed. Corridor number five of "A" deck, where Matt and his roommates lived, was known as "Hog Alley" and had acquired a ripe reputation for carefree conduct even before Tex Jarman added his talents.

The current "Mayor of Hog Alley" was an oldster named Bill Arensa. He was a brilliant scholar and seemed able to absorb the most difficult study spool in a single playing, but he had been in the *Randolph* an unusually long time—a matter of accumulated demerits.

One evening after supper, soon after arrival, Matt and Tex were attempting to produce a little harmony. Matt was armed with a comb and a piece of tissue paper; Tex had his harmonica. A bellow from across the hallway stopped them. "Open up in there! You youngsters—come busting out!"

Tex and Matt appeared as ordered. The Mayor looked them over. "No blood," he remarked. "I'd swear I heard someone being killed. Go back and get your noisemakers."

Arensa ushered them into his own room, which was crowded. He waved a hand around at the occupants. "Meet the Hog Alley People's Forum—Senator Mushmouth, Senator Filibuster, Senator Hidebound, Doctor Dogoodly, and the Marquis de Sade. Gentlemen, meet Commissioner Wretched and Professor Farflung." The oldster went into his study cubicle.

"What's your name, Mister?" said one of the cadets, addressing Tex.

"Jarman, sir."

"And yours?"

"We've got no time for those details," announced Arensa, returning bearing a guitar. "That number you gentlemen were working on—let's try it again. Brace yourself for the down beat . . . and a one, and a two!"

Thus was born the Hog Alley band. It grew to seven pieces and started working on a repertoire to be presented at a ship's entertainment. Matt dropped out when he became eligible for the space polo league, as he could not spare time for both—his meager talent was no loss to the band.

Nevertheless he remained in the orbit of the oldster. Arensa adopted all four of them, required them to report to his room from time to time, and supervised their lives. However, he never placed them on the report. By comparing notes with other youngster cadets on this point, Matt discovered that he and his friends were well off. They attended numerous sessions of the "Forum," first by direction, later from choice. The staple recreation in the *Ran-*

dolph, as it is in all boarding schools, was the bull session. The talk ranged through every possible subject and was kept spiced by Arensa's original and usually radical ideas.

However, no matter what was discussed, the subject usually worked around to girls and then broke up with the unstartling conclusion: "There's no sense in talking about it—there aren't any girls in the *Randolph*. Let's turn in."

Almost as entertaining was the required seminar in "Doubt." The course had been instituted by the present commandant and resulted from his own observation that every military organization—with the Patrol no exception—suffered from an inherent vice. A military hierarchy automatically places a premium on conservative behavior and dull conformance with precedent; it tends to penalize original and imaginative thinking. Commodore Arkwright realized that these tendencies are inherent and inescapable; he hoped to offset them a bit by setting up a course that could not be passed without original thinking.

The method was the discussion group, made up of youngsters, oldsters, and officers. The seminar leader would chuck out some proposition that attacked a value usually regarded as axiomatic. From there on anything could be said.

It took Matt a while to get the hang of it. At his first session the leader offered: "Resolved: that the Patrol is a detriment and should be abolished." Matt could hardly believe his ears.

In rapid succession he heard it suggested that the past hundred years of Patrol-enforced peace had damaged the race, that the storm of mutations that followed atomic warfare were necessarily of net benefit under the inexorable laws of evolution, that neither the human race nor any of the other races of the system could expect to survive permanently in the universe if they deliberately forsook war, and that, in any case, the Patrol was made up of a bunch of self-righteous fatheads who mistook their own trained-in prejudices for the laws of nature.

Matt contributed nothing to the first discussion he attended.

The following week he heard both mother love and love of mother questioned. He wanted to reply, but, for the life of him, could think of no other answer than "Because!" Thereafter came attacks on monotheism as a desirable religious form, the usefulness of the scientific method, and the rule of the majority, in reaching decisions. He discovered that it was permissible to express opinions that were orthodox as well as ones that were unorthodox and began to join the debate by defending some of his own pet ideas.

At once he found his own unconscious assumptions that lay behind his opinions subjected to savage attack and found himself again reduced to a stubborn and unvoiced "Because!"

He began to catch on to the method and found that he could ask an innocent question that would undermine someone else's line of argument. From then on he had a good time.

He particularly enjoyed it after Girard Burke was assigned to his seminar. Matt would lie in wait until Girard would express some definite opinion, then jump him—always with a question; never with a statement. For some reason not clear to Matt, Burke's opinions were always orthodox; to attack them Matt was forced to do some original thinking.

But he asked Burke about it after class one day. "See here, Burke—I thought you were the bird with a new slant on everything?"

"Well, maybe I am. What about it?"

"You don't sound like it in 'Doubt.' "

Burke looked wise. "You don't catch me sticking my neck out."

"What do you mean?"

"Do you think our dear superiors are really interested in your bright ideas? Won't you ever learn to recognize a booby trap, son?"

Matt thought about it. "I think you're crazy." Nevertheless he chewed it over.

The days rolled past. The pace was so hard that there was little time to be bored. Matt shared the herd *credo* of all cadets that the *Randolph* was a madhouse, unfit for human habitation, sky junk, etc., etc.—but in fact he had no opinion of his own about the school ship; he was too busy. At first he had had some acute twinges of homesickness; thereafter it seemed to recede. There was nothing but the treadmill of study, drill, more study, laboratory, sleep, eat, and study again.

He was returning from the communications office, coming off watch late one night, when he heard sounds from Pete's cubicle. At first he thought Pete must be running his projector, studying late. He was about to bang on his door and suggest going up to the galley to wheedle a cup of cocoa when he became convinced that the sound was not a projector.

Cautiously he opened the door a crack. The sound was sobbing. He closed the door noiselessly and knocked on it. After a short silence Pete said, "Come in."

Matt went in. "Got anything to eat?"

"Some cookies in my desk."

Matt got them out. "You look sick, Pete. Anything wrong?"

"No. Nothing."

"Don't give me the space drift. Out with it."

Pete hesitated. "It's nothing. Nothing anybody can do anything about."

"Maybe so, maybe not. Tell me."

"There's nothing you can do. I'm *homesick*, that's all!"

"Oh—" Matt had a sudden vision of the rolling hills and broad farms of Iowa. He suppressed it. "That's bad, kid. I know how you feel."

"No, you don't. Why, you're practically *at* home—you can just step to a port and *see* it."

"That's no help."

"And it hasn't been so terribly long since you've been home. Me—it took me two years just to make the trip to Terra; there's no way of telling when I'll ever see home again." Pete's eyes got a faraway look; his voice became almost lyrical. "You don't know what it's like, Matt. You've never *seen* it. You know what they say: 'Every civilized man has two planets, his own and Ganymede.' "

"Huh?"

Pete did not even hear him. "Jupiter hanging overhead, filling half the sky—" He stopped. "It's beautiful, Matt. There's no place like it."

Matt found himself thinking about Des Moines in a late summer evening . . . with fireflies winking and the cicadas singing in the trees, and the air so thick and heavy you could cup it in your hand. Suddenly he hated the steel shell around him, with its eternal free-fall and its filtered air and its artificial lights. "Why did we ever sign up, Pete?"

"I don't know. I don't know!"

"Are you going to resign?"

"I can't. My father had to put up a bond to cover my passage both ways—if I leave voluntarily he's stuck for it."

Tex came in, yawning and scratching. "What's the matter with you guys? Can't you sleep? Don't you want anybody else to sleep?"

"Sorry, Tex."

Jarman looked them over. "You both look like your pet dog had died. What's the trouble?"

Matt bit his lip. "Nothing much. I'm homesick, that's all."

Pete spoke up at once. "That's not quite straight. I was the one that was pulling the baby act—Matt was trying to cheer me up."

Tex looked puzzled. "I don't get it. What difference does it make where you are so long as you aren't in Texas?"

"Oh, Tex, for heaven's sake!" Matt exploded.

"What's the matter? Did I say something wrong?" Tex looked from Matt to Pete. "Pete, you certainly are a mighty far piece away from your folks, I've got to admit. Tell you what—comes time we get some leave, you come home with me. I'll let you count the legs on a horse."

Pete grinned feebly. "And meet your Uncle Bodie?"

"Sho', sho'! Uncle Bodie'll tell you about the time he rode the twister, bareback. Is it a deal?"

"If you'll come to visit at my home someday. You, too, Matt."

"It's a deal." They shook hands all around.

The effects of the nostalgic binge with Pete might have worn off if another incident had not happened soon after. Matt went across the passage to Arensa's room, intending to ask the oldster for some help in a tricky problem in astrogation. He found the oldster packing. "Come in, Senator," said Arensa. "Don't clutter up the doorway. What's on your mind, son?"

"Uh, nothing, I guess. You got your ship, sir?" Arensa had been passed for outer duty the month before; he was now technically a "passed cadet" as well as an "oldster."

"No." He picked up a sheaf of papers, glanced at them, and tore them across. "But I'm leaving."

"Oh."

"No need to be delicate about it—I wasn't fired. I've resigned."

"Oh."

"Don't stare at me and say 'oh'! What's so odd about resigning?"

"Nothing. Nothing at all."

"You were wondering why, weren't you? Well, I'll tell you. I've had it, that's why. I've had it and I'm sick of it. Because, sonny, I have no wish to be a superman. My halo is too tight and I'm chucking it. Can you understand that?"

"Oh, I wasn't criticizing!"

"No, but you were thinking it. You stick with it, Senator. You're just the sort of serious-minded young squirt they want and need. But not for me—I'm not going to be an archangel, charging around the sky and brandishing a flaming sword. Did you ever stop to think what it would feel like to atom-bomb a city? Have you ever really *thought about it?*"

"Why, I don't know. It hasn't been necessary for the Patrol actually to *use* a bomb since they got it rolling right. I don't suppose it ever will be."

"But that's what you signed up for, just the same. It's your reason for being, my boy." He stopped and picked up his guitar. "Forget it. Now what can I do with this? I'll sell it to you cheap, Earth-side price."

"I couldn't even pay Earth-side prices right now."

"Take it as a gift." Arensa chucked it at him. "The Hog Alley band ought to have a gitter and I can get another. In thirty minutes I shall be in Terra Station, Senator, and six hours later I shall be back with the ground crawlers, the little people who don't know how to play God—and wouldn't want to!"

Matt couldn't think of anything to say.

It seemed odd thereafter not to have Arensa's bellowing voice across the passageway, but Matt did not have time to think about it. Matt's drill section in piloting was ordered to the Moon for airless-landing.

The section had progressed from scooters to drill in an A-6 utility rocket rigged for instruction. The cargo space of this ship— P.R.S. *Shakysides* to the cadets; drill craft #106 on the rolls of the *Randolph*—had been fitted as a dozen duplicate control rooms, similar in every visible detail to the real control rooms, to the last switch, dial, scope and key. The instruments in the duplicate rooms showed the same data as their twins in the master room but when a cadet touched a control in one of the instruction rooms, it had no effect on the ship; instead the operation was recorded on tape.

The pilot's operations were recorded, too, so that each student pilot could compare what he did with what he should have done, after having practiced under conditions identical with those experienced by the actual pilot.

The section had completed all it could learn from practice contacts at the *Randolph* and at Terra Station. They needed the hazard of a planet. The two-day trip to Moon Base was made in the *Shakysides* herself, under conditions only a little worse than those encountered by an emigrant.

Matt and his companions saw nothing of the Lunar colonies. There was no liberty; they lived for two weeks in pressurized underground barracks at the Base and went up to the field each day for landing drill, first in the dummy control rooms of the *Shakysides*, then in dual-controlled A-6 rockets for actual piloting.

Matt soloed at the end of the first week. He had the "feel" for piloting; given a pre-calculated flight plan he could make his craft respond. It was as natural to him as mathematical astrogation was difficult.

Soloing left him with time on his hands. He explored the Base and took a space-suited walk on the burned and airless Lunar plain. The student pilots were quartered in a corner of the marine barracks. Matt killed time by watching the space marines and chinning with the non-coms.

He liked the spit-and-polish style with which the space marines did things, the strutting self-confidence with which they handled themselves. There is no more resplendent sight in the solar system than an old space-marine sergeant in full dress, covered with stripes, hash marks, and ribbons, the silver at his temples matching the blazing sunburst on his chest. Matt began to feel dowdy in the one plain, insignialess uniform he had brought in his jump bag.

He enjoyed their frequent ceremonials. At first it startled him to hear a unit mustered without the ghostly repetition of the names of the Four—"Dahlquist! Martin! Rivera! Wheeler!"—but the marines had traditional rites of their own and more of them.

Faithful to his intention of swotting astrogation as hard as possible, Matt had brought some typical problems along. Reluctantly he tackled them one day. "Given: Departure from the orbit of Deimos, Mars, not earlier than 1200 Greenwich, 15 May 2087; chemical fuel, exhaust velocity 10,000 meters per second; destination, suprastratospheric orbit around Venus. Required: Most economical orbit to destination and quickest orbit, mass-ratios and times of departure and arrival for each. Prepare flight plan and designate check points, with pre-calculation for each point, using stars of 2nd magnitude or brighter. Questions: Is it possible to save time or fuel by tacking on the Terra-Luna pair? What known meteor drifts will be encountered and what evasive plans, if any, should be made? All answers must conform to space regulations as well as to ballistic principles."

The problem could not be solved in any reasonable length of time without machine calculation. However, Matt could set it up and then, with luck, sweet-talk the officer in charge of the Base's computation room into letting him use a ballistic integrator. He got to work.

The sweet voice of a bugle reached him, first call for changing the guard. He ignored it.

He was sweating over his preliminary standard approximation when the bugle again interrupted him with call-to-muster. It com-

pletely disrupted his chain of reasoning. Confounded problem!—
why would they assign such a silly problem anyhow? The Patrol
didn't fiddle around with chemical fuels and most economical
orbits—that was merchant service stuff.

Two minutes later he was watching guard mount, down in the
main hall under the barracks. When the band sounded off with
"Till the Suns are cold and the heavens dark—" Matt found himself choking up.

He stopped by the guard office, reluctant to get back to the
fussy complexities of mathematics. The new sergeant of the guard
was an acquaintance, Master Sergeant Macleod. "Come in, young
fellow, and rest yourself. Did you see the guard mount?"

"Thanks. Yes, I did. It's pretty wonderful to see."

"Know what you mean. Been doing it twenty years and I get
more of a bang out of it than I did when I was a recruit. How's
tricks? They keeping you busy?"

Matt grinned sheepishly. "I'm playing hooky. I should be
studying astrogation, but I get so darned sick of it."

"Don't blame you a bit. Figures make my head ache."

Matt found himself telling the older man his troubles.
Sergeant Macleod eyed him with sympathetic interest. "See here,
Mr. Dodson—you don't like that long-haired stuff. Why don't you
chuck it?"

"Huh?"

"You like the space marines, don't you?"

"Why, yes."

"Why not switch over and join a man's outfit? You're a likely
lad and educated—in a year I'd be saluting you. Ever thought
about it?"

"Why, no, I can't say that I have."

"Then do so. You don't belong with the Professors—you didn't
know that was what we call the Patrol, did you?—the 'Professors.' "

"I'd heard it."

"You had? Well, we work for the Professors, but we aren't of
them. We're . . . well, you've seen. Think it over."

Matt did think it over, so much so that he took the Mars-to-
Venus problem back with him, still unsolved.

It was no easier to solve for the delay, nor were other and more
complicated problems made any simpler by virtue of the idea,
buzzing in the back of his mind, that he need not belabor himself
with higher mathematics in order to be a spaceman. He began to

see himself decked out in the gaudy, cock-pheasant colors of the space marines.

At last he took it up with Lieutenant Wong. "You want to transfer to the marines?"

"Yes. I think so."

"Why?"

Matt explained his increasing feeling of frustration in dealing with both atomic physics and astrogation.

Wong nodded. "I thought so. But we knew that you would have tough sledding since you came here insufficently prepared. I don't like the sloppy work you've been doing since you came back from Luna."

"I've done the best I could, sir."

"No, you haven't. But you *can* master these two subjects and I will see to it that you do."

Matt explained, almost inaudibly, that he was not sure he wanted to. Wong, for the first time, looked vexed.

"Still on that? If you turn in a request for transfer, I won't okay it and I can tell you ahead of time that the Commandant will turn it down."

Matt's jaw muscles twitched. "That's your privilege, sir."

"Damn it, Dodson, it's not my privilege; it's my duty. You would never make a marine and I say so because I know you, your record, and your capabilities. You have a good chance of making a Patrol officer."

Matt looked startled. "Why couldn't I become a marine?"

"Because it's too easy for you—so easy that you would fail."

"Huh?"

"Don't say 'huh.' The spread in I.Q. between leader and follower should not be more than thirty points. You are considerably more than thirty points ahead of those old sergeants—don't get me wrong; they are fine men. But your mind doesn't work like theirs." Wong went on, "Have you ever wondered why the Patrol consists of nothing but officers—and student officers, cadets?"

"Mmm, no, sir."

"Naturally you wouldn't. We never wonder at what we grow up with. Strictly speaking, the Patrol is not a military organization at all."

"Sir?"

"I know, I know—you are trained to use weapons, you are under orders, you wear a uniform. But your purpose is not to fight, but to prevent fighting, by every possible means. The Patrol is not a fighting organization; it is the repository of weapons too dangerous to entrust to military men.

"With the development last century of mass-destruction weapons, warfare became all offense and no defense, speaking broadly. A nation could launch a horrific attack but it could not even protect its own rocket bases. Then space travel came along.

"The spaceship is the perfect answer in a military sense to the atom bomb, and to germ warfare and weather warfare. It can deliver an attack that can't be stopped—and it is utterly impossible to attack that spaceship from the surface of a planet."

Matt nodded. "The gravity gauge."

"Yes, the gravity gauge. Men on the surface of a planet are as helpless against men in spaceships as a man would be trying to conduct a rock-throwing fight from the bottom of a well. The man at the top of the well has gravity working for him.

"We might have ended up with the tightest, most nearly unbreakable tyranny the world has ever seen. But the human race got a couple of lucky breaks and it didn't work out that way. It's the business of the Patrol to see that it stays lucky.

"But the Patrol can't drop an atom bomb simply because some pipsqueak Hitler has made a power grab and might some day, when he has time enough, build spaceships and mass-destruction weapons. The power is too great, too awkward—it's like trying to keep order in a nursery with a loaded gun instead of a switch.

"The space marines are the Patrol's switch. They are the finest—"

"Excuse me, sir—"

"Yes?"

"I know how the marines work. They do the active policing in the System—but that's why I want to transfer. They're a more active outfit. They are—"

"—more daring, more adventurous, more colorful, more glamorous—and they don't have to study things that Matthew Dodson is tired of studying. Now shut up and listen; there is a lot you don't know about the set-up, or you wouldn't be trying to transfer."

Matt shut up.

"People tend to fall into three psychological types, all differently motivated. There is the type, motivated by economic factors, money . . . and there is the type motivated by 'face,' or pride. This type is a spender, fighter, boaster, lover, sportsman, gambler; he has a will to power and an itch for glory. And there is the professional type, which claims to follow a code of ethics rather than simply seeking money or glory—priests and ministers, teachers, scientists, medical men, some artists and writers. The idea is that such a man believes that he is devoting his life to some purpose more important than his individual self. You follow me?"

"I . . . think so."

"Mind you this is terrifically over-simplified. And don't try to apply these rules to non-terrestrials; they won't fit. The Martian is another sort of a cat, and so is the Venerian."

Wong continued, "Now we get to the point: The Patrol is meant to be made up exclusively of the professional type. In the space marines, every single man jack, from the generals to the privates, is or should be the sort who lives by pride and glory."

"Oh . . ."

Wong waited for it to sink in. "You can see it in the very uniforms; the Patrol wears the plainest of uniforms, the marines wear the gaudiest possible. In the Patrol all the emphasis is on the oath, the responsibility to humanity. In the space marines the emphasis is on pride in their corps and its glorious history, loyalty to comrades, the ancient virtues of the soldier. I am not disparaging the marine when I say that he does not care a tinker's damn for the political institutions of the Solar System; he cares only for his organization.

"But it's not your style, Matt. I know more about you than you do yourself, because I have studied the results of your psychological tests. You will never make a marine."

Wong paused so long that Matt said diffidently, "Is that all, sir?"

"Almost. You've got to learn astrogation. If deep-sea diving were the key to the Patrol's responsibility, it would be that that you would have to learn. But the key happens to be space travel. So—I'll lay out a course of sprouts for you. For a few weeks you'll do nothing but astrogate. Does that appeal to you?"

"No, sir."

"I didn't think it would. But when I get through with you, you'll be able to find your way around the System blindfolded. Now let me see—"

The next few weeks were deadly monotony but Matt made progress. He had plenty of time to think—when he was not bending over a calculator. Oscar and Tex went to the Moon together; Pete was on night shift in the power room. Matt kept sullenly and stubbornly at work—and brooded. He promised himself to stick it out until Wong let up on him. After that—well, he would have a leave coming up one of these days. If he decided to chuck it, why, lots of cadets never came back from their first leave.

In the meantime his work began to get the grudging approval of Lietuenant Wong.

At last Wong let up on him and he went back to a normal routine. He was settling into it when he found himself posted for an extra duty. Pursuant thereto, he reported one morning to the officer of the watch, received a briefing, memorized a list of names, and was issued a black armband. Then he went to the main airlock and waited.

Presently a group of scared and greenish boys began erupting from the lock. When his turn came, he moved forward and called out, "Squad seven! Where is the squad leader of squad seven?"

He got his charges rounded up at last and told the acting squad leader to follow along in the rear, then led them slowly and carefully down to "A" deck. He was glad to find when he got there that none of them had gotten lost. "This is your messroom," he told them. "We'll have lunch before long."

Something about the expression of one of them amused him. "What's the matter, Mister?" he asked the boy. "Aren't you hungry?"

"Uh, no, sir."

"Well, cheer up—you will be."

10.
QUIS CUSTODIET IPSOS CUSTODES?

Interplanetary patrol Cadet Matthew Dodson sat in the waiting room of Pikes Peak Catapult Station and watched the clock. He had an hour to wait before boarding the *New Moon* for Terra Station; meanwhile he was expecting his roommates.

It had been a good leave, he supposed; he had done everything he had planned to do—except joining the others at the Jarman ranch at the end; his mother had kicked up such a fuss at the idea.

Still, it had been a good leave. His space-burned face, lean and beginning to be lined, looked slightly puzzled. He had confided to no one his tentative intention of resigning while on leave. Now he was trying to remember just when and why it had ceased to be his intention.

He had been sent on temporary duty to the P.R.S *Nobel*, as assistant to the astrogator during a routine patrol of circum-Terra bomb-rockets. Matt had joined his ship at Moon Base and, at the conclusion of the patrol when the *Nobel* had grounded at Terra Base for overhaul, was detached with permission to take leave before reporting back to the *Randolph*. He had gone straight home.

The entire family met him at the station and copted him home. His mother had cried a little and his father had shaken hands very vigorously. It seemed to Matt that his kid brother had grown almost incredibly. It was good to see them, good to be back in the old family bus. Matt would have piloted the copter himself had not Billie, his brother, gone straight to the controls.

The house had been redecorated throughout. His mother obviously expected favorable comment and Matt had given it—but he hadn't really liked the change. It had not been what he had pictured. Besides that, the rooms seemed smaller. He decided that it must be the effect of redecorating; the house couldn't have shrunk!

His own room was filled with Bill's things, although Bill had been temporarily evicted to his old room, now turned into a hobby room for his mother. The new arrangements were sensible, reasonable—and annoying.

In thinking it over Matt knew that the changes at home had had nothing to do with his decision. Certainly not! Nor his father's remarks about posture, even though they had stuck in his craw—

He and his father had been alone in the living room, just before dinner, and Matt had been pacing up and down, giving an animated and, he believed, interesting account of the first time he had soloed. His father had taken advantage of a pause to say, "Stand up, son."

Matt stopped. "Sir?"

"You are all crouched over and seem to be limping. Does your leg still bother you?"

"No, my leg is fine."

"Then straighten up and square your shoulders. Look proud. Don't they pay any attention to your posture at school?"

"What's wrong with the way I was walking?"

Bill had appeared in the door just as the subject had come up. "I'll show you, Mattie," he had interrupted, and proceeded to slouch across the room in a grotesque exaggeration of a spaceman's relaxed and boneless glide. The boy made it look like the amble of a chimpanzee. "You walk like that."

"The devil I do!"

"The devil you don't."

"Bill!" said his father. "Go wash up and get ready for dinner. And don't talk that way. Go on, now!" When the younger son had left his father turned again to Matt and said, "I thought I was speaking privately, Matt. Honestly, it's not as bad as Bill makes out; it's only about half that bad."

"But—Look, Dad, I walk just like everybody else—among spacemen, I mean. It comes of getting used to free-fall. You carry yourself sort of pulled in, for days on end, ready to bounce a foot off a bulkhead, or grab with your hands. When you're back under weight, after days and weeks of that, you walk the way I do. 'Cat feet' we call it."

"I suppose it would have that effect," his father had answered reasonably, "but wouldn't it be a good idea to practice walking a little every day, just to keep in form?"

"In free-fall? But—" Matt had stopped, suddenly aware that there was no way to bridge the gap.

"Never mind. Let's go in to dinner."

There had been the usual round of family dinners with aunts and uncles. Everyone asked him to tell about school, about what it felt like to go out into space. But, somehow, they had not actually seemed very interested. Take Aunt Dora.

Great-aunt Dora was the current family matriarch. She had been a very active woman, busy with church and social work. Now she was bedfast and had been for three years. Matt called on her because his family obviously expected it. "She often complains to me that you don't write to her, Matt, and—"

"But, Mother, I don't have time to write to everyone!"

"Yes, yes. But she's proud of you, Matt. She'll want to ask you a thousand questions about everything. Be sure to wear your uniform—she'll expect it."

Aunt Dora had not asked a thousand questions; she had asked just one—why had he waited so long to come to see her? Thereafter Matt found himself being informed, in detail, on the shortcomings of the new pastor, the marriage chances of several female relatives and connections, and the states of health of several older women, many of them unknown to him, including details of operations and post-operative developments.

He was a bit dizzy when he escaped, pleading a previous date.

Yes, maybe that was it—it might have been the visit to Aunt Dora that convinced him that he was not ready to resign and remain in Des Moines. It could not have been Marianne.

Marianne was the girl who had made him promise to write regularly—and, in fact, he had, more regularly than had she. But he had let her know that he was coming home and she had organized a picnic to welcome him back. It had been jolly. Matt had renewed old acquaintances and had enjoyed a certain amount of hero worship from the girls present. There had been a young man there, three or four years older than Matt, who seemed unattached. Gradually it dawned on Matt that Marianne treated the newcomer as her property.

It had not worried him. Marianne was the sort of girl who never would get clearly fixed in her mind the distinction between a planet and a star. He had not noticed this before, but it and similar matters had come up on the one date he had had alone with her.

And she had referred to his uniform as "cute."

He began to understand, from Marianne, why most Patrol officers do not marry until their mid-thirties, after retirement.

The clock in Pikes Peak Station showed thirty minutes until up-ship. Matt began to worry that Tex's casual way might have caused the other three to miss connections, when he spotted them in the crowd. He grabbed his jump bag and went toward them.

They had their backs toward him and had not seen him as yet. He sneaked up behind Tex and said in a hoarse voice, "Mister—report to the Commandant's office."

Tex jumped into the air and turned completely around. "Matt! You horse-thief, don't scare me like that!"

"Your guilty conscience. Hi, Pete. Hello, Oscar."

"How's the boy, Matt? Good leave?"

"Swell."

"Here, too." They shook hands all around.

"Let's get aboard."

"Suits." They weighed in, had their passes stamped, and were allowed to proceed on up to where the *New Moon* stood upright and ready in the catapult cradle, her mighty wings outstretched. A stewardess showed them to their seats.

At the ten-minute warning Matt announced, "I'm going up for some makee-learnee. Anybody with me?"

"I'm going to sleep," denied Tex.

"Me, too," added Pete. "Nobody ever sleeps in Texas. I'm dead."

Oscar decided to come along. They climbed up to the control room and spoke to the captain. "Cadets Dodson and Jensen, sir—request permission to observe."

"I suppose so," the captain grunted. "Strap down." The pilot room of any licensed ship was open to all members of the Patrol, but the skippers on the Terra-to-Station run were understandably bored with the practice.

Oscar took the inspector's chair; Matt had to use deck pads and straps. His position gave him an excellent view of the co-pilot and mate, waiting at the airplane-type controls. If the rocket motor failed to fire, after catapulting, it would be the mate's business to fight the ship into level flight and bring her down to a deadstick landing on the Colorado prairie.

The captain manned the rocket-type controls. He spoke to the catapult control room, then sounded the siren. Shortly thereafter the ship mounted up the face of the mountain, at a bone-clamping six gravities. The acceleration lasted only ten seconds; then the ship was flung straight up at the sky, leaving the catapult at 1300 miles per hour.

They were in free-fall and climbing. The captain appeared to be taking his time about cutting in the jet; for a moment Matt held to the excited hope that an emergency landing was going to be necessary. But the jet roared on time.

When they had settled in their orbit and the jet was again silent, Matt and Oscar thanked the captain and went back to their proper seats. Tex and Pete were both asleep; Oscar followed suit at once. Matt decided that he must have missed quite a bit in letting himself be talked out of finishing his leave in Texas.

His thoughts went back to the problem he had been considering. Certainly he had not decided to stick simply because his own leave had been fairly quiet; he had never thought of home as being a night club, or a fair ground.

One night at dinner his father had asked him to describe just what it was that the *Nobel* did in circum-Terra patrol. He had tried to oblige. "After we lift from Moon Base we head for Terra on an elliptical orbit. As we approach the Earth we brake gradually and throw her into a tight circular orbit from pole to pole—"

"Why pole to pole? Why not around the equator?"

"Because, you see, the atom-bomb rockets are in pole-to-pole orbits. That's the only way they can cover the whole globe. If they were circling around the equator—"

"I understand that," his father had interrupted, "but your purpose, as I understand it, is to inspect the bomb rockets. If you—your ship—circled around the equator, you could just wait for the bomb rockets to come past."

"*You* may understand it," his mother had said to his father, "but *I* don't."

Matt looked from one to the other, wondering which one to answer—and how. "One at a time . . . please," he protested. "Dad, we can't just intercept the bombs; we have to sneak up on them, match orbits until you are right alongside it and making exactly the same course and speed. Then you bring the bomb inside and ship and inspect it."

"And of what does that inspection consist?"

"Just a sec, Dad. Mother, look here for a moment." Matt took an orange from the table's centerpiece. "The rocket bombs go round and round, like this, from pole-to-pole, every two hours. In the meantime the Earth is turning on its axis, once every twenty-four hours." Matt turned the orange slowly in his left hand while moving a finger of his right hand rapidly around it from top to bottom to simulate a pole-to-pole bomb. "That means that if a bomb passes over Des Moines on this trip, it will just about pass over the Pacific Coast on its next trip. In twenty-four hours it covers the globe."

"Goodness! Matthew, I wish you wouldn't talk about an atom bomb being over Des Moines, even in fun."

"In fun?" Matt had been puzzled. "As a matter of fact . . . let me think; we're about forty-two north and ninety-four west—" He glanced at his watch finger and studied for a few moments. "Jay-three ought to be along in about seven minutes—yes, it will be almost exactly overhead by the time you finish your coffee." Long weeks in the *Nobel*, plotting, calculating, and staring in radarscopes had gotten Matt so that he knew the orbits of circum-Terra prowler rockets a bit better than a farmer's wife knows her own chickens; Jay-three was an individual to him, one with fixed habits.

His mother was looking horrified. She spoke directly to her husband as if she expected him to do something about it. "John. . . . I don't like this. I don't like it, do you hear me? What if it should fall?"

"Nonsense, Catherine—it can't fall."

Matt's younger brother chortled. "Mom doesn't even know what holds the Moon up!"

Matt turned to his brother. "Who pushed your button squirt? Do *you* know what holds the Moon up?"

"Sure—gravity."

"Not exactly. Suppose you give me a quick tell, with diagrams."

The boy tried; his effort was hardly successful. Matt shut him off. "You know somewhat less about astronomy than the ancient Egyptians. Don't make fun of your elders. Now, look, Mother— don't get upset. Jay-three *can't* fall on us. It's in a free orbit that does not intersect the Earth—like smarty-pants here says, it can't fall down any more than the Moon can fall. Anyhow, if the Patrol was to bomb Des Moines tonight, at this time, it wouldn't use Jay-three for the very reason that it *is* overhead. To bomb a city you start with a rocket heading for your target and a couple of thousand miles away, because you have to signal its robot to start the jet and seek the target. You have to slow it down and bend it down. So it wouldn't be Jay-three; it would be—" He thought again.

"—Eye-two, or maybe Ache-one." He smiled wryly. "I got bawled out over Eye-two."

"Why?" demanded his brother.

"Matt, I don't think you have picked the right tack to quiet your mother's fears," his father said dryly. "I suggest we not talk about bombing cities."

"But I didn't—Sorry, Father."

"Catherine, there really is nothing to get worked up over—you might just as well be afraid of the local policeman. Matt, you were going to tell me about inspection. Why do the rockets have to be inspected?"

"I want to know why Mattie got bawled out!"

Matt cocked an eyebrow at his brother. "I might as well start by telling him, Dad—it has to do with inspection. Okay, Bill—I made a poor dive when we started to pick it up and had to come back on my suit jet and try again."

"What do you mean, Matthew?"

"He means—"

"Pipe down, Billie. Dad, you send a man out in a suit to insert the trigger guard and attach a line to the rocket so you can bring her inboard of the ship and work on her. I was the man. I made a bad push-off and missed the rocket entirely. She was about a hundred yards away and I guess I misjudged the distance. I turned over and found I was floating on past her. I had to jet back and try again."

His mother still seemed confused, but did not like what she heard. "Matthew! That sounds dangerous to me."

"Safe as houses, Mother. You *can't* fall, any more than the rocket can, or the ship. But it's embarrassing. Anyhow, I finally got a line on her and rode her back into the ship."

"You mean you were *riding* an atom bomb?"

"Shucks, Mother, it's safe—the tamper around the fission material stops most of the radioactivity. Anyhow, the exposure is short."

"But suppose it went off?"

"It can't go off. To go off it has to either crash into the ground with a speed great enough to slap the sub-critical masses together as fast as its trigger-gun could do it, or you have to fire the trigger-gun by radio. Besides that, I had inserted the trigger guard—that's nothing more nor less than a little crowbar, but when it's in place not even a miracle could set it off, because you can't bring the subcritical masses together."

"Maybe we had better drop this subject, Matt. It seems to make your mother nervous."

"But, Dad, she asked me."

"I know. But you still haven't told me what you inspect for."

"Well, in the first place, you inspect the bomb itself, but there's never anything wrong with the bomb. Anyhow, I haven't had the course for bomb-officer yet—he has to be a nucleonics engineer. You inspect the rocket motor, especially the fuel tanks. Sometimes you have to replace a little that has escaped through relief valves. But mostly you give her a ballistic check and check her control circuits."

"Ballistic check?"

"Of course, theoretically you ought to be able to predict where a prowler bomb would be every instant for the next thousand years. But it doesn't work out that way. Little things, the effect of the tidal bulges and the fact that the Earth is not a perfect uniform sphere and such, cause them to gradually wander a little away from the predicted orbits. After you find one and service it— they're never very far from where they ought to be—you correct the orbit by putting the whole ship in just precisely the proper trajectory and then put the rocket outside the ship again. Then you go after the next one."

"Clear enough. And these corrections have to be made often enough that a ship is kept busy just inspecting them?"

"Well, no, Dad, we inspect oftener than we really have to—but it keeps the ship and the crew busy. Keeps it from getting monotonous. Anyhow, frequent inspections keep you on the safe side."

"Sounds like a waste of taxpayers' money to inspect too often."

"But you don't understand—we're not there to inspect; we're there to *patrol*. The inspection ship is the ship that would deliver an attack in case anybody started acting up. We have to stay on patrol until the next ship relieves us, so we might as well inspect. Granted that you can bomb a city from Moon Base, you can do a better, more accurate job, with less chance of hitting the wrong people, from close by."

His mother was looking very upset. His father raised his eyebrows and said, "We've wandered back to the subject of bombing, Matt."

"I was simply answering your questions, sir."

"I'm afraid I asked the wrong question. Your mother is not able to take the answers impersonally. Catherine, there isn't the slightest chance of the North American Union being bombed. Tell her that, Matt—I think she'll believe you."

Matt had remained silent. His father had insisted, "Go ahead, Matt. Catherine, after all, it's *our* Patrol. For all practical purposes the other nations don't count. A majority of the Patrol officers are from North America. That's true, Matt, isn't it?"

"I've never thought about it. I guess so."

"Very well. Now, Catherine, you can't imagine Matt bombing Des Moines, now can you? And that is what it amounts to. Tell, her, Matt."

"But—Dad, you don't know what you are saying!"

"What? What's that, young man!"

"I—" Matt had looked around him, then had gotten up very suddenly and left the room.

His father came into his room some time later. "Matt?"

"Yes, sir?"

"Look, Matt, I let the conversation get out of hand tonight. I'm sorry and I don't blame you for getting upset. Your mother, you know. I try to protect her. Women get worked up so easily."

"It's all right, Dad. I'm sorry I walked out."

"No matter. Let's forget it. There's just one thing I feel we ought to get straight on. I know that you feel loyal to the Patrol and its ideals and it's good that you should, but—well, you are a little young still to see the political realities involved, but you must know that the Patrol could not bomb the North American Union."

"It would in a show down!"

"But there won't be any show down. Even if there were, you couldn't bomb your own people and neither could your shipmates."

Matt thought about it, fiercely. He remembered Commander Rivera—one of the Four, of the proud Tradition—how Rivera, sent down to reason with the official in his own capital, his very native city, had kept the trust. Suspecting that he might be held as hostage, he had left orders to go ahead with the attack unless he returned in person to cancel the orders. Rivera, whose body was decaying radioactive dust but whose name was mustered whenever a unit of the Patrol called the roll.

His father was still talking. "Of course, the Patrol has to patrol this continent just as it patrols all through the System. It would look bad, otherwise this is no reason to frighten women with an impossibility."

"I'd rather not talk about it, Dad."

Matt glanced at his watch and figured how long it would be until the *New Moon* reached Terra Station. He wished he could sleep, like the others. He was sure now what it was that had changed his mind about resigning and remaining in Des Moines. It was not a desire to emulate Rivera. No, it was an accumulation of things—all of them adding up to just one idea, that little Mattie didn't live there any more!

For the first few weeks after leave, Matt was too busy to fret. He had to get back into the treadmill, with more studying to do and less time to do it in. He was on the watch list for cadet officer of the watch now, and had more laboratory periods in electronics and nucleonics as well. Besides this he shared with other oldsters the responsibility for bringing up the youngster cadets. Before leave his evenings had usually been free for study, now he coached youngsters in astrogation three nights a week.

He was beginning to think that he would have to give up space polo, when he found himself elected captain of the Hog Alley team. Then he was busier than ever. He hardly thought about abstract problems until his next session with Lieutenant Wong.

"Good afternoon," his coach greeted him. "How's your class in astrogation?"

"Oh, that—It seems funny to be teaching it instead of flunking it."

"That's why you're stuck with it—you still remember what it was that used to stump you and why. How about atomics?"

"Well . . . I suppose I'll get by, but I'll never be an Einstein."

"I'd be amazed if you were. How are you getting along otherwise?" Wong waited.

"All right, I guess. Do you know, Mr. Wong—when I went on leave I didn't intend to come back."

"I rather thought so. That space-marines notion was just your way of dodging around, trying to avoid your real problem."

"Oh. Say, Mr. Wong—tell me straight. Are you a regular Patrol officer, or a psychiatrist?"

Wong almost grinned. "I'm a regular Patrol officer, Matt, but I've had the special training required for this job."

"Uh, I see. What was it I was running away from?"

"I don't know. You tell me."

"I don't know where to start."

"Tell me about your leave, then. We've got all afternoon."

"Yes, sir." Matt meandered along, telling as much as he could remember. "So you see," he concluded, "it was a lot of little things. I was home—but I was a stranger. We didn't talk the same language."

Wong chuckled. "I'm not laughing at you," he apologized. "It isn't funny. We all go through it—the discovery that there's no way to go back. It's part of growing up—but with spacemen it's an especially acute and savage process."

Matt nodded. "I'd already gotten that through my thick head. Whatever happens I won't go back—not to stay. I might go into the merchant service, but I'll stay in space."

"You're not likely to flunk out at this stage, Matt."

"Maybe not, but I don't know yet that the Patrol is the place for me. That's what bothers me."

"Well . . . can you tell me about it?"

Matt tried. He related the conversation with his father and his mother that had gotten them all upset. "It's this: if it comes to a show down, I'm expected to bomb my own home town. I'm not sure it's in me to do it. Maybe I don't belong here."

"Not likely to come up, Matt. Your father was right there."

"That's not the point. If a Patrol officer is loyal to his oath only when it's no skin off his own nose, then the whole system breaks down."

Wong waited before replying. "If the prospect of bombing your own town, your own family, didn't worry you, I'd have you out of this ship within the hour—you'd be an utterly dangerous man. The Patrol doesn't expect a man to have godlike perfection. Since men are imperfect, the Patrol works on the principle of calculated risk. The chance of a threat to the System coming from your home town in your lifetime is slight; the chance that you might be called on to carry out the attack is equally slight—you might be away on Mars. Taking the two chances together you have something close to zero.

"But if you did hit the jackpot, your commanding officer would probably lock you up in your room rather than take a chance on you."

Matt still looked troubled. "Not satisfied?" Wong went on. "Matt, you are suffering from a disease of youth—you expect moral problems to have nice, neat, black-and-white answers. Suppose you relax and let *me* worry about whether or not you have what it takes. Oh, some day you'll be caught in a squeeze and no one around to tell you the right answer. But *I* have to decide whether or not *you* can get the right answer when the problem comes along—and I don't even know what your problem will be! How would you like to be in my boots?"

Matt grinned sheepishly. "I wouldn't like it."

11.
P.R.S. AES TRIPLEX

Oscar, Matt, and Tex were gathered in their common room just before lunch when Pete bounced in. Literally so—he caromed off the door frame and zipped into the room, shouting, "Hey, fellows!"

Oscar grabbed his arms as he rebounded from the inner wall. "Cut your jet and ground—what's the excitement?"

Peter turned in the air and faced them. "The new 'Passed' list is posted!"

"Who's on it?"

"Don't know—just heard about it. Come on!"

They streamed after him. Tex came abreast of Matt and said, "I don't know why I should be getting in a sweat—*I* won't be on it."

"Pessimist!" They turned out of Hog Alley, went inboard three decks, and forward. There was a clot of cadets gathered around the bulletin board outside the watch office. They crowded in.

Pete spotted his own name at once. "Look!" The paragraph read: "Armand, Pierre—temporary duty P.R.S. *Charles' Wain*, rpt. Terr.St., dtch. Leda, Gnymd, d.&a.o."

"Look!" he repeated. "*I'm going home*—'delay and await orders.' "

Oscar patted his shoulder. "Congratulations, Pete—that's swell. Now if you will kindly get your carcass out of the way—"

Matt spoke up. "I'm on it!"

"What ship?" asked Tex.

"The *Aes Triplex.*"

Oscar turned at this. "*What* ship?"

"*Aes Triplex.*"

"Matt—that's *my* ship. We're shipmates, boy!"

Tex turned disconsolately away. "Just as I said—no 'Jarman.' I'll be here five years, ten years, fifteen years—old and grizzled. Promise to write on my birthday."

"Gee, Tex, I'm sorry!" Matt tried to swallow his own elation.

"Tex, did you look on the other half of the list?" Pete wanted to know.

"What other half? Huh?"

Pete pointed. Tex dove back into the swarm; presently he reappeared. "What do you know? They passed me!"

"Probably didn't want to expose another class of youngsters to you. What ship?"

"P.R.S. *Oak Ridge*. Say, you and Oscar got the same ship?"

"Yep—the *Aes Triplex*."

"Rank discrimination, that's what it is. Well, come on, we'll be late to lunch."

They ran into Girard Burke in the passageway. Tex stopped him. "No use bothering to look, Stinky. Your name's not on the list."

"What list? Oh, you mean the 'Passed' list. Don't bother me, children—you're talking to a free man."

"So they finally bounced you?"

"Like fun! Resignation accepted, effective today. I'm going in business with my father."

"Going to build sky junk, eh? I don't envy you."

"No, we're starting an export line, with our own ships. The next time you see me, just remember to address me as 'Captain.' " He moved away.

"I'll 'captain' him," Tex muttered. "I'll bet he resigned by request."

"Maybe not," conceded Matt. "Girard is a smooth character. Well, we've seen the last of him."

"And a good thing, too."

Tex was missing after lunch. He showed up after nearly two hours. "I worked it. Shake hands with your new shipmate."

"Huh? No fooling!"

"Fact. First I located Dvorak and convinced him that he would rather have a ship in the circum-Terra patrol than the *Aes Triplex*—so he could see his girl oftener. Then I went to see the Commandant and pointed out to him that you guys were used to having the benefit of my advice and would be lost without it. That's all there was to it. The Commandant saw the wisdom of my words and approved the swap with Dvorak."

"Not for that reason, I'll bet," Matt answered. "Probably he wanted me to continue to look out for you."

Tex took on an odd look. "Do you know, Matt, you aren't so far wrong."

"Really? I was just kidding."

"What he did say was that he thought Cadet Jensen would be a good influence on me. What do you think of that, Oscar?"

Oscar snorted. "If I've reached the place where I'm a good influence on anybody, it's time I cultivated some new vices."

"I'd be glad to help."

"I don't want you, I want your Uncle Bodie—there's a man of the world."

Three weeks later, at Moon Base, Oscar and Matt were settling into their stateroom in the *Aes Triplex*. Matt was not feeling his best; the previous evening at Tycho Colony had been late and noisy. They had taken the last possible shuttle to Moon Base.

The ship's phone in their room sounded; Matt answered it to get the squeal out of his ears. "Yes? Cadet Dodson speaking—"

"Officer of the watch. Is Jensen there too?"

"Yes, sir."

"Both of you report to the Captain."

"Aye aye, sir." Matt turned a troubled face to Oscar. "What'll I do, Oz? The rest of my uniforms are over at the base tailor shop—and this one I've got on looks as if I had slept in it."

"You did. Wear one of mine."

"Thanks, but it would fit me like socks on a rooster. Do you suppose I have time to run over and pick up my clean ones?"

"Hardly!"

Matt rubbed the stubble on his chin. "I ought to shave, anyhow."

"Look," said Oscar, "if I'm any judge of skippers, you'll do better to show up naked as an oyster and with a beard down to here, than to keep him waiting. Let's get going."

The door opened and Tex stuck his head in. "Say—did you guys get a call to report to the Old Man?"

"Yes—Tex, can you lend me a clean uniform?"

Tex could. Matt crossed the passageway to Tex's tiny room and changed. He belted in tightly at the waist, distributed the wrinkles in back, and hoped for the best. The three headed for the cabin.

"I'm glad I don't have to report by myself," Tex announced. "I'm nervous."

"Relax," Oscar advised. "Captain McAndrews is supposed to be a very human sort of a guy."

"Hadn't you heard? McAndrews is detached—busted his ankle. At the last minute the Department ordered Captain Yancey to command the expedition."

"Yancey!" Oscar let out a low whistle. "Oh, my sore feet!"

"What's the matter, Oscar?" Matt demanded. "You know him?"

"My father knew him. Father had the fresh-foods contract for the port at New Auckland when Yancey—Lieutenant Yancey, then—was portmaster." They stopped outside the commanding officer's cabin.

"That ought to give you an inside track."

"Not likely! They didn't get along."

"I wonder if I did right," Tex mused darkly, "when I wangled the swap from the *Oak Ridge?*"

"Too late to fret. Well, I guess we might—" Oscar stopped speaking, for the door in front of them suddenly opened and they found themselves facing the commanding officer. He was tall, wide-shouldered, and flat-hipped, and so handsome that he looked like a television star playing a Patrol officer.

"Well?" he snapped. "Don't stand chatting outside my door. Come in!"

They filed in silently. Captain Yancey sat down, facing them, and looked them over, one after the other. "What's the trouble, gentlemen?" he said presently. "Are you all struck dumb?"

Tex found his voice. "Cadet Jarman, sir, reporting to the Captain." Yancey's eyes flicked over to Matt.

Matt wet his lips. "Cadet Dodson, sir."

"Cadet Jensen, sir, reporting as ordered." The officer looked at Oscar sharply, then spoke to him in Venerian.

"Do these ears detect some echo of the speech of the Fair Planet?"

"It is true, thou old and wise one."

"Never could stand that silly talk," Yancey commented, relapsing into Basic. "I won't ask you where you are from, but—is your father in the provisions racket?"

"My father is a food wholesaler, sir."

"I thought so." The Captain continued to look at him for a moment, then turned to Matt. "Now, Mister, what is the idea of the masquerade? You look like a refugee from an emigrant ship."

Matt tried to explain; Yancey cut him short. "I'm not interested in excuses. I keep a taut ship. Remember that."

"Aye aye, sir."

The Captain settled back and struck a cigarette. "Now, gentlemen, you are no doubt wondering as to why I sent for you. I must admit to a slight curiosity as to the sort of product the old school is turning out. In my day, it was a real course of sprouts and no nonsense about it. But now I understand that the psychologists have taken over and the old rules are all changed."

He leaned forward and fixed Matt with his eyes. "They aren't changed here, gentlemen. In my ship, the old rules still obtain."

No one answered. Yancey waited, then went on, "The regulations state that you shall pay a social call on your commanding officer within twenty-four hours after reporting to a new ship or station. Please consider that the social call has commenced. Sit down, gentlemen. Mr. Dodson, you will find coffee over there on your left. Will you please favor me by pouring it?"

Forty minutes later they left, feeling quite confused. Yancey had demonstrated that he could put them most charmingly at their ease and had displayed a dry, warm wit and a gift for telling anecdotes. Matt decided that he liked him.

But just as they left Yancey glanced at his clock and said, "I'll see you later, Mr. Dodson—in fifteen minutes."

Once they were outside Tex demanded, "What's he want to see you for, Matt?"

"Can't you guess?" answered Oscar. "Look, Matt, I'll tear over to the tailor shop for you—you can't do that and shave, too, not in fifteen minutes."

"You're a lifesaver, Oz!"

P.R.S. *Aes Triplex* blasted from Moon Base thirteen hours later in a trajectory intended to produce an elliptical orbit with its far end in the asteroid belt. Her orders were to search for the missing P.R.S. *Pathfinder*. The *Pathfinder* had been engaged in radar-charting a sector of the asteroid belt for the Uranographic Office of the Patrol. Her mission had taken her beyond the range of ship-type radio; nevertheless she should have reported in by radio nearly six months earlier, at which time she should have been approaching conjunction with Mars. But Deimos Station, around Mars, had been unable to raise the *Pathfinder*; she was presumed lost.

The possible locations of the *Pathfinder* were a moving zone in space, defined by using geometry, ballistics, the characteristics of the ship, her mission, and her last reported location, course, and speed. This zone was divided into four sectors and the *Aes Triplex* was to search one sector while three other Patrol vessels covered the other sectors. The joint task was designated "Operation Samaritan" but each ship was independent as they necessarily would be too far apart to be commanded as a task force.

While searching, the rescue vessels would continue the *Pathfinder*'s mission of charting the space drift that clutters the asteroid belt.

In addition to the commanding officer and the three cadets, the company of the *Aes Triplex* included Commander Hartley Miller, executive officer and astrogator, Lieutenant Novak, Chief Engineer, Lieutenant Thurlow, Bomb Officer, Lieutenant Brunn, Communications Officer, Sublieutenants Peters, Gomez, and Cleary, assistant engineer and communications watch officers respectively, and Dr. Pickering, ship's surgeon, along to care for survivors—if any were found.

The ship contained no marines, unless one chooses to count Dr. Pickering, who was technically a staff corps member of the marines rather than a member of the Patrol. Every task in the ship would be performed by the officers or cadets. Time was when the lowliest subaltern in an infantry regiment had his personal servant, but servants are too expensive a luxury in terms of fuel and space and food to lift through millions of miles of space. Besides that, some few manual tasks are a welcome relief from boredom in the endless monotony of space; even the undesirable chore of cleaning the refresher was taken in turn by the entire ship's company, in accordance with custom, except for the Captain, the Executive Officer, and the Surgeon.

Captain Yancey assigned Lieutenant Thurlow as training officer who in turn set up the jobs of assistant astrogator, junior communication watch officer, junior assistant engineer, and assistant bomb officer and arranged a schedule of rotation among these— quite unnecessary—positions. It was also Mr. Thurlow's job to see to it that Matt, Oscar, and Tex made intensive use of the one study projector available to the cadets.

The Executive Officer assigned other tasks not directly concerned with formal training. Matt was appointed the ship's "farmer." As the hydroponics tanks supply both fresh air and green vegetables to a ship he was responsible for the ship's air-conditioning and shared with Lieutenant Brunn the tasks of the ship's mess.

Theoretically every ration taken aboard a Patrol vessel is pre-cooked and ready for eating as soon as it is taken out of freeze and subjected to the number of seconds, plainly marked on the package, of high-frequency heating required. Actually many Patrol officers fancy themselves as chefs. Mr. Brunn was one and his results justified his conceit—the *Aes Triplex* set a good table.

Matt found that Mr. Brunn expected more of the "farm" than that the green plants should scavenge carbon dioxide from the air and replace it with oxygen; the mess officer wanted tiny green scallions, fragrant fresh mint, cherry tomatoes, Brussels sprouts, new potatoes. Matt began to wonder whether it wouldn't have been simpler to have stayed in Iowa and grown tall corn.

When he started in as air-conditioning officer Matt was not even sure how to take a carbon-dioxide count, but shortly he was testing his growing solutions and adding capsules of salts with the confidence and speed of a veteran, thanks to Brunn and to spool #62A8134 from the ship's files—"Simplified Hydroponics for Spaceships, with Growth Charts and Additives Formulae." He began to enjoy tending his "farm."

Until human beings give up the habit of eating, spaceships on long cruises must carry about seven hundred pounds of food per man per year. The green plants grown in a ship's air-conditioner enable the stores officer to get around this limitation to some extent, as the growing plants will cycle the same raw materials—air, carbon dioxide, and water—over and over again with only the addition of quite small quantities of such salts as potassium nitrate, iron sulphate, and calcium phosphate.

The balanced economy of a spaceship is much like that of a planet; energy is used to make the cycles work but the same raw materials are used over and over again. Since beefsteak and many other foods can't be grown conveniently aboard ship some foods have to be carried and the ship tends to collect garbage, waste paper, and other trash. Theoretically this could be processed back into the cycles of balanced biological economy, but in practice this is too complicated.

However, *all* mass in an atomic powered ship can be used, if desired, as reaction mass, mass for the rocket jet. The radioactive materials in the power pile of an atom-powered ship are not themselves used up to any great extent; instead they heat other materials to extreme temperatures and expel them out the rocket tube at very high speeds, as a sort of "steam" jet.

Even though turnip greens and such can be used in the jet, the primary purpose of the "farm" is to take the carbon dioxide out of the air. For this purpose each man in the ship must be balanced by about ten square feet of green plant leaf. Lieutenant Brunn, with his steady demands for variety in fresh foods, usually caused Matt to have too much growing at one time; the air in the ship would get too fresh and the plants would start to fail for lack of carbon dioxide to feed on. Matt had to watch his CO_2 count and sometimes build it up by burning waste paper or plant cuttings.

Brunn kept a file of seeds in his room; Matt went there one "day" (ship's time) to draw out Persian melon seeds and set a crop. Brun told him to help himself. Matt rummaged away, then said, "For the love of Pete! Look at this, Mr. Brunn."

"Huh?" The officer looked at the package Matt held. The outside was marked, "Seeds, melon, Persian—jumbo fancy, stock #12-Q4728-a"; the envelope inside read "Seed, pansies, giant variegated."

Brunn shook his head. "Let that be a lesson, Dodson—never trust a stock clerk—or you'll wind up half way to Pluto with a gross of brass spittoons when you ordered blank spacecharts."

"What'll I substitute? Cantaloupe?"

"Let's grow some watermelon—the Old Man likes watermelon."

Matt left with watermelon seed but he took along the truant pansy seeds.

Eight weeks later he devised a vase of sorts by covering a bowl from the galley with the same sponge-cellulose sheet which was used to restrain the solutions used in his farming, thereby to keep said solutions from floating around the "farm" compartment during free fall. He filled his vase with water, arranged his latest crop therein, and clipped the whole to the mess table as a centerpiece.

Captain Yancey smiled broadly when he appeared for dinner and saw the gay display of pansies. "Well, gentlemen," he applauded, "this is most delightful. All the comforts of home!" He looked along the table at Matt. "I suppose we have you to thank for this, Mr. Dodson?"

"Yes, sir." Matt's ears turned pink.

"A lovely idea. Gentlemen, I move that we divest Mr. Dodson of the plebeian title of 'farmer' and designate him 'horticulturalist extraordinary.' Do I hear a second?" There were nine "ayes" and a loud "no" from Commander Miller. A second ballot, proposed by

the Chief Engineer, required the Executive Officer to finish his
meal in the galley.

Lieutenant Brunn explained the mishap that resulted in the
flower garden. Captain Yancey frowned. "You've checked the rest
of your supply of seeds, of course, Mr. Brunn?"

"Uh, no, sir."

"Then do so." Lieutenant Brunn immediately started to leave
the table. "—after dinner," added the Captain. Brunn resumed his
place.

"That puts me in mind of something that happened to me
when I was 'farmer' in the old *Percival Lowell*—the one before
the present one," Yancey went on. "We had touched at Venus
South Pole and had managed somehow to get a virus infection, a
sort of rust, into the 'farm'—don't look so superior, Mr. Jensen;
someday you'll come a cropper with a planet that is new to you!"

"Me, sir? I wasn't looking superior."

"No? Smiling at the pansies, no doubt?"

"Yes, sir."

"Hmmph! As I was saying, we got this rust infection and about
ten days out I didn't have any more farm than an Eskimo. I
cleaned the place out, sterilized, and reseeded. Same story. The infection was all through the ship and I couldn't chase it down. We
finished that trip on preserved foods and short rations and I wasn't
allowed to eat at the table the rest of the trip." He smiled to himself, then shouted at the galley door, "How you getting along in
there, Red?"

The Executive Officer appeared in the doorway, a spoon in
one hand, covered dish in the other. "Fine," he answered in a muffled voice, "I just ate your dessert, Captain."

Lieutenant Brunn shouted, "Hey! Commander! Stop! Don't!
Those berries are for breakfast."

"Too late." Commander Miller wiped his mouth.

"Captain?"

"Yes, Dodson?"

"What did you do about air-conditioning?"

"Well. Mister, what would you have done?"

Matt studied it. "Well, sir, I would have jury-rigged something
to take the Cee-Oh-Two out of the air."

"Precisely. I exhausted the air from an empty compartment,
suited up, and drilled a couple of holes to the outside. Then I did a
piping job to carry foul air out of the dark side of the ship in a

fractional still arrangement-freeze out the water first, then freeze
out the carbon dioxide. Pesky thing was always freezing up solid
and forcing me to tinker with it. But it worked well enough to get
us home." Yancey backed away from the table. "Hartley, if you're
through making a pig of yourself, let's run over that meteor-
layout. I've got an idea."

The ship was approaching the orbit of Mars and soon would
be in the comparatively hazardous zone of the asteroids and their
company of space drift. Matt was rotated, in turn, to assistant astrogator, but continued as ship's farmer. Tex looked him up one
day in the hydroponics compartment. "Hey! Hayseed—"

"Hey yourself, Tex."

"Got the south forty plowed yet? Looks like rain." Tex pretended to study the blinking lights used to stimulate plant growth,
then looked away. "Never mind—I'm here on business. The Old
Man wants to see you."

"Well, for heaven's sake, why didn't you say so, instead of
banging your choppers?" Matt stopped what he was doing and
hurriedly started climbing into his uniform. Because of the heat
and the humidity in the "farm" Matt habitually worked there bare
naked, both for comfort and to save his clothes.

"Well, I did tell you, didn't I?"

The Captain was in his cabin. "Cadet Dodson, sir."

"So I see." Yancey held up a sheet of paper. "Dodson, I've just
written a letter to the Department, to be transmitted as soon as we
are in radio contact, recommending that fresh flowers be grown in
all ships, as a means of stimulating morale. You are credited
therein as the originator of the idea."

"Er . . . thank you, sir."

"Not at all. Anything that relieves the tedium, the boredom,
the barrenness of life in deep space is in the interest of the Patrol.
We have enough people going space-happy as it is. Flowers are
considered good for psychotics on Earth; perhaps they will help to
keep spacemen from going wacky. Enough of that—I've a question to ask you."

"Yes, sir?"

"I want to know why in the devil you were spending your time
growing pansies when you are behind in your study schedule?"

Matt did not have anything to say.

"I've been looking over the reports Mr. Thurlow sends me and
I find that both Mr. Jensen and Mr. Jarman are covering more
ground than you are. In the past few weeks they have pulled 'way

ahead of you. It's a fine thing to have hobbies but your duty is to study."

"Yes, sir."

"I've marked your performance unsatisfactory for this quarter; you have the next quarter in which to make up the deficiency. By the way, have you made up your mind about your next move?"

Matt did a double-take, then realized that the Captain had changed the subject to chess; he and Matt were fighting it out for first place in the ship's tournament. "Uh, yes, sir—I've decided to take your pawn."

"I thought so." Yancey reached behind him; Matt heard the pieces click into their sockets as the Captain made the move on his own board. "Wait till you see what's going to happen to your queen!"

The speeds of the asteroids, flying boulders, rocks, sand, and space drift that infest the area between Mars and Jupiter vary from about fifteen miles per second near Mars to about eight miles per second near Jupiter. The orbits of this flying junkyard are erratically inclined to the plane of the ecliptic an average of about nine degrees and some of the orbits are quite eccentric as well.

All this means that a ship on a circular orbit, headed "east," or with the traffic, may expect the possibility of side-swiping collisions at relative speeds averaging two miles per second, with crashes remotely possible at double that speed.

Two miles per second is only about twice the muzzle velocity of a good sporting rifle. With respect to small stuff, sand and gravel, the *Aes Triplex* was built to take it. Before the ship reached the danger zone, an all-hands chore in space suits took place; armor-plate segments, as thick as the skin of the ship, were bolted over the ship's quartz ports, leaving only the eyes of the astrogational instruments and the radar antennae exposed.

To guard against larger stuff Captain Yancey set up a meteor-watch much tighter than is usual in most parts of space. Eight radars scanned all space through a global 360°. The only condition necessary for collision is that the other object hold a steady bearing—no fancy calculation is involved. The only action necessary then to avoid collision is to change your own speed, any direction, any amount. This is perhaps the only case where theory of piloting is simple.

Commander Miller put the cadets and the sublieutenants on a continuous heel-and-toe watch, scanning the meteor-guard 'scopes. Even if the human being failed to note a steady bearing the radars would "see" it, for they were so rigged that, if a "blip" burned in at one spot on the screen, thereby showing a steady bearing, an alarm would sound—and the watch officer would cut in the jet, fast!

However, even the asteroid belt is very empty space indeed; the chances were strongly against collision with anything larger than a grain of sand. The only difference in the *Aes Triplex*, aside from the increased work for the junior officers, was a ship's order directing all hands to strap down when sleeping, instead of floating loosely and comfortably about, so that the sleeper would not break his neck in case of sudden acceleration.

P.R.S. *Aes Triplex* was equipped with two jeeps, nestled in hangar pockets—quite ordinary short-range, chemically-powered rockets except that they were equipped with search radar as powerful as the ship's. When they reached their search area a pilot and co-pilot were assigned to each jeep—and a second crew also, as each rocket was to remain away from the ship a week at a time, then swap crews and go out again.

Lieutenants Brunn, Thurlow, and Novak, and Sublieutenant Peters were designated pilots. A cadet was assigned to each senior lieutenant and Sublieutenant Gomez was teamed with Sublieutenant Peters. Matt drew Lieutenant Thurlow.

Dr. Pickering took over the mess. That left Sublieutenant Cleary as "George," the man who does everything—an impossibility, since meteor-guard and search watches would have to be kept up. Consequently the two jeep crews not actually in space had to help out even during their week of rest.

Each Monday the ship placed the jeep rockets on station so that the three vessels would sweep the largest possible volume of space, with their search fields barely overlapping. The placement was made by the mother ship, so that the jeep would be left with full tanks in the unhappy event that she was not picked up—and thereby have enough fuel to shape an orbit toward the inner planets, if need be.

12.
P.R.S. *PATHFINDER*

Matt took along a supply of study spools on his first week of search intending to play them on the jeep's tiny, earphones-type viewer. He did not get much chance; four hours out of eight he had to keep his eyes glued to the search scopes. During the four hours off watch he had to sleep, eat, attend to chores, and study, if possible.

Besides that, Lieutenant Thurlow liked to talk.

The bomb officer was expecting Earth-side duty in postgraduate study at the end of the cruise. "And then I'll have to make up my mind, Matt. Do I stay in and make physics a part-time specialty, or resign and go in for research?"

"It depends on what you want to do."

"Trite but true. I think I want to be a scientist, full time—but after a few years the Patrol becomes a father and a mother to you. I don't know. That pile of rock is creeping up on us—I can see it through the port now."

"It is, eh?" Matt moved forward until he, too, could see the undersized boulder that Thurlow had been watching by radar. It was of irregular shape, a pattern of sunlight and sharp, dark shadow.

"Mister Thurlow," said Matt, "look—about the middle. Doesn't that look like striation to you?"

"Could be. Some specimens have been picked up that were definitely sedimentary rock. That was the first proof that the asteroids used to be a planet, you know."

"I thought that Goodman's integrations were the first proof?"

"Nope, you're switched around. Goodman wasn't able to run

his checks until the big ballistic computer at Terra Station was built."

"I knew that—I just had it backwards, I guess." The theory that the asteroids had once been a planet, between Mars and Jupiter, was denied for many years because their orbits showed no interrelation, i.e., if a planet had blown to bits the orbits should intersect at the point of the explosion. Professor Goodman, using the giant, strain-free computer, had shown that the lack of relationship was caused by the perturbations through the ages of the other planets acting on the asteroids.

He had assigned a date to the disaster, nearly half a billion years ago, and had calculated as well that most of the ruined planet had escaped from the System entirely. The debris around them represented about one per cent of the lost planet.

Lieutenant Thurlow measured the angular width of the fragment, noted its distance by radar, and recorded the result as gross size. The rock, large as it was, was too small to merit investigation of its orbit; it was simply included in the space-drift survey. Smaller objects were merely listed while collisions with minute particles were counted by an electronic circuit hooked to the hull of the jeep.

"The thing that bothers me," went on Thurlow, "about getting out is this— Matt, have you noticed the difference between people in the Patrol and people not in the Patrol?"

"Haven't I, though!"

"What is the difference?"

"The difference? Uh, why, we're spacemen and they're not. I guess it's a matter of how big your world is."

"Partly. But don't get carried away by mere size. A hundred million miles of empty space isn't significant—if it's empty. No, Matt, the split goes deeper. We've given the human race a hundred years of peace, and now there is no one left who remembers war. They've come to accept peace and comfort as the normal way of life. But it isn't. The human animal has millions of years of danger and starving and death behind him; the past century is just a flicker of an eyelash in his history. But only the Patrol seems aware of it."

"Would you abolish the Patrol?"

"Oh, my, no, Matt! But I wish there were some way to make people realize by how thin a barrier the jungle has been shut out. And another thing, too—" Thurlow grinned sheepishly. "—I wish they had some understanding of what we are. The taxpayer's hired man, that's what they think of us."

Matt nodded. "They think we're some sort of traffic cop. There is a man back home who sells used copters—asked me why Patrolmen should be pensioned when they retire. He said that he hadn't been able to sit back and take it easy at thirty-five and he didn't see why he should have to support somebody else who did." Matt looked puzzled. "At the same time he sort of glamorized the Patrol—wants his son to be a cadet. I don't understand it."

"That's it. To them we are a kind of expensive, useless prize pet—their property. They don't understand that we are not for hire. The sort of guardian you can hire is worth about as much as the sort of wife you can buy."

The following week Matt found time to look up what the ship's library afforded on the subject of the exploded planet. There was not much—dry statistics on sizes of asteroids, fragments, and particles, distributional and orbital data, Goodman's calculations summarized. Nothing at all about what he wanted to know—how it happened!—nothing but some fine-spun theories.

He took it up with Thurlow the next time they were out on Patrol. The lieutenant shrugged. "What do you expect, Matt?"

"I don't know, but more than I found."

"Our time scale is all wrong for us to learn much. Suppose you pick out one of the spools you've been studying—here, this one." The officer held out one marked "Social structures of the Martian aborigines." "Now suppose you examine a couple of frames in the middle. Can you reconstruct the thousands and thousands of frames that come before it, just by logic?"

"Naturally not."

"That's the situation. If the race manages to keep from blowing its top for a few million years, maybe we'll begin to find out some things. So far, we don't even know what questions to ask."

Matt was dissatisfied, but had no answer ready. Thurlow knit his brows. "Maybe we aren't built to ask the right questions. You know the Martian 'double-world' idea—"

"Certainly, but I don't understand it."

"Who does? Let's forget the usual assumption that a Martian is talking in religious symbols when he says that we live just on 'one side' while he lives on 'both sides.' Suppose that what he means is as real as butter and eggs, that he really does live in two worlds at the same time and that we are in the one he regards as unimportant. If you accept that, then it accounts for the Martian being unwilling to waste time talking with us, or trying to explain things to us. He isn't being stuffy, he's being reasonable. Would you waste time trying to explain rainbows to an earthworm?"

"The cases aren't parallel."

"Maybe they are to a Martian. An earthworm can't even see, much less have a color sense. If you accept the 'double world' as real, then to a Martian we just don't have the proper senses to be able to ask the right questions. Why bother with us?"

The radio squealed for attention. Thurlow glanced toward it and said, "Someone calling, Matt. See who it is and tell 'em we don't want any."

"Okay." Matt flipped the switch and answered, "Jeep One, *Triplex*—go ahead."

"*Triplex* calling," came Sublieutenant Cleary's familiar voice. "Stand by to be picked up."

"Huh? Cut the comedy—we're only three days out."

"Stand by to be picked up—official. Jeep Two has found the *Pathfinder*."

"The deuce you say! Did you hear that, Mr. Thurlow? Did you hear that?"

It was true; Peters and Gomez, in the other jeep, had discovered the missing ship, almost by accident. The *Pathfinder* was found anchored to a smallish asteroid about a mile in greatest dimension. Since it was a listed body, 1987-CD, the crew of the jeep had paid little attention to it, until its rotation brought the *Pathfinder* into view.

With fine consideration Captain Yancey had elected to pick up Thurlow and Dodson before rendezvousing with the second jeep. Once they were inside, the *Aes Triplex* moved toward 1987-CD and matched orbits. Sublieutenant Peters had elected to expend some of his get-away fuel and had matched orbits also.

Matt fidgeted while the second jeep was brought into the ship. He could see nothing, since the ports were covered, and for the moment had no assigned duties. With maddening deliberation Captain Yancey secured his ship to the *Pathfinder*, sending a line over by Sublieutenant Gomez. The rest of the ship's company was crowded into the control room. Tex and Matt took the opportunity to question Sublieutenant Peters.

"Couldn't tell much," he informed them. "Off hand, she looks undamaged, but the door of the lock was standing open."

"Any chance anyone is alive inside?" asked Tex.

"Possible. Hardly likely."

Captain Yancey looked around. "Pipe down," he ordered. "This is a control room, not a sewing circle." When he had finished he ordered Peters and Gomez to come with him; the three suited up and left the ship.

They were gone about an hour. When they returned the Captain called them all into the mess room. "I am sorry to tell you, gentlemen, that none of our comrades is alive."

He went on heavily, "There is not much doubt as to what happened. The outer armored door of the lock was open and undamaged. The inner door had been punched through by a missile about the size of my fist, producing explosive decompression in the connecting compartments. Apparently they had had the enormous bad luck to have a meteor enter the ship through the door just as it was opened."

"Wait a minute, Skipper," objected Miller. "Was every airtight door in the ship wide open? One rock shouldn't have done the trick."

"We couldn't get into the after part of the ship; it still holds pressure. But we could reconstruct what happened, because we could count the bodies—seven of them, the entire ship's company. They were all near the lock and not in spacesuits, except for one man in the lock—his suit was pierced by a fragment apparently. The others seem to have been gathered at the lock, waiting for him to come in." Yancey looked grave. "Red, I think we are going to have to put in a recommended technical order over this— something to require personnel to spread out while suit operations are going on, so that an accident to the lock won't affect the entire ship's company."

Miller frowned. "I suppose so, Captain. Might be awkward to comply with, sometimes, in a small ship."

"It's awkward to lose your breath, too. Now about the investigation—you'll be the president, Red, and Novak and Brunn will be your other two members. The rest of us will remain in the ship until the board has completed its work. When they have finished and have removed from the *Pathfinder* anything needed as evidence I will allow sufficient time for each of you to satisfy his curiosity."

"How about the surgeon, Captain? I want him for an expert witness."

"Okay, Red. Dr. Pickering, you go with the board."

The cadets crowded into the stateroom shared by Matt and Oscar. "Can you beat it?" said Tex. "Of all the cheap tricks! We have to sit in here, a week or ten days, maybe, while a board measures how big a hole there is in the door."

"Forget it, Tex," advised Oscar. "I figure the Old Man didn't want you carving your initials in things, or maybe snagging the busted door for a souvenir, before they found out what the score was."

"Oh, nuts!"

"Quit crabbing. He promised you that you could snoop around and take pictures and satisfy your ghoulish appeties as soon as the board is finished. In the meantime, enjoy the luxury of eight hours of sleep for a change. No watches, none of any sort."

"Say, that's right!" agreed Matt. "I hadn't thought about it, but there's no point in watching for rocks when you're tied down and can't duck."

"As the crew of the *Pathfinder* know only too well."

Last Muster was held for the *Pathfinder* on the following day. The bodies themselves had been sealed into a compartment of the dead ship; muster took place in the wardroom of the *Aes Triplex*. It was rather lengthy, as it was necessary to read the services of three different faiths before the Captain concluded with the Patrol's own all-inclusive farewell: "*Now we shape our orbit home—*"

It so happened that there were just enough persons present to answer the roll. The *Aes Triplex*'s company was a captain and eleven others. For the *Pathfinder* there were exactly eleven—six patrol officers, one civilian planetologist, and the Four who are present at every muster. Captain Yancey called off the *Pathfinder*'s roll and the others answered, one after the other, from Commander Miller down to Tex—while *The Long Watch*, muted down to a requiem, played softly over the ship's speaker system.

Matt found his throat almost too dry to answer. Tex's chubby cheeks ran with tears and he made no effort to wipe them.

Lieutenant Brunn was a source of information for the first couple of days of the investigation. He described the *Pathfinder* as in good shape, except for the damaged door. On the third day he suddenly shut up. "The Captain doesn't want the board's findings discussed until he has had time to study them."

Matt passed the word on to the others. "What's cooking?" demanded Tex. "What can there possibly be to be secret about?"

"How should I know?"

"I've got a theory," said Oscar.

"Huh? What? Spill it."

"The Captain wants to prove a man can't die of curiosity. He figures that you are a perfect test case."

"Oh, go soak your head."

Captain Yancey called them all together again the following day. "Gentlemen, I appreciate your patience. I have not wanted to discuss what was found in the *Pathfinder* until I had time to decide what should be done about it. It comes to this: the planetologist with the *Pathfinder*, Professor Thorwald, came to the unmistakable conclusion that the disrupted planet was inhabited."

The room started to buzz. "Quiet, please! There are samples of fossil-bearing rock in the *Pathfinder*, but there are other exhibits as well, which Professor Thorwald concluded—Dr. Pickering and Commander Miller and I concur—concluded to be artifacts, items worked by intelligent hands.

"That fact alone would be enough to send a dozen ships scurrying into the asteroid belt," he went on. "It is probably the most important discovery in System-study since they opened the diggings in Luna. But Professor Thorwald formed another conclusion even more startling. With the aid of the ship's bomb officer, using the rate-of-radioactive-decay method, he formed a tentative hypothesis that the planet—he calls it Planet Lucifer—was disrupted by artificial nuclear explosion. In other words, they did it themselves."

The silence was broken only by the soft sighing of the room's ventilators. Then Thurlow exploded, "But Captain, that's impossible!"

Captain Yancey looked at him. "Do you know all the answers, young man? I'm sure I don't."

"I'm sorry, sir."

"In this case I wouldn't even venture to have an opinion. I'm not competent. However, gentlemen, if it be true, as Professor Thorwald certainly thought it was, then I hardly need point out to you that we have more reason than ever to be proud of our Patrol—and our responsibility is even heavier than we had thought.

"Now to business—I am very reluctant to leave the *Pathfinder* where she is. Aside from sentimental reasons she is a ship of the Patrol and she is worth a good many millions. I think we can repair her and take her back."

13.
LONG WAY HOME

Matt took part in the rebuilding of the inner door of the *Pathfinder*'s airlock and the checks for airtightness, all under the careful eye of the chief engineer. There was little other damage inside the ship. The rock, or meteor, that had punched the gaping hole in the inner door had expended most of its force in so doing; an inner bulkhead had to be patched and a few dents smoothed. The outer, armored door was quite untouched; it was clear that the invader, by bad chance, had come in while the outer door was standing open.

The plants in the air-conditioner had died for lack of attention and carbon dioxide. Matt took over the job while the others helped in the almost endless chores of checking every circuit, every instrument, every gadget necessary to the ship's functioning. It was a job which should have been done at a repair base and could not have been accomplished if there had actually been much wrong.

Oscar and Matt squeezed an hour out of sleep to explore 1987-CD, a job that mixed mountain climbing with suit-jet work. The asteroid had a gravitational field, of course, but even a mass the size of a small mountain is negligible compared with that of a planet. They simply could not feel it; muscles used to opposing the tenacious pull of robust Terra made nothing of the frail pull of 1987-CD.

At last the *Pathfinder* was cast loose and her drive tested by a scratch crew consisting of Captain Yancey at the controls and Lieutenant Novak in the power room. The *Aes Triplex* lay off a few miles, waited until she blasted her jet for a few seconds, then joined her. The two ships tied together and Captain Yancey and the chief engineer came back into the *Aes Triplex*.

"She's all yours, Hartley," he announced. "Test her yourself, then take over when you are ready."

"If she suits you she suits me. With your permission, sir, I'll transfer my crew now."

"So? Very well, Captain—take command and carry out your orders. Log it, Mister," Captain Yancey added, over his shoulder to the officer of the watch.

Thirty minutes later the split crew passed out through the airlock of the *Aes Triplex* and into the airlock of the other. P.R.S. *Pathfinder* was back in commission.

Remaining with the *Aes Triplex* was Captain Yancey, Lieutenant Thurlow, now executive officer and astrogator, Sublieutenant Peters, now chief engineer, Cadet Jensen, chief communications officer, and Cadets Jarman and Dodson, watch officers, all departments— and Dr. Pickering, ship's surgeon.

Commander Miller, captain of the *Pathfinder*, had one less officer than Captain Yancey, but all of his officers were experienced; Captain Yancey had elected to burden himself with the cadets. He would have assumed command of the derelict himself and taken his chances with her, except for one point—the law did not permit it. He could place a master aboard her and put her back in commission, but there was no one present with authority to relieve him of his own ship—he was prisoner of his own unique status, commanding officer operating alone.

In her original flight plan it had been intended that the *Pathfinder* should make port at Deimos, Mars, when Mars overtook her and was in a favorable position. The delay caused by the disaster made the planned orbit quite out of the question; Mars would not be at the rendezvous. Furthermore Captain Yancey wanted to get the astounding evidence contained in the *Pathfinder* to Terra Base as quickly as possible; there was little point in sending it to the outpost on Mars' outer satellite.

Accordingly reaction mass was pumped from the *Aes Triplex* to the smaller ship until her tanks were full and a fast, fairly direct, though uneconomical, orbit to Earth was plotted for her. The *Aes Triplex*, using an economical "Hohmann"-type,* much longer orbit, would mosey in past the orbit of Mars, past the orbit of Earth

---

*Hohmann, Dr. Walter—*The Attainability of the Celestial Bodies*, Munich, 1925. This pioneer work in astrogation, written long before the flight of the *Kilroy Was Here*, remains the foundation work in its field. All subsequent work is refinement of basic principles set forth by Hohmann.

(Earth would not be anywhere close at the time), in still further, swinging around the Sun and out again, catching up with Earth nearly a year later than the *Pathfinder*. She had mass to accomplish this, even after replenishing the *Pathfinder*, but she was limited to time-wasting, but fuel-saving, orbits more usual to merchant vessels than to ships of the Patrol.

Matt, in one of his multiple roles as assistant astrogator, noticed a peculiarity of the orbit and called it to Oscar's attention. "Say, Oz, come and look at this—when we get to perihelion point, the other side of the Sun, we almost clip a cloud off your home town. See?"

Oscar looked over the charted positions. "Well, darn if we don't! What's the nearest approach?"

"Less than a hundred thousand miles. We'll tack on her a bit—the Old Man is a heller for efficient orbits, I find. Want to jump ship?"

"We'd be going a trifle fast for that," Oscar commented dryly.

"Oh, where's the old pioneer spirit? You could swipe one of the jeeps and be gone before you're missed."

"Gosh, I'd like to. It would be nice to have some leave." Oscar shook his head sadly and stared at the chart.

"I know what's eating on you—since you've been made the head of a department you've acquired a sense of responsibility. How does it feel to be one of the mighty?"

Tex had come into the chartroom while they were talking. He chipped in with, "Yeah, come on, Oz—tell your public."

Oscar's fair skin turned pink. "Quit riding me, you guys. It's not my fault."

"Okay, you can get up now. Seriously," Matt went on, "this is quite a break for all of us—acting ship's officers on what was supposed to be a training tour. You know what I think?"

"*Do* you think?" inquired Tex.

"Shut up. If we keep our noses clean and get any chance to show some stuff, it might mean brevet commissions for all of us."

"Captain Yancey give me a brevet?" said Tex. "A fat chance!"

"Well, Oscar almost certainly. After all, he *is* chief comm officer."

"I tell you that doesn't mean a thing," protested Oscar. "Sure, I've got the tag—with nobody to communicate with. We're out of range, except for the *Pathfinder*, and she's pulling away fast."

"We won't always be out of range."

"It won't make any difference. Can you see the Old Man letting me—or any of us—do anything without staring down the backs of our necks? Anyhow, I don't want a brevet. Suppose we got back and it wasn't confirmed? Embarrassing!"

"I'd jump at the chance," announced Tex. "It may be the only way I'll ever get one."

"Drop the orphan-child act, Tex. Suppose your Uncle Bodie heard you talking like that."

In fact, the atmosphere in the ship was very different, even though the Captain, or Lieutenant Thurlow, or both, supervised them very carefully. Captain Yancey took to calling them by their first names at mess and dropped the use of "cadet" entirely. He sometimes referred to the "ship's officers," using the term so that it plainly included the three cadets. But there was no suggestion of brevet rank made.

Out of the asteroid belt, out of radio range, and in interminable free fall, the ship's duties were light. The cadets had plenty of time to study, enough time for card games and bull sessions. Matt caught up with his assignments and reached the point where he was digging into the ship's library for advanced work, for the courses outlined for them when they left the *Randolph* had been intended for a short cruise.

The Captain set up a seminar series, partly to pass his own time and partly as a supplement to their education. It was supposed to illustrate various problems faced by a Patrol officer as a spaceman, or in his more serious role as a diplomatic representative. Yancey lectured well; the cadets found, too, that he could be drawn into reminiscence. It was both enjoyable and instructive and helped to pass the weary weeks.

At long, long last they were within radio range of Venus—and there was mail for all of them, messages that had been chasing them half around the Solar System. An official despatch from the Department congratulated the Commanding Officer on the recovery of the *Pathfinder* and commended the ship's company—this was entered, in due course, in the record of each. A private message from Hartley Miller told Captain Yancey that the trip home had been okay and that the long-hairs were tearing same over the contents of the ship. Yancey read this aloud to them.

In addition to letters from home, Matt received a wedding announcement from Marianne. He wondered if she had married the young man he had met at the picnic, but he could not be sure of the name—the whole thing seemed very remote. There was a letter, too, to all three cadets date-marked "Leda, Ganymede" from

Pete, of the having-a-wonderful-time-wish-you-were-here sort. "Lucky stiff!" said Tex.

" 'Touring the world'—phooey!"

Other messages poured in—ships' movements, technical orders, personnel changes, the accumulated minutiae of a large military organization—and a detailed resumé of the news of four planets from the time they had lost contact to the present.

Oscar found that Captain Yancey did not breathe on his neck in his duties as communications chief—but by then it did not surprise him. Oscar simply was the comm chief and had almost forgotten that he had ever been anything else.

He felt, however, that he was really confirmed in his office the day a message came in top cipher, the first not in "clear." He was forced to ask the Captain for the top-cipher machine, kept in the Captain's safe. It was turned over to him without comment.

Oscar was bug-eyed when he took the translated message to Yancey. It read: TRIPLEX—CAN YOU INVESTIGATE TROUBLE EQUATORIAL REGION VENUS—OPERATIONS.

Yancey glanced at it. "Tell the Executive Officer I want to see him, please. And don't discuss this."

"Aye aye, sir."

Thurlow came in somewhat mystified. "What's up, Captain?"

Yancey handed him the flimsy. The lieutenant read it and whistled.

"Can you see any way to comply?"

"You know how much reaction potential we have, Captain. We could manage a circular orbit. We can't land."

"That's the way I see it. I suppose we'll have to refuse— dammit, I'd rather take a whipping than send in a negate. Why did they pick on us? There must be half a dozen other ships better located."

"I don't think so, Captain. I think we are the only available ship. Have you studied the movements file?"

"Not especially. Why?"

"Well, the *Thomas Paine* should be the ship—but she's grounded at New Aukland for emergency repairs."

"I see. There ought to be a standing circum-Venus patrol— there'll have to be, some day." Yancey scratched his chin and looked unhappy.

"How about this, Captain—"

"Yes?"

"If we change course right now we could do it cheaply. Then

we could bring her in for atmospheric braking with no further expenditure. Then ease her down with the jet."

"Hmmm—how much margin?"

Lieutenant. Thurlow got a far-away look in his eyes, while he approximated a fourth-order solution in his head. Captain Yancey joined him in the trance, his lips moving soundlessly.

"Practically none, Captain. After you've steadied in circum, you'd have to dive in and accept atmospheric terminal speed, or close to it, before you blasted."

Yancey shook his head. "Into *Venus?* I'd as soon fly a broom on Walpurgis night. No, Mr. Thurlow, we'll just have to call them up and confess."

"Just a minute, Captain—they know we don't have marines."

"Of course."

"Then they don't expect us to deliver police action. What we *can* do is to send a jeep down."

"I've been wondering when you would work around to that. All right, Mr. Thurlow—it's yours. I hand it over reluctantly, but I can't seem to help it. Never had a mission of your own, have you?"

"No, sir."

"You're getting one young. Well, I'll ask Operations for the details while you're preparing the course change."

"Fine, sir! Does the Captain care to designate the cadet to go with me, or shall I pick him?"

"You're not going with just one, Lieutenant—you'll take all three. I want you to leave the jeep manned at all times and I want you to have an armed man at your elbow. The equatorial region of Venus—there is no telling what you'll run into."

"But that leaves you with no one but Peters, sir—not counting the surgeon, of course."

"Mr. Peters and I will make out all right. Peters plays a very good hand of cribbage."

Details from Operations were slight. The M.R.S. *Gary* had radioed for help claiming to be imperiled by a native uprising. She had given her position, then radio contact had been lost.

Yancey elected to use atmospheric braking in any case to save his reaction mass for future use—otherwise the *Aes Triplex* might have circled Venus until she could be succored. The ship's company spent a crowded, tiring fifty-six hours shut up in the control room while the ship dipped into the clouds of Venus and out again, a bit deeper and a bit slower on each round trip. The ship grew painfully hot and the time spent in free space on each lap was hardly enough to let her radiate what she picked up. Most of the ship was intolerably hot, for the control room and the "farm" were refrigerated at the expense of the other spaces. In space, there is no way to get rid of unwanted heat, permanently, except by radiation—and the kinetic energy difference between the original orbit and the circum-Venus orbit the Captain wanted had to be absorbed as heat, a piece at a time, then radiated into space.

But at the end of that time three hot, tired, but very excited, young men, with one a little older, were ready to climb into jeep no. 2.

Matt suddenly remembered something. "Oh, Doctor—Doctor Pickering!" The surgeon had spent a medically uneventful voyage writing a monograph entitled "Some Notes on Comparative Pathologies of the Inhabited Planets" and was now at loose ends. He had relieved Matt as "farmer."

"Yes, Matt?"

"Those new tomato plants—they have to be cross-pollenated three days from now. You'll do it for me? You won't forget?"

"Can do!"

Captain Yancey guffawed. "Get your feet out of the furrows, Dodson. Forget the farm—we'll look out for it. Now, gentlemen—" He looked around and caught their eyes. "Try to stay alive. I doubt very much if this mission warrants expending four Patrol officers."

As they filed in Tex dug Matt in the ribs. "Did you hear that, kid—'four Patrol officers.'"

"Yeah, but look what else he said."

Thurlow tucked his orders in his pouch. They were simple: proceed to latitude north two degrees seven, longitude two hundred twelve degrees zero; locate the *Gary* and investigate reported native uprising. Keep the peace.

The lieutenant settled himself and looked around at his crew. "Hold your hats, boys. Here we go!"

14.
"THE NATIVES ARE FRIENDLY ..."

With Thurlow at the controls and Matt in the co-pilot's seat the jeep started down. It started with an orbital speed of better than four miles per second, the speed of the *Aes Triplex* in her tight circular orbit around the equator of Venus. The lieutenant's purpose was to kill this speed exactly over his destination, then balance the jeep down on its tail. A jet landing was necessary, as the jeep had no wings.

He needed to do this precisely, with the least use of fuel. He was helped somewhat by riding "with the current" from west to east; the 940-mile-per-hour rotational speed of Venus at her equator was profit rather than loss. However, exact placement was another matter. A departure time was selected so that the entire descending curve would be on the day side of the planet in order to use the Sun as a reckoning point for placement in longitude; placement in latitude would have to depend on dead reckoning by careful choice of course.

The Sun is the only possible celestial body to use in air navigation at Venus, and even Sol is lost to the naked eye as soon as one is inside the planet-wide blanket of cloud. Matt "shot the Sun" by keeping one eye glued on the eye-piece of an infra-red adapter which had been fitted to the ship's octant, and was enabled thereby to coach his skipper from a prepared flight plan. It had not been considered practical to cut a cam for the automatic robot; too little was known about the atmospheric conditions to be expected.

When Matt informed his pilot that they were about thirty miles up, by radar, and approaching the proper longitude, as given by the infra-red image of the Sun, Thurlow brought the jeep down

toward their target, ever lower and slower, and finally braked her
with the jet to let her drop in a parabola distorted by air resistance.

They were enveloped in the ever-present Venerian clouds. The
pilot's port was utterly useless to them. Matt now started watching
the surface under them, using an infra-red-sensitive "cloud piercer."

Thurlow watched his radar altimeter, checking it against the
height-time plan for grounding.

"If we are going to dodge around any, it's got to be now," he
said quietly to Matt. "What do you see?"

"Looks fairly smooth. Can't tell much."

Thurlow sneaked a look. "It's not water, anyway—and it's not
forest. I guess we'll chance it."

Down they dropped, with Matt watching the ghostly infra-red-
produced picture narrowly at the end, ready to tell Thurlow to give
her full power if it were a meadow.

Thurlow eased off his jet—and cut it. There was a bump as if
they had fallen a couple of feet. They were down, landed on
Venus.

"Whew!" said the pilot and wiped sweat from his forehead. "I
don't want to have to try that every day."

"Nice landing, Skipper!" called out Oscar.

"Yea bo!" agreed Tex.

"Thanks, fellows. Well, let's get the stilts down." He punched
a stud on the control board. Like most rockets built for jet landings, the jeep was fitted with three stabilizing jacks which came
telescoping out of the craft's sides and slanting downward. Hydraulic pressure forced them down until they touched something
solid enough to hold them, whereupon the thrusting force was automatically cut off and they locked in place, propping the rocket
on three sides, tripod fashion, and holding it erect.

Thurlow waited until three little green lights appeared under
the stud controlling the stilts, then unclutched the jeep's stabilizing gyros. The jeep held steady, he unstrapped. "All right, men.
Let's take a look. Matt and Tex, stay inside. Oscar, if you don't
mind my mentioning it, since it's your home town, you should do
the honors."

"Right!" Oscar unstrapped and hurried to the lock. There was
no need to check the air, since Venus is man-inhabited, and all of
them, as members of the Patrol, had been immunized to the virulent Venerian fungi.

Thurlow crowded close behind him. Matt unstrapped and
came down to sit by Tex in the passenger rest Oscar had left. The

space around the lock was too limited in the little craft to make it worthwhile to do anything but wait.

Oscar stared out into the mist. "Well, how does it feel to be home?" asked Thurlow.

"Swell! What a beautiful, beautiful day!"

Thurlow smiled at Oscar's back and said, "Let's get the ladder down and see where we are." The access door was more than fifty feet above the jeep's fins, with no convenient loading elevator.

"Okay." Oscar turned and squeezed past Thurlow. The jeep settled suddenly on the side away from the door, seemed to catch itself, then started to fall over with increasing speed.

"The gyros!" yelled Thurlow. "Matt, clutch the gyros!" He tried to scramble past Oscar; they fouled each other, then the two fell sprawling backwards as the jeep toppled over.

At the pilot's yell Matt tried to comply—but he had been sprawled out, relaxing. He grabbed the sides of the rest, trying to force himself up and back to the control station, but the rest tilted backwards; he found himself "skinning the cat" out of it, and then was resting on the side of the craft, which was now horizontal.

Oscar and Thurlow were the first things he saw as he untangled himself. They were piled up on the inner wall of the ship, with Oscar mostly on top. Oscar started to get up—and stopped. "Eeeyowp!"

"You hurt, Oz?"

"My arm."

"What's the trouble?" This was Tex, who appeared from behind Matt, apparently untouched by the tumble.

Oscar helped himself up with his right arm, then tenderly felt his left forearm. "I don't know. A sprain—or a break, maybe. Eeee—ah! It's a break."

"Are you sure?" Matt stepped forward. "Let me see it."

"What's the matter with the skipper?" asked Tex.

"Huh?" said Matt and Oscar together. Thurlow had not moved. Tex went to him and knelt over him.

"Looks like he's knocked out cold."

"Throw some water over him."

"No, don't do that. Do—" The craft settled again. Oscar looked startled and said, "I think we had better get out of here."

"Huh? We can't," protested Matt. "We've got to bring Mr. Thurlow to."

Oscar did not answer him but started climbing up toward the open lock, now ten feet over their heads, swearing in Venerian as he struggled painfully and awkwardly, using one hand, from strut to brace. "'S'matter with old Oz?" asked Tex. "Acts like he's blown his top."

"Let him go. We've got to take care of the skipper." They knelt over Thurlow and gave him a quick, gentle examination. He seemed unhurt, but remained unconscious. "Maybe he's just had the breath knocked out of him," suggested Matt. "His heart beat is strong and steady."

"Look at this, Matt." It was a lump on the back of the lieutenant's head. Matt felt it gently.

"Didn't bash in his skull. He's just had a wallop on his noggin. He'll be all right—I think."

"I wish Doc Pickering was here."

"Yeah, and if fish had feet, they'd be mice. Quit worrying, Tex. Stop messing with him and give him a chance to come out of it naturally."

Oscar stuck his head down into the open door. "Hey, you guys! Come up out of there—and fast!"

"What for?" asked Matt. "Anyhow, we can't—we got to stay with the boss, and he's still out cold."

"Then carry him!"

"How? Piggy-back?"

"Any way—but *do it!* The ship is sinking!"

Tex opened his mouth, closed it again, and dived toward a small locker. Matt yelled. "Tex—get a line!"

"What do you think I'm doing? Ice-skating?" Tex reappeared with a coil of thin, strong line used in warping the little craft in to her mother ship. "Easy now—lift him as I slip it under his chest."

"We ought to make a proper sling. We might hurt him."

"No time for that!" urged Oscar from above them. "Hurry!"

Matt swarmed up to the door with the end of the line while Tex was still fastening the loop under the armpits of the unconscious man. A quick look around was enough to confirm Oscar's prediction; the jeep lay on her side with her fins barely touching solid ground. The nose was lower than the tail and sinking in thin, yellow mud. The mud stretched away into the mist, like a flat field, its surface carpeted with a greenish-yellow fungus except for a small space adjacent to the ship where the ship, in falling, had splashed a gap in the surface.

Matt had no time to take the scene in; the mud was almost up to the door. "Ready down there?"

"Ready. I'll be right up."

"Stay where you are and steady him. I think I can handle him." Thurlow weighed one hundred forty pounds, Earth-side; his Venus weight was about one hundred and seventeen. Matt straddled the door and took a strain on the line.

"I can give you one hand, Matt," Oscar said anxiously.

"Just stay out of my way." With Matt pulling and Tex pushing and steadying from below, they got the limp lieutenant over the lip of the door and laid out on the rocket.

The craft lurched again as a tail fin slid off the bank. "Let's get going, troops," Matt urged. "Oz, can you get up on that bank by yourself?"

"Sure."

"Then do so. We'll leave the line on the skipper and chuck the end to you and you can hang onto it with your good hand. That way, if he goes in the mud, we can haul him out."

"Quit talking and get busy." Oscar trotted the length of the craft, taking the end of the line with him. He made it to the bank by stepping from a tail fin.

Matt and Tex had no trouble carrying Thurlow as far as the fins, but the last few feet, from fins to bank, were awkward. They had to work close to the jet tube, still sizzling hot, and balance themselves in a trough formed by a fin and the converging side of the ship. They finally made it by letting Oscar take most of the lieutenant's weight by hauling from the bank with his one good arm.

When they had gotten Thurlow laid out on the turf Matt jumped back aboard the jeep. Oscar shouted at him. "Hey, Matt— where do you think you're going?"

"Back inside."

"Don't do it. Come back here." Matt hesitated, Oscar added, "That's an order, Matt."

Matt answered, "I'll only be a minute. We've got no weapons and no survival kits. I'll duck in and toss them out."

"Don't try it." Matt stood still a moment, balanced between Oscar's unquestioned seniority and the novelty of taking direct orders from his roommate. "Look at the door, Matt," Oscar added. "You'd be trapped."

Matt looked. The far end of the door was already in the mud and a steady stream was slopping into the ship, like molasses. As he looked the jeep rolled about a quarter turn, seeking a new stability. Matt made it to the bank in one flying leap.

He looked back and saw that the door was out of sight; a big bubble formed and *plopped!*—and then another. "Thanks, Oz!"

They stood and watched as the tail slid away from the bank. A cloud of steam came up and joined the mist as the jet tube hit the wetness; then the tail lifted and the jeep was almost vertical, upside down, for a few moments, with only her after end showing above the slime.

She sank slowly. Presently there was nothing but bubbles in the mud and a ragged break in the false lawn to show where it had been.

Matt's chin was trembling. "I should have stayed at the controls. I could have caught her on her gyros."

"Nonsense," said Oscar. "He didn't tell you to stay put."

"I should have known better."

"Quit beating yourself with it. The procedures say it's the pilot's business. If there was any doubt in his mind he should have left her stabilized on gyro until he inspected. Right now we got to take care of him, so cut out the post-mortem."

"Okay." Matt knelt down and tried Thurlow's pulse. It was still steady. "Nothing we can do for him at the moment but let him rest. Let's see your arm."

"Okay, but take it easy. Ouch!"

"Sorry. I'm afraid I'll have to hurt you; I've never actually set a bone before."

"I have," said Tex, "out on the range. Here you go, Oz old boy—lie down on your back. And relax—it's going to hurt."

"Okay. Only I thought that down in Texas you just shot 'em." Oscar managed to smile.

"Just for broken legs. Broken arms we usually save. Matt, you whip up a couple of splints. Got a knife?"

"Yep."

"Good thing—I don't have. Better take your blouse off first, Oscar." With help Jensen complied; Tex placed a foot in Oscar's left armpit, grasped his left hand in both of his, and gave a steady tug.

Oscar yelped. "I think that did it," said Tex. "Matt, hurry up with those splints."

"Coming." Matt had found a clump of grass, twelve to fifteen feet tall and superficially similar to Earth-side bamboo. He cut about a dozen lengths as thick as his little finger and around fifteen inches long, brought them back and gave them to Tex. "Will these do?"

"I guess so. Here goes your blouse, Oscar." Tex attempted to tear strips from the garment, then gave up. "Golly, that stuff is tough. Gimme your knife, Matt."

Ten minutes later Oscar was adequately splinted and bandaged, with what remained of his blouse rigged as a sling. Tex took off his own blouse and sat down on it, for the turf was damp and the day was hot and muggy as only Venus can be. "That's done," he said, "and the skipper hasn't blinked an eye. That leaves you holding the sack, Oz—when do we have lunch?"

"A fine question, that." Oscar wrinkled his brows. "First, let's see what we've got to work with. Turn out your pouches."

Matt had his knife. Oscar's pouch contained nothing of significance. Tex contributed his harmonica. Oscar looked worried. "Fellows, do you suppose I'm justified in looking through Mr. Thurlow's pouch?"

"I think you ought to," said Tex. "I've never seen anybody stay out so long."

"I agree," added Matt. "I think we had better admit he's got a concussion and assume that he's going to be out of the running for a while. Go ahead, Oscar."

Thurlow's pouch contained some personal items that they skipped over quickly, the orders to the expedition, and a second knife—which had set in its handle a small, ornamental, magnetic compass. "Golly, I'm glad to find that item. I've been wondering how we would ever find our way back to this spot without natives to guide us."

"Who wants to?" asked Tex. "It doesn't seem to have any attractions for me."

"The jeep is here."

"And the *Triplex* is somewhere over your head. One is about as close as the other—to a pedestrian, meaning me."

"Look, Tex—somehow we've got to get that firecracker out of the mud and put her back into commission. Otherwise we stay here for life."

"Huh? I'd been depending on you, the old Venerian hand, to lead us back to civilization."

"You don't know what you're saying. Maybe you can walk five or six thousand miles through swamps, and sink holes, and cane brake; I can't. Just remember that there isn't a permanent settlement, not even a plantation, more than five hundred miles from either one of the poles. You know Venus isn't really explored—I know about as much about this neck of the woods as you know about Tibet."

"I wonder what in the world the *Gary* was doing here?" Matt commented.

"Search me."

"Say!" said Tex. "Maybe we can get home in the *Gary*."

"Maybe we can, but we haven't even found the *Gary* yet. Consequently if we find we can't, just as soon as we carry out these orders—" Oscar held up the paper he had taken from Thurlow's pouch. "—we've got to find some way to haul the jeep out of the sinkhole."

"With our own little pink patty-paws?" inquired Tex. "And what's that about our orders? We don't seem to be in very good shape to go around quelling riots, putting down insurrection, and generally throwing our weight about. We haven't even got a bean shooter, much less a bean. Come to think about it, if I had a bean, I'd eat it."

"Oscar's right," agreed Matt. "We're here; we've got a mission to perform; we've got to carry it out. That's what Mr. Thurlow would say. After that comes trying to figure out a way to get back."

Tex stood up. "I should have gone into the cattle business. Okay, Oscar—what next?"

"The first thing is for you and Matt to build a litter to carry the boss. We've got to find open water and I don't want to split up the party."

The same clump of cane grass that furnished splints provided material for a litter frame. Using both knives Matt and Tex cut two seven-foot lengths as thick as their upper arms. The stuff was light and, in that thickness, satisfactorily stiff. They slipped the poles through the sleeves of their blouses, then notched in cross pieces near each end. There was a wide gap in the middle which they wound about with the line salvaged from the jeep.

The result was a sloppy piece of work, but serviceable. Thurlow was still unconscious. His breathing was shallow but his pulse was still steady. They lifted him onto the stretcher and set out, with Oscar in the lead, compass in hand.

For about an hour they tramped through swampy land, splashing through mud, getting welts from the undergrowth, and pursued by clouds of insects. At last Matt called out, "Oz! We've just got to have some rest."

Jensen turned around. "Okay—this is the end of the line, anyhow. Open water."

They crowded forward and joined him. Beyond the cane brake, perfectly flat and calm under the fog, was a pond or lake. Its size was uncertain as the far shore was lost in the mist.

They tramped out a spot to put the litter down, then Oscar bent over the water and slapped it—*Slap!—Slap!—Slap, slap, slap—Slap, slap!*

"What do we do now?"

"We wait—and pray. Thank goodness the natives are usually friendly."

"Do you think they can help us?"

"If they want to help I'll lay you even money that they can snake the jeep out of that muck and polish it clean in three days."

"You really think so? I knew the Venerians were friendly but a job like that—"

"Don't underrate the Little People. They don't look like us but don't let that throw you."

Matt squatted down and started fanning the insects away from the unconscious officer. Presently Oscar slapped the water again, in the same pattern.

"Looks like nobody's home, Oz."

"I hope you're wrong, Tex. Most of Venus is supposed to be inhabited, but this might be a tabu spot."

A triangular head, large as a collie's, broke water about ten feet from them. Tex jumped. The Venerian regarded him with shiny, curious eyes. Oscar stood up. *"Greetings, thou whose mother was my mother's friend."*

The Venerian turned her attention to Oscar. *"May thy mother rest happily."* She surface-dived and disappeared almost without a ripple.

"That's a relief," said Oscar. "Of course they say this planet has only one language but this is the first time I've put it to a test."

"Why did it leave?"

"Gone back to report, probably. And don't say 'it,' Matt; say 'she.'"

"It's a difference that could only matter to another Venerian."

"Well, it's a bad habit, anyway." Oscar squatted down and waited.

After a time made longer by insects, heat, and sultriness the water was broken in a dozen places at once. One of the amphibians climbed gracefully up on the bank and stood up. She came about to Matt's shoulder. Oscar repeated the formal greeting. She looked him over. *"My mother tells me that she knows thee not."*

"Doubtless being busy with important thoughts she has forgotten."

"Perhaps. Let us go to my mother and let her smell thee."

"Thou art gracious. Canst thou carry my sibling?" Oscar

pointed to Thurlow. *"Being ill, 'she' cannot close 'her' mouth to the waters."*

The Venerian agreed. She called one of her followers to her side and Oscar joined the consultation, illustrating how Thurlow's mouth must be covered and his nose pinched together *"—lest the waters return 'her' to 'her' mother's mother's mother."* The second native argued but agreed.

Tex was getting more and more round-eyed. "See here, Matt," he said urgently in Basic, "surely you're not figuring on going under water?"

"Unless you want to stay here until the insects eat you up, you've got to. Just take it easy, let them tow you, and try to keep your lungs full. When they dive you may have to stay under several minutes."

"I don't like it either," said Matt.

"Shucks, I visited my first Venerian home when I was nine. They know you can't swim the way they do. At least the ones around the colonies know it," he admitted doubtfully.

"Maybe you had better impress them with it."

"I'll try."

The leader cut him short with assurances. She gave a sharp command and six of her party placed themselves by the cadets, two to each man. Three others took over Thurlow, lifting him and sliding him into the water. One of them was the one who had been instructed.

Oscar called out, "Take it easy, fellows!" Matt felt little hands urging him into the lake. He took a deep breath and stepped off into the water.

The water closed over his head. It was blood warm and fresh. He opened his eyes, saw the surface, then his head broke water again. The little hands grasped his sides and propelled him along, swimming strongly. He told himself to relax and stop fighting it.

After a while it even began to seem pleasant, once he was sure that the little creatures did not intend to pull him under. But he remembered Oscar's advice and tried to watch out for a dive. Luckily, he saw the trio of which Tex was the middle go under; he gulped air just in time.

They went down and down, until his eardrums hurt, then forward. By the time they started up the pains in his chest were almost unbearable. He was fighting a reflex to open his mouth and breathe anything, even water, when they broke surface again.

There were three more of the lung-searing passages under wa-

ter; when they broke water for the last time Matt saw that they
were no longer outdoors.

The cave—if it was a cave—was about a hundred feet long
and less than half as wide. In the center of it was the water entrance through which they had come. It was lighted from above,
rather dimly, from some sort of glowing, orange clusters.

Most of this he noticed after he pulled himself up on the bank.
His first impression was a crowd of Venerians surrounding the
pool. They were obviously curious about their guests and chattered among themselves. Matt picked up a few words of it and
heard a reference to *"—slime spawn—"* which annoyed him.

The three with Thurlow broke water. Matt pulled away from
his custodians and helped drag him onto dry land. He was frantic
for a moment when he could not find the lieutenant's pulse; then
he located it. It was fast and fluttery.

Thurlow opened his eyes and looked at him. "Matt—the
gyros . . ."

"It's all right, Lieutenant. Just take it easy."

Oscar was standing over him. "How is he Matt?"

"Coming out of it, it looks like."

"Maybe the immersion did him good."

"It didn't do me any good," asserted Tex. "I swallowed about a
gallon of water on that last one. Those little frogs are *careless*."

"They're more like seals," said Matt.

"They're neither one," Oscar cut in sharply. "They're *people*.
Now," he went on, "to try to set up some friendly relations." He
turned around, looking for the leader of the group.

The crowd separated, leaving an aisle to the pool. An amphibian, walking alone, but followed by three others, came slowly
down this aisle toward them. Oscar faced her. *"Greetings, most
worthy mother of many."*

She looked him slowly up and down, then spoke, but not to
him. *"As I thought. Take them away."*

Oscar started to protest, but it did him no good. Four of the little people closed in around him. Tex yelled at him. "How about it,
Oz? Let 'em have it?"

"No!" Oscar called back. "Don't resist."

Three minutes later they were herded into a small room that
was almost completely dark, the gloom being broken only by a
single sphere of the orange light. After depositing Thurlow on the
floor the little people went away, closing the door after them by

drawing across it a curtain. Tex looked around him, trying to adjust his eyes to the dim light, and said, "About as cozy as a grave. Oz, you should have let us put up a scrap. I'll bet we could have licked the whole caboodle of 'em."

"Don't be silly, Tex. Suppose we had managed it—a possibility which I doubt, but suppose we had: how would you like to try to swim your way out of here?"

"I wouldn't try it. We'd dig a tunnel up to the surface—we've got two knives."

"Maybe you would; I wouldn't attempt it. The Little People generally built their cities underneath lakes."

"I hadn't thought of that angle—say, that's bad." Tex studied the ceiling as if wondering when it would give way. "Look, Oz, I don't think we're under the lake, or the walls of this dungeon would be damp."

"Huh uh, they're good at this sort of thing."

"Well—okay, so they've got us. I'm not beefing, Oz—your intentions were good—but it sure looks like we should 'a' taken our chances in the jungle."

"For Pete's sake, Tex!—haven't I got enough to worry about without you second-guessing me? If you're not beefing, then stop beefing."

There was a short silence, then Tex said, "Excuse me, Oscar. My big mouth."

"Sorry. I shouldn't have lost my temper. My arm hurts."

"Oh. How's it doing? Didn't I set it right?"

"I think you did a good job on it, but it aches. And it's beginning to itch, under the wrappings—makes me edgy. What are you doing, Matt?"

After checking on Thurlow's condition—unchanged—Matt had gone to the door and was investigating the closure. The curtain he found to be a thick, firm fabric of some sort, fastened around the edges. He was trying his knife on it when Oscar spoke to him.

"Nothing," he answered. "This stuff won't cut."

"Then quit trying to and relax. We don't want to get out of here—not yet, anyway."

" 'Speak for yourself, John.' Why don't we?"

"That's what I've been trying to tell Tex. I won't say this is a pleasure resort but we are about eight hundred per cent better off than we were a couple of hours ago, in every way."

"How?"

"Have you got any idea of what it means to spend a night in the jungle here, with nothing at all to shut it out? When it gets dark and the slime worms come up and start nibbling at your toes? Maybe we could live through a night of it, or even two nights, by being active and very, very lucky—but how about him?" Oscar gestured at Thurlow's still form. "That's why I made it our first business to find natives. We're safe, even if we are locked up."

Matt shivered. The slime worms have no teeth; instead they excrete an acid that dissolves what they wish to sample. They average about seven feet long. "You've sold me."

Tex said, "I wish my Uncle Bodie was here."

"So do I—he'd keep you shut up. I'm not anxious to get out of here until we've had something to eat and some sleep. Then maybe the boss will be back on his feet and will know what to do next."

"What makes you think they'll feed us?"

"I don't know that they will, but I think they will. If they are anything like the same breed of cat as the natives around the polar colonies, they'll feed us. To keep another creature shut up without feeding it is a degree of orneriness they just wouldn't think of." Oscar groped for words. "You have to know them to understand what I mean, but the Little People don't have the cussedness in them that humans have."

Matt nodded. "I know that they are described as being a gentle, unwarlike race. I can't imagine becoming really fond of them, but the spools I studied showed them as friendly."

"That's just race prejudice. A Venerian is easier to like than a man."

"Oz, that's not fair," Tex protested. "Matt hasn't got any race prejudice and neither have I. Take Lieutenant Peters—did it make any difference to us that he's as black as the ace of spades?"

"That's not the same thing—a Venerian is *really* different. I guess you have to be brought up with them, like I have, to take them for granted. But everything about them is different—for instance, like the fact that you never lay eyes on anything but females."

"Say, how about that, Oz? Are there really male Venerians, or is it just a superstition?"

"Sure there are—the Little People are unquestionably bisexual. But I doubt if we'll ever get a picture of one or a chance to examine one. The guys who claim to have seen one are mostly liars," he added, "because their stories never add up."

"Why do you suppose they are so touchy about it?"

"Why won't a Hindu eat beef? There doesn't have to be any

reason for it. I go for the standard theory; the males are little and helpless and have to be protected."

"I'm glad I'm not a Venerian," Matt commented.

"Might not be such a bad life," Tex asserted. "Me—I could use a little coddling right now."

"Don't go taking me for an authority on Venerians," warned Oscar. "I was born here, but I wasn't born *here*." He patted the floor. "I know the polar region natives, the sort around my own home town—and that's just about the only sort anybody knows."

"You think that makes such a difference?" Matt wanted to know.

"I think we're lucky to be able to talk with them at all—even if the accent does drive me wild. As for other differences—look, if the only humans you had ever met were Eskimos, how far would that get you in dealing with the mayor of a Mexican town? The local customs would all be different."

"Then maybe they won't feed us, after all," Tex said mournfully.

But they were fed, and shortly. The curtain was thrust back, something was deposited on the floor, and the door was closed again.

There was a platter of some lumpish substance, color and texture indeterminate in the dim light, and an object about the size and shape of an ostrich egg. Oscar took the platter and sniffed at it, then took a small piece and tasted it. "It's all right," he announced. "Go ahead and eat."

"What is it?" inquired Tex.

"It's . . . well, never mind. Eat it. It won't hurt you and it will keep you alive."

"But what is it? I want to know what I'm eating."

"Permit me to point out that you eat this or go hungry. I don't care which. If I told you, your local prejudices would get in your way. Just pretend it's garbage and learn to love it."

"Aw, quit horsing around, Oz."

But Oscar refused to be drawn into any further discussion. He ate rapidly until he had finished his share, glanced at Thurlow and said reluctantly, "I suppose we ought to leave some for him."

Matt tried the stuff. "What's it like?" asked Tex.

"Not bad. Reminds me of mashed soybeans. Salty—it makes me thirsty."

"Help yourself," suggested Oscar.

"Huh? Where? How?"

"The drinking bladder, of course." Oscar handed him the "ostrich egg." It was soft to Matt's touch, despite its appearance. He held it, looking puzzled.

"Don't know how to use it? Here—" Oscar took it, looked at the ends, and selected one, which he placed to his lips.

"There!" he said, wiping his lips. "Try it. Don't squeeze too hard, or you'll get it all over you." Matt tried it and got a drink of water. It was a bit like using a nursing bottle.

"It's a sort of a fish's gizzard," explained Oscar, "and spongy inside. Oh, don't look squeamish, Tex! It's sterile."

Tex tried it gingerly, then gave in and tackled the food. After a while they all sat back, feeling considerably better. "Not bad," admitted Tex, "but do you know what I'd like? A stack of steaming hotcakes, tender and golden brown—"

"Oh, shut up!" said Matt.

"—with melted butter and just swimming in maple syrup. Okay, I'll shut up." He unzipped his pouch and took out his harmonica. "Well, what d'yuh know! Still dry." He tried a couple of notes, then broke into a brilliant execution of *The Cross-Eyed Pilot*.

"Hey, stop that," said Oscar. "This is a sort of a sick room, you know."

Tex turned a troubled glance at the patient. "You think he can hear it?"

Thurlow turned and muttered in his sleep. Matt bent over him. *"J'ai soif,"* the lieutenant mumbled, then repeated distinctly, *"J'ai soif."*

"What did he say?"

"I don't know."

"It sounded like French to me. Either of you guys savvy French?"

"Not me."

"Nor me," Matt concurred. "Why would he talk French? I always thought he was North American; he spoke Basic like one."

"Maybe he was French-Canadian." Tex knelt beside him and felt his forehead. "He seems sort of feverish. Maybe we should give him some water."

"Okay." Oscar took the bladder and put it to Thurlow's lips; he squeezed gently so that a little welled out. The injured man worked his lips and then began to suck on it, without appearing to wake up. Presently he let it fall from his mouth. "There," said Oscar, "maybe he'll feel better now."

"Are we going to save that for him?" asked Tex, eyeing the remainder of the food.

"Go ahead and eat it, if you want it. It turns rancid a few hours after it's . . . well, it turns rancid."

"I don't believe I want any more," Tex decided.

They had been sleeping an undetermined length of time when a noise awakened them—a voice, unquestionably human. "Hey!" it demanded, *"where art thou taking me? I insist that thou take me to see thy mother!"*

The noise was right at their door. *"Quell thy tongue!"* answered a native accent; the curtain was shoved aside and someone was pushed into the room before the door was again closed.

"Hello there!" called out Oscar.

The figure spun around. "Men . . ." he said, as if he could not believe it. "Men!" He began to sob.

"Hello, Stinky," said Tex. "What are you doing here?"

It was Girard Burke.

There was considerable confusion for the next several moments. Burke alternated between tears and uncontrollable shaking. Matt, who had awakened last, had trouble sorting out what was going on from the fantasy he had been dreaming, and everybody talked at once, all asking questions and none of them answering.

"Quiet!" commanded Oscar. "Let's get this straight. Burke, as I understand it, you were in the *Gary?*"

"I'm skipper of the *Gary.*"

"Huh? Well, I'll be switched. Come to think of it, we knew the captain of the *Gary* was named Burke, but it never occurred to anybody that it could be Stinky Burke. Who would be crazy enough to trust you with a crate, Stinky?"

"It's my own ship—or, anyhow, my father's. And I'll thank you to call me Captain Burke, not 'Stinky.' "

"Okay, Captain Stinky."

"But how did he get here?" Matt wanted to know, still trying to catch up.

"He's just explained that," said Tex. "He's the guy that yelled for help. But what beats me is that it should happen to be us—it's like dealing out a bridge hand and getting thirteen spades."

"Oh, I don't know," objected Oscar. "It's a coincidence, but not a very startling one. He's a spaceman, he hollers for help, and naturally the Patrol responds. It happened to be us. It's about as likely, or as unlikely, as running across your piano teacher on the downtown streets of your home town."

"I don't have a piano teacher," objected Tex.

"Skip it. Neither do I. Now I think—"

"Wait a minute," broke in Burke, "do I gather that you were sent here, in answer to my message?"

"Certainly."

"Well, thank heaven for that—even if you guys were stupid enough to stumble right into it. Now tell me—how many are there in the expedition and how are they equipped? This is going to be a tough nut to crack."

"Huh? What are you talking about, Stinky? This *is* the expedition, right in front of you."

"*What?* This is no time to joke. I sent for a regiment of marines, equipped for amphibious operations."

"Maybe you did, but this is what you got—total. Lieutenant Thurlow is in command, but he got a crack on the skull so I'm temporarily filling in for him. You can talk to me—what's the situation?"

Burke seemed dazed by the knowledge. He stared without speaking. Oscar went on, "Snap out of it, Stinky. Give us the data, so we can work out an operation plan."

"Huh? Oh, it's no use. It's utterly hopeless."

"What's so hopeless? The natives seem friendly, on the whole. Tell us what the difficulty was, so we can work it out with them."

"Friendly!" Burke gave a bitter laugh. "They killed all of my men. They're going to kill me. And they'll kill you."

15.
PIE WITH A FORK

"*Okay,*" *agreed Oscar.* "Now that that's settled, I still want to know the score. Suppose you pull yourself together, Burke, and tell us what happened?"

The merchant rocketship *Gary*, built by "Reactors Ltd." and transferred to the family corporation "System Enterprises," was a winged rocket especially fitted for point-to-point operations on Venus. The elder Mr. Burke had placed his son in command, backing him up with an experienced crew; the purpose of the trip was to investigate a tip concerning ores of the trans-uranic elements.

The tip had been good; the ores were present in abundance. Young Burke had then undertaken to negotiate exploitation rights with the local Venerian authorities in order to hold the valuable claim against other exploiters who were sure to follow.

He had not been able to interest the local "mother of many" in his wishes; the swamp he wanted, she gave Burke to understand, was tabu. However, he was able to intrigue her into visiting the *Gary*. Once aboard the ship he again tried to get her to change her mind. When she turned him down again he had refused to allow her to leave the rocket ship.

"You mean you kidnapped her," said Matt.

"Nothing of the sort. She came aboard of her own free will. I just didn't get up and open the door for her and went on arguing."

"Oh, yeah?" commented Oscar. "How long did this go on?"

"Not very long."

"Exactly how long? You might as well tell me; I'll find out from the natives."

"Oh, well! Overnight—what's so criminal about that?"

"I don't know just how criminal it is here. On Mars, as I learned in school and as I'm sure you did too, the punishment would be to stake you out on the desert, unprotected, for exactly the same length of time."

"Hell's bells—I didn't hurt her. I'm not that silly. I wanted her co-operation."

"So you twisted her arm to get it. You held her prisoner, in effect kidnapped her by enticement and held her for ransom. Okay— you kept her overnight. What happened when you let her go?"

"That's what I'm trying to tell you. I never got a chance to turn her loose. I was going to, of course, but—"

"Sez you!"

"Don't get sarcastic. The next morning they attacked the ship. There must have been thousands of the beasts."

"So you turned her loose?"

"I was afraid to. I figured as long as we held her nothing much could happen to us. But I was wrong—they poured something on the door that ate it right away and they were in the ship before we could stop them. They killed my crew, just overran them—but we must have gotten at least twice as many of them, the brutes!"

"How come you're still breathing?"

"I locked myself in the comm room and sent out the call for help that got you here. They didn't find me there until they went through the ship, compartment by compartment. I must have passed out from the fumes when they melted their way in— anyhow I woke up while they were bringing me here."

"I see." Oscar sat a while and thought, his knees pulled up under his chin. "This is your first time on Venus, Stinky?"

"Well, yes."

"I thought so. It's apparent that you didn't know just how stubborn and difficult the Little People can be if you start pushing them around."

Burke looked wry. "I know now. That's why I distinctly called for a regiment of marines. I can't imagine what the Department was thinking about, to send three cadets and a watch officer. Of all the brass-hatted stupidity! My old man will raise plenty of Cain about it when I get back."

Tex gave a snort of disgust. "Did you think the Patrol was invented to keep a jughead like you from having to pay for his fun?"

"Why, you—"

"Quiet, Burke. And never mind the side remarks, Tex. This is an investigation, not a debate. You know the Patrol never sends marines until they've tried negotiation, Burke."

"Sure, that's why I specified marines. I wanted them to cut the red tape and get some action."

"You were kidding yourself. And there's no point in talking about what you'll do when you get back. We don't know yet that we can get back."

"That's true." Burke chewed his lip and thought about it. "Look here, Jensen, you and I were never very chummy in school, but that's unimportant now; we're in the same boat and we've got to stick together. I've got a proposition. You know these frogs better than I do—"

"People, not 'frogs.' "

"Okay, you know the natives. If you can manage to square this and get me out of here, I can cut you in on—"

"Careful there, Burke!"

"Don't get on your high horse. Just hear me out, will you? Just listen. Do I have free speech or don't I?"

"Let him talk, Oz," advised Tex. "I like to watch his tonsils."

Oscar held his tongue, Burke went on, "I wasn't going to suggest anything that would smirch your alabaster character. After all, you're here to get me out of this; it's my business if I want to offer a reward. Now this swamp we staked out is loaded with the stuff—trans-uranics, all the way from element 97 through 104. I don't have to tell you what that means—101 and 103 for jet-lining alloys; 100 for cancer therapy—not to mention the catalyzing uses. Why, there's millions in catalysts alone. I'm no hog; I'll cut you *all* in . . . say for ten per cent apiece."

"Is that all you have to say?"

"Not quite. If you can work it so that they'll let us go and leave us alone while we jury-rig some repairs on the *Gary* so that we can get away with a load this trip, I'll make it twenty per cent. You'll like the *Gary*; she's the sweetest job in the System. But if that won't work and you can get me back in your ship it's still worth ten per cent."

"Are you through?"

"Yes."

"I can answer for all of us. If I didn't consider the source, I'd be insulted."

"Fifteen per cent. There's no need to get shirty; after all, it's absolutely free just for doing what you were ordered down here to do anyhow."

"Oz," said Matt, "do we have to listen to this tripe?"

"Not any more of it," decided Jensen. "He's had his say. Burke, I'll keep this factual and leave my personal opinions out of it. You can't hire the Parol, you know that. In—"

"I wasn't offering to hire you, I was just trying to do you a favor, show my appreciation."

"I've got the floor. In the second place, we haven't got a ship, not at present."

"Huh? What's that?" Burke seemed startled.

Oscar gave him a quick resumé of the fate of the jeep. Burke looked both amazed and terribly, bitterly disappointed. "Well, of all the gang of stupes! Just forget that offer; you haven't got anything to sell."

"I've already forgotten it and you had better be glad I have. Let me point out that we wouldn't have been making a jet-landing in a jungle if you hadn't made an ass of yourself and then called for help. However, we hope to recover the jeep if I can manage to smooth out the trouble you've caused—and that's no small job."

"Well, of course if you can square things and get your ship back, the offer stands."

"Stop talking about that clumsy piece of bribery! We can't possibly promise you anything, even if we wanted to. We've got our mission to carry out."

"Okay—your mission is to get me out of here. It comes to the same thing; I was just being generous."

"Our mission isn't anything of the sort. Our prime mission is what the prime mission of the Patrol always is: to keep the peace. Our orders read to investigate a reported native uprising—there isn't any—and 'keep the peace.' There's not a word about springing Girard Burke from the local jail and giving him a free ride home."

"But—"

"I'm not through. You know how the Patrol works as well as I do. It acts in remote places and a Patrol officer has to use his own judgment, being guided by the Tradition—"

"Well, if it's precedent you're looking for, you've got to—"

"Shut up! Precedent is merely the assumption that somebody else, in the past with less information, nevertheless knows better than the man on the spot. If you had gotten any use out of the time you spent as a cadet, you'd know that the Tradition is something very different. To follow a tradition means to do things in the same grand style as your predecessors; it does not mean to do the same things."

"Okay, okay—you can skip the lecture."

"I need some information from you. Had the Little People here ever seen a man before you came along?"

"Uh . . . why, they knew about men, a little anyhow. Of course there was Stevens."

"Who was Stevens?"

"Mineralogist, working for my old man. He did the quickie survey that caused us to bring the *Gary* in. Oh, there was his pilot, too."

"And those are the only men these natives have encountered, aside from the crew of the *Gary?*"

"So far as I know, yes."

"Have they ever heard of the Patrol?"

"I doubt it—yes, they have, too. At least the boss mother seemed to know the native word for it."

"Hmm . . . that rather surprises me. So far as I know the Patrol has never had any occasion to land this near the equator—and if it had I think Captain Yancey would have briefed us about it."

Burke shrugged. Oscar went on, "It affects what we're to do. You've stirred up a mess, Burke. With the discovery of valuable minerals here, there will be more men coming along. The way you've started things off there could be more and more trouble, until there was nothing but guerrilla warfare between the natives and the men, everywhere you looked. It might even spread to the poles. It's the Patrol's business to stamp out such things before they get started and that's what I construe our mission here to be. I've got to apologize and smooth it over and do my darnedest to correct a first bad impression. Can you give me any more information, anything at all, that might help me when I try it?"

"I don't think so. But go ahead—soft-soap the old girl any way you can. You can even pretend to take me away from here under arrest if it will do any good. Say, that might be a good idea! I'll be agreeable to it just as long as I get out."

Oscar shook his head. "I might take you out under arrest, if she wants it that way. But as far as I can see you are a perfectly legal prisoner here for a crime under the local customs."

"What in the world are you talking about?"

"I might point out that what you've admitted doing is a crime anywhere. You can be tried for it on Terra if she wants it that way.

But it really doesn't matter to me, one way or the other. It's no business of the Patrol."

"But you can't leave me here!"

Oscar shrugged. "That's the way I see it. Lieutenant Thurlow might snap out of it at any time, then you could take it up with him. As long as I'm in charge I'm not going to jeopardize the Patrol's mission to try to help you get away with murder—and I do mean murder!"

"But—" Burke looked wildly around him. "Tex! Matt! Are you going to let him side up with those frog-people against a *man?*"

Matt gave him a stony-eyed stare. Tex said, "Button your lip, Stinky."

Oscar added, "Yes, do. And go to sleep. My arm hurts and I don't want to be bothered any more with you tonight."

The room quieted down at once, even though none of them got to sleep quickly. Matt lay awake a long time, worrying out their predicament, wondering whether or not Oscar could convince the frog mother—he thought of her as such—of the innocence of their intentions, and repeatedly blaming himself for the disaster to the jeep. Presently he fell into an exhausted sleep.

He was awakened by a moaning sound. It brought him wide awake at once and to the lieutenant's side. He found Tex already awake with him. "What is it?" he asked. "Is he worse?"

"He keeps trying to say something," Tex answered.

Thurlow's eyes came open and he looked up at Matt. *"Maman,"* he said querulously. *"Maman—pourquoi fait-il nuit ainsi?"*

Oscar joined them. "What's he saying?"

"Sounds like he's calling for his momma," said Tex. "The rest is just gibberish."

"Where did that bladder get to? We could give him a drink." It was found and again the patient drank, then seemed to drop at once to sleep. "You guys go back to sleep," said Oscar. "I want to snag a word with the guard that brings us our next meal and try to get to see the big mother. He's got to have some medical attention, somehow."

"I'll take the watch, Oz," Matt offered.

"No, I can't sleep very well anyhow. This darn thing itches." He held up his damaged arm.

"Well—all right."

Matt was still awake when the curtain opened. Oscar had been sitting cross-legged at the door, waiting; as the native shoved inside a platter of food, he thrust his arm into the opening.

"*Remove thy arm,*" said the native emphatically.

"*Attend thou me,*" insisted Oscar. "*I must have speech with thy mother.*"

"*Remove thy arm.*"

"*Thou wilt carry my message?*"

"*Remove thy arm!*"

Oscar did so and the curtain was hurriedly secured. Matt said, "Doesn't look as if they intended to powwow with us, does it, Oz?"

"Keep your shirt on," Oscar answered. "Breakfast. Wake up the others."

It was the same dull fodder as before. "Split it five ways, Tex," Oscar directed. "The lieutenant may snap out of it and be hungry."

Burke looked at it and sniffed. "I'm sick of that stuff. I don't want any."

"Okay, split it four ways." Tex nodded and did so.

They ate; presently Matt sat back, burped reflectively, and said, "You know, while I could use some orange juice and coffee, that stuff's not bad."

"Did I ever tell you," asked Tex, "about the time my Uncle Bodie got incarcerated in the jail at Juarez?—by mistake, of course."

"Of course," agreed Oscar. "What happened?"

"Well, they fed him nothing but Mexican jumping beans. He—"

"Didn't they upset him?"

"Not a bit. He ate as many as he could and a week later he jumped over a twelve foot wall and bounced home."

"Having met your Uncle Bodie, I can well believe it. What do you suppose he would do under these circumstances?"

"Obvious. He'd make love to the old girl and inside of three days he'd be head man around here."

"I think I'll have some breakfast after all," announced Burke.

"You'll leave that chow for the lieutenant," Oscar said firmly. "You had your chance."

"You've got no authority over me."

"There are two reasons why you are wrong."

"So? What are they?"

"Matt and Tex."

Tex stood up. "Shall I clip him, boss?"

"Not yet."

"Oh, shucks!"

"Anyhow," objected Matt. "I get first crack—I'm senior to you, Tex."

"Pulling rank on me, eh? Why you unspeakable rat!"

"Mister Rat, if you please. Yep, in this instance I claim rank."

"But this is a social occasion."

"Shut up, you guys," instructed Oscar. "Neither of you is to clip him unless he gets to sniffing around that food dish."

There was a noise at the door, the curtain was pushed back and a native announced, *"My mother will see thee. Come."*

"Myself alone, or me and my sisters?"

"All of you. Come."

However, when Burke attempted to pass through the door two of the little creatures pushed him back inside. They continued to restrain him while four others picked up Lieutenant Thurlow and carried him outside. The numerous party set out down the passageway.

"I wish they would light these rabbit nests," Tex complained, after stumbling.

"It's light enough to their eyes," Oscar answered.

"Natch," agreed Tex, "but a fat lot of good that does me. *My* eyes don't see infra-red."

"Then pick up your big feet."

They were taken to another large room, not the entrance hall, for it contained no pool of water. An amphibian, the same who had viewed them and ordered them taken away on their arrival, sat on a raised platform at the far end of the room. Only Oscar recognized her as such; to the others she looked like the rest.

Oscar quickened his pace and drew ahead of his escort. *"Greetings, thou old and wise mother of many."*

She sat up and looked at him steadily. The room was very quiet. On every side the little folk waited, looking first from the earthlings to their chief executive, then back again. Matt felt that somehow the nature of her answer would show them their fate.

"Greetings." She had chucked the ball back to Oscar by refusing to assign him any title at all, good or bad. *"Thou sought speech with me. Thou may speak."*

"What manner of city is thine? Have I, perhaps, journeyed so far that manners are no longer observed?" The Venerian word meant much more than "manners"; it referred to the entire obligatory code of custom by which the older and stronger looked out for the weaker and younger.

The entire audience stirred. Matt wondered if Oscar had overplayed his hand. The expression of the leader changed but Matt had no way of reading it. *"My city and my daughters live ever by custom—"* She used a more inclusive term, embracing tabus and other required acts, as well as the law of assistance. *"—and I have never before heard it suggested that we fail in performance."*

"I hear thee, gracious mother of many, but thy words confuse me. We come, my 'sisters' and I, seeking shelter and help for ourselves and our 'mother,' who is gravely ill. I myself am injured and am unable to protect my younger 'sisters.' What have we received in thy house? Thou hast deprived us of our freedom; our 'mother' lies unattended and failing. Indeed we have not even been granted the common decency of personal rooms in which to eat."

A noise rose from the spectators which Matt correctly interpreted as the equivalent of a shocked gasp. Oscar had deliberately used the offensive word *"eat,"* instead of talking around it. Matt was sure now that Oscar had lost his judgment.

If so, Oscar went on to confirm it. *"Are we fish, that such should be done to us? Or are the customs such among thy daughters?"*

"We follow the customs," she said shortly, and even Matt and Tex could interpret the anger in her voice. *"It was my understanding that thy breed had no decencies. It will be corrected."* She spoke sharply in an aside to one of her staff; the little creature trotted away. *"As to thy freedom, what I had done was lawful for it was to protect my daughters."*

"To protect thy daughters? From what? From my ailing 'mother'? Or from my injured arm?"

"Thy sister who knows no customs has forfeited thy freedom."

"I hear thy words, wise mother, but I understand them not."

The amphibian seemed nonplused. She inquired specifically about Burke, naming him by his terrestrial tag, calling it "Captain-Burke," as one word. Oscar assured her that Burke was no "daughter" of Oscar's "mother," nor of Oscar's "mother's mother."

The matriarch considered this. *"If we return you to the upper waters will you leave us?"*

"What of my 'mother'?" asked Oscar. *"Wouldst thou cast 'her' forth thus ailing, to die and to be destroyed by the creatures of the slime?"* On this occasion he carefully avoided the Venerian expression for "to be eaten."

The mother-of-many had Thurlow carried up to the dais on which she sat. Several of the little folk gathered around him and examined him, speaking to each other in high, lisping whispers.

Presently the matriarch herself joined the consultation, then spoke again. *"Thy mother sleeps."*

"It is a sickly sleep. 'Her' head was injured by a blow." Oscar joined the group and showed them the lump on the back of Thurlow's head. They compared it with Oscar's own head, running gentle, inquisitive little hands through his blond hair. There was more lisping chatter; Matt found himself unable to follow even what he could hear; most of the words were strange.

"My learned sisters tell me that they dare not take thy mother's head apart for fear that they could not get it back together," announced the mother-of-many.

"Well, that's a relief!" Tex said out of the corner of his mouth.

"Old Oz wouldn't let them anyhow," Matt whispered.

The leader gave instructions and four of her "daughters" picked up the unconscious officer and started carrying him out of the room. Tex called out, "Hey, Oz—do you think that's safe?"

"It's all right," Oscar called back, then explained to the matriarch, *"My 'sister' feared for the safety of our 'mother.' "*

The creature made a gesture that reminded Matt suddenly of his great-aunt Dora—she positively sniffed. *"Tell her that her nose need not twitch!"*

"She says not to get in an uproar, Tex."

"I heard her. Okay, you're the boss," Tex answered, and then muttered, "My nose, indeed!"

When Thurlow had been removed the leader turned toward them again. *"May thy dreams be of daughters."*

"May thy dreams be as pleasant, gracious mother."

"We will speak again." She gathered herself up to a lordly four feet and left the chamber. When she was gone the group of escorts conducted the cadets out of the council hall but by a different passageway than that from which they had come. The group stopped presently at another doorway. The guide in charge wished them farewell with the same formula as the matriarch. A curtain was drawn but it was not fastened, a point that Matt immediately checked. He turned to Oscar.

"I've got to hand it to you, Oz. Anytime you get tired of the Patrol and don't want to run for prime minister of the System, I can book you for a swell job, selling snow to Eskimos. For you it would be a cinch."

"Matt's not just fanning the air," agreed Tex. "Oscar, you were wonderful. Uncle Bodie couldn't have handled the old gal any slicker."

"That's high praise, Tex. I'll admit to being relieved. If the Little People weren't so downright decent it wouldn't have worked."

The living room of their apartment—there were two rooms—was about the size of the room they had been in, but was more comfortable. There was a softly padded, wide couch running around the wall. In the center of the room was a pool of water, black under the dim light. "Oz, do you suppose that bathtub connects with the outside?" Tex wanted to know.

"They almost always do."

Matt became interested. "Maybe we could swim out."

"Go ahead and try it. Don't get lost in the dark and remember not to swim under water more than half the distance you can hold your breath." Oscar smiled cynically.

"I see your point."

"Anyhow, we want to stay until we've gotten over the last hurdle."

Tex wandered on into the second room. "Hey, Oz—come look at this."

Matt and Oscar joined him. There were rows of little closets down each side, ten in all, each with its own curtain. "Oh, yes, our eating booths."

"That reminds me," said Matt. "I thought you had wrecked everything, Oz, when you started talking about eating. But you pulled out of it beautifully."

"I didn't pull out of it; I did it on purpose."

"Why?"

"It was a squeeze play. I had to shock them with the idea that they were indecent, or looked that way to us. It established us as 'people,' from their point of view. After that it was easy." Oscar went on. "Now that we are accepted as people, we've got to be awfully careful not to undo it. I don't like to eat in one of these dark little cubbyholes any better than you do, but we don't dare take a chance of being seen eating—you don't dare even fail to draw the curtain, as one of them might come popping in. Remember, eating is the only sort of privacy they observe."

"I get you," agreed Tex. "Pie with a fork."

"Huh?"

"Never mind—it's a painful memory. But Matt and I won't slip."

16.
P.R.S. *ASTARTE*

Oscar was summoned again the next day into the presence of the city's chief magistrate and started laying the foundation, in a leisurely, indirect fashion, for formal diplomatic relations in the future. He began by getting her story of the trouble with the *Gary* and its skipper. It was much as Burke had admitted it to be, although from a different viewpoint.

Oscar had inquired casually as to why the swamp Burke wanted was tabu. He was worried that he might be invading religious matters but he felt that he needed to know—it was a dead certainty that others would be along, in due course, to attempt to exploit the trans-uranic ores; if the Patrol was to prevent further breaches of the peace the matter must be investigated.

The matriarch answered without hesitation; the swamp was tabu because the ore muds were poisonous.

Oscar felt the relief of a man who has just been told that it will not be necessary to lose a leg, after all. The ores were understandably poisonous; it was a matter that the Patrol could undoubtedly negotiate—conditional or practical tabus had been overcome many times with natives. He tabled the matter, as something to be taken up at a later time by the appropriate experts.

In a later interview he sounded her out on the subject of the Patrol. She had heard of it, in a fashion, apparently—she used the native word given by the polar-region natives to all colonial government, a word meaning "guardians of the customs" or "keepers of the law."

The native meaning was quite useful to Oscar, for he found it impossible to get over to her the idea that the Patrol was intended to prevent war—"war" was a concept she had never heard of!

But her conservative mind was naturally prejudiced in favor of any organization tagged as "guardians of the customs." Oscar approached it from that viewpoint. He explained to her that more of his own kind would be arriving; therefore the "great mother of many" of his own people had sent them as messengers to propose that a "mother" from Oscar's people be sent to aid her in avoiding friction.

She was receptive to the idea as it fitted her own experience and concepts. The groups of natives near the polar colonies were in the habit of handling their foreign affairs by exchanging "mothers"—actually judges—who ruled on matters arising out of differences in custom; Oscar had presented the matter in the same terms.

He had thus laid the groundwork for a consulate, extraterritorial courts, and an Earthman police force; the mission, as he saw it, was complete—provided he could get back to base and report before other prospectors, mining engineers, and boomers of all sorts started showing up.

Only then had he spoken to her of getting back—to have her suggest that he remain permanently as "mother" for his people. (The root word translated as "mother" is used for every position of authority in the Venerian speech; the modifiers and the context give the word its current meaning.)

The proposal left Oscar temporarily speechless. "I didn't know what to say next," he confessed later. "From her point of view she was honoring me. If I turned it down, it might offend her and crab the whole deal."

"Well, how did you talk your way out of it?" Tex wanted to know. "Or did you?"

"I think so. I explained as diplomatically as possible that I was too young for the honor and that I was acting as *'mother'* only because Thurlow was laid up and that, in any case, my *'great mother of many'* had other work which I was obliged, by custom, to carry out."

"I guess that held her."

"I think she just filed it away as a point to negotiate. The Little People are great negotiators; you'll have to come to New Auckland some time and listen to the proceedings of a mixed court."

"Keep to the point," suggested Matt.

"That *is* to the point—they don't fight; they just argue until

somebody gives in. Anyhow, I told her that we had to get Thurlow
back where he could get surgical attention. She understood that all
right and expressed regret for the steenth time that her own little
girls couldn't do the trick. But she had a suggestion for curing the
boss."

"Yes?" demanded Matt. "What was it?" Matt had appointed
himself Thurlow's caretaker, working with the amphibian healers
who now had him as a professional responsibility. He had taught
them to take his pulse and to watch his respiration; now there was
always one of the gentle creatures squatting on the end of Thurlow's couch, watching him with grave eyes. They seemed gen-
uinely distressed at not being able to help him; the lieutenant had
remained in a semi-coma, coming out of it enough occasionally
that it had been possible to feed him and give him water, but never
saying anything that the cadets could understand. Matt found that
the little nurses were quite unsqueamish about feeding a helpless
person; they accepted offensive necessities with the same gal-
lantry as a human nurse.

But Thurlow, while he did not die, did not get any better.

"The old girl's suggestion was sort of radical, but logical. She
suggested that her healers take Burke's head apart first, to see how
it was made. Then they could operate on the boss and fix him."

"*What?*" said Matt.

Tex was having trouble controlling himself. He laughed so
hard he strangled, then got hiccoughs and had to be pounded on
the back. "Oh, boy!" he finally exploded, tears streaming down
his cheeks, "this is wonderful. I can't wait to see Stinky's face.
You haven't told him, have you?"

"No."

"Then let me. Dibs on the job."

"I don't think we ought to tell him," objected Oscar. "Why
kick him when he's down?"

"Oh, don't be so noble! It won't hurt any to let him know that
his social rating is 'guinea pig.' "

"She really hates him, doesn't she?" Matt commented.

"Why shouldn't she?" Tex answered. "A dozen or more of her
people dead—do you expect her to regard it as a schoolboy
prank?"

"You've both got her wrong," Oscar objected. "She doesn't
hate him."

"Huh?"

"Could you hate a dog? Or a cat—"

"Sure could," said Tex. "There was an old tomcat we had once—"

"Pipe down and let me finish. Conceding your point, you can hate a cat only by placing it on your own social level. She doesn't regard Burke as . . . well, as *people* at all, because he doesn't follow the customs. We're 'people' to her, because we do, even though we look like him. But Burke in her mind is just a dangerous animal, like a wolf or a shark, to be penned up or destroyed—but not hated or punished.

"Anyhow," he went on, "I told her it wouldn't do, because we had an esoteric and unexplainable but unbreakable religious tabu that interfered—that blocked her off from pressing the point. But I told her we'd like to use Burke's ship to get the lieutenant back. She gave it to me. We go out tomorrow to look at it."

"Well, for crying out loud—why didn't you say so, instead of giving all this build-up?"

They had made much the same underwater trip as on entering the city, to be followed by a longish swim and a short trip overland. The city mother herself honored them with her company.

The *Gary* was everything Burke had claimed for her, modern, atomic-powered, expensively outfitted and beautiful, with sharp wings as graceful as a swallow's.

She was also a hopeless wreck.

Her hull was intact except the ruined door, which appeared to have been subjected to great heat, or an incredible corrosive, or both. Matt wondered how it had been done and noted it as still another indication that the Venerians were not the frog-seal-beaver creatures his Earth-side prejudices had led him to think.

The inside of the ship had looked fairly well, too, until they started checking over the controls. In searching the ship the amphibians, to whom even a common door latch was a puzzle, had simply burned their way through impediments—including the access hatch to the ship's autopilot and gyro compartment. The circuits of the ship's nervous system were a mass of fused and melted junk.

Nevertheless they spent three hours convincing themselves that it would take the resources of a dockyard to make the ship fly again. They gave up reluctantly at last and started back, their spirits drooping.

Oscar had at once taken up with the city mother the project of recovering the jeep. He had not mentioned it before as the *Gary* seemed the better bet. Language difficulties would have hampered him considerably—their hostesses had no word for "vehicle," much less a word for "rocket ship"—but the *Gary* gave him something to point to wherewith to explain.

When she understood what he was driving at she gave orders which caused the party to swim to the point where the cadets had first been picked up. The cadets made sure of the spot by locating the abandoned litter and from there Oscar had led them back to the sinkhole that was the grave of the jeep. There he acted out what had happened, showing her the scar in the bank where the jeep had balanced and pacing off on the bank the dimensions of the ship.

The mother-of-many discussed the problem with her immediate staff while the cadets waited, ignored rather than excluded. Then she abruptly gave the order to leave; it was getting on in the late afternoon and even the Venerians do not voluntarily remain out in the jungle overnight.

That had ended the matter for several days. Oscar's attempts to find out what, if anything, was being done about the jeep were brushed off as one might snub a persistent brat. It left them with nothing to do. Tex played his harmonica until threatened with a ducking in the room's center pool. Oscar sat around, nursing his arm and brooding. Matt spent much of his time watching over Thurlow and became well acquainted with the nurses who never left him, especially one bright-eyed cheerful little thing who called herself "Th'wing."

Th'wing changed his viewpoint about Venerians. At first he regarded her much as he might a good and faithful, and unusually intelligent dog. By degrees he began to think of her as a friend, an interesting companion—and as "people." He had tried to tell her about himself and his own kind and his own world. She had listened with alert interest, but without ever taking her eyes off Thurlow.

Matt was forced willy-nilly into the concepts of astronomy—and came up against a complete block. To Th'wing there was the world of water and swamp and occasional dry land; above that was the endless cloud. She knew the Sun, for her eyes, perceptive to infra-red, could see it, even though Matt could not, but she thought of it as a disc of light and warmth, not as a star.

As for other stars, none of her people had ever seen them and the idea did not exist. The notion of another planet was not ridiculous; it was simply incomprehensible—Matt got nowhere.

He told Oscar about it. "Well, what did you expect?" Oscar

had wanted to know. "All the natives are like that. They're polite but they think you are talking about your religion."

"The natives around the colonies, too?"

"Same deal."

"But they've seen rocket ships, some of 'em, anyhow. Where do they think we come from? They must know we haven't been here always."

"Sure they know that—but the ones at South Pole think we came originally from North Pole and the ones around North Pole are sure we came from South Pole—and it's no use trying to tell them anything different."

The difficulty was not one-sided. Th'wing was continually using words and concepts which Matt could not understand and which could not be straightened out even with Oscar's help. He began to get hazily the idea that Th'wing was the sophisticated one and that he, Matt, was the ignorant outlander. "Sometimes I think," he told Tex, "that Th'wing thinks that I am an idiot studying hard to become a moron—but flunking the course."

"Well, don't let it throw you, kid. You'll be a moron, yet, if you just keep trying."

On the morning fifteen Venus days after their arrival the mother of the city sent for them and had them taken to the site of the jeep. They stood on the same bank where they had climbed ashore from the sinking ship, but the scene had changed. A great hole stretched out at their feet; in it the jeep lay, three-quarters exposed. A swarm of Venerians crawled over it and around it like workmen in a dockyard.

The amphibians had begun by adding something to the thin yellow mud of the sinkhole. Oscar had tried to get the formula for the additive, but even his command of the language was useless—the words were strange. Whatever it was, the effect was to turn the almost-liquid mud into a thick gel which became more and more stiff the longer it was exposed to air. The little folk had carved it away from the top as fast as it consolidated; the jeep was now surrounded by the sheer walls of a caisson-like pit. A ramp led up on the shoreward side and a stream of the apparently tireless little creatures trotted up it, bearing more jelled blocks of mud.

The cadets had climbed down into the pit to watch, talking in high spirits about the prospects of putting the jeep back into commission and jetting out again, until the Venerian in charge of the work had urged them emphatically to go up out of the pit and stay out of the way. They joined the city mother and waited.

"Ask her how she expects to get it up out of there, Oz," Tex suggested. Oscar did so.

"Tell thy impatient daughter to chase her fish and I will chase mine."

"No need for her to be rude about it," Tex complained.

"What did she say?" inquired the mother-of-many.

" *'She' thanks thee for the lesson,"* Oscar prevaricated.

The Little People worked rapidly. It was evident that the ship would be entirely free before the day was far advanced—and clean as well; the outside shone now and a steady procession of them had been pouring in and out of the door of the ship, bearing cakes of jellied mud. In the last hour the routine had changed; the little workers came out bearing distended bladders. The clean-up squad was at work.

Oscar watched them approvingly. "I told you they would lick it clean."

Matt looked thoughtful. "I'm worried, Oz, about the possibility that they will mess with something on the control board and get into trouble."

"Why?" The leads are all sealed away. They can't hurt anything. You locked the board when you left it, didn't you?"

"Yes, of course."

"Anyhow, they can't fire the jet when she's in that attitude even if you hadn't."

"That's true. Still, I'm worried."

"Well, let's take a look, then. I want to talk to the foreman in any case. I've got an idea."

"What idea?" asked Tex.

"Maybe they can get her upright in the pit. It seems to me we could take off from there and never have to drag her out. Might save several days." They went down the ramp and located the Venerian in charge, then Matt and Tex went inside the ship while Oscar stayed to talk over his idea.

It was hard to believe that the pilot room had lately been choked with filthy, yellow mud. A few amphibians were still working in the after end of the room; elsewhere the compartment was clean.

Matt climbed to the pilot's seat and started inspecting. He noticed first that the sponge-rubber eyeguards for the infra-red viewer were missing. This was not important, but he wondered what had happened to them—did the little folk have the vice of souvenir snitching? He filed away the suspicion, and attempted a dry run on the controls, without firing the jet.

Nothing operated—nothing at all.

He looked the board over more carefully. To a casual inspection it was clean, bright, in perfect order, but he now perceived many little pits and specks. He dug at one with a finger nail, something came away. He worked at it a bit more and produced a tiny hole into the interior of the control board. It gave him a sick feeling at the pit of his stomach. "Say, Tex—come here a minute. I've got something."

"You think you've got something," Tex answered in muffled tones. "Wait till you've seen this."

He found Tex with a wrench in his hand and a cover plate off the gyro compartment. "After what happened to the *Gary* I decided to check this first. Did you ever see such a mess?"

The mud had gotten in. The gyros, although shut down, were of course still spinning when the ship had gone into the sink-hole and normally would have coasted for days; they should still have been spinning when Tex removed the cover. Instead they had ground to a stop against the mud—burned to a stop.

"We had better call Oscar," Matt said dully.

With Oscar's help they surveyed the mess. Every instrument, every piece of electronic equipment had been invaded. Nonmetallic materials were missing completely; thin metal sheets such as instrument cases were riddled with pinholes. "I can't understand what did it," Oscar protested, almost in tears.

Matt asked the Venerian in charge of the work. She did not understand him at first; he pointed out the pinholes, whereupon she took a lump of the jelled mud and mashed it flat. With a slender finger she carefully separated out what seemed to be a piece of white string, a couple of inches long. *This is the source of thy troubles.*

"Know what it is, Oz?"

"Some sort of worm. I don't recognize it. But I wouldn't expect to; the polar regions are nothing like this, thank goodness."

"I suppose we might as well call off the working party."

"Let's don't jump the gun. There might be some way to salvage the mess. We've *got* to."

"Not a chance. The gyros alone are enough. You can't raise ship in a wingless job without gyros. It's impossible."

"Maybe we could clean them up and get them to working."

"Maybe you could—I can't. The mud got to the *bearings*, Oz."

Jensen agreed regretfully. The gyros, the finest precision

equipment in a ship, were no better than their bearings. Even an instrument maker in a properly equipped shop would have thrown up his hands at gyros abused as these had been.

"We've at least got to salvage some electronic equipment and jury-rig some sort of a sending set. We've got to get a message through."

"You've seen it. What do you think?"

"Well—we'll pick out the stuff that seems in the best shape and take it back with us. They'll help us with the stuff."

"What sort of shape will it be in after an hour or so in the water? No, Oz, the thing to do is to lock up the door, once the last of the filth is out and come back and work here."

"Okay, we'll do that." Oscar called to Tex, who was still snooping around. He arrived swearing.

"What now, Tex?" Oscar asked wearily.

"I thought maybe we could at least take some civilized food back with us, but those confounded worms bored into the cans. Every ration in the ship is spoiled."

"Is that all?"

" 'Is that all? Is that all?' the man says! What do you want? Flood, pestilence, and earthquakes?"

But it was not all—further inspection showed another thing which would have dismayed them had they not already been as low in spirit as they could get. The jeep's jet ran on liquid hydrogen and liquid oxygen. The fuel tanks, insulated and protected from direct radiation, could retain fuel for long periods, but the warm mud had reached them and heated them; the expanding gases had bled out through relief valves. The jeep was out of fuel.

Oscar looked this situation over stonily. "I wish the *Gary* had been chemically powered," he finally commented.

"What of it?" Matt answered. "We couldn't raise ship if we had all the juice this side of Jupiter."

The mother-of-many had to be shown before she was convinced that there was anything wrong with the ship. Even then, she seemed only half convinced and somehow vexed with the cadets for being unsatisfied with the gift of their ship back. Oscar spent much of the return journey trying to repair his political fences with her.

Oscar ate no dinner that night. Even Tex only picked at his food and did not touch his harmonica afterwards. Matt spent the evening silently sitting out a watch in Thurlow's room.

* * *

The mother-of-many sent for all three of them the next morning. After formal exchange of greetings she commenced, *"Little mother, is it true that thy Gary is indeed dead, like the other Gary?"*

"It is true, gracious mother."

"Is it true that without a Gary thou canst not find thy way back to thine own people?"

"It is true, wise mother of many; the jungle would destroy us."

She stopped and gestured to one of her court. The "daughter" trotted to her with a bundle half as big as the bearer. The city mother took it and invited, or commanded, the cadets to join her on the dais. She commenced unwrapping. The object inside seemed to have more bandages than a mummy. At long last she had it uncovered and held it out to them. "Is this thine?"

It was a large book. On the cover, in large ornate letters, was:

LOG
of
the
Astarte

Tex looked at it and said, "Great leaping balls of fire! It can't be."

Matt stared and whispered, "It must be. The lost first expedition. They didn't fail—*they got here.*"

Oscar stared and said nothing at all until the city mother repeated her question impatiently. *"Is this thine?"*

"Huh? What? Oh, sure! *Wise and gracious mother, this thing belonged to my 'mother's mother's mother.' We are her 'daughters.'"*

"Then it is thine."

Oscar took it from her and gingerly opened the brittle pages. They stared at the original entry for "raise ship"—but most especially at the year entry in the date column—"1971." "Holy Moses!" breathed Tex. "Look at that—just look at it. More than a hundred years ago."

They thumbed through it. There was page after page of one line entries of "free fall, position according to plan" which they skipped over rapidly, except for one: "Christmas day. Carols were sung after the mid-day meal."

It was the entries after grounding they were after. They were forced to skim them as the mother-of-many was beginning to show impatience: "—climate no worse than the most extreme terrestrial tropics in the rainy season. The dominant life form seems to be a large amphibian. This planet is definitely possible of colonization."

"—the amphibians have considerable intelligence and seem to talk with each other. They are friendly and an attempt is being made to bridge the semantic gap."

"—Hargraves has contracted an infection, apparently fungoid, which is unpleasantly reminiscent of leprosy. The surgeon is treating it experimentally."

"—after the funeral muster Hargraves' room was sterilized at 400°."

The handwriting changed shortly thereafter. The city mother was growing so obviously discontented that they glanced only at the last two entries: "—Johnson continues to fail, but the natives are very helpful—"

"—my left hand is now useless. I have made up my mind to decommission the ship and take my chances in the hands of the natives. I shall take this log with me and add to it, if possible."

The handwriting was firm and clear; it was their own eyes that blurred it.

The mother-of-many immediately ordered up the party used to ferry the humans in and out of the city. She was not disposed to stop to talk and, once the journey began, there was no opportunity to until they reached dry land.

"Look here, Oz," Tex started in, as soon as he had shaken off the water, "do you really think she's taking us to the *Astarte?*"

"Could be. Probably is."

"Do you think there is a chance that we will find the ship intact?" asked Matt.

"Not a chance. Not a chance in this world. On one point alone, she couldn't possibly have any fuel left in her tanks. You saw what happened to the jeep. What do you think a century has done to the *Astarte?*" He paused and looked thoughtful. "Anyhow, I'm not going to get my hopes up, not again. I couldn't stand it, three times. That's too many."

"I guess you're right," agreed Matt. "It won't do to get excited. She's probably a mound of rust under a covering of vines."

"Who said anything about not getting excited?" Oscar answered. "I'm so excited I can hardly talk. But don't think of the *Astarte* as a possible way to get back; think of her historically."

"*You* think of it that way," said Tex. "I'm a believer and a hoper. I want to get out of this dump."

"Oh, you'll get out! They'll come find us some day—and then they'll finish the mission we flubbed."

"Look," answered Tex, "couldn't we go off duty and not think about the mission just for the next quarter of a mile? These insects are something fierce—you think about Oscar and I'll think about Mother Jarman's favorite son. I wish I was back in the good old *Triplex*."

"You were the guy that was always beefing that the *Triplex* was a madhouse."

"So I was wrong. I can be big about it."

They came to one of the rare rises in the level of the ground, all of ten feet above water level. The natives started to whisper and lisp excitedly among themselves. Matt caught the Venerian word for *"tabu."* "Did you get that, Oz?" he said in Basic. "Tabu."

"Yes. I don't think she told them where she was taking them."

The column stopped and spread out; the three cadets moved forward, pushing rank growth aside and stepped in a clearing.

In front of them, her rakish wings festooned in vines and her entire hull sheathed in some translucent substance, was the Patrol Rocket Ship *Astarte*.

17.
HOTCAKES FOR BREAKFAST

The city mother was standing near the door of the *Astarte*, underneath the starboard wing. Two of her people were working at the door, using bladders to squirt some liquid around the edges. The translucent layer over the hull melted away wherever the liquid touched it. They grasped a free edge of the skin stuff and began to peel it away. "Look at that," said Tex. "Do you see what they've done? The ship is *Venusized.*"

His use of the term was loose; an item that has been "planetized" is one that has been rendered stable against certain typical conditions of the planet concerned, as defined by tests of the Bureau of Standards—for example, an item listed in the colonial edition of the Sears & Montgomery catalog as "Venusized" is thereby warranted to resist the excessive humidity, the exotic fungi, and certain of the planet's pests. The *Astarte* was merely encased in a sheath.

"Looks like it," agreed Oscar, his voice carefully restrained. "Sort of a spray-gun job."

"Five gets you ten it never saw a spray gun. The Venerians did it." Tex slapped at an insect. "You know what this means, Oz?"

"I'm way ahead of you. Don't get your hopes up. And don't try to get mine up, either. A hundred years is a long time."

"Oz, you don't get any fun out of life."

The little workers were having difficulties. The top of the door was much higher than they could reach; they were now trying to form two-high pyramids, but, having no shoulders to speak of, they were hardly built for the job. Matt said to Oscar, "Couldn't we give them a hand with that?"

"I'll see." Oscar went forward and suggested that the cadets take over the job of squirting on the solvent. The mother person looked at him.

"Canst thou grow a new hand, if needed?"

Oscar admitted that he could not.

"Then do not tamper with that which thou dost not understand."

Using their own methods the natives soon had the door cleared. It was latched but not locked; the door refused to open for a moment, then gave suddenly. They scrambled up into the airlock. "Wait a minute," Matt whispered. "Hadn't we better go easy? We don't know that the infection that got them is necessarily dead."

"Don't be silly," Tex whispered back. "If your immunizations hadn't worked, you'd have been a sick chicken long ago."

"Tex is right, Matt. And there's no need to whisper. Ghosts can't hear."

"How do you know?" objected Tex. "Are you a doctor of ghostology?"

"I don't believe in ghosts."

"I do. Once my Uncle Bodie stayed overnight—"

"Let's get on inside," Matt insisted.

The passageway beyond the inner door was dark, save for the light that filtered in through the lock. The air had a strange odor, not precisely foul but lifeless—old.

The control room beyond was dimly but adequately lighted; the light from outside filtered softly through the sheathing that still covered the quartz pilot's port. The room was very cramped. The cadets were used to roomy modern ships; the *Astarte*'s wings gave her a false impression of great size. Inside she was smaller than the jeep.

Tex began humming something about "—stout-hearted men—," then broke off suddenly. "Look at the darned thing!" he said. "Just look at it. To think they actually made an interplanetary jump in it. Look at that control board. Why, she's as primitive as a rowboat. And yet they took the chance. Puts you in mind of Columbus and the *Santa Maria.*"

"Or the Viking ships," suggested Matt.

"There were men in those days," agreed Oscar, not very originally but with great sincerity.

"You can say that louder," commented Tex. "There's no getting around it, fellows; we were born too late for the age of adventure. Why, they weren't even heading for the listed port; they just blasted off into the dark and trusted to luck that they could get back."

"They didn't get back," Oscar said softly.

"Let's talk about something else," Matt requested. "I'm covered with goose pimples as it is."

"Okay," Oscar concurred, "I'd better get back and see what her royal nibs is doing anyway." He left, to return almost at once, accompanied by the city mother. "She was just waiting to be invited," he called out ahead of them, in Basic, "and huffy at being forgotten. Help me butter her up."

The native official turned out to be helpful; except for the control room the other spaces were dark, even to her. She stepped to the door made known her wants, and returned with one of the glowing orange spheres they used for lighting. It was a poor excuse for a flashlight, but about as effective as a candle.

Everywhere the ship was orderly and clean, save for a faint film of dust. "Say what you like, Oscar," commented Matt, "I'm beginning to get my hopes up. I don't believe there is anything wrong with her. It looks as if the crew had just gone out for a walk. We may be able to put her in commission."

"I'm ready to throw in with Oscar," Tex objected. "I've lost my enthusiasm—I'd rather go over Niagara Falls in a barrel."

"*They* flew her," Matt pointed out.

"Sure they did—and my hat's off to them. But it takes heroes to fly a box as primitive as this and I'm not the hero type."

The mother-of-many lost interest presently and went outside. Tex borrowed the orange sphere and continued to look around while Matt and Oscar gave the control room a careful going over. Tex found a locker containing small, sealed packages marked "Personal effects of Roland Hargraves," "Personal effects of Rupert H. Schreiber," and other names. He put them back carefully.

Oscar shouted for him presently. "I think we had better get going. Her nibs hinted that when she left."

"Come see what I've found. Food!"

Matt and Oscar came to the door of the galley storeroom. "Do you suppose any of it is any good?" asked Matt.

"Why not? It's all canned. Jigger for me and we'll find out." Tex operated with a can opener. "Phewey!" he said presently. "Anybody want to sample some embalmed corned beef hash? Throw it outside, Matt, before it stinks up the place."

"It already has."

"But look at this!" Tex held up a can marked: *Old Plantation Hotcake Flour*. "This won't be spoiled—hotcakes for breakfast, troops. I can hardly wait."

"What good are flapjacks without syrup?"

"All the comforts of home—half a dozen cans of it." He produced one marked: *Genuine Vermont Maple Syrup, unadulterated.*

Tex wanted to take some back with them. Oscar vetoed it, on both practical and diplomatic grounds. Tex suggested that they remain in the ship, not go back. "Presently, Tex, presently," Oscar agreed. "You forgot about Lieutenant Thurlow."

"So I did. Close my big mouth."

"Speaking of Mr. Thurlow," put in Matt, "you've given me an idea. He won't touch much of that native hash, even when he seems to come pretty far out of it. How about that sugar syrup? I could feed it to him from a drinking bladder."

"It can't hurt him and it might help," decided Oscar. "We'll take half the syrup back with us." Tex picked the cans up, Matt tucked a can opener in his pouch, and they went outside.

Matt was pleased to find Th'wing on watch in Thurlow's room when they got back; she would be easier to deal with than the other nurses. He explained to her what he had in mind, in polite circumlocutions. She accepted a can Matt had opened and tasted, beforehand, and turned her back apologetically while she tasted it.

She spat it out. *"Art thou sure that this will not harm thy ailing mother?"*

Matt understood her hesitation, since Venerian diet runs to starch and protein, not to sugar. He assured her that Thurlow would be helped thereby. They transferred the contents to a bladder.

The cadets talked over what they should do about the *Astarte* after dinner that night. Matt insisted that she could be made to fly; Tex remained of the opinion that they would be silly to attempt it. "She might get high enough to crash—no higher."

Oscar listened, then said, "Matt, did you check the tanks?" Matt admitted that he had. "Then you know there isn't any fuel."

"Then why are you arguing?" Tex interrupted. "The matter is settled."

"No, it's not, announced Oscar. "We'll try to fly her."

"Huh?"

"She can't fly and we'll try anyhow," Oscar went on.

"But why?"

"Okay—here's why. If we just sit here long enough, the Patrol will come along and find us, won't they?"

"Probably," agreed Matt.

"Absolute certainty. That's the way the Patrol works. They won't let us down. Look at the search for the *Pathfinder*—four ships, month after month. If their mishap hadn't killed them, the Patrol would have brought them back alive. We're still alive and we are somewhere near our original destination. They'll find us— the delay simply means they aren't sure we are lost yet; we haven't been out of touch so very long. Anyhow, we knew there wasn't a ship ready at either North Pole or South Pole to attempt an equatorial search, or we wouldn't have gotten the mission in the first place, so it may take a while before they can come for us. But they'll come."

"Then why not wait?" insisted Tex.

"Two reasons. The first is the boss—we've got to get him to a proper hospital before he just fades away and dies."

"And kill him in the take off."

"Maybe. That wouldn't faze him, is my guess. The second reason is—*we* are the Patrol."

"Huh? Come again."

"It's agreed that the Patrol wouldn't give up looking for us. Okay, if that's the sort of an outfit the Patrol is and we are part of the Patrol, then when they find us, they'll find us doing our level best to pull out unassisted, not sitting on our fat fannies waiting for a lift."

"I get you," said Tex. "I was afraid your busy little brain would figure that out, given time. Very well—mark me down as a reluctant hero. I think I'll turn in; this hero business is going to be sweaty and wearing."

It was indeed sweaty. The Venerians continued to be helpful but the actual work of attempting to outfit a ship for space had to be done entirely by the humans. With the permission of the city mother Oscar transferred their headquarters to the *Astarte*. Thurlow was not moved, but arrangements were made for one cadet to be ferried each day back to the city, to report on Thurlow and to bring food back. There were few supplies left in the *Astarte* which were still edible.

However the pancake mix turned out to be usable. Tex had gadgeted together an oil burner of sorts—they had no electrical power as yet—and had charged the contraption with a fish oil ob-

tained from the natives. Over this he baked his hotcakes. They
were noticeably inferior to any that any of the three had ever
tasted, for the flour had aged and changed flavor. They showed little tendency to rise.

But they were hotcakes and they were drowned in maple
syrup. It was a ceremony, at the beginning of each working day,
held on the sly behind a locked door, lest one of their puritanical
friends be offended.

They embarked on a systematic campaign to vandalize each of
the other ships for anything at all that might prove useful in outfit-
ting the *Astarte*. In this, too, they were dependent on the natives;
Matt or Tex could pick out what was wanted, but it took the little
folk to move anything several miles through swamp and water and
unmarked jungle.

They talked of the flight as if they really expected to make it.
"You give me radar," Matt told Oscar, "any sort of approach radar,
so that I've got a chance to land, and I'll set her down somewhere
at South Pole. You can forget about the astrogational junk; it'll be
dead reckoning."

They had settled on New Auckland, South Pole, as their nom-
inal destination. North Pole would have been equally reasonable,
but Oscar was a southern colonial, which decided it.

Oscar had promised the radar, not knowing quite how he could
manage it. The *Gary* was the only hope; her communications
room had been wrecked but Oscar had hopes of salvaging her
belly radar. He set about doing it, while swearing at the impossibility of doing delicate work with one arm in a sling.

Little from the jeep was worth salvaging and none of it was
entirely intact. Oscar had tried at first to use the radar equipment
of the *Astarte*, but had given up—a century of difference in tech-
nology baffled him. Not only were the electronic circuits of the
Astarte vastly more complicated and equally less efficient than the
gear he had been brought up with but the nomenclature was
different—the markings, for example, on a simple resistor were
Greek to him.

As for radio circuits the only sending installation actually fit to
operate was a suit walky-talky from the *Gary*.

Nevertheless there came a morning when they had done what
they could do. Tex was dealing out hotcakes. "It looks to me," he
said, "as if we were ready to go, if we had some 'go' juice."

"How do you figure that," asked Matt. "The control board isn't
even hooked to the jet."

"What of it? I'm going to have to throttle by hand anyhow. I'm going to take that big piece of tubing we pulled out of the *Gary* and string it from you back to me, at the jet throttle. You can shout down it and if I like it I'll do it."

"And if you don't like it?"

"Then I'll do something else. Easy on that syrup, Oz; it's the very last."

Oscar stopped himself, syrup can in midair. "Oh, I'm sorry, Tex. Here—let me slop some from my plate onto yours."

"Don't bother. It was just a reflex remark. To tell the truth, I'm sick of hotcakes. We've had them every day now for more than two weeks, with nothing to break the monotony but hash à la native."

"I'm sick of them, too, but it didn't seem polite to say so, with you doing the cooking." Oscar pushed back his plate. "I don't mind the syrup running out."

"But it hasn't—" Matt stopped.

"Something bite you, Matt?"

"No, I—nothing." He continued to look thoughtful.

"Close your mouth, then. Say, Oz, if we had some 'go' juice for the *Tart,* what would you pick?"

"Monatomic hydrogen."

"Why pick the one thing she can't burn? I'd settle for alcohol and oxygen."

"As long as you haven't got it, why not wish for the best?"

"Because we agreed to play this game for keeps. Now we've got to go through the motions of trying to make some fuel, from now till they find us. That's why I say alcohol and oxygen. I'll whomp up some sort of a still and start cooking alky while you and Matt figure out how to produce liquid oxygen with just your bare hands and a ship's equipment."

"How long do you figure it will take you to distil several tons of alcohol with what you can rig up?"

"That's the beauty of it. I'll still be working away at it, like a good little boy, busy as a moonshiner, when they come to rescue us. Say, did I ever tell you about Uncle Bodie and the moonshiners? It seems—"

"Look here," interrupted Matt, "how would you go about cooking up some maple syrup—here?"

"Huh? Why fret about it? We're sick of hotcakes."

"So am I, but I want to know how you can make maple syrup right here. Or, rather, how the natives can do it?"

"Are you nuts, or is this a riddle?"

"Neither one. I just remembered something I had overlooked. You said there wasn't any more maple syrup, and I was about to say that there was still plenty in Thurlow's room." Two days before, it had been Matt's turn to go into the city. As usual he had visited Thurlow's sickroom. His friend Th'wing had been on watch and had left him alone with the lieutenant for twenty minutes or so.

During the interval the patient had roused and Matt had wished to offer him a drink; there were several drinking bladders at hand.

The first one Matt picked up turned out to be charged with maple syrup, and so did the next and the next—the entire row, in fact. Then he found the one he wanted, lying on the couch. "I didn't think anything about it at the time—I was busy with the lieutenant. But this is what bothers me: He's been taking quite a lot of the syrup; you might say he's been living on nothing else. I opened the first can when we first took it to him, and I opened both the other cans myself, as needed—Th'wing couldn't cope with the can opener. So I know that the syrup was almost gone."

"Where did the rest of the syrup come from?"

"Why, I suppose the natives made it," answered Oscar. "It wouldn't be too hard to get sugar from some of the plants around here. There's a sort of grass somewhat like sugar cane, up near the Poles; they could find something of the sort."

"But, Oz, this was *maple* syrup!"

"Huh? It couldn't be. Your taster has gone haywire."

"It was maple, I tell you."

"Well, what if it was—mind you, I don't concede that you can get the true maple flavor this side of Vermont, but what difference does it make?"

"I think we've been overlooking a bet. You were talking about distilling alcohol; I'll bet the natives can supply alcohol in any quantities."

"Oh." Oscar thought about it. "You're probably right. They are clever about things like that—that gunk they use to jell mud and those solvents they cleaned the *Tart* with. Kitchen chemists."

"Maybe they aren't kitchen chemists. Maybe they are the real thing."

"Huh?" said Tex. "What do you mean, Matt?"

"Just what I said. We want 'go' juice for the *Tart*—maybe if we just had sense enough to ask the mother-of-many for it, we'd get it."

Oscar shook his head. "I wish you were right, Matt. Nobody has more respect for the Little People than I have, but there isn't a rocket fuel we can use that doesn't involve one or more liquefied gases. We might even make them understand what we needed but they wouldn't have the facilities for it."

"Why are you so sure?"

"Well, shucks, Matt, liquid oxygen—even liquid air—calls for high pressures and plenty of power, and high-pressure containers for the intermediate stages. The Little People make little use of power, they hardly use metal."

"They don't use power, eh? How about those orange lights?"

"Well, yes, but that can't involve much power."

"Can you make one? Do you know how they work?"

"No, but—"

"What I'm trying to get at is that there may be more ways of doing engineering than the big, muscley, noisy ways we've worked out. You've said yourself that we don't really know the natives, not even around the poles. Let's at least ask!"

"I think he's got something there, Oz," said Tex. "Let's ask."

Oscar was looking very thoughtful. "I've realized for some time that our friends here were more civilized than the ones around the colonies, but I couldn't quite put my finger on it."

"What *is* civilization?"

"Never mind the philosophy—let's get going." Oscar unlocked the ship's outer door and spoke to a figure, waiting in what was to her bright sunlight and busy looking at the pictures in a 1971 *Saturday Evening Post*. "Hey, girlie! *Wouldst thou graciously conduct us to the home of thy mother?*"

It *was* maple syrup. Both Tex and Oscar agreed. Th'wing explained quite readily that, when the supply ran low, they had made more, using the original terrestrial stuff as a sample.

Oscar went to see the city mother, taking with him a bottle of grain alcohol salvaged from the medical supplies of the *Gary*. Matt and Tex had to sweat it out, for it had been agreed that Oscar did best with her nibs when not accompanied. He returned after more than two hours, looking stunned.

"What gives, Oz? What did you find out?" Matt demanded.

"It's bad news," said Tex. "I can tell from your face."

"No, it's not bad news."

"Then spill it, man, spill it—you mean they can do it?"

Oscar swore softly in Venerian. "They can do anything!"

"Back off and try again," advised Tex. "They can't play a harmonica. I know; I let one try. Now tell us."

"I started in by showing her the ethyl alcohol and tried to explain that we still had a problem and asked her if her people could make the stuff. She seemed to think it was a silly question—just sniffed it and said they could. Then I positively strained myself trying to act out liquid oxygen, first telling her that there were two different things in air, one inert and one active. The best I could do was to use their words for 'living' and 'dead.' I told her I wanted the living part to be like water. She cut me off and sent for one of her people. They talked back and forth for several minutes and I swear I could understand only every second or third word and could not even get the gist of it. It was a part of their language totally new to me. Then the other old girl leaves the room.

"We waited. She asked me if we would be leaving soon if we got what we wanted. I said, yes if— Then she asked me to do her the favor of taking Burke along; she was apologetic about it but firm. I said we would."

"I'm glad of that," said Matt. "I despise Stinky's insides, but it sticks in my craw to leave him to die here. He ought to have a trial."

"Keep quiet, Matt," said Tex. "Who cares about Stinky? Go on, Oscar."

"After quite a wait, the other old girl came back, with a bladder—just an ordinary bladder by the appearance, but darker than a drinking bladder. Her nibs hands it to me and asks me if this is what I wanted. I said sorry but I did not want water. She squeezed a few drops out on my hand." Oscar held out his hand. "See that? It burned me."

"It actually was liquid oxygen?"

"That or liquid air. I didn't have any way to test. I think it was oxygen. But get this—the bladder wasn't even cold. And it didn't fume until she squeezed out the drops. The other gal was carrying it around as casually as you'd carry a hot-water bottle."

Oscar stared off into space a moment. "It beats me," he said. "The only thing I can think of is catalyst chemistry—they must have catalyst chemistry down to the point where they can do things without fuss that we do with heat and pressure."

"Why try to figure it out?" asked Tex. "You'll probably get the wrong answer. Just let it go that they've forgotten more about chemistry than we'll ever learn. And we get the 'go' juice."

* * *

For two days a steady procession of little folk had formed a double line from the water's edge to the *Astarte*, bearing full bladders toward the ship and returning with empty ones. Thurlow was already abroad, still attended by his patient little nurses. Burke was brought to the ship under escort and turned loose. The cadets let him alone, which seemed to disconcert him. He looked the ship over—it was the first he had heard of it—and finally sought out Jensen.

"If you think I'm going to ride in that flying coffin you're greatly mistaken."

"Suit yourself."

"Well, what are you going to do about it?"

"Nothing. You can stay in the jungle, or try to persuade the city mother to take you back."

Burke considered it. "I think I'll stay with the frogs. If you get through, you can tell them where I am and have them come get me."

"I'll tell them where you are all right and all the rest of it, too."

"You needn't think you can scare me." Burke went away.

He returned shortly. "I've changed my mind. I'm coming with you."

"You mean they wouldn't have you."

"Well—yes."

"Very well," answered Cadet Jensen, "the local authorities having declined jurisdiction, I arrest you under the colonial code titled 'Relations with Aborigines,' charges and specifications to be made known to you at your arraignment and not necessarily limited to the code cited. You are warned that anything you say may be used in evidence against you."

"You can't do this!"

"Matt! Tex! Take him in and strap him down."

"With pleasure!" They strapped him to an acceleration rest mounted in the galley, where, they had agreed, he would be the least nuisance. Done, they reported it to Jensen."

"See here, Oz," Matt added, "do you think you can make any charges stick against him?"

"I rather doubt it, unless they allow our hearsay under a 'best evidence' rule. Of course he ought to be strung up higher than the Milky Way, but the best I expect is to get his license revoked and his passport lifted. The Patrol will believe our story and that's enough for those items."

Less than an hour later Thurlow's nurses left the ship and the cadets said good-by to the mother-of-many, a flowery, long-winded business in which Oscar let himself be trapped into promising to return some day. But at last he closed the outer door and Tex clamped it. "Are you sure they understand how to keep clear of our blast?" asked Matt.

"I paced off the safety line with her myself and heard her give the orders. Quit worrying and get to your station."

"Aye aye, sir."

Matt and Oscar went forward, Oscar with the ancient log tucked in his sling. Tex took station at the hand throttles. Oscar sat down in the co-pilot's chair and opened the log to the page of the last entry. He took a stub of pencil that he had found in the galley, wet it in his mouth, entered the date, and wrote in a large hand:

He paused and said to Matt, "I still think we ought to shift the command."

"Stow it," said Matt. "If Commodore Arkwright can command the *Randolph* with his lights gone, you can command the *Tart* with a busted wing."

"Okay, if that's the way you want it." He continued to write,

O. Jensen, acting captain
M. Dodson, pilot and astrogator
W. Jarman, chief engineer
Lt. R. Thurlow, passenger (*sick list*)
G. Burke, passenger, civilian (*prisoner*)

"Muster the crew, Mister."

"Aye aye, sir. Call your name, too, Oz?"

"Sure, it's a short list as it is."

"How about Stinky?"

"Of course not! I've got him billed as cargo."

Matt took a deep breath and, speaking close to the speaking tube so that Tex could hear, called out: "Lieutenant Thurlow!"

Oscar replied, "I answer for him." He glanced back at the lieutenant, strapped in the inspector's rest where they could keep an eye on him. Thurlow opened his eyes with the puzzled, questioning look he always showed on the rare occasions when he seemed to be aware of anything.

"Jensen!"

"Here."

"Jarman!"

"Here!" Tex called back, his voice muffled and hollow through the tube.

Matt said, "Dodson present," then wet his lips and hesitated.

"Dahlquist!"

Oscar was about to reply when Thurlow's voice came from behind them: "I answer for him."

"Martin!" Matt went on mechanically, too startled to stop.

"I answer for him," said Oscar, his eyes on Thurlow.

"Rivera!"

"I answer for him," came Tex's voice.

"Wheeler!"

"Wheeler's here too," Tex answered again. "They're all here, Matt. We're ready."

"Complement complete, Captain."

"Very well, sir."

"How is he, Oz?"

"He's closed his eyes again. Raise ship when ready."

"Aye aye, sir. According to plan—*raise ship!*" He grasped the wing controls and waited. The *Astarte* reared on her belly jets, drove up and forward and into the mists of Venus.

18.
IN THE COMMANDANT'S OFFICE

Passed Cadets Dodson and Jarman, freshly detached from the P.R.S. *Pegasus*, at Terra Station out from New Auckland, climbed out of the *Randolph*'s scooter and into the *Randolph* herself. Cadet Jensen was not with them; Oscar, on despatch authorization from the Academy, had been granted six months for leave at home, with the understanding that he would be ordered to temporary duty in the course of it, to accompany the first consul to the equatorial regions to his station and assist in establishing liaison.

Matt and Tex showed their orders to the officer of the watch and left with him the inevitable copies. He gave them their rooming assignments—in Hog Alley, in a room with a different number but otherwise like the one they had had. "Seems like we never left it," remarked Tex, as he unpacked his jump bag.

"Except it seems funny not to have Oz and Pete around."

"Yeah, I keep expecting Oz to stick his head in and ask if we'd like to team up with him and Pete."

The room phone sounded, Tex answered.

"Cadet Jarman?"

"Speaking."

"The Commandant's compliments—you are to report to his office at once."

"Aye aye, sir." He switched off and continued to Matt. "They don't waste much time, do they?" He looked thoughtful and added, "You know what I think?"

"Maybe I can guess."

"Well, this quick service looks promising. And we *did* do quite a job, Matt. There's no getting around to it."

"I guess so. Bringing in the *Astarte*, a hundred and eight years overdue, was something—even if we had dragged it in on wheels it still would be something. I won't start calling you 'Lieutenant' just yet, but—he might commission us."

"Keep your fingers crossed. How do I look?"

"You aren't pretty, but you look nineteen times better than you did when we grounded at South Pole. Better get moving."

"Right." Tex left and Matt waited nervously. Presently the call he expected came in, telling him, too, to report to the Commandant.

He found that Tex was still inside. Rather than fidget under the eyes of others in the Commandant's outer office, he chose to wait in the passageway. After a while, Tex came out. Matt went up to him eagerly. "How about it?"

Tex gave him an odd look. "Just go on in."

"You can't talk?"

"We'll talk later. Go on in."

"Cadet Dodson!" someone called from the outer office.

"On deck," he called back. A couple of moments later he was in the presence of the Commandant.

"Cadet Dodson, reporting as ordered, sir."

The Commandant turned his face toward him and Matt felt again the eerie feeling that Commodore Arkwright could see him better than could an ordinary, sighted man. "Oh, yes, Mr. Dodson. At ease." The elder Patrolman reached unerringly for a clip on his desk. "I've been looking over your record. You've made up your deficiency in astrogation and supplemented it with a limited amount of practical work. Captain Yancey seems to approve of you, on the whole, but notes that you are sometimes absent-minded, with a tendency to become pre-occupied with one duty to the expense of others. I don't find that very serious—in a young man."

"Thank you, sir."

"It was not a compliment, just an observation. Now tell me, what would you do if—" Forty-five minutes later Matt caught his breath sufficiently to realize that he had been subjected to a very searching examination. He had come into the Commandant's office feeling nine feet tall, four feet wide, and completely covered with hair. The feeling had passed.

The Commandant paused for a moment as if thinking, then went on, "When will you be ready to be commissioned, Mr. Dodson?"

Matt strangled a bit, then managed to answer, "I don't know, sir. Three or four years, perhaps."

"I think a year should suffice, if you apply yourself. I'm sending you down to Hayworth Hall. You can catch the shuttle from the Station this afternoon.

"The usual delay for leave, of course," he added.

"That's fine, sir!"

"Enjoy yourself. I have an item here for you—" The blind man hesitated a split second, then reached for another clip. "—a copy of a letter from Lieutenant Thurlow's mother. Another copy has been placed in your record."

"Uh, how is the lieutenant, sir?"

"Completely recovered, they tell me. One more thing before you go—"

"Yes, sir."

"Let me have some notes on what troubles you ran into in recommissioning the *Astarte*, emphasizing what you had to learn as you went along—especially any mistakes you made."

"Uh, aye aye, sir."

"Your notes will be considered in revising the manual on obsolete equipment. No hurry about it—do it when you come back from leave."

Matt left the Commandant's presence feeling only a fraction the size he had when he had gone in, yet he felt curiously elated rather than depressed. He hurried to the room he shared with Tex and found him waiting. Tex looked him over. "I see you've had it."

"Check."

"Hayworth Hall?"

"That's it." Matt looked puzzled. "I don't understand it. I went in there honestly convinced that I was going to be commissioned. But I feel wonderful. Why is that?"

"Don't look at me. I feel the same way, and yet I can't remember that he had a kind word to say. The whole business on Venus he just tossed off."

Matt said, "That's it!"

"What's what?"

" 'He just tossed it off.' That's why we feel good. He didn't make anything of it because he didn't expect anything less— *because we are Patrolmen!*"

"Huh? Yes, that's it—that's exactly it! Like he was thirty-second degree and we were first degree, but members of the same lodge." Tex started to whistle.

"I feel better," said Matt. "I felt good before, but now I feel better, now that I understand why. Say—one other thing."

"What?"

"You didn't tell him about the fight I had with Burke in New Auckland, did you?"

"Of course not." Tex was indignant.

"That's funny. I didn't tell anybody but you, and I could have sworn that no one saw it. I planned it that way."

"He knew about it?"

"He sure did."

"Was he sore?"

"No. He said he realized that Burke was out on bond and that I was on leave and he had no wish to invade my private life—but he wanted to give me a word of advice."

"Yeah? What was it?"

"Never lead with my left."

Tex looked amazed, then thoughtful. "I think he was telling you not to lead with your chin, too."

"Probably." Matt started repacking his jump bag. "When's the next scooter for the Station?"

"About thirty minutes. Say, Matt, you've got leave of course?"

"Check."

"How about picking up my invitation to spend a few weeks on the Jarman spread? I want you to meet my folks—and Uncle Bodie."

"Uncle Bodie, by all means. But Tex?"

"Yeah?"

"Hotcakes for breakfast?"

"No hotcakes."

"It's a deal."

"Shake."

RED
PLANET

For TISH

1.
WILLIS

The thin air of Mars was chill but not really cold. It was not yet winter in southern latitudes and the daytime temperature was usually above freezing.

The queer creature standing outside the door of a dome-shaped building was generally manlike in appearance, but no human being ever had a head like that. A thing like a coxcomb jutted out above the skull, the eye lenses were wide and staring, and the front of the face stuck out in a snout. The unearthly appearance was increased by a pattern of black and yellow tiger stripes covering the entire head.

The creature was armed with a pistol-type hand weapon slung at its belt and was carrying, crooked in its right arm, a ball, larger than a basketball, smaller than a medicine ball. It moved the ball to its left arm, opened the outer door of the building and stepped inside.

Inside was a very small anteroom and an inner door. As soon as the outer door was closed the air pressure in the anteroom began to rise, accompanied by a soft sighing sound. A loudspeaker over the inner door shouted in a booming bass, "Well? Who is it? Speak up! Speak up!"

The visitor placed the ball carefully on the floor, then with both hands grasped its ugly face and pushed and lifted it to the top of its head. Underneath was disclosed the face of an Earth-human boy. "It's Jim Marlowe, Doc," he answered.

"Well, come in. Come in! Don't stand out there chewing your nails."

"Coming." When the air pressure in the anteroom had equalized with the pressure in the rest of the house the inner door opened automatically. Jim said, "Come along, Willis," and went on in.

The ball developed three spaced bumps on its lower side and followed after him, in a gait which combined spinning, walking, and rolling. More correctly, it careened, like a barrel being manhandled along a dock. They went down a passage and entered a large room that occupied half the floorspace of the circular house plan. Doctor MacRae looked up but did not get up. "Howdy, Jim. Skin yourself. Coffee on the bench. Howdy, Willis," he added and turned back to his work. He was dressing the hand of a boy about Jim's age.

"Thanks, Doc. Oh—hello, Francis. What are you doing here?"

"Hi, Jim. I killed a water-seeker, then I cut my thumb on one of its spines."

"Quit squirming!" commanded the doctor.

"That stuff stings," protested Francis.

"I meant it to. Shut up."

"How in the world did you do that?" persisted Jim. "You ought to know better than to touch one of those things. Just burn 'em down and burn 'em up." He zipped open the front of his outdoor costume, peeled it off his arms and legs and hung it on a rack near the door. The rack held Francis's suit, the headpiece of which was painted in bright colors like an Indian brave's war paint, and the doctor's suit, the mask of which was plain. Jim was now stylishly and appropriately dressed for indoors on Mars—bare naked save for bright red jockey shorts.

"I did burn it," explained Francis, "but it moved when I touched it. I wanted to get the tail to make a necklace."

"Then you didn't burn it right. Probably left it full of live eggs. Who're you making a necklace for?"

"None of your business. And I did so burn the egg sac. What do you take me for? A tourist?"

"Sometimes I wonder. You know those things don't die until sundown."

"Don't talk nonsense, Jim," the doctor advised. "Now, Frank, I'm going to give you an anti-toxin shot. 'Twon't do you any good but it'll make your mother happy. Long about tomorrow your thumb will swell up like a poisoned pup; bring it back and I'll lance it."

"Am I going to lose my thumb?" the boy asked.

"Nope. But you'll do your scratching with your left hand for a few days. Now, Jim, what brings you here? Bellyache?"

"No, Doc. It's Willis."

"Willis, eh? He looks pert enough to me." The doctor stared down at the creature. Willis was at his feet, having come up to watch the dressing of Frank's thumb. To do so he had protruded three eye stalks from the top of his spherical mass. The stalks stuck up like thumbs, in an equal-sided triangle, and from each popped a disturbingly human eye. The little fellow turned around slowly on his tripod of bumps, or pseudopeds, and gave each of his eyes a chance to examine the doctor.

"Get me a cup of Java, Jim," commanded the doctor, then leaned over and made a cradle of his hands. "Here, Willis—upsi-daisy!" Willis gave a little bounce and landed in the doctor's hands, withdrawing all protuberances as he did so. The doctor lifted him to the examining table; Willis promptly stuck out legs and eyes again. They stared at each other.

The doctor saw a ball covered with thick, close-cropped fur, like sheared sheepskin, and featureless at the moment save for supports and eye stalks. The Mars creature saw an elderly male Earthman almost completely covered with wiry grey-and-white hair. The hair was thin on top, thick on chin and cheeks, moder-ately thick to sparse on chest and arms and back and legs. The middle portion of this strange, unMartian creature was concealed in snow-white shorts. Willis enjoyed looking at him.

"How do you feel, Willis?" inquired the doctor. "Feel good? Feel bad?"

A dimple showed at the very crown of the ball between the stalks, dilated to an opening. "Willis fine!" he said. His voice was remarkably like Jim's.

"Fine, eh?" Without looking around the doctor added, "Jim! Wash those cups again. And this time, sterilize them. Want every-body around here to come down with the pip?"

"Okay, Doc," Jim acknowledged, and added to Francis, "You want some coffee, too?"

"Sure. Weak, with plenty of cow."

"Don't be fussy." Jim dipped into the laboratory sink and managed to snag another cup. The sink was filled with dirty dishes. Nearby a large flask of coffee simmered over a bunsen burner. Jim washed three cups carefully, put them through the sterilizer, then filled them.

Doctor MacRae accepted a cup and said, "Jim, this citizen says he's okay. What's the trouble?"

"I know he says he's all right, Doc, but he's not. Can't you ex-amine him and find out?"

"Examine him? How, boy? I can't even take his temperature because I don't know what his temperature ought to be. I know as much about his body chemistry as a pig knows about patty-cake. Want me to cut him open and see what makes him tick?"

Willis promptly withdrew all projections and became as featureless as a billiard ball. "Now you've scared him," Jim said accusingly.

"Sorry." The doctor reached out and commenced scratching and tickling the furry ball. "Good Willis, nice Willis. Nobody's going to hurt Willis. Come on, boy, come out of your hole."

Willis barely dilated the sphincter over his speaking diaphragm. "Not hurt Willis?" he said anxiously in Jim's voice.

"Not hurt Willis. Promise."

"Not cut Willis?"

"Not cut Willis. Not a bit."

The eyes poked out slowly. Somehow he managed an expression of watchful caution, though he had nothing resembling a face. "That's better," said the doctor. "Let's get to the point, Jim. What makes you think there's something wrong with this fellow, when he and I can't see it?"

"Well, Doc, it's the way he behaves. He's all right indoors, but outdoors— He used to follow me everywhere, bouncing around the landscape, poking his nose into everything."

"He hasn't got a nose," Francis commented.

"Go to the head of the class. But now, when I take him out, he just goes into a ball and I can't get a thing out of him. If he's not sick, why does he act that way?"

"I begin to get a glimmering," Doctor MacRae answered. "How long have you been teamed up with this balloon?"

Jim thought back over the twenty-four months of the Martian year. "Since along toward the end of Zeus, nearly November."

"And now here it is the last of March, almost Ceres, and the summer gone. That suggest anything to your mind?"

"Uh, no."

"You expect him to go hopping around through the snow? We migrate when it gets cold; he lives here."

Jim's mouth dropped open. "You mean he's trying to hibernate?"

"What else? Willis's ancestors have had a good many millions of years to get used to the seasons around here; you can't expect him to ignore them."

Jim looked worried. "I had planned to take him with me to Syrtis Minor."

"Syrtis Minor? Oh, yes, you go away to school this year, don't you? You, too, Frank."

"You bet!"

"I can't get used to the way you kids grow up. It was just last week I was painting your thumb to keep you from sucking it."

"I never sucked my thumb!" Francis answered.

"No? Then it was some other kid. Never mind. I came to Mars so that the years would be twice as long, but it doesn't seem to make any difference."

"Say, Doc, how old are you?" inquired Francis.

"Mind your own business. Which one of you is going to study medicine and come back to help me with my practice?"

Neither one answered. "Speak up, speak up!" urged the doctor. "What are you going to study?"

Jim said, "Well, I don't know. I'm interested in aerography*, but I like biology, too. Maybe I'll be a planetary economist, like my old man."

"That's a big subject. Ought to keep you busy a long time. You, Frank?"

Francis looked slightly embarrassed. "Well, uh—shucks, I still think I'd like to be a rocket pilot."

"I thought you had outgrown that." Doctor MacRae looked almost shocked.

"Why not?" Francis answered doggedly. "I might make it."

"That's just what I'd be afraid of. See here, Frank, do you really want to live a life bound around with rules and regulations and discipline?"

"Mmmm . . . I want to be a pilot. I know that."

"On your own head be it. Me, I left Earth to get away from all that nonsense. Earth has gotten so musclebound with laws that a man can't breathe. So far, there's still a certain amount of freedom on Mars. When that changes—"

" 'When that changes' what, Doc?"

"Why, I'll go find another planet that hasn't been spoiled, naturally. Speaking of such things, you younkers go to school before the colony migrates, don't you?" Since Earth-humans do not hi-

---

*Aerography: equivalent to "geography" for Earth. From "Ares" Greek for Mars.

bernate, it was necessary that the colony migrate twice each Martian year. The southern summer was spent at Charax, only thirty degrees from the southern pole; the colony was now about to move to Copais in Utopia, almost as far to the north, there to remain half a Martian year, or almost a full Earth year.

There were year-around establishments near the equator—New Shanghai, Marsport, Syrtis Minor, others—but they were not truly colonies, being manned mainly by employees of the Mars Company. By contract and by charter the Company was required to provide advanced terrestrial education on Mars for colonials; it suited the Company to provide it only at Syrtis Minor.

"We go next Wednesday," said Jim, "on the mail scooter."

"So soon?"

"Yes, and that's what worries me about Willis. What ought I to do, Doc?"

Willis heard his name and looked inquiringly at Jim. He repeated, in exact imitation of Jim, "What ought I to do, Doc?"

"Shut up, Willis—"

" 'Shut up, Willis.' " Willis imitated the doctor just as perfectly.

"Probably the kindest thing would be to take him out, find him a hole, and stuff him in it. You can renew your acquaintance when he's through hibernating."

"But, Doc, that means I'll lose him! He'll be out long before I'm home from school. Why, he'll probably wake up even before the colony comes back."

"Probably." MacRae thought about it. "It won't hurt him to be on his own again. It's not a natural life he leads with you, Jim. He's an individual, you know; he's not property."

"Of course he's not! He's my friend."

"I can't see," put in Francis, "why Jim sets such store by him. Sure, he talks a lot, but most of it is just parrot stuff. He's a moron, if you ask me."

"Nobody asked you. Willis is fond of me, aren't you, Willis? Here, come to papa." Jim spread his arms; the little Martian creature hopped into them and settled in his lap, a warm, furry mass, faintly pulsating. Jim stroked him.

"Why don't you ask one of the Martians?" suggested MacRae.

"I tried to, but I couldn't find one that was in a mood to pay any attention."

"You mean you weren't willing to wait long enough. A Martian will notice you if you're patient. Well, why don't you ask *him*? He can speak for himself."

"What should I say?"

"I'll try it. Willis!"

Willis turned two eyes on the doctor; MacRae went on, "Want to go outdoors and go to sleep?"

"Willis not sleepy."

"Get sleepy outdoors. Nice and cold, find hole in ground. Curl up and take good long sleep. How about it?"

"No!" The doctor had to look sharply to see that it was not Jim who had answered; when Willis spoke for himself he always used Jim's voice. Willis's sound diaphragm had no special quality of its own, any more than has the diaphragm of a radio loudspeaker. It was much like a loudspeaker's diaphragm, save that it was part of a living animal.

"That seems definite, but we'll try it from another angle. Willis, do you want to stay with Jim?"

"Willis stay with Jim." Willis added meditatively, "Warm!"

"There's the key to your charm, Jim," the doctor said dryly. "He likes your blood temperature. But *ipse dixit*—keep him with you. I don't think it will hurt him. He may live fifty years instead of a hundred, but he'll have twice as much fun."

"Do they normally live to be a hundred?" asked Jim.

"Who knows? We haven't been around this planet long enough to know such things. Now come on, get out. I've got work to do." The doctor eyed his bed thoughtfully. It had not been made in a week; he decided to let it wait until wash day.

"What does *'ipse dixit'* mean, Doc?" asked Francis.

"It means, 'He sure said a mouthful.' "

"Doc," suggested Jim, "Why don't you have dinner with us tonight? I'll call mother. You, too, Frank."

"Huh uh," Frank denied. "I'd better not. My mother says I eat too many meals with you folks."

"My mother, if she were here, would undoubtedly say the same thing," admitted the doctor. "Fortunately I am free of her restraining influence. Call your mother, Jim."

Jim went to the phone, tuned out two colonial housewives gossiping about babies, and finally reached his home on an alternate frequency. When his mother's face appeared on the screen he explained his wish. "Delighted to have the doctor with us," she said. "Tell him to hurry along, Jimmy."

"Right away, Mom!" Jim switched off and reached for his outdoor suit.

"Don't put it on," advised MacRae. "It's too chilly out. We'll go through the tunnels."

"It's twice as far," objected Jim.

"We'll leave it up to Willis. Willis, how do you vote?"

"Warm," said Willis smugly.

2.
SOUTH COLONY, MARS

South Colony was arranged like a wheel. The administration building was the hub; tunnels ran out in all directions and buildings were placed over them. A rim tunnel had been started to join the spokes at the edge of the wheel; thus far a forty-five degree arc had been completed.

Save for three Moon huts erected when the colony was founded and since abandoned, all the buildings were shaped alike. Each was a hemispherical bubble of silicone plastic, processed from the soil of Mars and blown on the spot. Each was a double bubble, in fact; first one large bubble would be blown, say thirty or forty feet across; when it had hardened, the new building would be entered through the tunnel and an inner bubble, slightly smaller than the first, would be blown. The outer bubble, "polymerized"— that is to say, cured and hardened, under the rays of the sun; a battery of ultra-violet and heat lamps cured the inner. The walls were separated by a foot of dead air space, which provided insulation against the bitter sub-zero nights of Mars.

When a new building had hardened a door would be cut to the outside and a pressure lock installed; the colonials maintained about two-thirds Earth-normal pressure indoors for comfort and the pressure on Mars is never as much as half of that. A visitor from Earth, not conditioned to the planet, will die without a respirator. Among the colonists only Tibetans and Bolivian Indians will venture outdoors without respirators and even they will wear the snug elastic Mars suits to avoid skin hemorrhages.

Buildings had not even view windows, any more than a modern building in New York has. The surrounding desert, while beautiful, is monotonous. South Colony was in an area granted by the Martians, just north of the ancient city of Charax—there is no need to give the Martian name since an Earthman can't pronounce it—and between the legs of the double canal Strymon. Again we follow colonial custom in using the name assigned by the immortal Dr. Percival Lowell.

Francis accompanied Jim and Doctor MacRae as far as the junction of the tunnels under city hall, then turned down his own tunnel. A few minutes later the doctor and Jim—and Willis—ascended into the Marlowe home. Jim's mother met them; Doctor MacRae bowed, a bow made no less courtly by bare feet, and a grizzled, hairy chest: "Madame, I am again imposing on your good nature."

"Fiddlesticks, Doctor. You are always welcome at our table."

"I would that I had the character to wish that you were not so superlative a cook, that you might know the certain truth: it is yourself, my dear, that brings me here."

Jim's mother blushed. She was wearing a costume that a terrestrial lady might choose for sunbathing or gardening and was a very pretty sight, although Jim was certainly not aware of it. She changed the subject, "Jim, hang up your pistol. Don't leave it on the sofa where Oliver can get it."

Jim's baby brother, hearing his name, immediately made a dash for the pistol. Jim and his sister Phyllis both saw this, both yelled, "Ollie!"—and were immediately mimicked by Willis, who performed the difficult trick, possible only to an atonal diaphragm, of duplicating both voices simultaneously.

Phyllis was nearer; she grabbed the gun and slapped the child's hands. Oliver began to cry, reinforced by Willis. "Children!" said Mrs. Marlowe, just as Mr. Marlowe appeared in the door.

"What's all the ruckus?" he inquired mildly.

Doctor MacRae picked up Oliver, turned him upside down, and sat him on his shoulders. Oliver forgot that he was crying. Mrs. Marlowe added, "Nothing darling. I'm glad you're home. Children, go wash for dinner, all of you."

The second generation trooped out. Phyllis said, "Take the charges out of your gun, Jimmy, and let me practice with it."

"You're too young for a gun."

"Pooh! I can't outshoot you." This was very nearly true and not to be borne; Phyllis was two years younger than Jim and female besides.

"Girls are just target shooters. If you saw a water-seeker, you'd scream."

"I would, huh? We'll go hunting together and I'll bet you two credits that I score first."

"You haven't got two credits."

"I have, too."

"Then how was it you couldn't lend me a half credit yesterday?"

Phyllis changed the subject. Jim hung up his weapon in his cupboard and locked it. Presently they were back in the living room, to find that their father was home and dinner ready.

Phyllis waited for a lull in grown-up talk to say, "Daddy?"

"Yes, Puddin'? What is it?"

"Isn't it about time I had a pistol of my own?"

"Eh? Plenty of time for that later. You keep up your target practice."

"But, look, Daddy—Jim's going away and that means that Ollie can't ever go outside unless you or mother have time to take him. If I had a gun, I could help out."

Mr. Marlowe wrinkled his brow. "You've got a point. You've passed all your tests, haven't you?"

"You know I have!"

"What do you think, my dear? Shall we take Phyllis down to city hall and see if they will license her?"

Before Mrs. Marlowe could answer Doctor MacRae muttered something into his plate. The remark was forceful and probably not polite.

"Eh? What did you say, Doctor?"

"I said," answered MacRae, "that I was going to move to another planet. At least that's what I meant."

"Why? What's wrong with this one? In another twenty years we'll have it fixed up good as new. You'll be able to walk outside without a mask."

"Sir, it is not the natural limitations of this globe that I object to; it is the pantywaist nincompoops who rule it—These ridiculous regulations offend me. That a free citizen should have to go before a committee, hat in hand, and pray for permission to bear arms—fantastic! Arm your daughter, sir, and pay no attention to petty bureaucrats."

Jim's father stirred his coffee. "I'm tempted to. I really don't know why the Company set up such rules in the first place."

"Pure copy-cattism. The swarming beehives back on Earth have similar childish rules; the fat clerks that decide these things cannot imagine any other conditions. This is a frontier community; it should be free of such."

"Mmmm . . . probably you're right, Doctor. Can't say that I disagree with you, but I'm so busy trying to get on with my job that I really don't have time to worry about politics. It's easier to comply than to fight a test case." Jim's father turned to his wife. "If it's all right with you, my dear, could you find time to arrange for a license for Phyllis?"

"Why, yes," she answered doubtfully, "if you really think she's old enough." The doctor muttered something that combined "Danegeld" and the "Boston Tea Party" in the same breath. Phyllis answered:

"Sure, I'm old enough, Mother. I'm a better shot than Jimmy."

Jim said, "You're crazy as a spin bug!"

"Mind your manners, Jim," his father cautioned. "We don't speak that way to ladies."

"Was she talking like a lady? I ask you, Dad."

"You are bound to assume that she is one. Drop the matter. What were you saying, Doctor?"

"Eh? Nothing that I should have been saying, I'm sure. You said something earlier about another twenty years and we could throw away our respirators; tell me: is there news about the Project?"

The colony had dozens of projects, all intended to make Mars more livable for human beings, but *the* Project always meant the atmosphere, or oxygen, project. The pioneers of the Harvard-Carnegie expedition reported Mars suitable for colonization except for the all-important fact that the air was so thin that a normal man would suffocate. However they reported also that many, many billions of tons of oxygen were locked in the Martian desert sands, the red iron oxides that give Mars its ruddy color. The Project proposed to free this oxygen for humans to breathe.

"Didn't you hear the Deimos newscast this afternoon?" Mr. Marlowe answered.

"Never listen to newscasts. Saves wear and tear on the nervous system."

"No doubt. But this was good news. The pilot plant in Libya is in operation, successful operation. The first day's run restored nearly four million tons mass of oxygen to the air—and no breakdowns."

Mrs. Marlowe looked startled. "Four million tons? That seems a tremendous lot."

Her husband grinned. "Any idea how long it would take that

one plant at that rate to do the job, that is, increase the oxygen pressure by five mass-pounds per square inch?"

"Of course I haven't. But not very long I should think."

"Let me see—" His lips moved soundlessly. "Uh, around two hundred thousand years—Mars years, of course."

"James, you're teasing me!"

"No, I'm not. Don't let big figures frighten you, my dear; of course we won't depend on one plant; they'll be scattered every fifty miles or so through the desert, a thousand mega-horsepower each. There's no limit to the power available, thank goodness; if we don't clean up the job in our lifetimes, at least the kids will certainly see the end of it."

Mrs. Marlowe looked dreamy. "That would be nice, to walk outside with your bare face in the breeze. I remember when I was a little girl, we had an orchard with a stream running through it—" She stopped.

"Sorry we came to Mars, Jane?" her husband asked softly.

"Oh, no! This is my home."

"Good. What are you looking sour about, Doctor?"

"Eh? Oh, nothing, nothing! I was just thinking about the end result. Mind you, this is fine work, all of it—hard work, good work, that a man can get his teeth into. But we get it done and what for? So that another two billion, three billion sheep can fiddle around with nonsense, spend their time scratching themselves and *baa*ing. We should have left Mars to the Martians. Tell me, sir, do you know what television was used for when it first came out?"

"No. How would I?"

"Well, I didn't see it myself of course, but my father told me about it. It seems—"

"Your *father*? How old was he? When was he born?"

"My grandfather, then. Or it may have been my great grandfather. That's beside the point. They installed the first television sets in cocktail bars—amusement places—and used them to watch wrestling matches."

"What's a 'wresting match'?" demanded Phyllis.

"An obsolete form of folk dancing," explained her father. "Never mind. Granting your point, Doctor, I see no harm—"

"What's 'folk dancing'?" persisted Phyllis.

"You tell her, Jane. She's got me stumped."

Jim looked smug. "It's when folks dance, silly."

"That's near enough," agreed his mother.

Doctor MacRae stared. "These kids are missing something. I think I'll organize a square-dancing club. I used to be a pretty good caller, once upon a time."

Phyllis turned to her brother. "Now I suppose you'll tell me that square dancing is when a square dances."

Mr. Marlowe raised his eyebrows. "I think the children have all finished, my dear. Couldn't they be excused?"

"Yes, surely. You may leave, my dears. Say 'Excuse me, please,' Ollie." The baby repeated it, with Willis in mirror chorus.

Jim hastily wiped his mouth, grabbed Willis, and headed for his own room. He like to hear the doctor talk but he had to admit that the old boy could babble the most fantastic nonsense when other grown-ups were around. Nor did the discussion of the oxygen project interest Jim; he saw nothing strange nor uncomfortable about wearing his mask. He would feel undressed going outdoors without it.

From Jim's point of view Mars was all right the way it was, no need to try to make it more like Earth. Earth was no great shakes anyway. His own personal recollection of Earth was limited to vague memories from early childhood of the emigrants' conditioning station on the high Bolivian plateau—cold, shortness of breath, and great weariness.

His sister trailed after him. He stopped just inside his door and said, "What do you want, shorty?"

"Uh, Jimmy—I'm sorry I said I could shoot better than you can. I can't really."

"Huh? What are you leading up to?"

"Well. . . . Lookie, Jimmy, seeing as I'm going to have to take care of Willis after you're gone away to school, maybe it would be a good idea for you to sort of explain it to him, so he would do what I tell him."

Jim stared. "Whatever gave you the notion I was going to leave him behind?"

She stared back. "But you are! You'll *have* to. You can't take him to school. You ask mother."

"Mother hasn't anything to do with it. She doesn't care what I take to school."

"You just ask her. They don't allow pets at school. I heard her talking with Frank Sutton's mother about it just yesterday."

"Willis isn't a pet. He's a, he's a—"

"He's a what?"

"He's a friend, that's what he is: a friend!"

"Well, he's a friend of mine, too—aren't you, Willis? Anyhow, I think you're mean."

"You always think I'm mean if I don't cater to your every wish!"

"Not to me—to Willis. This is Willis's home; he's used to it. He'll be homesick away at school."

"He'll have me!"

"Not most of the time, he won't. You'll be in class. Willis wouldn't have anything to do but sit and mope. You ought to leave him here with me—with us—where he'd be happy."

Jim straightened himself up. "I'm going to find out about this, right away." He walked back into the living compartment and waited aggressively to be noticed. Shortly his father turned toward him.

"Yes? What is it, Jim? Something eating on you?"

"Uh, well—look, Dad, is there any doubt about Willis going with me when I go away to school?"

His father looked surprised. "It had never occurred to me that you would consider taking him."

"Huh? Why not?"

"Well, school is hardly the place for him."

"Why?"

"Well, you wouldn't be able to take care of him properly. You'll be awfully busy."

"Willis doesn't take much care. He never makes messes. Just feed him every month or so and give him a drink about once a week and he doesn't ask for anything else. Why can't I take him, Dad?"

Mr. Marlowe looked baffled; he turned to his wife. She started in, "Now, Jimmy darling, we don't want you to—"

Jim interrupted, "Mother, every time you want to talk me out of something you start out, 'Jimmy darling'!"

Her mouth twitched but she kept from smiling. "Sorry, Jim. Perhaps I do. What I was trying to say was this: we want you to get off to a good start at school. I don't believe that having Willis on your hands will help any. As a matter of fact Mrs. Sutton was telling me just the other day that she had heard that pets were not allowed. She said—"

"How does she know anything about it?"

"Well, she had been talking with the Resident's wife."

Jim was stumped for the moment. The wife of the Resident Agent of the Mars Company for South Colony undoubtedly had better sources of information than he had. But he was not ready to give up. "Look, Mother. Look, Dad. You both saw the pamphlet the school sent me, telling me what to do and what to bring and when to show up and so forth. If either one of you can find anything anywhere in those instructions that says I can't take Willis with me, I'll shut up like a Martian. Is that fair?"

Mrs. Marlowe looked inquiringly at her husband. He looked back at her with the same appeal for help in his expression. He was acutely aware that Doctor MacRae was watching both of them, not saying a word but wearing an expression of sardonic amusement.

Mr. Marlowe shrugged. "Take Willis along, Jim. But he's your problem."

Jim's face broke out in a grin. "Thanks, Dad!" He left the room quickly in order not to give his parents time to change their minds.

Mr. Marlowe banged his pipe on an ashtray and glowered at Doctor MacRae. "Well, what are you grinning at, you ancient ape? You think I'm too indulgent, don't you?"

"Oh, no, not at all! I think you did perfectly right."

"You think that pet of Jim's won't cause him trouble at school?"

"On the contrary. I have some familiarity with Willis's peculiar social habits."

"Then why do you say I did right?"

"Why shouldn't the boy have trouble? Trouble is the normal condition for the human race. We were raised on it. We thrive on it."

"Sometimes, Doctor, I think that you are, as Jim would put it, crazy as a spin bug."

"Probably. But since I am the only medical man around, I am not likely to be committed for it. Mrs. Marlowe, could you favor an old man with another cup of your delicious coffee?"

"Certainly, Doctor." She poured for him, then went on. "James, I am not sorry you decided to let Jim take Willis. It will be a relief."

"Why, dear? Jim was correct when he said that the little beggar isn't much trouble."

"Well, he isn't really. But—I just wish he weren't so truthful."

"So? I thought he was the perfect witness in settling the children's squabbles?"

"Oh, he is. He'll play back anything he hears as accurately as a transcriber. That's the trouble." She looked upset, then chuckled. "You know Mrs. Pottle?"

"Of course."

The doctor added, "How can one avoid it? I, unhappy man, am in charge of her 'nerves'."

Mrs. Marlowe asked, "Is she actually sick, Doctor?"

"She eats too much and doesn't work enough. Further communication is forbidden by professional ethics."

"I didn't know you had any."

"Young lady, show respect for my white hairs. What about this Pottle female?"

"Well, Luba Konski had lunch with me last week and we got to talking about Mrs. Pottle. Honest, James, I didn't say much and I did not know that Willis was under the table."

"He was?" Mr. Marlowe covered his eyes. "Do go on."

"Well, you both remember that the Konskis housed the Pottles at North Colony until a house was built for them. Sarah Pottle has been Luba's pet hate ever since, and Tuesday Luba was giving me some juicy details on Sarah's habits at home. Two days later Sarah Pottle stopped by to give me advice on how to bring up children. Something she said triggered Willis—I knew he was in the room but I didn't think anything of it—and Willis put on just the wrong record and I couldn't shut him up. I finally carried him out of the room. Mrs. Pottle left without saying good-bye and I haven't heard from her since."

"That's no loss," her husband commented.

"True, but it got Luba in Dutch. No one could miss Luba's accent and Willis does it better than she does herself. I don't think Luba minds, though—and you should have heard Willis's playback of Luba's description of how Sarah Pottle looks in the morning—and what she does about it."

"You should hear," answered MacRae, "Mrs. Pottle's opinions on the servant problem."

"I have. She thinks it's a scandal that the Company doesn't import servants for us."

The doctor nodded. "With collars riveted around their necks."

"That woman! I can't see why she ever became a colonist."

"Didn't you know?" her husband said. "They came out here expecting to get rich in a hurry."

"Hummph!"

Doctor MacRae got a far-away look. "Mrs. Marlowe, speaking

as her physician, it might help me to hear what Willis has to say about Pottle, distaff. Do you suppose he would recite for us?"

"Doctor, you're an old fraud, with a taste for gossip."

"Granted. I like also eavesdropping and window peeping."

"You're shameless."

"Again granted. My nerves are relaxed. I haven't felt ashamed in years."

"Willis may just give a thrilling account of the children's chit-chat for the past two weeks."

"Perhaps if you coaxed him?"

Mrs. Marlowe suddenly dimpled. "It won't hurt to try." She left the room to fetch Jim's globular friend.

3.
GEKKO

Wednesday morning dawned clear and cold, as mornings have a habit of doing on Mars. The Suttons and the Marlowes, minus Oliver, were gathered at the Colony's cargo dock on the west leg of Strymon canal, ready to see the boys off.

The temperature was rising and the dawn wind was blowing firmly, but it was still at least thirty below. Strymon canal was a steel-blue, hard sheet of ice and would not melt today in this latitude. Resting on it beside the dock was the mail scooter from Syrtis Minor, its boat body supported by razor-edged runners. The driver was still loading it with cargo dragged from the warehouse on the dock. The two families waited nearby.

The tiger stripes on Jim's mask, the war paint on Frank's, and a rainbow motif on Phyllis's made the young people easy to identify. The adults could be told apart only by size, shape, and manner; there were two extras, Doctor MacRae and Father Cleary. The priest was talking in low, earnest tones to Frank.

He turned presently and spoke to Jim. "Your own pastor asked me to say good-bye to you, son. Unfortunately the poor man is laid up with a touch of Mars throat. He would have come anyhow had I not hidden his mask." The protestant chaplain, as well as the priest, was a bachelor; the two clergy shared a house.

"Is he very sick?" asked Jim.

"Not that sick. He'll not die till I convert him. But take his blessing—and mine too." He offered his hand.

Jim dropped his travel bag, shifted his ice skates and Willis over to his left arm and shook hands. There followed an awkward silence. Finally Jim said, "Why don't you all go inside before you freeze to death?"

"Yeah," agreed Francis. "That's a good idea."

"I think the driver is about ready now," Mr. Marlowe countered. "Well, son, take care of yourself. We'll see you at migration." He shook hands solemnly.

"So long, Dad."

Mrs. Marlowe put her arms around him, pressed her mask against his and said, "Oh, my little boy—you're too young to go away from home!"

"Oh, mother, please!" But he hugged her. Then Phyllis had to be hugged. The driver called out:

"'Board!'"

"'Bye everybody!'" Jim turned away, felt his elbow caught.

It was the doctor. "Keep your nose clean, Jim. And don't take any guff off of anybody."

"Thanks, Doc." Jim turned and presented his school authorization to the driver while the doctor bade Francis good-bye.

The driver looked it over. "Both deadheads, eh? Well, seeing as how there aren't any pay passengers this morning you can ride in the observatory." He tore off his copy; Jim climbed inside and went up to the prized observation seats behind and above the driver's compartment. Frank joined him.

The craft trembled as the driver jacked the runners loose from the ice, then with a roar from the turbine and a soft, easy surge the car got under way. The banks flowed past them and melted into featureless walls as the speed picked up. The ice was mirror smooth; they soon reached cruising speed of better than two hundred fifty miles per hour. Presently the driver removed his mask; Jim and Frank, seeing him, did likewise. The car was pressurized now by an air ram faced into their own wind of motion; it was much warmer, too, from the air's compression.

"Isn't this swell?" said Francis.

"Yeah. Look at Earth."

Their mother planet was riding high above the Sun in the northeastern sky. It blazed green against a deep purple background. Close to it, but easy to separate with the naked eye, was a lesser, pure white star—Luna, Earth's moon. Due north of them, in the direction they were going, Deimos, Mars' outer moon, hung no more than twenty degrees above the horizon. Almost lost in the rays of the sun, it was a tiny pale disc, hardly more than a dim star and much outshone by Earth.

Phobos, the inner moon, was not in sight. At the latitude of Charax it never rose more than eight degrees or so above the northern horizon and that for an hour or less, twice a day. In the daytime it was lost in the blue of the horizon and no one would be so foolhardy as to watch for it in the bitter night. Jim did not remember ever having seen it except during migration between colonies.

Francis looked from Earth to Deimos. "Ask the driver to turn on the radio," he suggested. "Deimos is up."

"Who cares about the broadcast?" Jim answered. "I want to watch." The banks were not so high now; from the observation dome he could see over them into the fields beyond. Although it was late in the season the irrigated belt near the canal was still green and getting greener as he watched, as the plants came out of the ground to seek the morning sunlight.

He could make out, miles away, an occasional ruddy sand dune of the open desert. He could not see the green belt of the east leg of their canal; it was over the horizon.

Without urging, the driver switched on his radio; music filled the car and blotted out the monotonous low roar of the turbo-jet. It was terrestrial music, by Sibelius, a classical composer of another century. Mars colony had not yet found time to develop its own arts and still borrowed its culture. But neither Jim nor Frank knew who the composer was, nor cared. The banks of the canal had closed in again; there was nothing to see but the straight ribbon of ice; they settled back and daydreamed.

Willis stirred for the first time since he had struck the outer cold. He extended his eye stalks, looked inquiringly around, then commenced to beat time with them.

Presently the music stopped and a voice said: "This is station D-M-S, the Mars Company, Deimos, *circum* Mars. We bring you now by relay from Syrtis Minor a program in the public interest. Doctor Graves Armbruster will speak on 'Ecological Considerations involved in Experimental Artificial Symbiotics as related to—' "

The driver promptly switched the radio off.

"I would like to have heard that," objected Jim. "It sounded interesting."

"Oh, you're just showing off," Frank answered. "You don't even know what those words mean."

"The deuce I don't. It means—"

"Shut up and take a nap." Taking his own advice Frank lay

back and closed his eyes. However he got no chance to sleep. Willis had apparently been chewing over, in whatever it was he used for a mind, the program he had just heard. He opened up and started to play it back, woodwinds and all.

The driver looked back and up, looked startled. He said something but Willis drowned him out. Willis bulled on through to the end, even to the broken-off announcement. The driver finally made himself heard. "Hey, you guys! What yuh got up there? A portable recorder?"

"No, a bouncer."

"A what?"

Jim held Willis up so that the driver could see him. "A bouncer. His name is Willis."

"You mean *that* thing is a recorder?"

"No, he's a bouncer. As I said, his name is Willis."

"This I got to see," announced the driver. He did something at his control board, then turned around and stuck his head and shoulders up into the observation dome.

Frank said, "Hey! You'll wreck us."

"Relax," advised the driver. "I put her on echo-automatic. High banks for the next couple o' hundred miles. Now what is this gismo? When you brought it aboard I thought it was a volleyball."

"No, it's Willis. Say hello to the man, Willis."

"Hello, man," Willis answered agreeably.

The driver scratched his head. "This beats anything I ever saw in Keokuk. Sort of a parrot, eh?"

"He's a bouncer. He's got a scientific name, but it just means 'Martian roundhead'. Never seen one before?"

"No. You know, bud, this is the screwiest planet in the whole system."

"If you don't like it here," asked Jim, "why don't you go back where you came from?"

"Don't go popping off, youngster. How much will you take for the gismo? I got an idea I could use him."

"Sell Willis? Are you crazy?"

"Sometimes I think so. Oh, well, it was just an idea." The driver went back to his station, stopping once to look back and stare at Willis.

The boys dug sandwiches out of their travel bags and munched them. After that Frank's notion about a nap seemed a good idea. They slept until wakened by the car slowing down. Jim sat up, blinked, and called down, "What's up?"

"Coming into Cynia Station," the driver answered. "Lay over until sundown."

"Won't the ice hold?"

"Maybe it will. Maybe it won't. The temperature's up and I'm not going to chance it." The car slid softly to a stop, then started again and crawled slowly up a low ramp, stopped again. "All out!" the driver called. "Be back by sundown—or get left." He climbed out; the boys followed.

Cynia Station was three miles west of the ancient city of Cynia, where west Strymon joins the canal Oeroe. It was merely a lunchroom, a bunkhouse, and a row of pre-fab warehouses. To the east the feathery towers of Cynia gleamed in the sky, seemed almost to float, too beautifully unreal to be solid.

The driver went into the little inn. Jim wanted to walk over and explore the city; Frank favored stopping in the restaurant first. Frank won out. They went inside and cautiously invested part of their meager capital in coffee and some indifferent soup.

The driver looked up from his dinner presently and said, "Hey, George! Ever see anything like that?" He pointed to Willis.

George was the waiter. He was also the cashier, the hotel keeper, the station agent, and the Company representative. He glanced at Willis. "Yep."

"You did, huh? Where? Do you suppose I could find one?"

"Doubt it. You see 'em sometimes, hanging around the Martians. Not many of 'em." He turned back to his reading—a *New York Times*, more than two years old.

The boys finished, paid their bills, and prepared to go outside. The cook-waiter-station-agent said, "Hold on. Where are you kids going?"

"Syrtis Minor."

"Not that. Where are you going right now? Why don't you wait in the dormitory? Take a nap if you like."

"We thought we would kind of explore around outside," explained Jim.

"Okay. But stay away from the city."

"Why?"

"Because the Company doesn't allow it, that's why. Not without permission."

"How do we get permission?" Jim persisted.

"You can't. Cynia hasn't been opened up to exploitation yet." He went back to his reading.

Jim was about to continue the matter but Frank tugged at his sleeve. They went outside together. Jim said, "I don't think he has any business telling us we can't go to Cynia."

"What's the difference? He thinks he has."

"What'll we do now?"

"Go to Cynia, of course. Only we won't consult his nibs."

"Suppose he catches us?"

"How can he? He won't stir off that stool he's warming. Come on."

"Okay." They set out to the east. The going was not too easy; there was no road of any sort and all the plant growth bordering the canal was spread out to its greatest extent to catch the rays of the midday sun. But Mars' low gravity makes walking easy work even over rough ground. They came shortly to the bank of Oeroe and followed it to the right, toward the city.

The way was easy along the smooth stone of the bank. The air was warm and balmy even though the surface of the canal was still partly frozen. The sun was high; they were the better part of a thousand miles closer to the equator than they had been at daybreak.

"Warm," said Willis. "Willis want down."

"Okay," Jim agreed, "but don't fall in."

"Willis not fall in." Jim put him down and the little creature went skipping and rolling along the bank, with occasional excursions into the thick vegetation, like a puppy exploring a new pasture.

They had gone perhaps a mile and the towers of the city were higher in the sky when they encountered a Martian. He was a small specimen of his sort, being not over twelve feet tall. He was standing quite still, all three of his legs down, apparently lost in contemplation of the whichness of what. The eye facing them stared unblinkingly.

Jim and Frank were, of course, used to Martians and recognized that this one was busy in his "other world"; they stopped talking and continued on past him, being careful not to brush against his legs.

Not so Willis. He went darting around the Martian's peds, rubbing against them, then stopped and let out a couple of mournful croaks.

The Martian stirred, looked around him, and suddenly bent and scooped Willis up.

"Hey!" yelled Jim. "Put him down!"

No answer.

Jim turned hastily to Frank. "You talk to him, Frank. I'll never be able to make him understand me. Please!" Of the Martian dominant language Jim understood little and spoke less. Frank was somewhat better, but only by comparison. Those who speak Martian complain that it hurts their throats.

"What'll I say?"

"Tell him to put Willis down! Or, so help me, I'll burn his legs off!"

"Oh, now, Jim, you wouldn't do anything like *that*. It would get your whole family in trouble."

"If he hurts Willis, I sure will!"

"Grow up. Martians never hurt anybody."

"Well, tell him to put Willis down, then."

"I'll try." Frank screwed up his mouth and got to work. His accent, bad at best, was made worse by the respirator and by nervousness. Nevertheless he clucked and croaked his way through a phrase that seemed to mean what Jim wanted. Nothing happened.

He tried again, using a different idiom; still nothing happened. "It's no good, Jim," he admitted. "Either he doesn't understand me or he doesn't want to bother to listen."

Jim shouted, "Willis! Hey, Willis! Are you all right?"

"Willis fine!"

"Jump down! I'll catch you."

"Willis fine."

The Martian wobbled his head, seemed to locate Jim for the first time. He cradled Willis in one arm; his other two arms came snaking suddenly down and enclosed Jim, one palm flap cradling him where he sat down, the other slapping him across the belly. Jim was unable to get at his gun, which was just as well.

He felt himself lifted and held and then he was staring into a large liquid Martian eye which stared back at him. The Martian "man" rocked his head back and forth and let each of his eyes have a good look.

It was the closest Jim had ever been to a Martian; he did not care for it. Worse, the little supercharger on the top of Jim's mask compressed not only the thin air, but also the body odor of the native; the stench was overpowering. Jim tried to wiggle away, but the fragile-appearing Martian was stronger than he was.

Suddenly the Martian's voice boomed out from the top of his head. Jim could not understand what was being said although he spotted the question symbol at the beginning of the phrase. But the Martian's voice had a strange effect on him. Croaking and uncouth though it was, it was filled with such warmth and sympathy and friendliness that the native no longer frightened him. Instead he seemed like an old and trusted friend. Even the stink of his kind no longer troubled Jim.

The Martian repeated the question.

"What did he say, Frank?"

"I didn't get it. Shall I burn him?" Frank stood uneasily by, his gun drawn, but apparently unsure what to do.

"No, no! He's friendly, but I can't understand him."

The Martian spoke again; Frank listened. "He's inviting you to go with him, I think."

Jim hesitated a split second. "Tell him okay."

"Jim, are you crazy?"

"It's all right. He means well. I'm sure of it."

"Well—all right." Frank croaked the phrase of assent.

The native gathered up one leg and strode rapidly away toward the city. Frank trotted after. He tried his best to keep up, but the pace was too much for him. He paused, gasping, then shouted, "Wait for me," his voice muffled by his mask.

Jim tried to phrase a demand to stop, gave up, then got an inspiration. "Say, Willis—Willis boy. Tell him to wait for Frank."

"Wait for Frank?" Willis said doubtfully.

"Yes. Wait for Frank."

"Okay." Willis hooted at his new friend; the Martian paused and dropped his third leg. Frank came puffing up.

The Martian removed one arm from Jim and scooped up Frank with it. "Hey!" Frank protested. "Cut it out."

"Take it easy," advised Jim.

"But I don't want to be carried. Judas—what a smell! Pew!"

"Smell? Don't be a sissy. He smells better than you do."

Frank's reply was disturbed by the Martian starting up again. Thus burdened, he shifted to a three-legged gait in which at least two legs were always on the ground. It was bumpy but surprisingly fast. Finally Frank managed to say, "Repeat that last crack when we get down and I'll show you who smells bad."

"Forget it," urged Jim. "Where do you suppose he is taking us?"

"To the city I guess." Frank added, "We don't want to miss the scooter."

"We've got hours yet. Quit worrying."

The Martian said nothing more but continued slogging toward Cynia. Willis was evidently as happy as a bee in a flower shop. Jim settled down to enjoying the ride. Now that he was being carried with his head a good ten feet above ground his view was much improved; he could see over the tops of the plants growing by the canal and beyond them to the iridescent towers of Cynia. The towers were not like those of Charax; no two Martian cities looked alike. It was as if each were a unique work of art, each expressing the thoughts of a different artist.

Jim wondered why the towers had been built, what they were good for, how old they were?

The canal crops spread out around them, a dark green sea in which the Martian waded waist deep. The broad leaves were spread flat to the sun's rays, reaching greedily for life-giving radiant energy. They curled aside as the native's body brushed them, to spread again as he passed.

The towers grew much closer; suddenly the Martian stopped and set the two boys down. He continued to carry Willis. Ahead of them, almost concealed by overhanging greenery, a ramp slanted down into the ground and entered a tunnel arch. Jim looked at it and said, "Frank, what do you think?"

"Gee, I don't know." The boys had been inside the cities of Charax and Copais, but only in the abandoned parts and at ground level. They were not allowed time to fret over their decision; their guide started down the slope at a good clip.

Jim ran after him, shouting, "Hey, Willis!"

The Martian stopped and exchanged a couple of remarks with Willis; the bouncer called out, "Jim wait."

"Tell him to put you down."

"Willis fine. Jim wait." The Martian started up again at a pace that Jim could not possibly match. Jim went disconsolately back to the start of the ramp and sat down on the ledge thereof.

"What are you going to do?" demanded Frank.

"Wait, I suppose. What else can I do? What are *you* going to do?"

"Oh, I'll stick. But I'm not going to miss the scooter."

"Well, neither am I. We couldn't stay here after sundown anyhow."

"You aint whistling!" The precipitous drop in temperature at sunset on Mars is almost all the weather there is, but it means death by freezing for an Earth human unless he is specially clothed and continuously exercising.

They sat and waited and watched spin bugs skitter past. One stopped by Jim's knee, a little tripod of a creature, less than an inch high; it appeared to study him. He touched it; it flung out its limbs and whirled away. The boys were not even alert, since a water-seeker will not come close to a Martian settlement; they simply waited.

Perhaps a half hour later the Martian—or, at least, *a* Martian of the same size—came back. He did not have Willis with him. Jim's face fell. But the Martian said, "Come with me," in his own tongue, prefacing the remark with the question symbol.

"Do we or don't we?" asked Frank.

"We do. Tell him so." Frank complied. The three started down. The Martian laid a great hand flap on the shoulders of each boy and herded them along. Shortly he stopped and picked them up. This time they made no objection.

The tunnel seemed to remain in full daylight even after they had penetrated several hundred yards underground. The light came from everywhere but especially from the ceiling. The tunnel was large by human standards but no more than comfortably roomy for Martians. They passed several other natives; if another was moving their host always boomed a greeting, but if he was frozen in the characteristic trance-like immobility no sound was made.

Once their guide stepped over a ball about three feet in diameter. Jim could not make out what it was at first, then he did a double take and was still more puzzled. He twisted his neck and looked back at it. It *couldn't be*—but it was!

He was gazing at something few humans ever see, and no human ever wants to see: a Martian folded and rolled into a ball, his hand flaps covering everything but his curved back. Martians—modern, civilized Martians—do not hibernate, but at some time remote eons in the past their ancestors must have done so, for they are still articulated so that they can assume the proper, heat-conserving, moisture-conserving globular shape, if they wish.

They hardly ever so wish.

For a Martian to roll up is the moral equivalent of an Earthly duel to the death and is resorted to only when that Martian is offended so completely that nothing less will suffice. It means: I cast you out, I leave your world, I deny your existence.

The first pioneers on Mars did not understand this, and, through ignorance of Martian values, offended more than once. This delayed human colonization of Mars by many years; it took the most skilled diplomats and semanticians of Earth to repair the unwitting harm. Jim stared unbelievingly at the withdrawn Martian and wondered what could possibly have caused him to do that to an entire city. He remembered a grisly tale told him by Doctor MacRae concerning the second expedition to Mars. "So this dumb fool," the doctor had said, "a medical lieutenant he was, though I hate to admit it—this idiot grabs hold of the beggar's flaps and tries to unroll him. Then it happened."

"What happened?" Jim had demanded.

"He disappeared."

"The Martian?"

"No, the medical officer."

"Huh? How did he disappear?"

"Don't ask me; I didn't see it. The witnesses—four of 'em, with sworn statements—say there he was and then there he wasn't. As if he had met a boojum."

"What's a 'boojum'?" Jim had wanted to know.

"You modern kids don't get any education, do you? The boojum is in a book; I'll dig up a copy for you."

"But *how* did he disappear?"

"Don't ask me. Call it mass hypnosis if it makes you feel any better. It makes me feel better, but not much. All I can say is that seven-eighths of an iceberg never shows." Jim had never seen an iceberg, so the allusion was wasted on him—but he felt decidedly *not* better when he saw the rolled up Martian.

"Did you see that?" demanded Frank.

"I wish I hadn't," said Jim. "I wonder what happened?"

"Maybe he ran for mayor and lost."

"It's nothing to joke about. Maybe he—*Sssh!*" Jim broke off. He caught sight of another Martian, immobile, but not rolled up; politeness called for silence.

The Martian carrying them made a sudden turn to the left and entered a hall; he put them down. The room was very large to them; to Martians it was probably suitable for a cozy social gathering. There were many of the frames they use as a human uses a chair and these were arranged in a circle. The room itself was circular and domed; it had the appearance of being outdoors for the domed ceiling simulated Martian sky, pale blue at the horizon, increasing to warmer blue, then to purple, and reaching purple-black with stars piercing through at the highest point of the ceiling.

A miniature sun, quite convincing, hung west of the meridian. By some trick of perspective the pictured horizons were apparently distant. On the north wall Oeroe seemed to flow past.

Frank's comment was, "Gee whiz!"; Jim did not manage that much.

Their host had placed them by two resting frames. The boys did not attempt to use them; stepladders would have been more comfortable and convenient. The Martian looked first at them, then at the frames, with great sorrowful eyes. He left the room.

He came back very shortly, followed by two others; all three were carrying loads of colorful fabrics. They dumped them down in a pile in the middle of the room. The first Martian picked up Jim and Frank and deposited them gently on the heap.

"I think he means, 'Draw up a chair,' " commented Jim.

The fabrics were not woven but were a continuous sheet, like cobweb, and almost as soft, though much stronger. They were in all hues of all colors from pastel blue to deep, rich red. The boys sprawled on them and waited.

Their host relaxed himself on one of the resting frames; the two others did the same. No one said anything. The two boys were decidedly not tourists; they knew better than to try to hurry a Martian. After a bit Jim got an idea; to test it he cautiously raised his mask. Frank snapped, "Say! What 'cha trying to do? Choke to death?"

Jim left his mask up. "It's all right. The pressure is up."

"Huh? It can't be. We didn't come through a pressure lock."

"Have it your own way." Jim left his mask up. Seeing that he did not turn blue, gasp, nor become slack featured, Frank ventured to try it himself. He found himself able to breathe without trouble. To be sure, the pressure was not as great as he was used to at home and it would have seemed positively stratospheric to an Earthling, but it was enough for a man at rest.

Several other Martians drifted in and unhurriedly composed themselves on frames. After a while Frank said, "Do you know what's going on, Jim?"

"Uh—maybe."

"No 'maybes' about it. It's a 'Growing-together.' "

"Growing together" is an imperfect translation of a Martian idiom which names their most usual social event—in bald terms, just sitting around and saying nothing. In similar terms, violin music has been described as dragging a horse's tail across the dried gut of a cat. "I guess you're right," agreed Jim. "We had better button our lips."

"Yeah."

For a long time nothing was said. Jim's thoughts drifted away, to school and what he would do there, to his family, to things in the past. He came back presently to personal self-awareness and realized that he was happier than he had been in a long time, with no particular reason that he could place. It was a quiet happiness; he felt no desire to laugh nor even to smile, but he was perfectly relaxed and content.

He was acutely aware of the presence of the Martians, of each individual Martian, and was becoming even more aware of them with each drifting minute. He had never noticed before how beautiful they were. "Ugly as a native" was a common phrase with the colonials; Jim recalled with surprise that he had even used it himself, and wondered why he ever had done so.

He was aware, too, of Frank beside him and thought about how much he liked him. Staunch—that was the word for Frank, a good man to have at your back. He wondered why he had never told Frank that he liked him.

Mildly he missed Willis, but was not worried about him. This sort of a party was not Willis's dish; Willis liked things noisy, boisterous, and unrefined. Jim put aside the thought of Willis, lay back, and soaked in the joy of living. He noted with delight that the unknown artist who had designed this room had arranged for the miniature sun to move across the ceiling just as the true Sun moved across the sky. He watched it travel to the west and presently begin to drop toward the pictured horizon.

There came a gentle booming behind him—he could not catch the words—and another Martian answered. One of them unfolded himself from his resting stand and ambled out of the room. Frank sat up and said, "I must have been dreaming."

"Did you go to sleep?" asked Jim. "I didn't."

"The heck you didn't. You snored like Doc MacRae."

"Why, I wasn't even asleep."

"Says you!"

The Martian who had left the room returned. Jim was sure it was the same one; they no longer looked alike to him. He was carrying a drinking vase. Frank's eyes bulged out. "Do you suppose they are going to serve us *water*?"

"Looks like," Jim answered in an awed voice.

Frank shook his head. "We might as well keep this to ourselves; nobody'll ever believe us."

"Yeah. You're right."

The ceremony began. The Martian with the vase announced his own name, barely touched the stem of the vase and passed it on. The next Martian gave his name and also simulated drinking. Around the circle it came. The Martian who had brought them in, Jim learned, was named "Gekko"; it seemed a pretty name to Jim and fitting. At last the vase came around to Jim; a Martian handed it to him with the wish, "May you never suffer thirst." The words were quite clear to him.

There was an answering chorus around him: "May you drink deep whenever you wish!"

Jim took the vase and reflected that Doc said that the Martians didn't have anything that was catching for humans. "Jim Marlowe!" he announced, placed the stem in his mouth and took a sip.

As he handed it back he dug into his imperfect knowledge of the dominant language, concentrated on his accent and managed to say, "May water ever be pure and plentiful for you." There was an approving murmur that warmed him. The Martian handed the vase to Frank.

With the ceremony over the party broke up in noisy, almost human chatter. Jim was trying vainly to follow what was being said to him by a Martian nearly three times his height when Frank said, "Jim! You see that sun? We're going to miss the scooter!"

"Huh? That not the real Sun; that's a toy."

"No, but it matches the real Sun. My watch says the same thing."

"Oh, for Pete's sake! Where's Willis? Gekko—where's Gekko?"

Gekko, on hearing his name, came over; he clucked inquiringly at Jim. Jim tried very hard to explain their trouble, tripped over syntax, used the wrong directive symbols, lost his accent entirely. Frank shoved him aside and took over. Presently Frank said, "They'll get us there before sunset, but Willis stays here."

"Huh? They can't do that!"

"That's what the man says."

Jim thought. "Tell them to bring Willis here and ask *him*."

Gekko was willing to do that. Willis was carried in, placed upon the floor. He waddled up to Jim and said, "Hi, Jim boy! Hi, Frank boy!"

"Willis," said Jim, earnestly, "Jim is going away. Willis come with Jim?"

Willis seemed puzzled. "Stay here. Jim stay here. Willis stay here. Good."

"Willis," Jim said frantically, "Jim has *got* to go away. Willis come with Jim?"

"Jim go?"

"Jim go."

Willis almost seemed to shrug. "Willis go with Jim," he said sadly.

"Tell Gekko." Willis did so. The Martian seemed surprised, but there was no further argument. He gathered up both boys and the bouncer and started for the door. Another larger Martian— tagged "G'kuro" Jim recalled—relieved Gekko of Frank and tailed along behind. As they climbed the tunnel Jim found suddenly that he needed his mask; Frank put his on, too.

The withdrawn Martian was still cluttering the passageway; both their porters stepped over it without comment.

The sun was very low when they got to the surface. Although a Martian cannot be hastened his normal pace makes very good time; the long-legged pair made nothing of the three miles back to Cynia station. The sun had just reached the horizon and the air was already bitter when the boys and Willis were dumped on the dock. The two Martians left at once, hurrying back to the warmth of their city.

"Good-bye, Gekko!" Jim shouted. "Good-bye, G'kuro!"

The driver and the station master were standing on the dock; it was evident that the driver was ready to start and had been missing his passengers. "What in the world?" said the station master.

"We're ready to go," said Jim.

"So I see," said the driver. He stared at the retreating figures. He blinked and turned to the agent. "We should have left that stuff alone, George. I'm seeing things." He added to the boys, "Well, get aboard."

They did so and climbed up to the dome. The car clumped down off the ramp to the surface of the ice, turned left onto Oeroe canal and picked up speed. The Sun dropped behind the horizon; the landscape was briefly illuminated by the short Martian sunset. On each bank the boys could see the plants withdrawing for the night. In a few minutes the ground, so lush with vegetation a half hour before, was bare as the true desert.

The stars were out, sharp and dazzling. Soft curtains of aurora hung over the skyline. In the west a tiny steady light rose and fought its way upwards against the motion of the stars. "There's Phobos," said Frank. "Lookie!"

"I see it," Jim answered. "It's cold. Let's turn in."

"Okay. I'm hungry."

"I've got some sandwiches left." They munched one each,

then went down into the lower compartment and crawled into bunks. In time the car passed the city Hesperidum and turned west-northwest onto the canal Erymanthus, but Jim was unaware of it; Jim was dreaming that Willis and he were singing a duet for the benefit of amazed Martians.

"All out! End of the line!" The driver was prodding them.
"Huh?"
"Up you come, shipmate. This is it—Syrtis Minor."

4.
LOWELL ACADEMY

"Dear Mother and Dad,

"The reason I didn't phone you when we got in Wednesday night was that we didn't get in until Thursday morning. When I tried to phone on Thursday the operator told me that Deimos had set for South Colony and then I knew it would be about three days until I could relay a call through Deimos and a letter would get there sooner and save you four and a half credits on a collect phone call. Now I realize that I didn't get this letter off to you right away and maybe you're not going to get it until after I would have been able to make a phone call if I had made it but what you probably don't realize is how busy they keep you at school and how many demands there are on a fellow's time and anyhow you probably heard from Frank's mother that we had gotten here all right and anyway you look at it I still saved you four and one half credits by not making that phone call.

"I can just hear Phyllis saying that I am just hinting that the half-and-four I saved should be turned over to me but I am not doing anything of the sort because I wouldn't do anything like that and besides I've still got some of the money left that you gave me before I left as well as part of my birthday money and with careful management I will not need any more until you all come through here at Migration even though everything costs more here than it does at home. Frank says it's because they always jack the prices up for the tourist trade but there aren't any tourists around now and won't be until the *Albert Einstein* gets in next week. Anyway if you simply split the difference with me you would still be a clear two and a quarter credits ahead.

"The reason we didn't get here Wednesday night was because the driver decided the ice might not hold so we laid over at Cynia Station and Frank and I just fooled around and killed time until sunset.

"Frank and I have been allowed to room together and we've got a dandy room. It was meant for just one boy and only has one study desk but we're mostly taking the same subjects and lots of time we can use the projector together. I am talking this letter into the study desk recorder because tonight is Frank's night to help out in the kitchen and all I've got left to study is a little bit of history and I'm saving that to do it with Frank when he comes back. Professor Steuben says that he does not know what they are going to do if they keep getting more students here with no more room, hang them on hooks maybe but he is just joking. He jokes a lot and everybody likes him and will be sorry when he leaves on the *Albert Einstein* and the new headmaster takes over.

"Well that's all for now because Frank just got back and we had better get to work because tomorrow we have a quiz on system history.
"Your loving son,
"James Madison Marlowe, Jr.
"P.S. Frank just told me that he didn't write his folks either and he wonders if you would mind phoning his mother and telling her that he is all right and would she please send his camera right away, he forgot it.
P.P.S. Willis sends his love. I just asked him.
P.P.P.S. Tell Phyllis that the girls here are dyeing their hair in stripes. I think it looks silly.
"JIM"

If Professor Otto Steuben, M.A., Ll.D., had not retired, Jim's life at Lowell Academy would have been different. But retire he did and went back to San Fernando Valley for a well-earned rest. The entire school went to Marsport to see him off. He shook hands all around and wept a little and commended them to the care of Marquis Howe, recently arrived from Earth and now taking over.

When Jim and Frank got back from the space port they found the first arrivals gathered around the bulletin board. They crowded in and read the item that was drawing the crowd:

SPECIAL NOTICE

All students are required to keep themselves and their quarters neat and orderly at all times. The supervision of these matters by student monitors has not proved satisfactory. Therefore formal inspections by the Headmaster will be held each week. The first such inspection will be at ten hundred, Saturday, the 7th of Ceres.

(signed)
M. Howe, Headmaster

"Well, for crying out loud!" Frank burst out. "What d'you think of that, Jim?"

Jim stared at it darkly. "I think that today is the sixth of Ceres."

"Yeah, but what's the idea? He must think that this is a school of correction." Frank turned to one of the older students, who had, until now, been monitor of their corridor. "Anderson, what do you think about it? Can he do that?"

"I don't know. I really don't know. It seems to me that our rooms and so forth are our private business."

"What do you intend to do about it?"

"Me?" The young man thought a while before replying, "I've got just one more semester to my degree, then I'm out of here. I think I'll just sit tight, keep my mouth shut, and sweat it out."

"Huh? That's easy enough for you to say but I've got twelve semesters staring me in the face. What am I? A criminal?"

"That's your problem, fellow." The older student left.

One of the boys in the crowd seemed undisturbed by the notice. He was Herbert Beecher, son of the Company's Resident Agent General and a newcomer both to Mars and to the school. One of the other boys noticed his smirk. "What are you looking smug about, tourist?" he demanded. "Did you know about this ahead of time?"

"Certainly I did."

"I'll bet you thought it up."

"No, but my old man says you guys have been getting away with it for a long time. My old man says that Stoobie was too soft to put any discipline into this school. My old man says that—"

"Nobody cares what your old man says. Beat it!"

"You better not talk about my old man that way. I'll—"

"Beat it before I clip you one!"

Young Beecher eyed his antagonist—a red-headed lad named Kelly—and decided that he meant it. He faded out of sight.

"He can afford to grin," Kelly said bitterly, "he lives in his old man's quarters. This thing only gets at those of us who have to live in the school. It's rank discrimination, that's what it is!" About a third of boys were day students, mostly sons of Company employees who were stationed at Syrtis Minor. Another third were migratory colonials and the balance were the children of terrestrials at the outlying stations, especially those employed on the atmosphere project. Most of these last were Bolivians and Tibetans, plus a few Eskimos. Kelly turned to one of them. "How about it, Chen? Are we going to put up with this?"

The Asiatic's broad face showed no expression. "It is not worth getting excited about."

"Huh? You mean you won't stand up for your rights?"

"These things pass."

Jim and Frank went back to their room but continued to discuss it. "Frank," asked Jim, "what's behind this? Do you suppose they're pulling the same stunt over in the girls' school?"

"I could call up Dolores Montez and find out."

"Mmm . . . don't bother. I don't suppose it matters. The question is: what are we going to do about it?"

"What can we do about it?"

"I don't know. I wish I could ask Dad about this. He always told me to stand up for my rights . . . but maybe he would say that this is just something I should expect. I don't know."

"Look," suggested Frank, "why don't we ask our fathers?"

"You mean call 'em up tonight? Is there relay tonight?"

"No, don't call 'em up; that costs too much. We'll wait till our folks come through here at migration; that's not so very long now. If we're going to make a fuss, we've got to have our folks here to back us up, or we won't get any place with it. Meantime, we sit tight and do what he asks us. It may not amount to anything."

"Now you're talking sense." Jim stood up. "I suppose we might as well try to get this dump tidied up."

"Okay. Say, Jim, I just thought of something. Isn't the chairman of the Company named Howe?"

"John W. Howe," agreed Jim. "What about it?"

"Well, the head is named Howe, too."

"Oh." Jim shook his head. "Doesn't mean anything. Howe is a very common name."

"I'll bet it does mean something. Doc MacRae says you have to be somebody's cousin to get any of the juicy Company appointments. Doc says that the Company setup is just one big happy family, playing-you-tickle-me-and-I'll-kiss-you and that the idea that it is a non-profit corporation is the biggest joke since women were invented."

"Hmm . . . Well, I wouldn't know. Where shall I put this junk?"

Slips were distributed at breakfast the next morning giving what was described as "Official Arrangement of Rooms for Inspection"; the job the boys had done the night before had to be done over. Since Headmaster Howe's instructions failed to consider the possibility that two boys might be living in a one-boy room the rearranging was not easy; they were not ready by ten o'clock. However it was nearly two hours later that the Headmaster got around to their cubicle.

He poked his head inside, seemed about to leave, then came inside. He pointed to their outdoors suits, hanging on hooks by the clothes locker. "Why haven't you removed those barbaric decorations from your masks?"

The boys looked startled; Howe went on, "Haven't you looked at the bulletin board this morning?"

"Er—no, sir."

"Do so. You are responsible for anything posted on the bulletin board." He shouted toward the door. "Orderly!"

One of the older students appeared in the doorway. "Yes, sir."

"Weekend privileges suspended for these two pending satisfaction of inspection requirements. Five demerits each." Howe looked around. "This room is unbelievably cluttered and untidy. Why didn't you follow the prescribed diagram?"

Jim stuttered, tongue-tied by the evident unfairness of the question. Finally he got out, "This is supposed to be a single room. We did the best we could."

"Don't resort to excuses. If you don't have room to store things neatly, get rid of the excess baggage." For the first time his eye lit on Willis, who, at the sight of strangers, had retreated to a corner and hauled in all out-rigging. Howe pointed at him. "Athletic equipment must be stored on tops of lockers or left in the gymnasium. It must *not* be thrown in corners."

Jim started to answer; Frank kicked him in a shin. Howe went on lecturing as he moved toward the door. "I realize that you young people have been brought up away from civilization and have not had the benefits of polite society, but I shall do my best to remedy that. I intend that this school shall, above all other things, turn out civilized young gentlemen." He paused at the door and added, "When you have cleaned up those masks, report to my office."

When Howe was out of earshot Jim said, "What did you kick me for?"

"You dumb idiot, he thought Willis was a ball."

"I know; I was just about to set him right."

Frank looked disgusted. "Don't you know enough to let well enough alone? You want to keep Willis, don't you? He would have whipped up some rule making him contraband."

"Oh, he couldn't do that!"

"The heck he couldn't! I'm beginning to see that Stoobie kept our pal Howe from exercising his full talents. Say, what did he mean: 'demerits'?"

"I don't know, but it doesn't sound good." Jim took down his respirator mask, looked at the gay tiger stripes. "You know, Frank, I don't think I want to become a 'civilized young gentleman'."

"You and me both!"

They decided to take a quick look at the bulletin board before they got into any more trouble, rather than fix the masks at once. They went to the entrance foyer and did so. On the board was pinned:

NOTICE TO STUDENTS

1. The practice of painting respirator masks with so-called identification patterns will cease. Masks will be plain and each student will letter his name neatly in letters one inch high across the chest and across the shoulders of his outdoors suit.

2. Students are required to wear shirts and shoes or slippers at all times and places except in their own rooms.

3. Pets will not be kept in dormitory rooms. In some cases, where the animals are of interest as scientific specimens, arrangements may be made to feed and care for pets in the biology laboratory.

4. Food must not be kept in dormitory rooms. Students receiving food packages from parents will store them with the commissary matron and reasonable amounts may be withdrawn immediately after meals, except Saturday morning breakfast. Special permission may be obtained for "sweets parties" during recreation hours on occasions such as birthdays, etc.

5. Students denied weekend privileges for disciplinary reasons may read, study, compose letters, play musical instruments, or listen to music. They are not permitted to play cards, visit in other students' rooms, nor leave the school area for any reason.

6. Students wishing to place telephone calls will submit a written request on the approved form and will obtain key to the communications booth at the main office.

(signed) M. Howe, Headmaster

Jim whistled. Frank said, "Would you look at that, Jim? Would you, now? Do you suppose we have to get permission to scratch? What does he take us for?"

"Search me."

"Frank, I haven't *got* a shirt."

"Well, I can lend you a sweat shirt until you can buy some. But take a look at paragraph three—you'd better get busy."

"Huh? What about it?" Jim reread it.

"You'd better go butter up the bio teacher, so you can make arrangements for Willis."

"What?" Jim simply had not connected the injunction concerning pets with Willis; he did not think of Willis as a pet. "Oh, I can't do that, Frank. He'd be terribly unhappy."

"Then you had better ship him home and let your folks care for him."

Jim looked balky. "I won't do it. I won't!"

"Then what are you going to do?"

"I don't know." He thought about it. "I won't do anything about it. I'll just keep him under cover. Old lady Howe doesn't even know I've got him."

"Well . . . you might get away with it, so long as nobody snitches on you."

"I don't think any of the fellows would do that."

They went back to their room and attempted to remove the decorations from their masks. They were not very successful; the paint had bitten into the plastic and they succeeded only in smearing the colors around. Presently a student named Smythe stuck his head in the door. "Clean up your masks for you?"

"Huh? It can't be done; the colors have soaked in."

"You're the umpteenth to find that out. But, from the goodness of my heart and a willingness to be of public service, I will paint your mask over to match the original shade—at a quarter credit per mask."

"I thought there was a catch in it," Jim answered.

"Do you want it, or don't you? Hurry up, my public is waiting."

"Smitty, you would sell tickets to your grandmother's funeral." Jim produced a quarter credit.

"That's an idea. How much do you think I could charge?" The other boy produced a can of lacquer and a brush, rapidly painted out Jim's proud design, using a pigment that was a fair match for the olive-drab original shade. "There! It'll dry in a couple of minutes. How about you, Sutton?"

"Okay, bloodsucker," Frank agreed.

"Is that any way to talk about your benefactor? I've got a heavy date over on the girls' side and here I am spending my precious Saturday helping you out." Smythe made equally rapid work of Frank's mask.

"Spending your time raising money for your date, you mean," amended Jim. "Smitty, what do you think of these trick rules the new Head has thought up? Should we knuckle under, or make a squawk?"

"Squawk? What for?" Smythe gathered up his tools. "There's a brand-new business opportunity in each one, if you only had the wit to see it. When in doubt, come see Smythe—special services at all hours." He paused at the door. "Don't mention that deal about tickets to my grandmother's funeral; she'd want a cut on it before she kicks off. Granny is a very shrewd gal with a credit."

"Frank," remarked Jim when Smythe was gone, "there is something about that guy I don't like."

Frank shrugged. "He fixed us up. Let's check in and get off the punishment list."

"Right. He reminds me of something Doc used to say. 'Every law that was ever written opened up a new way to graft.'"

"That's not necessarily so. My old man says Doc is a crackpot. Come on."

They found a long line waiting outside the Headmaster's office. They were finally ushered in groups of ten. Howe gave their masks a brief glance each, then started in to lecture. "I hope that this will be a lesson to you young gentlemen not only in neatness, but in alertness. Had you noticed what was posted on the bulletin board you would have been, each of you, prepared for inspection. As for the dereliction itself, I want you to understand that this lesson far transcends the matter of the childish and savage designs you have been using on your face coverings."

He paused and made sure of their attention. "There is actually no reason why colonial manners should be rude and vulgar and, as head of this institution, I intend to see to it that whatever defects there may have been in your home backgrounds are repaired. The first purpose, perhaps the only purpose, of education is the building of character—and character can be built only through discipline. I flatter myself that I am exceptionally well prepared to undertake this task; before coming here I had twelve years experience as a master at the Rocky Mountains Military Academy, an exceptionally fine school, a school that produced *men*."

He paused again, either to catch his breath or let his words soak in. Jim had come in prepared to let a reprimand roll off his back, but the schoolmaster's supercilious attitude and most especially his suggestion that a colonial home was an inferior sort of environment had gradually gotten his dander up. He spoke up. "Mr. Howe?"

"Eh? Yes? What is it?"

"This is not the Rocky Mountains; it's Mars. And this isn't a military academy."

There was a brief moment when it seemed as if Mr. Howe's surprise and anger might lead him to some violence, or even to apoplexy. After a bit he contained himself and said through tight lips, "What is your name?"

"Marlowe, sir. James Marlowe."

"It would be a far, far better thing for you, Marlowe, if it were a military academy." He turned to the others. "The rest of you may go. Weekend privileges are restored. Marlowe, remain behind."

When the others had left Howe said, "Marlowe, there is nothing in this world more offensive than a smart-aleck boy, an ungrateful upstart who doesn't know his place. You are enjoying a fine education through the graciousness of the Company. It ill behooves you to make cheap wisecracks at persons appointed by the Company to supervise your training and welfare. Do you realize that?"

Jim said nothing. Howe said sharply, "Come! Speak up, lad— admit your fault and make your apology. Be a man!"

Jim still said nothing. Howe drummed on the desk top; finally he said, "Very well, go to your room and think it over. You have the weekend to think about it."

When Jim got back to his room Frank looked him over and shook his head admiringly. "Boy, oh boy!" he said, "aint you the reckless one."

"Well, he needed to be told."

"He sure did. But what are your plans now? Are you going to cut your throat, or just enter a monastery? Old Howie will be gunning for you every minute from here on out. Matter of fact, it won't be any too safe to be your roommate."

"Confound it, Frank, if that's the way you feel, you're welcome to find another roommate!"

"Easy, easy! I won't run out on you. I'm with you to the end. 'Smiling, the boy fell dead.' I'm glad you told him off. I wouldn't have had the courage to do it myself."

Jim threw himself across the bunk. "I don't think I can stand this place. I'm not used to being pushed around and sneered at, just for nothing. And now I'm going to get it double. What can I do?"

"Derned if I know."

"This was a nice place under old Stoobie. I thought I was going to like it just fine."

"Stoobie was all right. And Howe is a prime stinker. But what *can* you do, Jim, except shut up, take it, and hope he will forget it?"

"Look, nobody else likes it either. Maybe if we stood together we could make him slow up."

"Not likely. You were the only one who had the guts to speak up. Shucks, *I* didn't even back you up—and I agreed with you a hundred per cent."

"Well, suppose we all sent letters to our parents?"

Frank shook his head. "You couldn't get them all to—and some pipsqueak would snitch. Then you would be in the soup, for inciting to riot or some such nonsense. Anyhow," he went on, "just what could you say in a letter that you could put your finger on and prove that Mr. Howe was doing something he had no right to? I know what my old man would say."

"What would he say?"

"Many's the time he's told me stories about the school he went to back Earthside and what a rough place it was. I think he's a little bit proud of it. If I tell him that Howie won't let us keep cookies in our room, he'll just laugh at me. He'd say—"

"Dawggone it, Frank, it's not the rule about food in our rooms; it's the whole picture."

"Sure, sure. *I* know it. But try to tell my old man. All we can tell is little things like that. It'll have to get a lot worse before you could get our parents to do anything."

Frank's views were confirmed as the day wore on. As the news spread student after student dropped in on them, some to pump Jim's hand for having bearded the Headmaster, some merely curious to see the odd character who had had the temerity to buck vested authority. But one two-pronged fact became apparent: while no one liked the new school head and all resented some or all of his new "disciplinary" measures, no one was anxious to join up in what was assumed to be a foregone lost cause.

One of the senior boys summed it up. "Get wise to yourself, kid. A man wouldn't go into school teaching if he didn't enjoy exercising cheap authority. It's the natural profession of little Napoleons."

"Stoobie wasn't like that!"

"Stoobie was an exception. Most of them like rules just for the sake of rules. It's a fact of nature, like frost at sundown. You have to get used to it."

On Sunday Frank went out into Syrtis Minor—the terrestrial settlement, not the nearby Martian city. Jim, under what amounted to room arrest, stayed in their room, pretended to study and talked to Willis. Frank came back at supper time and announced, "I brought you a present." He chucked Jim a tiny package.

"You're a pal! What is it?"

"Open it and see."

It was a new tango recording, made in Rio and direct from Earth via the *Albert Einstein*, titled *¿Quién Es La Señorita?* Jim was inordinately fond of Latin music; Frank had remembered it.

"Oh, boy!" Jim went to the study desk, threaded the tape into the speaker, and got ready to enjoy it. Frank stopped him.

"There's the supper bell. Better wait."

Reluctantly Jim complied, but he came back and played it several times during the evening until Frank insisted that they study. He played it once more just before lights-out.

The dormitory corridor had been dark and quiet for perhaps fifteen minutes when *¿Quién Es La Señorita?* started up again. Frank sat up with a start. "What the deuce? Jim—don't play that now!"

"I'm not," protested Jim. "It must be Willis. It has to be Willis."

"Well, shut him up. Choke him. Put a pillow over his head."

Jim switched on the light. "Willis boy—hey, Willis! Shut up that racket!" Willis probably did not even hear him. He was standing the middle of the floor, beating time with his eye stalks, and barrelling on down the groove. His rendition was excellent, complete with marimbas and vocal chorus.

Jim picked him up. "Willis! Shut up, fellow."

Willis kept on beating it out.

The door bust open and framed Headmaster Howe. "Just as I thought," he said triumphantly, "no consideration for other people's rights and comforts. Shut off that speaker. And consider yourself restricted to your room for the next month."

Willis kept on playing; Jim tried to hide him with his body. "Didn't you hear my order?" demanded Howe. "I said to shut off that music." He strode over to the study desk and twisted the speaker switch. Since it was already shut off full, all he accomplished was breaking a fingernail. He suppressed an unschoolmasterly expression and stuck the finger in his mouth. Willis worked into the third chorus.

Howe turned around. "How do you have this thing wired?" he snapped. Getting no answer, he stepped up to Jim and said, "What are you hiding?" He shoved Jim aside, looked at Willis with evident disbelief and distaste. "What is *that*?"

"Uh, that's Willis," Jim answered miserably, raising his voice to be heard.

Howe was not entirely stupid; it gradually penetrated that the music he had been hearing came out of the curious-looking, fuzzy sphere in front of him.

"And what is 'Willis', may I ask?"

"Well, he's a . . . a bouncer. A sort of a Martian." Willis picked this moment to finish the selection, breathe a liquid contralto *buenas noches,* and shut up—for the moment.

"A bouncer? I've never heard of one."

"Well, not very many have seen one, even among the colonists. They're scarce."

"Not scarce enough. Sort of a Martian parrot, I assume."

"Oh, no!"

"What do you mean, 'Oh, no'?"

"He's not a bit like a parrot. He talks, he thinks—he's my friend!"

Howe was over his surprise and recalling the purpose of his visit. "All that is beside the point. You saw my order about pets?"

"Yes, but Willis is not a pet."

"What is he, then?"

"Well, he *can't* be a pet. Pets are animals; they're property. Willis isn't property; he's . . . well, he's just Willis."

Willis picked this time to continue with the next thing he had heard after the last playing of the tango. "Boy, when I hear that music," he remarked in Jim's voice, "I don't even remember that old stinker Howe."

"I can't forget him," Willis went on in Frank's voice. "I wish I had had the nerve to tell him off the same time you did, Jim. You know what? I think Howe is nuts, I mean really nuts. I'll bet he was a coward when he was a kid and it's twisted him inside."

Howe turned white. Frank's arm-chair psychoanalyzing had hit dead center. He raised his hand as if to strike, then dropped it again, uncertain what to strike. Willis hastily withdrew all protuberances and became a smooth ball.

"I say it's a pet," he said savagely, when he regained his voice. He scooped Willis up and headed for the door.

Jim started after him. "Say! Mr. Howe—you can't take Willis!"

The Headmaster turned. "Oh, I can't, can't I? You get back to bed. See me in my office in the morning."

"If you hurt Willis, I'll . . . I'll . . ."

"You'll what?" He paused. "Your precious pet won't be hurt. Now you get back in that bed before I thrash you." He turned again and left without stopping to see whether or not his order had been carried out.

Jim stood staring at the closed door, tears streaming down his cheeks, sobs of rage and frustration shaking him. Frank came over and put a hand on him. "Jim. Jim, don't take on so. You heard him promise not to hurt Willis. Get back into bed and settle it in the morning. At the very worst you'll have to send Willis home."

Jim shook off the hand. "I should have burned him," he muttered. "I should have burned him down where he stood."

"Suppose you did? Want to spend the rest of your life in an asylum? Don't let him get your goat, fellow; if he gets you angry, you'll do something silly and then he's got you."

"I'm already angry."

"I know you are and I don't blame you. But you've got to get over it and use your head. He was laying for you—you saw that. No matter what he does or says you've got to keep cool and outsmart him—or he gets you in wrong."

"I suppose you're right."

"I know I'm right. That's what Doc would say. Now come to bed."

Neither one of them got much sleep that night. Toward morning Jim had a nightmare that Howe was a withdrawn Martian whom he was trying to unroll—against his better judgment.

There was a brand-new notice on the bulletin board at breakfast time. It read:

IMPORTANT NOTICE

All students possessing personal weapons will turn them in at the main office for safekeeping. Weapons will be returned on request whenever the student concerned is leaving the limits of the school and the adjoining settlement. The practice of wearing sidearms in areas where there is no actual danger from Martian *fauna* will cease.

(signed) M. Howe, Headmaster

Jim and Frank read it together. "This is the worst one yet," said Jim. "The right to bear arms is guaranteed. Doc says it's the basis of all freedom."

Frank studied it. "Do you know what I think?"

"No. What?"

"I think he's afraid of you personally."

"Me? Why?"

"Because of what happened last night. There was murder in your eye and he saw it. I think he wants to pull your teeth. I don't think he gives a hoot about the rest of us hanging on to our heaters."

"You really think so?"

"I do. The question is: what are you going to do about it?"

Jim thought about it. "I'm not going to give up my gun. Dad wouldn't want me to. I'm sure of that. Anyhow, I'm licensed and I don't have to."

"Neither will I. But we had better think up a wrinkle before you have to go see him this morning."

The wrinkle showed up at breakfast—the student named Smythe. Frank spoke to Jim about it in a low voice; together they accosted the student after breakfast and brought him to their room. "Look, Smitty," began Jim, "you're a man with lots of angles, aren't you?"

"Mmm . . . could be. What's up?"

"You saw that notice this morning?"

"Sure. Who didn't? Everybody is grousing about it."

"Are you going to turn in your gun?"

"I did before breakfast. What do I need a gun for around here? I've got a brain."

"In that case you won't be called in about it. Now just supposing that you were handed two packages to take care of. You won't open them and you won't know what's in them. Do you think you could find a safe, a *really* safe place to keep them and still be able to give them back on short notice?"

"I don't suppose you want me to tell anybody about these, uh, packages?"

"Nope. Nobody."

"Hmm . . . . this sort of service comes high."

"How high?"

"Well, now, I couldn't afford to do it for less than two credits a week."

"That's too much," Frank put in sharply.

"Well—you're friends of mine. I'll make you a flat rate of eight credits for the rest of the year."

"Too much."

"Six credits then, and I won't go lower. You've got to pay for the risk."

"It's a deal," Jim said before Frank could bargain further.

Smythe left with a bundle before Jim reported to the Headmaster's office.

5.
LITTLE PITCHERS HAVE BIG EARS

Headmaster Howe kept Jim waiting thirty minutes before admitting him. When he was finally let in, Jim saw that Howe seemed to be quite pleased with himself. He glanced up. "Yes? You asked to see me?"

"You told me to see you, sir."

"I did? Let me see now, what is your name?"

He darn well knows my name, Jim said savagely to himself; *he's trying to get my goat.* He recalled Frank's solemn warning not to lose his temper. "James Marlowe, sir," he answered evenly.

"Oh, yes." The headmaster picked up a list from his desk. "I suppose you have come in to surrender your gun. Turn it over."

Jim shook his head. "I didn't come in for that."

"You didn't? Well, that's beside the point. You've seen the order; give me your gun."

Jim shook his head again. "I don't have a gun."

"Why did you come here without it? Go back to your room and fetch it. Quickly—I give you three minutes."

"No," said Jim slowly, "I've already told you that I haven't got a gun."

"You mean you haven't one in your room?"

"That's what I said."

"You're lying."

Jim counted slowly to twenty, then answered, "You know that I have no gun, or you wouldn't dare say that."

Howe stared at him for what seemed a long time, then stepped into his outer office. He returned shortly and appeared to have regained his cockiness. "Now, Marlowe, you said you wanted to see me about something else?"

"You told me to see you. About Willis."

"Willis? Oh, yes, the Martian roundhead." Howe smiled with his lips. "An interesting scientific specimen."

Howe added nothing more. The silence kept up so long that Jim began to realize that the Headmaster intended to force him to make any moves. Jim had already resigned himself to the idea that it would be impossible to keep Willis at the school any longer. He said, "I've come to get him. I'm going to take him out in town and arrange to send him home."

Howe smiled more broadly. "Oh, you are? And pray tell me how you are going to do that when you are restricted to the school for the next thirty days?"

Frank was still warning him; Jim could almost hear him. He answered, "All right, sir, I'll get somebody to do it for me—today. Now, please, can I have Willis?"

Howe leaned back and crossed his fingers over his stomach. "You bring up a most interesting point, Marlowe. You said last night that this creature is not a pet."

Jim was puzzled. "Yes?"

"You were quite emphatic about it. You said that he wasn't your property, but your friend. That's right, isn't it?"

Jim hesitated. He could feel that a trap was being built for him, but he was not sure what sort. "What if I did?"

"Did you say that, or didn't you? Answer me!"

"Well—yes."

Howe leaned forward. "In that case, what are you doing in here demanding that I turn this creature over to you? You have no claim on him."

"But—but—" Jim stopped, at a loss for words. He had been tricked with words, slippery words; he did not know how to answer them. "You can't do that!" he blurted out. "You don't own him, either! You have no right to keep him locked up."

Howe carefully fitted his finger tips together. "That is a matter still to be determined. Although you have waived all claim to him, it may be that the creature is property nevertheless—in which case he was found on the school grounds and I may take title to him on behalf of the school, as a scientific specimen."

"But—You can't do that; that's not fair! If he belongs to anybody, he belongs to me! You've got no right to—"

"Silence!" Jim shut up; Howe went on more quietly, "Don't tell me what I can or cannot do. You forget that I am *in loco parentis* to you. Any rights that you may have are vested in me, just as if I were your own father. As to the disposition of this creature, I am looking into it; I expect to see the Agent General this afternoon. In due course you will be informed of the outcome."

The Latin phrase confused Jim, as it was intended to; but he did catch one point in Howe's statement and snatched at it. "I'm going to tell my father about this. You can't get away with it."

"Threats, eh?" Howe smiled sourly. "Don't bother to ask for the key to the communications booth; I don't propose to have students phoning their parents every time I tell them to wipe their noses. Send your father a letter—but let me hear it before you send it." He stood up. "That is all. You may go. No—wait." He went again to his outer office, to return almost immediately. He seemed quite angry.

"Where did you hide that gun?" he demanded.

Jim had had time to regain some portion of calm. He said nothing. "Answer me!" insisted the Headmaster.

Jim answered slowly, "You've already called me a liar once on that subject; I won't say anything."

Howe looked at him. "Get to your room!" Jim got out.

Frank was waiting. "I don't see any blood," he announced, looking Jim over. "How did it go?"

"Oh, that so-and-so! That filthy, filthy so-and-so!"

"Bad, eh?"

"Frank, he won't let me have Willis."

"He's going to make you send him home? But you expected that."

"No, not that. He won't let me have him at all. He used a lot of double-talk but all it meant was that he had him and meant to keep him." Jim seemed about to break down and blubber. "Poor little Willis—you know how timid he is. Frank, what'll I do?"

"I don't get it," Frank answered slowly. "He can't keep Willis, not for keeps. Willis belongs to you."

"I told you he used a lot of double-talk—but that's what he means to do just the same. How am I going to get him back? Frank, I've just got to get him back."

Frank did not answer; Jim looked around disconsolately and noticed the room for the first time. "What happened here?" he asked. "The place looks like you had tried to wreck it."

"Oh, that. I started to tell you. While you were gone, a couple of Howie's stooges searched the joint."

"Huh?"

"Trying to find our guns. I just played dumb."

"They did, did they?" Jim appeared to make up his mind. "I've got to find Smythe." He headed for the door.

"Hey, wait—what d'you want to find Smitty for?"

Jim looked back and his face was very old. "I'm going to get my gun and go back there and get Willis."

"Jim! You're crazy!"

Jim did not answer but continued toward the door.

Frank stuck out a foot, tripped him and landed on his back as he went down. He grabbed Jim's right arm and twisted it behind his back. "Now you just rest there," he told Jim, "until you quiet down."

"Let me up."

"You got some sense in your head?"

No answer. "Okay," Frank went on, "I can sit here just as long as you want to. Let me know when you've quieted down." Jim started to struggle; Frank twisted his arm until he yelped and relaxed.

"That's better," said Frank. "Now listen to me: you're a nice guy, Jim, but you go off half-cocked. Suppose you do get your gun and suppose you manage to scare old Howie into coughing up Willis. How long are you going to keep him? You know how long? Just long enough for him to call in some Company police. Then they lock you up and take Willis away from you again. And you'll never see Willis again, not to mention the trouble and grief you'll cause your folks."

There followed a considerable silence. Finally Jim said, "Okay, let me up."

"You've given up the idea of waving your gun around?"

"Yeah."

"On your honor? Solemn promise?"

"Yes, I promise."

Frank let him up and brushed him off. Jim rubbed his arm and said, "You needn't have twisted it so hard."

"You're a fine one to complain; you ought to thank me. Now grab your notebook; we're going to be late to chemistry lab."

"I'm not going."

"Don't be silly, Jim. No use to pile up a bunch of cuts and maybe flunk just because you're sore at the Head."

"That's not the idea. I'm quitting, Frank. I won't stay in this school."

"What? Don't be hasty, Jim. I know how you feel, but it's here or nowhere. Your folks can't afford to send you back to Earth for school."

"Then it's nowhere. I won't stay here. I'm going to hang around just long enough to find some way to get my hands on Willis, then I'm going home."

"Well . . ." Frank stopped to scratch his head. "It's your problem. But see here—you might as well come on to chem lab. It won't hurt you any and you don't intend to leave this minute anyhow."

"No."

Frank looked worried. "Will you promise me to stay right here and not do anything rash till I get back?"

"Why should you worry?"

"Promise me, Jim, or I cut lab, too."

"Oh, all right, all right! Go ahead."

"Right!" Frank dashed away.

When Frank got back he found Jim sprawled on his bunk. "Asleep?"

"No."

"Figured out what you are going to do?"

"No."

"Anything you want?"

"No."

"Your conversation is brilliant," Frank commented and sat down at the study desk.

"Sorry." Nothing was heard from Howe the rest of that day. Frank managed to persuade Jim to attend classes the next day by pointing out that he did not want to invite attention to himself while he was waiting for an opportunity to grab Willis.

Tuesday also passed without word from Howe. Tuesday night, perhaps two hours after lights-out, Frank suddenly woke up. Someone was stirring in the room. "Jim!" he called out softly.

Dead silence. Keeping quiet himself Frank reached out and switched on the light. Jim was standing near the door. "Jim," complained Frank, "why didn't you answer me? You trying to scare me to death?"

"Sorry."

"What's up? What are you doing out of bed?"

"Never mind. You go on back to sleep."

Frank climbed out of bed. "Oh, no! Not while you've got that wild look in your eye. Now tell papa."

Jim waved him away. "I don't want to mix you up in this. Go on back to bed."

"Think you're big enough to make me? Now cut out the foolishness and give. What are your plans?"

Reluctantly Jim explained. It seemed likely to him that Headmaster Howe had Willis locked up somewhere in his office. Jim planned to break in and attempt a rescue. "Now you go back to bed," he finished. "If they question you, you don't know anything; you slept all night."

"Let you tackle it alone? Not likely! Anyhow you need somebody to jigger for you." Frank started fumbling around in their locker.

"I don't want any help. What are you looking for?"

"Laboratory gloves," answered Frank. "You're going to get help whether you want it or not, you thumb-fingered idiot. I don't want you caught."

"What do you want gloves for?"

"Ever hear of fingerprints?"

"Sure, but he'll know who did it—and I don't care; I'll be gone."

"Sure, he'll know, but he may not be able to prove it. Here, put these on." Jim accepted the gloves and with them he tacitly accepted Frank's help in the adventure.

Burglary is not common on Mars and locks are unusual items. As for night watchmen, manpower is not transported through millions of miles of space simply to be used to watch the silent corridors of a boys' school. The principal hazard that Jim and Frank faced in getting to the school's offices was the chance of running into some restless student going to the washroom after hours.

They moved as silently as possible and scouted each stretch of corridor before entering it. In a few minutes they were at the outer door of the offices without—they hoped—having been seen. Jim tried the door; it was locked. "Why do they bother to lock this?" he whispered.

"On account of guys like you and me," Frank told him. "Go back to the corner and keep your eyes peeled." He attacked the latch with his knife.

"Okay." Jim went to the passageway intersection and kept lookout. Five minutes later Frank hissed at him; he went back "What's the matter?"

"Nothing's the matter. Come on." Frank had the outer door open.

They tiptoed through the outer office, past recording desks and high stacked spool files to an inner door marked: Marquis Howe—HEADMASTER—*Private*.

The lettering on the door was new—and so was the lock. The lock was no mere gesture, capable of being picked or sprung with a knife; it was a combination type, of titanium steel, and would have looked more at home on a safe.

"Think you can open it?" Jim asked anxiously.

Frank whistled softly. "Don't be silly. The party is over, Jim. Let's see if we can get back to bed without getting caught."

"Maybe we can get the door off its hinges."

"It swings the wrong way. I'd rather try to cut a hole through the partition." He moved aside, knelt down, and tried the point of his knife on the wall.

Jim looked things over. There was an air-conditioning duct running from the corridor through the room they were in and to the wall of the headmaster's office. The hole for the duct was almost as wide as his shoulders; if he could unscrew the holding flanges and let the duct sag out of the way—

No, he could not even get up to it; there was nothing to use as a ladder. The file cabinets were fastened to the floor, he found.

There was a small grille set in the bottom of the door, to permit the exhaust air to escape from the inner office. It could not be removed, nor would the hole left be large enough to be of use, but he lay down and tried to peer through it. He could see nothing; the room beyond was dark.

He cupped his hands over it and called out, "Willis! Oh, Willis! Willis boy—"

Frank came over and said urgently, "Cut that out. Are you trying to get us caught?"

"Sh!" Jim put his ear to the grille.

They both heard a muffled reply: "Jim boy! Jim!"

Jim replied, "Willis! Come here, Willis!" and listened. "He's in there," he said to Frank. "Shut up in something."

"Obviously," agreed Frank. "Now will you quiet down before somebody comes?"

"We've got to get him out. How are you making out with the wall?"

"No good. There's heavy wire mesh set in the plastic."

"Well, we've got to get him out. What do we do?"

"We don't do a darn thing," asserted Frank. "We're stymied. We go back to bed."

"You can go back to bed if you want to. I'm going to stay here and get him out."

"The trouble with you, Jim, is that you don't know when you are licked. Come on!"

"No. Sh!" He added, "Hear anything?"

Frank listened, "I hear something. What is it?"

It was a scraping noise from inside the inner office. "It's Willis, trying to get out," Jim stated.

"Well, he can't. Let's go."

"No." Jim continued to listen at the grille. Frank waited impatiently, his spirit of adventure by now more than satisfied. He was stretched between a reluctance to run out on Jim and an anxiety to get back to his room before they were caught. The scraping noise continued.

After a while it stopped. There was a soft *plop!* as if something soft but moderately heavy had fallen a foot or so, then there was a slight scurrying sound, almost beyond hearing.

"Jim? Jim boy?"

"Willis!" yelped Jim. The bouncer's voice had come to him from just beyond the grille.

"Jim boy take Willis home."

"Yes, yes! Stay there, Willis; Jim has to find a way to get Willis out."

"Willis get out." The bouncer stated it positively.

"Frank," Jim said urgently, "if we could just find something to use as a crowbar, I could bust that grille out of its frame. I think maybe Willis could squeeze through."

"We've got nothing like that. We've got nothing but our knives."

"Think, fellow, think! Is there anything in our room, anything at all?"

"Not that I know of." The scraping noise had resumed; Frank added, "What's Willis up to?"

"I guess he's trying to get the door open. We've got to find some way to open it for him. Look, I'll boost you up on my shoulders and you try to take the collar off that air duct."

Frank looked the situation over. "No good. Even if we get the duct down, there'll be a grille set in the other side of the wall."

"How do you know?"

"There always is."

Jim shut up. Frank was certainly correct and he knew it. The scraping sound had continued, still continued. Frank dropped on one knee and put his head close to the grille. He listened.

"Take it easy," he advised Jim after a moment. "I think maybe Willis is making out all right by himself."

"What do you mean?"

"That's a cutting sound if I ever heard one."

"Huh? Willie can't get through a door. Many's the time I've locked him up, back home."

"Maybe. Maybe not. Maybe he just didn't want to get out bad enough." The scraping sound was more distinct now.

A few minutes later a fine circular line began to show around the grille, then the portion of the door enclosed by the line fell toward them. For an instant Willis could be seen through the hole. Sticking out from his tubby body was a clawed pseudolimb eight inches long and an inch thick. "What's that?" demanded Frank.

"Darned if I know. He never did anything like *that* before."

The strange limb withdrew, disappeared inside his body, and the fur closed over the spot, leaving no sign that it had ever existed. Willis proceeded to change his shape, until he was more nearly watermelon-shaped than globular. He oozed through the hole. "Willis out," he announced proudly.

Jim snatched him up and cradled him in his arms. "Willis! Willis, old fellow."

The bouncer cuddled in his arms. "Jim boy lost," he said accusingly. "Jim went away."

"Yes, but not ever again. Willis stay with Jim."

"Willis stay. Good."

Jim rubbed his cheek against the little fellow's fur. Frank cleared his throat. "If you two love birds are through necking, it might be a good idea to pop back into our hole."

"Yeah, sure." The trip back to their room was made quickly and, so far as they could detect, without arousing attention. Jim dumped Willis on his bed and looked around. "I wonder just what I should try to take? I'll have to get hold of Smitty and get my gun."

"Hold on," said Frank. "Don't get ahead of yourself. You don't really have to go, you know."

"Huh?"

"I didn't hurt the outer lock; we never touched Stinky's private lock. All there is to show for Willis' escape is a hole that we obviously couldn't get through—and another one like it, probably, in Stinky's desk. He can't prove a thing. You can arrange to ship Willis back and we can just sit tight."

Jim shook his head. "I'm leaving. Willis is just part of it. I wouldn't stay in a school run by Howe if you paid me to."

"Why be hasty, Jim?"

"I'm not being hasty. I don't blame you for staying; in another year you can take the rocket pilot candidate exams and get out. But if you should happen to bust the exams, I'll bet you don't stick here until graduation."

"No, I probably won't. Have you figured out how you are going to get away without Howe stopping you? You don't dare leave until daylight; it is too cold until then."

"I'll wait until daylight and just walk out. If Howe tries to stop me, so help me, I'll blast him."

"The idea," Frank said dryly, "is to get away, not to stir up a gun battle. What you want to do is to pull a sneak. I think we had a better find a way to keep you under cover until that can be arranged. The chances ought to be good after noon."

Jim was about to ask Frank why he thought the chances would be good after noon when Willis repeated the last three words. First he repeated them in Frank's voice, then he said them again in rich, fruity accents of an older man. "Good afternoon!" he intoned.

"Shut up, Willis."

Willis said it again, "Good afternoon, Mark. Sit down, my boy. Always happy to see you."

"I've heard that voice," said Frank, puzzlement in his tones.

"Thank you, General. How do you do, sir?" Willis went on, now in the precise, rather precious tones of Headmaster Howe.

"I know!" said Frank. "I've heard it on broadcast; it's Beecher, the Resident Agent General."

"Sh—" said Jim, "I want to listen." Willis continued, again in the fruity voice:

"Not bad, not too bad for an old man."

"Nonsense, General, you're not old."—Howe's voice again.

"Kind of you to say so, my boy," Willis went on. "What have you in the bag? Contraband?"

Willis repeated Howe's sycophantic laugh. "Hardly. Just a scientific specimen—a rather interesting curiosity I confiscated from one of the students."

There was a short pause, then the fruity voice said, "Bless my boots! Mark, wherever did you find this creature?"

"I just told you, sir," came Howe's voice. "I was forced to take it away from one of the students."

"Yes, yes—but do you have any idea of *what* you've got?"

"Certainly, sir; I looked it up. *Areocephalopsittacus Bron—*"

"Spare me the learned words, Mark. It's a roundhead, a Martian roundhead. That's not the point. You say you got this from a student; do you think you could buy it from him?" the fruity voice continued eagerly.

Howe's voice answered slowly, "I hardly think so, sir. I am fairly sure he wouldn't want to sell." He hesitated, then went on, "Is it important?"

"Important? That depends on what you mean by 'important'," answered the voice of the Resident Agent General. "Would you say that sixty thousand credits was important? Or even seventy thousand? For that is what I am sure the London zoo will pay for him, over and above the cost of getting him there."

"Really?"

"Really. I have a standing order from a broker in London at fifty thousand credits; I've never been able to get him one. I'm sure the price can be boosted."

"Indeed?" Howe agreed cautiously. "That would be a fine thing for the Company, wouldn't it?"

There was a brief silence, then a hearty laugh. "Mark, my boy, you slay me. Now see here—you are hired to run the school, aren't you?"

"Yes."

"And I'm hired to look out for the interests of the Company, right? We put in a good day's work and earn our pay; that leaves eighteen hours a day that belong to each of us, personally. Are you hired to find strange specimens?"

"No."

"Neither am I. Do you understand me?"

"I think I do."

"I'm sure you do. After all, I know your uncle quite well; I'm sure he wouldn't have sent his nephew out here without explaining the facts of life to him. He understands them very well himself, I can assure you. The fact is, my boy, that there are unlimited opportunities in a place such as this for a smart man, if he will just keep his eyes and ears open. Not graft, you understand." Willis paused.

Jim started to say something; Frank said, "Shut up! We don't want to miss any of this."

The Resident's voice continued, "Not graft at all. Legitimate business opportunities that are the natural concomitants of our office. Now about this student: what will it take to convince him he should sell? I wouldn't offer him too much or he will become suspicious. We mustn't have that."

Howe was slow in replying. "I am almost certain he won't sell, General, but there is another way, possibly."

"Yes? I don't understand you."

The boys heard Howe explain his peculiar theory of ownership with respect to Willis. They could not see Beecher dig Howe in the ribs but they could hear his choked laughter. "Oh, that is rich! Mark, you slay me, you really do. Your talents are wasted as a schoolteacher; you should be a Resident."

"Well," Howe's voice replied, "I hardly expect to teach school all my life."

"You won't, you won't. We'll find an agency for you. After all, the school will be smaller and of less importance after the non-migration policy goes into effect."

("What's he talking about?" whispered Frank—"Quiet!" Jim answered.)

"Is there any news about that?" Howe wanted to know.

"I expect to hear from your uncle momentarily. You might stop in again this evening, my boy; I may have news."

The remainder of the conversation was of no special interest, but Willis plowed on with it nevertheless. The boys listened until Howe had made his farewell, after which Willis shut up.

Jim was frothing. "Put Willis in a zoo! Why, the very idea! I hope he does catch me leaving; I'd welcome an excuse to take a shot at him!"

"Easy, fellow! I wonder," Frank went on, "what that business was about a 'non-migration' policy?"

"I thought he said 'immigration'."

"I'm sure it was 'non-migration'. What time is it?"

"About three."

"We've got three hours, more or less. Jim, let's see what else we can coax out of Willis. I've got a hunch it may be important."

"Okay." Jim picked the fuzz ball up and said, "Willis old fel-

low, what else do you know? Tell Jim everything you've heard—
*every*thing."

Willis was happy to oblige. He reeled off bits of dialog for the
next hour, most of it concerned with unimportant routine of the
school. At last the boys were rewarded by hearing again the unc-
tuous tones of Gaines Beecher:

"Mark, my boy—"

"Oh—come in, General. Sit down. Happy to see you."

"I just stopped by to say that I have gotten a despatch from
your dear uncle. He added a postscript sending his regards to
you."

"That's nice. Thank you, sir."

"Not at all. Close that door, will you?" Willis put in sound effects of a door being closed. "Now we can talk. The despatch, of
course, concerned the non-migration policy."

"Yes?"

"I am happy to say that the board came around to your uncle's
point of view. South Colony will stay where it is; this next ship
load and the one following it will go to North Colony, where the
new immigrants will have nearly twelve months of summer in
which to prepare for the northern winter. What are you chuckling
about?"

"Nothing important, sir. One of the students, a great lout
named Kelly, was telling me today what his father was going to do
to me when he came through here at migration. I am looking forward to seeing his face when he learns that his father will not
show up."

"You are not to tell him anything of the sort," the Resident's
voice said sharply.

"Eh?"

"I want all this handled with the least possible friction. No one
must know until the last possible moment. There are hotheads
among the colonials who will oppose this policy, even though it
has already been proved that, with reasonable precautions, the
dangers of a Martian winter are negligible. My plan is to postpone
migration two weeks on some excuse, then postpone it again. By
the time I announce the change it will be too late to do anything
but comply."

"Ingenious!"

"Thank you. It's really the only way to handle colonials, my
boy. You haven't been here long enough to know them the way I

do. They are a neurotic lot, most of them failures back on Earth, and they will drive you wild with their demands if you are not firm with them. They don't seem to understand that all that they are and all that they have they owe directly to the Company. Take this new policy: if you let the colonists have their own way, they would continue to follow the sun, like so many rich playboys—and at the Company's expense."

Willis shifted to Howe's voice. "I quite agree. If their children are any guide, they are a rebellious and unruly lot."

"Really shiftless," agreed the other voice. "You must be firm with them. I must be going. Oh, about that, uh, specimen: you have it in a safe place?"

"Yes indeed, sir. Locked in this cabinet."

"Hmm . . . it might be better to bring it to my quarters."

"Hardly necessary," Howe's voice denied. "Notice the lock on that door? It will be safe."

There were good-byes said and Willis shut up.

Frank cursed steadily and bitterly under his breath.

6.
FLIGHT

Jim shook him by the shoulder. "Snap out of it and help me. I'm going to be late."

"That fat slug," Frank said softly, "I wonder how he would like to tackle a winter at Charax? Maybe he'd like to stay inside for eleven or twelve months at a time—or go outside when it's a hundred below. I'd like to see him freeze to death—slowly."

"Sure, sure," agreed Jim. "But give me a hand."

Frank turned suddenly and took down Jim's outdoors suit. He flung it at him, then took down his own and started climbing rapidly into it. Jim stared. "Hey—what yuh doin'?"

"I'm going with you."

"Huh?"

"Think I'm going to sit here and do lessons when somebody is planning to trick my mother into being forced to last out a high-latitude winter? My own mother? Mom's got a bad heart; it would kill her." He turned and started digging things out of the locker. "Let's get moving."

Jim hesitated, then said, "Sure, Frank, but how about your plans? If you quit school now you'll never be a rocket pilot."

"The deuce with that! This is more important."

"I can warn everybody of what's up just as well as two of us can."

"The matter is settled, I tell you."

"Okay. Just wanted to be sure you knew your own mind. Let's go." Jim climbed into his own suit, zipped it up, tightened the straps, and then started picking over his belongings. He was forced to throw away a large part, as he wanted Willis to travel in his bag.

He picked up Willis. "Look, fellow," he said, "we're going home. I want you to ride inside here, where it's nice and warm."

"Willis go for ride?"

"Willis go for ride. But I want you to stay inside and not say one word until I take you out. Understand?"

"Willis not talk?"

"Willis not talk at all, not till Jim takes him out."

"Okay, Jim boy." Willis thought about it and added, "Willis play music?"

"No! Not a sound, not a word. No music. Willis close up and stay closed up."

"Okay, Jim boy," Willis answered in aggrieved tones and promptly made a smooth ball of himself. Jim dropped him into the bag and zipped it.

"Come on," said Frank. "Let's find Smitty, get our guns, and get going."

"The Sun won't be up for nearly an hour."

"We'll have to risk it. Say, how much money have you got?"

"Not much. Why?"

"Our fare home, dope."

"Oh—" Jim had been so preoccupied with other matters that he had not thought about the price of a ticket. The trip to the school had been free, of course, but they had no travel authorization for this trip; cash would be required.

They pooled resources—not enough for one ticket, much less than enough for two. "What'll we do?" asked Jim.

"We'll get it out of Smitty."

"How?"

"We'll get it. I'll tear off his arm and beat him over the head with it if I have to. Let's go."

"Don't forget your ice skates."

Smythe roomed alone, a tribute to his winning personality. When they shook him, he wakened quickly and said, "Very well, officer, I'll go quietly."

"Smitty," said Jim, "we want our—we want those packages."

"I'm closed for the night. Come back in the morning."

"We got to have them *now.*"

Smythe got out of bed. "There's an extra charge for night service, of course." He stood on his bunk, removed the grille from his air intake, reached far inside, and hauled out the wrapped guns.

Jim and Frank tore off the wrappings and belted their guns on. Smythe watched them with raised eyebrows. Frank added, "We've got to have some money." He named the amount.

"Why come to me?"

"Because I know you've got it."

"So? And what do I get in return? A sweet smile?"

"No." Frank got out his slide rule, a beautiful circular instrument with twenty-one scales. "How much for that?"

"Mmm—six credits."

"Don't be silly! It cost my father twenty-five."

"Eight, then. I won't be able to get more than ten for it."

"Take it as security for fifteen."

"Ten, cash. I don't run a pawn shop." Jim's slide rule went for a smaller amount, then both their watches, followed by lesser items at lower prices.

At last they had nothing left to sell but their skates, and both boys refused the suggestion although they were still twelve credits short of what they needed. "You've just got to trust us for the rest, Smitty," Frank told him.

Smythe studied the ceiling. "Well, seeing what good customers you've been, I might add that I also collect autographs."

"Huh?"

"I'll have both of yours, on one I.O.U., at six per cent—per month. The security will be the pound of flesh nearest your heart."

"Take it," said Jim.

Finished, they started to leave. Smythe said, "My crystal ball tells me that you gentlemen are about to fade away. How?"

"Just walk out," Jim told him.

"Hmm . . . it does not seem to have come to your attention that the front door is now locked at nights. Our friend and mentor, Mr. Howe, unlocks it himself when he arrives in the morning."

"You're kidding!"

"Go see for yourself."

Frank tugged Jim's arm. "Come on. We'll bust it down if we have to."

"Why do things the hard way?" inquired Smythe. "Go out through the kitchen."

"You mean the back door's not locked?" demanded Frank.

"Oh, it's locked all right."

"Then quit making silly suggestions."

"I should be offended at that," Smythe answered, "but I consider the source. While the back door is locked, it did not occur to brother Howe to install a lock on the garbage dump."

"The *garbage* dump," exploded Jim.

"Take it or leave it. It's your only way to sneak out."

"We'll take it," decided Frank. "Come on, Jim."

"Hold on," put in Smythe. "One of you can operate the dump for the other, but who's going to do it for the second man? He's stuck."

"Oh, I see." Frank looked at him. "You are."

"And what am I offered?"

"Confound you, Smitty how would you like a lump on the head? You've already taken us for everything but our eyeteeth."

Smythe shrugged. "Did I refuse? After all, I told you about it. Very well, I'll chalk it up to overhead—good will, full measure, advertising. Besides, I don't like to see my clients fall afoul of the law."

They went quickly to the school's large kitchen. Smythe's cautious progress through the corridors showed long familiarity with casual disregard of rules. Once there, Smythe said, "All right, who goes first?"

Jim eyed the dump with distaste. It was a metal cylinder, barrel-size, laid on its side in the wall. It could be rotated on its main axis by means of a lever set in the wall; a large opening in it permitted refuse to be placed in it from inside the building, then removed from the outside, without disturbing the pressurization of the building—the simplest sort of a pressure lock. The interior showed ample signs of the use for which it was intended. "I'll go first," he volunteered and settled his mask over his face.

"Wait a second," said Frank. He had been eyeing the stocks of canned foods racked around the room. Now he dumped spare clothing from his bag and started replacing it with cans.

"Hurry up," Smythe insisted. "I want to get back to my beddy-bye before the morning bell rings."

"Yes, why bother?" protested Jim. "We'll be home in a few hours."

"Just a hunch. Okay, I'm ready."

Jim climbed into the dump, drawing up his knees and clutching his bag to his chest. The cylinder rotated around him; he felt a sudden drop in pressure and a bitter cold draft. Then he was picking himself up from the pavement of the alley behind the school.

The cylinder creaked back to the loading position; in a moment Frank landed beside him. Jim helped him up. "Boy, are you a mess!" he said, brushing at a bit of mashed potato that clung to his chum's suit.

"So are you, but there's no time to worry about it. Gee, but it's cold!"

"It'll be warmer soon. Let's go." The pink glow of the coming Sun was already lighting the eastern sky, even though the air was still midnight cold. They hurried down the alley to the street in back of the school and along it to the right. This portion of the city was entirely terrestrial and could have been a city in Alaska or Norway, but beyond them, etched against the lightening sky, were the ancient towers of Syrtis Minor, denying the Earthlike appearance of the street.

They came, as they had planned, to a tributary canal and sat down to put on their skates. They were racers, with 22-inch razor-like blades, intended for speed alone. Jim finished first and lowered himself to the ice. "Better hurry," he said. "I almost froze my behind."

"You're telling me!"

"This ice is almost too hard to take an edge."

Frank joined him; they picked up their bags and set out. A few hundred yards away the little waterway gave into the Grand Canal of the city; they turned into it and made speed for the scooter station. Despite the exercise they were tingling with cold by the time they got to it.

They went through the pressure door and inside. A single clerk was on duty there. He looked up and Frank went to him. "Is there a scooter to South Colony today?"

"In about twenty minutes," said the clerk. "You want to ship those bags?"

"No, we want tickets." Frank handed over their joint funds.

Silently the clerk attended to the transaction. Jim heaved a sigh of relief; scooters to the colony did not run every day. The chance that they might have to keep out of sight for a day or more and then try to get away without encountering Howe had been eating at him.

They took seats in the back of the station and waited. Presently Jim said, "Frank, is Deimos up?"

"I didn't notice. Why?"

"Maybe I can get a call through to home."

"No money."

"I'll put it through collect." He went to the booth opposite the clerk's desk; the clerk looked up but said nothing. Inside, he signalled the operator. Subconsciously he had been worrying about getting word to his father ever since Willis had spilled the secret of the so-called non-migration policy.

The screen lighted up and a pleasant-appearing young woman with the fashionable striped hair appeared therein. "I'd like to call South Colony," he said.

"No relay until later this morning," she informed him. "Would you like to record a delayed message?"

He was stopped; delayed messages were not accepted on a collect basis. "No, thank you, I'll try later," he fibbed and switched off.

The clerk was tapping on the booth's door. "The driver is ready for you," he told Jim. Jim hurriedly settled his mask in place and followed Frank out through the pressure door. The driver was just closing the baggage compartment of the scooter. He took their tickets and the two boys got aboard. Again they were the only passengers; they claimed the observation seats.

Ten minutes later, tired of staring almost into a rising Sun, Jim announced, "I'm sleepy. I think I'll go down."

"I think I'll ask the driver to turn on the radio," said Frank.

"Oh, the heck with that. We've both had a hard night. Come on."

"Well—all right." They went into the lower compartment, found bunks, and crawled in. In a few minutes they both were snoring.

The scooter, leaving Syrtis Minor at sunrise, kept ahead of the daily thaw and did not have to lay over at Hesperidum. It continued south and reached Cynia about noon. So far advanced was the season that there was no worry about the ice holding from Cynia south to Charax; Strymon canal would not thaw again until the following spring.

The driver was pleased to have kept his schedule. When Deimos rose toward the end of the morning's run he relaxed and switched on his radio. What he heard caused him to make a quick check of his passengers. They were still asleep; he decided not to do anything about it until he reached Cynia station.

On reaching there he hurried inside. Jim and Frank were awakened by the scooter stopping but did not get out. Presently the driver came back and said, "Meal stop. Everybody out."

Frank answered, "We're not hungry."

The driver looked disconcerted. "Better come in anyhow," he insisted. "It gets pretty cold in the car when she's standing still."

"We don't mind." Frank was thinking that he would dig a can

of something out of his bag as soon as the driver had left; from suppertime the night before until noon today seemed a long time to his stomach.

"What's the trouble?" the driver continued. "Broke?" Something in their expressions caused him to continue, "I'll stake you to a sandwich each."

Frank refused but Jim interceded. "Don't be silly, Frank. Thank you, sir. We accept."

George, the agent and factotum of Cynia station, looked at them speculatively and served them sandwiches without comment. The driver bolted his food and was quickly through. When he got up, the boys did so, too. "Just take it easy," he advised them. "I've got twenty, thirty minutes' work, loading and checking."

"Can't we help you?" asked Jim.

"Nope. You'd just be in the way. I'll call you when I'm ready."

"Well—thanks for the sandwich."

"Don't mention it." He went out.

Less than ten minutes later there came faintly to their ears the sound of the scooter starting up. Frank looked startled and rushed to the traffic-checking window. The car was already disappearing to the south. Frank turned to the agent. "Hey, he didn't wait for us!"

"Nope."

"But he said he'd call us."

"Yep." The agent resumed reading.

"But—but *why*," insisted Frank. "He told us to wait."

The agent put down his newspaper. "It's like this," he said, "Clem is a peaceable man and he told me that he wasn't a cop. He said he would have no part in trying to arrest two strapping, able-bodied boys, both wearing guns."

"What!"

"That's what I said. And don't go to fiddling around with those heaters. You'll notice I ain't wearing my gun; you can take the station apart for all of me."

Jim had joined Frank at the counter. "What's this all about?" he asked.

"You tell me. All I know is, there's a call out to pick you up. You're charged with burglary, theft, truancy, destruction of company property—pretty near everything but committing a nuisance in the canal. Seems like you are a couple of desperate characters—though you don't look the part."

"I see," said Frank slowly. "Well, what are you going to do about it?"

"Nothing. Nothing at all. 'Long about tomorrow morning a special scooter will arrive and I presume there will be force enough aboard her to subdue a couple of outlaws. In the meantime do as you please. Go outside. Wander around. When you get chilly, come back inside." He went back to his reading.

"I see. Come along, Jim." They retreated to the far corner of the room for a war conference. The agent's attitude was easily understood. Cynia station was almost literally a thousand miles from anywhere; the station itself was the only human habitation against the deadly cold of night.

Jim was almost in tears. "I'm sorry, Frank. If I hadn't been so darned anxious to eat, this wouldn't have happened."

"Don't be so tragic about it," Frank advised him. "Can you imagine us shooting it out with a couple of innocent bystanders and hijacking the scooter? I can't."

"Uh—no. I guess you're right."

"Certainly I am. What we've got to decide is what to do next."

"I know one thing; I'm not going to let them drag me back to school."

"Neither am I. What's more important, we've got to get word to our folks about the deal that's being cooked up against them."

"Say, look—maybe we can phone now!"

"Do you think he—" Frank nodded toward the agent "—would let us?"

"Maybe. Maybe not. We've still got our guns—and I can be pushed just so far." Jim got up and went to the agent. "Any objection to us using the phone?"

The agent did not even glance up. "Not a bit. Help yourself."

Jim went into the booth. There was no local exchange; the instrument was simply a radio link to the relay station on the outer moon. A transparency announced that Deimos was above the horizon; seeing this, Jim punched the call button and asked for linkage to South Colony.

There was an unusually long delay, then a sweetly impersonal voice announced, "Due to circumstances beyond our control calls are not being accepted from Cynia station to South Colony."

Jim started to ask if Deimos were visible at South Colony, since he knew that line-of-sight was essential to radio transmission on Mars—indeed, it was the only sort of radio transmission he was familiar with—but the relay station had switched off and made no answer when he again punched the call button. He left the booth and told Frank about it.

"Sounds like Howe has fixed us," Frank commented. "I don't believe there is a breakdown. Unless—"

"Unless what?"

"Unless there is more to it than that. Beecher may be rigging things to interfere with messages getting through until he's put over his scheme."

"Frank, we've got to get word to our folks. See here, I bet we could hole up with the Martians over at Cynia. After all, they offered us water and—"

"Suppose we could. Where does that get us?"

"Let me finish. We can mail a letter from here, giving our folks all the details and telling them where we are hiding. Then we could wait for them to come and get us."

Frank shook his head. "If we mail a letter from here, old frozen face over there is bound to know it. Then, when the cops show up and we are gone, he turns it over to them. Instead of our folks getting it, it goes back to Howe and Beecher."

"You really think so? Nobody has any right to touch private mail."

"Don't be a little innocent. Howe didn't have any right to order us to give up our guns—but he did. No, Jim, we've got to carry this message ourselves."

On the wall opposite them was a map of the area served by Cynia station. Frank had been studying it idly while they talked. Suddenly he said, "Jim, what's that new station south of Cynia?"

"Huh? Where do you mean?"

"There." Frank pointed. Inked on the original map was a station on west Strymon, south of them.

"That?" said Jim. "That must be one of the shelters for the Project." The grand plan for restoring oxygen to Mars called for setting up, the following spring, a string of processing plants in the desert between Cynia and Charax. Some of the shelters had been completed in anticipation of the success of plant number one in Libya.

"It can't be much over a hundred miles away."

"A hundred and ten, maybe," Jim commented, looking at the scale.

Frank got a far-away look in his eyes. "I think I can skate that far before dark. Are you game?"

"What? Are you crazy? We'd still be better than seven hundred miles from home."

"We can skate better than two hundred miles a day," answered Frank. "Aren't there more shelters?"

"The map doesn't show any." Jim thought. "I *know* they've finished more than one; I've heard Dad talking about it."

"If we had to, we could skate all night and sleep in the daytime. That way we wouldn't freeze."

"Hmm . . . I think you're kidding yourself. I saw a man once who was caught out at night. He was stiff as a board. All right, when do we start?"

"Right now."

They picked up their bags and headed for the door The agent looked up and said, "Going somewhere?"

"For a walk."

"Might as well leave your bags. You'll be back."

They did not answer but went on out the door. Five minutes later they were skating south on west Strymon.

"Hey, Jim!"

"Yeah?"

"Let's stop for a minute. I want to sling my bag."

"Just what I was thinking." Their travel bags unbalanced them and prevented proper arm motion and any real speed. But skating was a common form of locomotion; the bags had straps which permitted them to be slung as haversacks. Jim opened his before he put it on; Willis extended his eye stalks and looked at him reproachfully. "Jim boy gone long time."

"Sorry, old fellow."

"Willis not talk."

"Willis can talk all he wants to now. Look, if I leave the bag open a little bit so that you can see, will you manage not to fall out?"

"Willis want out."

"Can't do that; I'm going to take you for a fine ride. You won't fall out?"

"Willis not fall out."

"Okay." He slung the bag and they set out again.

They picked up speed. With fast ice, little air resistance, and the low Martian gravity the speed of a skater on Mars is limited by his skill in stroking. Both of the boys were able. Willis let out a "Whee!" and they settled down to putting miles behind them.

The desert plateau between Cynia and Charax is higher than the dead sea bottom between Cynia and the equator. This drop is used to move the waters of the southern polar cap across the desert to the great green belt near the equator. In midwinter the southern ice cap reaches to Charax; the double canal of Strymon, which starts at Charax, is one of the principal discharge points for the polar cap when it melts in the spring.

The boys were starting at the lower end of the canal's drop; the walls of the canal reached high above their heads. Furthermore the water level—or ice level—was low because the season was late autumn; the water level would be much higher during spring flood. There was nothing to see but the banks of the canal converging ahead of them, the blue sky beyond, and the purple-black sky overhead. The Sun was behind them and a bit west of meridian; it was moving north toward northern summer solstice. Seasons do not lag on Mars as much as they do on Earth; there are no oceans to hold the heat and the only "flywheel" of the climate is the freezing and melting of the polar caps.

With nothing to see the boys concentrated on skating, heads down and shoulders swinging.

After many miles of monotonous speed Jim grew careless; the toe of his right runner caught on some minor obstruction in the ice. He went down. His suit saved him from ice burns and he knew how to fall safely, but Willis popped out of his bag like a cork from a bottle.

The bouncer, true to instinct, hauled in all excrescences at once. He hit as a ball and rolled; he traveled over the ice for several hundred yards. Frank threw himself into a hockey stop as soon as he saw Jim tumble. He stopped in a shower of ice particles and went back to help Jim up. "You all right?"

"Sure. Where's Willis?"

They skated on and recovered the bouncer who was now standing on his tiny legs and waiting for them. "Whoopee!" yelled Willis as they came up. "Do it again!"

"Not if I can help it," Jim assured him and stuffed him back in the bag. "Say, Frank how long have we been traveling?"

"Not over three hours," Frank decided, after a glance at the Sun.

"I wish I had my watch," complained Jim. "We don't want to overrun the shelter."

"Oh, we won't come to it for another couple of hours, at least."

"But what's to keep us from passing right by it? We can't see over these banks."

"Want to turn around and go back?"

"No."

"Then quit worrying."

Jim shut up but continued to worry. Perhaps that was why he noticed the only indication of the shelter when they came to it, for Frank skated on past it. It was merely a ramp down the bank. There were such ramps every few miles, as ancient as the canals themselves, but this one had set above it an overhanging beam, as if to support a hoist. Jim spotted it as terrestrial workmanship.

He stopped. Frank skated on ahead, noticed presently that Jim was not following him and came back. "What's up?" he called out.

"I think this is it."

"Hmm . . . could be." They removed their skates and climbed the ramp. At the top, set back a short distance from the bank, was one of the bubble-shaped buildings which are the sign anywhere on Mars of the alien from Earth. Beyond it a foundation had been started for the reducing plant. Jim heaved a big sigh. Frank nodded and said, "Just about where we expected to find it."

"And none too soon," added Jim. The Sun was close to the western horizon and dropping closer as they watched.

There was, of course, no one in the shelter; no further work would be done at this latitude until the following spring. The shelter was unpressurized; they simply unlatched the outer door, walked through the inner door without delay. Frank groped for the light switch, found it, and lighted up the place—the lighting circuit was powered by the building's atomic-fuel power pack and did not require the presence of men.

It was a simple shelter, lined with bunks except for the space occupied by the kitchen unit. Frank looked around happily. "Looks like we've found a home from home, Jim."

"Yep." Jim looked around, located the shelter's thermostat, and cut it in. Shortly the room became warmer and with it there was a soft sighing sound as the building's pressure regulator, hooked in with the thermostat, started the building's supercharger. In a few minutes the boys were able to remove their masks and finally their outdoors suits as well.

Jim poked around the kitchen unit, opening cupboards and peering into shelves. "Find anything?" asked Frank.

"Nary a thing. Seems like they could have left at least a can of beans."

"Now maybe you're glad I raided the kitchen before we left. Supper in five minutes."

"Okay, so you've got a real talent for crime," acknowledged Jim. "I salute you." He tried the water tap. "Plenty of water in the tanks," he announced.

"Good!" Frank answered. "That saves me having to go down and chip ice. I need to fill my mask. I was dry the last few miles." The high coxcomb structure on a Mars mask is not only a little supercharger with its power pack, needed to pressurize the mask; it is also a small water reservoir. A nipple in the mask permits the wearer to take a drink outdoors, but this is a secondary function. The prime need for water in a Mars mask is to wet a wick through which the air is forced before it reaches the wearer's nose.

"You were? Well, for crying out loud—don't you know better than to drink yourself dry?"

"I forgot to fill it before we left."

"Tourist!"

"Well, we left in kind of a hurry, you know."

"How long were you dry?"

"I don't know exactly," Frank evaded.

"How's your throat?"

"All right. A little dry, maybe."

"Let me see it," Jim persisted, coming closer.

Frank pushed him away. "I tell you it's all right. Let's eat."

"Well—okay."

They dined off canned corned beef hash and went promptly to bed. Willis snuggled up against Jim's stomach and imitated his snores.

Breakfast was more of the same, since there was some hash left and Frank insisted that they not waste anything. Willis had no breakfast since he had eaten only two weeks before, but he absorbed nearly a quart of water. As they were about to leave Jim held up a flashlight. "Look what I found."

"Well, put it back and let's go."

"I think I'll keep it," Jim answered, stuffing it in his bag. "We might have a use for it."

"We won't and it's not yours."

"For criminy's sake, I'm not swiping it; I'm just borrowing it. This is an emergency."

Frank shrugged. "Okay, let's get moving." A few minutes later they were on the ice and again headed south. It was a beautiful day, as Martian days almost always are; when the Sun was high enough to fill the slot of the canal it was almost balmy, despite the late season. Frank spotted the tell-tale hoisting beam of a Project shelter around midday and they were able to lunch inside, which saved them the tedious, messy, and unsatisfactory chore of trying to eat through the mouth valve of a respirator mask. The shelter was a twin of the first but no foundation for the plant had as yet been built near it.

As they were preparing to leave the shelter Jim said, "You look sort of flushed, Frank. Got a fever?"

"That's just the bloom of health," Frank insisted. "I'm fine." Nevertheless he coughed as he put on his mask. "Mars throat," Jim thought but said nothing as there was nothing that he could do for Frank.

Mars throat is not a disease in itself; it is simply an extremely dry condition of the nose and throat which arises from direct exposure to Martian air. The humidity on Mars is usually effectively zero; a throat dehydrated by it is wide open to whatever disease organisms there may be present in the human throat at the time. The result is usually a virulent sore throat.

The afternoon passed without incident. As the Sun began to drop toward the skyline it seemed possible that home was not much more than five hundred miles away. Jim had watched Frank closely all afternoon. His chum seemed to be skating as strongly as ever; perhaps, he decided, the cough was just a false alarm. He skated up alongside Frank. "I guess we had better start watching for a shelter."

"Suits me."

Soon they passed another of the ramps built by long-dead Martians, but there was no hoisting beam above it nor any other sign of terrestrial activity. The banks, though somewhat lower now, were still too high to see over. Jim stepped up the stroke a bit; they hurried on.

They came to another ramp, but again there was nothing to suggest that a shelter might be above it. Jim stopped. "I vote we take a look up on the bank," he said. "We *know* they build the shelters by the ramps and they may have taken the hoist down for some reason."

"It would just be wasting valuable time," Frank protested. "If we hurry, we can get to another ramp before dark."

"Well, if you say so—" Jim shoved off and picked up speed.

The next ramp was the same story; Jim stopped again. "Let's take a look," he pleaded. "We can't possibly reach the next one before sundown."

"Okay." Frank stopped over and tugged at his skates.

They hurried up the bank and reached the top. The slanting rays of the Sun showed nothing but the vegetation bordering the canal.

Jim felt ready to bawl through sheer weariness and disappointment. "Well, what do we do now?" he said.

"We go back down," Frank answered, "and keep going until we find it."

"I don't think we could spot one of those hoist beams in the dark."

"Then we keep going," Frank said grimly, "until we fall flat on our faces."

"More likely we'll freeze."

"Well, if you want my opinion," Frank replied, "I think we're washed up. I, for one, can't keep going all night, even if we don't freeze."

"You don't feel good?"

"That's putting it mildly. Come on."

"All right."

Willis had climbed out of the bag and up on Jim's shoulder, in order to see better. Now he bounced to the ground and rolled away. Jim snatched at him and missed. "Hey! Willis! Come back here!"

Willis did not answer. Jim started after him. His progress was difficult. Ordinarily he would have gone under the canal plants, but, late in the day as it was, most of them had lowered almost to knee height preparatory to withdrawing into the ground for the night. Some of the less hardy plants were already out of sight, leaving bare patches of ground.

The vcgctation did not seem to slow up Willis but Jim found it troublesome; he could not catch the little scamp. Frank shouted, "'Ware water-seekers! Watch where you put your feet!" Thus warned, Jim proceeded more carefully—and still more slowly. He stopped. "Willis! Oh, Willis! Come back! Come back, dawggone it, or we'll go away and leave you." It was a completely empty threat.

Frank came crashing up and joined him. "We can't hang around up here, Jim."

"I know it. Wouldn't you know that he would pull a stunt like this just at the wrong time?"

"He's a pest, that's what he is. Come on."

Willis's voice—or, rather, Jim's voice as used by Willis—reached them from a distance. "Jim boy! Jim! Come here!"

Jim struggled through the shrinking vegetation with Frank after him. They found the bouncer resting at the edge of an enormous plant, a desert cabbage quite fifty yards across. The desert cabbage is not often found near the canals; it is a weed and not tolerated in the green sea bottoms of the lower latitudes, though it may be found in the deserts miles from any surface water.

The western half of this specimen was still spread out in a semicircular fan, flat to the ground, but the eastern half was tilted up almost vertically, its flat leaves still reaching greedily for the Sun's rays to fuel the photosynthesis by which plants live. A hardy plant, it would not curl up until the Sun was gone completely, and it would not withdraw into the ground at all. Instead it would curl into a tight ball, thus protecting itself from the cold and incidentally simulating, on giant scale, the Earth plant for which it was named.

Willis sat by the edge of the half that was flat to the ground. Jim reached for him.

Willis bounced up on the edge of the desert cabbage and rolled toward the heart of the plant. Jim stopped and said, "Oh, Willis, darn your eyes, come back here. Please come back."

"Don't go after him," warned Frank. "That thing might close up on you. The Sun is almost down."

"I won't. Willis! Come back!"

Willis called back, "Come here, Jim boy."

"*You* come *here*."

"Jim boy come here. Frank come here. Cold there. Warm here."

"Frank, what'll I do?"

Willis called again. "Come, Jim boy. Warm! Stay warm all night."

Jim stared. "You know what, Frank? I think he means to let it close up on him. And he wants us to join him."

"Sounds that way."

"Come, Jim! Come, Frank!" Willis insisted. "Hurry!"

"Maybe he knows what he's doing," Frank added. "Like Doc says, he's got instincts for Mars and we haven't."

"But we can't go inside a cabbage. It would crush us."

"I wonder."

"Anyhow, we'd suffocate."

"Probably." Frank suddenly added, "Do as you like, Jim. I can't skate any farther." He set one foot on a broad leaf—which flinched under the contact—and strode steadily toward the bouncer. Jim watched him for a moment and then ran after them.

Willis greeted them ecstatically. "Good boy, Frank! Good boy, Jim! Stay nice and warm all night."

The Sun was slipping behind a distant dune; the sunset wind whipped coldly at them. The far edges of the plant lifted and began to curl toward them. "We still could get out if we jumped, Frank," Jim said nervously.

"I'm staying." Nevertheless Frank eyed the approaching leaves apprehensively.

"We'll smother."

"Maybe. That's better than freezing."

The inner leaves were beginning to curl faster than the outer leaves. Such a leaf, four feet wide at its widest and at least ten feet long, raised up back of Jim and curved in until it touched his shoulder. Nervously he struck at it. The leaf snatched itself away, then slowly resumed its steady progress toward him. "Frank," Jim said shrilly, "they'll smother us!"

Frank looked apprehensively at the broad leaves, now curling up all around them. "Jim," he said, "sit down. Spread your legs wide. Then take my hands and make an arch."

"What for?"

"So that we'll take up as much space as possible. Hurry!"

Jim hurried. With elbows and knees and hands the two managed to occupy a roughly spherical space about five feet across and a little less than that high. The leaves closed down on them, seemed to feel them out, then settled firmly against them, but not, however, with sufficient pressure to crush them. Soon the last open space was covered and they were in total darkness. "Frank," Jim demanded, "we can move now, can't we?"

"No! give the outside leaves a chance to settle into place."

Jim kept still for quite a long while. He knew that considerable time had passed for he spent the time counting up to one thousand. He was just starting on his second thousand when Willis stirred in the space between his legs. "Jim boy, Frank boy—nice and warm, huh?"

"Yeah, Willis," he agreed. "Say, how about it, Frank?"

"I think we can relax now." Frank lowered his arms; the inner leaf forming the ceiling immediately above him at once curled down and brushed him in the dark. He slapped at it instinctively; it retreated.

Jim said, "It's getting stuffy already."

"Don't worry about it. Take it easy. Breathe shallowly. Don't talk and don't move and you'll use up less oxygen."

"What difference does it make whether we suffocate in ten minutes or an hour? This was a crazy thing to do, Frank; any way you figure it we can't last till morning."

"Why can't we? I read in a book that back in India men have let themselves be buried alive for days and even weeks and were still alive when they were dug up. Fakers, they called them."

" 'Fakers' is right! I don't believe it."

"I read it in a book, I tell you."

"I suppose you think that anything that's printed in a book is true?"

Frank hesitated before replying, "It had better be true because it's the only chance we've got. Now will you shut up? If you keep yapping, you'll use up what air there is and kill us both off and it'll be your fault."

Jim shut up. All that he could hear was Frank's breathing. He reached down and touched Willis; the bouncer had withdrawn all his stalks. He was a smooth ball, apparently asleep. Presently Frank's breathing changed to rasping snores.

Jim tried to sleep but could not. The utter darkness and the increasing deadness of the air pressed down on him like a great weight. He wished again for his watch, lost to Smythe's business talent; if he only knew what time it was, how long it was until sunrise, he felt that he could stand it.

He became convinced that the night had passed—or had almost passed. He began to expect the dawn and with it the unrolling of the giant plant. When he had been expecting it "any minute now" for a time that he estimated at two hours, at least, he became panicky. He knew how late in the season it was; he knew also that desert cabbages hibernated by the simple method of remaining closed through the winter. Apparently Frank and he had had the enormous bad luck to take shelter in a cabbage on the very night on which it started its hibernation.

Twelve long months from now, more than three hundred days in the future, the plant would open to the spring Sun and release them—dead. He was sure of it.

He remembered the flashlight he had picked up in the first Project shelter. The thought of it stimulated him, took his mind off his fears for the moment. He leaned forward, twisted around and tried to get at his bag, still strapped to his shoulders.

The leaves about him closed in; he struck at them and they shrank away. He was able to reach the torch, drag it out, and turn it on. Its rays brightly illuminated the cramped space. Frank stopped snoring, blinked, and said, "What's the matter?"

"I just remembered this. Good thing I brought it, huh?"

"Better put it out and go to sleep."

"It doesn't use up any oxygen. I feel better with it on."

"Maybe you do, but as long as you stay awake *you* use up more oxygen."

"I suppose so." Jim suddenly recalled what had been terrifying him before he got out the light. "It doesn't make any difference." He explained to Frank his conviction that they were trapped forever in the plant.

"Nonsense!" said Frank.

"Nonsense yourself! Why didn't it open up at dawn?"

"Because," Frank said, "we haven't been in here more than an hour."

"What? Says you."

"Says me. Now shut up and let me sleep. Better put out that light." Frank settled his head again on his knees.

Jim shut up but did not turn out the light. It comforted him. Besides, the inner leaves which had shown an annoying tendency to close in on the tops of their heads now had retreated and flattened themselves firmly against the dense wall formed by the outer layers of leaves. Under the mindless reflex which controlled the movements of the plant they were doing their best to present maximum surface to the rays from the flashlight.

Jim did not analyse the matter; his knowledge of photosynthesis and of heliotropism was sketchy. He was simply aware that the place seemed roomier in the light and that he was having less trouble with the clinging leaves. He settled the torch against Willis, who had not stirred, and tried to relax.

It actually seemed less stuffy with the light on. He had the impression that the pressure was up a little. He considered trying to take off his mask but decided against it. Presently, without knowing it, he drifted off to sleep.

He dreamed and then dreamt that he was dreaming. Hiding in the desert cabbage had been only a fantastic, impossible dream; school and Headmaster Howe had merely been nightmares; he was home, asleep in his bed, with Willis cuddled against him. Tomorrow Frank and he would start for Syrtis Minor to enter school.

It had simply been a nightmare, caused by the suggestion that

Willis be taken away from him. They were planning to take Willis away from him! They couldn't do that; he wouldn't let them!

Again his dream shifted; again he defied Headmaster Howe; again he rescued Willis and fled—and again they were locked away in the heart of a desert plant.

He knew with bitter certainty that it would always end like this. This was the reality, to be trapped and smothering in the core of a hibernating giant weed—to die there.

He choked and muttered, tried to wake up, then slipped into a less intolerable dream.

7.
PURSUED

Tiny Phobos, inner moon of Mars, came out of eclipse and, at breakneck speed, flew west to east into the face of the rising Sun. The leisurely spin of its ruddy primary, twenty-four and a half hours for each rotation, presently brought the rays of that Sun to east Strymon, then across the bank of desert between the twin canals and to the banks of west Strymon. The rays struck a great ball perched near the eastern bank of that canal, a desert cabbage closed against the cold.

The plant stirred and unfolded. The sunward half of the plant opened flat to the ground; the other half fanned itself open like a spread peacock's tail to catch the almost horizontal rays. In so doing it spilled something out of its heart and onto the flat portion—two human bodies, twisted and stiff, clad garishly in elastic suits and grotesque helmets.

A tiny ball spilled out with them, rolled a few yards over the thick green leaves, and stopped. It extended eye stalks and little bumps of legs and waddled back to the sprawled bodies. It nuzzled up against one.

It hesitated, nuzzled again, then settled back and let out a thin wailing in which was compounded inconsolable grief and an utter sense of loss.

Jim opened one bloodshot eye. "Cut out that infernal racket," he said crossly.

Willis shrieked, "Jim boy!" and jumped upon his stomach, where he continued to bounce up and down in an ecstasy of greeting.

Jim brushed him off, then gathered him up in one arm. "Calm down. Behave yourself. Ouch!"

"What's the matter, Jim boy?"

"My arm's stiff. Ooo—ouch!" Further efforts had shown Jim that his legs were stiff as well. Also his back. And his neck.

"What's the matter with you?" demanded Frank.

"Stiff as board. I'd do better to skate on my hands today. Say—"

"Say what?"

"Maybe we don't skate. I wonder if the spring floods have started?"

"Huh? What are you gibbering about?" Frank sat up, slowly and carefully.

"Why, the spring floods, of course. Somehow we lasted through the winter, though I don't know how. Now we—"

"Don't be any sillier than you have to be. Look where the Sun is rising."

Jim looked. Martian colonials are more acutely aware of the apparent movements of the Sun than any Earthbound men, except, possibly, the Eskimos. All he said was, "Oh . . ." then added, "I guess it was a dream."

"Either that or you are even nuttier than usual. Let's get going." Frank struggled to his feet with a groan.

"How do you feel?"

"Like my own grandfather."

"I mean, how's your throat?" Jim persisted.

"Oh, it's all right." Frank promptly contradicted himself by a fit of coughing. By great effort he controlled it shortly; coughing while wearing a respirator is a bad idea. Sneezing is worse.

"Want some breakfast?"

"I'm not hungry now," Frank answered. "Let's find a shelter first, so we can eat in comfort."

"Okay." Jim stuffed Willis back into the bag, discovered by experiment that he could stand and walk. Noticing the flashlight, he tucked it in with Willis and followed Frank toward the bank. The canal vegetation was beginning to show; even as they walked the footing grew more tangled. The green plants, still stiff with night cold, could not draw away quickly as they brushed through them.

They reached the bank. "The ramp must be about a hundred yards off to the right," Frank decided. "Yep—I see it. Come on."

Jim grabbed his arm and drew him back. "'Smatter?" demanded Frank.

"Look on up the canal, north."

"Huh? Oh!" A scooter was proceeding toward them. Instead of the two hundred fifty miles per hour or more that such craft usually make, this one was throttled down to a minimum. Two men were seated on top of it, out in the open.

Frank drew back hastily. "Good boy, Jim," he approved. "I was just about to walk right into them. I guess we had better let them get well ahead."

"Willis good boy, too," Willis put in smugly.

"Let them get ahead, my foot!" Jim answered. "Can't you see what they're doing?"

"Huh?"

"They're following our tracks!"

Frank looked startled but did not answer. He peered cautiously out. "Look out!" Jim snapped. "He's got binoculars." Frank ducked back. But he had seen enough; the scooter had stopped at approximately the spot where they had stopped the night before. One of the men on top was gesturing through the observation dome at the driver and pointing to the ramp.

Canal ice was, of course, never cleaned of skate marks; the surface was renewed from time to time by midday thaws until the dead freeze of winter set in. However, it was unlikely that anyone but the two boys had skated over this stretch of ice, so far from any settlement, any time in months. The ice held scooter tracks, to be sure, but, like all skaters, Jim and Frank had avoided them in favor of untouched ice.

Now their unmistakable spoor lay for any to read from Cynia station to the ramp near them.

"If we head back into the bushes," Jim whispered. "We can hide until they go away. They'll never find us in this stuff."

"Suppose they don't go away. Do you want to spend another night in the cabbage?"

"They're bound to go away eventually."

"Sure but not soon enough. They know we went up the ramp; they'll stay and they'll search, longer than we can hold out. They can afford to; they've got a base."

"Well, what do we do?"

"We head south along the bank, on foot, at least as far as the next ramp."

"Let's get going, then. They'll be up the ramp in no time."

With Frank in the lead they dog-trotted to the south. The plants along the bank were high enough now to permit them to go under; Frank held a course about thirty feet in from the bank. The gloom under the spreading leaves and the stems of the plants themselves protected them from any distant observation.

Jim kept an eye out for snake worms and water-seekers and cautioned Willis to do likewise. They made fair time. After a few minutes Frank stopped, motioned for silence, and they both listened. All that Jim could hear was Frank's rasping breath; if they were being pursued, the pursuers were not close.

They were at least two miles south of the ramp when Frank stopped very suddenly. Jim bumped into him and the two almost tumbled into the thing that had caused Frank to stop—another canal. This one ran east and west and was a much narrower branch of the main canal. There were several such between Cynia and Charax. Some of them joined the east and west legs of Strymon canal; some merely carried water to local depressions in the desert plateau.

Jim stared down into the deep and narrow gash. "For the love of Mike! We nearly took a header."

Frank did not answer. He sank down to his knees, then sat and held his head. Suddenly he was overcome by a spasm of coughing. When it was over, his shoulders still shook, as if he were racked by dry sobs.

Jim put a hand on his arm. "You're pretty sick, aren't you, fellow?"

Frank did not answer. Willis said, "Poor Frank boy," and tut-tutted.

Jim stared again at the canal, his forehead wrinkled. Presently Frank raised his head and said, "I'm all right. It just got me for a moment—running into the canal and all and realizing it had us stopped. I was so tired."

Jim said, "Look here, Frank, I've got a new plan. I'm going to follow this ditch off to the east until I find some way to get down into it. You're going to go back and give yourself up—"

"*No!*"

"Wait till I finish! This makes sense. You're too sick to keep going. If you stay out here, you're going to die. You might as well admit it. Somebody's got to get the word to our folks—me. You go back, surrender, and then give them a song and dance about how I went that way—any way but this way. If you make it good, you can stall them and keep them chasing their tails for a full day and give me that much head start. In the mean time you lay around in the scooter, warm and safe, and tonight you're in bed in the infirmary at school. There—doesn't that make sense?"

"No."

"Why not? You're just being stubborn."

"No," repeated Frank, "it's no good. In the first place I won't turn myself over to them. I'd rather die out here—"

"Nuts!"

"Nuts yourself. In the second place, a day's start will do you no good. Once they are sure you aren't where I say you are, they'll just go back to combing the canal, by scooter. They'll pick you up tomorrow."

"But—well, what is the answer then?"

"I don't know, but it's not that." He was seized again by coughing.

Neither one of them said anything for several minutes. At last Jim said, "What kind of a scooter was that?"

"The usual cargo sort, a Hudson Six Hundred I think. Why?"

"Could it turn around on that ice down there?"

Frank looked down into the small canal. Its sides sloped in toward the bottom; the water level was so low that the ice surface was barely twenty feet across. "Not a chance," he answered.

"Then they won't try to search this branch by scooter—at least not in *that* scooter."

"I'm way ahead of you," put in Frank. "You figure we'll cross to east Strymon and go home that way. But how do you know this cut runs all the way through? You remember the map that well?"

"No, I don't. But there is a good chance it does. If it doesn't, it will run most of the way across and we'll just have to hoof it the rest of the way."

"After we get to the east leg it will still be five hundred miles or so to Charax. This leg has shelters on it, even if we did miss the one last night."

"We've got just as good a chance of finding project shelters on east leg as on west leg," Jim answered. "The Project starts next spring on both sides. I know—Dad's talked about it enough. Anyhow, we can't use this leg any further; they're searching it—so why beat your choppers about it? The real question is: can you skate? If you can't, I still say you ought to surrender."

Frank stood up. "I'll skate," he said grimly. "Come on."

They went boldly along the stone embankment, convinced that

their pursuers were still searching the neighborhood of the ramp. They were three or four miles further east when they came to a ramp leading down to the ice. "Shall we chance it?" asked Jim.

"Sure. Even if they send a man in on skates I doubt if he would come this far with no tracks to lead him on. I'm tired of walking." They went down, put on their skates, and started. Most of the kinks from their uncomfortable night had been smoothed out by walking; it felt good to be on the ice again. Jim let Frank set the pace; despite his illness he stroked right into it and pushed the miles behind them.

They had come perhaps forty miles when the banks began to be noticeably lower. Jim, seeing this, got a sick feeling that the little canal was not cross-connecting from west to east leg, but merely a feeder to a low spot in the desert. He kept his suspicion to himself. At the end of the next hour it was no longer necessary to spare his chum; the truth was evident to them both. The banks were now so low that they could see over them and the ice ahead no longer disappeared into the blue sky but dead-ended in some fashion.

They came to the dead end presently, a frozen swamp. The banks were gone; the rough ice spread out in all directions and was bordered in the distance by green plants. Here and there, canal grass, caught by the freeze, stuck up in dead tufts through the ice.

They continued east, skating where they could and picking their way around bits of higher ground. At last Frank said, "All out! End of the line!" and sat down to take off his skates.

"I'm sorry, Frank."

"About what? We'll leg it the rest of the way. It can't be so many miles."

They set out through the surrounding greenery, walking just fast enough to let the plants draw out their way. The vegetation that surrounded the marsh was lower than the canal plants, hardly shoulder high, and showed smaller leaves. After a couple of miles of this they found themselves out on the sand dunes.

The shifting, red, iron-oxide sands made hard walking and the dunes, to be climbed or skirted, made it worse. Jim usually elected to climb them even if Frank went around; he was looking for a dark green line against the horizon that would mark east Strymon. It continued to disappoint him.

Willis insisted on getting down. First he gave himself a dust bath in the clean sand; thereafter he kept somewhat ahead of Jim, exploring this way and that and startling the spin bugs. Jim had just topped a dune and was starting down the other side when he heard an agonized squeak from Willis. He looked around.

Frank was just coming around the end of the dune and Willis was with him, that is to say, Willis had skittered on ahead. Now the bouncer was standing dead still. Frank apparently had noticed nothing; he was dragging along in a listless fashion, his head down.

Charging straight at them was a water-seeker.

It was a long shot, even for a match marksman. The scene took on a curious unreality to Jim. It seemed as if Frank were frozen in his tracks and as if the water-seeker itself were strolling slowly toward his victims. Jim himself seemed to have all the time in the world to draw, take a steady, careful bead, and let go his first charge.

It burned the first two pairs of legs off the creature; it kept coming.

Jim sighted on it again, held the stud down. His beam, held steadily on the centerline of the varmit, sliced it in two as if it had run into a buzz saw. It kept coming until its two halves were no longer joined, until they fell two ways, twitching. The great scimitar claw on the left half stopped within inches of Willis.

Jim ran down the dune. Frank, no longer a statue, actually had stopped. He was standing, blinking at what had been a moment before the incarnation of sudden and bloody death. He looked around as Jim came up. "Thanks," he said.

Jim did not answer but kicked at a trembling leg of the beast. "The filthy, filthy thing!" he said intensely. "Cripes, how I hate them. I wish I could burn every one on Mars, all at once." He walked on up along the body, located the egg sac, and carefully blasted every bit of it.

Willis had not moved. He was sobbing quietly. Jim came back, picked him up, and popped him in the travel bag. "Let's stick together from here on," he said. "If you don't feel like climbing, I'll go around."

"Okay."

"Frank!"

"Uh? Yes, what is it, Jim?" Frank's voice was listless.

"What do you see ahead?"

"Ahead?" Frank tried manfully to make his eyes focus, to chase the fuzz from them. "Uhh, it's the canal, the green belt I mean. I guess we made it."

"And what else? Don't you see a tower?"

"What? Where? Oh, there—Yes, I guess I do. It's a tower all right."

"Well, for heaven's sake, don't you know what that means? Martians!"

"Yeah, I suppose so."

"Well, show some enthusiasm!"

"Why should I?"

"They'll take us in, man! Martians are good people; you'll have a warm place to rest, before we go on."

Frank looked a bit more interested, but said nothing. "They might even know Gekko," Jim went on. "This is a real break."

"Yeah, maybe so."

It took another hour of foot-slogging before the little Martian town was reached. It was so small that it boasted only one tower, but to Jim it was even more beautiful than Syrtis Major. They followed its wall and presently found a gate.

They had not been inside more than a few minutes when Jim's hopes, so high, were almost as low as they could be. Even before he saw the weed-choked central garden, the empty walks and silent courts had told him the bad truth: the little town was deserted.

Mars must once have held a larger native population than it does today. Ghost cities are not unknown and even the greater centers of population, such as Charax, Syrtis Major and Minor, and Hesperidum, have areas which are no longer used and through which tourists from Earth may sometimes be conducted. This little town, apparently never of great importance, might have been abandoned before Noah laid the keel of his ship.

Jim paused in the plaza, unwilling to speak. Frank stopped and sat down a metal slab, its burnished face bright with characters that an Earthly scholar would have given an arm to read. "Well," said Jim, "rest a bit, then I guess we had better find a way to get down onto the canal."

Frank answered dully, "Not for me. I've come as far as I can."

"Don't talk that way."

"I'm telling you, Jim, that's how it is."

Jim puzzled at it. "I tell you what—I'll search around. These places are always honeycombed underneath. I'll find a place for us to hole up over night."

"Just as you like."

"You just stay here." He started to leave, then suddenly became aware that Willis was not with him. He then recalled that the bouncer had jumped down when they entred the city. "Willis—where's Willis?"

"How would I know?"

"I've got to find him. Oh, Willis! Hey, Willis! Come, boy!" His voice echoed around the dead square.

"Hi, Jim!"

It was Willis, rightly enough, his voice reaching Jim from some distance. Presently he came into sight. But he was not alone; he was being carried by a Martian.

The Martian came near them, dropped his third leg, and leaned down. His voice boomed gently at Jim. "What's he saying, Frank?"

"Huh? Oh, I don't know. Tell him to go away."

The Martian spoke again. Jim abandoned the attempt to use Frank as a translator and concentrated on trying to understand. He spotted the question symbol, in the inverted position; the remark was an invitation or a suggestion of some sort. Following it was the operator of motion coupled with some radical that meant nothing to Jim.

He answered it with the question symbol alone, hoping that the native would repeat himself. Willis answered instead. "Come along, Jim boy—fine place!"

Why not? he said to himself and answered, "Okay, Willis." To the Martian he replied with the symbol of general assent, racking his throat to produce the unEarthly triple guttural required. The Martian repeated it, inverted, then picked up the leg closest to them and walked rapidly away without turning around. He had gone about twenty-five yards when he seemed to notice that he was not being followed. He backed up just as rapidly and used the general inquiry symbol in the sense of "What's wrong?"

"Willis," Jim said urgently, "I want him to carry Frank."

"Carry Frank boy?"

"Yes, the way Gekko carried him."

"Gekko not here. This K'boomch."

"His name is K'boomk?"

"Sure—K'boomch," Willis agreed, correcting Jim's pronunciation.

"Well, I want K'boomch to carry Frank like Gekko carried him."

Willis and the Martian mooed and croaked at each other for a moment, then Willis said, "K'boomch wants to know does Jim boy know Gekko."

"Tell him we are friends, water friends."

"Willis already tell him."

"How about Frank?" But it appeared that Willis had already told his new acquaintance about that, too, for K'boomch enclosed Frank in two palm flaps and lifted him up. Frank opened his eyes, then closed them. He seemed indifferent to what happened to him.

Jim trotted after the Martian, stopping only to grab up Frank's skates from where he had abandoned them on the metal slab. The Martian led him into a huge building that seemed even larger inside than out, so richly illuminated in glowing lights were the walls. The Martian did not tarry but went directly into an archway in the far wall; it was a ramp tunnel entrance, leading down.

The Martians appear never to have invented stair steps, or more likely never needed them. The low surface gravity of Mars, only 38% of that of Earth, permits the use of ramps which would be disastrously steep on Earth. The Martian led Jim down a long sequence of these rapid descents.

Presently Jim discovered, as he had once before under Cynia city, that the air pressure had increased. He raised his mask with a feeling of great relief; he had not had it off for more than twenty-four hours. The change in pressure had come abruptly; he knew from this that it had not resulted from descent alone, nor had they come deep enough to make any great difference in pressure.

Jim wondered how the trick was accomplished. He decided that it had pressure locks beat all hollow.

They left the ramps and entered a large domed chamber, evenly lighted from the ceiling itself. Its walls were a continuous series of archways. K'boomch stopped and spoke again to Jim, another inquiry in which he used the name Gekko.

Jim reached into his memory and carefully phrased a simple declaration: "Gekko and I have shared water. We are friends."

The Martian seemed satisfied; he led the way into one of the side rooms and placed Frank gently on the floor. The door closed behind them, sliding silently into place. It was a smallish room, for Martians, and contained several resting frames. K'boomch arranged his ungainly figure on one of them.

Suddenly Jim felt heavy and sat down rather unexpectedly on the floor. The feeling persisted and with it a slight giddiness; he stayed seated. "Are you all right, Frank?" he asked.

Frank muttered something. His breathing seemed labored and rough. Jim took off Frank's mask and touched his face; it was hot. There was nothing that he could do for Frank at the moment.

The heavy feeling continued. The Martian did not seemed disposed to talk and Jim did not feel up to attempting a conversation in the dominant tongue in any case. Willis had withdrawn into a ball. Jim lay down beside Frank, closed his eyes, and tried not to think.

He felt a moment of lightness, almost of vertigo, then felt heavy again and wondered what he was coming down with. He lay still for a few more minutes, to be disturbed presently by the native bending over him and speaking. He sat up and discovered that he felt fine again. K'boomch scooped up Frank and they left the room.

The great domed chamber outside looked the same, except that it now held a crowd of Martians, thirty or more of them. When K'boomch and his two burdens, followed by Jim, came out the archway one of them separated himself from the group and stepped forward. He was rather short as Martians go. "Jim-Marlowe," he stated, with the vocative symbol.

"Gekko!" yelled Jim, echoed by Willis.

Gekko bent over him. "My friend," he boomed softly in his own tongue. "My little, crippled friend." He raised Jim up and carried him away, the other Martians retreating to make way.

Gekko moved rapidly through a series of tunnels. Jim, looking back, could see that K'boomch and the rest of his party were close behind, so he let matters drift. Gekko turned presently into a medium-sized chamber and put Jim down. Frank was deposited by him. Frank blinked his eyes and said, "Where are we?"

Jim looked around. The room held several resting frames, set in a circle. The ceiling was domed and simulated the sky. On one wall a canal flowed past, in convincing miniature. Elsewhere on the curved wall was the silhouette of a Martian city, feathery towers floating in the air. Jim knew those towers, knew of what city they were the signature; Jim knew this room.

It was the very room in which he had "grown together" with Gekko and his friends.

"Oh, my gosh, Frank—we're back in Cynia."

"Huh?" Frank sat up suddenly, glared around him—then lay back down and shut his eyes tightly.

Jim did not know whether to laugh or to cry. All that effort! All their striving to escape and to get home, Frank's gallant refusal to give up in the face of sickness and body weariness, the night in the desert cabbage—and here they were not three miles from Cynia station.

8.
THE OTHER WORLD

Jim set up housekeeping—or hospital-keeping—in the smallest room that Gekko could find for him. There had been a "growing together" immediately after their arrival. On its conclusion Jim had found, as before, that his command of the dominant tongue was improved. He had made Gekko understand that Frank was sick and needed quiet.

Gekko offered to take over Frank's care, but Jim refused. Martian therapy might cure Frank—or it might kill him. He asked instead for a plentiful supply of drinking water—his right, now that he was a "water friend," almost a tribal brother—and he asked for the colorful Martian silks that had been used by the boys in place of resting frames. From these silks Jim made a soft bed for Frank and a nest nearby for himself and Willis. He bedded Frank down, roused him enough to get him to drink deeply of water, and then waited for his friend to get well.

The room was quite comfortably warm; Jim took off his outdoors suit, stretched, and scratched. On second thought he peeled off Frank's elastic suit as well and covered him with a layer of flame-colored cloth. After that he dug into Frank's travel bag and looked over the food supply. Up to now he had been too busy and too tired to worry about his stomach; now the very sight of the labels made him drool. He picked out a can of synthetic orange juice, vitamin fortified, and a can of simulated chicken filet. The latter had started life in a yeast tank at North Colony, but Jim was used to yeast proteins and the flavor was every bit as tempting as white breast of chicken. Whistling, he got out his knife and got busy.

Willis had wandered off somewhere but he did not miss him. Subconsciously he was not disposed to worry about Willis while they were both in a native city; the place was filled with an atmosphere of peace and security. In fact Jim hardly thought about his patient until he had finished and wiped his mouth.

Frank was still sleeping but his breathing was noisy and his face still flushed. The air in the room, though warm and of satisfactory pressure, was Mars dry. Frank got a handkerchief from his bag, wet it, and put it over Frank's face. From time to time he moistened it again. Later he got another handkerchief, doused it, and tied it around his own face.

Gekko came in with Willis tagging along. "Jim-Marlowe," he stated and settled himself. "Gekko," Jim answered and went on with moistening Frank's face cloth. The Martian remained so quiet for so long that Jim decided that he must have retreated into his "other world" but, when Jim looked at him, Gekko's eyes showed lively, alert interest.

After a long wait he asked Jim what he was doing and why.

Jim tried to explain that his kind must breathe water as well as air but his Martian vocabulary, despite the "growing together," was not up to the strain it placed on it. He gave up and there was another long silence. Eventually the Martian left, Willis with him.

Presently Jim noticed that the face cloths, both his and Frank's, were not drying out rapidly. Shortly they were hardly drying at all. He took off his, as it made him uncomfortable, and decided that it must be uncomfortable for Frank as well; he stopped using them entirely.

Gekko returned. After only ten minutes of silence he spoke, showing thereby almost frantic haste for his kind. He wanted to know if the water that flies with the air was now sufficient? Jim assured him that it was and thanked him. After twenty minutes or so of silence Gekko again left. Jim decided to go to bed. It had been a long, hard day and the previous night could hardly be called a night of rest. He looked around for some way to switch off the light but could find none. Giving up, he lay down, pulled a polychrome sheet up to his chin, and went to sleep.

Sometime during his sleep Willis returned. Jim became aware of it when the little fellow snuggled up against his back. Sleepily, Jim reached behind and petted him, then went back to sleep.

"Hey, Jim—wake up."

Blearily Jim opened his eyes, and closed them. "Go away."

"Come on. Snap out of it. I've been awake the past two hours, while you snored. I want to know some things."

"What do you want to know? Say—how do you feel?"

"Me?" said Frank. "I feel fine. Why shouldn't I? Where are we?"

Jim looked him over. Frank's color was certainly better and his voice sounded normal, the hoarseness all gone. "You were plenty sick yesterday," he informed him. "I think you were out of your head."

Frank wrinkled his forehead. "Maybe I was. I've sure had the darnedest dreams. There was a crazy one about a desert cabbage—"

"That was no dream."

"What?"

"I said that was no dream, the desert cabbage—nor any of the rest of it. Do you know where we are?"

"That's what I was asking you."

"We're in Cynia, that's where we are. We—"

"In *Cynia*?"

Jim tried to give Frank a coherent account of the preceding two days. He was somewhat hampered by the item of their sudden translation from far up the canal back to Cynia, because he did not understand it clearly himself. "I figure it's a sort of a subway paralleling the canal. You know—a subway, like you read about."

"Martians don't do that sort of engineering."

"Martians built the canals."

"Yes, but that was a long, long time ago."

"Maybe they built the subway a long time ago. What do you know about it?"

"Well—nothing, I guess. Never mind. I'm hungry. Anything left to eat?"

"Sure." Jim got up. In so doing he woke Willis, who extended his eyes, sized up the situation, and greeted them. Jim picked him up, scratched him, and said, "What time did you come in, you tramp?" then suddenly added, "Hey!"

" 'Hey' what?" asked Frank.

"Well, would you look at *that*?" Jim pointed at the tumbled silks.

Frank got up and joined him. "Look at what? Oh—"

In the hollow in which Willis had been resting were a dozen small, white spheroids, looking like so many golf balls.

"What do you suppose they are?" asked Jim.

Frank studied them closely. "Jim," he said slowly, "I think you'll just have to face it. Willis isn't a boy; he's a she."

"Huh? Oh, no!"

"Willis good boy," Willis said defensively.

"See for yourself," Frank went on to Jim. "Those are eggs. If Willis didn't lay them, you must have."

Jim looked bewildered, then turned to Willis. "Willis, did you lay those eggs? Did you?"

"Eggs?" said Willis. "What Jim boy say?"

Jim set him down by the nest and pointed. "Did you lay those?"

Willis looked at them, then figuratively shrugged his shoulders and washed his hands of the whole matter. He waddled away. His manner seemed to say that if Jim chose to make a fuss over some eggs or whatever that just happened to show up in the bed, well, that was Jim's business; Willis would have none of it.

"You won't get anything out of him," Frank commented. "I suppose you realize this makes you a grandfather, sort of."

"Don't be funny!"

"Okay, forget the eggs. When do we eat? I'm starved."

Jim gave the eggs an accusing glance and got busy on the commissary. While they were eating Gekko came in. They exchanged grave greetings, then the Martian seemed about to settle himself for another long period of silent sociability—when he caught sight of the eggs.

Neither of the boys had ever seen a Martian hurry before, nor show any signs of excitement. Gekko let out a deep snort and left the room at once, to return promptly with as many companions as could crowd into the room. They all talked at once and paid no attention to the boys.

"What goes on here?" asked Frank, as he crowded against a wall and peered through a thicket of legs.

"Blessed if I know."

After a while they calmed down a little. One of the larger Martians gathered up the eggs with exaggerated care and clutched them to him. Another picked up Willis and they all trooped out.

Jim stood hesitantly at the door and watched them disappear. "I'd like to find Gekko and ask him about it," he fretted.

"Nuts," said Frank. "Let's finish breakfast."

"Well . . . all right."

Once the meal was over, Frank opened the larger question. "Okay, so we are in Cynia. We've still got to get home and fast.

The question is: how do we go about it? Now as I see it, if these Martians could bring us back here so fast, they can turn around and put us back where they found us and then we can head home up the east leg of Strymon. How does that strike you?"

"It sounds all right, I guess," Jim answered, "but—"

"Then the first thing to do is to find Gekko and try to arrange it, without fiddling around."

"The first thing to do," Jim contradicted, "is to find Willis."

"Why? Hasn't he caused enough trouble? Leave him; he's happy here."

"Frank, you take entirely the wrong attitude toward Willis. Didn't he get us out of a jam? If it hadn't been for Willis, you'd be coughing your lungs out in the desert."

"If it hadn't been for Willis, we wouldn't have been in that jam in the first place."

"Now that's not fair. The truth is—"

"Skip it, skip it. Okay, go find Willis."

Jim left Frank to clean up the litter of breakfast and set out. Although he was never able thereafter to give a fully coherent account of just what happened to him on this errand, certain gross facts are clear. He started by looking for Gekko, asking for him of the first Martian he met in the corridors by the barbarous expedient of voicing the general inquiry followed by Gekko's name.

Jim was not and probably never would be a competent linguist, but his attempt worked. The first Martian he encountered took him to another, as an Earthly citizen might lead a foreigner to a policeman. This Martian took him to Gekko.

Jim had no great trouble in explaining to Gekko that he wanted Willis returned to him. Gekko listened, then explained gently that what Jim wanted was impossible.

Jim started over again, sure that his own poor command of the language had caused misunderstanding. Gekko let him finish, then made it quite clear that he understood correctly what it was that Jim wanted, but that Jim could not have it—could not have Willis. No. Gekko was sorrowful to have to refuse his friend with whom he had shared the pure water of life, but this thing could not be.

Under the direct influence of Gekko's powerful personality Jim understood most of what was said and guessed the rest. Gekko's refusal was unmistakable. It is not important that Jim did not have his gun with him; Gekko could not inspire the hatred in him that Howe did. For one thing Gekko's warm sympathy poured over him in a flood; nevertheless Jim was thunderstruck, indignant, and quite unable to accept the verdict. He stared up at the Martian for a long moment. Then he walked away abruptly, not choosing his direction and shouting for Willis as he did so. "Willis! Oh, Willis! Here, Willis boy—come to Jim!"

The Martian started after him, each stride three of Jim's. Jim ran, still shouting. He turned a corner, came face-to-face with three natives and darted between their legs and beyond. Gekko got into a traffic jam with them which required the time-wasting exercise of Martian protocol to straighten out. Jim got considerably ahead.

He stuck his head into every archway he came to and shouted. One such led into a chamber occupied by Martians frozen in that trancelike state they call visiting the "other world." Jim would no more have disturbed a Martian in a trance, ordinarily, than an American western frontier child would have teased a grizzly—but he was in no shape to care or notice; he shouted in there, too, thereby causing an unheard-of and unthinkable disturbance. The least response was violent trembling; one poor creature was so disturbed that he lifted abruptly all of his legs and fell to the floor.

Jim did not notice; he was already gone, shouting into the next chamber.

Gekko caught up with him and scooped him up with two great hand flaps. "Jim-Marlowe!" he said. "Jim-Marlowe, my friend—"

Jim sobbed and beat on the Martian's hard thorax with both his fists. Gekko endured it for a moment, then wrapped a third palm flap around Jim's arms, securing him. Jim looked wildly up at him. "Willis," he said in his own language, "I want Willis. You've got no right!"

Gekko cradled him and answered softly, "I have no power. This is beyond me. We must go to the other world." He moved away. Jim made no answer, tired by his own outburst. Gekko took a ramp downward, then another and another. Down and down he went, much deeper than Jim had ever been before, deeper perhaps than any terrestrial had ever been. On the upper levels they passed other Martians; farther down there were none.

At last Gekko halted in a small chamber far underground. It was exceptional in that it was totally without decoration; its plain, pearl-grey walls seemed almost unMartian. Gekko laid Jim on the floor here and said, "This is a gate to the other world."

Jim picked himself up. "Huh?" he said. "What do you mean?" and then carefully rephrased the question in the dominant tongue. He need not have bothered; Gekko did not hear him.

Jim craned his neck and looked up. Gekko stood utterly motionless, all legs firmly planted. His eyes were open but lifeless.
Gekko had crossed over into the "other world."

"For the love of Mike," Jim fretted, "he sure picks a sweet
time to pull a stunt like that." He wondered what he ought to do,
try to find his way to upper levels alone or wait for Gekko. Natives
were reputed to be able to hold a trance for weeks at a time, but
Doc MacRae had pooh-poohed such stories.

He decided to wait for a while at least and sat down on the
floor, hands clasped around his knees. He felt considerably
calmed down and in no special hurry, as if Gekko's boundless
calm had flowed over into him while the native had carried him.

After a while, an indefinitely long while, the room grew
darker. Jim was not disturbed; he was vastly content, feeling again
the untroubled happiness that he had known in his two experi-
ences of "growing together."

A tiny light appeared at a great distance in the darkness and
grew. But it did not illuminate the small pearl-grey room; it built
up an outdoor scene instead. It was as if a stereo-movie projector
were being used to project New Hollywood's best work, in full,
natural color. That it was not an importation from Earth Jim knew,
for the scene, while utterly realistic, had no slick commercial finish, no plot.

He seemed to be seeing a grove of canal plants from a viewpoint about a foot off the ground. The viewpoint shifted steadily
and erratically as if the camera were being trucked on a very low
dolly here and there through the stalks of the canal plants. The
viewpoint would shift quickly for a few feet, stop, then change direction and move again, but it never got very far off the ground.
Sometimes it would wheel in a full circle, a panorama of three
hundred and sixty degrees.

It was during one of these full rotations that he caught sight of
a water-seeker.

It would not have been strange if he had not recognized it as
such, for it was enormously magnified. As it charged in, it filled
the entire screen. But it was impossible not to recognize those
curving scimitar claws, the grisly horror of the gaping sucker orifice, those pounding legs—and most particularly the stomach-
clutching revulsion the thing inspired. Jim could almost smell it.

The viewpoint from which he saw it did not change; it was
frozen to one spot while the foul horror rushed directly at him in
the final death charge. At the last possible instant, when the thing

filled the screen, something happened. The face—or where the face should have been—disappeared, went to pieces, and the creature collapsed in a blasted ruin.

The picture was wiped out completely for a few moments, replaced by whirling colored turmoil. Then a light, sweet voice said, "Well, aren't you the cute little fellow!" The picture built up again as if a curtain had been lifted and Jim stared at another face almost as grotesque as the faceless horror it replaced.

Although this face occupied the whole screen and was weirdly distorted, Jim had no trouble in placing it as a colonial's respirator mask. What startled him almost out of the personal unawareness with which he was accepting this shadow show was that he recognized the mask. It was decorated with the very tiger stripes that Smythe had painted out for a quarter credit; it was his own, as it used to be.

He heard his own voice say, "You're too little to be wandering around by yourself; another one of those vermin might really get you. I think I'll take you home."

The scene went swinging through the canal growth at a greater height, bobbling up and down to the boy's steps. Presently the point of view came out into open country and showed in the distance the star-shaped layout and bubble domes of South Colony.

Jim adjusted to the idea of watching himself, hearing himself, and accepted the notion of seeing things from Willis's viewpoint. The record was quite unedited; it pushed forward in a straight line, a complete recollection of everything Willis had seen and heard from the time Jim had first taken him under his protection. Willis's visual recollections were not entirely accurate; they seemed to be affected by his understanding of what he saw and how used to it he was. Jim—the "Jim" in the shadow show—at first seemed to have three legs; it was some time before the imaginary excrescence vanished. Other actors, Jim's mother, old Doc MacRae, Frank, developed from formless shapes to full, though somewhat distorted, representations.

On the other hand, every sound was heard with great clarity and complete accuracy. As Jim listened and watched he found that he was savoring sounds of every sort and most especially voices with a new and rich delight.

Most especially he enjoyed seeing himself as Willis saw him. With affection and warm humor he saw himself stripped of dignity but clothed in a lively regard; he was loved but not respected. He, Jim himself, was a great bumbling servant, helpful but maddeningly unreliable in his attentions, like a poorly trained dog. As for other human beings, they were curious creatures, harmless on the whole, but unpredictable traffic hazards. This bouncer-eye view of people amused Jim mightily.

Day by day and week by week the account unfolded, even to the periods of dark and quiet when Willis chose to sleep or was shut up. It carried on to Syrtis Minor and into a bad time when Jim was missing. Howe appeared as a despised voice and a pair of legs; Beecher was a faceless nonentity. It continued, step by step, and somehow Jim was neither tired nor bored. He was simply in the continuity and could no more escape from it than could Willis—nor did it occur to him to try. At last it wound up in the Martian city of Cynia and ended in a period of dark and quiet.

Jim stretched his cramped legs; the light was returning. He looked around but Gekko was still deep in his trance. He looked back and found that a door had opened in what had appeared to be blank wall. He looked through and into a room beyond, decorated as Martian rooms so frequently are in careful imitation of an outdoor scene—lush countryside more like the sea bottoms south of Cynia than like the desert.

A Martian was in the room. Jim was never able afterwards to visualize him completely for his face and particularly his eyes compelled attention. An Earthling has no good way to estimate the age of a Martian yet Jim had the unmistakable impression that this Martian was very old—older than his father, older even than Doc MacRae.

"Jim Marlowe," the native said in clear tones. "Welcome, Jim Marlowe, friend of my people and friend of mine. I give you water." He spoke in Basic English, in an accent vaguely familiar.

Jim had never heard a Martian speak an Earthly tongue before, but he knew that some of them did speak Basic. It was a relief to be able to answer in his own speech. "I drink with you. May you ever enjoy pure and plentiful water."

"I thank you, Jim Marlowe." No actual water was used and none was needed. There followed a polite period of quiet, during which Jim thought about the Martian's accent. It was oddly familiar; it put him in mind of his father's voice, again it sounded like Doc MacRae.

"You are troubled, Jim Marlowe. Your unhappiness is ours. How may I help you?"

"I don't want anything," Jim answered, "except to go home

and take Willis with me. They took Willis away. They shouldn't have done that."

The silence that followed was even longer than before. At last the Martian answered, "When one stands on the ground, one may not see over the horizon—yet Phobos sees all horizons." He hesitated a moment before the word "Phobos." As if in afterthought he added, "Jim Marlowe, I have but lately learned your tongue. Forgive me if I stumble."

"Oh, you speak it beautifully!" Jim said quite sincerely.

"The words I know; the pictures are not clear. Tell me, Jim Marlowe, what is the london-zoo?"

Jim had to ask him to repeat it before it was clear that the Martian asked about the London Zoo. Jim tried to explain, but broke off before he had finished elaborating the idea. The Martian radiated such cold, implacable anger that Jim was frightened.

After a time the Martian's mood changed abruptly and Jim was again bathed in a warm glow of friendliness that poured out of his host like rays from the Sun and was as real as sunshine to Jim. "Jim Marlowe, twice you have saved the little one whom you call 'Willis' from—" He used first a Martian term not known to Jim, then changed it to "water-seekers." "Have you killed many such?"

"Uh, quite a few, I guess," Jim answered, then added, "I kill 'em whenever I see 'em. They're getting too smart to hang around the colonies much."

The Martian appeared to be thinking this over, but when he got around to answering he had again changed the subject. "Jim Marlowe, twice, perhaps three times, you have saved the little one; once, perhaps twice, our little one has saved you. Each time you have grown closer together. Day by day you have grown together until neither one of you is complete without the other. Do not leave here, Jim Marlowe. Stay. You are welcome in my house, a son and a friend." He had said "daughter" first, instead of "son," then corrected it without any comic effect nor loss of emphasis.

Jim shook his head. "I have to go home. In fact I have to go home right away. It's a mighty kind offer and I want to thank you but—" He explained as clearly as he could the threat to the welfare of the colony and the urgent need for him to carry the message. "If you please, sir, we—my friend and I—would like to be taken back where K'boomch found us. Only I want Willis back before we go."

"You wish to go back to the city where you were found? You do not wish to go home?"

Jim explained that Frank and he would go home from there. "Now, sir, why don't you ask Willis whether or not he wants to stay or to go home with me?"

The old Martian sighed exactly as Jim's father had been known to sigh after a fruitless family discussion. "There is a law of life and a law of death and both are the law of change. Even the hardest rock is worn away by the wind. You understand, my son and friend, that even if the one you call Willis returns with you, there will come a time when the little one *must* leave you?"

"Uh, yes, I guess so. You mean Willis can come home with me?"

"We will speak to the one you call Willis."

The old one spoke to Gekko, who stirred and muttered in his sleep. Then the three of them wound back up the ramps, with Gekko carrying Jim and the old one following a little behind.

They stopped in a chamber about halfway up to the surface. The room was dark when they reached it but it became illuminated as soon as the party entered. Jim saw that the place was lined, floor to ceiling, with little niches and each niche contained a bouncer, as similar, each to the other, as identical twins.

The little fellows raised their eye stalks when the light came on and peered interestedly around. From somewhere in the room came a shout of "Hi, Jim boy!"

Jim looked around but could not pick out the bouncer that had spoken. Before he could do anything about it the phrase had echoed around the room, "Hi, Jim boy! Hi, Jim boy! Hi, Jim boy!" each time in Jim's own voice, as borrowed by Willis.

Jim turned back to Gekko in bewilderment. "Which one is Willis?" he demanded, forgetting to speak in the dominant tongue.

The chorus started up again, "Which one is Willis? Which one is Willis? Which—Which—Which one is Willis?"

Jim stepped out into the middle of the room. "Willis!" he commanded, "come to Jim."

Off to his right a bouncer popped out from a middle tier, landed on the floor, and waddled up to him. "Pick up Willis," it demanded. Gratefully, Jim did so.

"Where Jim boy been?" Willis wanted to know.

Jim scratched the bouncer. "You wouldn't understand if I told you. Look, Willis—Jim is about to go home. Does Willis want to go home with him?"

"Jim go?" Willis said doubtfully, as if the unrelenting echoing chorus had made it hard for him to understand.

"Jim go home, right away. Is Willis coming or is Willis going to stay here?"

"Jim go; Willis go," the bouncer announced, stating it as a law of nature.

"Okay, tell Gekko that."

"Why?" Willis asked suspiciously.

"Tell Gekko that, or you'll get left behind. Go on, tell him."

"Okay." Willis addressed Gekko in a series of clucks and croaks. Neither the old Martian nor Gekko made any comment; Gekko picked up the two smaller creatures and the procession continued on up toward the surface. Gekko put them down outside the room assigned to Frank and Jim. Jim carried Willis inside.

Frank looked up as they came in. He was sprawled on the silks and, arranged beside him on the floor, was a meal, as yet untouched. "Well, I see you found him," he commented. "It sure took you long enough."

Jim was suddenly overcome with remorse. He had been gone goodness knows how long. Days? Weeks? That moving picture thing had covered months, in detail. "Gee, Frank, I'm sorry," he apologized. "Were you worried about me?"

"Worried? What for? I just didn't know whether or not to wait lunch on you. You must have been gone at least three hours."

Three hours? Jim started to object that it had been more like three weeks, then thought better of it. He recalled that he had not eaten while away, nor did he feel anything more than normally hungry.

"Uh—Yeah, sure. Sorry. Look, do you mind waiting lunch a bit longer?"

"Why? I'm starved."

"Because we're leaving, that's why. Gekko and another native are waiting to take us back to that town where K'boomch found us."

"Well—Okay!" Frank stuffed his mouth full and started to pull on his outdoors suit.

Jim imitated him, both as to eating and dressing. "We can finish lunch in the subway dingus," he said, mumbling with his mouth full. "Don't forget to fill your mask reservoir."

"Don't worry. I won't pull that stunt twice." Frank filled his tank and Jim's, took a big drink of water, and offered the rest to Jim. Moments later they slung their skates over their shoulders and were ready to leave. The party filed through ramps and corridors to the "subway station" hall and stopped at one of the archways.

The old Martian went inside, but, somewhat to Jim's surprise, Gekko bade them good-bye. They parted with ritualistic exchange of courtesies appropriate to water friends, then Frank and Jim, with Willis, went inside and the door closed behind them.

The car started up at once. Frank said, "Wups! What is this?" and sat down suddenly. The old Martian, secure on the resting frame, said nothing. Jim laughed.

"Don't you remember the last ride?"

"Not very well. Say, I feel heavy."

"So do I. That's part of the ride. Now how about a bite to eat? It may be a long time before we get another decent meal."

"You ain't whistlin'." Frank got out the remainder of their lunch. When they had finished Frank thought about it and opened another can. Before they had had a chance to eat its contents—cold baked beans and surrogate pork—his stomach suddenly did a flip-flop. "Hey!" he yelped. "What's happened?"

"Nothing. It was like that last time."

"I thought we had plowed into something."

"Nope, it's all right, I tell you. Hand me over some of those beans." They ate the beans and waited; after a time the feeling of extra weight left them and Jim knew that they had arrived.

The door of the car compartment opened and they stepped out into a circular hall exactly like the one they had left. Frank looked around in disappointment. "Say, Jim—we haven't gone anyplace. There's some mistake."

"No, there's not." He turned, intending to speak to the old Martian, but the archway door behind them was already closed. "Oh, that's too bad," he said.

"What's too bad? That they gave us a run-around?"

"They didn't give us a run-around; it's just that this room looks like the one back in Cynia. You'll see when we get up to the surface. No, I was saying 'too bad' because I let—" Jim hesitated, realizing that he had never gotten the old Martian's name. "—because I let the old fellow, not Gekko, the other one, get away without saying good-bye."

"Who?"

"You know, the other one. The one that rode with us."

"What do you mean, the other one? I didn't see anybody but Gekko. And nobody rode with us; we were in there by ourselves."

"Huh? You must be blind."

"You must be nuts."

"Frank Sutton, do you mean to stand there and tell me you didn't see the Martian that rode with us?"

"You heard me the first time."

Jim took a deep breath. "Well, all I've got to say is: if you hadn't had your face buried in your food the whole time and had looked around you occasionally, you'd see more. How in—"

"Forget it, forget it," Frank interrupted, "before you get me sore. There were six Martians, if you like it that way. Let's get on up and outside and see what the score is. We're wasting time."

"Well, all right." They started up the ramps. Jim was very silent; the incident bothered him more than it did Frank.

Partway up they were forced to adjust their masks. Ten minutes or so thereafter they reached a room into which the sunlight came flooding; they hurried through it and outdoors.

A moment later it was Frank's turn to be puzzled and uncertain. "Jim, I know I was light-headed at the time but wasn't, uh— wasn't that town we started from just a one-tower burg?"

"It was."

"This one isn't."

"No, it isn't."

"We're lost."

"That's right."

9.
POLITICS

They were in a large enclosed courtyard, such as characterizes many Martian buildings. They could make out the tops of the towers of the city, or some of them, but their view was much restricted.

"What do you think we ought to do?" asked Frank.

"Mmm . . . try to find a native and see if we can find out where we've landed. I wish I hadn't let the old fellow get away from us," Jim added. "He spoke Basic."

"You still harping on that?" said Frank. "Anyway I don't think our chances are good; this place looks utterly deserted. You know what I think? I think they've just dumped us."

" 'I think they've just dumped us,' " agreed Willis.

"Shut up. They wouldn't do that," Jim went on to Frank in worried tones. He moved around and stared over the roof of the building. "Say, Frank—"

"Yeah?"

"You see those three little towers, just alike? You can just make out their tips."

"Yeah? What about them?"

"I think I've seen them before."

"Say, I think I have, too!"

They began to run. Five minutes later they were standing on the city wall and there was no longer any doubt about it; they were in the deserted part of Charax. Below them and about three miles away were the bubble domes of South Colony.

Forty minutes of brisk walking, varied with dog-trotting, got them home.

* * *

They split up and went directly to their respective homes. "See you later!" Jim called to Frank and hurried away to his father's house. It seemed to take forever for the pressure lock to let him through. Before the pressure had equalized he could hear his mother, echoed by his sister, inquiring via the announcing speaker as to who was at the door, please?—he decided not to answer but to surprise them.

Then he was inside, facing Phyllis whose face was frozen in amazement—only to throw herself around his neck while shouting, "Mother! Mother! Mother! It's Jim! It's Jim!" and Willis was bouncing around the floor and chorusing "It's Jim! It's Jim!" and his mother was crowding Phyl aside and hugging him and getting his face wet with her tears and Jim himself wasn't feeling any too steady.

He managed to push them away presently. His mother stood back a little and said, "Just let me look at you, darling. Oh, my poor baby! Are you all right?" She was ready to weep again.

"Sure, I'm all right," Jim protested. "Why shouldn't I be? Say, is Dad home?"

Mrs. Marlowe looked suddenly apprehensive. "No, Jim, he's at work."

"I've got to see him right away. Say, Mom, what are you looking funny about?"

"Why, because—Uh, nothing. I'll call your father right away." She went to the phone and called the ecological laboratory. He could hear her guarded tones: "Mr. Marlowe? Dear, this is Jane. Could you come home right away?" and his father's reply, "It wouldn't be convenient. What's up? You sound strange."

His mother glanced over her shoulder at Jim. "Are you alone? Can I be overheard?" His father answered, "What's the matter? Tell me." His mother replied, almost in a whisper, "He's home."

There was a short silence. His father answered, "I'll be there right away."

In the meantime Phyllis was grilling Jim. "Say, Jimmy, what in the world have you been doing?"

Jim started to answer, thought better of it. "Kid, you wouldn't believe me if I told you."

"I don't doubt that. But what *have* you been doing? You've sure got folks in a stew."

"Never mind. Say, what day is it?"

"Saturday."

"Saturday the what?"

"Saturday the fourteenth of Ceres, of course."

Jim was startled. Four days? Only four days since he had left Syrtis Minor? Then as he reviewed it in his mind, he accepted it. Granting Frank's assertion that the time he had spent down under Cynia was only three hours or so, the rest added up. "Gee! I guess I'm in time then."

"What do you mean, 'in time'?"

"Huh? Oh, you wouldn't understand it. Wait a few years."

"Smarty!"

Mrs. Marlowe came away from the phone. "Your father will be right home, Jim."

"So I heard. Good."

She looked at him. "Are you hungry? Is there anything you would like?"

"Sure, fatted calf and champagne. I'm not really hungry, but I could stand something. How about some cocoa? I've been living on cold stuff out of cans for days."

"Cocoa there shall be."

"Better eat what you can now," put in Phyllis. "Maybe you won't get what you want to eat when—"

"Phyllis!"

"But, Mother, I was just going to say that—"

"Phyllis—keep quiet or leave the room."

Jim's sister subsided with muttering. Shortly the cocoa was ready and while Jim was drinking it his father came in. His father shook hands with him soberly as if he were a grown man. "It's good to see you home, Son."

"It feels mighty good to be home, Dad." Jim gulped the rest of the cocoa. "But look, Dad, I've got a lot to tell you and there isn't any time to waste. Where's Willis?" He looked around. "Anybody see where he went?"

"Never mind Willis. I want to know—"

"But Willis is essential to this, Dad. Oh, Willis! Come here!" Willis came waddling out of the passageway; Jim picked him up.

"All right; you've got Willis," Mr. Marlowe said. "Now pay attention. What is this mess you are in, son?"

Jim frowned. "It's a little hard to know where to start."

"There's a warrant out for you and Frank!" blurted out Phyllis.

Mr. Marlowe said, "Jane, will you please try to keep your daughter quiet?"

"Phyllis, you heard what I said before!"

"Aw, Mother, everybody knows it!"

"Possibly Jim did not know it."

Jim said, "Oh, I guess I did. They had cops chasing us all the way home."

"Frank came with you?" asked his father.

"Oh, sure! But we gave 'em the slip. Those Company cops are stupid."

Mr. Marlowe frowned. "See here, Jim—I'm going to call up the Resident and tell him you are here. But I'm not going to let you surrender until something a lot more definite is shown to me than I have seen so far, and certainly not until we've had your side of the matter. When you do surrender, Dad will go along with you and stick by you."

Jim sat up straight. "Surrender? What are you talking about, Dad?"

His father suddenly looked very old and tired. "Marlowes don't run away from the law, Son. You know I'll stick by you no matter what you've done. But you've got to face up to it."

Jim looked at his father defiantly. "Dad, if you think Frank and I have beaten our way across better than two thousand miles of Mars just to give up when we get here—well, you've just got another think coming. And anybody that tries to arrest me is going to find it a hard job." His right hand, almost instinctively, was hovering around the place where his holster ordinarily hung. Phyllis was listening round-eyed; his mother was quietly dripping tears.

His father said, "Son, you can't take that attitude."

Jim said, "Can't I? Well, I do. Why don't you find out what the score is before you talk about giving me up?" His voice was a bit shrill.

His father bit his lip. His mother said, "Please, James—why don't you wait and hear what he has to say?"

"Of course I want to hear what he has to say," Mr. Marlowe answered irritably. "Didn't I say that? But I can't let my own son sit there and declare himself an outlaw."

"Please, James!"

"Speak your piece, Son."

Jim looked around. "I don't know as I'm so anxious to, now," he said bitterly. "This is a fine homecoming. You all act like I was a criminal or something."

"I'm sorry, Jim," his father said slowly. "Let's keep first things first. Tell us what happened."

"Well . . . all right. But wait a minute—Phyllis said there was a warrant out for me. For what?"

"Well . . . truancy—but that's not important. Actions to the prejudice of good order and discipline at the school and I myself don't know what they mean by that. It doesn't worry me. But the real charges are burglary and theft—and another one they tacked on a day later, escaping arrest."

"Escaping arrest? That's silly! They never caught us."

"So? How about the others?"

"Theft is silly, too. I didn't steal anything from *him*—Howe, I mean, Headmaster Howe—he stole Willis from *me*. And then he laughed at me when I tried to get him back! I'll 'theft' him!" If he ever shows up around me, I'll burn him down!"

"Jim!"

"Well, I will!"

"Go on with your story."

"The burglary business has got something to it. I busted in to his office, or tried to. But he can't prove anything. I'd like to see him show how I could crawl through a ten-inch round hole. And we didn't leave any fingerprints." He added, "Anyhow, I had a right to. He had Willis locked up inside. Say, Dad, can't we swear out a warrant against Howe for stealing Willis? Why should he have it all his own way?"

"Wait a minute, now. You've got me confused. If you have a cause for action against the headmaster, I'll certainly back you up in it. But I want to get things straight. What hole? Did you cut a hole in the headmaster's door?"

"No, Willis did."

"Willis! How can he cut anything?"

"Darned if I know. He just grew an arm with a sort of a claw on the end and cut his way out. I called to him and out he came."

Mr. Marlowe rubbed his forehead. "This gets more confusing all the time. How did you boys get here?"

"By subway. You see—"

"By subway!"

Jim looked thwarted. His mother put in, "James dear, I think perhaps he could tell his story better if we just let him tell it straight through, without interrupting."

"I think you are right," Mr. Marlowe agreed. "I'll reserve my questions. Phyllis, get me a pad and pencil."

Thus facilitated, Jim started over and told a reasonably consecutive and complete story, from Howe's announcement of military-school inspections to their translation via Martian "subway" from Cynia to Charax. When Jim had done, Mr. Marlowe pulled his chin. "Jim, if you didn't have a life-time reputation for stubborn honesty, I'd think you were romancing. As it is, I have to believe it, but it is the most fantastic thing I ever heard."

"You still think I ought to surrender?"

"Eh? No, no—this puts it in a different light. You leave it up to Dad. I'll call the Resident and—"

"Just a second, Dad."

"Eh?"

"I didn't tell you all of it."

"What? You must, Son, if I am to—"

"I didn't want to get my story fouled up with another issue entirely. I'll tell you, but I want to know something. Isn't the colony supposed to be on its way by now?"

"It was supposed to have been," agreed his father. "Migration would have started yesterday by the original schedule. But there has been a two-week postponement."

"That's not a postponement, Dad; that's a frame-up. The Company isn't going to allow the colony to migrate this year. They mean to make us stay here all through the winter."

"What? Why, that's ridiculous, Son; a polar winter is no place for terrestrials. But you are mistaken, it's just a postponement; the Company is revamping the power system at North Colony and is taking advantage of an unusually late winter to finish it before we get there."

"I'm telling you, Dad, that's just a stall. The plan is to keep the colony here until it's too late and force you to stay here through the winter. I can prove it."

"How?"

"Where's Willis?" The bouncer had wandered off again, checking up on his domain.

"Never mind Willis. You've made an unbelievable charge. What makes you think such a thing?"

"But I've got to have Willis to prove it. Here, boy! Come to Jim." Jim gave a rapid summary of what he had learned through Willis's phonographic hearing, following which he tried to get Willis to perform.

Willis was glad to perform. He ran over almost all of the boys' conversation of the past few days, repeated a great amount of

Martian speech that was incomprehensible out of context, and sang *¿Quién Es La Señorita?* But he could not, or would not, recall Beecher's conversation.

Jim was still coaxing him when the phone sounded. Mr. Marlowe said, "Phyllis, answer that."

She trotted back in a moment. "It's for you, Daddy."

Jim shut Willis up; they could hear both ends of the conversation. "Marlowe? This is the Resident Agent. I hear that boy of yours has turned up."

Jim's father glanced over his shoulder, hesitated. "Yes. He's here."

"Well, keep him there. I'm sending a man over to pick him up."

Mr. Marlowe hesitated again. "That's not necessary, Mr. Kruger. I'm not through talking with him. He won't go away."

"Come, come, Marlowe—you can't interfere with orderly legal processes. I'm executing that warrant at once."

"You are? You just think you are." Mr. Marlowe started to add something, thought better of it, and switched off. The phone sounded again almost at once. "If that's the Resident," he said, "I won't speak to him. If I do, I'll say something I'll regret."

But it was not; it was Frank's father. "Marlowe? Jamie, this is Pat Sutton." The conversation showed that each father had gotten about to the same point with his son.

"We were just about to try to get something out of Jim's bouncer," Mr. Marlowe added. "It seems he overheard a pretty damning conversation."

"Yes, I know," agreed Mr. Sutton. "I want to hear it, too. Hold it till we get there."

"Fine. Oh, by the way—friend Kruger is out to arrest the kids right away. Watch out."

"How well I know it; he just called me. And I put a flea in his ear. 'Bye now!"

Mr. Marlowe switched off, then went to the front door and locked it. He did the same to the door of the tunnels. He was none too soon; the signal showing that someone had entered the pressure lock came on shortly. "Who is it?" called out Jim's father.

"Company business!"

"What sort of Company business and who is it?"

"This is the Resident's proctor. I've come for James Marlowe, Junior."

"You might as well go away again. You won't get him." There

was a whispered exchange outside the door, then the lock was rattled.

"Open up that door," came another voice. "We have a warrant."

"Go away. I'm switching off the speaker." Mr. Marlowe did so.

The pressure lock indicator showed presently that the visitors had left, but shortly it indicated occupancy again. Mr. Marlowe switched the speaker back on. "If you've come back, you might as well leave," he said.

"What sort of a welcome is this, Jamie my boy?" came Mr. Sutton's voice.

"Oh, Pat! Are you alone?"

"Only my boy Francis and that's all."

They were let in. "Did you see anything of proctors?" Mr. Marlowe inquired.

"Yep, I ran into 'em."

"Pop told them that if they touched me he'd burn their legs off," Frank said proudly, "and he would, too."

Jim caught his father's eye. Mr. Marlowe looked away. Mr. Sutton went on, "Now what's this about Jim's pet having evidence for us? Let's crank him up and hear him talk."

"We've been trying to," Jim said. "I'll try again. Here, Willis—" Jim took him in his lap. "Now, look, Willis, do you remember Headmaster Howe?"

Willis promptly became a featureless ball.

"That's not the way to do it," objected Frank. "You remember what set him off before. Hey, Willis." Willis extended his eyes. "Listen to me, chum. 'Good afternoon. Good afternoon, Mark,' Frank continued in a fair imitation of the Agent General's rich, affected tones. " 'Sit down, my boy.' "

" 'Always happy to see you,' " Willis continued in exact imitation of Beecher's voice. He went on from there, reciting perfectly the two conversations he had overheard between the headmaster and the Resident Agent General, and including the meaningless interlude between them.

When he had finished and seemed disposed to continue with all that had followed up to the present moment, Jim shut him off.

"Well," said Jim's father, "what do you think of it, Pat?"

"*I* think it's terrible," put in Jim's mother.

Mr. Sutton screwed up his face. "Tomorrow I am taking myself down to Syrtis Minor and there I shall take the place apart with my two hands."

"An admirable sentiment," agreed Mr. Marlowe, "but this is a matter for the whole colony. I think our first step should be to call a town meeting and let everyone know what we are up against."

"Humph! No doubt you are right but you'll be taking all the fun out of it."

Mr. Marlowe smiled. "I imagine there will be excitement enough to suit you before this is over. Kruger isn't going to like it—and neither is the Honorable Mr. Gaines Beecher."

Mr. Sutton wanted Dr. MacRae to examine Frank's throat and Jim's father decided, over Jim's protest, that it would be a good idea to have him examine Jim as well. The two men escorted the boys to the Doctor's house. There Mr. Marlowe instructed them, "Stay here until we get back, kids. I don't want Kruger's proctors picking you up."

"I'd like to see them try!"

"Me, too."

"I don't want them to try; I want to settle the matter first. We're going over to the Resident's office and offer to pay for the food you kids appropriated and, Jim, I'll offer to pay for the damage Willis did to Headmaster Howe's precious door. Then—"

"But, Dad, we oughn't to pay for that. Howe shouldn't have locked him up."

"I agree with the kid," said Mr. Sutton. "The food, now, that's another matter. The boys took it; we pay for it."

"You're both right," agreed Mr. Marlowe, "but it's worth it to knock the props out of these ridiculous charges. Then I'm going to swear out a warrant against Howe for attempting to steal, or enslave, Willis. What would you say it was, Pat? Steal, or enslave?"

"Call it 'steal'; you'll not be raising side issues, then."

"All right. Then I shall insist that he consult the planet office before taking any action. I think that will stop his clock for the time being."

"Dad," put in Jim, "you aren't going to tell the Resident that we've found out about the migration frame-up, are you? He would just turn around and call Beecher."

"Not just yet, though he's bound to know at the town meeting. He won't be able to call Beecher then; Deimos sets in two hours." Mr. Marlowe glanced at his watch. "See you later, boys. We've got things to do."

Doctor MacRae looked up as they came in. "Maggie, bar the door!" he called out. "We've got two dangerous criminals."

"Howdy, Doc."

"Come in and rest yourselves. Tell me all about it."

It was fully an hour later that MacRae said, "Well, Frank, I suppose I had better look you over. Then I'll have a look at you, Jim."

"There's nothing wrong with me, Doc."

"How would like a clout in the head? Start some more coffee while I take care of Frank." The room was well stocked with the latest diagnostic equipment, but MacRae did not bother with it. He tilted Frank's head back, told him to say *aaaah!*, thumped his chest, and listened to his heart. "You'll live," he decided. "Any kid who can hitchhike from Syrtis to Charax will live a long time."

" 'Hitchhike'?" asked Frank.

"Beat your way. It's an expression that was used way back when women wore skirts. Your turn, Jim." He took even less time to dispose of Jim. Then the three friends settled back to visit.

"I want to know more about this night you spent in the cabbage head," Doc announced. "Willis I can understand, since any Martian creature can tuck his tail in and live indefinitely without air. But by rights you two laddie bucks should have smothered. The plant closed up entirely?"

"Oh, yes," Jim assured him, then related the event in more detail. When he got to the point about the flashlight MacRae stopped him.

"That's it, that's it. You didn't mention that before. The flashlight saved your lives, son."

"Huh? How?"

"Photosynthesis. You shine light on green leaf and it can no more help taking in carbon dioxide and giving off oxygen than you can help breathing." The doctor stared at the ceiling, his lips moving while he figured. "Must have been pretty stuffy, just the same; you were short on green leaf surface. What kind of a torch was it?"

"A G.E. 'Midnight Sun.' It *was* stuffy, terribly."

"A 'Midnight Sun' has enough candle power to do the trick. Hereafter I'll carry one if I'm going further than twenty feet from my front stoop. It's a good dodge."

"Something that still puzzles me," said Jim, "is how I could see a movie that covered every bit of the time I've had Willis, minute by minute, without missing anything, and have it turn out to be only three or four hours."

"That," Doc said slowly, "is not nearly so mysterious as the other matter, the matter of *why* you were shown this."

"Huh?"

"I've wondered about that, too," put in Frank. "After all, Willis is a pretty insignificant creature—take it easy, Jim! What was the point in running over his biography for Jim? What do you think, Doc?"

"The only hypothesis I've got on that point is so wildly fantastic that I'll keep it to myself, thank you. But on the point of time, Jim—can you think of any way to photograph a person's memories?"

"Uh, no."

"I'll go further and state flatly that it is impossible. Yet you described *seeing* what Willis *remembered*. That suggest anything to you?"

"No," admitted Jim, "it's got me stumped. But I *did* see it."

"Sure, you did—because seeing takes place in the brain and not in the eye. I can close my eyes and 'see' the Great Pyramid shimmering in the desert heat. I can see the donkeys and hear the porters yelling at the tourists. See 'em? Shucks, I can smell 'em— but it's just my memory."

Jim looked thoughtful but Frank looked incredulous. "Say, Doc, what are you talking about? You never saw the Great Pyramid; it was blown up in World War III." Frank was, of course, correct as to his historical facts; the eastern allies should never have used the Pyramid of Cheops as a place to stockpile atom bombs.

Doctor MacRae looked annoyed. "Can't you permit a man a figure of speech? You tend to your own business. Now back to what I was saying, Jim. When only one hypothesis covers the facts, you've got to accept it. You saw what the old Martian wanted you to see. Call it hypnosis."

"But—But—" Jim was wildly indignant; it felt like an attack on his very inner being. "But I *did* see it, I tell you. I was there."

"I'll string along with Doc," Frank told him. "You were still seeing things on the trip back."

"How would you like a punch in the nose? The old boy did so make the trip back with us; if you had kept your eyes open, you would have seen him."

"Easy, there," cautioned Doc, "if you lugs want to fight, go outside. Has it occurred to you that both of you might be right?"

"What? How could we be?" objected Frank.

"I don't like to put words to it, but I can tell you this: I've lived long enough to know that man does not live by bread alone and that the cadaver I perform an autopsy on is not the man himself."

The most wildly impossible philosophy of all is materialism. We'll leave it at that."

Frank was about to object again when the lock signalled visitors; the boys' parents were back. "Come in, come in, gentlemen," the doctor roared. "You're just in time. We were having a go at solipsism. Pull up a pulpit and take part. Coffee?"

"Solipsism, is it?" said Mr. Sutton. "Francis, pay no mind to the old heathen. You listen to what Father Cleary tells you."

"He'll pay no mind to me anyhow," MacRae answered. "That's the healthy thing about kids. How did you make out with the Lord High Executioner?"

Mr. Marlowe chuckled. "Kruger was fit to be tied."

The called meeting of the colonists took place that evening in the town hall, central building of the star-shaped group. Mr. Marlowe and Mr. Sutton, having sponsored the meeting, arrived early. They found the meeting-room doors closed and Kruger's two proctors posted outside. Mr. Marlowe ignored the fact that they had been attempting to arrest Frank and Jim only a few hours ago; he offered them a civil good evening and said, "Let's get the place opened up. People will be arriving any minute now."

The proctors did not move. The senior of them, a man named Dumont, announced, "There'll be no meeting tonight."

"What? Why not?"

"Mr. Kruger's orders."

"Did he say why?"

"No."

"This meeting," Mr. Marlowe told him, "has been properly called and will be held. Stand aside."

"Now, Mr. Marlowe, don't make things tough for yourself. I've got my orders and—"

Mr. Sutton crowded forward. "Let me handle him, Jamie." He hitched at his belt. Behind the men, Frank glanced at Jim with a grin and hitched at *his* belt. All four of them were armed, as were the proctors; the two fathers had decided not to depend on Kruger's self-restraint while waiting for instructions from Syrtis Minor about the warrant.

Dumont looked nervously at Sutton. The colony had no real police force; these two were clerks in the Company's office and proctors only by Kruger's deputization. "You people have got no call to be running around armed to the teeth, inside the colony," he complained.

"Oh, so that's it?" Mr. Sutton said sweetly. "Well, this job calls for no gun. Here, Francis—hold my heater." With empty holster he advanced on them. "Now would you like to be tossed out gently or would you prefer to bounce?"

For years before coming to Mars Mr. Sutton had used something other than his engineering degree to dominate tough construction gangs. He was not much bigger than Dumont but immeasurably tougher. Dumont backed into his cohort and stepped on his toes. "Now see here, Mr. Sutton, you've no—Hey! Mr. Kruger!"

They all looked around. The Resident was approaching. He took in the scene and said briskly, "What's this? Sutton, are you interfering with my men?"

"Not a bit of it," denied Mr. Sutton. "They were interfering with me. Tell them to stand aside."

Kruger shook his head. "The meeting is canceled."

Mr. Marlowe stepped forward. "By whom?"

"*I* canceled it."

"By what authority? I have the approval of all councilors and will, if necessary, get you the names of twenty colonists." Twenty colonists could call a meeting without permission from the council, under the colony's rules.

"That's beside the point. The rule reads that meetings are to consider matters 'of public interest'; it cannot be construed as 'of public interest' to agitate about criminal indictments in advance of trial—and I won't let you take advantage of the rules to do so. After all, I have the final word. I do not intend to surrender to mob rule and agitation."

A crowd was forming, colonists come to the meeting. Marlowe said, "Are you through?"

"Yes, except to say that these others and you yourself should return to your quarters."

"They will do as they please—and so will I. Mr. Kruger, I am amazed to hear you say that a civil-rights case is not of public interest. Our neighbors here have boys who are still under the care, if you call it that, of Headmaster Howe; they are interested in how their sons are treated. However, that is not the purpose of the meeting. I give you my word that neither Mr. Sutton nor I intend to ask the colony to take any action about the charges against our sons. Will you accept that and withdraw your proctors?"

"What is the purpose, then?"

"It's a matter of urgent interest to every member of the colony. I'll discuss it inside."

"Hummph!"

By this time several councilors were in the crowd. One of them, Mr. Juan Montez, stepped forward. "Just a minute. Mr. Marlowe, when you called me about this meeting, I had no notion that the Resident objected."

"The Resident has no option in the matter."

"Well, that's never come up before. He does have a veto over actions of meetings. Why don't you tell us what the meeting is for?"

"Don't give in, Jamie!" It was Doctor MacRae; he shouldered forward. "What kind of nincompoop are you, Montez? I'm sorry I voted for you. We meet when it suits us, not when Kruger says we may. How about it, folks?"

There was a murmur of approval. Mr. Marlowe said, "I wasn't going to tell him, Doc. I want everybody here and the doors closed when I talk."

Montez went into a huddle with other councilors. Out of it came Hendrix, the chairman. "Mr. Marlowe, just to keep things regular, will you tell the council why you want this meeting?"

Jim's father shook his head. "You okayed the meeting. Otherwise I would have collected twenty signatures and forced a meeting. Can't you stand up to Kruger?"

"We don't need them, Jamie," MacRae assured him. He turned to the crowd, now growing fast. "Who wants a meeting? Who wants to hear what Marlowe has to tell us?"

"I do!" came a shout.

"Who's that? Oh—Kelly. All right, Kelly and I make two. Are there eighteen more here who don't have to ask Kruger for permission to sneeze? Speak up."

There was another shout and another. "That's three—and four." Seconds later MacRae called off the twentieth; he turned to the Resident. "Get your stooges out of that doorway, Kruger."

Kruger sputtered. Hendrix whispered with him, then motioned the two proctors away. They were only too happy to treat this as a relayed order from Kruger; the crowd poured into the hall.

Kruger took a seat in the rear; ordinarily he sat on the platform.

Jim's father found that none of the councilors cared to preside; he stepped to the platform himself. "Let's elect a chairman," he announced.

"You run it, Jamie," It was Doc MacRae.

"Let's have order, please. Do I hear a nomination?"

"Mr. Chairman—"

"Yes, Mr. Konski?"

"I nominate you."

"Very well. Now let's have some others." But there were none; he kept the gavel by unanimous consent.

Mr. Marlowe told them that news had come to him which vitally affected the colony. He then gave the bald facts about how Willis had come into Howe's hands. Kruger stood up. "Marlowe!"

"Address the chair, please."

"Mr. Chairman," Kruger acceded sourly, "you said this meeting was not to stir up sympathy for your son. You are simply trying to keep him from having to take his medicine. You—"

Mr. Marlowe pounded his gavel. "You're out of order. Sit down."

"I won't sit down. You had the bare-faced gall to—"

"Mr. Kelly, I appoint you sergeant-at-arms. Keep order. Pick your own deputies."

Kruger sat down. Mr. Marlowe went on, "This meeting has nothing to do with the charges against my son and Pat Sutton's boy, but the news I have came through them. You've all seen Martian roundheads—bouncers, the kids call them, and you know their amazing ability to repeat sounds. Probably most of you have heard my son's pet perform. It happened that this particular roundhead was within hearing when some things were discussed that we all need to know about. Jim—bring your pet here."

Jim, feeling self-conscious, mounted the platform and sat Willis on the speaker's table. Willis looked around and promptly battened down all hatches. "Jim," his father whispered urgently, "snap him out of it."

"I'll try," agreed Jim. "Come on, boy. Nobody's going to hurt Willis. Come out; Jim wants to talk to you."

His father said to the audience, "These creatures are timid. Please be very quiet," then, "How about it, Jim?"

"I'm trying."

"Confound it, we should have made a recording."

Willis chose this minute to come out of hiding. "Look, Willis boy," Jim went on, "Jim wants you to talk. Everybody is waiting for Willis to talk. Come on, now. 'Good afternoon. Good afternoon, Mark.'"

Willis picked it up. " 'Sit down, my boy. Always happy to see you.' " He went on, reeling off the words of Howe and Beecher.

Somebody recognized Beecher's voice; there was a muffled exclamation as he passed his knowledge on. Mr. Marlowe made frantic shushing signs.

Presently, as Beecher was expounding by proxy his theory of "legitimate graft," Kruger got up. Kelly placed hands on his shoulders and pushed him down. Kruger started to protest; Kelly placed a hand over Kruger's mouth. He then smiled; it was something he had been wanting to do ever since Kruger had first been assigned to the colony.

The audience got restless between the two significant conversations; Mr. Marlowe promised by pantomime that the best was yet to come. He need not have worried; Willis, once wound up, was as hard to stop as an after-dinner speaker.

There was amazed silence when he had finished, then a murmur that became a growl. It changed to uproar as everyone tried to talk at once. Marlowe pounded for order and Willis closed up. Presently Andrews, a young technician, got the floor.

"Mr. Chairman . . . we know how important this is, *if* it's true—but how reliable is that beastie?"

"Eh? I don't think it's possible for one of them to repeat other than *verbatim*. Is there a psychological expert present who might give us an opinion? How about you, Dr. Ibañez?"

"I agree, Mr. Marlowe. A roundhead can originate speech on its mental level, but a speech such as we just heard is something it has listened to. It repeats parrot-fashion exactly what it has heard. I doubt if such a 'recording,' if I may call it that, may be modified after it has been impressed on the animal's nervous system; it's an involuntary reflex—complicated and beautiful, but reflex nevertheless."

"Does that satisfy you, Andy?"

"Uh, no. Everybody knows that a bouncer is just a superparrot and not smart enough to lie. But is that the Resident General's voice? It sounds like it, but I've only heard him over the radio."

Someone called out, "It's Beecher. I had to listen to his drivel often enough, when I was stationed at Syrtis."

Andrews shook his head. "Sure, it sounds like him, but we've got to *know*. It could be a clever actor."

Kruger had been quiet, in a condition resembling shock. The

revelation had come as a surprise to him, too, as Beecher had not dared trust anyone on the spot. But Kruger's conscience was not easy; there were tell-tale signs in his own despatch file that Willis's report was correct; migration required a number of routine orders from the planet office. He was uncomfortably aware that none of the proper groundwork had been laid if, as was the official claim, migration were to take place in less than two weeks.

But Andrews's comment gave him a straw to clutch. Standing, he said, "I'm glad somebody has sense enough not to be swindled. How long did it take you to teach him that, Marlowe?"

Kelly said, "Shall I gag him, chief?"

"No. This has to be met. I suppose it's a matter of whether or not you believe my boy and his chum. Do any of you wish to question them?"

A long, lean, lanky individual unfolded himself from a rear seat. "I can settle it."

"Eh? Very well, Mr. Toland, you have the floor."

"Got to get some apparatus. Take a few minutes." Toland was an electronic engineer and sound technician.

"Oh—I think I see what you mean. You'll need a comparison model of Beecher's voice, won't you?"

"Sure. But I've got all I need. Every time Beecher made a speech, Kruger wanted it recorded."

Volunteers were found to help Toland, then Marlowe suggested that it was time for a stretch. At once Mrs. Pottle stood up. "Mr. Marlowe!"

"Yes, Mrs. Pottle. Quiet, everybody."

"I for one will not remain here one minute longer and listen to this nonsense! The idea of making such charges against dear Mr. Beecher! To say nothing of what you let that awful man Kelly do to Mr. Kruger! And as for that beast—" She pointed to Willis. "It is utterly unreliable, as I know full well." She paused to snort, then said, "Come, dear," to Mr. Pottle, and started to flounce out.

"Stop her, Kelly!" Mr. Marlowe went on quietly, "I had hoped that no one would try to leave until we reached a decision. If the colony decides to act it may be to our advantage to keep it as a surprise. Will the meeting authorize me to take steps to see that no scooter leaves the colony until you have made up your minds about the issue?"

There was just one "no," from Mrs. Pottle. "Conscript some help, Mr. Kelly," Marlowe ordered, "and carry out the will of the meeting."

"Right, chief!"

"You can go now, Mrs. Pottle. Not you, Mr. Kruger." Mr. Pottle hesitated in bewilderment, then trotted after his wife.

Toland returned and set up his apparatus on the platform. With Jim's help, Willis was persuaded to perform again, this time into a recorder. Shortly Toland held up his hand. "That's enough. Let me find some matching words." He selected "colony," "company," "afternoon," and "Martian" because they were easy to find in each recording, Willis's and an identified radio speech of the Resident General. Each he checked with care, throwing complex standing waves on the bright screen of an oscilloscope, waves that earmarked the peculiar timbre of an individual's voice as certainly as a fingerprint would identify his body.

At last he stood up. "It's Beecher's voice," he said flatly.

Jim's father again had to pound for order. When he had got it, he said, "Very well—what is your pleasure?"

Someone shouted, "Let's lynch Beecher." The chairman suggested that they stick to practical objectives.

Someone else called out, "What's Kruger got to say about it?"

Marlowe turned to Kruger. "Mr. Resident Agent, you speak for the Company. What about it?"

Kruger wet his lips. "If one assumes that that beast is actually reporting statements of the Agent General—"

"Quit stalling!"

"Toland proved it!"

Kruger's eyes darted around; he was faced with a decision impossible for a man of his temperament. "Well, it's really no business of mine," he said angrily. "I'm about to be transferred."

MacRae got up. "Mr. Kruger, you are custodian of our welfare. You mean to say you won't stand up for our rights?"

"Well, now, Doctor, I work for the Company. If this is its policy—and I'm not admitting it—you can't expect me to go against it."

"I work for the Company, too," the Doctor growled, "but I didn't sell myself to it, body and soul." His eyes swept the crowd. "How about it, folks? Shall we throw him out on his ear?"

Marlowe had to bang for order. "Sit down, Doctor. We haven't time to waste on trivia."

"Mr. Chairman—"

"Yes, Mrs. Palmer?"

"What do you think we ought to do?"

"I would rather that suggestions came from the floor."

"Oh, nonsense—you've known about it longer than we have; you must have an opinion. Speak up."

Marlowe saw that her wish was popular. "Very well, I speak for myself and Mr. Sutton. By contract we are entitled to migrate and the Company is obligated to let us. I say go ahead and do so, at once."

"I so move!"

"I second!"

"Question!"—"Question!"

"Is there debate?" asked Marlowe.

"Just a moment, Mr. Chairman—" The speaker was one Humphrey Gibbs, a small precise individual. "—we are acting hastily and, if I may say so, not in proper procedure. We have not exhausted our possible reliefs. We should communicate with Mr. Beecher. It may be that there are good reasons for this change in policy—"

"How are *you* going to like a hundred below!"

"Mr. Chairman, I really must insist on order."

"Let him have his say," Marlowe ordered.

"As I was saying, there may be good reasons, but the Company board back on Earth is perhaps not fully aware of conditions here. If Mr. Beecher is unable to grant us relief, then we should communicate with the board, reason with them. But we should not take the law into our own hands. If worst comes to worst, we have a contract; if forced to do so, we can always sue." He sat down.

MacRae got up again. "Anybody mind if I talk? I don't want to hog the proceedings." Silence gave approval; he went on, "So this pantywaist wants to sue! With the temperature outside a hundred and thirty below by the time he has 'exhausted his means'—and us!—and with the rime frost a foot deep on the ground he wants it put on some judge's calendar, back on Earth, and hire a lawyer!

"If you want a contract enforced, you have to enforce it yourself. You know what lies behind this; it showed up last season when the Company cut down on the household allowance and started charging excess baggage. I warned you then—but the board was a hundred million miles away and you paid rather than fight. The Company hates the expense of moving us, but more important they are bloody anxious to move more immigrants in here faster than we can take them; they think they see a cheap way out by keeping both North Colony and South Colony filled up all the time, instead of building more buildings. As Sister Gibbs put it, they don't realize the conditions here and they don't know that we can't do effective work in the winter.

"The question is not whether or not we can last out a polar winter; the Eskimo caretakers do that every season. It isn't just a matter of contract; it's a matter of whether we are going to be free men, or are we going to let our decisions be made for us on another planet, by men who have never set foot on Mars!

"Just a minute—let me finish! We are the advance guard. When the atmosphere project is finished, millions of others will follow. Are they going to be ruled by a board of absentee owners on Terra? Is Mars to remain a colony of Earth? Now is the time to settle it!"

There was dead silence, then scattered applause. Marlowe said, "Is there more debate?"

Mr. Sutton got up. "Doc has something there. It was never in my blood to love absentee landlords."

Kelly called out, "Right you are, Pat!"

Jim's father said, "I rule that subject out of order. The question before the house is to migrate, at once, and nothing else. Are you ready for the question?"

They were—and it was carried unanimously. If any refrained from voting, at least they did not vote against. That matter settled, by another ballot they set up an emergency committee, the chairman to hold power subject to review by the committee, and the committee's decisions to be subject to review by the colony.

James Marlowe, Senior, was elected chairman. Dr. MacRae's name was proposed but he refused to let it be considered. Mr. Marlowe got even with him by sticking him on the committee.

South Colony held at the time five hundred and nine persons, from the youngest baby to old Doc MacRae. There were eleven scooters on hand; enough but barely enough to move everyone at one time, provided they were stacked almost like freight and each person was limited to a few pounds only of hand baggage. A routine migration was usually made in three or more sections, with extra scooters provided from Syrtis Minor.

Jim's father decided to move everyone at once and hope that events would permit sending back for personal possessions. The squawks were many, but he stood by his guns, the committee ratified and no one tried to call a town meeting. He set dawn Monday as the zero hour.

Kruger was allowed to keep his office; Marlowe preferred to

run the show from his own. But Kelly, who remained a sort of *de facto* chief of police, was instructed to keep a constant watch over him. Kelly called Marlowe Sunday afternoon. "Hey, chief, what do you know? A couple of Company cops just arrived by scooter to take your boy and the Sutton kid back to Syrtis."

Marlowe considered it. Kruger must have phoned Beecher the moment he heard that the boys were home, he decided. "Where are they now?"

"Right here, in Kruger's office. *We* arrested *them*."

"Bring them over. I'd like to question them."

"Right."

They showed up shortly, two very disgruntled men, disarmed and escorted by Kelly and an assistant. "That's fine, Mr. Kelly. No, no need to stay—I'm armed."

When Kelly and his deputy had left, one of the Company men said, "You can't get away with this, you know."

"You're not hurt," Marlowe said reasonably, "and you'll get your guns back presently. I just want to ask you some questions." But all he had gotten out of them, several minutes later, was a series of begrudged negative answers. The intracolony phone sounded again; Kelly's face appeared on the screen. "Chief? You wouldn't believe it—"

"Wouldn't believe what?"

"That old fox Kruger has skipped in the scooter those two birds came in on. I didn't even know he could drive."

Marlowe's calm face concealed his feelings. After a short time he answered, "Departure time is stepped up to sundown, today. Drop everything and get the word around." He consulted a chart. "That's two hours and ten minutes from now."

The squawks were louder even than before; nevertheless as the Sun touched the horizon, the first scooter got underway. The rest followed at thirty second intervals. As the Sun disappeared the last one shoved off and the colony was headed north on its seasonal migration.

10.
"WE'RE BOXED IN!"

Four of the scooters were older types and slower, less than two hundred miles per hour top speed. They were placed in the van as pacesetters. Around midnight one of them developed engine trouble; the column had to slow down. About 3 a.m. it quit completely; it was necessary to stop and distribute its passengers among the other scooters—a cold and risky business.

MacRae and Marlowe climbed back into the headquarters car, last in the column. The doctor glanced at his watch. "Planning to stop in Hesperidum now, Skipper?" he asked as the scooter started up. They had passed Cynia station without stopping; Hesperidum lay a short distance ahead, with Syrtis Minor some seven hundred miles beyond it.

Marlowe frowned. "I don't want to. If we lay over at Hesperidum, that means waiting until sundown for ice and a full day's loss of time. With Kruger ahead of us that gives Beecher a whole day in which to figure out a way to stop us. If I were sure the ice would hold after sunrise long enough for us to get there—" He stopped and chewed his lip.

Back at South Colony it was early winter and the canal ice would remain hard until spring, but here they were already close to the equator; the canals froze every night and thawed every day under the extreme daily changes in temperature permitted by Mars' thin blanket of air. North of the equator, where they were headed, the spring floods from the melting northern polar cap had already started; ice formed in the flooding canal currents at night, but it was floe ice, riding with the current, and night clouds helped to save the daytime heat.

"Suppose you do go on through, what's your plan, Skipper?" MacRae persisted.

"Go straight to the boat basin, ramp the scooters, and load whatever boats are there. As soon as the ice is rotten enough for the boats to break through it, start them north. I'd like to have a hundred and fifty or so of us out of Syrtis Minor and headed north before Beecher recovers from his surprise. I haven't any real plan except to keep forcing events so that *he* doesn't have time to plan, either. I want to hand him a set of accomplished facts."

MacRae nodded. "Audacity, that's the ticket. Go ahead with it."

"I want to, but I'm afraid of the ice. If a scooter breaks through there'll be people killed—and my fault."

"Your drivers are smart enough to spread out in echelon once the Sun is up. Jamie, I found out a long time ago that you have to take some chances in this life. Otherwise you are just a vegetable, headed for the soup pot." He paused and peered out past the driver. "I see a light ahead that ought to be Hesperidum. Make up your mind, Jamie."

Marlowe did not answer. After a time the light was behind them.

When the Sun came up Marlowe had his driver cut out of column and take the lead. It was near nine when they passed Syrtis Minor scooter station, without stopping. They ploughed on past the space port and turned right into the boat basin that marked the terminus of the main canal from the north. Marlowe's driver drove onto the ramp while he was still lowering his crawling gear, with no respect for his runners. The lead car crawled far along the ramp and parked; the others closed in behind it.

Out of the headquarters car climbed Marlowe, Kelly, and MacRae, followed by Jim, carrying Willis. Other scooter doors opened and people started getting out. "Tell them to get back into their cars, Kelly," Mr. Marlowe snapped. Hearing this, Jim placed himself behind his father and tried to avoid attracting attention.

Marlowe stared angrily at the basin. There was not a boat in it. Across the basin one small launch was drawn up on skids, its engine dismounted. Finally Marlowe turned to MacRae. "Well, Doc, I'm up a tree; how do I get down?"

"You are no worse off than if you had stopped at Hesperidum."

"And no better."

A man came out of one of the row of warehouses ringing the basin and approached them. "What's all this?" he inquired, staring at the parked scooters. "A circus?"

"It's the seasonal migration."

"Wondered when you folks were coming through. Hadn't heard anything about it."

"Where are all the boats?"

"Still spread out here and there, at the Project camps mostly, I suppose. Not my responsibility. Better call the traffic office."

Marlowe frowned again. "At least you can tell me where the temporary quarters are." To take care of the relays of colonists a warehouse was always set aside at each migration and fitted up as a barracks; the one Company hostelry, Hotel Marsopolis, had only twenty beds.

The man looked puzzled. "Now that you mention it, I don't know of any such preparations being made. Looks like the schedule was kind of fouled up, doesn't it?"

Marlowe swore, realizing his question had been foolish. Beecher, of course, had made no preparations for a migration he did not intend to permit. "Is there a phone around here?"

"Inside, in my office—I'm the warehouse storekeeper. Help yourself."

"Thanks," said Marlowe and started off. MacRae followed him.

"What's your plan, son?"

"I'm going to call Beecher."

"Do you think that's wise?"

"Confound it, I've got to get those people out of those cars. There are young babies in there—and women."

"They're safe."

"Look, Doc, Beecher has got to do *something* about it, now that we're here."

MacRae shrugged. "You're the cook."

Marlowe argued his way past several secretaries and finally got Beecher on the screen. The Agent General looked out at him without recognition. "Yes? Speak up, my good man, what is this urgent business?"

"My name is Marlowe. I'm executive chairman of the colonists from South Colony. I want to know—"

"Oh, yes! The famous Mr. Marlowe. We saw your tattered army coming through." Beecher turned away and said something in an aside. Kruger's voice answered him.

"Well, now that we are here, what are you going to do about us?"

"Do? Isn't that obvious? As soon as the ice forms tonight you can all turn around and go back where you came from. All except you—you stay here for trial. And your son, if I recall correctly."

Marlowe held his temper. "That isn't what I mean. I want living space, with cooking and toilet accommodations, for five hundred people."

Beecher waved the problem away. "Let them stay where they are. A day won't hurt them. Teach them a lesson."

Marlowe started to answer, thought better of it and switched off. "You were right, Doc. There was no point in talking with him."

"Well—no harm done, either."

They went outside, there to find that Kelly had strung a line of his deputies around the scooters. "After you went inside, Boss, I got uneasy, so I stationed some of the boys around."

"You're a better general than I am," Marlowe told him. "Any trouble?"

"One of Beecher's cops showed up, but he went away again."

"Why didn't you grab him?" asked MacRae.

"Well, I wanted to," Kelly answered, "but he kept going when I yelled at him. I couldn't stop him without shooting, so I let him go."

"Should have winged him," said MacRae.

"Should I have?" Kelly said to Marlowe. "I was tempted to, but I didn't know where we stood. Is this a shooting war, or is it just a row with the Company?"

"You did right," Marlowe assured him. "There will be no shooting unless Beecher starts it." MacRae snorted. Marlowe turned to him. "You disagree?"

"Jamie, you put me in mind of a case I ran into in the American West. A respected citizen shot a professional gun-thrower in the back. When asked why he didn't give the other chap a chance to draw, the survivor said, 'Well, he's dead and I'm alive and that's how I wanted it to be.' Jamie, if you use sportsmanship on a known scamp, you put yourself at a terrible disadvantage."

"Doctor, this is no time to swap stories. I've got to get these people safely housed and at once."

"That's my point," persisted MacRae. "Finding housing isn't the first thing to do."

"What is is, then?"

"Set up a task force of your best shots and send them over to grab Beecher and the Company offices. I volunteer to lead it."

Marlowe gestured angrily. "Out of the question. At present we are a group of citizens going about our lawful occasions. One move like that and we're outlaws."

MacRae shook his head. "You don't see the logic of the actions you've already taken. You know that water runs downhill, but you think—praise God!—it'll never reach the bottom. In Beecher's books you are an outlaw now. All of us."

"Nonsense, we're just enforcing our contract. If Beecher behaves, we'll behave."

"I'm telling you, son—the way to grasp a nettle is firmly."

"Doctor MacRae, if you are so sure how this matter should be conducted, why did you refuse to accept leadership?"

MacRae turned red. "I beg your pardon, sir. What are your orders?"

"You know Syrtis better than I do. Where is a building we can commandeer as a barracks?"

Jim decided that this was a good time to come out of hiding. "Dad," he said, coming around in front of him, "I know where we are and the school is—"

"Jim, I've no time to chat. Get in the car."

"But, Dad, it's only about ten minutes' walk!"

"I think he's got something," put in the doctor. "The school will have real beds for the kids, and a kitchen."

"Hmmm . . . very well. Possibly we should use both schools and put the women and small children in the girls' school."

"Jamie," advised the doctor, "at the risk of getting my ears batted down again, I say 'no.' Don't divide your forces."

"I didn't really want to. Kelly!"

"Yes, sir."

"Get them all out and put a deputy in charge of each car party to keep them together. We're moving out."

"Right."

There is very little foot traffic in the streets of the Earth settlement at Syrtis Minor; pedestrians prefer to go by tunnel. The few they did meet seemed startled but no one bothered them.

The pressure lock at the school's front door could hold about twenty people at a time. As the outer door opened after the second load, Howe stepped out. Even with his mask on it could be seen that he was angry. "What is the meaning of this?" he demanded.

Willis took one look at him and closed up. Jim got behind his father. Marlowe stepped forward. "We're sorry but we've got to use the school as an emergency shelter."

"You can't do that. Who are you, anyway?"

"My name is Marlowe. I'm in charge of the migration."

"But—" Howe turned suddenly, pushed his way through the crowd and went inside.

Nearly thirty minutes later Marlowe, MacRae, and Kelly went inside with the last party. Marlowe directed Kelly to station guards on the inside at each door. MacRae considered suggesting a string of armed guards around the outside of the building, but he held his tongue.

Mr. Sutton was waiting for Marlowe in the entrance hall. "A news flash from Mrs. Palmer, Chief—she says to tell you that chow will be ready in about twenty minutes."

"Good! I could use a bite myself."

"And the school's regular cook is sulking in the dining room. She wants to talk to you."

"You deal with her. Where is Howe?"

"Derned if I know. He went through here like a destroying angel."

A man pressed forward through the crowd—the entrance hall was jammed, not only with colonists but with students, each of whom wanted to see the excitement. Reunions were going on all around, between parents and sons. Kelly was pounding a slightly smaller replica of himself on the back, and was himself being pounded. The babble was deafening. The man who had forced his way forward put his mouth to Marlowe's ear and said, "Mr. Howe is in his office. He's locked himself in; I've just come from trying to see him."

"Let him stay," decided Marlowe. "Who are you?"

"Jan van der Linden, instructor here in natural sciences. Who, may I ask, are you?"

"Name's Marlowe. I'm supposed to be in charge of this mad house. Look here, could you round up the boys who live outside the school? We are going to have to stay here for a day or two at least. I'm sorry but it's necessary. There can't very well be any classes; you might as well send the town boys home—and the teachers, too."

The teacher looked doubtful. "Mr. Howe won't like me doing it without his say-so."

"It's necessary. I'm going to do it in any case but you can speed things up and help me put an end to this riot. I take full responsibility."

Jim saw his mother through the crowd and did not wait to hear the outcome. She was leaning against the wall, holding Oliver and looking very tired, almost sick. Phyllis was standing close to her. Jim wormed his way through the crowd. "Mother!"

She looked up. "What is it, Jimmy?"

"You come with me."

"Oh, Jimmy—I'm too tired to move."

"Come on! I know a place where you can lie down." A few minutes later he had the three in the room abandoned by Frank and himself: it was, as he had guessed, still unoccupied. His mother sank down on his bunk. "Jimmy, you're an angel."

"You just take it easy. Phyl can bring you something to eat when it's ready. Uh, there's a toilet right across the hall. I'm going back and see what's going on." He started to leave, then hesitated. "Phyl—would you take care of Willis for me?"

"Why? I want to see what's doing, too."

"You're a girl; you'd better stay out from under foot."

"Well, I like that! I guess I've got just as much business—"

"Stop it, children. Jimmy, we'll take care of Willis. Tell your father where we are."

Jim delivered his mother's message, then found himself rather late in the chow line. By the time he had gone through for seconds as well, and eaten same, he discovered that most of the colonists were gathered in the school auditorium. He went in, spotted Frank and Doctor MacRae standing against the rear wall and squeezed over to them.

His father was pounding for order, using the butt of his gun as a gavel. "Mr. Linthicum has the floor."

The speaker was a man about thirty with an annoyingly aggresssive manner. "I say Doctor MacRae is right; we shouldn't fool around. We've got to have boats to get to Copais. Right? Beecher won't give 'em to us. Right? But all the actual force Beecher has is a squad of cops. Right? Even if he deputizes every man in Syrtis he only has maybe a hundred to a hundred and fifty guns. Right? We've got twice that many or more right here. Besides which Beecher won't be able to get all the local employees to fight us. So what do we do? We go over and grab him by the neck and force him to do right by us. Right?" He sat down triumphantly.

MacRae muttered, "Heaven defend me from my friends."

Several tried to speak; Marlowe picked one out. "Mr. Gibbs has the floor."

"Mr. Chairman . . . neighbors . . . I have rarely heard a more rash and provocative speech. You persuaded us, Mr. Marlowe, to embark on this reckless adventure, a project of which, I must say, I never approved—"

"You came along!" someone shouted.

"Order!" called Marlowe. "Get to the point, Mr. Gibbs."

". . . but in which I acceded rather than oppose the will of the majority. Now the hasty and ill-tempered would make matters worse with outright violence. But now that we are here, at the seat of government, the obvious thing to do is to petition for redress of grievances."

"If you mean by that to ask Beecher for transportation to Copais, Mr. Gibbs, I've already done that."

Gibbs smiled thinly. "Forgive me, Mr. Marlowe, if I say that the personality of the petitioner sometimes affects the outcome of the petition? I understand we have here, Mr. Howe, the Headmaster of this school and a person of some influence with the Resident Agent General. Would it not be wise to seek his help in approaching the Resident?"

Mr. Sutton shouted, "He's the last man on Mars I'd let speak for me!"

"Address the chair, Pat," Marlowe cautioned. "Personally, I feel the same way, but I won't oppose it if that's what the crowd wants. But," he continued, addressing the audience, "is Howe still here? I haven't seen him."

Kelly stood up. "Oh, he's here all right; he's still holed up in his office. I've talked to him twice through his ventilator, I've promised him a honey of a beating if he will only do me the favor of coming out and standing up to me like a man."

Mr. Gibbs looked scandalized. "Well, really!"

"It's a personal matter involving my boy," explained Kelly.

Marlowe banged the table. "I imagine Mr. Kelly will waive his privilege if you folks really want Howe to speak for you. Do I hear a motion?" Gibbs proposed it; in the end only he and the Pottles voted for it.

After the vote Jim said, "Dad?"

"Address the chair, son. What is it?"

"Er, Mr. Chairman—I just got an idea. I was wondering, since we haven't got any boats, just maybe we could get to Copais the way Frank and I got back to Charax—that is, if the Martians would help us." He added, "If folks wanted us to, I guess Frank and I could go back and find Gekko and see what could be done about it."

There was a moment of silence, then murmurs of "What's he talking about?" and unresponsive replies. Although almost all of the colonists had heard some version of the two boys' story, it was the simple fact that it had not been believed, as told, or had been ignored or discounted. The report ran counter to experience and most of the colonists were as bogged down in "common sense" as their relatives back on Earth. The necessary alternative, that the boys had crossed eight hundred and fifty miles of open country without special shelter equipment, simply had not been examined by them; the "common sense" mind does not stoop to logic.

Mr. Marlowe frowned. "You've brought up an entirely new possibility, Jim." He thought a moment. "We don't know that the natives have these conveyances between here and Copais—"

"I'll bet they have!"

"—and we don't know that they would let us ride in them even if they have."

"But, Dad, Frank and I—"

"A point of order, Mr. Chairman!" It was Gibbs again. "Under what rules do you permit children to speak in the councils of adult citizens?"

Mr. Marlowe looked embarrassed and annoyed. Doctor MacRae spoke up. "Another point of order, Mr. Chairman. Since when does this cream puff—" He motioned at Gibbs.

"Order, Doctor."

"Correction. I mean this fine upstanding male citizen, Mr. Gibbs, get the notion that Frank and Jim and the other gun-toting men their age ain't citizens? I might mention in passing that I was a man grown when this Gibbs party was still wetting his diapers—"

"Order!"

"Sorry. I mean even before he had reached that stage. Now as I see it, this is a frontier society and any man old enough to fight is a man and must be treated as such—and any girl old enough to cook and tend babies is an adult, too. Whether you folks know it yet or not, you are headed into a period when you'll have to fight for your rights. The youngsters will do most of the fighting; it behooves you to treat them accordingly. Twenty-five may be the right age for citizenship in a moribund, age-ridden society like that back on Earth, but we aren't bound to follow customs that aren't appropriate to our needs here."

Mr. Marlowe banged his gun. "I declare this subject out of order. Jim, see me after the meeting. Has anyone any specific action to propose that can be carried out at this time? Do we negotiate, or do we resort to force of numbers?"

Mr. Konski addressed the chair and said, "I favor taking what we have to have, if necessary, but it may not be necessary. Wouldn't it be well for you, Mr. Marlowe, to phone Mr. Beecher again? You could point out to him that we have force enough to do as we see fit; perhaps he will see reason. In fact, I so move."

The motion was put and carried; Mr. Marlowe suggested that someone else speak for them, but was turned down. He left the rostrum and went out into the hall to the communications booth. It was necessary to break the lock Howe had placed on it.

Beecher seemed excessively pleased with himself. "Ah, yes—my good friend, Marlowe. You've called to give yourself up I assume?"

Marlowe glanced around at the half dozen colonists crowded into the open door of the booth, then explained civilly to Beecher the purpose of his call.

"Boats to Copais?" Beecher laughed. "Scooters will be ready at nightfall to take the colonists—back to South Colony. You may tell them that all who are ready to go at that time will escape the consequences of their hasty actions. Not you, of course."

"The purpose of this call was to point out to you that we are considerably larger in numbers than the largest force you can possibly drum up here in Syrtis Minor. We intend to carry out the contract. If you crowd us into using force to get our rights, force we will use."

Beecher sneered through the TV screen. "Your threats do not move me, Marlowe. Surrender. Come out one at a time and unarmed, hands up."

"Is that your last word?"

"One more thing. You are holding Mr. Howe a prisoner. Let him go at once, or I shall see to it that you are prosecuted for kidnapping."

"Howe? He's not a prisoner; he's free to leave at any time."

Beecher elaborated. Marlowe answered, "That's a private matter between Kelly and Howe. You can call Howe in his office and tell him so."

"You must give him safe conduct out of the building," Beecher insisted.

Marlowe shook his head. "I'm not going to interfere in a private quarrel. Howe is safe where he is; why should I bother? Beecher, I am offering you one more chance to provide boats peacefully."

Beecher stared at him and switched off.

Kelly said, "Maybe you should have thrown me to the wolves, Chief."

Marlowe scratched his chin. "I don't think so. I can't conscientiously hold a hostage—but I have a feeling that this building is safer with Howe in it. I don't know just what Beecher has—so far as I know there isn't a bomb nor any other heavy weapon of any sort in Syrtis—but I would like to know what makes him so confident."

"He's bluffing."

"I wonder." Marlowe went back in and reported the conversation to all the colonists.

Mrs. Pottle stood up. "Well, *we* are accepting Mr. Beecher's gracious offer at once! As for holding poor Mr. Howe a prisoner— why, the very idea! I hope that you are properly punished, and that ungentlemanly Mr. Kelly as well. Come, dear!" Again she made a grand exit, with Mr. Pottle trotting after her.

Marlowe said, "Any more who want to surrender?"

Gibbs stood up, looked around uncertainly, and followed them. No one spoke until he had left, then Toland stood up and said, "I move that we organize ourselves for action."

"Second!"—"Second the motion!"

No one wanted to debate it; it was carried. Toland then proposed that Marlowe be elected captain of the forces, with power to appoint officers. It, too, was carried.

At this point Gibbs came stumbling back into the room, his face white, his hands trembling. "They're dead! They're dead!" he cried.

Marlowe found it impossible to restore order. Instead he crowded into the circle around Gibbs and demanded, "Who's dead? What happened?"

"The Pottles. Both of them. I was almost killed myself." He quieted down enough to tell his story; the three had assumed their masks and gone out through the lock. Mrs. Pottle, without bothering to look around her, had stomped out into the street, her husband a close shadow. As soon as they had stepped clear of the archway they had both been blasted. Their bodies lay out in the street in front of the school. "It's your fault," Gibbs finished shrilly, looking at Marlowe. "You got us into this."

"Just a moment," said Marlowe, "did they do the things Beecher demanded? Hands up, one at a time, and so forth? Was Pottle wearing his gun?"

Gibbs shook his head and turned away. "That's not the point," MacRae said bitterly. "While we've been debating, Beecher has boxed us in. We can't get out."

11.
BESEIGED

It was maddeningly true, as a cautious investigation soon proved. Both the front and back exits were covered by gunmen—Beecher's police, supposedly—who were able to blast anyone emerging from the building without themselves being under fire. The air-lock nature of the doors made a rush suicidal.

The school was at a distance from the settlement's dwellings; it was not connected by tunnel. Nor had it any windows. Men and women, boys and girls, the colony listed hundreds of licensed gun wearers—and yet a handful of gun fighters outside, as few as two, could keep them holed up.

Under the influence of Doc MacRae's bellowing voice the assembly got back to work. "Before I go ahead with organizing," Marlowe announced, "does anyone else want to surrender? I'm fairly sure that the Pottles were shot because they blundered out without notice. If you shout and wave something white, I think your surrender will be accepted."

He waited. Presently a man got up with his wife, and then another. A few more trickled out. They left in dead silence.

When they were gone Captain Marlowe went on with the details of organizing. Mrs. Palmer he confirmed as head of commissary, Doc he designated as executive officer, Kelly he appointed permanent officer of the watch, responsible for the interior guard. Sutton and Toland were given the job of devising some sort of a portable screen to block the enfilading fire that had dropped Mr. and Mrs. Pottle. Jim followed all this with excited interest until, after the appointment of platoon leaders, it became evident that his father did not intend to use boys as combatants. The students from the school were organized into two platoons, designated as reserve, and dismissed.

Jim hung around, trying to get a word with his father. At last he managed to catch his eye. "Dad—"

"Don't bother us now, Jim."

"But, Dad, you *told* me to see you about the business of getting the Martians to help us get to Copais."

"The Martians? Oh—" Mr. Marlowe thought about it, then said, "Forget about it, Jim. Until we can break out of here, neither that scheme, nor any other, will work. Now let us be. Go see how your mother is doing."

Thus brushed off, Jim turned disconsolately away. As he was leaving Frank fell in step with him, and locked arms. "Do you know, Jim, sometimes you aren't as full of guff as you are other times."

Jim eyed him suspiciously. "If that's a compliment—thanks."

"Not a compliment, Jim, merely justice. Seldom as I approve of one of your weary notions, this time I am forced to admit that you had a bright idea."

"Quit making a speech and get to the point."

"Very well. Point: when you suggested getting the Martians to help us you were firing on all jets."

"Huh? Well, thanks for the applause, but I don't see it myself. As Dad pointed out, there's nothing we can do about it until we find some way to break out of here and slap old Beecher down. Then I suppose we won't need their help."

"You're supposing too fast. Let's, as Doc would say, analyse the situation. In the first place, your father got us boxed in here—"

"You lay off my father!"

"I wasn't picking on your father. Your father is a swell guy and my old man says that he is a swell scientist, too. But by behaving like a gentleman he got us cornered in here and we can't get out. Mind you, I'm not blaming him, but that's the situation. So what are they going to do about it? Your old man tells my old man and that drip Toland to work out a shield, some sort of armor, that will let us get out the door and into the open where we can fight. Do you think they'll have any luck?"

"Well, I hadn't thought about it."

"I have. They are going to get exactly no place. Now Dad is a good engineer with a lot of savvy. You give him equipment and materials and he'll build you anything. But what's he got to work with now? For equipment he's got the school workshop and you know what a sad mess that is. The Company never spent any real money on equipping it; it's about right for making book ends. Materials? What are they going to make a shield out of? Dining-room tabletops? A heater would cut through a tabletop like soft cheese."

"Oh, there must be something around they can use."

"You name it."

"Well, what do you want us to do?" Jim said in exasperation. "Surrender?"

"Certainly not. The old folks are stuck in a rut. Here's where we show finesse—using your idea."

"Quit calling it my idea. I haven't got any idea."

"Okay, I'll take all the credit. We get word to Gekko that we need help. He's our water friend; he'll see to it."

"How can Gekko help us? Martians don't fight."

"That's right, but, as it says in geometry, what's the corollary? Human beings never fight Martians, *never*. Beecher can't risk offending the Martians. Everybody knows what a terrible time the Company had persuading the Martians that it was all right to let us settle here in the first place. Now just suppose that about twenty or thirty Martians—or even one—came stomping up to the front door of this place: what do Beecher's cops do?"

"Huh?"

"They cease fire, that's what they do—and we come swarming out. That's what Gekko can do for us. He can fix it so that Beecher is forced to call off his gun toters."

Jim thought about it. There was certainly merit in what Frank had to say. Every human who set foot on Mars had it thoroughly drummed into him that the natives must not be interfered with, provoked, nor their customs violated—nor, above all things, hurt. The strange and distressing history of the first generation of contact with the Martians had resulted in this being the first law of the extraterritorial settlements on Mars. Jim could not imagine Beecher violating this rule—nor could he imagine one of the Company police doing so. In normal times the principal duty of the police was the enforcement of this rule, particularly with respect to tourists from Earth, who were never allowed to come in contact with natives.

"There is just one thing wrong with your idea, Frank. Supposing Gekko and his friends were willing to come to our rescue, how in the name of mud are we going to let him know that we need help? We can't just call him on the phone."

"No, we can't—but that is where you come in. *You* can send him a message."

"How?"

"Willis."

"You're crazy!"

"Am I now? Suppose you go out that front door—*fsst!* You're fertilizer. But suppose Willis goes out? Who's going to shoot a bouncer?"

"I don't like it. Willis might get hurt."

"If we just sit tight and do nothing, you'll wish he was dead. Beecher will sell him to the London Zoo."

Jim considered this unpleasant probability, then answered, "Anyhow, your scheme is full of holes. Even if he gets outside safely, Willis couldn't find Gekko and couldn't be depended on to deliver a message. He'd be just as likely to sing or recite some of Doc's bum jokes. I've got a better idea."

"Convince me."

"I'll bet that Beecher's plug-uglies didn't think to keep watch on the garbage dump. I'll deliver the message to Gekko myself."

Frank thought it over. "No good. Even if they aren't really watching the dump, they can see you from the corner where they are watching the back door. They'd nail you before you could scramble to your feet."

"I'll wait till dark."

"Mmmm . . . could work. Only I'll do it. I'm faster on my feet than you are."

"Look who's talking!"

"All right, all right! We'll *both* do it—an hour apart." Frank went on, "But that doesn't cut Willis out of it. He'll try it, too. One of us might get through. Now wait a minute—you underrate your little pal. We'll teach him just what he's to say. That'll be easy. Then you tell him to go over into the native city, and stop the first Martian he meets and recite his piece. The Martian does the rest because we'll put it all into the message. The only question is whether or not Willis is bright enough to do as you tell him and go over into Syrtis Minor proper. I've got grave doubts about that."

Jim bristled. "You're always trying to make out that Willis is stupid. He's not; you just don't understand him."

"Okay, then he can find his way over to the city and deliver the message. Or can't he?"

"Well—I don't like it."

"Which do you prefer, to take a small risk with Willis or to have your mother and your baby brother have to spend the winter at South Colony?"

Jim chewed his lip in a manner just like his father. "All right—
we'll try it. Let's go get Willis."

"Don't get in a rush. Neither you nor I know the native language well enough to whip up just what we want to say. But Doc
does. He'll help us."

"He's the only one of the grown-ups I'd want to trust with this
anyhow. Come on."

They found MacRae easily enough, but were not able to speak
with him at once. He was in the communications booth, bellowing
at the screen. They could hear his half of the conversation. "I want
to talk to Doctor Rawlings. Well, get him, get him—don't sit there
chewing your pencil! Tell him it's Doctor MacRae. . . . Ah, good
day, Doctor! . . . No, I just got here . . . How's business, Doctor?
Still cremating your mistakes? . . . Well, don't we all . . . Sorry, I
can't; I'm locked up . . . Locked up, I said . . . —L . . . O . . .
C . . . K . . . E . . . D up, like a disorderly drunk . . . No reason,
none at all. It's that simian moron, Beecher . . . Yes, hadn't you
heard? The entire colony, penned up in the little red school-
house . . . shoots us down if we so much as stick our noses out . . .
No, I'm not joking. You know Skinny Pottle—he and his wife
were killed not two hours ago. Burned down in cold blood, never
had a chance . . . Damn it, man, I don't joke. Come see for yourself and find out what kind of a madman you have ruling you here.
The cadavers were still out in the street in front of the school the
last time I looked. We don't dare drag them in and lay them out
decently . . . I said—" The screen suddenly went blank. MacRae
swore and fiddled with the controls. Nothing happened.

Presently, by experiment, he realized the instrument had been
cut off completely. He came out, shrugging. "Well, they finally
caught on to me," he remarked to the room in general, "but I
talked to three key men."

"What were you doing, Doc?" asked Jim.

"Starting a little backfire, some fifth column activity behind
Beecher's lines. There are good people everywhere, son, but you
have to spell it out for them."

"Oh. Look, Doc, could you spare us some time?"

"What for? Your father has a number of things for me to do,
Jim."

"This is important." They got MacRae aside and explained to
him their plans.

MacRae looked thoughtful. "It just might work. It's worth a
whirl. That notion of making use of Martian inviolability is posi-

tively Machiavellian, Frank; you should go into politics. However, about the other stunt—the garbage-can paratrooper act—if you ask your father, he'll veto it."

"Can't you ask him? He'll listen to you."

"I said '*If* you ask your father,' you idjut. Do I have to wipe your nose for you?"

"Oh. I get you."

"About the other matter—chase up the little beastie and meet me in classroom 'C'; I'm using it as an office."

Jim and Frank left to do so. Jim found his mother and Oliver asleep, his sister and Willis gone. He had started to leave when his mother woke up. "Jimmy?"

"I didn't mean to wake you, Mother. Where's Phyl? I want to find Willis."

"Your sister is in the kitchen, I think, helping out. Isn't Willis here? He was here on the bed with baby and me."

Jim looked around again, but found no sign of Willis. "I'll go ask Phyl. Maybe she came back and got him."

"He can't have wandered far. I'm sorry, Jim."

"I'll find him."

He went to the kitchen, found his sister. "How would I know?" she protested. "He was there with mother when I left."

"I asked you to look out for him."

"And I left him with mother—they wanted me to help out here. Don't go looking at me."

Jim joined Frank. "Darn it, they've let him wander off. He might be any place. We'll just have to search."

One hour and hundreds of inquiries later they were convinced that, if the bouncer was in the school, he had found a very special hiding place. Jim was so annoyed that he had forgotten completely the essential danger that they were all in. "That's what comes of trusting women," he said bitterly. "Frank, what'll I do now?"

"Search me."

They were in the far end of the building from their former room. They started back toward it on the chance that Willis might have come back. As they were passing through the entrance hall, Jim stopped suddenly. "I heard him!"

They both listened. "Open up!" came a replica of Jim's voice. "Let Willis in!" The voice came through the door's announcing speaker.

Jim darted for the pressure lock, was stopped by the guard. "Hey," he protested, "open the lock. That's Willis."

"More likely it's a trap. Stand back."

"Let him in. That's Willis, I tell you." The guard ignored him, but threw the switch that caused the lock to cycle. He cleared everybody back out of range, then cautiously watched the door from one side, gun drawn.

The inner door opened and Willis waddled through.

Willis was bland about the whole thing. "Jim go away. Everybody go away. Willis go for walk."

"How did you get outdoors?"

"Went out."

"But how?" Willis apparently could see nothing difficult about that; he did not amplify.

"Maybe he went out when the Pottles did?" suggested Frank.

"Maybe. Well, I guess it doesn't matter."

"Go see people," Willis offered. He named off a string of native names, then added, "Fine time. Water friends. Give Willis good water, big drink." He made lipsmacking noises in imitation of Jim, although he had no lips himself.

"You had a drink just a week ago," Jim said accusingly.

"Willis good boy!" Willis countered.

"Wait a minute," said Frank. "He was with *Martians*."

"Huh? I don't care if he was with Cleopatra; he shouldn't run away."

"But don't you see? He can get to the natives; he already has. All we've got to do is to be sure he carries a message for them to pass on to Gekko."

The point, relayed to MacRae, increased his interest. The three composed a message in English for MacRae to translate. "Greetings," it began, "this is a message from Jim Marlowe, water friend of Gekko of the city of—" Here they inserted the unspellable and almost unpronounceable Martian name of Cynia. "Whoever you may be, friend of my friend, you are implored to send this word at once to Gekko. I am in great trouble and I need your help." The message went on to tell in detail the nature of the trouble, who was responsible, and what they hoped would be done about it. Telegraphic simplicity was not attempted, since Willis's nervous system could hold a thousand words as easily as ten.

MacRae translated it, then drilled Jim in reading it, after which they attempted to impress on Willis what he was to do. Willis was willing, but his consistently slap-happy, feather-brained approach to any problem exasperated them all almost to hysteria. At last it seemed fairly likely that he might carry out his assignment; at least (a) when asked what he was to do he would answer, "go see friends," and (b) when asked what he would tell them he would (usually) answer by reciting the message.

"It just might work," decided MacRae. "We know the Martians have some means of rapid communication, even though we've never known what sort. If our plump friend doesn't forget what he is doing and why he is making the trip . . ."

Jim took him to the front door. On MacRae's authorization the guard let them through. Jim checked Willis again while the lock was cycling; the bouncer appeared to be sure of his instructions, although his answers showed his usual mental leapfrog.

Jim hung back in the doorway, out of the line of fire, while Willis rolled off the stoop. The Pottles still lay where they had fallen; Willis looked at them curiously, then took up a zig-zag course down the street and disappeared from Jim's view, cut off as he was by the door frame. Jim wished mightily then that he had had the foresight to bring along a mirror to use as a periscope. Finally he screwed up his courage, lay down, and peeked around the edge of the door at the bottommost part.

Willis was well down the street and nothing had happened to him. Far down the street some sort of cover had been set up. Jim stuck his head out an inch farther, trying to see what it was, when the corner of the door frame above him gave off a puff of smoke and he felt the electric tingle of a near miss. He jerked his head hastily back and reentered the lock.

He had an all-gone feeling at the pit of his stomach and a conviction that he would never see Willis again.

12.
"DON'T SHOOT!"

The rest of the day passed wearily for Jim and Frank. There was nothing they could do about their own plan until after dark. In the meantime discussions were taking place among colonial leaders, but they were held behind closed doors and the boys were definitely not invited.

Supper was a welcome diversion, both because they were hungry and because it meant that the kitchen would presently be deserted and the way left open to the garbage dump. Or so they thought. They found that, in practice, the womenfolk running the kitchen first took a leisurely time to clean the place up, then seemed disposed to sit around all night, drinking coffee and talking.

The boys found excuses to come into the kitchen, excuses that got thinner every trip and which began to arouse Mrs. Palmer's suspicions.

Finally Jim followed another boy in, wondering what he would say this time, when he heard the other boy say, "Mrs. Palmer, Captain Marlowe sends his regards and wants to know if it would be too much trouble to keep a night watch for coffee and sandwiches for the men on guard."

"Why, no," Jim heard her say, "we'll be glad to do that. Henrietta, will you go out and find some volunteers? I'll take the first stint."

Jim backed out and went to where Frank awaited him. "What's the chances?" asked Frank. "Does it look like they're going to break up any time soon?"

Jim told him what the chances were—or, rather, were not.

Frank swore, using a couple of words that Jim had not heard before, and noted down for future use. "What'll we do, Jim?"

"I don't know. Maybe when it's down to just one of them on duty, she'll go out occasionally."

"Maybe we could get her out with some song and dance."

"Maybe. Maybe we could tell her that she's wanted in the headquarters room. That ought to do it."

They were still discussing it when the lights went out.

The place was suddenly completely dark, as dark as the inside of a rock. Worse than that, there was a disturbing utter silence. Jim had just realized that the complete emptiness of sound resulted from the ending of the noise of circulating air, from the stopping of the supercharger on the roof, when a woman began to scream.

She was joined by another, in a higher key. Then there were voices everywhere in the darkness, questioning, complaining, soothing.

Down the hall from where the boys loitered a light sprang out and Jim heard his father's voice. "Quiet, everybody. Don't get excited. It's just a power failure. Be patient."

The light moved toward them, suddenly hit them. "You boys get to bed." Jim's father moved on. Down the passage in the other direction they could hear Doc's bellow, ordering people to shut up and calm down.

Jim's father came back. This time he was saying, "Into your suits, everybody. Have your respirators on your head. We hope to correct this in a few minutes, but we don't want anybody hurt. Now don't get excited; this building will hold pressure for half an hour at least. There's plenty of time to get ready for thin air, even if it takes a while to correct the trouble."

Other lights sprang up here and there; shortly the passageways throughout the building, if not the rooms, were adequately lighted. The corridors were crowded with dim shapes, struggling into their outdoors suits. Jim and Frank, planning as they were to attempt to go outside, had long been in their suits, armed, and with respirators at the ready. "Maybe this is a good time," suggested Frank.

"Nope," Jim answered. "They're still in the kitchen. I can see a light."

MacRae came down the corridor; Jim stopped him. "Doc, how long do you think it will be until they get the lights on?"

MacRae said, "Are you kidding?"

"What do you mean, Doc?"

"The lights aren't coming on. This is one of Beecher's stunts. He's pulled the switch on us, at the power house."

"Are you sure?"

"There's no failure—we've checked it. I'm surprised Beecher didn't do it hours ago—in his shoes, I would have done it five minutes after we moved in. But don't you birds go blabbing, Jim; your Pop has his hands full keeping the custard heads from blowing their tops." He moved on.

In spite of Captain Marlowe's reassuring words the true state of things was soon common knowledge. The pressure dropped slowly, so slowly that it was necessary to warn everyone to adjust their respirators, lest oxygen starvation sneak up on the unwary. After that it was hardly possible to maintain the fiction that the power loss was temporary, to be corrected any minute now. The temperature in the building fell slowly; there was no danger of them freezing in the closed and insulated building—but the night chill penetrated.

Marlowe set up headquarters in the entrance hall in a circle of light cast by a single torch. Jim and Frank loitered there, discreetly back in the shadows, unwilling to miss what might be going on and quite unwilling to go to bed as ordered. . . . as Frank pointed out to Jim, the only beds they had were occupied, by Mrs. Marlowe, Phyllis, and Oliver. Neither of them had given up the idea of attempting the garbage chute route, but they knew in their hearts that the place was too stirred up to give them the privacy they would require.

Joseph Hartley, one of the colony's hydroponists, came up to Marlowe. His wife was behind him, carrying their baby daughter in a pressurized crib, its supercharger sticking up above the clear plastic shell of it like a chimney. "Mr. Marlowe—I mean Captain Marlowe—"

"Yes?"

"You've got to do something. Our kid can't stand this. She's coming down with croup and we can't get at her to help her."

MacRae crowded forward. "You should have brought her to me, Joe." He looked the baby over, through the plastic, then announced, "The kid seems to be doing all right."

"She's sick, I tell you."

"Hmm—I can't make much of an examination when I can't get at her. Can't take her temperature, but she doesn't seem to be in any real danger."

"You're just trying to soothe me down," Hartley said angrily. "You can't tell anything about it when she is in a sealed crib."

"Sorry, son," the doctor answered.

"A fat lot of good it does to be sorry! Somebody's got to *do* something. This can't—" His wife plucked at his sleeve; he turned away and they went into a huddle. Shortly he turned back. "Captain Marlowe!"

"Yes, Mr. Hartley."

"The rest of you can do as you like. I've had enough. I've got my wife and baby to think about."

"The decision is yours," Marlowe said stiffly and turned away in abrupt dismissal.

"But—" said Hartley and stopped, aware that Marlowe was no longer paying any attention to him. He looked uncertain, like a man who wants someone to argue him out of his resolution. His wife touched his arm; he turned then and they went together to the front entrance.

Marlowe said to MacRae, "What do they expect of me? Miracles?"

MacRae answered, "Exactly, boy. Most people never grow up. They expect papa to get 'em the pretty Moon." The doctor went on, "Just the same, Joe accidentally told the truth. We've got to do something."

"I don't see what we can do until Sutton and Toland get some results."

"You can't wait any longer for them, son. We've got to crush out of here anyway. Theoretically a man can live for days in a respirator. Practically, it won't work and that is what Beecher is counting on. You can't keep several hundred people crouching here in the dark and the cold, wearing masks to stay alive, not indefinitely. You're going to have a panic on your hands."

Marlowe looked weary, even through his mask. "We can't tunnel out. We can't get out at all, except through the doors. And they've got those doors zeroed. It's suicide."

"It's got to be done, son. I'll lead the rush."

Marlowe sighed. "No, I will."

"In a pig's eye! You've got a wife and kids. I've got nobody and I've been living on borrowed time so long I've lost track."

"It's my privilege. That's settles it."

"We'll see."

"I said that settles it, sir!"

The argument was left unfinished; the inner door to the pressure lock opened again and Mrs. Hartley stumbled inside. She was clutching the tiny crib and sobbing wildly.

It was the case of the Pottles and Gibbs all over again. When MacRae was able to make something out of her sobs, it appeared that they had been very cautious, had waited, had shouted their intention to surrender, and had displayed a light. There had been no answer, so they had shouted again, then Hartley had stepped off the threshold with his hands up and his wife shining the light on him.

He had been struck down as soon as he stepped out the door.

MacRae turned her over to the women, then went out to reconnoiter. He came back in almost at once. "Somebody get me a chair," he demanded, and looked around. "You, Jim—skedaddle."

"What's up?" asked Marlowe.

"Let you know in a moment. I suspect something."

"Be careful."

"That's why I want the chair."

Jim came back with one; the doctor went through the pressure lock again. He came back in about five minutes later. "It's a booby trap," he stated.

"What do you mean?"

"Beecher didn't try to keep men outdoors all night—at least I don't think so. It's automatic. They've put an electric-eye grid across the door. When you break it, a bolt comes across, right where you'd be if you walked through it." He displayed half a dozen deep burns through the chair.

Marlowe examined them. "But that's not the important point," MacRae went on. "It's automatic but it's inflexible. It hits about two feet above the step and about four feet. A man could crawl through it—if his nerves were steady."

Marlowe straightened up. "Show me."

They came back, with the chair still more burned, in a few minutes. "Kelly," Marlowe said briskly, "I want twenty volunteers to make a sortie. Pass the word around."

There were at least two hundred volunteers; the problem was to weed them down. Both Frank and Jim tried to get in on it; Jim's father refused to take any but grown, unmarried men—except himself. MacRae he refused.

The doctor pulled Jim back and whispered to him. "Hold your horses. In a few minutes I'll be boss."

The raiding party started into the lock. Marlowe turned to MacRae. "We'll head for the power plant. If we are gone more than two hours, you are on your own." He went into the lock and closed the door.

As soon as the door was closed, MacRae said, "Okay, twenty more volunteers."

Kelly said, "Aren't you going to wait two hours?"

"You tend to your knitting! When I'm out of here, you're in charge." He turned and nodded to Jim and Frank. "You two come along." MacRae had his party in short order, had apparently selected them in his mind before Marlowe left. They filed into the lock.

Once the outer door was open MacRae flashed his torch into the street. The Pottles and the unfortunate Joseph Hartley lay where they had fallen, but no other bodies littered the street. MacRae turned around and said, "Gimme that chair. I'll demonstrate the gimmick." He stuck it out into the door. Instantly two bolts cut across the doorway, parallel to the ground. After they were gone and the eye was still dazzled by their brilliance, two soft violet paths of ionization marked where they had been and then gradually dispersed.

"You will note," said the doctor, as if he were lecturing medical students, "that it does not matter where the chair is inserted." He again shoved the chair into the opening, moved it up and down. The bolts repeated at split-second intervals, but always at the same places, about knee high and chest high.

"I think it is best," continued the doctor, "to maintain the attack. Then you can see where you are. First man!"

Jim gulped and stepped forward—or was shoved, he was not sure which. He eyed the deadly fence, stooped over, and with awkward and infinite care stepped through. He went on out into the street. "Get moving!" the doctor ordered. "Spread out."

Jim ran up the street, feeling very much alone but terribly excited. He paused short of the end of the building and cautiously looked around the corner. Nothing either way—he stopped and waited in the darkness, ready to blast anything that moved.

Ahead of him and to the left he could see the curious structure which had almost cost him the top of his head many hours before. It was clear now that the bolts were coming from it.

Some one came up behind him. He whirled and heard a voice yelp, "Don't shoot! It's me—Frank."

"How about the others?"

"They're coming—I think."

A light flashed at the building ahead, beyond the shield from which the bolts came. Frank said, "I think somebody came out there."

"Can you see him? Do you think we ought to shoot?"

"I don't know."

Someone else was pounding up the street behind them. Up ahead, from near the spot where Frank had thought he had seen a man a heater flashed out in the darkness; the beam passed them.

Jim's gun answered by pure reflex; he nailed the spot from which the flash had come. "You got him," said Frank. "Good boy!"

"I did?" said Jim. "How about the guy behind me?" He found that he was trembling.

"Here he is now."

"Who shot at me?" the newcomer said. "Where are they?"

"Nowhere at the moment," Frank answered. "Jim nailed him." Frank tried to peer into the mask; the night was too dark. "Who is it?"

"Smitty."

Both Frank and Jim gave exclamations of surprise—it was Smythe, the practical man. "Don't look at me like that," Smythe said defensively. "I came along at the last minute—to protect my investment. You guys owe me money."

"I think Jim just paid it off," suggested Frank.

"Not on your life! That's another matter entirely."

"Later, later," said Frank. Others were coming up. Presently MacRae came puffing up and roared, "I told you bird-brains to spread out!" He caught his breath and said, "We tackle the Company main offices. Dogtrot—and don't bunch together."

"Doc," said Jim, "there are some in that building up ahead."

"Some what?"

"Somebody that shoots at us, that's what."

"Oh. Hold it, everybody." MacRae gave them hoarse instructions, then said, "Got it, everybody?"

"Doc," asked Frank, "how about the gun over there? Why don't we wreck it first?"

"I must be getting old," said MacRae. "Anybody here enough of a technician to sneak up on it and pull its teeth?"

A faceless figure in the darkness volunteered. "Go ahead," Doc told him. "We'll cover you from here." The colonial trotted ahead, swung around behind the shield covering the stationary automatic blaster, and stopped. He worked away for several minutes, then there was a white flash, intensely bright. He trotted back.

"Shorted it out. Bet I blew every overload breaker in the power house."

"Sure you fixed it?"

"You couldn't dot an 'i' with it now."

"Okay. You—" MacRae grabbed one of his squad by the arm. "—tear back and tell Kelly that allee allee out's in free. You—" He indicated the chap who had wrecked the gun. "—go around in back and see what you can do with the setup back there. You two guys cover him. The rest of you follow me—the building ahead, according to plan."

Jim's assignment called for sneaking along the face of the building and taking a covering position about twenty feet short of the doorway. His way led him over the ground where the man had been at whom he had shot. There was no body on the pavement; he wondered if he had missed. It was too dark to look for blood.

MacRae gave his covering troops time to reach their stations, then made a frontal assault with six to back him up, among them Frank. The doctor himself walked up to the building entrance, tried the outer door. It opened. Motioning the assault group to join him, he went in. The outer door of the building's lock closed on them.

Jim huddled against the icy wall, eyes wide, ready to shoot. It seemed a cold eternity that he waited; he began to fancy that he could see some traces of dawn in the east. At last he saw silhouettes ahead, raised his gun, then identified one as Doc's portly figure.

MacRae had the situation in hand. There were four disarmed prisoners; one was being half carried by two others. "Take 'em back to the school," Doc ordered one of his group. "Shoot the first one of them who makes a funny move. And tell whoever is in charge back there now to lock 'em up. Come on, men. We've got our real job ahead."

There came a shout behind them; MacRae turned. Kelly's voice called, "Doc! Wait for baby!" He came running up and demanded, "What are the plans?" Behind him, men were pouring out of the school and up the street.

MacRae took a few minutes to recast things on the basis of more guns. One of the platoon leaders, a civil engineer named Alvarez, was left in charge at the school with orders to maintain a guard outside the building and to patrol the neighborhood with scouts. Kelly was assigned the task of capturing the communications building which lay between the settlement and the space port. It was an important key to control of the whole situation, since it housed not only the local telephone exchange but also the radio link to Deimos and thence to all other outposts on Mars—and also the radar beacons and other aids for incoming ships from Earth.

MacRae reserved for himself the job of taking the planet office—the main offices on Mars of the Company, Beecher's own headquarters. The Resident Agent General's personal apartment was part of the same building; the doctor expected to come to grips with Beecher himself.

MacRae sent a squad of men to reinforce Marlowe at the power house, then called out, "Let's go, before we all freeze to death. Chop, chop!" He led the way at a ponderous trot.

Jim located Frank in the group and joined him. "What took you guys so long in that building?" he asked. "Was there a fight?"

"Took so long?" said Frank. "We weren't inside two minutes."

"But you must have—"

"Cut out that chatter back there!" called out Doc. Jim shut up and pondered it.

MacRae had them cross the main canal on ice, avoiding the arching bridge as a possible trap. They crossed in pairs, those behind covering those crossing; in turn they who had crossed spread out and covered those yet to come. The crossing held a nightmarish, slow-motion quality; while on the ice a man was a perfect target—yet it was impossible to hurry. Jim longed for his skates.

On the far side the doctor gathered them together in the shadow of a warehouse. "We'll swing around to the east and avoid the dwellings," he told them in a hoarse whisper. "From here on, *quiet!*—for your life. We won't split up because I don't want you shooting each other in the dark." He set forth a plan to surround the building and cover all exits, while MacRae himself and about half their numbers tried to force an entrance at the main door.

"When you get around in back and make contact," MacRae warned the two who were to lead the flanking and covering moves, "you may have one deuce of a time telling friend from foe. Be careful. The word is "Mars'; the answer is 'Freedom'."

Jim was in the assault party. Doc stationed six of them in fan shape around the door, at an easy twenty-five yards range, and had them take cover where available. Three of them were on the open ramp in front of the door; he had them lie down and steady their guns. "In case of doubt—shoot," he instructed them. "Come on, the rest of you."

Jim was included in the last order. MacRae walked up to the

outer door and tried it; it was locked. He pressed the signal switch and waited.

Nothing happened. MacRae pressed the switch again and called out mildly to the speaker grille, "Let me in. I have an important message for the Resident."

Still nothing happened. MacRae changed his tone to pretended exasperation. "Hurry up, please! I'm freezing to death out here."

The door remained dark and silent. MacRae changed his manner to belligerence. "Okay, Beecher, open up! We've got the place surrounded and we're ready to blast in the door. You have thirty seconds till we set off the charge."

The seconds ticked away. Doc muttered to Jim, "I wish it were the truth," then raised his voice and said, "Time's up, Beecher. This is it."

The door hissed as the compressed air in the lock began to escape to the outside; the lock was starting to cycle. MacRae motioned them back a little; they waited, not breathing, all guns drawn and aimed at the point where the door would begin to open.

Then it was open and a single figure stood in it, the lock's light shining behind him. "Don't shoot!" said a firm, pleasant voice. "It's all right. It's all over."

MacRae peered at the figure. "Why, Doctor Rawlings!" he said. "Bless your ugly face."

13.
"IT'S AN ULTIMATUM."

Rawlings himself had spent half the night locked up, along with half a dozen other prominent citizens who had attempted to reason with Beecher. As the story got around, especially the matter of the deaths of the Pottles, Beecher found himself with no support at all, save from his own clique of sycophants and toadies and the professional, largely disinterested support of the Company's police.

Even Kruger cracked up under the strain, tried to get Beecher to reverse himself—and was stuffed in with the other dissidents, which by then included the chief engineer of the power plant. But it was Doctor Rawlings who talked the guard placed over them into risking his job and letting them go—the doctor was treating the guard's wife.

"I don't think Beecher would ever stand trial, even if we had him back on Earth," MacRae remarked about the matter to Rawlings and Marlowe. "What do you think, Doctor?" The three were seated in the outer offices of the planet office building. Marlowe had come there after getting word at the power house from MacRae and had gotten busy at once, writing despatches to the Project camps and the other outlying activities, including North Colony itself, trying to round up boats. He had then tried, red-eyed and uncertain from lack of sleep, to compose a suitable report to Earth, until MacRae had interrupted him and insisted that he rest.

"Paranoia?" said Rawlings.

"A clear case."

"My opinion, too. I've seen suggestive indications of it, but the case was not fully developed until his will was crossed. He must be hospitalized—and restrained." Doctor Rawlings glanced over his shoulder at a closed door. Behind it was Beecher.

"Certainly, certainly," agreed MacRae, "but speaking non-professionally, I'd rather see the no-good so-and-so hang. Paranoia is a disorder contracted only by those of fundamentally bad character."

"Now, Doctor," protested Rawlings.

"That's my opinion," insisted MacRae, "and I've seen a lot of cases, in and out of hospitals."

Marlowe put down his coffee cup and wiped his mouth. "All that is as may be. I think I'll stretch out on one of these desks for a couple of hours. Doc, will you see that someone wakes me?"

"Certainly," agreed MacRae, having no intention of allowing the man to be disturbed until he was fully rested. "Don't worry."

Jim and the others were back at the school where they were to remain until boats could be gotten to take them to Copais. Mrs. Palmer was bustling around with her assistants, getting a mammoth breakfast for weary men and boys. Jim himself was dead tired and hungry but much too excited to think about sleeping, even though dawn had broken outside.

He had just received a cup of coffee and was blowing on it when Smythe showed up. "Say, I understand you really did kill that cop that took a pot shot at me."

"No," Jim denied, "he's in the infirmary now, just wounded. I've seen him."

Smythe looked troubled. "Oh, shucks," he said finally, "it won't happen more than once in a lifetime. Here's your I.O.U."

Jim stared at him. "Smitty, you're sick."

"Probably. Better take it."

Jim reached back into his subconscious memory and quoted his father. "No, thanks. Marlowes pay their debts."

Smythe looked at him, then said, "Oh, the heck with you, you ungracious twerp!" He tore the I.O.U. into small pieces and stalked away.

Jim looked wonderingly after him. "Now what was he sore about?" He decided to look up Frank and tell him about it.

He found Frank but had no time to tell him about it; a shout came through the crowd: "Marlowe! Jim Marlowe!"

"Captain Marlowe's at the planet office," someone answered.

"Not him, the kid," the first voice replied. "Jimmy Marlowe! You're wanted up front, right away."

"Coming," yelled Jim. "What for?" He pushed his way toward the entrance, Frank behind him.

The man who had paged him let him get close before he answered, "You won't believe it—I don't myself. Martians."

Jim and Frank hurried outside. Gathered in front of the school door were more than a dozen Martians. Gekko was there, and G'kuro, but not K'booch. Nor could Jim make out the old one whom he thought of as "head man" of Gekko's tribe. Gekko spotted them and said in his own speech, "Greetings, Jim-Marlowe, greetings, Frank-Sutton, friends sealed with water."

Another voice called out from one of Gekko's palm flaps, "Hi, Jim boy!" Willis had come home with the bacon, a little late perhaps, but successfully.

Another voice boomed mellowly. Gekko listened, then said, "Where is he who stole our little one?"

Jim, uncertain of the dominant tongue, at best, was not sure that he had understood. "Huh?"

"He wants to know where Howe is," said Frank and answered in fluent, fairly accurate Martian. Howe was still where he had taken refuge, still afraid to face Kelly, despite repeated invitations.

Gekko indicated that he would come into the building. Amazed, but cooperative, the boys led him in. Gekko was forced to fold himself into a shape resembling a hat rack to get into the lock but he managed it; the lock was large. Inside, the sensation caused by his appearance was like that which might have resulted from introducing an elephant into a church. People gave way before him.

The door to the outer office was even more of a squeeze than the air lock, but Gekko made it, with Jim and Frank trailing him. Gekko handed Willis to Jim, then gently explored the handle of the door to Howe's office with a hand flap. Suddenly he pulled and the door came away, not only the lock broken but the door wrenched completely off its hinges. He squatted down further, completely filling the door frame.

The boys looked at each other; Willis closed up. They heard Howe saying "What's the meaning of this? Who are—"

Then Gekko stood up as well as he could in a room intended for humans and started for the outer door. The boys hesitated; Frank said, "Let's see what he did to him." He stepped to the wrecked door and looked in. "I don't see him. Hey, Jim—he's not in here at all."

Nor was he.

They hurried after Gekko and reached him at the air lock. No one stopped Gekko; no one stopped them. The repeated indoctrination concerning Martians swept a path before them. Outside Gekko turned to them. "Where is the other one, who would do harm to the little one?"

Frank explained that Beecher was some distance away and not available. "You will show us," announced Gekko and picked them both up. Another Martian relieved him of Frank.

Jim felt himself cradled in the soft palm flaps, even as Willis was still cradled in Jim's arms. Willis extended his eyes, looked around and remarked, "Fine ride, huh?" Jim was not sure.

The Martians ambled through town at an easy eight miles an hour, over the bridge, and to the planet offices. The pressure lock there was higher and larger than that at the school; the entire party went inside. The ceiling of the building's foyer was quite high enough for even the tallest Martian. Once they were inside Gekko set Jim down, as did the Martian carrying Frank.

There had been the same scurrying surprise as at the school. MacRae came out and looked the situation over without excitement. "What's all this jamboree?" he asked.

"They want to talk to Beecher," Frank explained.

MacRae raised his eyebrows, then spoke in clear Martian. One of them answered him; they conversed back and forth. "Okay, I'll get him," agreed MacRae, then repeated it in Martian. He went into the offices. He returned in a few minutes, pushing Beecher in front of him, and followed by Rawlings and Marlowe. "Some people to see you," MacRae said and gave Beecher a shove that carried him out onto the floor of the foyer.

"This is the one?" inquired the Martian spokesman.

"This is verily the one."

Beecher looked up at them. "What do you want me for?" he said in Basic. The Martians moved so that they were on all sides of him. "Now you get away from me!" he said. They moved in slowly, tightening the circle. Beecher attempted to break out of it; a great hand flap was placed in his way.

They closed in further. Beecher darted this way and that, then he was concealed completely from the spectators by a screen of palm flaps. "Let me out!" he was heard to shout. "I didn't do anything. You've got no right to—" His voice stopped in a scream.

The circle relaxed and broke up. There was no one inside it, not even a spot of blood on the floor.

The Martians headed for the door. Gekko stopped and said to Jim, "Would you return with us, my friend?"

"No—oh, no," said Jim. "I have to stay here," then remembered to translate.

"And the little one?"

"Willis stays with me. That's right, isn't it, Willis?"

"Sure, Jim boy."

"Then tell Gekko so." Willis complied. Gekko said farewell sadly to the boys and to Willis and went on out the lock.

MacRae and Rawlings were in whispered, worried conference at the spot where Beecher had last been seen; Captain Marlowe was looking sleepy and confused and listening to them. Frank said, "Let's get out of here, Jim."

"Right."

The Martians were still outside. Gekko saw them as they came out, spoke to one of his kind, then said, "Where is the learned one who speaks our speech? We would talk with him."

"I guess they want Doc," said Frank.

"Is that what he meant?"

"I think so. We'll call him." They went back inside and dug MacRae out of a cluster of excited humans. "Doc," said Frank, "they want to talk with you—the Martians."

"Eh?" said MacRae. "Why me?"

"I don't know."

The doctor turned to Marlowe. "How about it, Skipper? Do you want to sit in on this?"

Mr. Marlowe rubbed his forehead. "No, I'm too confused to try to handle the language. You take it."

"Okay." MacRae went for his suit and mask, let the boys help dress him, and then did not deny them when they tagged along. However, once outside, they held back and watched from a distance.

MacRae walked down to the group standing on the ramp and addressed them. Voices boomed back at him. He entered the group and the boys could see him talking, answering, gesticulating with his hands. The conference continued quite a long time.

Finally MacRae dropped his arms to his sides and looked tired. Martian voices boomed in what was plainly farewell, then the whole party set out at a rapid, leisurely pace for the bridge and their own city. MacRae plodded back up the ramp.

In the lock Jim demanded, "What was it all about, Doc?"

"Eh? Hold your peace, son."

Inside MacRae took Marlowe's arm and led him toward the

office they had pre-empted. "You, too, Rawlings. The rest of you get about your business." Nevertheless the boys tagged along and MacRae let them come in. "You might as well hear it; you're in it up to your ears. Mind that door, Jim. Don't let anyone open it."

"Now what is it?" asked Jim's father. "What are you looking so grim about?"

"They want us to leave."

"Leave?"

"Get off Mars, go away, go back to Earth."

"What? Why do they suggest that?"

"It's not a suggestion; it's an order, an ultimatum. They aren't even anxious to give us time enough to get ships here from Earth. They want us to leave, every man jack, woman, and child; they want us to leave right away—and they aren't fooling!"

14.
WILLIS

Four days later Doctor MacRae stumbled into the same office. Marlowe still looked tired, but this time it was MacRae who looked exhausted. "Get these other people out of here, Skipper."

Marlowe dismissed them and closed the door. "Well?"

"You got my message?"

"Yes."

"Is the Proclamation of Autonomy written? Did the folks go for it?"

"Yes, it's written—we cribbed a good deal from the American Declaration of Independence I'm afraid, but we wrote one."

"I'm not interested in the rhetoric of the thing! How about it?"

"It's ratified. Easily enough here. We had quite a few startled queries from the Project camps, but it was accepted. I guess we owe Beecher a vote of thanks on that; he made independence seem like a fine idea."

"We owe Beecher nothing! He nearly got us all killed."

"Just how do you mean that?"

"I'll tell you—but I want to know about the Declaration. I had to make some promises. It's gone off?"

"Radioed to Chicago last night. No answer yet. But let me ask the questions: were you successful?"

"Yes." MacRae rubbed his eyes wearily. "We can stay. 'It was a great fight, Maw, but I won.' They'll let us stay."

Marlowe got up and started to set up a wire recorder. "Do you want to talk it into the record and save having to go over it again?"

MacRae waved it away. "No. Whatever formal report I make will have to be very carefully edited. I'll try to tell you about it first." He paused and looked thoughtful. "Jamie, how long has it been since men first landed on Mars? More than fifty Earth years, isn't it? I believe I have learned more about Martians in the past few hours than was learned in all that time. And yet I don't know anything about them. We kept trying to think of them as human, trying to force them into our molds. But they aren't human; they aren't anything like us at all."

He added, "They had interplanetary flight millions of years back . . . had it and gave it up."

"What?" said Marlowe.

"It doesn't matter. It's not important. It's just one of the things I happened to find out while I was talking with the old one, the same old one with whom Jim talked. By the way, Jim was seeing things; he's not a Martian at all."

"Wait a minute—what is he, then?"

"Oh, I guess he's a native of Mars all right, but he isn't what you and I mean by a Martian. At least he didn't look like one to me."

"What did he look like? Describe him."

MacRae looked puzzled. "Uh, I *can't*. Maybe Jim and I each saw what he wanted us to see. Never mind. Willis has to go back to the Martians and rather soon."

"I'm sorry," Marlowe answered. "Jim won't like that, but it's not a high price to pay if it pleases them."

"You don't understand, you don't understand at all. Willis is the key to the whole thing."

"Certainly he's been mixed up in it," agreed Marlowe, "but why the key?"

"Don't call Willis 'he'; call him 'she.' There—I did it myself. Habit."

"I don't care what sex the little beast is. Go on."

MacRae rubbed his temples. "That's the trouble. It's very complicated and I don't know where to start. Willis *is* important and it does matter that he's a she. Look, Jamie, you'll go down in history as the father of your country, no doubt, but, between ourselves, Jim should be credited for being the savior of it. It was directly due to Jim and Willis—Willis's love for Jim and Jim's staunch befriending of him—that the colonists are alive today instead of pushing up daisies. The ultimatum to get off this globe represented a concession made to Jim; they had intended to exterminate us."

Marlowe's mouth dropped open. "But that's impossible! Martians wouldn't do anything like that!"

"Could and would," MacRae stated flatly. "They've been having doubts about us for a long time. Beecher's notion of shipping Willis off to a zoo pushed them over the edge—but Jim's relationship to Willis pulled them back again. They compromised."

"I can't believe that they would," protested Marlowe, "nor can I see how they could."

"*Where's Beecher?*" MacRae said bluntly.

"Mmm . . . yes."

"So don't talk about what they can or can't do. We don't know anything about them . . . not *any*thing."

"I can't argue with you. But can you clear up some of this mystery about Jim and Willis? Why do they care? After all, Willis is just a bouncer."

"I don't think I can clear it up," MacRae admitted, "but I can sure lace it around with some theories. Do you know Willis's Martian name? Do you know what it means?"

"I didn't know he had one—I mean 'she'."

"It reads: 'In whom the hopes of a world are joined.' That suggest anything to you?"

"Gracious, no! Sounds like a name for a messiah, not a bouncer."

"Maybe you aren't joking. On the other hand, I may have translated it badly. Maybe it means 'Young Hopeful,' or merely 'Hope.' Maybe Martians go in for poetical meanings, like we do. Take my name, 'Donald.' Means 'World Ruler.' My parents sure muffed that one. Or maybe Martians enjoy giving bouncers fancy names. I once knew a Pekinese called, believe it or not, 'Grand Champion Manchu Prince of Belvedere.' " MacRae looked suddenly startled. "Do you know, I just remembered that dog's family-and-fireside name was Willis!"

"You don't say!"

"I do say." The doctor scratched the stubble on his chin and reflected that he should shave one of these weeks. "But it's not even a coincidence. I suggested the name 'Willis' to Jim in the first place; I was probably thinking of the Peke. Engaging little devil, with a pop-eyed way of looking at you just like Willis—our Willis. Which is to say that neither one of Willis's names necessarily means anything."

He sat so long without saying anything that Marlowe said, "You aren't clearing up the mystery very fast. You think that Willis's real name does mean something, don't you?—else you wouldn't have brought it up."

MacRae sat up with a jerk. "I do. I do indeed. I think Willis is sort of a Martian crown princess. Now wait a minute—don't throw anything. I won't get violent. That's a farfetched figure of speech. What do *you* think Willis is?"

"Me?" said Marlowe. "I think he's an example of exotic Martian *fauna*, semi-intelligent and adapted to his environment."

"Big words," complained the doctor. "*I* think he is what a Martian is before he grows up."

Marlowe looked pained. "There is no similarity of structure. They're as different as chalk and cheese."

"Granted. What's the similarity between a caterpillar and a butterfly?"

Marlowe opened his mouth and closed it. "I don't blame you," MacRae went on, "we never think of such metamorphosis in connection with higher types, whatever a 'higher type' is. But I think that is what Willis is and it appears to be why Willis has to go back to his people soon. He's in the nymph stage; he's about to go into a pupal stage—some sort of a long hibernation. When he comes out he'll be a Martian."

Marlowe chewed his lip. "There's nothing unreasonable about it—just startling."

"Everything about Mars is startling. Another thing: we've never been able to find anything resembling sex on this planet— various sorts of species conjugation, yes, but no sex. It appears to me that we missed it. I think that all the nymph Martians, the bouncers, are female; all of the adults are male. They change. I use the terms for want of better ones, of course. But if my theory is correct—and mind you, I'm not saying it is—then it might explain *why* Willis is such an important personage. Eh?"

Marlowe said wearily, "You ask me to assimilate too much at once."

"Emulate the Red Queen. I'm not through. I think the Martians have still another stage, the stage of the 'old one' to whom I talked—and I think it's the strangest one of all. Jamie, can you imagine a people having close and everyday relations with Heaven—*their* heaven—as close and matter of fact as the relations between, say, the United States and Canada?"

"Doc, I'll imagine anything you tell me to."

"We speak of the Martian 'other world'; what does it mean to you?"

"Nothing. Some sort of a trance, such as the East Indians indulge in."

"I ask you because I talked, so they told me, to someone in the 'other world'—the 'old one' I mean. Jamie, I think I negotiated our new colonizing treaty with a *ghost*.

"Now just keep your seat," MacRae went on. "I'll tell you why. I was getting nowhere with him so I changed the subject. We were talking Basic, by the way; he had picked Jim's brains. He knew every word that Jim might know and none that Jim couldn't be expected to know. I asked him to assume, for the sake of argument, that we were to be allowed to stay—in which case, would the Martians let us use their subway system to get to Copais? I rode one of those subways to the conference. Very clever—the acceleration is always *down*, as if the room were mounted on gymbals. The old one had trouble understanding what I wanted. Then he showed me a globe of Mars—very natural, except that it had no canals. Gekko was with me, just as he was with Jim. The old one and Gekko had a discussion, the gist of which was *what year was I at?* Then the globe changed before my eyes, bit by bit. I saw the canals crawl across the face of Mars. *I saw them being built*, Jamie.

"Now I ask you," he concluded, "what kind of a being is it that has trouble remembering which millenium he is in? Do you mind if I tag him a ghost?"

"I don't mind anything," Marlowe assured him. "Maybe we're all ghosts."

"I've given you one theory, Jamie; here is another: bouncers are Martians and Old Ones are entirely separate races. Bouncers are third class citizens, Martians are second class citizens, and the real owners we never see, because they live down underneath. They don't care what we do with the surface as long as we behave ourselves. We can use the park, we can even walk on the grass, but we mustn't frighten the birds. Or maybe the 'old one' was just hypnosis that Gekko used on me, maybe it's bouncers and Martians only, with bouncers having some fanatical religious significance to Martians, the way Hindus feel about cows. You name it."

"I can't," said Marlowe. "I'm satisfied that you managed to negotiate an agreement that permits us to stay on Mars. I suppose it will be years before we understand the Martians."

"You are putting it mildly, Jamie. The white man was still studying the American Indian, trying to find out what makes him tick, five hundred years after Columbus—and the Indian and the European are both *men*, like as two peas. These are *Martians*.

We'll never understand them; we aren't even headed in the same direction."

MacRae stood up. "I want to get a bath and some sleep. . . . after I see Jim."

"Just a minute. Doc, do you think we'll have any real trouble making this autonomy declaration stick?"

"It's got to stick. Relations with the Martians are eight times as delicate as we thought they were; absentee ownership isn't practical. Imagine trying to settle issues like this one by taking a vote back on Earth among board members that have never even *seen* a Martian."

"That's not what I mean. How much opposition will we run into?"

MacRae scratched his chin again. "Men have had to fight for their liberties before, Jamie. I don't know. It's up to us to convince the folks back on Earth that autonomy is necessary. With the food and population problem back on Earth being what it is, they'll do anything necessary—once they realize what we're up against—to keep the peace and continue migration. They don't want anything to hold up the Project."

"I hope you're right."

"In the long run I have to be right. We've got the Martians pitching on our team. Well, I'm on my way to break the news to Jim."

"He's not going to like it," said Jim's father.

"He'll get over it. Probably he'll find another bouncer and teach him English and call him Willis, too. Then he'll grow up and not make pets of bouncers. It won't matter." He looked thoughtful, and added, "But what becomes of Willis? I wish I knew."

Jim took it well. He accepted MacRae's much expurgated explanation and nodded. "I guess if Willis has to hibernate, well, that's that. When they come for him, I won't make any fuss. It was just that Howe and Beecher didn't have any *right* to take him."

"That's the slant, son. But it's right for him to go with the Martians because they know how to take care of him, when he needs it. You saw that when you were with them."

"Yes." Jim added, "Can I visit him?"

"He won't know you. He'll be asleep."

"Well—look, when he wakes up, will he know me?"

MacRae looked grave. He had asked the old one the same question. "Yes," he answered truthfully, "he'll have all his memory intact." He did not give Jim the rest of the answer—that the transition period would last more than forty Earth years.

"Well, that won't be so bad. I'm going to be awfully busy in school right now, anyhow."

"That's the spirit."

Jim looked up Frank and they went to their old room, vacant of womenfolk at the moment. Jim cradled Willis in his arms and told Frank what Doc had told him. Willis listened, but the conversation was apparently over the little Martian's depth; Willis made no comment.

Presently Willis became bored with it and started to sing. The selection was the latest Willis had heard, the tango Frank had presented to Jim: *¿Quién Es La Señorita?*

When it was over Frank said, "You know, Willis sounds exactly like a girl when he sings that."

Jim chuckled. *¿Quién Es La Señorita?*, Willis?"

Willis managed to look indignant. "Willis fine boy!" she insisted.

FARMER
IN THE
SKY

For Sandy

1.
EARTH

Our troop had been up in the High Sierras that day and we were late getting back. We had taken off from the camp field on time but Traffic Control swung us 'way east to avoid some weather. I didn't like it; Dad usually won't eat if I'm not home.

Besides that, I had had a new boy shoved off on me as co-pilot; my usual co-pilot and assistant patrol leader was sick, so our Scoutmaster, Mr. Kinski, gave me this twerp. Mr. Kinski rode in the other copter with the Cougar Patrol.

"Why don't you put on some speed?" the twerp wanted to know.

"Ever hear of traffic regulations?" I asked him.

The copter was on slave-automatic, controlled from the ground, and was cruising slowly, down a freight lane they had stuck us in.

The twerp laughed. "You can always have an emergency. Here—I'll show you." He switched on the mike. "Dog Fox Eight Three, calling traffic—"

I switched it off, then switched on again when Traffic answered and told them that we had called by mistake. The twerp looked disgusted. "Mother's good little boy!" he said in sticky sweet tones.

That was just the wrong thing to say to me. "Go aft," I told him, "and tell Slats Keifer to come up here."

"Why? He's not a pilot."

"Neither are you, for my money. But he weighs what you do and I want to keep the crate trimmed."

He settled back in his seat. "Old Man Kinski assigned me as co-pilot; here I stay."

I counted to ten and let it ride. The pilot compartment of a ship in the air is no place for a fight. We had nothing more to say to each other until I put her down on North Diego Platform and cut the tip jets.

I was last one out, of course. Mr. Kinski was waiting there for us but I didn't see him; all I saw was the twerp. I grabbed him by the shoulder. "Want to repeat that crack now?" I asked him.

Mr. Kinski popped up out of nowhere, stepped between us and said, "Bill! Bill! What's the meaning of this?"

"I—" I started to say that I was going to slap the twerp loose from his teeth, but I thought better of it.

Mr. Kinski turned to the twerp. "What happened, Jones?"

"I didn't do anything! Ask anybody."

I was about to say that he could tell that to the Pilots' Board. Insubordination in the air is a serious matter. But that "Ask anybody" stopped me. Nobody else had seen or heard anything.

Mr. Kinski looked at each of us, then said, "Muster your patrol and dismiss them, Bill." So I did and went on home.

All in all, I was tired and jumpy by the time I got home. I had listened to the news on the way home; it wasn't good. The ration had been cut another ten calories—which made me still hungrier and reminded me that I hadn't been home to get Dad's supper. The newscaster went on to say that the Spaceship *Mayflower* had finally been commissioned and that the rolls were now opened for emigrants. Pretty lucky for them, I thought. No short rations. No twerps like Jones.

And a brand new planet.

George—my father, that is—was sitting in the apartment, looking over some papers. "Howdy, George," I said to him, "eaten yet?"

"Hello, Bill. No."

"I'll have supper ready right away." I went into the pantry and could see that he hadn't eaten lunch, either. I decided to fix him a plus meal.

I grabbed two Syntho-Steaks out of the freezer and slapped them in quickthaw, added a big Idaho baked potato for Dad and a smaller one for me, then dug out a package of salad and let it warm naturally.

By the time I had poured boiling water over two soup cubes and over coffee powder the steaks were ready for the broiler. I transferred them, letting it cycle at medium rare, and stepped up the gain on the quickthaw so that the spuds would be ready when the steaks were—then back to the freezer for a couple of icekreem cake slices for dessert.

The spuds were ready. I took a quick look at my ration accounts, decided we could afford it, and set out a couple of pats of butterine for them. The broiler was ringing; I removed the steaks, set everything out, and switched on the candles, just as Anne would have done.

"Come and get it!" I yelled and turned back to enter the calorie and point score on each item from the wrappers, then shoved the wrappers in the incinerator. That way you never get your accounts fouled up.

Dad sat down as I finished. Elapsed time from scratch, two minutes and twenty seconds—there's nothing hard about cooking; I don't see why women make such a fuss about it. No system, probably.

Dad sniffed the steaks and grinned. "Oh boy! Bill, you'll bankrupt us."

"You let me worry," I said. "I'm still plus for this quarter." Then I frowned. "But I won't be, next quarter, unless they quit cutting the ration."

Dad stopped with a piece of steak on its way to his mouth. "Again?"

"Again. Look, George, I don't get it. This was a good crop year and they started operating the Montana yeast plant besides."

"You follow all the commissary news, don't you, Bill?"

"Naturally."

"Did you notice the results of the Chinese census as well? Try it on your slide rule."

I knew what he meant—and the steak suddenly tasted like old rubber. What's the use in being careful if somebody on the other side of the globe is going to spoil your try? "Those darned Chinese ought to quit raising babies and start raising food!"

"Share and share alike, Bill."

"But—" I shut up. George was right, he usually is, but somehow it didn't seem fair. "Did you hear about the *Mayflower?*" I asked to change the subject.

"What about the *Mayflower?*" Dad's voice was suddenly cautious, which surprised me. Since Anne died—Anne was my mother—George and I have been about as close as two people can be.

"Why, she was commissioned, that's all. They've started picking emigrants."

"So?" There was that cautious tone again. "What did you do to-day?"

"Nothing much. We hiked about five miles north of camp and Mr. Kinski put some of the kids through tests. I saw a mountain lion."

"Really? I thought they were all gone."

"Well, I thought I saw one."

"Then you probably did. What else?"

I hesitated, then told him about this twerp Jones. "He's not even a member of our troop. How does he get that way, interfering with my piloting?"

"You did right, Bill. Sounds as if this twerp Jones, as you call him, was too young to be trusted with a pilot's license."

"Matter of fact, he's a year older than I am."

"In my day you had to be sixteen before you could even go up for your license."

"Times change, George."

"So they do. So they do."

Dad suddenly looked sad and I knew he was thinking about Anne. I hastily said, "Old enough or not, how does an insect like Jones get by the temperament-stability test?"

"Psycho tests aren't perfect, Bill. Neither are people." Dad sat back and lit his pipe. "Want me to clean up tonight?"

"No, thanks." He always asked; I always turned him down. Dad is absent-minded; he lets ration points get into the incinerator. When I salvage, I really salvage. "Feel like a game of cribbage?"

"I'll beat the pants off you."

"You and who else?" I salvaged the garbage, burned the dishes, followed him into the living room. He was getting out the board and cards.

His mind wasn't really on the game. I was around the corner and ready to peg out before he was really under way. Finally he put down his cards and looked square at me. "Son——"

"Huh? I mean, 'Yes, George?' "

"I've decided to emigrate in the *Mayflower*."

I knocked over the cribbage board. I picked it up, eased my throttle, and tried to fly right. "That's swell! When do we leave?"

Dad puffed furiously on his pipe. "That's the point, Bill. You're not going."

I couldn't say anything. Dad had never done anything like this to me before. I sat there, working my mouth like a fish. Finally I managed, "Dad, you're joking."

"No, I'm not, Son."

"But why? Answer me that one question: why?"

"Now see here, Son——"

"Call me 'Bill'."

"Okay, Bill. It's one thing for me to decide to take my chances with colonial life but I've got no right to get *you* off to a bad start. You've got to finish your education. There are no decent schools on Ganymede. You get your education, then when you're grown, if you want to emigrate, that's your business."

"That's the reason? That's the *only* reason? To go to *school?*"

"Yes. You stay here and take your degree. I'd like to see you take your doctor's degree as well. Then, if you want to, you can join me. You won't have missed your chance; applicants with close relatives there have priority."

"No!"

Dad looked stubborn.

So did I, I guess. "George, I'm telling you, if you leave me behind, it won't do any good. I won't go to school. I can pass the exams for third class citizenship right now. Then I can get a work permit and——"

He cut me short. "You won't need a work permit. I'm leaving you well provided for, Bill. You'll——"

" 'Well provided for'! Do you think I'd touch a credit of yours if you go away and leave me? I'll live on my student's allowance until I pass the exams and get my work card."

"Bring your voice down, Son!" He went on, "You're proud of being a Scout, aren't you?"

"Well—yes."

"I seem to remember that Scouts are supposed to be obedient. And courteous, too."

That one was pretty hot over the plate. I had to think about it. "George——"

"Yes, Bill?"

"If I was rude, I'm sorry. But the Scout Law wasn't thought up to make it easy to push a Scout around. As long as I'm living in your home I'll do what you say. But if you walk out on me, you don't have any more claim on me. Isn't that fair?"

"Be reasonable, Son. I'm doing it for your own good."

"Don't change the subject, George. Is that fair or isn't it? If you go hundreds of millions of miles away, how can you expect to run my life after you're gone? I'll be on my own."

"I'll still be your father."

"Fathers and sons should stick together. As I recall, the fathers that came over in the original *Mayflower* brought their kids with them."

"This is different."

"How?"

"It's further, incredibly further—and dangerous."

"So was that move dangerous—half the Plymouth Rock colony died the first winter; everybody knows that. And distance doesn't mean anything; what matters is how long it takes. If I had had to walk back this afternoon, I'd still be hiking next month. It took the Pilgrims sixty-three days to cross the Atlantic or so they taught me in school—but this afternoon the caster said that the *Mayflower*—will reach Ganymede in sixty days. That makes Ganymede closer than London was to Plymouth Rock."

Dad stood up and knocked out his pipe. "I'm not going to argue, Son."

"And I'm not, either." I took a deep breath. I shouldn't have said the next thing I did say, but I was mad. I'd never been treated this way before and I guess I wanted to hurt back. "But I can tell you this: you're not the only one who is sick of short rations. If you think I'm going to stay here while you're eating high on the hog out in the colonies, then you had better think about it again. *I* thought we were partners."

That last was the meanest part of it and I should have been ashamed. That was what he had said to me the day after Anne died, and that was the way it had always been.

The minute I said it I knew why George had to emigrate and I knew it didn't have anything to do with ration points. But I didn't know how to unsay it.

Dad stared. Then he said slowly, "You think that's how it is? That I want to go away so I can quit skipping lunch to save ration points?"

"What else?" I answered. I was stuck in a groove; I didn't know what to say.

"Hmm . . . well, if you believe that, Bill, there is nothing I can say. I think I'll turn in."

I went to my room, feeling all mixed up inside. I wanted Mother around so bad I could taste it and I knew that George felt the same way. She would never have let us reach the point where we were actually shouting at each other—at least I had shouted. Besides that, the partnership was busted up, it would never be the same.

I felt better after a shower and a long massage. I knew that the partnership couldn't really be busted up. In the long run, when George saw that I had to go, he wouldn't let college stand in the way. I was sure of that—well, pretty sure at least.

I began to think about Ganymede.

Ganymede!

Why, I had never even been out to the Moon!

There was a boy in my class who had been born on the Moon. His parents were still there; he had been sent home for schooling. He gave himself airs as a deep-space man. But Luna was less than a quarter of a million miles away; you could practically throw rocks at it. It wasn't self-supporting; Moon Colony had the same rations as Earth. It was really part of Earth. But *Ganymede!*

Let's see—Jupiter was half a billion miles away, more or less, depending on the time of year. What was the tiny distance to the Moon compared with a jump like that?

Suddenly I couldn't remember whether Ganymede was Jupiter's third moon or fourth. And I just had to know. There was a book out in the living room that would tell and more besides— Ellsworth Smith's *A Tour of Earth's Colonies*. I went out to get it.

Dad hadn't gone to bed. He was sitting up, reading. I said, "Oh—hello," and went to look for the book. He nodded and went on reading.

The book wasn't where it should have been. I looked around and Dad said, "What are you looking for, Bill?"

Then I saw that he was reading it. I said, "Oh, nothing. I didn't know you were using it."

"This?" He held it up.

"It doesn't matter. I'll find something else."

"Take it. I'm through with it."

"Well . . . All right—thanks." I took it and turned away.

"Just a minute, Bill."

I waited. "I've come to a decision, Bill. I'm not going."

"Huh?"

"You were right about us being partners. My place is here."

"Yes, but—Look, George, I'm sorry I said what I did about rations. I know that's not the reason. The reason is—well, you've *got* to go." I wanted to tell him I knew the reason was Anne, but if I said Anne's name out loud I was afraid I'd bawl.

"You mean that you are willing to stay behind—and go to school?"

"Uh—" I wasn't quite ready to say that; I was dead set on going myself. "I didn't quite mean that. I meant that I know why you want to go, why you've *got* to go."

"Hmm . . ." He lit his pipe, making a long business of it. "I see. Or maybe I don't." Then he added, "Let's put it this way, Bill. The partnership stands. Either we both go, or we both stay—unless you decide of your own volition that you will stay to get your degree and join me out there later. Is that fair?"

"Huh? Oh, yes!"

"So let's talk about it later."

I said goodnight and ducked into my room quick. William, my boy, I told myself, it's practically in the bag—if you can just keep from getting soft-hearted and agreeing to a split up. I crawled into bed and opened the book.

Ganymede was Jupiter-III; I should have remembered that. It was bigger than Mercury, much bigger than the Moon, a respectable planet, even if it was a moon. The surface gravity was one third of Earth-normal; I would weigh about forty-five pounds there. First contacted in 1985—which I knew—and its atmosphere project started in 1998 and had been running ever since.

There was a stereo in the book of Jupiter as seen from Ganymede—round as an apple, ruddy orange, and squashed on both poles. And big as all outdoors. Beautiful. I fell asleep staring at it.

Dad and I didn't get a chance to talk for the next three days as my geography class spent that time in Antarctica. I came back with a frostbitten nose and some swell pix of penguins—and some revised ideas. I had had time to think.

Dad had fouled up the account book as usual but he had remembered to save the wrappers and it didn't take me long to straighten things out. After dinner I let him beat me two games, then said, "Look, George——"

"Yes?"

"You know what we were talking about?"

"Well, yes."

"It's this way. I'm under age; I can't go if you won't let me. Seems to me you ought to, but if you don't, I won't quit school. In any case, you ought to go—you *need* to go—you know why. I'm asking you to think it over and take me along, but I'm not going to be a baby about it."

Dad almost looked embarrassed. "That's quite a speech, Son.

You mean you're willing to let me go, you stay here and go to school, and not make a fuss about it?"

"Well, not 'willing'—but I'd put up with it."

"Thanks." Dad fumbled in his pouch and pulled out a flat photo. "Take a look at this."

"What is it?"

"Your file copy of your application for emigration. I submitted it two days ago."

2.
THE GREEN-EYED MONSTER

<hr>

I wasn't much good in school for the next few days. Dad cautioned me not to get worked up over it; they hadn't approved our applications as yet. "You know, Bill, ten times as many people apply as can possibly go."

"But most of them want to go to Venus or Mars. Ganymede is too far away; that scares the sissies out."

"I wasn't talking about applications for all the colonies; I meant applications for Ganymede, specifically for this first trip of the *Mayflower*."

"Even so, you can't scare me. Only about one in ten can qualify. That's the way it's always been."

Dad agreed. He said that this was the first time in history that some effort was being made to select the best stock for colonization instead of using colonies as dumping grounds for misfits and criminals and failures. Then he added, "But look, Bill, what gives you the notion that you and I can necessarily qualify? Neither one of us is a superman."

That rocked me back on my heels. The idea that we might not be good enough hadn't occurred to me. "George, they couldn't turn us *down!*"

"They could and they might."

"But how? They need engineers out there and you're tops. Me—I'm not a genius but I do all right in school. We're both healthy and we don't have any bad mutations; we aren't color blind or bleeders or anything like that."

"No bad mutations *that we know of,*" Dad answered. "However, I agree that we seem to have done a fair job in picking our grandparents. I wasn't thinking of anything as obvious as that."

"Well, what, then? What could they possibly get us on?"

He fiddled with his pipe the way he always does when he doesn't want to answer right away. "Bill, when I pick a steel alloy for a job, it's not enough to say, 'Well, it's a nice shiny piece of metal; let's use it.' No, I take into account a list of tests as long as your arm that tells me all about that alloy, what it's good for and just what I can expect it to do in the particular circumstances I intend to use it. Now if you had to pick people for a tough job of colonizing, what would you look for?"

"Uh . . . I don't know."

"Neither do I. I'm not a social psychometrician. But to say that they want healthy people with fair educations is like saying that I want steel rather than wood for a job. It doesn't tell what sort of steel. Or it might not be steel that was needed; it might be titanium alloy. So don't get your hopes too high."

"But—well, look, what can we *do* about it?"

"Nothing. If we don't get picked, then tell yourself that you are a darn good grade of steel and that it's no fault of yours that they wanted magnesium."

It was all very well to look at it that way, but it worried me. I didn't let it show at school, though. I had already let everybody know that we had put in for Ganymede; if we missed—well, it would be sort of embarrassing.

My best friend, Duck Miller, was all excited about it and was determined to go, too.

"But how can you?" I asked. "Do your folks want to go?"

"I already looked into that," Duck answered. "All I have to have is a grown person as a sponsor, a guardian. Now if you can tease your old man into signing for me, it's in the bag."

"But what will *your* father say?"

"He won't care. He's always telling me that when he was my age he was earning his own living. He says a boy should be self reliant. Now how about it? Will you speak to your old man about it—tonight?"

I said I would and I did. Dad didn't say anything for a moment, then he asked: "You really want Duck with you?"

"Sure I do. He's my best friend."

"What does his father say?"

"He hasn't asked him yet," and then I explained how Mr. Miller felt about it.

"So?" said Dad. "Then let's wait and see what Mr. Miller says."

"Well—look, George, does that mean that you'll sign for Duck if his father says it's okay?"

"I meant what I said, Bill. Let's wait. The problem may solve itself."

I said, "Oh well, maybe Mr. and Mrs. Miller will decide to put in for it, too, after Duck gets them stirred up."

Dad just cocked an eyebrow at me. "Mr. Miller has, shall we say, numerous business interests here. I think it would be easier to jack up one corner of Boulder Dam than to get him to give them up."

"You're giving up *your* business."

"Not my business, my professional practice. But I'm not giving up my profession; I'm taking it with me."

I saw Duck at school the next day and asked him what his father had said.

"Forget it," he told me. "The deal is off."

"Huh?"

"My old man says that nobody but an utter idiot would even think of going out to Ganymede. He says that Earth is the only planet in the system fit to live on and that if the government wasn't loaded up with a bunch of starry-eyed dreamers we would quit pouring money down a rat hole trying to turn a bunch of bare rocks in the sky into green pastures. He says the whole enterprise is doomed."

"You didn't think so yesterday."

"That was before I got the straight dope. You know what? My old man is going to take me into partnership. Just as soon as I'm through college he's going to start breaking me into the management end. He says he didn't tell me before because he wanted me to learn self reliance and initiative, but he thought it was time I knew about it. What do you think of that?"

"Why, that's pretty nice, I suppose. But what's this about the 'enterprise being doomed'?"

" 'Nice', he calls it! Well, my old man says that it is an absolute impossibility to keep a permanent colony on Ganymede. It's a perilous toehold, artificially maintained—those were his exact words—and someday the gadgets will bust and the whole colony will be wiped out, every man jack, and then we will quit trying to go against nature."

We didn't talk any more then as we had to go to class. I told Dad about it that night. "What do you think, George?"

"Well, there is something in what he says——"

"Huh?"

"Don't jump the gun. If everything went sour on Ganymede at once and we didn't have the means to fix it, it would revert to the state we found it in. But that's not the whole answer. People have a funny habit of taking as 'natural' whatever they are used to—but there hasn't been any 'natural' environment, the way they mean it, since men climbed down out of trees. Bill, how many people are there in California?"

"Fifty-five, sixty million."

"Did you know that the first four colonies here starved to death? 'S truth! How is it that fifty-odd million can live here and not starve? Barring short rations, of course."

He answered it himself. "We've got four atomic power plants along the coast just to turn sea water into fresh water. We use every drop of the Colorado River and every foot of snow that falls on the Sierras. And we use a million other gadgets. If those gadgets went bad—say a really big earthquake knocked out all four atomic plants—the country would go back to desert. I doubt if we could evacuate that many people before most of them died from thirst. Yet I don't think Mr. Miller is lying awake nights worrying about it. He regards Southern California as a good 'natural' environment.

"Depend on it, Bill. Wherever Man has mass and energy to work with and enough savvy to know how to manipulate them, he can create any environment he needs."

I didn't see much of Duck after that. About then we got our preliminary notices to take tests for eligibility for the Ganymede colony and that had us pretty busy. Besides, Duck seemed different—or maybe it was me. I had the trip on my mind and he didn't want to talk about it. Or if he did, he'd make some crack that rubbed me the wrong way.

Dad wouldn't let me quit school while it was still uncertain as to whether or not we would qualify, but I was out a lot, taking tests. There was the usual physical examination, of course, with some added wrinkles. A *g* test, for example—I could take up to eight gravities before I blacked out, the test showed. And a test for low-pressure tolerance and hemorrhaging—they didn't want people who ran to red noses and varicose veins. There were lots more.

But we passed them. Then came the psycho tests which were a

lot worse because you never knew what was expected of you and half the time you didn't even know you were being tested. It started off with hypno-analysis, which really puts a fellow at a disadvantage. How do you know what you've blabbed while they've got you asleep?

Once I sat around endlessly waiting for a psychiatrist to get around to seeing me. There were a couple of clerks there; when I came in one of them dug my medical and psycho record out of file and laid it on a desk. Then the other one, a red-headed guy with a permanent sneer, said, "Okay, Shorty, sit down on that bench and wait."

After quite a while the redhead picked up my folder and started to read it. Presently he snickered and turned to the other clerk and said, "Hey, Ned—get a load of this!"

The other one read what he was pointing to and seemed to think it was funny, too. I could see they were watching me and I pretended not to pay any attention.

The second clerk went back to his desk, but presently the redhead went over to him, carrying my folder, and read aloud to him, but in such a low voice that I couldn't catch many of the words. What I did catch made me squirm.

When he had finished the redhead looked right at me and laughed. I stood up and said, "What's so funny?"

He said, "None of your business, Shorty. Sit down."

I walked over and said, "Let me see that."

The second clerk stuffed it into a drawer of his desk. The redhead said, "Mamma's boy wants to see it, Ned. Why don't you give it to him?"

"He doesn't really want to see it," the other one said.

"No, I guess not." The redhead laughed again and added, "And to think he wants to be a big bold colonist."

The other one looked at me while chewing a thumbnail and said, "I don't think that's so funny. They could take him along to cook."

This seemed to convulse the redhead. "I'll bet he looks cute in an apron."

A year earlier I would have poked him, even though he outweighed me and outreached me. That "Mamma's boy" remark made me forget all about wanting to go to Ganymede; I just wanted to wipe the silly smirk off his face.

But I didn't do anything. I don't know why; maybe it was from riding herd on that wild bunch of galoots, the Yucca Patrol—Mr.

Kinski says that anybody who can't keep order without using his fists can't be a patrol leader under him.

Anyhow I just walked around the end of the desk and tried to open the drawer. It was locked. I looked at them; they were both grinning, but I wasn't. "I had an appointment for thirteen o'clock," I said. "Since the doctor isn't here, you can tell him I'll phone for another appointment." And I turned on my heel and left.

I went home and told George about it. He just said he hoped I hadn't hurt my chances.

I never did get another appointment. You know what? They weren't clerks at all; they were psychometricians and there was a camera and a mike on me the whole time.

Finally George and I got notices saying that we were qualified and had been posted for the *Mayflower,* "subject to compliance with all requirements."

That night I didn't worry about ration points; I really set us out a feast.

There was a booklet of the requirements mentioned. "Satisfy all debts"—that didn't worry me; aside from a half credit I owed Slats Keifer I didn't have any. "Post an appearance bond"— George would take care of that. "Conclude any action before any court of superior jurisdiction"—I had never been in court except the Court of Honor. There were a flock of other things, but George would handle them.

I found some fine print that worried me. "George," I said, "It says here that emigration is limited to families with children."

He looked up. "Well, aren't we such a family? If you don't mind being classified as a child."

"Oh. I suppose so. I thought it meant a married couple and kids."

"Don't give it a thought."

Privately I wondered if Dad knew what he was talking about.

We were busy with innoculations and blood typing and immunizations and I hardly got to school at all. When I wasn't being stuck or being bled, I was sick with the last thing they had done to me. Finally we had to have our whole medical history tattooed on us—identity number, Rh factor, blood type, coag time, diseases you had had, natural immunities and inoculations. The girls and the women usually had it done in invisible ink that showed up only under infra-red light, or else they put it on the soles of their feet.

They asked me where I wanted it, the soles of my feet? I said no, I don't want to be crippled up; I had too much to do. We compromised on putting it where I sit down and then I ate standing up for a couple of days. It seemed a good place, private anyhow. But I had to use a mirror to see it.

Time was getting short; we were supposed to be at Mojave Space Port on 26 June, just two weeks away. It was high time I was picking out what to take. The allowance was fifty-seven and six-tenths pounds per person and had not been announced until all our body weights had been taken.

The booklet had said, "Close your terrestrial affairs as if you were dying." That's easy to say. But when you die, you can't take it with you, while here we could—fifty-seven-odd pounds of it.

The question was: what fifty-seven pounds?

My silkworms I turned over to the school biology lab and the same for the snakes. Duck wanted my aquarium but I wouldn't let him; twice he's had fish and twice he's let them die. I split them between two fellows in the troop who already had fish. The birds I gave to Mrs. Fishbein on our deck. I didn't have a cat or a dog; George says ninety floors up is no place to keep junior citizens— that's what he calls them.

I was cleaning up the mess when George came in. "Well," he says, "first time I've been able to come into your room without a gas mask."

I skipped it; George talks like that. "I still don't know what to do," I said, pointing at the heap on my bed.

"Microfilmed everything you can?"

"Yes, everything but this picture." It was a cabinet stereo of Anne, weighing about a pound and nine ounces.

"Keep that, of course. Face it, Bill, you've got to travel light. We're pioneers."

"I don't know what to throw out."

I guess I looked glum for he said, "Quit feeling sorry for your-self. Me, I've got to give up *this*—and that's tough, believe me." He held out his pipe.

"Why?" I asked. "A pipe doesn't weigh much."

"Because they aren't raising tobacco on Ganymede and they aren't importing any."

"Oh. Look, George, I could just about make it if it weren't for my accordion. But it licks me."

"Hmm . . . Have you considered listing it as a cultural item?"

"Huh?"

"Read the fine print. Approved cultural items are not covered by the personal weight schedule. They are charged to the colony."

It had never occurred to me that I might have anything that would qualify. "They wouldn't let me get away with it, George!"

"Can't rule you out for trying. Don't be a defeatist."

So two days later I was up before the cultural and scientific board, trying to prove that I was an asset. I knocked out *Turkey in the Straw*, Nehru's *Opus 81*, and the introduction to Morgenstern's *Dawn of the 22nd Century*, as arranged for squeeze boxes. I gave them *The Green Hills of Earth* for an encore.

They asked me if I liked to play for other people and told me politely that I would be informed as to the decision of the board ... and about a week later I got a letter directing me to turn my accordion over to the Supply Office, Hayward Field. I was in, I was a "cultural asset"!

Four days before blast-off Dad came home early—he had been closing his office—and asked me if we could have something special for dinner; we were having guests. I said I supposed so; my accounts showed that we would have rations to turn back.

He seemed embarrassed. "Son———"

"Huh? Yes, George?"

"You know that item in the rules about families?"

"Uh, yes."

"Well, you were right about it, but I was holding out on you and now I've got to confess. I'm getting married tomorrow."

There was a sort of roaring in my ears. Dad couldn't have surprised me more if he had slapped me.

I couldn't say anything. I just stood there, looking at him. Finally I managed to get out, "But, George, you can't do that!"

"Why not, Son?"

"How about Anne?"

"Anne is dead."

"But—But—" I couldn't say anything more; I ducked into my room and locked myself in. I lay on the bed, trying to think.

Presently I heard Dad trying the latch. Then he tapped on the door and said, "Bill?"

I didn't answer. After a while he went away. I lay there a while longer. I guess I bawled, but I wasn't bawling over the trouble with Dad. It seemed the way it did the day Anne died, when I couldn't get it through my head that I wouldn't ever see her again. Wouldn't ever see her smile at me again and hear her say, "Stand tall, Billy."

And I would stand tall and she would look proud and pat my arm.

How could George do it? How could he bring some other woman into Anne's home?

I got up and had a look at myself in the mirror and then went in and set my 'fresher for a needle shower and a hard massage. I felt better afterwards, except that I still had a sick feeling in my stomach. The 'fresher blew me off and dusted me and sighed to a stop. Through the sound it seemed to me I could hear Anne speaking to me, but that must have been in my head.

She was saying, "Stand tall, Son." I got dressed again and went out.

Dad was messing around with dinner and I do mean messing. He had burned his thumb on the shortwave, don't ask me how. I had to throw out what he had been fiddling with, all except the salad. I picked out more stuff and started them cycling. Neither of us said anything.

I set the table for three and Dad finally spoke. "Better set it for four, Bill. Molly has a daughter, you know."

I dropped a fork. "Molly? You mean Mrs. Kenyon?"

"Yes. Didn't I tell you? No, you didn't give me a chance to."

I knew her all right. She was Dad's draftsman. I knew her daughter, too—a twelve-year-old brat. Somehow, it being Mrs. Kenyon made it worse, indecent. Why, she had even come to Anne's Farewell and had had the nerve to cry.

I knew now why she had always been so chummy with me whenever I was down at Dad's office. She had had her eye on George.

I didn't say anything. What was there to say?

I said "How do you do?" politely when they came in, then went out and pretended to fiddle with dinner. Dinner was sort of odd. Dad and Mrs. Kenyon talked and I answered when spoken to. I didn't listen. I was still trying to figure out how he could do it. The brat spoke to me a couple of times but I soon put her in her place.

After dinner Dad said how about all of us going to a show? I begged off, saying that I still had sorting to do. They went.

I thought and thought about it. Any way I looked at it, it seemed like a bad deal.

At first I decided that I wouldn't go to Ganymede after all, not if they were going. Dad would forfeit my bond, but I would work hard and pay it back—I wasn't going to owe *them* anything!

Then I finally figured out why Dad was doing it and I felt some better, but not much. It was too high a price.

Dad got home late, by himself, and tapped on my door. It wasn't locked and he came in. "Well, Son?" he said.

" 'Well' what?"

"Bill, I know that this business comes as a surprise to you, but you'll get over it."

I laughed, though I didn't feel funny. Get over it! Maybe he could forget Anne, but I never would.

"In the meantime," he went on, "I want you to behave yourself. I suppose you know you were as rude as you could be without actually spitting in their faces?"

"Me rude?" I objected. "Didn't I fix dinner for them? Wasn't I polite?"

"You were as polite as a judge passing sentence. And as friendly. You needed a swift kick to make you remember your manners."

I guess I looked stubborn. George went on, "That's done; let's forget it. See here, Bill—in time you are going to see that this was a good idea. All I ask you to do is to behave yourself in the meantime. I don't ask you to fall on their necks; I do insist that you be your own normal, reasonably polite and friendly self. Will you try?"

"Uh, I suppose so." Then I went on with, "See here, Dad, why did you have to spring it on me as a surprise?"

He looked embarrassed. "That was a mistake. I suppose I did it because I knew you would raise Cain about it and I wanted to put it off."

"But I would have understood if you had only *told* me. I know why you want to marry her——"

"Eh?"

"I should have known when you mentioned that business about rules. You have to get married so that we can go to Ganymede——"

"What?"

I was startled. I said, "Huh? That's right, isn't it? You told me so yourself. You said——"

"I said nothing of the sort!" Dad stopped, took a deep breath, then went on slowly, "Bill, I suppose you possibly could have gathered that impression—though I am not flattered that you could have entertained it. Now I'll spell out the true situation: Molly and I are not getting married in order to emigrate. We are emigrating because we are getting married. You may be too young to understand it, but I love Molly and Molly loves me. If I wanted to stay here, she'd stay. Since I want to go, she wants to go. She's wise enough to understand that I need to make a complete break with my old background. Do you follow me?"

I said I guessed so.

"I'll say goodnight, then."

I answered, "Goodnight." He turned away, but I added, "George—" He stopped.

I blurted out. "You don't love Anne any more, do you?"

Dad turned white. He started back in and then stopped. "Bill," he said slowly, "it has been some years since I've laid a hand on you—but this is the first time I ever wanted to give you a thrashing."

I thought he was going to do it. I waited and I had made up my mind that if he touched me he was going to get the surprise of his life. But he didn't come any nearer; he just closed the door between us.

After awhile I took another shower that I didn't need and went to bed. I must have lain there an hour or more, thinking that Dad had wanted to hit me and wishing that Anne were around to tell me what to do. Finally I switched on the dancing lights and stared at them until they knocked me out.

Neither one of us said anything until breakfast was over and neither of us ate much, either. Finally Dad said, "Bill, I want to beg your pardon for what I said last night. You hadn't done or said anything to justify raising a hand to you and I had no business thinking it or saying it."

I said, "Oh, that's all right." I thought about it and added, "I guess I shouldn't have said what I did."

"It was all right to say it. What makes me sad is that you could have thought it. Bill, I've never stopped loving Anne and I'll never love her any less."

"But you said—" I stopped and finished, "I just don't get it."

"I guess there is no reason to expect you to." George stood up. "Bill, the ceremony is at fifteen o'clock. Will you be dressed and ready about an hour before that time?"

I hesitated and said, "I won't be able to, George. I've got a pretty full day."

His face didn't have any expression at all and neither did his voice. He said, "I see," and left the room. A bit later he left the apartment. A while later I tried to call him at his office, but the autosecretary ground out the old stall about "Would you like to record a message?" I didn't. I figured that George would be home some time before fifteen hundred and I got dressed in my best. I even used some of Dad's beard cream.

He didn't show up. I tried the office again, and again, got the "Would-you-like-to-record-a-message?" routine. Then I braced myself and looked up the code on Mrs. Kenyon.

He wasn't there. Nobody was there.

The time crawled past and there was nothing I could do about it. After a while it was fifteen o'clock and I knew that my father was off somewhere getting married but I didn't know where. About fifteen-thirty I went out and went to a show.

When I got back the red light was shining on the phone. I dialed playback and it was Dad: "Bill I tried to reach you but you weren't in and I can't wait. Molly and I are leaving on a short trip. If you need to reach me, call Follow Up Service, Limited, in Chicago—we'll be somewhere in Canada. We'll be back Thursday night. Goodbye." That was the end of the recording.

Thursday night—blast-off was Friday morning.

3.
SPACE SHIP *BIFROST*

Dad called me from Mrs. Kenyon's—I mean from Molly's—apartment Thursday night. We were both polite but uneasy. I said yes, I was all ready and I hoped they had had a nice time. He said they had and would I come over and we would all leave from there in the morning.

I said I hadn't known what his plans were, so I had bought a ticket to Mojave port and had reserved a room at Hotel Lancaster. What did he want me to do?

He thought about it and said, "It looks like you can take care of yourself, Bill."

"Of course I can."

"All right. We'll see you at the port. Want to speak to Molly?"

"Uh, no, just tell her hello for me."

"Thanks, I will." He switched off.

I went to my room and got my kit—fifty-seven and fifty-nine hundredths pounds; I couldn't have added a clipped frog's hair. My room was bare, except for my Scout uniform. I couldn't afford to take it, but I hadn't thrown it away yet.

I picked it up, intending to take it to the incinerator, then stopped. At the physical exam I had been listed at one hundred thirty-one and two tenths pounds mass in the clothes I would wear for blast off.

But I hadn't eaten much the last few days.

I stepped into the 'fresher and onto the scales—one hundred twenty-nine and eight tenths. I picked up the uniform and stepped back on the scales—one hundred thirty-two and five tenths.

William, I said, you get no dinner, you get no breakfast, and you drink no water tomorrow morning. I bundled up my uniform and took it along.

The apartment was stripped. As a surprise for the next tenant I left in the freezer the stuff I had meant to eat for supper, then switched all the gadgets to zero except the freezer, and locked the door behind me. It felt funny; Anne and George and I had lived there as far back as I could remember.

I went down to subsurface, across town, and caught the In-Coast tube for Mojave. Twenty minutes later I was at Hotel Lancaster in the Mojave Desert.

I soon found out that the "room" I had reserved was a cot in the billiard room. I trotted down to find out what had happened.

I showed the room clerk the 'stat that said I had a room coming to me. He looked at it and said, "Young man, have you ever tried to bed down six thousand people at once?"

I said no, I hadn't.

"Then be glad you've got a cot. The room you reserved is occupied by a family with nine children."

I went.

The hotel was a madhouse. I couldn't have gotten anything to eat even if I hadn't promised myself not to eat; you couldn't get within twenty yards of the dining room. There were children underfoot everywhere and squalling brats galore. There were emigrant families squatting in the ball room. I looked them over and wondered how they had picked them; out of a grab bag?

Finally I went to bed. I was hungry and got hungrier. I began to wonder why I was going to all this trouble to hang on to a Scout uniform I obviously wasn't going to use.

If I had had my ration book I would have gotten up and stood in line at the dining room—but Dad and I had turned ours in. I still had some money and thought about trying to find a free-dealers; they say you can find them around a hotel. But Dad says that "free-dealer" is a fake word; they are black marketeers and no gentleman will buy from them.

Besides that I didn't have the slightest idea of how to go about finding one.

I got up and got a drink and went back to bed and went through the relaxing routine. Finally I got to sleep and dreamed about strawberry shortcake with real cream, the kind that comes from cows.

I woke up hungry but I suddenly remembered that this was it!—my last day on Earth. Then I was too excited to be hungry. I got up, put on my Scout uniform and my ship suit over it.

I thought we would go right on board. I was wrong.

First we had to assemble under awnings spread out in front of the hotel near the embarking tubes. It wasn't air conditioned outside, of course, but it was early and the desert wasn't really hot yet. I found the letter "L" and sat down under it, sitting on my baggage. Dad and his new family weren't around yet; I began to wonder if I was going to Ganymede by myself. I didn't much care.

Out past the gates about five miles away, you could see the ships standing on the field, the *Daedalus* and the *Icarus,* pulled off the Earth-Moon run for this one trip, and the old *Bifrost* that had been the shuttle rocket to Supra-New-York space station as far back as I could remember.

The *Daedalus* and the *Icarus* were bigger but I hoped I would get the *Bifrost*; she was the first ship I ever saw blast off.

A family put their baggage down by mine. The mother looked out across the field and said, "Joseph, which one is the *Mayflower*?"

Her husband tried to explain to her, but she still was puzzled. I nearly burst, trying to keep from laughing. Here she was, all set to go to Ganymede and yet she was so dumb she didn't even know that the ship she was going in had been built out in space and couldn't land anywhere.

The place was getting crowded with emigrants and relatives coming to see them off, but I still didn't see anything of Dad. I heard my name called and turned around and there was Duck Miller. "Gee, Bill," he said, "I thought I'd missed you."

"Hi, Duck. No, I'm still here."

"I tried to call you last night but your phone answered 'service discontinued,' so I hooked school and came up."

"Aw, you shouldn't have done that."

"But I wanted to bring you this." He handed me a package, a whole pound of chocolates. I didn't know what to say.

I thanked him and then said, "Duck, I appreciate it, I really do. But I'll have to give them back to you."

"Huh? Why?"

"Weight. Mass, I mean. I can't get by with another ounce."

"You can carry it."

"That won't help. It counts just the same."

He thought about it and said, "Then let's open it."

I said, "Fine," and did so and offered him a piece. I looked at them myself and my stomach was practically sitting up and begging. I don't know when I've been so hungry.

I gave in and ate one. I figured I would sweat it off anyhow; it was getting hot and I had my Scout uniform on under my ship suit—and that's no way to dress for the Mojave Desert in June! Then I was thirstier than ever, of course; one thing leads to another.

I went over to a drinking fountain and took a very small drink. When I came back I closed the candy box and handed it back to Duck and told him to pass it around at next Scout meeting and tell the fellows I wished they were going along. He said he would and added, "You know, Bill, I wish I was going. I really do."

I said I wished he was, too, but when did he change his mind? He looked embarrassed but about then Mr. Kinski showed up and then Dad showed up, with Molly and the brat—Peggy—and Molly's sister, Mrs. van Metre. Everybody shook hands all around and Mrs. van Metre started to cry and the brat wanted to know what made my clothes so bunchy and what was I sweating about?

George was eyeing me, but about then our names were called and we started moving through the gate.

George and Molly and Peggy were weighed through and then it was my turn. My baggage was right on the nose, of course, and then I stepped on the scales. They read one hundred and thirty-one and one tenth pounds—I could have eaten another chocolate.

"Check!" said the weightmaster, then he looked up and said, "What in the world have you got on, son?"

The left sleeve of my uniform had started to unroll and was sticking out below the half sleeve of my ship suit. The merit badges were shining out like signal lights.

I didn't say anything. He started feeling the lumps the uniform sleeves made. "Boy," he said, "you're dressed like an arctic explorer; no wonder you're sweating. Didn't you know you weren't supposed to wear anything but the gear you were listed in?"

Dad came back and asked what the trouble was? I just stood there with my ears burning. The assistant weightmaster got into the huddle and they argued what should be done. The weightmaster phoned somebody and finally he said, "He's inside his weight limit; if he wants to call that monkey suit part of his skin, we'll allow it. Next customer, please!"

I trailed along, feeling foolish. We went down inside and climbed on the slide strip, it was cool down there, thank goodness. A few minutes later we got off at the loading room down under the rocket ship. Sure enough, it was the *Bifrost,* as I found out when the loading elevator poked above ground and stopped at the passenger port. We filed in.

They had it all organized. Our baggage had been taken from us in the loading room; each passenger had a place assigned by his weight. That split us up again; I was on the deck immediately under the control room. I found my place, couch 14-D, then went to a view port where I could see the *Daedalus* and the *Icarus*.

A brisk little stewardess, about knee high to a grasshopper, checked my name off a list and offered me an injection against dropsickness. I said no, thanks.

She said, "You've been out before?"

I admitted I hadn't; she said, "Better take it."

I said I was a licensed air pilot; I wouldn't get sick. I didn't tell her that my license was just for copters. She shrugged and turned away. A loudspeaker said, "The *Daedalus* is cleared for blasting." I moved up to get a good view.

The *Daedalus* was about a quarter of a mile away and stood up higher than we did. She had fine lines and was a mighty pretty sight, gleaming in the morning sunshine. Beyond her and to the right, clear out at the edge of the field, a light shone green at the traffic control blockhouse.

She canted slowly over to the south, just a few degrees.

Fire burst out of her base, orange, and then blinding white. It splashed down into the ground baffles and curled back up through the ground vents. She lifted.

She hung there for a breath and you could see the hills shimmer through her jet. And she was gone.

Just like that—she was gone. She went up out of there like a scared bird, just a pencil of white fire in the sky, and was gone while we could still hear and feel the thunder of her jets inside the compartment.

My ears were ringing. I heard someone behind me say, "But I haven't had breakfast. The Captain will just have to wait. Tell him, Joseph."

It was the woman who hadn't known that the *Mayflower* was a space-to-space ship. Her husband tried to hush her up, but he didn't have any luck. She called over the stewardess. I heard her answer, "But, madam, you can't speak to the Captain now. He's preparing for blast-off."

Apparently that didn't make any difference. The stewardess finally got her quiet by solemnly promising that she could have breakfast after blast-off. I bent my ears at that and I decided to put in a bid for breakfast, too.

The *Icarus* took off twenty minutes later and then the speaker said, "All hands! Acceleration stations—prepare to blast off." I went back to my couch and the stewardess made sure that we were all strapped down. She cautioned us not to unstrap until she said we could. She went down to the deck below.

I felt my ears pop and there was a soft sighing in the ship. I swallowed and kept swallowing. I knew what they were doing: blowing the natural air out and replacing it with the standard helium-oxygen mix at half sea-level pressure. But the woman—the same one—didn't like it. She said, "Joseph, my head aches. Joseph, I can't breathe. Do something!"

Then she clawed at her straps and sat up. Her husband sat up, too, and forced her back down.

The *Bifrost* tilted over a little and the speaker said, "Minus three minutes!"

After a long time it said, "Minus two minutes!"

And then "Minus one minute!" and another voice took up the count:

"Fifty-nine! Fifty-eight! Fifty-seven!"

My heart started to pound so hard I could hardly hear it. But it went on: "—thirty-five! Thirty-four! Thirty-three! Thirty-two! Thirty-one! *Half!* Twenty-nine! Twenty-eight!"

And it got to be: *"Ten!"*

And "Nine!"

"Eight!

"Seven!

"And six!

"And five!

"And four!

"And three!

"And two——"

I never did hear them say "one" or "fire" or whatever they said. About then something fell on me and I thought I was licked. Once, exploring a cave with the fellows, a bank collapsed on me and I had to be dug out. It was like that—but nobody dug me out.

My chest hurt. My ribs seemed about to break. I couldn't lift a finger. I gulped and couldn't get my breath.

I wasn't scared, not really, because I knew we would take off with a high *g,* but I was awfully uncomfortable. I managed to turn my head a little and saw that the sky was already purple. While I watched, it turned black and the stars came out, millions of stars. And yet the Sun was still streaming in through the port.

The roar of the jets was unbelievable but the noise started to die out almost at once and soon you couldn't hear it at all. They say the old ships used to be noisy even after you passed the speed of sound; the *Bifrost* was not. It got as quiet as the inside of a bag of feathers.

There was nothing to do but lie there, stare out at that black sky, try to breathe, and try not to think about the weight sitting on you.

And then, so suddenly that it made your stomach turn flip-flops, you didn't weigh anything at all.

4.
CAPTAIN DELONGPRE

Let me tell you that the first time you fall is no fun. Sure, you get over it. If you didn't you would starve. Old space hands even get so they like it—weightlessness, I mean. They say that two hours of weightless sleep is equal to a full night on Earth. I got used to it, but I never got to like it.

The *Bifrost* had blasted for a little more than three minutes. It seemed lots longer because of the high acceleration; we had blasted at nearly six *g*. Then she was in free orbit for better than three hours and we fell the whole time, until the Captain started to maneuver to match orbits with the *Mayflower*.

In other words we fell straight up for more than twenty thousand miles.

Put that way, it sounds silly. Everybody knows that things don't fall *up*; they fall *down*.

Everybody knew the world was flat, too.

We fell up.

Like everybody, I had had the elements of space ballistics in grammar school physics, and goodness knows there have been enough stories about how you float around in a spaceship when it's in a free orbit. But, take it from me, you don't really believe it until you've tried it.

Take Mrs. Tarbutton—the woman who wanted breakfast. I suppose she went to school like everybody else. But she kept insisting that the Captain had to do something about it. What he could do I don't know; find her a small asteroid, maybe.

Not that I didn't sympathize with her—or with myself, I

guess. Ever been in an earthquake? You know how everything you ever depended on suddenly goes back on you and *terra firma* isn't *firma* any longer? It's like that, only much worse. This is no place to review grammar school physics but when a spaceship is in a free trajectory, straight up or any direction, the ship and everything in it moves along together and you *fall,* endlessly—and your stomach darn near falls out of you.

That was the first thing I noticed. I was strapped down so that I didn't float away, but I felt weak and shaky and dizzy and as if I had been kicked in the stomach. Then my mouth filled with saliva and I gulped and I was awfully sorry I had eaten that chocolate.

But it didn't come up, not quite.

The only thing that saved me was no breakfast. Some of the others were not so lucky. I tried not to look at them. I had intended to unstrap as soon as we went free and go to a port so I could look at Earth, but I lost interest in that project entirely. I stayed strapped down, and concentrated on being miserable.

The stewardess came floating out the hatch from the next deck, shoved herself along with a toe, checked herself with a hand at the center stanchion, and hovered in the air in a swan dive, looking us over. It was very pretty to watch if I'd been in shape to appreciate it.

"Is everybody comfy?" she said cheerfully.

It was a silly remark but I suppose nurses get that way. Somebody groaned and a baby on the other side of the compartment started to cry. The stewardess moved over to Mrs. Tarbutton and said, "You may have breakfast now. What would you like? Scrambled eggs?"

I clamped my jaw and turned my head away, wishing she would shut up. Then I looked back. She had paid for that silly remark—and she had to clean it up.

When she was through with Mrs. Tarbutton I said, "Uh—oh, Miss——"

"Andrews."

"Miss Andrews, could I change my mind about that drop-sick injection?"

"Righto, chum," she agreed, smiling, and whipped out an injector from a little kit she had at her belt. She gave me the shot. It burned and for a moment I thought I was going to lose the chocolate after all. But then things quieted down and I was almost happy in a miserable sort of way.

She left me and gave shots to some others who had kidded

themselves the same way I had. Mrs. Tarbutton she gave another
sort of shot to knock her out entirely. One or two of the hardier
souls unstrapped themselves and went to the ports; I decided I was
well enough to try it.

It's not as easy as it looks, this swimming around in free fall. I
undid the safety belts and sat up; that's all I meant to do. Then I
was scrambling in the air, out of control, trying frantically to grasp
at anything.

I turned over in the air and cracked the back of my head
against the underside of the control room deck and saw stars, not
the ones out the ports—some of my own. Then the deck with the
couches on it was approaching me slowly.

I managed to grab a safety belt and came to anchor. The
couch it belonged to was occupied by a little plump man. I said,
"Excuse me."

He said, "Don't mention it," and turned his face away, looking
as if he hated me. I couldn't stay there and I couldn't even get
back to my own couch without grabbing handholds on other
couches that were occupied, too, so I pushed off again, very gently this time, and managed to grab hold when I bumped against the
other deck.

It had handholds and grab lines all over it. I didn't let go again,
but pulled myself along, monkey fashion, to one of the ports.

And there I got my first view of Earth from space.

I don't know what I expected, but it wasn't what I expected.
There it was, looking just like it does in the geography books, or
maybe more the way it does in the station announcements of
Super-New-York TV station. And yet it was different. I guess I
would say it was like the difference between being told about a
good hard kick in the rear and actually being kicked.

Not a transcription. Alive.

For one thing it wasn't prettily centered in a television screen;
it was shouldering into one side of the frame of the port, and the
aft end of the ship cut a big chunk out of the Pacific Ocean. And it
was moving, shrinking. While I hung there it shrunk to about half
the size it was when I first got there and got rounder and rounder.
Columbus was right.

From where I was it was turned sideways; the end of Siberia,
then North America, and finally the north half of South America
ran across from left to right. There were clouds over Canada and
the eastern part of the rest of North America; they were the
whitest white I ever saw—whiter than the north pole cap. Right

opposite us was the reflection of the Sun on the ocean; it hurt my eyes. The rest of the ocean was almost purple where there weren't clouds.

It was so beautiful my throat ached and I wanted to reach out and touch it.

And back of it were stars, even brighter and bigger and more of them than the way they look from Little America.

Pretty soon there were more people crowding around, trying to see, and kids shoving and their mothers saying, "Now, now, darling!" and making silly remarks themselves. I gave up. I pulled myself back to my couch and put one belt around me so I wouldn't float away and thought about it. It makes you proud to know that you come from a big, fancy planet like that. I got to thinking that I hadn't seen all of it, not by a long sight, in spite of all the geography trips I had made and going to one Scout round-up in Switzerland and the time George and Anne and I went to Siam.

And now I wasn't going to see any more of it. It made me feel pretty solemn.

I looked up; there was a boy standing in front of me. He said, "What's the trouble, William, my boy? Dropsick?"

It was that twerp Jones. You could have knocked me out with a feather. If I had known he was going to emigrate, I would have thought twice about it.

I asked him where in the world he had come from.

"The same place you did, naturally. I asked you a question."

I informed him that I was not dropsick and asked him whatever gave him that silly notion. He reached out and grabbed my arm and turned it so that the red spot the injection had made showed. He laughed and I jerked my arm away.

He laughed again and showed me his arm; it had a red spot on it, too. "Happens to the best of us," he said. "Don't be shy about it."

Then he said, "Come on. Let's look around the joint before they make us strap down again."

I went along. He wasn't what I would pick for a buddy but he was a familiar face. We worked our way over to the hatch to the next deck. I started to go through but Jones stopped me. "Let's go into the control room," he suggested.

"Huh? Oh, they wouldn't let us!"

"Is it a crime to try? Come on." We went back the other way and through a short passage. It ended in a door that was marked: CONTROL ROOM—STAY OUT! Somebody had written under it: *This means you!!!* and somebody else had added: *Who? Me?*

Jones tried it; it was locked. There was a button beside it; he pushed it.

It opened and we found ourselves staring into the face of a man with two stripes on his collar. Behind him was an older man with four stripes on his; he called out, "Who is it, Sam? Tell 'em we're not in the market."

The first man said, "What do you kids want?"

Jones said, "Please, sir, we're interested in astrogation. Could we have permission to visit the control room?"

I could see he was going to chuck us out and I had started to turn away when the older man called out, "Oh, shucks, Sam, bring 'em in!"

The younger fellow shrugged and said, "As you say, Skipper."

We went in and the Captain said, "Grab on to something; don't float around. And don't touch anything, or I'll cut your ears off. Now who are you?"

We told him; he said, "Glad to know you, Hank—same to you, Bill. Welcome aboard." Then he reached out and touched the sleeve of my uniform—it had come loose again. "Son, your underwear is showing."

I blushed and told him how I happened to be wearing it. He laughed and said, "So you swindled us into lifting it anyway. That's rich—eh, Sam? Have a cup of coffee."

They were eating sandwiches and drinking coffee—not from cups, of course, but from little plastic bags like they use for babies. The bags even had nipples on them. I said no, thanks. While the shot Miss Andrews gave me had made me feel better, it hadn't made me feel that much better. Hank Jones turned it down, too.

The control room didn't have a port in it of any sort. There was a big television screen forward on the bulkhead leading to the nose, but it wasn't turned on. I wondered what Mrs. Tarbutton would think if she knew that the Captain couldn't see where we were going and didn't seem to care.

I asked him about the ports. He said ports were strictly for tourists. "What would you do with a port if you had one?" he asked. "Stick your head out the window and look for road signs? We can see anything we need to see. Sam, heat up the video and show the kids."

"Aye aye, Skipper." The other chap swam over to his couch and started turning switches. He left his sandwich hanging in the air while he did so.

I looked around. The control room was circular and the end

we came in was bigger than the other end; it was practically up in the nose of the ship and the sides sloped in. There were two couches, one for the pilot and one for the co-pilot, flat against the wall that separated the control room from the passenger compartments. Most of the space between the couches was taken up by the computer.

The couches were fancier than the ones the passengers had; they were shaped to the body and they lifted the knees and the head and back, like a hospital bed, and there were arm rests to support their hands over the ship's controls. An instrument board arched over each couch at the middle, where the man in the couch could see the dials and stuff even when his head was pushed back into the cushions by high *g*.

The TV screen lighted up and we could see Earth; it filled most of the screen. "That's 'View Aft'," the co-pilot said, "from a TV camera in the tail. We've got 'em pointing in all directions. Now we'll try 'View Forward'." He did, but it didn't amount to anything, just a few tiny little dots that might have been stars. Hank said you could see more stars out a port.

"You don't use it to look at stars," he answered. "When you need to take a star sight, you use the coelostats. Like this." He lay back on the couch and reached behind his head, pulling an eye piece arrangement over his face until the rubber guard fitted over one eye without lifting his head off the couch. "Coelostat" is just a trick name for a telescope with a periscope built into it. He didn't offer to let us look through it, so I looked back at the instrument board. It had a couple of radar presentations, much like you'll find in any atmosphere ship, even in a copter, and a lot of other instruments, most of which I didn't understand, though some of them were pretty obvious, like approach rate and throat temperature and mass ratio and ejection speed and such.

"Watch this," said the co-pilot. He did something at his controls; one of the tiny blips on the TV screen lit up very brightly, blinked a few times, then died away. "That was Supra-New-York; I triggered her radar beacon. You are not seeing it by television; it's radar brought on to the same screen." He fiddled with the controls again and another light blinked, two longs and a short. "That's where they're building the *Star Rover*."

"Where's the *Mayflower*?" Hank asked.

"Want to see where you're going, eh?" He touched his controls again; another light came on, way off to one side, flashing in groups of three.

I said it didn't look much like we were going there. The Captain spoke up. "We're taking the long way round, past the fair grounds. That's enough, Sam. Lock your board."

We all went back where the Captain was still eating. "You an Eagle Scout?" he asked me. I said yes and Hank said he was too.

"How old were you when you made it?" he wanted to know. I said I had been thirteen, so Hank said twelve, whereupon the Captain claimed he had made it at eleven. Personally I didn't believe either one of them.

The Captain said so now we were going out to Ganymede; he envied both of us. The co-pilot said what was there to envy about that?

The Captain said, "Sam, you've got no romance in your soul. You'll live and die running a ferry boat."

"Maybe so," the co-pilot answered, "but I sleep home a lot of nights."

The Captain said pilots should not marry. "Take me," he said, "I always wanted to be a deep-spaceman. I was all set for it, too, when I was captured by pirates and missed my chance. By the time I had the chance again, I was married."

"You and your pirates," said the co-pilot.

I kept my face straight. Adults always think anybody younger will swallow anything; I try not to disillusion them.

"Well, all that's as may be," said the Captain. "You two young gentlemen run along now. Mr. Mayes and I have got to fake up a few figures, or we'll be landing this bucket in South Brooklyn."

So we thanked him and left.

I found Dad and Molly and the Brat in the deck aft of my own. Dad said, "Where have you been, Bill? I've been looking all over the ship for you."

I told them, "Up in the control room with the Captain."

Dad looked surprised and the Brat made a face at me and said, "Smarty, you have not. Nobody can go up there."

I think girls should be raised in the bottom of a deep, dark sack until they are old enough to know better. Then when it came time, you could either let them out or close the sack and throw them away, whichever was the best idea.

Molly said, "Hush, Peggy."

I said, "You can just ask Hank. He was with me. We——" I looked around but Hank was gone. So I told them what had happened, all but the part about pirates.

When I finished the Brat said, "I want to go into the control room, too."

Dad said he didn't think it could be arranged. The Brat said, "Why not? Bill went."

Molly said hush again. "Bill is a boy and older than you are." The Brat said it wasn't fair.

I guess she had something there—but things hardly ever are. Dad went on, "You should feel flattered, Bill, being entertained by the famous Captain DeLongPre."

"Huh?"

"Maybe you are too young to remember it. He let himself be sealed into one of the robot freighters used to jump thorium ore from the lunar mines—and busted up a ring of hijackers, a gang the newscasters called the 'Ore Pirates.' "

I didn't say anything.

I wanted to see the *Mayflower* from space, but they made us strap down before I could locate it. I got a pretty good view of Supra-New-York though; the *Mayflower* was in the 24-hour orbit the space station rides in and we were closing almost directly on it when the word came to strap down.

Captain DeLongPre was quite some pilot. He didn't fiddle around with jockeying his ship into the new groove; he gave one long blast on the jet, the right time, the right amount, and the right direction. As it says in the physics book, "every one-plane correction-of-orbit problem which can be solved at all, can be solved with a single application of acceleration"—provided the pilot is good enough.

He was good enough. When we went weightless again, I looked over my shoulder out a port and there was the *Mayflower,* with the Sun gleaming on her, large as life and not very far away. There was the softest sort of a correction bump and the loud-speaker sang out, "Contact completed. You may unstrap."

I did and went to the port from which we could see the *Mayflower.* It was easy to see why she could never land; she had no airfoils of any sort, not even fins, and she was the wrong shape—almost spherical except that one side came out to a conical point.

She looked much too small—then I realized that a little bulge that was sticking out past her edge at one point was actually the bow of the *Icarus,* unloading on the far side. Then suddenly she was enormous and the little flies on her were men in space suits.

One of them shot something at us and a line came snaking across. Before the knob on the end of it quite reached us there was a bright purple brush discharge from the end of it and every hair on my head stood straight up and my skin prickled. A couple of the women in the compartment squealed and I heard Miss Andrews soothing them down and telling them that it was just the electrical potential adjusting between the two ships. If she had told them it was a bolt of lightning she would have been just as correct, but I don't suppose that would have soothed them.

I wasn't scared; any kid who had fooled around with radio or any sort of electronics would have expected it.

The knob on the line clunked against the side of the ship and after a bit the little line was followed by a heavier line and then they warped us together, slowly. The *Mayflower* came up until she filled the port.

After a bit my ears popped and the loudspeaker said, "All hands—prepare to disembark."

Miss Andrews made us wait quite a while, then it was our deck's turn and we pulled ourselves along to the deck we had come in by. Mrs. Tarbutton didn't come along; she and her husband were having some sort of a discussion with Miss Andrews.

We went right straight out of our ship, through a jointed steel drum about ten feet long, and into the *Mayflower*.

5.
CAPTAIN HARKNESS

Do you know the worst thing about spaceships? They smell bad.

Even the *Mayflower* smelled bad and she was brand new. She smelled of oil and welding and solvents and dirty, sweaty smells of all the workmen who had lived in her so long. Then we came, three shiploads of us, most of us pretty whiff with that bad odor people get when they're scared or very nervous. My stomach still wasn't happy and it almost got me.

The worst of it is that there can't be very good 'freshers in a ship; a bath is a luxury. After the ship got organized we were issued tickets for two baths a week, but how far does that go, especially when a bath means two gallons of water to sponge yourself off with?

If you felt you just *had* to have a bath, you could ask around and maybe buy a ticket from somebody who was willing to skip one. There was one boy in my bunk room who sold his tickets for four weeks running until we all got sick of it and gave him an unscheduled bath with a very stiff brush. But I'm getting ahead of myself.

And you couldn't burn your clothes either; you had to *wash* them.

When we first got into the *Mayflower* it took them maybe half an hour to get us all sorted out and into our acceleration couches. The people from the *Daedalus* and the *Icarus* were supposed to be stowed away by the time we got there, but they weren't and the passageways were traffic jams. A traffic jam when everybody is floating, and you don't know which end is up, is about eight times as confusing as an ordinary one.

There weren't any stewardesses to get us straight, either; there were emigrants instead, with signs on their chests reading SHIP'S AIDE—but a lot of them needed aid themselves; they were just as lost as anybody else. It was like amateur theatricals where the ushers don't know how to find the reserved seats.

By the time I was in the bunk room I was assigned to and strapped down there were bells ringing all over the place and loudspeakers shouting: "Prepare for acceleration! Ten minutes!"

Then we waited.

It seemed more like half an hour. Presently the count-off started. I said to myself, William, if the blast-off from Earth was rugged, this is going to knock the teeth right out of your head. I knew what we were going to build up to—better than ninety-three miles per second. That's a third of a million miles an hour! Frankly I was scared.

The seconds ticked away; there was a soft push that forced me down against the cushions—and that was all. I just lay there; the ceiling was the ceiling again and the floor was under me, but I didn't feel extra heavy, I felt fine.

I decided that was just the first step; the next one would be a dilly.

Up overhead in the bunk room was a display screen; it lighted up and I was looking into the face of a man with four collar stripes; he was younger than Captain DeLongPre. He smiled and said, "This is your Captain speaking, friends—Captain Harkness. The ship will remain at one gravity for a little more than four hours. I think it is time to serve lunch, don't you?"

He grinned again and I realized that my stomach wasn't bothering me at all—except that I was terribly hungry. I guess he knew that all of us ground hogs would be starving to death as soon as we were back to normal weight. He went on:

"We'll try to serve you just as quickly as possible. It is all right for you to unstrap now, sit up, and relax, but I must ask you to be very careful about one thing:

"This ship is precisely balanced so that the thrust of our drive passes exactly through our center of gravity. If that were not so, we would tend to spin instead of moving in a straight line—and we might fetch up in the heart of the Sun instead of at Ganymede.

"None of us wants to become an impromptu barbecue, so I will ask each of you not to move unnecessarily from the neighborhood of your couch. The ship has an automatic compensator for a limited amount of movement, but we must not overload it—so get permission from your ship's aide before moving as much as six inches from your present positions."

He grinned again and it was suddenly a most unpleasant grin. "Any one violating this rule will be strapped down by force—and the Captain will assign punishment to fit the crime after we are no longer under drive."

There wasn't any ship's aide in our compartment; all we could do was wait. I got acquainted with the boys in the bunkroom, some older, some younger. There was a big, sandy-haired boy about seventeen, by the name of Edwards—"Noisy" Edwards. He got tired of waiting.

I didn't blame him; it seemed like hours went past and still nothing to eat. I thought we had been forgotten.

Edwards had been hanging around the door, peering out. Finally he said, "This is ridiculous! We can't sit here all day. I'm for finding out what's the hold up. Who's with me?"

One of the fellows objected, "The Captain said to sit tight."

"What if he did? And what can he do if we don't? We aren't part of the crew."

I pointed out that the Captain had authority over the whole ship, but he brushed me off. "Tommyrot! We got a right to know what's going on—and a right to be fed. Who's coming along?"

Another boy said, "You're looking for trouble, Noisy."

Edwards stopped; I think he was worried by the remark but he couldn't back down. Finally he said, "Look, we're supposed to have a ship's aide and we haven't got one. You guys elect me ship's aide and I'll go bring back chow. How's that?"

Nobody objected out loud. Noisy said, "Okay, here I go."

He couldn't have been gone more than a few seconds when a ship's aide showed up carrying a big box of packaged rations. He dealt them out and had one left over. Then he counted the bunks. "Weren't there twenty boys in here?" he asked.

We looked at each other but nobody said anything. He pulled out a list and called our names. Edwards didn't answer, of course, and he left, taking Noisy's ration with him.

Then Noisy showed up and saw us eating and wanted to know where his lunch was. We told him; he said, "For the love of Mike! Why didn't you guys save it for me? A fine bunch you turned out to be." And he left again.

He came back shortly, looking mad. A ship's aide followed him and strapped him down.

We had about reached the teeth-picking stage when the screen on the ceiling lit up again and there was the Moon. It looked as if we were headed right toward it and coming up fast. I began to wonder if Captain Harkness had dropped a decimal point.

I lay back on my couch and watched it grow. After a while it looked worse. When it had grown until it filled the screen and more and it seemed as if we couldn't possibly miss, I saw that the mountains were moving past on the screen from right to left. I breathed a sigh of relief; maybe the Old Man knew what he was doing after all.

A voice came over the speaker: "We are now passing the Moon and tacking slightly in so doing. Our relative speed at point of closest approach is more than fifty miles per second, producing a somewhat spectacular effect."

I'll say it was spectacular! We zipped across the face of the Moon in about half a minute, then it faded behind us. I suppose they simply kept a TV camera trained on it, but it looked as if we had dived in, turned sharply, and raced out again. Only you don't make sharp turns at *that* speed.

About two hours later they stopped gunning her. I had fallen asleep and I dreamed I was making a parachute jump and the chute failed to open. I woke up with a yell, weightless, with my stomach dropping out of me again. It took me a moment to figure out where I was.

The loudspeaker said: "End of acceleration. Spin will be placed on the ship at once."

But it did not happen all at once; it happened very slowly. We drifted toward one wall and slid down it toward the outer wall of the ship. That made what had been the outer wall the floor; we stood on it—and the side with the bunks on it was now a wall and the side with the TV screen on it, which had been the ceiling, was now the opposite wall. Gradually we got heavier.

Noisy was still strapped to his couch; the ship's aide had moved the buckles so that he could not reach them himself. Now he was up against the wall, hanging on the straps like a papoose. He began to yell for us to help him down.

He was not in any danger and he could not have been too uncomfortable, for we weren't up to a full gravity, not by a whole lot. It turned out later that the Captain had brought the spin up to one-third g and held it there, because Ganymede has one-third g. So there wasn't any urgent need to turn Noisy loose.

Nor was there any rush to do so. We were still discussing it and some of the fellows were making comical remarks which

Noisy did not appreciate when the same ship's aide came in, un-strapped Noisy, and told all of us to follow him.

That's how I happened to attend Captain's mast.

"Captain's mast" is a sort of court, like when in ancient times the lord of the countryside would sit and dispense the high and middle justice. We followed the aide, whose name was Dr. Archibald, to Captain Harkness's cabin. There were a lot of other people waiting there in the passage outside the cabin. Presently Captain Harkness came out and Noisy was the first case.

We were all witnesses but the Captain didn't question but a few of us; I wasn't questioned. Dr. Archibald told about finding Noisy wandering around the ship while we were under accelera-tion and the Captain asked Noisy if he had heard the order to stay at his bunk?

Noisy beat around the bush a good deal and tried to spread the blame on all of us, but when the Captain pinned him down he had to admit that he had heard the order.

Captain Harkness said, "Son, you are an undisciplined lunk. I don't know what sort of trouble you'll run into as a colonist, but so far as my ship is concerned, you've had it."

He mused for a moment, than added, "You say you did this be-cause you were hungry?"

Noisy said yes, he hadn't had anything since breakfast and he still hadn't had his lunch.

"Ten days bread and water," said the Captain. "Next case."

Noisy looked as if he couldn't believe his ears.

The next case was the same thing, but a woman—one of those large, impressive ones who run things. She had had a row with her ship's aide and had stomped off to tell the Captain about it personally—while we were under acceleration.

Captain Harkness soon cut through the fog. "Madam," he said, with icy dignity, "by your bull-headed stupidity you have en-dangered the lives of all of us. Do you have anything to say for yourself?"

She started a tirade about how "rude" the aide had been to her and how she never heard of anything so preposterous in her life as this kangaroo court, and so forth, and so forth. The Captain cut her short.

"Have you ever washed dishes?" he asked.

"Why, no!"

"Well, you are going to wash dishes—for the next four hun-dred million miles."

6.

$E = MC^2$

I looked up dad after they let us go. It was like finding a needle in a haystack but I kept asking and presently I found him. Molly and he had a room to themselves. Peggy was there and I thought she was rooming with them, which annoyed me some, until I saw that there were only two couches and realized that Peggy must be in a dormitory. It turned out that all the kids over eight were in dormitories.

Dad was busy unclamping their couches and moving them to what was the floor, now that the ship was spinning. He stopped when I came in and we sat around and talked. I told him about Captain's mast. He nodded. "We saw it in the screen. I didn't notice your shining face, however."

I said I hadn't been called on.

"Why not?" Peggy wanted to know.

"How should I know?" I thought about mast for a bit and said, "Say, George, the skipper of a ship in space is just about the last of the absolute monarchs, isn't he?"

Dad considered it and said, "Mmm . . . no, he's a constitutional monarch. But he's a monarch all right."

"You mean we have to bow down to him and say 'Your Majesty'?" Peggy wanted to know.

Molly said, "I don't think that would be advisable, Peg."

"Why not? I think it would be fun."

Molly smiled. "Well, let me know how you make out. I suspect that he will just turn you over his knee and paddle you."

"Oh, he wouldn't dare! I'd scream."

I wasn't so sure. I remembered those four hundred million

miles of dirty dishes. I decided that, if the Captain said "Frog," I'd hop.

If Captain Harkness was a monarch, he didn't seem anxious to rule; the first thing he had us do was to hold an election and set up a ship's council. After that we hardly laid eyes on him.

Everybody over eighteen could vote. The rest of us got to vote, too; we were told to set up a junior council—not that it was ever good for anything.

But the senior council, the *real* council, ran the ship from then on. It even acted as a court and the Captain never handed out punishments again. Dad told me that the Captain reviewed everything that the council did, that he *had* to, to make it legal—but I never heard of him overruling their decisions.

And you know what the first thing was that that council did—after setting up meal hours and simple things like that? They decided we had to go to school!

The junior council promptly held a meeting and passed a resolution against it, but it didn't mean anything. We had school, just the same.

Peggy was on the junior council. I asked her why she didn't resign if she wasn't going to do anything. I was just teasing—as a matter of fact she put up quite a battle for us.

School wasn't so bad, though. There is very little to do in space and when you've seen one star you've seen 'em all. And the first thing we had in school was a tour of the ship, which was all right.

We went in groups of twenty and it took all day—"day" by ship's time, I mean. The *Mayflower* was shaped like a ball with a cone on one side—top shaped. The point of the cone was her jet—although Chief Engineer Ortega, who showed us around, called it her "torch."

If you count the torch end as her stern, then the round end, her bow, was where the control room was located; around it were the Captain's cabin and the staterooms of the officers. The torch and the whole power plant space were cut off from the rest of the ship by a radiation shield that ran right through the ship. From the shield forward to the control room was a big cargo space. It was a cylinder more than a hundred feet in diameter and was split up into holds. We were carrying all sorts of things out to the colony—earth moving machinery, concentrated soil cultures, instruments, I don't know what all.

Wrapped around this central cylinder were the decks for living, "A" deck just inside the skin of the ship, "B" deck under it, and "C" deck just inside that, with "D" deck's ceiling being the outer wall of the cargo space. "D" deck was the mess rooms and galley and recreation rooms and sick bay and such; the three outer decks were bunk rooms and staterooms. "A" deck had steps in it every ten or fifteen feet because it was fitted into the outer curve of the ship; this made the ceilings in it of various heights. The furthest forward and furthest aft on "A" deck were only about six feet between floor and ceiling and some of the smaller kids lived in them, while at the greatest width of the ship the ceilings in "A" deck must have been twelve or thirteen feet high.

From inside the ship it was hard to see how it all fitted together. Not only was it all chopped up, but the artificial gravity we had from spinning the ship made directions confusing—anywhere you stood on a deck it seemed level, but it curved sharply up behind you and in front of you. But you never came to the curved part; if you walked forward it was still level. If you walked far enough you looped the loop and came back to where you started, having walked clear around the ship.

I never would have figured it out if Mr. Ortega hadn't drawn a sketch for us.

Mr. Ortega told us that the ship was spinning three and six-tenths revolutions per minute or two hundred and sixteen complete turns an hour, which was enough to give "B" deck a centrifugal force of one-third g. "B" deck was seventy-five feet out from the axis of the *Mayflower*; "A" deck where I lived was further out and you weighed maybe a tenth more there, while "C" deck caught about a tenth less. "D" deck was quite a lot less and you could make yourself dizzy if you stood up suddenly in the mess room.

The control room was right on the axis; you could float in it even when the ship was spinning—or so they told me; I never was allowed inside.

Spinning the ship had another odd effect: all around us was "down." I mean to say that the only place you could put a view port was in the floor plates of "A" deck and that's where they were, four of them—big ones, each in its own compartment.

Mr. Ortega took us into one of these view galleries. The view port was a big round quartz plate in the floor, with a guard rail around it.

The first ones into the room went up to the guard rail and then backed away from it quick and two of the girls squealed. I pushed forward and got to the rail and looked down . . . and I was staring straight into the very bottom of the universe, a million trillion miles away and all of it *down*.

I didn't shy away—George says I'm more acrobat than acrophobe—but I did sort of grip the railing. Nobody wants to fall that far. The quartz was surface-treated so that it didn't give off reflections and it looked as if there were nothing at all between you and Kingdom Come.

The stars were reeling across the hole from the ship spinning, which made it worse. The Big Dipper came swinging in from the left, passed almost under me, and slid away to the right—and a few seconds later it was back again. I said, "This is where I came in," and gave up my place so that someone else could have a look, but nobody seemed anxious to.

Then we went through the hydroponics plant, but there wasn't anything fancy about that—just enough plants growing to replace the oxygen we used up breathing. Eel grass, it was mostly, but there was a vegetable garden as well. I wondered how they had gotten it going before they had the passengers aboard? Mr. Ortega pointed to a CO_2 fitting in the wall. "We had to subsidize them, of course."

I guess I should have known it; it was simple arithmetic.

The Chief led us back into one of the mess rooms, we sat down, and he told us about the power plant.

He said that there had been three stages in the development of space ships: first was the chemical fuel rocket ship that wasn't very different from the big German war rockets used in the Second World War, except that they were step rockets. "You kids are too young to have seen such rockets," he said, "but they were the biggest space ships ever built. They had to be big because they were terribly inefficient. As you all know, the first rocket to reach the Moon was a four-stage rocket. Its final stage was almost as long as the *Mayflower*—yet its pay load was less than a ton.

"It is characteristic of space ship development that the ships have gotten smaller instead of bigger. The next development was the atom-powered rocket. It was a great improvement; steps were no longer necessary. That meant that a ship like the *Daedalus* could take off from Earth without even a catapult, much less step rockets, and cruise to the Moon or even to Mars. But such ships still had the shortcomings of rockets; they depended on an atomic power plant to heat up reaction mass and push it out a jet, just as their predecessors depended on chemical fuel for the same purpose.

"The latest development is the mass-conversion ship, such as the *Mayflower*, and it may be the final development—a mass-conversion ship is theoretically capable of approaching the speed of light. Take this trip: we accelerated at one gravity for about four hours and twenty minutes which brought us up to more than ninety miles a second. If we had *held* that drive for a trifle less than a year, we would approach the speed of light.

"A mass-conversion ship has plenty of power to do just that. At one hundred per cent efficiency, it would use up about one per cent of her mass as energy and another one per cent as reaction mass. That's what the *Star Rover* is going to do when it is finished."

One of the younger kids was waving his hand. "Mister Chief Engineer?"

"Yes, son?"

"Suppose it goes on a few weeks longer and *passes* the speed of light?"

Mr. Ortega shook his head. "It can't."

"Why not, sir?"

"Eh, how far have you gone in mathematics, sonny?"

"Just through grammer school calculus," the kid answered.

"I'm afraid there is no use in trying to explain it, then. Just take it from me that the big brains are sure it can't be done."

I had worried about that very point more than once. Why *can't* you go faster than light? I know all that old double-talk about how the Einstein equations show that a speed faster than light is a meaningless quantity, like the weight of a song or the color of a sound, because it involves the square root of minus one—but all of that is just theory and if the course we had in history of science means anything at all, it means that scientists change their theories about as often as a snake changes his skin. I stuck up my hand.

"Okay," he says. "You with the cowlick. Speak up."

"Mr. Ortega, admitting that you can't pass the speed of light, what would happen if the *Star Rover* got up close to the speed of light—and then the Captain suddenly stepped the drive up to about six g and held it there?"

"Why, it would——— No, let's put it this way———" He broke off and grinned; it made him look real young. "See here, kid, don't ask me questions like that. I'm an engineer with hairy ears, not a mathematical physicist." He looked thoughtful and added, "Truthfully, I don't know what would happen, but I would sure give a pretty to find out. Maybe we would find out what the square root of minus one looks like—from the inside."

He went on briskly, "Let's go on about the *Mayflower*. You probably know that when the original *Star Rover* failed to come back, the *Mayflower* was designed to be the *Star Rover II,* but the design was obsolete before they ever started putting her together. So they shifted the name over to the new intersteller ship, the *Star Rover III,* renamed this one the *Mayflower* and grabbed her for the colonial service.

"You kids should consider how lucky you are. Up to now, emigrants to Ganymede have had to spend two years and nine months in space, just to get there. You're making it in two months."

"Couldn't we go faster?" somebody wanted to know.

"We could," he told us. "But we don't need to and it runs up the astrogation and control difficulties. In these new ships the power plant has gotten 'way ahead of the instrumentation. Be patient; your grandchildren will make the trip in a week, blasting at one *g* all the way. There'll be so many ships they'll have to have traffic cops and maybe we can come close to shipping out as many people as there are extras born each year.

"Enough about that," he went on. "Who here can tell me what 'E equals M C squared' means?"

I could have answered but I had already spoken up once and it doesn't do to get a reputation for apple polishing. Finally one of the older kids said, "It means that mass can be converted into energy."

"Right!" Mr. Ortega agreed. "The first real demonstration of that was the atom bomb they set off 'way back in 1945 at Alamogordo, New Mexico. That was a special case; they still didn't know how to control it; all they could do was to make one whale of a big bang. Then came the uranium power plants, but that still didn't amount to much because it was a very special case and only a microscopic percentage of the mass was converted into energy. It wasn't until Kilgore's energy transformation equations—don't worry about them; you'll study them when you are older if you are interested—it wasn't until Kilgore showed how it could be done that we had any idea of *how* to do what Dr. Einstein's energy-mass equation said, clear back in 1905.

"And we still didn't know how to control it. If we were going to turn mass into energy, we needed more mass with which to surround the reaction, a very special sort of mass that would not turn into energy when we didn't want it to and would hold the reaction where we wanted it. Ordinary metal wouldn't do; one might as well use soft butter.

"But the Kilgore equations showed how to do that, too, when they were read correctly. Now has anyone here any notion of how much energy you get when you convert a chunk of mass into raw energy?"

Nobody knew. "It's all in that one equation," he said, "good old Doc Einstein's 'E equals M C squared.' It comes out that one gram of mass gives nine times ten to the twentieth power ergs." He wrote it down for us: 1 gm. = 9×10^{20} ergs.

"Doesn't look like much, does it?" he said. "Now try it this way:" He wrote down

900,000,000,000,000,000,000 ergs.

"Read it off. Nine hundred thousand million billion ergs. It still doesn't mean much, does it? Figures like that are impossible to comprehend. The nuclear physicists keep a barrel of zeroes around handy the way a carpenter does a keg of nails.

"I'll try once more," he went on. "A pound of mass, any old mass, say a pound of feathers, when converted into energy equals *fifteen billion* horsepower-hours. Does that give anyone a notion of why the *Mayflower* was assembled out in an orbit and will never ever land anywhere?"

"Too hot," somebody said.

" 'Too hot' is an understatement. If the *Mayflower* had blasted off from Mojave space port the whole Los Angeles Borough of the City of Southern California would have been reduced to a puddle of lava and people would have been killed by radiation and heat from Bay City to Baja California. And that will give you an idea of why the shielding runs right through the ship between here and the power plant, with no way at all to get at the torch."

We had the misfortune to have Noisy Edwards along, simply because he was from the same bunk room. Now he spoke up and said, "Suppose you have to make a repair?"

"There is nothing to go wrong," explained Mr. Ortega. "The power plant has no moving parts of any sort."

Noisy wasn't satisfied. "But suppose something did go wrong, how would you fix it if you can't get at it?"

Noisy has an irritating manner at best; Mr. Ortega sounded a little impatient when he answered. "Believe me, son, even if you could get at it, you wouldn't want to. No indeed!"

"Humph!" said Noisy. "All I've got to say is, if there isn't any way to make a repair when a repair is needed, what's the use in sending engineer officers along?"

You could have heard a pin drop. Mr. Ortega turned red, but all he said was, "Why, to answer foolish questions from youngsters like yourself, I suppose." He turned to the rest of us. "Any more questions?"

Naturally nobody wanted to ask any then. He added, "I think that's enough for one session. School's out."

I told Dad about it later. He looked grim and said, "I'm afraid Chief Engineer Ortega didn't tell you the whole truth."

"Huh?"

"In the first place there is plenty for him to do in taking care of the auxiliary machinery on this side of the shield. But it is possible to get at the torch, if necessary."

"Huh? How?"

"There are certain adjustments which could conceivably have to be made in extreme emergency. In which case it would be Mr. Ortega's proud privilege to climb into a space suit, go outside and back aft, and make them."

"You mean——"

"I mean that the assistant chief engineer would succeed to the position of chief a few minutes later. Chief engineers are very carefully chosen, Bill, and not just for their technical knowledge."

It made me feel chilly inside; I didn't like to think about it.

7.
SCOUTING IN SPACE

Making a trip in a space ship is about the dullest way to spend time in the world, once the excitement wears off. There's no scenery, nothing to do, and no room to do it in. There were nearly six thousand of us crowded into the *Mayflower* and that doesn't leave room to swing a cat.

Take "B" deck—there were two thousand passengers sleeping in it. It was 150 feet across—fore and aft, that is—and not quite 500 feet around, cylinder fashion. That gives about forty square feet per passenger, on the average, but a lot was soaked up in stairs, passageways, walls, and such. It worked out that each one had about room enough for his bunk and about that much left over to stand on when he wasn't sleeping.

You can't give a rodeo in that kind of space; you can't even get up a game of ring-around-the-rosy.

"A" deck was larger and "C" deck was smaller, being nearer the axis, but they averaged out the same. The council set up a staggered system to get the best use out of the galley and the mess rooms and to keep us from falling over each other in the 'freshers. "A" deck was on Greenwich time; "B" deck was left on zone plus-eight time, or Pacific West Coast time; and "C" deck drew zone minus-eight time, Philippine time. That would have put us on different days, of course, but the day was always figured officially on Greenwich time; the dodge was just to ease the pressure on eating facilities.

That was really all we had to worry about. You would wake up early, not tired but bored, and wait for breakfast. Once breakfast was over, the idea was to kill time until lunch. All afternoon you could look forward to the terrific excitement of having dinner.

I have to admit that making us go to school was a good plan; it meant that two and a half hours every morning and every afternoon was taken care of. Some of the grown ups complained that the mess rooms and all the spare space was always crowded with classes, but what did they expect us to do? Go hang on sky hooks? We used up less space in class than if we had been under foot.

Still, it was a mighty odd sort of school. There were some study machines in the cargo but we couldn't get at them and there wouldn't have been enough to go around. Each class consisted of about two dozen kids and some adult who knew something about something. (You'd be surprised how many adults don't know anything about anything!) The grown up would talk about what he knew best and the kids would listen, then we would ask questions and he would ask questions. No real examinations, no experiments, no demonstrations, no stereos.

Dad says this is the best kind of a school, that a university consists of a log with a teacher on one end and a pupil on the other. But Dad is a sort of romantic.

Things got so dull that it was hardly worth while to keep up my diary, even if I had been able to get microfilm, which I wasn't.

Dad and I played an occasional game of cribbage in the evening—somehow Dad had managed to squeeze the board and a pack of cards into his weight allowance. Then he got too busy with technical planning he was doing for the council and didn't have time. Molly suggested that I teach her to play, so I did.

After that I taught Peggy to play and she pegged a pretty sharp game, for a girl. It worried me a little that I wasn't being loyal to Anne in getting chummy with Peg and her mother, but I decided that Anne would want me to do just what I did. Anne was always friendly with everybody.

It still left me with time on my hands. What with only one-third gravity and no exercise I couldn't sleep more than six hours a night. The lights were out eight hours but they didn't make us go to bed, not after the trouble they had with it the first week. I used to fool around the corridors after lights out, usually with Hank Jones, until we both would get sleepy. We talked a lot. Hank turned out not to be such a bad guy as long as you kept him trimmed down to size.

I still had my Scout suit with me and kept it folded up in my bunk. Hank came in one morning while I was making up my bunk and noticed it. "See here, William," he said, "why do you hang on to that? Let the dead past bury its dead."

"I don't know," I admitted. "Maybe there will be Scouting on Ganymede."

"Not that I ever heard of."

"Why not? There is Scouting on the Moon."

"Proves nothing," he answered.

But it got us to talking about it and Hank got a brilliant idea. Why not start up Scouting right now, in the *Mayflower?*

We called a meeting. Peggy spread the word around for us, through the junior council, and we set it for fifteen-thirty that same afternoon, right after school. Fifteen-thirty Greenwich, or "A" deck time, that is. That made it seven-thirty in the morning for the "B" deck boys and a half hour before mid-night for the fellows on "C" deck. It was the best we could do. "B" deck could hurry through breakfast and get to the meeting if they wanted to and we figured that those who were really interested from "C" would stay up for the meeting.

I played my accordion while they were drifting in because Hank's father said that you needed music to warm up a meeting before it got down to work. The call had read "all Scouts and former Scouts;" by fifteen-forty we had them packed in and spilling into the corridors, even though we had the use of the biggest mess room. Hank called them to order and I put away my accordion and acted as Scribe *pro tem,* having borrowed a wire recorder from the Communications Officer for the purpose.

Hank made a little speech. I figure him for politics when he grows up. He said that all of us had enjoyed the benefits, the comradeship, and the honorable traditions of Scouting on Earth and it seemed a shame to lose them. He said that the Scouting tradition was the tradition of the explorer and pioneer and there could be no more fitting place and time for it than in the settlement of a new planet. In fact the spirit of Daniel Boone demanded that we continue as Scouts.

I didn't know he had it in him. It sounded good.

He stopped and slipped me the wink. I got up and said that I wanted to propose a resolution. Then I read it—it had been a lot longer but we cut it down. It read: "Be it resolved—we the undersigned, Scouts and former Scouts of many jurisdictions and now passengers in the good ship *Mayflower,* having as our purpose to continue the Scouting tradition and to extend the Scouting trail out to the stars, do organize ourselves as the Boy Scouts of Ganymede in accordance with the principles and purpose of Scouting and in so doing do reaffirm the Scout Law."

Maybe it was flowery but it sounded impressive; nobody laughed. Hank said, "You have heard the resolution; what is your pleasure? Do I hear a second?"

He surely did; there were seconds all over the place. Then he asked for debate.

Somebody objected that we couldn't call ourselves the Boy Scouts of Ganymede because we weren't on Ganymede yet. He got a chilly reception and shut up. Then somebody else pointed out that Ganymede wasn't a star, which made that part about "Carrying the Scouting trail out to the stars" nonsense.

Hank told him that was poetic license and anyhow going out to Ganymede was a step in the right direction and that there would be more steps; what about the *Star Rover III?* That shut *him* up.

The worst objection was from "Millimetre" Muntz, a weary little squirt too big for his britches. He said, "Mr. Chairman, this is an outlaw meeting. You haven't any authority to set up a new Scouting jurisdiction. As a member in good standing of Troop Ninety-Six, New Jersey, I object to the whole proceeding."

Hank asked him just what authority he thought Troop Ninety-Six, New Jersey, had out around the orbit of Mars? Somebody yelled, "Throw him out!"

Hank banged on the mess table. "It isn't necessary to throw him out—but, since Brother Millimetre thinks this is not a proper meeting, then it isn't proper for him to take part in it. He is excused and the chair will recognize him no further. Are you ready to vote?"

It was passed unanimously and then Hank was elected organizational chairman. He appointed a flock of committees, for organization and for plans and programs and for credentials and tests and for liaison, and such. That last was to dig out the men in the ship who had been troop masters and commissioners and things and get a Court of Honor set up. There were maybe a dozen of the men passengers at the meeting, listening. One of them, a Dr. Archibald who was an aide on "A" deck, spoke up.

"Mr. Chairman, I was a Scoutmaster in Nebraska. I'd like to volunteer my services to this new organization."

Hank looked him straight in the eye. "Thank you, sir. Your application will be considered."

Dr. Archibald looked startled, but Hank went smoothly on, "We want and need and will appreciate the help of all you older

Scouts. The liaison committee is instructed to get the names of any who are willing to serve."

It was decided that we would have to have three troops, one for each deck, since it wasn't convenient to try to meet all at the same time. Hank asked all the Explorer Scouts to stand up. There were too many of them, so he asked those who were Eagles to remain standing. There were about a dozen of us.

Hank separated us Eagles by decks and told us to get busy and organize our troops and to start by picking an acting senior patrol leader. "A" deck had only three Eagles, me, Hank, and a kid from another bunk room whom I hadn't met before, Douglas MacArthur Okajima. Doug and Hank combined on me and I found myself tagged with the job.

Hank and I had planned to finish the meeting with setting up exercises, but there just wasn't room, so I got out my accordion again and we sang *The Scouting Trail* and followed it with *The Green Hills of Earth*. Then we took the oath together again:

"Upon my honor I will do my best to do my duty to God and my planet, and to keep myself physically fit, mentally alert, and morally straight."

After that the meeting busted up.

For a while we held meetings every day. Between troop meetings and committee meetings and Explorer meetings and patrol leader meetings we didn't have time to get bored. At first the troops were just "A" troop, "B" troop, and "C" troop, after the decks, but we wanted names to give them some personality. Anyhow I wanted a name for my troop; we were about to start a membership drive and I wanted something with more oomph to it than " 'A' deck troop."

Somebody suggested "The Space Rats" but that was voted down, and somebody else suggested "The Mayflowers"; they didn't bother to vote on that; they simply sat on him.

After that we turned down "The Pilgrims," "Deep Space Troop," "Star Rovers," and "Sky High." A kid named John Edward Forbes-Smith got up. "Look," he said, "we're divided into three troops on the basis of the time zones we use, aren't we? "B" deck has California time; "C" deck has Philippine time; and we have Greenwich or English time. Why don't we pick names that will show that fact? We could call ourselves the Saint George Troop."

Bud Kelly said it was a good idea as far as it went but make it Saint Patrick instead of Saint George; after all, Dublin was on

Greenwich time, too, and Saint Patrick was a more important saint.

Forbes-Smith said, "Since when?"

Bud said, "Since always, you limey——" So we sat on both of them, too, and it was decided not to use saints. But Johnny Edwards had a good idea, just the same; we settled on the Baden-Powell Troop, Boy Scouts of Ganymede, which tied in with the English time zone and didn't offend anybody.

The idea took hold; "C" deck picked Aguinaldo as a name and "B" deck called themselves the Junipero Serra Troop. When I heard that last I was kind of sorry our deck didn't have California time so that we could have used it. But I got over it; after all "Baden-Powell" is a mighty proud name, too.

For that matter they were all good names—scouts and explorers and brave men, all three of them. Two of them never had a chance to be Scouts in the narrow, organized meaning, but they were all Scouts in the wider sense—like Daniel Boone.

Dad says there is a lot in a name.

As soon as they heard about what we were doing the girls set up Girl Scouting, too, and Peggy was a member of the Florence Nightingale Troop. I suppose there was no harm in it, but why do girls copy what the boys do? We were too busy to worry about them, though; we had to revamp Scouting activities to fit new conditions.

We decided to confirm whatever ranks and badges a boy had held in his former organization—permanent rankings, I mean, not offices. Having been a patrol leader or a scribe didn't mean anything, but if you were an Eagle on Earth, you stayed one in the B.S.G.; if you were a Cub, then you were still a Cub. If a boy didn't have records—and about half of them didn't—we took his Scout oath statement as official.

That was simple; working over the tests and the badges was complicated. After all you can't expect a boy to pass bee-keeping when you haven't any bees.

(It turned out that there *were* several swarms of bees sleep-frozen in the cargo, but we didn't have the use of them.)

But we could set up a merit badge in hydroponics and give tests right there in the ship. And Mr. Ortega set up a test for us in spaceship engineering and Captain Harkness did the same for ballistics and astrogation. By the end of the trip we had enough new tests to let a boy go up for Eagle Scout, once we had a Court of Honor.

That came last. For some reason I couldn't figure Hank had kept putting off the final report of the liaison committee, the committee which had as its job getting Scout Masters and Commissioners and such. I asked him about it, but he just looked mysterious and said that I would see.

I did see, eventually. At last we had a joint meeting of all three troops to install Scout Masters and dedicate the Court of Honor and such. And from then on the adults ran things and we went back to being patrol leaders at the most. Oh well—it was fun while it lasted.

8.
TROUBLE

When we were fifty-three days out and about a week to go to reach Ganymede, Captain Harkness used the flywheel to precess the ship so that we could see where we were going—so that the passengers could see, that is; it didn't make any difference to his astrogation.

You see, the axis of the *Mayflower* had been pointed pretty much toward Jupiter and the torch had been pointed back at the Sun. Since the view ports were spaced every ninety degrees around the sides, while we had been able to see most of the sky, we hadn't been able to see ahead to Jupiter nor behind to the Sun. Now he tilted the ship over ninety degrees and we were rolling, so to speak, along our line of flight. That way, you could see Jupiter and the Sun both, from any view port, though not both at the same time.

Jupiter was already a tiny, ruddy-orange disc. Some of the boys claimed they could make out the moons. Frankly, I couldn't, not for the first three days after the Captain precessed the ship. But it was mighty fine to be able to see Jupiter.

We hadn't seen Mars on the way out, because Mars happened to be on the far side of the Sun, three hundred million miles away. We hadn't seen anything but the same old stars you can see from Earth. We didn't even see any asteroids.

There was a reason for that. When we took off from the orbit of Supra-New-York, Captain Harkness had not aimed the *Mayflower* straight for where Jupiter was going to be when we got there; instead he had lifted her north of the ecliptic high enough to give the asteroid belt a wide berth. Now anybody knows that meteors are no real hazard in space. Unless a pilot does deliberately foolish things like driving his ship through the head of a comet it is almost impossible to get yourself hit by a meteor. They are too far between.

On the other hand the asteroid belt has more than its fair share of sky junk. The older power-pile ships used to drive straight through the belt, taking their chances, and none of them was ever hit to amount to anything. But Captain Harkness, having literally all the power in the world, preferred to go around and play it safe. By avoiding the belt there wasn't a chance in a blue moon that the *Mayflower* would be hit.

Well, it must have been a blue moon. We were hit.

It was just after reveille, "A" deck time, and I was standing by my bunk, making it up. I had my Scout uniform in my hands and was about to fold it up and put it under my pillow. I still didn't wear it. None of the others had uniforms to wear to Scout meetings so I didn't wear mine. But I still kept it tucked away in my bunk.

Suddenly I heard the goldarnest noise I ever heard in my life. It sounded like a rifle going off right by my ear, it sounded like a steel door being slammed, and it sounded like a giant tearing yards and yards of cloth, all at once.

Then I couldn't hear anything but a ringing in my ears and I was dazed. I shook my head and looked down and I was staring at a raw hole in the ship, almost between my feet and nearly as big as my fist. There was scorched insulation around it and in the middle of the hole I could see blackness—then a star whipped past and I realized that I was staring right out into space.

There was a hissing noise.

I don't remember thinking at all. I just wadded up my uniform, squatted down, and stuffed it in the hole. For a moment it seemed as if the suction would pull it on through the hole, then it jammed and stuck and didn't go any further. But we were still losing air. I think that was the point at which I first realized that we *were* losing air and that we might be suffocated in vacuum.

There was somebody yelling and screaming behind me that he was killed and alarm bells were going off all over the place. You couldn't hear yourself think. The air-tight door to our bunk room slid across automatically and settled into its gaskets and we were locked in.

That scared me to death.

I know it has to be done. I know that it is better to seal off one compartment and kill the people who are in it than to let a whole ship die—but, you see, *I* was in that compartment, personally. I guess I'm just not the hero type.

I could feel the pressure sucking away at the plug my uniform made. With one part of my mind I was recalling that it had been advertised as "tropical weave, self ventilating" and wishing that it had been a solid plastic rain coat instead. I was afraid to stuff it in any harder, for fear it would go all the way through and leave us sitting there, chewing vacuum. I would have passed up desserts for the next ten years for just one rubber patch, the size of my hand.

The screaming had stopped; now it started up again. It was Noisy Edwards, beating on the air-tight door and yelling, "Let me out of here! *Get me out of here!*"

On top of that I could hear Captain Harkness's voice coming through the bull horn. He was saying, "H-twelve! Report! H-twelve! Can you hear me?"

On top of that everybody was talking at once.

I yelled: "Quiet!" at the top of my voice—and for a second or so there *was* quiet.

Peewee Brunn, one of my Cubs, was standing in front of me, looking big-eyed. "What happened, Billy?" he said.

I said, "Grab me a pillow off one of the bunks. Jump!"

He gulped and did it. I said, "Peel off the cover, quick!"

He did, making quite a mess of it, and handed it to me—but I didn't have a hand free. I said, "Put it down on top of my hands."

It was the ordinary sort of pillow, soft foam rubber. I snatched one hand out and then the other, and then I was kneeling on it and pressing down with the heels of my hands. It dimpled a little in the middle and I was scared we were going to have a blowout right through the pillow. But it held. Noisy was screaming again and Captain Harkness was still asking for somebody, *anybody,* in compartment H-12 to tell him what was going on. I yelled *"Quiet!"* again, and added, "Somebody slug Noisy and shut him up."

That was a popular idea. About three of them jumped to it. Noisy got clipped in the side of the neck, then somebody poked him in the pit of his stomach and they swarmed over him. "Now everybody keep quiet," I said, "and keep on keeping quiet. If Noisy lets out a peep, slug him again." I gasped and tried to take a deep breath and said, "H-twelve, reporting!"

The Captain's voice answered, "What is the situation there?"

"There is a hole in the ship, Captain, but we got it corked up."

"How? And how big a hole?"

I told him and that is about all there was to it. They took a while to get to us because—I found this out afterward—they isolated that stretch of corridor first, with the air-tight doors, and that meant they had to get everybody out of the rooms on each side of us and across the passageway. But presently two men in space suits opened the door and chased all the kids out, all but me. Then they came back. One of them was Mr. Ortega. "You can get up now, kid," he said, his voice sounding strange and far away through his helmet. The other man squatted down and took over holding the pillow in place.

Mr. Ortega had a big metal patch under one arm. It had sticky padding on one side. I wanted to stay and watch him put it on but he chased me out and closed the door. The corridor outside was empty but I banged on the air-tight door and they let me through to where the rest were waiting. They wanted to know what was happening but I didn't have any news for them because I had been chased out.

After a while we started feeling light and Captain Harkness announced that spin would be off the ship for a short time. Mr. Ortega and the other man came back and went on up to the control room. Spin was off entirely soon after that and I got very sick. Captain Harkness kept the ship's speaker circuits cut in on his conversations with the men who had gone outside to repair the hole, but I didn't listen. I defy anybody to be interested in anything when he is drop sick.

Then spin came back on and everything was all right and we were allowed to go back into our bunk-room. It looked just the same except that there was a plate welded over the place where the meteorite had come in.

Breakfast was two hours late and we didn't have school that morning.

That was how I happened to go up to Captain's mast for the second time. George was there and Molly and Peggy and Dr. Archibald, the Scoutmaster of our deck, and all the fellows from my bunk room and all the ship's officers. The rest of the ship was cut in by visiplate. I wanted to wear my uniform but it was a mess—torn and covered with sticky stuff. I finally cut off the merit badges and put it in the ship's incinerator.

The First Officer shouted, "Captain's Mast for punishments

and rewards!" Everybody sort of straightened up and Captain Harkness walked out and faced us. Dad shoved me forward.

The Captain looked at me. "William Lermer?" he said.

I said, "Yessir."

He said, "I will read from yesterday's log: 'On twenty-one August at oh-seven-oh-four system standard, while cruising in free fall according to plan, the ship was broached by a small meteorite. Safety interlocks worked satisfactorily and the punctured volume, compartment H-twelve, was isolated with no serious drop in pressure elsewhere in the ship.

" 'Compartment H-twelve is a bunk room and was occupied at the time of the emergency by twenty passengers. One of the passengers, William J. Lermer, contrived a makeshift patch with materials at hand and succeeded in holding sufficient pressure for breathing until a repair party could take over.

" 'His quick thinking and immediate action unquestionably saved the lives of all persons in compartment H-twelve.' "

The Captain looked up from the log and went on, "A certified copy of this entry, along with depositions of witnesses, will be sent to Interplanetary Red Cross with recommendation for appropriate action. Another copy will be furnished you. I have no way to reward you except to say that you have my heart-felt gratitude. I know that I speak not only for the officers but for all the passengers and most especially for the parents of your bunk mates."

He paused and waggled a finger for me to come closer. He went on in a low voice, to me alone, "That really was a slick piece of work. You were on your toes. You have a right to feel proud."

I said I guessed I had been lucky.

He said, "Maybe. But that sort of luck comes to the man who is prepared for it."

He waited a moment, then said, "Lermer, have you ever thought of putting in for space training?"

I said I suppose I had but I hadn't thought about it very seriously. He said, "Well, Lermer, if you ever do decide to, let me know. You can reach me care of the Pilots' Association, Luna City."

With that, mast was over and we went away, George and I together and Molly and Peggy following along. I heard Peggy saying, "That's *my* brother."

Molly said, "Hush, Peggy. And don't point."

Peggy said, "Why not? He *is* my brother—well, isn't he?"

Molly said, "Yes, but there's no need to embarrass him."

But I wasn't embarrassed.

* * *

Mr. Ortega looked me up later and handed me a little, black, twisted piece of metal, about as big as a button. "That's all there was left of it," he said, "but I thought you would like to have it— pay you for messing up your Scout suit, so to speak."

I thanked him and said I didn't mind losing the uniform; after all, it had saved my neck, too. I looked at the meteorite. "Mr. Ortega, is there any way to tell where this came from?"

"Not really," he told me, "though you can get the scientific johnnies to cut it up and then express an opinion—if you don't mind them destroying it."

I said no, I'd rather keep it—and I have; I've still got it as a pocket piece. He went on, "It's either a bit of a comet or a piece of the Ruined Planet. We can't tell which because where we were there shouldn't have been either one."

"Only there was," I said.

"As you say, there was."

"Uh, Mr. Ortega, why don't they put enough armor on a ship to stop a little bitty thing like this?" I remembered what the skin of the ship looked like where it had been busted; it seemed awful thin.

"Well, now, in the first place, this meteor is a real giant, as meteors go. In the second place—do you know anything about cosmic rays, Bill?"

"Uh, not much, I guess."

"You undoubtedly know that the human body is transparent to primary cosmic radiation and isn't harmed by it. That is what we encounter out here in space. But metal is not completely transparent to it and when it passes through metal it kicks up all sorts of fuss—secondary and tertiary and quaternary cosmic radiation. The stuff cascades and it is *not* harmless, not by a darn sight. It can cause mutations and do you and your descendants a lot of harm. It adds up to this: a man is safest in space when he has just enough ship around him to keep the air in and ultraviolet out."

Noisy didn't have much to say around the compartment for the next couple of days and I thought maybe he had learned his lesson. I was wrong. I ran into him in one of the lower passageways when there was nobody else around. I started to go around him but he stepped in my way. "I want to talk to you," he said.

"Okay," I answered. "What's on your mind?"

"You think you're pretty smart, don't you?"

I didn't like the way he said it, nor what he said. I said, "I don't *think* I'm smart; I *am* smart." He made me tired.

"Pretty cocky, aren't you? You think I ought to be kissing your hand and telling you how grateful I am for saving my life, don't you?"

I said, "Oh, yeah? If that's what is worrying you, you can just skip it; I didn't do it for *you*."

"I know that," he answered, "and I'm *not* grateful, see?"

"That's fine with me," I told him. "I wouldn't want a guy like you being grateful to me."

He was breathing hard. "I've had just about enough of you," he said slowly. And the next thing I knew I had a mouthful of knuckles and I was down.

I got up cautiously, trying to surprise him. But it was no good; he knocked me down again. I tried to kick him while I was down, but he danced out of my way.

The third time he hit me I stayed down. When I quit seeing stars he was gone—and I hadn't managed to lay a finger on him. I never was any good in a fight; I'm still talking when I ought to be slugging.

I went to a scuttlebutt and bathed my face. Hank ran across me there and asked me what in the world I had been doing. I told him I had run into a door. I told Dad the same thing.

Noisy didn't bother me any more and we never had anything to say to each other again. I lay awake a long time that night, trying to figure it out. I didn't get it. The chap who thought up that malarkey about "my strength is as the strength of ten because my heart is pure" certainly had never met Noisy Edwards. For my taste Noisy was a no good so-and-so and I wished I had been able to use his face to stuff the hole the meteor made. I thought about a number of ways to fix him, but none of them was any good. As Dad says, sometimes there just isn't any cure for a situation.

9.
THE MOONS OF JUPITER

Nothing much happened until it was time to make our approach to Jupiter, except that a four-year-old kid turned up missing. The kid's parents searched all around and they passed the word from the control room for everybody to keep an eye open but they still couldn't find him.

So we had a chance to try out the Scouts' emergency organization. The ship's officers couldn't search the ship, since there was just the Captain and two watch officers and Mr. Ortega and his assistant chief. Captain Harkness supplied plans to each of the Scoutmasters and we went through that ship like a kid searching his clothes for a half credit. We turned the kid up, all right, in about twenty minutes. Seems the little devil had snuck into the hydroponics room while it was being serviced and had got himself locked in.

While he was in there he had got thirsty and had tried to drink the solutions they raise the plants in—had drunk some, in fact. The result was just about what you would expect. It didn't do him any real harm but, boy, was that place a mess!

I was talking to Dad about it that night over a game. Peggy had a Girl Scout meeting and Molly was off somewhere; we were alone for once. The baby's mother had raised particular Ned, just as if there had really been something wrong—I mean, what can happen in a space ship? The kid couldn't fall overboard.

Dad said her reaction was perfectly natural.

I said, "See, here, George, does it seem to you that some of the emigrants don't have what it takes to be colonists?"

"Mmmm . . . possibly."

I was thinking of Noisy but the ones I mentioned were Mrs. Tarbutton, who gave up and didn't even come along, and that female—Mrs. Grigsby—who got in trouble and had to wash dishes. And another fellow named Saunders who was continually in trouble with the council for trying to live his own life, wild and free, no matter what it did to the rest of us. "George, how did those characters get past the psycho tests?"

George stopped to peg fifteen-four, then said, "Bill, haven't you ever heard of political influence?"

All I said was, "Huh?"

"It's a shocking thought I know, but you are old enough to get used to the world as it is, instead of the way it ought to be. Take a hypothetical case: I don't suppose that a niece of a state councilor would be very likely to fail the psycho tests. Oh, she might fail the first tests, but a review board might find differently—if the councilor really wanted her to pass."

I chewed this over a while. It did not sound like George; he isn't the cynical type. Me, I'm cynical, but George is usually naïve. "In that case, George, there is no use in having psycho tests at all, not if people like that can sneak past."

"Contrariwise. The tests are usually honest. As for those who sneak past, it doesn't matter. Old Mother Nature will take care of them in the long run. Survivors survive." He finished dealing and said, "Wait till you see what I'm going to do to you this hand. You haven't a chance."

He always says that. I said, "Anybody who would use public office like that ought to be impeached!"

George said mildly, "Yep. But don't burn out your jets, son; we've got human beings, not angels, to work with."

On the twenty-fourth of August Captain Harkness took spin off and started bringing us in. We decelerated for better than four hours and then went into free fall about six hundred thousand miles out from Jupiter and on the opposite side from where Ganymede was then. Weightlessness still wasn't any fun but this time we were ready and everyone got shots for it who wanted them. I took mine and no nonsense.

Theoretically the *Mayflower* could have made it in one compound maneuver, ending up at the end of deceleration in a tight circular orbit around Ganymede. Practically it was much better to sneak in easy and avoid any more trouble with meteorites—with the "false rings," that is.

Of course Jupiter doesn't have rings like Saturn, but it does have quite a lot of sky junk traveling around in the same plane as its moons. If there were enough of it, it would show up like Saturn's rings. There isn't that much, but there is enough to make a pilot walk on eggs coming in. This slow approach gave us a fine front seat for a tour of Jupiter and its satellites.

Most of this stuff we were trying to avoid is in the same plane as Jupiter's equator, just the way Saturn's rings are—so Captain Harkness brought us in *over the top* of Jupiter, right across Jupiter's north pole. That way, we never did get in the danger zone until we had curved down on the other side to reach Ganymede— and by then we were going fairly slow.

But we weren't going slow when we passed over Jupiter's north pole, no indeedy! We were making better than thirty miles a second and we were close in, about thirty thousand miles. It was quite a sight. Jupiter is ninety thousand miles thick; thirty thousand miles is close—too close for comfort.

I got one good look at it for about two minutes from one of the view ports, then had to give up my place to somebody who hadn't had a turn yet and go back to the bunk room and watch through the vision screen. It was an odd sight; you always think of Jupiter with equatorial bands running parallel across it. But now we were looking at it end on and the bands were circles. It looked like a giant archery target, painted in orange and brick red and brown— except that half of it was chewed away. We saw it in half moon, of course.

There was a dark spot right at the pole. They said that was a zone of permanent clear weather and calm and that you could see clear down to the surface there. I looked but I couldn't see anything; it just looked dark.

As we came over the top, Io—that's satellite number one— suddenly came out of eclipse. Io is about as big as the Moon and was about as far away from us at the time as the Moon is from the Earth, so it looked about Moon size. There was just black sky and then there was a dark, blood red disc and in less than five minutes it was brilliant orange, about the color of Jupiter itself. It simply popped up, like magic.

I looked for Barnard's satellite while we were close in, but missed it. It's the little one that is less than one diameter from the surface of Jupiter—so close that it whirls around Jupiter in twelve hours. I was interested in it because I knew that the Jovian observatory was on it and also the base for Project Jove.

I probably didn't miss anything; Barnard's satellite is only about a hundred and fifty miles in diameter. They say a man can come pretty close to jumping right off it. I asked George about it and he said, no, the escape speed was about five hundred feet per second and who had been filling me up with nonsense?

I looked it up later; he was right. Dad is an absolute mine of useless information. He says a fact should be loved for itself alone.

Callisto was behind us; we had passed her on the way in, but not very close. Europa was off to the right of our course nearly ninety degrees; we saw her in half moon. She was more than four hundred thousand miles away and was not as pretty a sight as the Moon is from Earth.

Ganymede was straight ahead, almost, and growing all the time—and here was a funny thing; Callisto was silvery, like the Moon, but not as bright; Io and Europa were bright orange, as bright as Jupiter itself. Ganymede was downright dull!

I asked George about it; he came through, as usual. "Ganymede used to be about as bright as Io and Europa," he told me. "It's the greenhouse effect—the heat trap. Otherwise we wouldn't be able to live on it."

I knew about that, of course; the greenhouse effect is the most important part of the atmosphere project. When the 1985 expedition landed Ganymede had a surface temperature a couple of hundred degrees below zero—that's cold enough to freeze the milk of human kindness! "But look, George," I objected, "sure, I know about the heat trap, but why is it so dark? It looks like the inside of a sack."

"Light is heat; heat is light," he answered. "What's the difference? It's not dark on the ground; it goes in and doesn't come out—and a good thing, too."

I shut up. It was something new to me and I didn't understand it, so I decided to wait and not pound my teeth about it.

Captain Harkness slowed her down again as we came up to Ganymede and we got in one good meal while she was under drive. I never did get so I could eat at free fall, even with injections. He leveled her off in a tight circular orbit about a thousand miles up from Ganymede. We had arrived—just as soon as we could get somebody to come and get us.

It was on the trip down to Ganymede's surface that I began to suspect that being a colonist wasn't as glamorous and romantic as it had seemed back on Earth. Instead of three ships to carry us all at once, there was just one ship, the *Jitterbug,* and she would have fitted into one of the *Bifrost's* compartments. She could carry only ninety of us at a time and that meant a lot of trips.

I was lucky; I had to wait only three days in free fall. But I lost ten pounds.

While I waited, I worked, helping to stow the freight that the *Jitterbug* brought up each trip. At last it came our turn and we piled into the *Jitterbug.* She was terrible; she had shelves rather than decks—they weren't four feet apart. The air was stale and she hadn't been half way cleaned up since the last trip. There weren't individual acceleration couches; there were just pads covering the deck space and *we* covered the pads, shoulder to shoulder—and foot in your eye, for that matter.

The skipper was a loud-mouthed old female they called "Captain Hattie" and she kept bawling us out and telling us to hurry. She didn't even wait to make sure that we were all strapped down.

Fortunately it didn't take very long. She drove away so hard that for the first time except in tests I blacked out, then we dropped for about twenty minutes; she gunned her again, and we landed with a terrible bump. And Captain Hattie was shouting, "Out you come, you ground hogs! This is it."

The *Jitterbug* carried oxygen, rather than the helium-oxygen mix of the *Mayflower.* We had come down at ten pounds pressure; now Captain Hattie spilled the pressure and let it adjust to Ganymede normal, three pounds. Sure, three pounds of oxygen is enough to live on; that's all Earth has —the other twelve pounds are nitrogen. But a sudden drop in pressure like that is enough to make you gasp anyhow. You aren't suffocating but you feel as if you were.

We were miserable by the time we got out and Peggy had a nose bleed. There weren't any elevators; we had to climb down a rope ladder. And it was cold!

It was snowing; the wind was howling around us and shaking the ladder—the smallest kids they had to lower with a line. There was about eight inches of snow on the ground except where the splash of the *Jitterbug's* jet had melted it. I could hardly see, the wind was whipping the snow into my face so, but a man grabbed me by the shoulder, swung me around, and shouted, "Keep moving! Keep moving! Over that way."

I headed the way he pointed. There was another man at the edge of the blast clearing, singing the same song, and there was a path through the snow, trampled to slush. I could see some other people disappearing in the snow ahead and I took out after them, dogtrotting to keep warm.

It must have been half a mile to the shelter and cold all the way. We weren't dressed for it. I was chilled through and my feet were soaking wet by the time we got inside.

The shelter was a big hangarlike building and it was not much warmer, the door was open so much, but it was out of the weather and it felt good to be inside. It was jammed with people, some of them in ship suits and some of them Ganymedeans—you couldn't miss the colonial men; they were bearded and some of them wore their hair long as well. I decided that was one style I was not going to copy; I'd be smooth shaven, like George.

I went scouting around, trying to find George & Co. I finally did. He had found a bale of something for Molly to sit on and she was holding Peggy on her lap. Peg's nose had stopped bleeding. I was glad to see, but there were dried tears and blood and dirt on her face. She was a sight.

George was looking gloomy, the way he did the first few days without his pipe. I came up and said, "Hi, folks!"

George looked around and smiled and said, "Well, Bill, fancy meeting you here! How is it going?"

"Now that you ask me," I answered, "it looks like a shambles."

He looked gloomy again and said, "Oh, I suppose they will get things straightened out presently."

We didn't get a chance to discuss it. A colonist with snow on his boots and hair on his face stopped near us, put his little fingers to his lips, and whistled. "Pipe down!" he shouted. "I want twelve able-bodied men and boys for the baggage party." He looked around and started pointing. "You—and you—and you——"

George was the ninth "You"; I was the tenth.

Molly started to protest. I think George might have balked if she had not. Instead he said, "No, Molly, I guess it has to be done. Come on, Bill."

So we went back out into the cold.

There was a tractor truck outside and we were loaded in it standing up, then we lumbered back to the rocket site. Dad saw to it that I was sent up into the *Jitterbug* to get me out of the weather and I was treated to another dose of Captain Hattie's tongue; we couldn't work fast enough to suit her. But we got our baggage lowered finally; it was in the truck by the time I was down out of the ship. The trip back was cold, too.

Molly and Peggy were not where we had left them. The big room was almost empty and we were told to go on into another building through a connecting door. George was upset, I could see, from finding Molly gone.

In the next building there were big signs with arrows: MEN & BOYS—TO THE RIGHT and WOMEN & GIRLS—TO THE LEFT. George promptly turned to the left. He got about ten yards and was stopped by a stern-faced woman dressed like a colonial, in a coverall. "Back the other way," she said firmly. "This is the way to the ladies' dormitory."

"Yes, I know," agreed Dad, "but I want to find my wife."

"You can look for her at supper."

"I want to see her *now*."

"I haven't any facilities for seeking out any one person at this time. You'll have to wait."

"But—" There were several women crowding past us and going on inside. Dad spotted one from our deck in the *Mayflower*. "Mrs. Archibald!"

She turned around. "Oh—Mr. Lermer. How do you do?"

"Mrs. Archibald," Dad said intently, "could you find Molly and let her know that I'm waiting here?"

"Why, I'd be glad to try, Mr. Lermer."

"Thanks, Mrs. Archibald, a thousand thanks!"

"Not at all." She went away and we waited, ignoring the stern-faced guard. Presently Molly showed up without Peggy. You would have thought Dad hadn't seen her for a month.

"I didn't know what to do, dear," she said. "They said we had to come and it seemed better to get Peggy settled down. I knew you would find us."

"Where is Peggy now?"

"I put her to bed."

We went back to the main hall. There was a desk there with a man behind it; over his head was a sign: IMMIGRATION Service—INFORMATION. There was quite a line up at it; we took our place in the queue.

"How is Peggy?" Dad asked.

"I'm afraid she is catching a cold."

"I hope—" Dad said. "Ah, I HOPE—*Atchoo!*"

"And so are you," Molly said accusingly.

"I don't catch cold," Dad said, wiping his eyes. "That was just a reflex."

"Hmm—" said Molly.

The line up took us past a low balcony. Two boys, my age or older, were leaning on the rail and looking us over. They were colonials and one was trying to grow a beard, but it was pretty crummy.

One turned to the other and said, "Rafe, will you look at what they are sending us these days?"

The other said, "It's sad."

The first one pointed a thumb at me and went on, "Take that one, now—the artistic type, no doubt."

The second one stared at me thoughtfully. "Is it alive?" he asked.

"Does it matter?" the first one answered.

I turned my back on them, whereupon they both laughed. I hate self-panickers.

10.
THE PROMISED LAND

Mr. Saunders was ahead of us in line. He was crabbing about the weather. He said it was an outrage to expose people the way we had been. He had been with us on the working party, but he had not worked much.

The man at the desk shrugged. "The Colonial Commission set your arrival date; we had nothing to say about it. You can't expect us to postpone winter to suit your convenience."

"Somebody's going to hear about this!"

"By all means." The man at the desk handed him a form. "Next, please!" He looked at Dad and said, "What may I do for you, citizen?"

Dad explained quietly that he wanted to have his family with him. The man shook his head. "Sorry. Next case, please."

Dad didn't give up his place. "You can't separate a man and wife. We aren't slaves, nor criminals, nor animals. The Immigration Service surely has some responsibilities toward us."

The man looked bored. "This is the largest shipload we've ever had to handle. We've made the best arrangements we could. This is a frontier town, not the Astor."

"All I'm asking for is a minimum family space, as described in the Commission's literature about Ganymede."

"Citizen, those descriptions are written back on Earth. Be patient and you will be taken care of."

"Tomorrow?"

"No, not tomorrow. A few days—or a few weeks."

Dad exploded. "Weeks, indeed! Confound it, I'll build an igloo out on the field before I'll put up with this."

"That's your privilege." The man handed Dad a sheet of paper. "If you wish to lodge a complaint, write it out on this."

Dad took it and I glanced at it. It was a printed form—and it was addressed to the Colonial Commission *back on Earth!* The man went on, "Turn it in to me any time this phase and it will be ultramicrofilmed in time to go back with the mail in the *Mayflower.*"

Dad looked at it, snorted, crumpled it up, and stomped away. Molly followed him and said, "George! George! Don't be upset. We'll live through it."

Dad grinned sheepishly. "Sure we will, honey. It's the beauty of the system that gets me. Refer all complaints to the head office—half a billion miles away!"

The next day George's reflexes were making his nose run. Peggy was worse and Molly was worried about her and Dad was desperate. He went off somewhere to raise a stink about the way things were being handled.

Frankly, I didn't have it too bad. Sleeping in a dormitory is no hardship to me; I could sleep through the crack of doom. And the food was everything they had promised.

Listen to this: For breakfast we had corn cakes with syrup and real butter, little sausages, *real* ham, strawberries with cream so thick I didn't know what it was, tea, all the milk you could drink, tomato juice, honeydew melon, eggs—as many eggs as you wanted.

There was an open sugar bowl, too, but the salt shaker had a little sign on it; DON'T WASTE THE SALT.

There wasn't any coffee, which I wouldn't have noticed if George had not asked for it. There were other things missing, too, although I certainly didn't notice it at the time. No tree fruits, for example—no apples, no pears, no oranges. But who cares when you can get strawberries and watermelon and pineapples and such? There were no tree nuts, too, but there were peanuts to burn.

Anything made out of wheat flour was a luxury, but you don't miss it at first.

Lunch was choice of corn chowder or jellied consomme, cheese soufflé, fried chicken, corned beef and cabbage, hominy grits with syrup, egg plant *au gratin,* little pearl onions scalloped with cucumbers, baked stuffed tomatoes, sweet potato surprise, German-fried Irish potatoes, tossed endive, coleslaw with sour cream, pineapple and cottage cheese with lettuce. Then there was peppermint ice cream, angel berry pie, frozen egg nog, raspberry ice, and three kinds of pudding—but I didn't do too well on the desserts. I had tried to try everything, taking a little of this and a dab of that, and by the time desserts came along I was short on space. I guess I ate too much.

The cooking wasn't fancy, about like Scout camp, but the food was so good you couldn't ruin it. The service reminded me of camp, too—queueing up for servings, no table cloths, no napkins. And the dishes had to be washed; you couldn't throw them away or burn them—they were imported from Earth and worth their weight in uranium.

The first day they took the first fifty kids in the chow line and the last fifty kids to leave the mess hall and made them wash dishes. The next day they changed pace on us and took the middle group. I got stuck both times.

The first supper was mushroom soup, baked ham, roast turkey, hot corn bread with butter, jellied cold meats, creamed asparagus, mashed potatoes and giblet gravy, spinach with hard boiled egg and grated cheese, corn pudding, creamed peas and carrots, smothered lettuce and three kinds of salad. Then there was frozen custard and raisin pudding with hard sauce and Malaga and Thompson grapes and more strawberries with powdered sugar.

Besides that you could drop around to the kitchen and get a snack any time you felt like it.

I didn't go outside much the first three days. It snowed and although we were in Sun phase when we got there it was so murky that you couldn't see the Sun, much less Jupiter. Besides, we were in eclipse part of the time. It was as cold as Billy-be-switched and we still didn't have any cold weather clothes.

I was sent along with the commissary tractor once to get supplies over in town. Not that I saw much of the town—and not that Leda is much of a town, anyhow, to a person who has lived in Diego Borough—but I did see the hydroponics farms. There were three of them, big multiple sheds, named for what they grew in them, "Oahu," "Imperial Valley," and "Iowa." Nothing special about them, just the usual sort of soiless gardening. I didn't hang around because the flicker lighting they use to force the plants makes my eyes burn.

But I was interested in the tropical plants they grew in "Oahu"—I had never seen a lot of them before. I noticed that most of the plants were marked "M-G" while a few were tagged "N. T."

I asked one of the gardeners; he said that "M-G" meant "mutation-Ganymede" and the other meant "normal terrestrial."

I found out later that almost everything grown on Ganymede was a special mutation adapted to Ganymede conditions.

Beyond there was another of the big multiple sheds named "Texas"; it had real cows in it and was very interesting. Did you know a cow moves its lower jaw from side to side? And no matter what you've heard, there *is not* one teat that is especially for cream.

I hated to leave, but "Texas" shed smelled too much like a space ship. It was only a short dash through the snow to the Exchange where all of Leda's retail buying and selling takes place—big and little shops all under one roof.

I looked around, thinking I might take a present back to Peggy, seeing that she was sick. I got the shock of my life. The prices!

If I had had to buy in the Exchange the measly fifty-eight pounds of stuff they had let me bring with me, it would have cost—I'm telling the truth!—several *thousand* credits. Everything that was imported from Earth cost that kind of money. A tube of beard cream was two hundred and eighty credits.

There were items for sale made on Ganymede, hand work mostly, and they were expensive, too, though not nearly as expensive as the stuff brought up from Earth.

I crept out of that place in a hurry. As nearly as I could figure the only thing cheap on Ganymede was food.

The driver of the commissary tractor wanted to know where I had been when there was loading to do? "I should have left you behind to walk back," he groused. I didn't have a good answer so I didn't say anything.

They shut off winter soon after that. The heat trap was turned on full force, the skies cleared and it was lovely. The first view I got of the Ganymede sky was a little after dawn next Sun phase. The heat trap made the sky a pale green but Jupiter shone right through it, ruddy orange, and *big*. Big and beautiful—I've never gotten tired of looking at Jupiter!

A harvest moon looks big, doesn't it? Well, Jupiter from Ganymede is sixteen or seventeen times as wide as the Moon looks and it covers better than two hundred and fifty times as much sky. It hangs there in the sky, never rising, never setting, and you wonder what holds it up.

I saw it first in half-moon phase and I didn't see how it could be any more beautiful than it was. But the Sun crept across the sky and a day later Jupiter was a crescent and better than ever. At the middle of Sun phase we went into eclipse, of course, and Jupiter was a great red, glowing ring in the sky, brightest where the Sun had just passed behind it.

But the best of all is during dark phase.

Maybe I ought to explain how the phases work; I know I didn't understand it until I came to Ganymede. Ganymede is such a small planet and so close to its primary that it is tide-locked, just the way the Moon is; it keeps one face always toward Jupiter and therefore Jupiter does not move in the sky. The sun moves, the other Jovian moons move, the stars move—but not good old Jove; it just hangs there.

Ganymede takes just over an Earth week to revolve around Jupiter, so we have three and a half days of sunlight and then three and a half days of darkness. By Ganymede time the period of rotation is *exactly* one week; twenty-four Ganymede hours is one seventh of the period. This arrangement makes a Ganymede minute about a standard second longer than an Earth minute, but who cares? Except scientists, of course, and they have clocks that keep both sorts of time.

So here is the way a week goes on Ganymede: the Sun rises at Sunday midnight every week; when you get up Monday morning it's a little above the eastern horizon and Jupiter is in half-moon phase. The Sun keeps climbing higher and about suppertime on Tuesday it slides behind Jupiter and Ganymede is in eclipse; eclipse can last an hour or so up to a maximum of about three hours and a half. The stars come out and Jupiter shows that beautiful red ring effect because of its thick atmosphere. Then it's light again by bedtime Tuesday.

At noon on Thursday the Sun goes down and we start the dark phase; that's best of all. Jupiter's colors really show and the other moons are easier to see. They can be almost anywhere and in almost any combination.

Jupiter and its satellites is sort of a miniature solar system; from Ganymede you have a front seat for the show. There is always something new in the sky. Besides the eleven "historical" satellites ranging in size from Ganymede down to Jay-ten or Nicholson-Alpha, which is a ball of rock and ice only fifteen miles thick, there are maybe a dozen more a few miles or less in diameter but big enough to be called moons and heaven knows how many smaller than that. Sometimes these little ones come close enough to Ganymede to show discs; they mostly have very eccentric orbits. Any time there will be several that are conspicuous lights in the sky, like the planets are from Earth.

Io, and Europa, and Callisto are always discs. When Europa passes between Jupiter and Ganymede it is as big in the sky as the Moon is from Earth. It actually is as big as the Moon and at that time it is only about a quarter of a million miles away.

Then it swings around to the far side and is very much smaller—more than a million miles away and less than a quarter as wide. Io goes through the same sorts of changes, but it never gets as big.

When Io and Europa pass between Ganymede and Jupiter you can see them move with your naked eye, chasing their shadows or running ahead of them, depending on the phase. Io and Europa, being inside Ganymede's orbit, never get very far away from Jupiter. Io sticks within a couple of diameters of the big boy; Europa can get about sixty degrees away from it. Callisto is further out than Ganymede and goes all around the sky.

It's a show you never get tired of. Earth's sky is *dull*.

By six o'clock Saturday morning Jupiter would be in full phase and it was worthwhile to get up to see it. Not only was it the most gorgeous thing I had ever seen, but there was always the reverse eclipse, too, and you could see Ganymede's shadow, a little round black dot, crawling across old Jupiter's face. It gave you an idea of just how colossally *big* Jupiter was—there was the shadow of your whole planet on it and it wasn't anything more than a big freckle.

Jupiter is ninety thousand miles across the equator, eighty-four thousand from pole to pole. Ganymede is only a little better than three thousand.

For the next couple of days after full phase Jupiter would wane and at Sunday midnight it would be in half phase again, the Sun would rise and a new light phase would start. One thing I expected but didn't find was dim sunlight. Jupiter is a long way out; it gets only one twenty-seventh the sunlight that Earth does. I expected that we would always be in a sort of twilight.

It didn't work out that way. It seemed to me that the sunlight was just as bright as on Earth.

George says that this is an optical illusion and that it has to do with the way the human eye works, because the iris of the eye simply shuts out light it doesn't need. Bright desert sunlight back on Earth is maybe ten thousand foot-candles; the same thing on Ganymede is only four hundred foot-candles. But really good bright artificial light is only *twenty-five* foot candles and a "well-lighted" room is seldom that bright.

If you've got only a two-gallon bucket does it make any difference whether you fill it from the ocean or from a small pond? Sunlight on Ganymede was still more than the eye could accept, so it looked just as bright as sunlight on Earth.

I did notice, however, that it was almost impossible to get a sunburn.

11.
"SHARE CROPPERS"

George got us a place to live when we had been there about a week, which was a lot better than most of the other immigrants did, but it didn't suit him and it didn't suit Molly and it didn't really suit me.

The trouble was he had to take a job as a staff engineer with the colonial government to get quarters for us—and that meant he would be too tied down to prove a piece of land for homestead. But it did carry private family quarters with it, if you could call two rooms twelve feet square a home.

It was like this: the colony was made up of homesteaders and townies. The townies worked for the government and lived in government-owned buildings—except for a very few who were in private trade. The townies included the Colonial Commission representative, Captain Hattie the pilot, the hydroponics engineers, the hospital staff, the engineers who ran the power plant and the heat trap, the staff of the local office of Project Jove, and everybody else who worked at anything but land farming. But most of the colonials were homesteaders and that's what George had meant us to be. Like most everybody, we had come out there on the promise of free land and a chance to raise our own food.

There was free land, all right, a whole planet of it. Putting up a house and proving a farm was another matter.

Here is the way it was supposed to work: A colonist comes out from Earth with his family and lands at Leda. The Colonial Commission gives him an apartment in town on arrival, helps him pick out a piece of land to improve and helps him get a house up on it. The Commission will feed him and his family for one Earth year—that is, two Ganymede years—while he gets a couple of acres under cultivation. Then he has ten G-years in which to pay back the Commission by processing at least twenty acres for the Commission—and he is allowed to process as much land for himself as for the Commission during the time he is paying what he owes. At the end of five Earth years he owns a tidy little farm, free and clear. After that, he can spread out and acquire more land, get into trade, anything he likes. He has his toehold and has paid off his debt.

The Colonial Commission had a big expensive investment in having started the atmosphere project and made the planet fit to live on in the first place. The land processed by the colonists was its return on the investment; the day would come when the Colonial Commission would own thousands of acres of prime farmland on Ganymede which it could then sell Earthside to later settlers . . . if you wanted to emigrate from Earth you would have to pay for the privilege and pay high. People like us would not be able to afford it.

By that time, although Ganymede would be closed to free immigration, Callisto would have an atmosphere and pioneers could move in there and do it all over again. It was what the bankers call "Self-liquidating," with the original investment coming from Earth.

But here is the way it actually did work out: when we landed there were only about thirty thousand people on Ganymede and they were geared to accept about five hundred immigrants an Earth year, which was about all the old-type ships could bring out. Remember, those power-pile ships took over five years for the round trip; it took a fleet of them to bring in that many a year.

Then the *Star Rover II* was renamed the *Mayflower* and turned over to the Colonial Commission, whereupon six thousand people were dumped on them all at once. We were about as welcome as unexpected overnight guests when there is sickness in the family.

The colonists had known, for a full Earth year, that we were coming, but they had not been able to protest. While Earth Sender can punch a message through to Ganymede anytime except when the Sun is spang in the way, at that time the best radio the colony could boast had to relay via Mars to reach Earth—and then only when Mars was at its closest approach to Jupiter—which it wasn't.

I've got to admit that they did what they could for us. There was plenty to eat and they had managed to fix up places for us to

620   FOUR FRONTIERS

sleep. The Immigrants' Receiving Station had formerly been split up into family apartments; they had torn out the partitions and used the partitions to build bunks for the big dormitories we were stacked in. They had moved their town hall and made it over into a mess hall and kitchen for us. We were in out of the weather and well fed, even if we were about as crowded as we had been in the *Mayflower.*

You may ask why, with a year to get ready, they had not built new buildings for us? Well, we asked the same thing, only we weren't asking, we were demanding, and we were sore about it!

They hadn't built new buildings because they could not. Before the Earthmen moved in, Ganymede was bare rock and ice. Sure, everybody knows that—but does everybody know what that means? I'm sure I didn't.

No lumber. No sheet metal. No insulation. No wires. No glass. No pipe. The settlers in North America built log cabins—no logs.

The big hydroponics sheds, the Receiving Station and a few other public buildings had been built with materials lifted a half a billion miles from Earth. The rest of Leda and every home-steader's farm house had been built the hard way, from country rock. They had done their best for us, with what they had.

Only we didn't appreciate it.

Of course we should not have complained. After all, as George pointed out, the first California settlers starved, nobody knows what happened to the Roanoke Colony, and the first two expeditions to Venus died to the last man. *We* were safe.

Anyhow, even if we had to put up with barracks for a while, there was all that free land, waiting for us.

On close inspection, it looked as if it would have to wait quite a while. That was why George had given in and taken a staff engineering job. The closest land to town open to homesteading was nine miles away. To find enough land for six thousand people meant that most of them would have to go about eighteen to twenty miles away.

"What's twenty miles? A few minutes by tube, an up-and-down hop for a copter—brother, have you ever *walked* twenty miles? And then walked back again?

It wasn't impossible to settle six thousand people that far from town; it was just difficult—and slow. The pioneer explorer used to set out with his gun and an axe; the settler followed by hitching his oxen to a wagonload of furniture and farm tools. Twenty miles meant nothing to them.

They weren't on Ganymede.

The colony had two tractor trucks; another had come in the *Mayflower*. That's all the transportation there was on the whole planet—not just to settle six thousand people but for the daily needs of thirty thousand people who were there ahead of us.

They explained it all to us at a big meeting of heads of families. I wasn't supposed to be there but it was held outdoors and there was nothing to stop me. The chief ecologist and the chief engineer of the planet were there and the chairman of the colony council presided. Here was the proposition:

What Ganymede really needed was not more farmers, but manufacturing. They needed prospectors and mines and mills and machine shops. They needed all the things you can make out of metal and which they simply could not afford to import from Earth. That's what they wanted us to work on and they would feed any of us who accepted, not just for a year, but indefinitely.

As for any who insisted on homesteading—well, the land was there; help ourselves. There wasn't enough processing machinery to go around, so it might be two or three years before any particular immigrant got a chance to process his first acre of ground.

Somebody stood up near the front of the crowd and yelled, "We've been swindled!"

It took Mr. Tolley, the chairman, quite a while to calm them down. When they let him talk again, he said, "Maybe you have been swindled, maybe you haven't. That's a matter of opinion. I'm quite willing to concede that conditions here are not the way they were represented to you when you left Earth. In fact——"

Somebody yelled. "That's mighty nice of you!" only the tone was sarcastic.

Mr. Tolley looked vexed. "You folks can either keep order, or I'll adjourn this meeting."

They shut up again and he went on. Most of the present homesteaders had processed more land than they could cultivate. They could use hired hands to raise more crops. There was a job waiting for every man, a job that would keep him busy and teach him Ganymede farming—and feed his wife and family—while he was waiting his turn to homestead.

You could feel a chill rolling over the crowd when the meaning of Mr. Tolley's words sunk in. They felt the way Jacob did when he had labored seven years and then was told he would have to labor another seven years to get the girl he really wanted. I felt it myself, even though George had already decided on the staff job.

A man spoke up. "Mr. Chairman!"

"Yes? Your name, please."

"Name of Saunders. I don't know how the rest of them feel, but I'm a farmer. Always have been. But I said 'farmer,' not sharecropper. I didn't come here to hire out to no boss. You can take your job and do what you see fit with it. I stand on my rights!"

There was scattered applause and the crowd began to perk up. Mr. Tolley looked at him and said, "That's your privilege, Mr. Saunders."

"Huh? Well, I'm glad you feel that way, Mr. Chairman. Now let's cut out the nonsense. I want to know two things: what piece of land am I going to get and when do I lay hands on some machinery to start putting it into condition?"

Mr. Tolley said, "You can consult the land office about your first question. As to the second, you heard the chief engineer say that he estimates the average wait for processing machinery will be around twenty-one months."

"That's too long."

"So it is, Mr. Saunders."

"Well, what do you propose to do about it?"

Mr. Tolley shrugged and spread his hands. "I'm not a magician. We've asked the Colonial Commission by urgent message going back on the *Mayflower* not to send us any more colonists on the next trip, but to send us machinery. If they agree, there may be some relief from the situation by next winter. But you have seen—all of you have already seen—that the Colonial Commission makes decisions without consulting us. The first trip of the *Mayflower* should have been all cargo; you folks should have waited."

Saunders thought about it. "Next winter, eh? That's five months away. I guess I can wait—I'm a reasonable man. But no sharecropping; that's out!"

"I didn't say you could start homesteading in five months, Mr. Saunders. It may be twenty-one months or longer."

"No, indeed!"

"Suit yourself. But you are confronted with a fact, not a theory. If you do have to wait and you won't work for another farmer, how do you propose to feed yourself and your family in the mean time?"

Mr. Saunders looked around and grinned, "Why, in that case,

Mr. Chairman, I guess the government will just have to feed us until the government can come through on its end of the deal. I know my rights."

Mr. Tolley looked at him as if he had just bitten into an apple and found Saunders inside. "We won't let your children starve," he said slowly, "but as for you, you can go chew rocks. If you won't work, you won't eat."

Saunders tried to bluster. "You can't get away with it! I'll sue the government and I'll sue you as the responsible government official. You can't——"

"*Shut up!*" Mr. Tolley went on more quietly, speaking to all of us. "We might as well get this point straight. You people have been enticed into coming out here by rosy promises and you are understandably disappointed. But your contract is with the Colonial Commission *back on Earth*. But you have no contract with the common council of Ganymede, of which I am chairman, and the citizens of Ganymede owe you nothing. We are trying to take care of you out of common decency.

"If you don't like what we offer you, don't start throwing your weight around with me; I won't stand for it. Take it up with the representative of the Immigration Service. That's what he is here for. Meeting's adjourned!"

But the immigration representative wasn't there; he had stayed away from the meeting.

12.
BEES AND ZEROES

We had been swindled all right. It was equally clear that there was no help for it. Some of the immigrants did see the Colonial Commission representative, but they got no comfort out of him. He had resigned, he said, fed up with trying to carry out impossible instructions five hundred million miles from the home office. He was going home as soon as his relief arrived.

That set them off again; if he could go home so could they. The *Mayflower* was still in orbit over us, taking on cargo. A lot of people demanded to go back in her.

Captain Harkness said no, he had no authority to let them deadhead half way across the system. So they landed back on the Commission representative, squawking louder than ever.

Mr. Tolley and the council finally settled it. Ganymede wanted no soreheads, no weak sisters. If the Commission refused to ship back those who claimed they were gypped and didn't want to stay, then the next shipload wouldn't even be allowed to land. The representative gave in and wrote Captain Harkness out a warrant for their passage.

We held a family powwow over the matter, in Peggy's room in the hospital—it had to be there because the doctors were keeping her in a room pressurized to Earth normal.

Did we stay, or did we go back? Dad was stuck in a rut. Back Earthside he at least had been working for himself; here he was just an employee. If he quit his job and elected to homestead, it meant working two or three G-years as a field hand before we could expect to start homesteading.

But the real rub was Peggy. In spite of having passed her physical examination Earthside she hadn't adjusted to Ganymede's low pressure. "We might as well face it," George said to Molly. "We've got to get Peg back to the conditions she's used to."

Molly looked at him; his face was as long as my arm. "George, you don't want to go back, do you?"

"That's not the point, Molly. The welfare of the kids comes first." He turned to me and added, "You're not bound by this, Bill. You are big enough to make up your own mind. If you want to stay, I am sure it can be arranged."

I didn't answer right away. I had come into the family get-together pretty disgusted myself, not only because of the run-around we had gotten, but also because of a run-in I had had with a couple of the Colonial kids. But you know what it was that swung me around? That pressurized room. I had gotten used to low pressure and I liked it. Peggy's room, pressurized to Earth normal, felt like swimming in warm soup. I could hardly breath. "I don't think I want to go back," I said.

Peggy had been sitting up in bed, following the talk with big eyes, like a little lemur. Now she said, "I don't want to go back, either!"

Molly patted her hand and did not answer her. "George," she said, "I've given this a lot of thought. You don't want to go back, I know. Neither does Bill. But we don't all have to go back. We can——"

"That's out, Molly," Dad answered firmly. "I didn't marry you to split up. If you have to go back, I go back."

"I didn't mean that. Peggy can go back with the O'Farrells and my sister will meet her and take care of her at the other end. She wanted me to leave Peggy with her when she found I was determined to go. It will work out all right." She didn't look at Peggy as she said it.

"But, Molly!" Dad said.

"No George," she answered, "I've thought this all out. My first duty is to you. It's not as if Peggy wouldn't be well taken care of; Phoebe will be a mother to her and——"

By now Peggy had caught her breath. "I don't *want* to go live with Aunt Phoebe!" she yelled and started to bawl.

George said, "It won't work, Molly."

Molly said, "George, not five minutes ago you were talking about leaving Bill behind, on his own."

"But Bill is practically a man!"

"He's not too old to be lonesome. And I'm not talking about

leaving Peggy alone; Phoebe will give her loving care. No, George, if the womenfolk ran home at the first sign of trouble there never would be any pioneers. Peggy has to go back, but I stay."

Peggy stopped her blubbering long enough to say, "I *won't* go back! I'm a pioneer, too—ain't I, Bill?"

I said, "Sure kid, sure!" and went over and patted her hand. She grabbed onto mine.

I don't know what made me say what I did then. Goodness knows the brat had never been anything but a headache, with her endless questions and her insistence that she be allowed to do anything I did. But I heard myself saying, "Don't worry, Peggy. If you go back, I'll go with you."

Dad looked at me sharply, then turned to Peggy. "Bill spoke hastily, Baby. You mustn't hold him to that."

Peggy said, "You did so mean it, didn't you, Bill?"

I was regretting it already. But I said, "Sure, Peggy."

Peggy turned back to Dad. "See? But it doesn't matter; we're not going back, not any of us. Please Daddy—I'll get well, I promise you I will. I'm getting better every day."

Sure, she was—in a pressurized room. I sat there, sweating, and wishing I had kept my big mouth shut. Molly said, "It defeats me, George. What do you think?"

"Mmmm——"

"Well?"

"Uh, I was thinking we could pressurize one room in our quarters. I could rig some sort of an impeller in the machine shop."

Peggy was suddenly all over her tears. "You mean I can get out of the hospital?"

"That's the idea, Sugar, if Daddy can work it."

Molly looked dubious. "That's no answer to our problems, George."

"Maybe not." Dad stood up and squared his shoulders. "But I have decided one thing: we all go, or we'll all stay. The Lermers stand together. That's settled."

Homesteading wasn't the only thing we had been mistaken about. There was Scouting on Ganymede even if the news hadn't gotten back to Earth. There hadn't been any meetings of the *Mayflower* troops after we landed; everybody had been just too busy to think about it. Organized Scouting is fun, but sometimes there just isn't time for it.

There hadn't been any meetings of the Leda Troop, either.

They used to meet in their town hall; now we had their town hall as a mess hall, leaving them out in the cold. I guess that didn't tend to make them feel chummy towards us.

I ran into this boy over in the Exchange. Just as he was passing me I noticed a little embroidered patch on his chest. It was a homemade job and not very good, but I spotted it. "Hey!" I said.

He stopped. " 'Hey' yourself! Were you yelling at me?"

"Uh, yes. You're a Scout, aren't you?"

"Certainly."

"So am I. My name's Bill Lermer. Shake." I slipped him the Scout grip.

He returned it. "Mine's Sergei Roskov." He looked me over. "You're one of the Johnny-Come-Latelies, aren't you?"

"I came over in the *Mayflower*," I admitted.

"That's what I meant. No offense—I was born Earthside, myself. So you used to be a Scout, back home. That's good. Come around to meeting and we'll sign you up again."

"I'm *still* a Scout," I objected.

"Huh? Oh, I get you—'Once a Scout, always a Scout.' Well, come around and we'll make it official."

That was a very good time for me to keep my lip zipped. But not me—oh, no! When comes the Tromp of Doom, I'll still be talking instead of listening. I said, "It's as official as it can be. I'm senior patrol leader, Baden-Powell Troop."

"Huh? You're kind of far away from your troop, aren't you?"

So I told him all about it. He listened until I was through, then said quietly, "And you laddie bucks had the nerve to call yourselves the 'Boy Scouts of Ganymede.' Anything else you would like to grab? You already have our meeting hall; maybe you'd like to sleep in our beds?"

"What do you mean?"

"Nothing." He seemed to be thinking it over. "Just a friendly warning, Bill——"

"Huh?"

"There is only one senior patrol leader around here—and you're looking right at him. Don't make any mistake about it. But come on around to meeting anyhow," he added. "You'll be welcome. We're always glad to sign up a new tenderfoot."

I went back to the Receiving Station and looked up Hank Jones and told him all about it. He looked at me admiringly. "William, old son," he said, "I've got to hand it to you. It takes real talent to louse things up that thoroughly. It's not easy."

"You think I've messed things up?"

"I hope not. Well, let's look up Doc Archibald and see what can be done."

Our troop master was holding clinic; we waited until the patients were out of the way, then went in. He said, "Are you two sick, or just looking for a ticket to gold brick?"

"Doc," I said, "we were wrong. There are so Scouts on Ganymede."

"So I know," he answered.

I said, "Huh?"

"Mr. Ginsberg and Mr. Bruhn and I have been negotiating with the senior Scout officials here to determine just how our troops will be taken into the parent organization. It's a bit complicated as there are actually more *Mayflower* Scouts than there are in the local troop. But they have jurisdiction, of course."

I said, "Oh."

"We'll have a joint meeting in a few days, after we get the rules ironed out."

I thought it over and decided I had better tell him what had happened, so I did.

He listened, not saying anything. Finally I said, "Hank seems to think I've messed things up. What do you think, Doc?"

"Mmmm—" he said. "Well, I hope he's wrong. But I think I may say you haven't helped the situation any."

I didn't know what to say. "Don't look so tragic about it," he urged. "You'll get well. Now run along and forget it. It may not make any difference."

But it did make a difference. Doc and the others had been pitching for our troops to be recognized as properly constituted troops, with all ratings acknowledged. But after Sergei spread the word around, the regular Ganymede Scouts all squawked that we were nothing but a bunch of tenderfeet, no matter what we had been back on Earth. The place for us to start was the bottom; if we were any good, we could prove it—by tests.

It was compromised; George says things like that are always compromised. Ratings were confirmed on probation, with one G-year to make up any tests that were different. Our troops were kept intact. But there was one major change:

All patrol leaders had to be from the original Ganymede Scouts; they were transferred from the Leda troop. I had to admit the justice of it. How could *I* be a patrol leader on Ganymede when I was still so green that I didn't know northwest from next week? But it didn't set well with the other fellows who had been patrol leaders when the word got around that I was responsible for the flies in the soup.

Hank talked it over with me. "Billy my boy," he told me, "I suppose you realize that you are about as popular as ants at a picnic?"

"Who cares?" I objected.

"You care. Now is the time for all good men to perform an *auto da fé*."

"What in great blazing moons is an *auto da fé*?"

"In this case it means for you to transfer to the Leda Troop."

"Have you gone crazy? You know what those guys think of us, especially me. I'd be lucky to get away with my life."

"Which just goes to show how little you know about human nature. Sure, it would be a little rough for a while, but it's the quickest way to gain back some respect."

"Hank, you really are nuts. In that troop I really would be a tenderfoot—and how!"

"That's just the point," Hank went on quietly. "We're all tenderfeet—only here in our own troop it doesn't show. If we stay here, we'll keep on being tenderfeet for a long time. But if we transfer, we'll be with a bunch who really know their way around—and some of it will rub off on us."

"Did you say 'we'?"

"I said 'we'."

"I catch on. You want to transfer, so you worked up this gag about how I ought to do so, so you would have company. A fine chum you are!"

He just grinned, completely unembarrassed. "Good old Bill! Hit him in the head eight or nine times and he can latch on to any idea. It won't be so bad, Bill. In precisely four months and nine days we won't be tenderfeet; we'll be old timers."

"Why the exact date?"

"Because that is the due date of the *Mayflower on* her next trip—as soon as *they* arrive *they'll* be the Johnny-Come-Latelies."

"Oh!"

Anyhow, we did it—and it was rough at first, especially on me . . . like the night they insisted that I tell them how to be a hero. Some twerp had gotten hold of the meteorite story. But the hazing wasn't too bad and Sergei put a stop to it whenever he caught them at it. After a while they got tired of it.

Sergei was so confounded noble about the whole thing that I wanted to kick him.

The only two merit badges to amount to anything that stood in the way of my getting off probation and back up to my old rating of Eagle Scout were agronomy and planetary ecology, Ganymede style. They were both tough subjects but well worth studying. On Ganymede you had to know them to stay alive, so I dug in.

Ecology is the most involved subject I ever tackled. I told George so and he said possibly politics was worse—and on second thought maybe politics was just one aspect of ecology. The dictionary says ecology is "the science of the interrelations of living organisms and their environment." That doesn't get you much, does it? It's like defining a hurricane as a movement of air.

The trouble with ecology is that you never know where to start because everything affects everything else. An unseasonal freeze in Texas can affect the price of breakfast in Alaska and that can affect the salmon catch and that can affect something else. Or take the old history book case: the English colonies took England's young bachelors and that meant old maids at home and old maids keep cats and the cats catch field mice and the field mice destroy the bumble bee nests and bumble bees are necessary to clover and cattle eat clover and cattle furnish the roast beef of old England to feed the soldiers to protect the colonies that the bachelors emigrated to, which caused the old maids.

Not very scientific, is it? I mean you have too many variables and you can't put figures to them. George says that if you can't take a measurement and write it down in figures you don't know enough about a thing to call what you are doing with it "science" and, as for him, he'll stick to straight engineering, thank you.

But there were some clear cut things about applied ecology on Ganymede which you could get your teeth into. Insects, for instance—on Ganymede, under no circumstances do you step on an insect. There were no insects on Ganymede when men first landed there. Any insects there now are there because the bionomics board planned it that way and the chief ecologist okayed the invasion. He wants that insect to stay right where it is, doing whatever it is that insects do; he wants it to wax and grow fat and raise lots of little insects.

Of course a Scout doesn't go out of his way to step on anything but black widow spiders and the like, anyhow—but it really brings it up to the top of your mind to know that stepping on an insect carries with it a stiff fine if you are caught, as well as a very pointed lecture telling you that the colony can get along very nicely without *you* but the insects are necessary.

Or take earthworms. I *know* they are worth their weight in uranium because I was buying them before I was through. A farmer can't get along without earthworms.

Introducing insects to a planet isn't as easy as it sounds. Noah had less trouble with his animals, two by two, because when the waters went away he still had a planet that was suited to his load. Ganymede isn't Earth. Take bees—we brought bees in the *Mayflower* but we didn't turn them loose; they were all in the shed called "Oahu" and likely to stay there for a smart spell. Bees need clover, or a reasonable facsimile. Clover would grow on Ganymede but our real use for clover was to fix nitrogen in the soil and thereby refresh a worn out field. We weren't planting clover yet because there wasn't any nitrogen in the air to fix—or not much.

But I am ahead of my story. This takes us into the engineering side of ecology. Ganymede was bare rock and ice before we came along, cold as could be, and no atmosphere to speak of—just traces of ammonia and methane. So the first thing to do was to give it an atmosphere men could breathe.

The material was there—ice. Apply enough power, bust up the water molecule into hydrogen and oxygen. The hydrogen goes up—naturally—and the oxygen sits on the surface where you can breathe it. That went on for more than fifty years.

Any idea how much power it takes to give a planet the size of Ganymede three pressure-pounds of oxygen all over its surface?

Three pressure-pounds per square inch means nine mass pounds, because Ganymede has only one third the surface gravitation of Earth. That means you have to start with nine pounds of ice for every square inch of Ganymede—and that ice is *cold* to start with, better than two hundred degrees below zero Fahrenheit.

First you warm it to the freezing point, then you melt it, then you dissociate the water molecule into oxygen and hydrogen—not in the ordinary laboratory way by electrolysis, but by extreme heat in a mass converter. The result is three pressure pounds of oxygen and hydrogen mix for that square inch. It's not an explosive mixture, because the hydrogen, being light, sits on top and the boundary layer is too near to being a vacuum to maintain burning.

But to carry out this breakdown takes power and plenty of it— 65,000 Btus for each square inch of surface, or for each nine pounds of ice, whichever way you like it. That adds up; Ganymede may be a small planet but it has 135,000,000,000,000,000 square inches of surface. Multiply that by 65,000 Btus for each square inch, then convert British thermal units to ergs and you get:

92,500,000,000,000,000,000,000,000,000,000 ergs.

Ninety-two-and-a-half million billon *quadrillion* ergs! That figure is such a beauty that I wrote it down in my diary and showed it to George.

He wasn't impressed. George said that all figures were the same size and nobody but a dimwit is impressed by strings of zeroes. He made me work out what the figure meant in terms of mass-energy, by the good old $E=MC^2$ formula, since mass-energy converters were used to give Ganymede its atmosphere.

By Einstein's law, one gram mass equals 9×10^{20} ergs, so that fancy long figure works out to be 1.03×10^{11} grams of energy, or 113,200 tons. It was ice, mostly, that they converted into energy, some of the same ice that was being turned into atmosphere— though probably some country rock crept in along with the ice. A mass converter will eat anything.

Let's say it was all ice; that amounts to a cube of ice a hundred and sixty feet on an edge. That was a number I felt I could understand.

I showed my answer to George and he still was not impressed. He said I ought to be able to understand one figure just as easily as the other, that both meant the same thing, and both figures were the same size.

Don't get the idea that Ganymede's atmosphere was made from a cube of ice 160 feet on a side; that was just the mass which had to be converted to energy to turn the trick. The mass of ice which was changed to oxygen and hydrogen would, if converted back into ice, cover the *entire planet* more than *twenty feet deep*— like the ice cap that used to cover Greenland.

George says all that proves is that there was a lot of ice on Ganymede to start with and that if we hadn't had mass converters we could never have colonized it. Sometimes I think engineers get so matter of fact that they miss a lot of the juice in life.

With three pressure-pounds of oxygen on Ganymede and the heat trap in place and the place warmed up so that blood wouldn't freeze in your veins colonists could move in and move around without wearing space suits and without living in pressure chambers. The atmosphere project didn't stop, however. In the first place, since Ganymede has a low escape speed, only 1.8 miles per second compared with Earth's 7m/s, the new atmosphere would gradually bleed off to outer space, especially the hydrogen, and would be lost—in a million years or so. In the second place, nitrogen was needed.

We don't need nitrogen to breathe and ordinarily we don't think much about it. But it takes nitrogen to make protein—muscle. Most plants take it out of the ground; some plants, like clover and alfalfa and beans, take it out of the air as well and put it back into the ground. Ganymede's soil was rich in nitrogen; the original scanty atmosphere was partly ammonia—but the day would come when we would have to put the nitrogen back in that we were taking out. So the atmosphere project was now turned to making nitrogen.

This wasn't as simple as breaking up water; it called for converting stable isotope oxygen-16 into stable isotope nitrogen-14, an energy consuming reaction probably impossible in nature—or so the book said—and long considered theoretically impossible. I hadn't had any nucleonics beyond high school physics, so I skipped the equations. The real point was, it could be done, in the proper sort of a mass-energy converter, and Ganymede would have nitrogen in her atmosphere by the time her fields were exhausted and had to be replenished.

Carbon dioxide was no problem; there was dry ice as well as water ice on Ganymede and it had evaporated into the atmosphere long before the first homesteader staked out a claim.

Not that you can start farming with oxygen, carbon dioxide, and a stretch of land. That land was *dead*. Dead as Christopher Columbus. Bare rock, sterile, no life of any sort—and there never had been any life in it. It's a far piece from dead rock to rich, warm, black soil crawling with bacteria and earthworms, the sort of soil you have to have to make a crop.

It was the job of the homesteaders to make the soil.

See how involved it gets? Clover, bees, nitrogen, escape speed, power, plant-animal balance, gas laws, compound interest laws, meteorology—a mathematical ecologist has to think of *everything* and think of it ahead of time. Ecology is explosive; what seems like a minor and harmless invasion can change the whole balance. Everybody has heard of the English sparrow. There was the Australian jack rabbit, too, that darn near ate a continent out of house and home. And the Caribbean mongoose that killed the chickens it was supposed to protect. And the African snail that almost ruined the Pacific west coast before they found a parasite to kill it.

You take a harmless, useful insect, plant, or animal to Ganymede and neglect to bring along its natural enemies and after a couple of seasons you'll wish you had imported bubonic plague instead.

But that was the chief ecologist's worry; a farmer's job was engineering agronomy—making the soil and then growing things in it.

That meant taking whatever you came to—granite boulders melted out of the ice, frozen lava flows, pumice, sand, ancient hardrock—and busting it up into little pieces, grinding the top layers to sand, pulverizing the top few inches to flour, and finally infecting the topmost part with a bit of Mother Earth herself—then nursing what you had to keep it alive and make it spread. It wasn't easy.

But it was interesting. I forgot all about my original notion of boning up on the subject just to pass a merit badge test. I asked around and found out where I could see the various stages going on and went out and had a look for myself. I spent most of one light phase just looking.

When I got back to town I found that George had been looking for me. "Where in blazes have you been?" he wanted to know.

"Oh, just out and around," I told him, "seeing how the 'steaders do things."

He wanted to know where I had slept and how I had managed to eat? "Bill, it's all very well to study for your merit badges but that's no reason to turn into a tramp," he objected. "I guess I have neglected you lately—I'm sorry." He stopped and thought for a moment, then went on, "I think you had better enter school here. It's true they haven't much for you, but it would be better than running around at loose ends."

"George?"

"Yes, that's probably the best—huh?"

"Have you completely given up the idea of homesteading?"

Dad looked worried. "That's a hard question, Bill. I still want us to, but with Peggy sick—it's difficult to say. But our name is still in the hat. I'll have to make up my mind before the drawing."

"Dad, I'll prove it."

"Eh?"

"You keep your job and take care of Peggy and Molly. I'll make us a farm."

13.
JOHNNY APPLESEED

The drawing of our division took place three weeks later; the next day George and I walked out to see what we had gotten. It was west of town out through Kneiper's Ridge, new country to me; I had done my exploring east of town, toward the power plant, where most of the proved land was located.

We passed a number of farms and some of them looked good, several acres in cultivation, green and lush, and many more acres already chewed level. It put me in mind of Illinois, but there was something missing. I finally figured out what it was—no trees.

Even without trees it was beautiful country. On the right, north of us, were the foothills of the Big Rock Candy Mountains. Snow-covered peaks thrust up beyond them, twenty or thirty miles away. On the left, curving in from the south and closer than it came to Leda, was Laguna Serenidad. We were a couple of hundred feet higher than the lake. It was a clear day and I tried to see the far shore, but I couldn't be sure.

It was a mighty cheerful scene. Dad felt it, too. He strode along, whistling "Beulah Land" off key. I get my musical talent from Anne.

He broke off and said, "Bill, I envy you."

I said, "We'll all be together yet, George. I'm the advance guard." I thought a bit and said, "George, do you know what the first thing I raise is going to be—after I get some food crops in?"

"What?"

"I'm going to import some seed and raise you some tobacco."

"Oh, no, Son!"

"Why not?" I knew he was touched by it, because he called me 'Son'. "I could do it, as well as not."

"It's a kind thought, but we'll have to stick to the main chance. By the time we can afford that, I will have forgotten how to light a pipe. Honest, I don't miss it."

We slogged along a bit further, not saying anything but feeling close together and good. Presently the road played out. Dad stopped and took his sketch map out of his pouch. "This must be about it."

The sketch showed where the road stopped, with just a dotted line to show where it would be, some day. Our farm was outlined on it, with the nearest corner about half a mile further along where the road ought to be and wasn't. By the map, the edge of our property—or what would be ours if we proved it—ran along the north side of the road about a quarter of a mile and from there back toward the foothills. It was marked "Plot 117-H-2" and had the chief engineer's stamp on it.

Dad was staring at where the road ended. There was a lava flow right across it, high as my head and rough as a hard winter in Maine. "Bill," he said, "How good an Indian are you?"

"Fair, I guess."

"We'll have to try to pace it off and hold a straight line due west."

But it was almost impossible to do it. We struggled and slipped on the lava and made detours. Lava looks soft and it isn't. Dad slipped and skinned his shin and I discovered that I had lost track of how many paces we had come. But presently we were across the flow and in a boulder field. It was loose rubble, from pieces the size of a house down to stuff no bigger than your fist—stuff dropped by the ice when it melted and formed Laguna Serenidad.

George says that Ganymede must have had a boisterous youth, covered with steam and volcanoes.

The boulder field was somewhat easier going but it was even harder to hold a straight line. After a bit Dad stopped. "Bill," he said, "do you know where we are?"

"No," I admitted, "but we aren't really lost. If we head back east we are bound to come to proved ground."

"Perhaps we had better."

"Wait a minute." There was a particularly big boulder ahead of us. I picked a way and managed to scramble to the top with nothing worse than a cut on my hand. I stood up. "I can see the road," I told Dad. "We're north of where we ought to be. And I think maybe we've come too far." I marked a spot with my eye and came down.

We worked south the amount I thought was right and then headed east again. After a bit I said, "I guess we missed it, George. I'm not much of an Indian."

He said, "So? What's this?" He was a little ahead of me and had stopped.

It was a cairn with a flat rock on top. Painted on it was: "117-H-2, SE corner."

We had been on our farm for the past half hour; the big boulder I had climbed up on was on it.

We sat down on a fairly flat rock and looked around. Neither of us said anything for a while; we were both thinking the same thing: if this was a farm, I was my own great uncle.

After a bit Dad muttered something. I said, "What did you say?"

"Golgotha," he said out loud. "Golgotha, the place of skulls." He was staring straight ahead.

I looked where he was looking; there was a boulder sitting on top of another and the way the sun caught it, it *did* look like a skull. It leered at us.

It was so darn quiet you could hear your hair grow. The place was depressing me. I would have given anything to hear something or see something move. Anything—just a lizard darting out from behind a rock, and I could have kissed it.

But there were no lizards here and never had been.

Presently Dad said, "Bill, are you sure you want to tackle this?"

"Sure I'm sure."

"You don't have to, you know. If you want to go back to Earth and go to M.I.T., I could arrange it for the next trip."

Maybe he was thinking that if I went back, I could take Peggy with me and she would be willing to go. Maybe I should have said something about it. But didn't; I said, "Are you going back?"

"No."

"Neither am I." At the moment is was mostly stubbornness. I had to admit that our "farm" wasn't flowing with milk and honey; in fact it looked grim. Nobody but a crazy hermit would want to settle down in such a spot.

"Think it over, Bill."

"I've thought it over."

We sat there a while longer, not saying anything, just thinking long thoughts. Suddenly we were almost startled out of our boots by somebody yodelling at us. A moment before I had been wishing to hear just anything, but when it came it was like unexpectedly encountering a clammy hand in the dark.

We both jumped and Dad said, "What in the——?" I looked around. There was a large man coming toward us. In spite of his size he skipped through the rocks like a mountain goat, almost floating in the low gravity. As he got closer I knew I had seen him before; he was on the Court of Honor, a Mr. Schultz.

Dad waved to him and pretty soon he reached us. He stood half a head taller than Dad and would have made the pair of us, he was so big. His chest was as thick as my shoulders were broad and his belly was thicker than that. He had bushy, curly red hair and his beard spread out over his chest like a tangle of copper springs. "Greetings, citizens," he boomed at us, "my name is Johann Schultz."

Dad introduced us and he shook hands and I almost lost mine in his. He fixed his eyes on me and said, "I've seen you before, Bill."

I said I guessed he had, at Scout meetings. He nodded and added, "A patrol leader, no?"

I admitted that I used to be. He said, "And soon again," as if the matter were all settled. He turned to Dad. "One of the kinder saw you going past on the road, so Mama sent me to find you and bring you back to the house for tea and some of her good coffee cake."

Dad said that was very kind but that we didn't want to impose. Mr. Schultz didn't seem to hear him. Dad explained what we were there for and showed him the map and pointed out the cairn. Mr. Schultz nodded four or five times and said, "So we are to be neighbors. Good, good!" He added to Dad "My neighbors call me John, or sometimes 'Johnny'." Dad said his name was George and from then on they were old friends.

Mr. Schultz stood by the cairn and sighted off to the west and then north to the mountains. Then he scrambled up on a big boulder where he could see better and looked again. We went up after him.

He pointed to a rise west of us. "You put your house so, not too far from the road, but not on it. And first you work this piece in here and next season you work back further toward the hills." He looked at me and added. "No?"

I said I guessed so. He said, "It is good land, Bill. You will make a fine farm." He reached down and picked up a piece of rock and rubbed it between his fingers. "Good land," he repeated.

He laid it down carefully, straightened up, and said, "Mama will be waiting for us."

Mama was waiting for us, all right, and her idea of a piece of coffee cake was roughly what they used to welcome back the Prodigal Son. But before we got into the house we had to stop and admire the Tree.

It was a real tree, an apple tree, growing in a fine bluegrass lawn out in front of his house. Furthermore it was bearing fruit on two of its limbs. I stopped and stared at it.

"A beauty, eh, Bill?" Mr. Schultz said, and I agreed. "Yes," he went on, "it's the most beautiful tree on Ganymede—you know why? Because it's the *only* tree on Ganymede." He laughed uproariously and dug me in the ribs as if he had said something funny. My ribs were sore for a week.

He explained to Dad all the things he had had to do to persuade it to grow and how deep down he had had to go to prepare for it and how he had had to channel out to drain it. Dad asked why it was bearing only on one side. "Next year we pollenate the other side," he answered, "and then we have Stark's Delicious. And Rome Beauties. This year, Rhode Island Greenings and Winesaps." He reached up and picked one. "A Winesap for you, Bill."

I said thanks and bit into it. I don't know when I've tasted anything so good.

We went inside and met Mama Schultz and four or five other Schultzes of assorted sizes, from a baby crawling around in the sand on the floor up to a girl as old as I was and nearly as big. Her name was Gretchen and her hair was red like her father's, only it was straight and she wore it in long braids. The boys were mostly blond, including the ones I met later.

The house was mainly a big living room, with a big table down the middle of it. It was a solid slab of rock, maybe four feet wide and twelve or thirteen feet long, supported by three rock pillars. A good thing it was rock, the way Mama Schultz loaded it down.

There were rock slab benches down the long sides and two real chairs, one at each end, made out of oil drums and padded with stuffed leather cushions.

Mama Schultz wiped her face and hands on her apron and shook hands and insisted that Dad sit down in her chair; she wouldn't be sitting down much, she explained. Then she turned back to her cooking while Gretchen poured tea for us.

The end of the room was the kitchen and was centered around a big stone fireplace. It had all the earmarks of being a practical fireplace—and it was, as I found out later, though of course nothing had ever been burned in it. It was really just a ventilation hole. But Papa Schultz had wanted a fireplace so he had a fireplace. Mama Schultz's oven was set in the side of it.

It was faced with what appeared to be Dutch tile, though I couldn't believe it. I mean, who is going to import anything as useless as ornamental tile all the way from Earth? Papa Schultz saw me looking at them and said, "My little girl Kathy paints good, huh?" One of the medium-sized girls blushed and giggled and left the room.

I had the apple down to a very skinny core and was wondering what to do with it in that spotless room when Papa Schultz stuck out his hand. "Give it to me, Bill."

I did. He took out his knife and very gently separated out the seeds. One of the kids left the room and fetched him a tiny paper envelope in which he placed the seeds and then sealed it. He handed it to me. "There, Bill," he said. "I have only one apple tree, but you have eight!"

I was sort of surprised, but I thanked him. He went on, "That place just this side of where you will build your house—if you will fill that gully from the bottom, layer by layer, building your soil as you go, with only a very little 'pay dirt' you will have a place that will support a whole row of trees. When your seedlings are big, we'll bud from my tree."

I put them very carefully in my pouch.

Some of the boys drifted in and washed up and soon we were all sitting around the table and digging into fried chicken and mashed potatoes and tomato preserves and things. Mama Schultz sat beside me and kept pressing food on me and insisting that I wasn't eating enough to keep body and soul together which wasn't true.

Afterwards I got acquainted with the kids while George and Papa Schultz talked. Four of the boys I knew; they were Scouts. The fifth boy, Johann junior—they called him "Yo"—was older than I, almost twenty, and worked in town for the chief engineer. The others were Hugo and Peter, both Cubs, then Sam, and then Vic, who was an Explorer Scout, same as I was. The girls were the baby, Kathy and Anna, who seemed to be twins but weren't, and Gretchen. They all talked at once.

Presently Dad called me over. "Bill, you know we don't rate a chance at a rock crusher for several months."

"Yes," I said, somewhat mystified.

"What are your plans in the meantime?"

"Uh, well, I don't know exactly. Study up on what I'll have to do."

"Mmm . . . Mr. Schultz has very kindly offered to take you on as a farm hand in the meantime. What do you think of the idea?"

14.
LAND OF MY OWN

Papa Schultz needed a field hand about as much as I need four ears, but that didn't keep me from moving in. In that family everybody worked but the baby and you could count on it that she would be washing dishes as soon as she was up off the floor. Everybody worked all the time and seemed to enjoy it. When the kids weren't working they were doing lessons and the boys were punished when they weren't up on their lessons by being required to stay in from the fields.

Mama would listen to them recite while she cooked. Sometimes she listened to lessons in things I'm pretty sure she never had studied herself, but Papa Schultz checked up on them, too, so it didn't matter.

Me, I learned about pigs. And cows. And chickens. And how you breed pay dirt to make more pay dirt. "Pay dirt" is the stuff that is actually imported from Earth, concentrated soil cultures with the bacteria and so forth in it you have to have to get a field alive.

There was an awful lot to learn. Take cows, now—half the people you meet can't tell their left hands from their right so who would think that a cow would care about such things? But they do, as I found out when I tried to milk one from the left.

Everything was stoop labor around the place, as primitive as a Chinese farm. The standard means of transportation was a wheelbarrow.

I learned not to sneer at a wheelbarrow after I priced one at the Exchange.

The total lack of power machinery wasn't through lack of

power; the antenna on the farm house roof could pick up as much power as necessary—but there wasn't any machinery. The only power machinery in the colony belonged to the whole colony and was the sort of thing the colony absolutely couldn't get along without, like rock chewers and the equipment for the heat trap and the power plant itself.

George explained it this way: every load that was sent up from Earth was a compromise between people and cargo. The colonists were always yapping for more machinery and fewer immigrants; the Colonial Commission always insisted on sending as many people as possible and holding the imports down to a minimum.

"The Commission is right, of course," he went on. "If we have people, we'll get machinery—we'll make it ourselves. By the time you have a family of your own, Bill, immigrants will arrive here bare-handed, no cargo at all, and we'll be able to outfit a man with everything from plastic dishes for his cupboard to power cultivators for his fields."

I said, "If they wait until I have a family, they'll have a long wait. I figure a bachelor travels faster and further."

Dad just grinned, as if he knew something I didn't know and wouldn't tell. I had walked into town to have dinner with him and Molly and the kid. I hadn't seen much of them since I went to work for Papa Schultz. Molly was teaching school, Peggy couldn't come out to the farm, of course, and Dad was very busy and very excited over a strike of aluminum oxides twenty miles east of town. He was in the project up to his ears and talking about having sheet aluminum on sale in another G-year.

As a matter of fact, cultivating a farm by stoop labor wasn't too bad, not on Ganymede. Low gravity was a big help; you didn't wear yourself out just dragging your own carcass around. I grossed a hundred and forty-two mass pounds, what with the way Mama Schultz stuffed me; that meant I weighed less than fifty pounds, field boots and all. A wheelbarrow was similarly light when loaded.

But the real advantage that made the work easy was something you might not guess.

No weeds.

No weeds at all; we had very carefully not imported any. Once the land was built, making a crop was darn near a case of poking a seed into the ground and then stepping back quick before the stalk shot up and hit you in the eye.

Not that we didn't work. There is plenty of work around a

farm even with no weeds to worry about. And a light wheelbarrow load simply meant that we piled three times as much on. But we had fun, too; I never met a family that laughed so much.

I brought my squeeze box out from town and used to play it after supper. We would all sing, with Papa Schultz booming away on his own and leaving it up to the rest of us to find the key he was singing in. We had fun.

It turned out that Gretchen was an awful tease when she got over being shy. But I could always get her goat by pretending that her head was on fire and either warming my hands over her hair or threatening to pour water on her before she burned the place down.

The day finally came when it was my turn to have the colony's crushers work on my land and I was almost sorry to see it arrive; I had had such a nice time at the Schultz's. But by then I could caponize a rooster or plant a row of corn; I still had a lot to learn, but there wasn't any good reason why I shouldn't start making my own farm.

Dad and I had had to prepare our farm for the crusher by dynamiting the biggest boulders. A crusher will choke on anything much bigger than a barrel but it will handle up to that size very nicely. Dynamite is cheap, thank goodness, and we used plenty of it. The raw material is nitroglycerine which we didn't have to import from Earth, the glycerine being refined from animal fats and the nitric acid being a synthetic byproduct of the atmosphere project.

Dad spent two weekends with me, making medium-sized ones out of big ones, then decided it was safe to trust me to set powder by myself and I finished the job. There was a little stream of melted snow water coming down from the hills at the far side of our property; we blew out a new bed for it to lead it close to the place where the house would go. We left it dry for the time being, with a natural rock dam to blow up later. One fair-sized hill we moved entirely and blew it into a gully on the lake side of the land. *Big* charges that took and I almost got fitted for a halo through underestimating how far some of the stuff would throw.

It was easy work and lots of fun. I had a vibro-drill, borrowed from the engineer's office; you could sink a charge hole with it twenty feet into rock as easily as you could sink a hot knife into butter. Then drop in the powder, fill the rest of the hole with rock dust, light the fuse, and run like the dickens!

But the most fun was blowing up that rock that looked like a grinning skull. I fixed it properly, it and its leer!

We had a visitor while we were dynamiting the land. Dad and I had just knocked off for lunch one day when Saunders, "The One-Man Lobby"—that's George's name for him—showed up. We invited him to share what we had; he had brought nothing but his appetite.

He complained about this and that. Dad tried to change the subject by asking him how he was getting along with his blasting. Saunders said it was slow work. Dad said, "You have the crusher the day after us, don't you?"

Saunders admitted it and said he wanted to borrow some powder; he was running short of time. Dad let him have it, though it meant another trip out from town, after work, for him the next day. Saunders went on, "I've been looking this situation over, Mr. Lermer. We're tackling it all wrong."

George said, "So?"

Saunders said, "Yes, indeedy! Now in the first place this blasting ought not to be done by the homesteader; it should be done by trained crews, sent out by the government. It's really part of the contract anyway; we're supposed to receive processed land."

Dad said mildly that, while that might be a nice idea, he didn't know where they would find enough trained crews to do the work for fifteen hundred new farms.

"Let the government hire them!" Mr. Saunders answered. "Bring them in from Earth for that purpose. Now, see here, Mr. Lermer, you are in the chief engineer's office. You ought to put in a word for the rest of us."

George picked up the vibro and got ready to set a charge. Presently he answered, "I'm afraid you've come to the wrong party. I'm in an entirely different department."

I guess Mr. Saunders saw he was off on the wrong tack for he went on, "In the second place, I have been looking into the matter of the soil, or what they call 'soil'—again they are off on the wrong foot." He kicked a rock. "This stuff isn't good for anything. You can't grow anything in stuff like that."

"Naturally not," agreed Dad. "You have to make soil first."

"That's just what I'm getting at," Saunders went on. "You have to have soil—good, black, rich soil. So they tell us to breed it, a square foot at a time. Plough garbage into it, raise earthworms—I don't know how many tomfool stunts."

"Do you know of a better way?"

"You bet you I do! That's just what I'm getting at. Here we are, piddling along, doing things the way a bunch of bureaucrats who never made a crop tell us to, all for a few inches of second-rate soil—when there are millions of cubic feet of the richest sort of black soil going begging."

Dad looked up sharply. "Where?"

"In the Mississippi Delta, that's where! Black soil goes down there for hundreds of feet."

We both looked at him, but he was quite serious about it. "Now here's what you've got to have—Level the ground off, yes. But after that spread real Earth soil over the rock to a depth of at least two feet; then it will be worth while to farm. As it is, we are just wasting our time."

Dad waited a bit before answering, "Have you figured out what this would cost?"

Mr. Saunders brushed that aside. "That's not the point; the point is, that's what we've got to have. The government wants us to settle here, doesn't it? Well, then, if we all stick together and insist on it, we'll get it." He jerked his chin triumphantly.

George started to say something, then stopped. He patted rock dust in on top of his charge, then straightened up and wiped the sweat off his beard. "Listen, citizen," he said, "can't you see that we are busy? I'm about to light this fuse; I suggest that you back away out of danger."

"Huh?" said Saunders. "How big a charge is it? How far?"

If he had kept his eyes open, he would have seen how big a charge it was and known how far to give back. Dad said, "Oh, say a mile and a half—or even two miles. And keep backing."

Saunders looked at him, snorted disgustedly, and stalked away. We backed out of range and let her blow. While we were setting the next charge I could see George's lips moving. After a while he said, "Figuring gumbo mud conservatively at a hundred pounds per cubic foot it would take one full load of the *Mayflower* to give Mr. Saunders alone the kind of a farm he would like to have handed to him. At that rate it would take just an even thousand G-years—five hundred Earth years—for the *Mayflower* to truck in top-soil for farms for our entire party."

"You forgot the *Covered Wagon*," I said brightly.

George grinned. "Oh, yes! When the *Covered Wagon* is commissioned and in service we could cut it down to two hundred and fifty years—provided no new immigrants came in and there was a ban on having babies!" He frowned and added, "Bill, why is it that some apparently-grown men never learn to do simple arithmetic?" I didn't know the answer, so he said, "Come on, Bill, let's get on with our blasting. I'm afraid we'll just have to piddle along in our inefficient way, even if it doesn't suit our friend Saunders."

The morning the crusher was scheduled to show up I was waiting for it at the end of the road. It came breezing down the road at twenty miles an hour, filling it from side to side. When it came to the wall of lava, it stopped. I waved to the operator; he waved back, then the machine grunted a couple of times, inched forward, and took a bite out of the lava.

Lava didn't bother it; it treated it like peanut brittle. A vibro-cutter built into its under carriage would slice under the flow like a housewife separating biscuit from a pan, the big steel spade on the front of the thing would pry under and crack the bite off, and the conveyor would carry the chunk up into the jaws.

The driver had a choice of dropping the chewed up material under the rear rollers or throwing it off to the side. Just now he was throwing it away, leaving the clean slice made by the vibro-cutter as a road bed—a good road, a little dusty but a few rains would fix that.

It was terrifically noisy but the driver didn't seem to mind. He seemed to enjoy it; there was a good breeze taking the dust away from him and he had his anti-silicosis mask pushed up on his forehead, showing the grin on his face.

By noon he was down to our place and had turned in. We had a bite to eat together, then he started in levelling a farm for me—five acres, the rest would have to wait. At that I was lucky for I was to get land to work months ahead of the original schedule. The second trip of the *Mayflower* had brought in three more crushers and very few immigrants, just enough to replace those who had given up and gone back out of our party, that being the compromise the town council had worked out with the Colonial Commission.

The racket was still worse when the crusher bit into hard rock, instead of lava, but it was music to me and I didn't get tired of watching. Every bite was a piece of land to me. At suppertime the second-shift driver showed up with Dad. We watched together for a while, then Dad went back to town. I stayed. About midnight I went over into a stretch that was not to be processed now, found a big rock to keep the Sun out of my eyes and lay down for a quick nap.

Then the relief driver was shaking me and saying, "Wake up, kid—you got a farm."

I stood up and rubbed my eyes and looked around. Five acres, with just enough contour for drainage and a low hummock in the middle where the house would sit. I had a farm.

The next logical thing to do would have been to get the house up, but, under the schedule, I rated the use of a cud-chewer for the following week. A cud-chewer is a baby rock crusher. It uses a power pack instead of an antenna, it is almost fool proof and anybody can run one, and it finishes up what the crusher starts. It is small and low-powered compared with a crusher. The colony had about forty of them.

The crusher left loose rubble several feet deep in pieces as big as my fist. The cud-chewer had a fork spade on the front of it, several sizes of spade forks, in fact. The coarse fork went down into the loose rocks about eighteen inches and picked up the big ones. These drifted back into the hopper as the machine moved forward and were busted into stuff about the size of walnuts.

When you had been over the ground once with the coarse fork, you unshipped it and put on the medium fork and reset the chewing rollers. This time you went down only ten inches and the result was gravel. Then you did it again for medium-fine and then fine and when you were done the upper six inches or so was rock flour, fine as the best loam—still dead, but ready to be bred into life.

Round and round and round, moving forward an inch at a time. To get real use out of your time allotment the cud-chewer had to be moving twenty-four hours a day until they took it away from you. I stayed at it all through the first day, eating my lunch in the saddle. Dad spelled me after supper and Hank came out from town and we alternated through the night—light phase it was, actually, it being Monday night.

Papa Schultz found me asleep with my head on the controls late next afternoon and sent me back to his house to get some real sleep. Thereafter one of the Schultzes always showed up when I had been at it alone for four or five hours. Without the Schultzes I don't know how Dad and I would have gotten through the dark phase of that week.

But they did help and by the time I had to pass the cud-chewer along I had nearly three and a half acres ready to be seeded with pay dirt.

Winter was coming on and I had my heart set on getting my house up and living in it during the winter month, but to do so I really had to hump. I had to get some sort of a holding crop in or the spring thaw would wash my top soil away. The short Ganymede year is a good idea and I'm glad they run it that way; Earth's winters are longer than necessary. But it keeps you on the jump.

Papa Schultz advised grass; the mutated grass would grow in sterile soil much like growing things in hydroponic solutions. The mat of rootlets would hold my soil even if the winter killed it and the roots would furnish something through which the infection could spread from the "pay dirt."

Pay dirt is fundamentally just good black soil from Earth, crawling with bacteria and fungi and microscopic worms—everything you need but the big fishing worms; you have to add those. However, it wouldn't do simply to ship Earth dirt to Ganymede by the car load. In any shovelful of loam there are hundreds of things, plant and animal, you need for growing soil—but there are hundreds of other things you don't want. Tetanus germs. Plant disease viruses. Cut worms. Spores. Weed seeds. Most of them are too small to be seen with the naked eye and some of them can't even be filtered out.

So to make pay dirt the laboratory people back on Earth would make pure cultures of everything they wanted to keep in the way of bacteria, raise the little worms under laboratory conditions, do the same for fungi and everything else they wanted to save—and take the soil itself and kill it deader than Luna, irradiate it, bake it, test it for utter sterility. Then they would take what they had saved in the way of life forms and put it back into the dead soil. That was "pay dirt," the original pay dirt. Once on Ganymede the original stuff would be cut six ways, encouraged to grow, then cut again. A hundred weight of pay dirt supplied to a 'steader might contain a pound of Terra's own soil.

Every possible effort was made to "limit the invasion," as the ecologists say, to what was wanted. One thing that I may not have mentioned about the trip out was the fact that our clothes and our baggage were sterilized during the trip and that we ourselves were required to take a special scrub before we put our clothes back on. It was the only good bath I got the whole two months, but it left me smelling like a hospital.

The colony's tractor trucks delivered the pay dirt I was entitled to in order to seed my farm; I left the Schultz place early that morning to meet them. There is difference of opinion as to the best way to plant pay dirt; some 'steaders spread it all over and take a chance on it dying; some build up little pockets six or eight feet apart, checker board style . . . safe but slow. I was studying the matter, my mind not made up, when I saw something moving down the road.

It was a line of men, pushing wheelbarrows, six of them. They got closer and I could see that it was all the male Schultzes. I went out to meet them.

Every one of those wheelbarrows was loaded with garbage and all for me!

Papa Schultz had been saving it as a surprise for me. I didn't know what to say. Finally I blurted out, "Gee, Papa Schultz, I don't know when I'll be able to pay you back!"

He looked fierce and said, "Who is speaking of paying back when we have compost running out of our ears yet?" Then he had the boys dump their loads down on top of my pay dirt, took a fork and began mixing it as gently as Mama Schultz folding in beaten egg white.

He took charge and I didn't have to worry about the best way to use it. In his opinion—and you can't bet that I didn't buck it!— what we had was good for about an acre and his method was to spread it through the soil. But he did not select one compact acre; he laid out strips, seven of them, a couple of hundred yards long each and stretching across my chewed soil thirty-five or forty feet apart. Each of us took a wheelbarrow—their six and my one—and distributed the mix along each line.

When that was done and cairns had been set to show where the strips ran, we raked the stuff into the rock dust five or six feet on each side of each line. Around noon Mama and Gretchen showed up, loaded down, and we stopped and had a picnic.

After lunch Yo had to go back to town but he had almost finished his strip. Papa had finished his and proceeded to help Hugo and Peter who were too small to swing a good rake. I dug in and finished mine soon enough to be able to finish what Yo had left. Dad showed up at the end of the day, expecting to help me all evening—it was light phase and you could work as late as you could stand up under it—but there was nothing left to do. And he didn't know how to thank them either.

I like to think that we would have gotten the farm made anyhow, without the Schultzes, and maybe we would have—but I'm sure not sure. Pioneers need good neighbors.

The following week I spent working artificial nitrates from the colony's power pile into the spaces between the strips—not as good as pay dirt from Earth, but not as expensive, either.

Then I tackled sowing the grass, by hand, just like in the Bible, and then raking it gently in. That old pest Saunders showed up. He still did so every now and then, but never when Dad was around. I guess he was lonely. His family was still in town and he was camping out in a ten-foot rock shed he had built. He wasn't really making a farm, not properly; I couldn't figure out what he was up to. It didn't make sense.

I said, "Howdy," and went on with my work.

He watched me, looking sour, and finally said, "You still bent on breaking your heart on this stuff, aren't you, youngster?"

I told him I hadn't noticed any wear and tear on my pump, and anyhow, wasn't he making a farm, too?

He snorted. "Not likely!"

"Then what *are* you doing?"

"Buying my ticket, that's what."

"Huh?"

"The only thing you can sell around this place is improved land. I'm beating them at their own game, that's what. I'll get that land in shape to unload it on some other sucker and then me and mine are heading straight back for that ever-lovin' Earth. And that's just what you'll be doing if you aren't an utter fool. You'll never make a farm here. It can't be done."

I was getting very tired of him but I'm short on the sort of point-blank guts it takes to be flatly rude. "Oh, I don't know," I said. "Look at Mr. Schultz—he's got a good farm."

Saunders snorted again. "You mean 'Johnny Appleseed'?"

"I mean Mr. Johann Schultz."

"Sure, sure—Johnny Appleseed. That's what everybody calls him in town. He's nuts. You know what he did? He gave me a handful of apple seeds and acted like he had handed me the riches of Solomon."

I stopped raking. "Well, hadn't he?"

Saunders spat on the ground between us. "He's a clown."

I lifted up the head of the rake. I said, "Mr. Saunders, you are standing on my land, my property. I'll give you just two shakes to get off it and never set foot on it again!"

He backed away and said, "Hey! You stop that! Watch what you are doing with that rake!"

I said, "Git!"

He got.

The house was a problem. Ganymede has little quakes all the time. It has to do with "isostasy" which doesn't mean a thing but "equal-pressure" when you get right down to it, but it's the science of how the mountains balance the seas and the gravitation of a planet all comes out even.

It has to do with tidal strains, too, which is odd, since Ganymede doesn't have any tides; the Sun is too far away to matter and Ganymede always keeps the same face toward Jupiter. Oh, you can detect a little tide on Laguna Serenidad when Europa is closest to Ganymede and even a trifle from Callisto and Io, but what I mean is it doesn't have *tides*—not like the Pacific Ocean.

What it does have is a frozen tidal strain. The way Mr. Hooker, the chief meteorologist, explains it is that Ganymede was closer to Jupiter when it cooled off and lost its rotation, so that there is a tidal bulge in the planet itself—sort of a fossil tidal bulge. The Moon has one, you know.

Then we came along and melted off the ice cap and gave Ganymede an atmosphere. That rearranged the pressures everywhere and the isostatic balance is readjusting. Result: little quakes all the time.

I'm a California boy; I wanted a quakeproof house. Schultzes had a quakeproof house and it seemed like a good idea, even though there had never been a quake heavy enough to knock a man down, much less knock a house down. On the other hand most of the colonists didn't bother; it is hard to make a rock house really quakeproof.

Worse than that, it's expensive. The basic list of equipment that a 'steader is promised in his emigration contract reads all right, a hoe, a spade, a shovel, a wheelbarrow, a hand cultivator, a bucket, and so forth down the list—but when you start to farming you find that is only the beginning and you've got to go to the Exchange and buy a lot of other stuff. I was already in debt a proved acre and a half, nearly, before the house ever went up.

As usual we compromised. One room had to be quake proof because it had to be air tight—Peggy's room. She was getting better all the time, but she still couldn't take low pressure for any length of time. If the family was going to move out to the farm, her bedroom had to be sealed, it had to have an air lock on it, and we had to have an impeller. All that runs into money.

Before I was through I had to pledge two more acres. Dad tried to sign for it but they told him bluntly that while a 'steader's credit was good, his wasn't. That settled the matter. We planned on one reinforced room and hoped to build on to it later. In the mean time the house would be a living room, ten by twelve, where

I would sleep, a separate bedroom too small to swing a cat for George and Molly, and Peggy's room. All but Peggy's room would be dry wall rock with a patent roof.

Pretty small, eh? Well, what's wrong with that? Abe Lincoln started with less.

I started in cutting the stone as soon as the seed was in. A vibro-saw is like a vibro-drill, except that it cuts a hair line instead of drilling a hole. When the power is on you have to be durned careful not to get your fingers or anything into the field, but it makes easy work of stone cutting. By the contract you got the use of one for forty-eight hours free and another forty-eight hours, if you wanted it, at a reduced rate. I got my work lined up and managed to squeeze it into the two free days. I didn't want to run up any more debt, because there was another thing I was hankering for, come not later than the second spring away—flicker flood lights. Papa Schultz had them for his fields and they just about doubled his crops. Earth plants aren't used to three and half days of darkness, but, if you can tickle them during the dark phase with flicker lights, the old photosynthesis really gets in and humps itself.

But that would have to wait.

The patrol got the house up—the patrol I was in, I mean, the Auslanders. It was a surprise to me and yet it wasn't, because everybody has a house raising; you can't do it alone. I had already taken part in six myself—not just big-heartedness, don't get me wrong. I had to learn how it was done.

But the patrol showed up before I had even passed the word around that I was ready to hold a house raising. They came swinging down our road; Sergei marched them up to where the house was to be, halted them, and said to me, "Bill, are your Scout dues paid up?" He sounded fierce.

I said, "You know they are."

"Then you can help. But don't get in our way." Suddenly he grinned and I knew I had been framed. He turned to the patrol and shouted, "House raising drill! Fall out and fall to."

Suddenly it looked like one of those TV comedies where everything has been speeded up. I never saw anybody work the way they did. Let me tell you it doesn't take Scout uniforms to make Scouts. None of us ever had uniforms; we couldn't afford special clothes just for Scouting.

Besides the Auslanders there was Vic Schultz and Hank Jones, both from the Hard Rock patrol and Doug Okajima, who wasn't even of our troop but still with the Baden-Powell. It did my heart good. I hadn't seen much of the fellows lately; during light phase I always worked too late to get in to meetings; during dark phase a cold nine miles into town after supper is something to think twice about.

I felt sheepish to realize that while I might have forgotten them, they hadn't forgotten me, and I resolved to get to meetings, no matter how tired I was. And take the tests for those two merit badges, too—the very first chance I got.

That reminded me of another item of unfinished business, too—Noisy Edwards. But you can't take a day off just to hunt somebody up and poke him in the snoot, not when you are making a farm. Besides it wouldn't hurt anything for me to put on another ten pounds; I didn't want it to be a repetition of the last time.

Dad showed up almost immediately with two men from his office and he took charge of bracing and sealing Peggy's room. The fact that he showed up at all let me know that he was in on it—which he admitted. It had been Sergei's idea and that was why Dad had put me off when I said it was about time to invite the neighbors in.

I got Dad aside. "Look, George," I said, "how in nation are we going to feed 'em?"

"Don't worry about it," he said.

"But I do worry about it!" Everybody knows it's the obligation of the 'steader whose house is being raised to provide the victuals and I had been taken by surprise.

"I said not to," he repeated. And presently I knew why; Molly showed up with Mama Schultz, Gretchen, Sergei's sister Marushka, and two girls who were friends of Peggy—and what they were carrying they couldn't have carried on Earth. It was a number one picnic and Sergei had trouble getting them back to work after lunch.

Theoretically, Molly had done the cooking over at the Schultz's but I know Mama Schultz—anyhow, let's face it, Molly wasn't much of a cook.

Molly had a note for me from Peggy. It read: "Dearest Billy, Please come into town tonight and tell me all about it. Pretty please!" I told Molly I would.

By eighteen o'clock that afternoon the roof was on and we had a house. The door wasn't hung; it was still down at the 'Change. And the power unit wasn't in and might not be for a week. But we had a house that would keep off the rain, and a pint-sized cow barn as well, even if I didn't own a cow.

15.
WHY DID WE COME?

According to my diary we moved into the house on the first day of spring.

Gretchen came over and helped me get ready for them. I suggested that we ask Marushka as well, since there would be lots of work to do. Gretchen said, "Suit yourself!" and seemed annoyed, so I didn't. Women are funny. Anyhow Gretchen is a right good worker.

I had been sleeping in the house ever since the raising and even before the technicians from the engineer's office had come and installed the antenna on the roof and rigged the lights and heat—but that was done before winter was started and I passed a comfortable month, fixing up the inside of the place and getting in a crop of ice for the summer. I stored the ice, several tons of it, in the gully at the side of the house, where I meant to plant apple trees just as soon as I could get fixed for it. The ice would keep there until I could build a proper cold cellar.

The first few months after the folks moved out are the happiest I can remember. We were together again and it was good. Dad still spent most of each dark phase in town, working on a part time basis, but that was quite as much because he was interested in the manufacturing project as it was to help pay off our debts. During light phase we worked almost around the clock, side by side or at least within earshot.

Molly seemed to like being a housewife. I taught her how to cook and she caught on real fast. Ganymede cooking is an art. Most things have to be cooked under pressure, even baked things, for water boils at just a little over a hundred and forty degrees. You can stir boiling water with your finger if you don't leave it in too long. Then Molly started learning from Mama Schultz but I didn't mind that; Mama Schultz was an artist. Molly got to be a really good cook.

Peg had to live in her room, of course, but we had hopes that she would be out soon. We had the pressure down to eight pounds, half oxygen and half nitrogen, and we usually all ate in her room. I still hated the thick stuff but it was worth while putting up with it so that the family could eat together. After a while I got so that I could change pressure without even an earache.

Peggy could come outside, too. We had brought her from town in a bubble stretcher—another thing bought on credit!—and Dad had fitted it with the gas apparatus from an old space suit he had salvaged from the Project Jove people. Peggy could get into the stretcher and shut herself in and we could bleed off the pressure in her room and take her outside where she could get some sunshine and look at the mountains and the lake and watch Dad and me work in the fields. The clear plastic of the bubble did not stop ultraviolet and it was good for her.

She was a skinny little runt and it was no trouble to move her around, even in the stretcher. Light phase, she spent a lot of time outdoors.

We had started with a broody hen and fifteen fertile eggs, and a pair of rabbits. Pretty soon we had meat of our own. We always let Peggy think that the fryers we ate came from the Schultzes and I don't think she ever caught on. At first I used to go to the Schultz farm every day for fresh milk for Peggy, but I got a chance, midsummer, to get a fresh two-year-old cow on tick at a reasonable price. Peggy named her Mabel and was much irked that she couldn't get at her to pet her.

We were on the move all the time. I still hadn't managed to take my merit badge tests and I hadn't done much better about getting in to Scout meetings. There was just too much to do. Building a pond, for example—Laguna Serenidad was being infected with plankton and algae but there weren't fish in it yet and it would be a long time, even after the fish were stocked, before fishing would be allowed. So we did fish-pond gardening, Chinese style, after I got the pond built.

And there were always crops to work on. My cover grass had taken hold all right and shortly after we moved in the soil seemed ready to take angle worms. Dad was about to send a sample into town for analysis when Papa Schultz stopped by. Hearing what we were about he took up a handful of the worked soil, crumbled it, smelled it, tasted it, and told me to go ahead and plant my worms. I did and they did all right; we encountered them from time to time in working the fields thereafter. You could see the stripes on the fields which had been planted with pay dirt by the way the grass came up. You could see that the infection was spreading, too, but not much. I had a lot of hard work ahead before the stripes would meet and blend together and then we could think about renting a cud-chewer and finishing off the other acre and a half, using our own field loam and our own compost heap to infect the new soil. After that we could see about crushing some more acres, but that was a long way away.

We put in carrots and lettuce and beets and cabbage and brussels sprouts and potatoes and broccoli. We planted corn between the rows. I would like to have put in an acre of wheat but it didn't make sense when we had so little land. There was one special little patch close to the house where we put in tomatoes and Hubbard squash and some peas and beans. Those were "bee" plants and Molly would come out and pollenate them by hand, a very tedious business. We hoped to have a hive of bees some day and the entomologists on the bionomics staff were practically busting their hearts trying to breed a strain of bees which would prosper out doors. You see, among other things, while our gravity was only a third Earth-normal, our air pressure was only a little better than a fifth Earth-normal and the bees resented it; it made flying hard work for them.

Or maybe bees are just naturally conservative.

I guess I was happy, or too tired and too busy to be unhappy, right up to the following winter.

At first winter seemed like a good rest. Aside from getting the ice crop in and taking care of the cow and the rabbits and the chickens there wasn't too much to do. I was tired out and cranky and didn't know it; Molly, I think, was just quietly, patiently exhausted. She wasn't used to farm life and she wasn't handy at it, the way Mama Schultz was.

Besides that, she wanted inside plumbing and it just wasn't in the cards for her to have it any time soon. I carried water for her, of course, usually having to crack ice in the stream to get it, but that didn't cover everything, not with snow on the ground. Not that she complained.

Dad didn't complain, either, but there were deep lines forming from his nose down to his mouth which his beard didn't cover entirely. But it was mostly Peggy.

When we first moved her out to the farm she perked up a lot. We gradually reduced the pressure in her room and she kept insisting that she was fine and teasing for a chance to go out without the bubble stretcher. We even tried it once, on Dr. Archibald's advice, and she didn't have a nose bleed but she was willing to get back in after about ten minutes.

The fact was she wasn't adjusting. It wasn't just the pressure; something else was wrong. She didn't *belong* here and she wouldn't *grow* here. Have you ever had a plant that refused to be happy where you planted it? It was like that.

She belonged back on Earth.

I suppose we weren't bad off, but there is a whale of a difference between being a rich farmer, like Papa Schultz, with heaps of cow manure in your barn yard and hams hanging in your cold cellar and every modern convenience you could want, even running water in your house, and being poor framers, like us, scratching for a toe hold in new soil and in debt to the Commission. It told on us and that winter we had time to brood about it.

We were all gathered in Peggy's room after lunch one Thursday. Dark phase had just started and Dad was due to go back into town; we always gave him a send off. Molly was darning and Peg and George were playing cribbage. I got out my squeeze box and started knocking out some tunes. I guess we all felt cheerful enough for a while. I don't know how I happened to drift into it, but after a bit I found I was playing *The Green Hills of Earth*. I hadn't played it in a long time.

I brayed through that fortissimo part about *"Out ride the sons of Terra; Far drives the thundering jet——"* and was thinking to myself that jets didn't thunder any more. I was still thinking about it when I went on into the last chorus, the one you play very softly: *"We pray for one last landing on the globe that gave us birth——"*

I looked up and there were tears running down Molly's cheeks.

I could have kicked myself. I put my accordion down with a squawk, not even finishing, and got up. Dad said, "What's the matter, Bill?"

I muttered something about having to go take a look at Mabel.

I went out into the living room and put on my heavy clothes and actually did go outside, though I didn't go near the barn. It

had been snowing and it was already almost pitch dark, though the
Sun hadn't been down more than a couple of hours. The snow had
stopped but there were clouds over head and you couldn't see
Jupiter.

The clouds had broken due west and let the sunset glow come
through a bit. After my eyes adjusted, by that tiny amount of
light I could see around me—the mountains, snow to their bases,
disappearing in the clouds, the lake, just a sheet of snow-covered
ice, and the boulders beyond our fields, making weird shapes in
the snow. It was a scene to match the way I felt; it looked like
the place where you might be sent for having lived a long and
sinful life.

I tried to figure out what I was doing in such a place.

The clouds in the west shifted a little and I saw a single bright
green star, low down toward the horizon, just above where the Sun
had set.

It was Earth.

I don't know how long I stood there. Presently somebody put a
hand on my shoulder and I jumped. It was Dad, all bundled up for
a nine-mile tramp through the dark and the snow.

"What's the matter, Son?" he said.

I started to speak, but I was all choked up and couldn't. Finally
I managed to say, "Dad, why did we come here?"

"Mmmm . . . you wanted to come. Remember?"

"I know," I admitted.

"Still, the real reason, the basic reason, for coming here was to
keep your grandchildren from starving. Earth is overcrowded,
Bill."

I looked back at Earth again. Finally I said, "Dad, I've made a
discovery. There's more to life than three square meals a day.
Sure, we can make crops here—this land would grow hair on a
billiard ball. But I don't think you had better plan on any grandchildren here; it would be no favor to them. I know when I've
made a mistake."

"You're wrong, Bill. *Your* kids will like this place, just the way
Eskimos like where they live."

"I doubt it like the mischief."

"Remember, the ancestors of Eskimos weren't Eskimos; they
were immigrants, too. If you send your kids back to Earth, for
school, say, they'll be homesick for Ganymede. They'll *hate*
Earth. They'll weigh too much, they won't like the air, they won't
like the climate, they won't like the people."

"Hmm—look, George, do you like it here? Are you glad we came?"

Dad was silent for a long time. At last he said, "I'm worried about Peggy, Bill."

"Yeah, I know. But how about yourself—and Molly?"

"I'm not worried about Molly. Women have their ups and downs. You'll learn to expect that." He shook himself and said, "I'm late. You go on inside and have Molly fix you a cup of tea. Then take a look at the rabbits. I think the doe is about to drop again; we don't want to lose the young 'uns." He hunched his shoulders and set off down toward the road. I watched him out of sight and then went back inside.

16.
LINE UP

Then suddenly it was spring and everything was all right.

Even winter seemed like a good idea when it was gone. We had to have winter; the freezing and thawing was necessary to develop the ground, not to mention the fact that many crops won't come to fruit without cold weather. Anyway, anybody can live through four weeks of bad weather.

Dad laid off his job when spring came and we pitched in together and got our fields planted. I rented a power barrow and worked across my strips to spread the living soil. Then there was the back-breaking job of preparing the gully for the apple trees. I had started the seeds soon after Papa Schultz had given them to me, forcing them indoors, first at the Schultz's, then at our place. Six of them had germinated and now they were nearly two feet tall.

I wanted to try them outdoors. Maybe I would have to take them in again next winter, but it was worth a try.

Dad was interested in the venture, too, not just for fruit trees, but for lumber. Wood seems like an obsolete material, but try getting along without it.

I think George had visions of the Big Rock Candy Mountains covered with tall straight pines . . . someday, someday.

So we went deep and built it to drain and built it wide and used a lot of our winter compost and some of our precious topsoil. There was room enough for twenty trees when we got through, where we planted our six little babies. Papa Schultz came over and pronounced a benediction over them.

Then he went inside to say hello to Peggy, almost filling her little room. George used to say that when Papa inhaled the pressure in the room dropped.

A bit later Papa and Dad were talking in the living room; Dad stopped me as I was passing through. "Bill," he asked, "how would you like to have a window about here?" He indicated a blank wall.

I stared. "Huh? How would we keep the place warm?"

"I mean a real window, with glass."

"Oh." I thought about it. I had never lived in a place with windows in my life; we had always been apartment dwellers. I had *seen* windows, of course, in country houses back Earthside, but there wasn't a window on Ganymede and it hadn't occurred to me that there ever would be.

"Papa Schultz plans to put one in his house. I thought it might be nice to sit inside and look out over the lake, light phase evenings," Dad went on.

"To make a home you need windows and fireplaces," Papa said placidly. "Now that we glass make, I mean to have a view."

Dad nodded. "For three hundred years the race had glazed windows. Then they shut themselves up in little air-conditioned boxes and stared at silly television pictures instead. One might as well be on Luna."

It was a startling idea, but it seemed like a good one. I knew they were making glass in town. George says that glassmaking is one of the oldest manufacturing arts, if not the oldest, and certainly one of the simplest. But I had thought about it for bottles and dishes, not for window glass. They already had glass buckets on sale at the 'Change, for about a tenth the cost of the imported article.

A view window—it was a nice idea. We could put one on the south and see the lake and another on the north and see the mountains. Why, I could even put in a skylight and lie on my bunk and see old Jupiter.

Stow it, William, I said to myself; you'll be building a whole house out of glass next. After Papa Schultz left I spoke to George about it. "Look," I said, "about this view window idea. It's a good notion, especially for Peggy's room, but the question is: can we afford it?"

"I think we can," he answered.

"I mean can we afford it without your going back to work in town? You've been working yourself to death—and there's no need to. The farm can support us now."

He nodded. "I had been meaning to speak about that. I've about decided to give up the town work, Bill—except for a class I'll teach on Saturdays."

"Do you have to do that?"

"Happens that I like to teach engineering, Bill. And don't worry about the price of the glass; we'll get it free—a spot of cumshaw coming to your old man for designing the glass works. 'The kine who tread the grain,'" he quoted. "Now you and I had better get busy; there is a rain scheduled for fifteen o'clock."

It was maybe three weeks later that the moons lined up. This is an event that almost never happens, Ganymede, Callisto, Io, and Europa, all perfectly lined up and all on the same side of Jupiter. They come close to lining up every seven hundred and two days, but they don't quite make it ordinarily. You see, their periods are all different, from less than two days for Io to more than two weeks for Callisto and the fractions don't work out evenly. Besides that they have different eccentricities to their orbits and their orbits aren't exactly in the same plane.

As you can see, a real line up hardly ever happens.

Besides that, *this* line up was a line up with the Sun, too; it would occur at Jupiter full phase. Mr. Hooker, the chief meteorologist, announced that it had been calculated that such a perfect line up would not occur again for more than two hundred thousand years. You can bet we were all waiting to see it. The Project Jove scientists were excited about it, too, and special arrangements had been made to observe it.

Having it occur at Jupiter full phase meant not only that a sixth heavenly body—the Sun—would be in the line up, but that we would be able to see it. The shadows of Ganymede and Callisto would be centered on Jupiter just as Io and Europa reached mid transit.

Full phase is at six o'clock Saturday morning; we all got up about four-thirty and were outside by five. George and I carried Peggy out in her bubble stretcher. We were just in time.

It was a fine, clear summer night, light as could be, with old Jupiter blazing overhead like a balloon on fire. Io had just barely kissed the eastern edge of Jupiter—"first contact" they call it. Europa was already a bit inside the eastern edge and I had to look sharp to see it. When a moon is not in full phase it is no trouble to pick it out while it's making its transit, but at full phase it tends to blend into the background. However, both Io and Europa are just a hair brighter than Jupiter. Besides that, they break up the pattern of Jupiter's bands and that lets you see them, too.

Well inside, but still in the eastern half—say about half way to Jupiter's center point—were the shadows of Ganymede and Callisto. I could not have told them apart, if I hadn't known that the one further east had to be Ganymede's. They were just little round black dots; three thousand miles or so isn't anything when it's plastered against Jupiter's eighty-nine thousand mile width.

Io looked a bit bigger than the shadows; Europa looked more than half again as big, about the way the Moon looks from Earth.

We felt a slight quake but it wasn't even enough to make us nervous; we were used to quakes. Besides that, about then Io "kissed" Europa. From then on, throughout the rest of the show, Io gradually slid underneath, or behind, Europa.

They crawled across the face of Jupiter; the moons fairly fast, the shadows in a slow creep. When we had been outside a little less than half an hour the two shadows kissed and started to merge. Io had slid halfway under Europa and looked like a big tumor on its side. They were almost halfway to center and the shadows were even closer.

Just before six o'clock Europa—you could no longer see Io; Europa covered it—as I was saying, Europa kissed the shadow, which by now was round, just one shadow.

Four or five minutes later the shadow had crawled up on top of Europa; they were all lined up—and I knew I was seeing the most extraordinary sight I would ever see in my life, Sun, Jupiter, and the four biggest moons all perfectly lined up.

I let out a deep breath: I don't know how long I had been holding it. "Gee whiz!" was all I could think of to say.

"I agree in general with your sentiments, Bill," Dad answered. "Molly, hadn't we better get Peggy inside? I'm afraid she is getting cold."

"Yes," agreed Molly. "I know I am, for one."

"I'm going down to the lake now," I said. The biggest tide of record was expected, of course. While the lake was too small to show much tide, I had made a mark the day before and I hoped to be able to measure it.

"Don't get lost in the dark," Dad called out. I didn't answer him. A silly remark doesn't require an answer.

I had gotten past the road and maybe a quarter of a mile beyond when it hit.

It knocked me flat on my face, the heaviest shake I had ever felt in my life. I've felt heavy quakes in California; they weren't a patch on this one. I lay face down for a long moment, digging into the rock with my finger nails and trying to get it to *hold still*.

The seasick roll kept up and kept up and kept up, and with it the noise—a deep bass rumble, deeper than thunder and more terrifying.

A rock rolled up against me and nipped my side. I got to my feet and managed to stay there. The ground was still swaying and the rumble kept on. I headed for the house, running—like dancing over shifting ice. I fell down twice and got up again.

The front end of the house was all caved in. The roof slanted down at a crazy angle. "George!" I yelled. "Molly! Where are you?"

George heard me and straightened up. He was on the other side of the house and now I saw him over the collapsed roof. He didn't say anything. I rushed around to where he stood. "Are you all right?" I demanded.

"Help me get Molly out——" he gasped.

I found out later that George had gone inside with Molly and Peggy, had helped get Peg out of the stretcher and back into her room, and then had gone outside, leaving Molly to get breakfast. The quake had hit while he was returning from the barn. But we didn't have time then to talk it over; we dug—moving slabs with our bare hands that had taken four Scouts, working together, to lay. George kept crying, "Molly! Molly! Where are you?"

She was lying on the floor beside the stone work bench that was penned in by the roof. We heaved it off her; George scrambled over the rubble and reached her. "Molly! Molly darling!"

She opened her eyes. "George!"

"Are you all right?"

"What happened?"

"Quake. Are you all right? Are you hurt?"

She sat up, made a face as if something hurt her, and said, "I think I—George! Where's Peggy? *Get Peggy!*"

Peggy's room was still upright; the reinforcements had held while the rest of the house had gone down around it. George insisted on moving Molly out into the open first, then we tackled the slabs that kept us from getting at the air lock to Peggy's room.

The outer door of the air lock was burst out of its gaskets and stood open, the wrong way. It was black inside the lock; Jupiter light didn't reach inside. I couldn't see what I was doing but when

I pushed on the inner door it wouldn't give. "Can't budge it," I told Dad. "Get a light."

"Probably still held by air pressure. Call out to Peggy to get in the stretcher and we'll bleed it."

"I need a light," I repeated.

"I haven't got a light."

"Didn't you have one with you?" *I* had had one; we always carried torches, outdoors in dark phase, but I had dropped mine when the quake hit. I didn't know where it was.

Dad thought about it, then climbed over the slabs. He was back in a moment. "I found it between here and the barn. I must have dropped it." He shined it on the inner door and we looked over the situation.

"It looks bad," Dad said softly. "Explosive decompression." There was a gap you could poke your fingers through between the top of the door and the frame; the door wasn't pressure held, it was jammed.

Dad called out, "Peggy! Oh, Peggy, darling—can you hear me?"

No answer. "Take the light, Bill—and stand aside." He reared back and then hit the door hard with his shoulder. It gave a bit but didn't open. He hit it again and it flew open, spilling him on his hands and knees. He scrambled up as I shined the light in past him.

Peggy lay half in and half out of bed, as if she had been trying to get up when she passed out. Her head hung down and a trickle of blood was dripping from her mouth on to the floor.

Molly had come in right behind us; she and Dad got Peggy into the stretcher and Dad brought the pressure up. She was alive; she gasped and choked and sprayed blood over us while we were trying to help her. Then she cried. She seemed to quiet down and go to sleep—or maybe fainted again—after we got her into the bubble.

Molly was crying but not making any fuss about it. Dad straightened up, wiped his face and said, "Grab on, Bill. We've got to get her into town."

I said, "Yes," and picked up one end. With Molly holding the light and us carrying, we picked our way over the heap of rock that used to be our house and got out into the open. We put the stretcher down for a moment and I looked around.

I glanced up at Jupiter; the shadows were still on his face and Io and Europa had not yet reached the western edge. The whole thing had taken less than an hour. But that wasn't what held my attention; the sky looked funny.

The stars were too bright and there were too many of them. "George," I said, "what's happened to the sky?"

"No time now——" he started to say. Then he stopped and said very slowly, "Great Scott!"

"What?" asked Molly. "What's the matter?"

"Back to the house, all of you! We've got to dig out all the clothes we can get at. And blankets!"

"What? Why?"

"The heat trap! The heat trap is gone—the quake must have gotten the power house."

So we dug again, until we found what we had to have. It didn't take long; we knew where things had to be. It was just a case of getting the rocks off. The blankets were for the stretcher; Dad wrapped them around like a cocoon and tied them in place. "Okay, Bill," he said. "Quick march, now!"

It was then that I heard Mabel bawl. I stopped and looked at Dad. He stopped too, with an agony of indecision on his face. "Oh, damn!" he said, the first time I had ever heard him really swear. "We can't just leave her to freeze; she's a member of the family. Come, Bill."

We put the stretcher down again and ran to the barn. It was a junk heap but we could tell by Mabel's complaints where she was. We dragged the roof off her and she got to her feet. She didn't seem to be hurt but I guess she had been knocked silly. She looked at us indignantly.

We had a time of it getting her over the slabs, with Dad pulling and me pushing. Dad handed the halter to Molly. "How about the chickens?" I asked, "And the rabbits?" Some of them had been crushed; the rest were loose around the place. I felt one—a rabbit—scurry between my feet.

"No time!" snapped Dad. "We can't take them; all we could do for them would be to cut their throats. Come!"

We headed for the road.

Molly led the way, leading and dragging Mabel and carrying the light. We needed the light. The night, too bright and too clear a few minutes before, was now suddenly overcast. Shortly we couldn't see Jupiter at all, and then you couldn't count your fingers in front of your face.

The road was wet underfoot, not rain, but sudden dew; it was getting steadily colder.

Then it did rain, steadily and coldly. Presently it changed to wet snow. Molly dropped back. "George," she wanted to know, "have we come as far as the turn off to the Schultz's?"

"That's no good," he answered. "We've got to get the baby into the hospital."

"That isn't what I meant. Oughtn't I to warn them?"

"They'll be all right. Their house is sound."

"But the cold?"

"Oh." He saw what she meant and so did I, when I thought about it. With the heat trap gone and the power house gone, every house in the colony was going to be like an ice box. What good is a power receiver on your roof with no power to receive? It was going to get colder and colder and colder. . . .

And then it would get colder again. And colder. . . .

"Keep moving," Dad said suddenly. "We'll figure it out when we get there."

But we didn't figure it out, because we never found the turn off. The snow was driving into our faces by then and we must have walked on past it. It was a dry snow now, little sharp needles that burned when they hit.

Without saying anything about it, I had started counting paces when we left the walls of lava that marked the place where the new road led to our place and out to the new farms beyond. As near as I could make it we had come about five miles when Molly stopped. "What's the matter?" yelled Dad.

"Dear," she said, "I can't find the road. I think I've lost it."

I kicked the snow away underfoot. It was made ground, all right—soft. Dad took the torch and looked at his watch. "We must have come about six miles," he announced.

"Five," I corrected him. "Or five and a half at the outside," I told him I had been counting.

He considered it. "We've come just about to that stretch where the road is flush with the field," he said. "It can't be more than a half mile or a mile to the cut through Kneiper's Ridge. After that we can't lose it. Bill, take the light and cast off to the right for a hundred paces, then back to the left. If that doesn't do it, we'll go further. And for heaven's sakes retrace your steps—it's the only way you'll find us in this storm."

I took the light and set out. To the right was no good, though I went a hundred and fifty paces instead of a hundred, I got back to them, and reported, and started out again. Dad just grunted; he was busy with something about the stretcher.

On the twenty-third step to the left I found the road—by stepping down about a foot, falling flat on my face, and nearly losing the light. I picked myself up and went back.

"Good!" said Dad. "Slip your neck through this."

"This" was a sort of yoke he had devised by retying the blankets around the stretcher so as to get some free line. With my neck through it I could carry the weight on my shoulders and just steady my end with my hands. Not that it was heavy, but our hands were getting stiff with cold. "Good enough!" I said, "But, look, George—let Molly take your end."

"Nonsense!"

"It isn't nonsense. Molly can do it—can't you, Molly? And you know this road better than we do; you've tramped it enough times in the dark."

"Bill is right, dear," Molly said at once. "Here—take Mabel."

Dad gave in, took the light and the halter. Mabel didn't want to go any further; she wanted to sit down, I guess. Dad kicked her in the rear and jerked on her neck. Her feelings were hurt; she wasn't used to that sort of treatment—particularly not from Dad. But there was no time to humor her; it was getting colder.

We went on. I don't know how Dad kept to the road but he did. We had been at it another hour, I suppose, and had left Kneiper's slot well behind, when Molly stumbled, then her knees just seemed to cave in and she knelt down in the snow.

I stopped and sat down, too; I needed the rest. I just wanted to stay there and let it snow.

Dad came back and put his arms around her and comforted her and told her to lead Mabel now; she couldn't get lost on this stretch. She insisted that she could still carry. Dad ignored her, just lifted the yoke business off her shoulders. Then he came back and peeled a bit of blanket off the bubble and shined the torch inside. He put it back into place. Molly said, "How is she?"

Dad said, "She's still breathing. She opened her eyes when the light hit them. Let's go." He got the yoke on and Molly took the light and the halter.

Molly couldn't have seen what I saw; the plastic of the bubble was frosted over on the inside. Dad hadn't seen Peggy breathe; he hadn't seen anything.

I thought about it for a long while and wondered how you would classify that sort of a lie. Dad wasn't a liar, that was certain—and yet it seemed to me that such a lie, right then, was better than the truth. It was complicated.

Pretty soon I forgot it; I was too busy putting one foot in front of the other and counting the steps. I couldn't feel my feet any longer.

Dad stopped and I bumped into the end of the stretcher. "Listen!" he said.

I listened and heard a dull rumble. "Quake?"

"No. Keep quiet." Then he added, "It's down the road. Off the road, everybody! Off to the right."

The rumble got louder and presently I made out a light through the snow, back the way we had come. Dad saw it, too, and stepped out on the road and started waving our torch.

The rumble stopped almost on top of him; it was a rock crusher and it was loaded down with people, people clinging to it all over and even riding the spade. The driver yelled, "Climb on! And hurry!"

Then he saw the cow and added, "No live stock."

"We've got a stretcher with my little girl in it," Dad shouted back to him. "We need help."

There was a short commotion, while the driver ordered a couple of men down to help us. In the mix up Dad disappeared. One moment Molly was holding Mabel's halter, then Dad was gone and so was the cow.

We got the stretcher up onto the spade and some of the men braced it with their backs. I was wondering what to do about Dad and thinking maybe I ought to jump off and look for him, when he appeared out of the darkness and scrambled up beside me. "Where's Molly?" he asked.

"Up on top. But where is Mabel? What did you do with her?"

"Mabel is all right." He folded his knife and put it in his pocket. I didn't ask any more questions.

17.
DISASTER

We *passed several* more people after that, but the driver wouldn't stop. We were fairly close into town and he insisted that they could make it on their own. His emergency power pack was running low, he said; he had come all the way from the bend in the lake, ten miles beyond our place.

Besides, I don't know where he would have put them. We were about three deep and Dad had to keep warning people not to lean on the bubble of the stretcher.

Then the power pack did quit and the driver shouted, "Everybody off! Get on in on your own." But by now we were actually in town, the outskirts, and it would have been no trouble if it hadn't been blowing a blizzard. The driver insisted on helping Dad with the stretcher. He was a good Joe and turned out to be—when I saw him in the light—the same man who had crushed our acreage.

At long, long last we were inside the hospital and Peggy was turned over to the hospital people and put in a pressurized room. More than that, she was alive. In bad shape, but alive.

Molly stayed with her. I would like to have stayed, too—it was fairly warm in the hospital; it had its own emergency power pack. But they wouldn't let me.

Dad told Molly that he was reporting to the chief engineer for duty. I was told to go to the Immigration Receiving Station. I did so and it was just like the day we landed, only worse—and colder. I found myself right back in the very room which was the first I had ever been in on Ganymede.

* * *

The place was packed and getting more packed every minute as more refugees kept pouring in from the surrounding country. It was cold, though not so bitterly cold as outside. The lights were off, of course; light and heat all came from the power plant for everything. Hand lights had been set up here and there and you could sort of grope your way around. There were the usual complaints, too, though maybe not as bad as you hear from immigrants. I paid no attention to any of them; I was happy in a dead beat sort of way just to be inside and fairly warm and feel the blood start to go back into my feet.

We stayed there for thirty-seven hours. It was twenty-four hours before we got anything to eat.

Here was the way it went: the metal buildings, such as the Receiving Station, stood up. Very few of the stone buildings had, which we knew by then from the reports of all of us. The Power Station was out, and with it, the heat trap. They wouldn't tell us anything about it except to say that it was being fixed.

In the mean time we were packed in tight as they could put us, keeping the place warm mainly by the heat from our bodies, sheep style. There were, they say, several power packs being used to heat the place, too, one being turned on every time the temperature in the room dropped below freezing. If so, I never got close to one and I don't think it ever did get *up* to freezing where I was.

I would sit down and grab my knees and fall into a dopey sleep. Then a nightmare would wake me up and I'd get up and pound myself and walk around. After a while I'd sit down on the floor and freeze my fanny again.

I seem to remember encountering Noisy Edwards in the crowd and waving my finger under his nose and telling him I had an appointment to knock his block off. I seem to remember him staring back at me as if he couldn't place me. But I don't know; I may have dreamed it. I thought I ran across Hank, too, and had a long talk with him, but Hank told me afterwards that he never laid eyes on me the whole time.

After a long time—it seemed a week but the records show it was eight o'clock Sunday morning—they passed us out some lukewarm soup. It was wonderful. After that I wanted to leave the building to go to the hospital. I wanted to find Molly and see how Peggy was doing.

They wouldn't let me. It was seventy below outside and still dropping.

About twenty-two o'clock the lights came on and the worst was over.

We had a decent meal soon after that, sandwiches and soup, and when the Sun came up at midnight they announced that anybody could go outside who cared to risk it. I waited until noon Monday. By then it was up to twenty below and I made a dash for it to the hospital.

Peggy was doing as well as could be expected. Molly had stayed with her and had spent the time in bed with her, huddling up to her to keep her warm. While the hospital had emergency heat, it didn't have the capacity to cope with any such disaster as had struck us; it was darn near as cold as the Receiving Station. But Peggy had come through it, sleeping most of the time. She even perked up enough to smile and say hello.

Molly's left arm was in a sling and splinted. I asked how that happened—and then I felt foolish. It had happened in the quake itself but I hadn't known it and George still didn't know about it; none of the engineers were back.

It didn't seem possible that she could have done what she did, until I recalled that she carried the stretcher only after Dad had rigged the rope yokes. Molly is all right.

They chased me out and I high-tailed it back to the Receiving Station and ran into Sergei almost at once. He hailed me and I went over to him. He had a pencil and a list and a number of the older fellows were gathered around him. "What's up?" I said.

"Just the guy I'm looking for," he said. "I had you down for dead. Disaster party—are you in?"

I was in, all right. The parties were made up of older Scouts, sixteen and up, and the younger men. We were sent out on the town's tractors, one to each road, and we worked in teams of two. I spotted Hank Jones as we were loading and they let us make up a team.

It was grim work. For equipment we had shovels and lists— lists of who lived on which farm. Sometimes a name would have a notation "known to be alive," but more often not. A team would be dropped off with the lists for three or four farms and the tractor would go on, to pick them up on the return trip.

Our job was to settle the doubt about those other names and— theoretically—to rescue anyone still alive.

We didn't find anyone alive.

The lucky ones had been killed in the quake; the unlucky ones had waited too long and didn't make it into town. Some we found on the road; they had tried to make it but had started too late. The worst of all were those whose houses hadn't fallen and had tried to stick it out. Hank and I found one couple just sitting, arms around each other. They were hard as rock.

When we found one, we would try to identify it on the list, then cover it up with snow, several feet deep, so it would keep for a while after it started to thaw. When we settled with the people at a farm, we rummaged around and found all the livestock we could and carried or dragged their carcasses down to the road, to be toted into town on the tractor and slapped into deep freeze. It seemed a dirty job to do, robbing the dead, but, as Hank pointed out, we would all be getting a little hungry by and by.

Hank bothered me a little; he was merry about the whole thing. I guess it was better to laugh about it, in the long run, and after a while he had me doing it. It was just too big to soak up all at once and you didn't dare let it get you.

But I should have caught on when we came to his own place. "We can skip it," he said, and checked off the list.

"Hadn't we better check for livestock?" I said.

"Nope. We're running short of time. Let's move on to the Millers' place."

"Did they get out?"

"I don't know. I didn't see any of them in town."

The Millers hadn't gotten out; we barely had time to take care of them before the tractor picked us up. It was a week later that I found out that both of Hank's parents had been killed in the quake. He had taken time to drag them out and put them into their ice cellar before he had headed for town.

Like myself, Hank had been outside when it hit, still looking at the line up. The fact that the big shock had occurred right after the line up had kept a lot of people from being killed in their beds—but they say that the line up caused the quake, triggered it, that is, with tidal strains, so I guess it sort of evens up. Of course, the line up didn't actually make the quake; it had been building up to it ever since the beginning of the atmosphere project. Gravity's books have got to balance.

The colony had had thirty-seven thousand people when the quake hit. The census when we finished it showed less than thirteen thousand. Besides that we had lost every crop, all or almost all the livestock. As Hank said, we'd all be a little hungry by and by.

They dumped us back at the Receiving Station and a second

group of parties got ready to leave. I looked for a quiet spot to try to get some sleep.

I was just dozing off, it seemed to me, when somebody shook me. It was Dad. "Are you all right, Bill?"

I rubbed my eyes. "I'm okay. Have you seen Molly and Peggy?"

"Just left them. I'm off duty for a few hours. Bill, have you seen anything of the Schultzes?"

I sat up, wide awake. "No. Have you?"

"No."

I told him what I had been doing and he nodded. "Go back to sleep, Bill. I'll see if there has been a report on them."

I didn't go to sleep. He was back after a bit to say that he hadn't been able to find out anything one way or another. "I'm worried, Bill."

"So am I."

"I'm going out and check up."

"Let's go."

Dad shook his head. "No need for us both. You get some sleep." I went along, just the same.

We were lucky. A disaster party was just heading down our road and we hitched a ride. Our own farm and the Schultz's place were among those to be covered on this trip; Dad told the driver that we would check both places and report when we got back to town. That was all right with him.

They dropped us at the turn off and we trudged up toward the Schultz's house. I began to get the horrors as we went. It's one thing to pile snow over comparative strangers; it's another thing entirely to expect to find Mama Schultz or Gretchen with their faces blue and stiff.

I didn't visualize Papa as dead; people like Papa Schultz don't die—they just go on forever. Or it feels like that.

But I still wasn't prepared for what we did find.

We had just come around a little hummock that conceals their house from the road. George stopped and said, "Well, the house is still standing. His quakeproofing held."

I looked at it, then I stared—and then I yelled. "Hey, George! *The Tree is gone!*"

The house was there, but the apple tree—"the most beautiful tree on Ganymede"—was missing. Just gone. I began to run.

We were almost to the house when the door opened. There stood Papa Schultz.

* * *

They were all safe, every one of them. What remained of the tree was ashes in the fireplace. Papa had cut it down as soon as the power went off and the temperature started to drop—and then had fed it, little by little, into the flames.

Papa, telling us about it, gestured at the blackened firebox. "Johann's folly, they called it. I guess they will not think old Appleseed Johnny quite so foolish now, eh?" He roared and slapped Dad on the shoulders.

"But your tree," I said stupidly.

"I will plant another, many others." He stopped and was suddenly serious. "But your trees, William, your brave little baby trees—they are dead, not?"

I said I hadn't seen them yet. He nodded solemnly. "They are dead of the cold. Hugo!"

"Yes, Papa."

"Fetch me an apple." Hugo did so and Papa presented it to me. "You will plant again." I nodded and stuck it in my pocket.

They were glad to hear that we were all right, though Mama clucked over Molly's broken arm. Yo had fought his way over to our place during the first part of the storm, found that we were gone and returned, two frost bitten ears for his efforts. He was in town now to look for us.

But they were all right, every one of them. Even their livestock they had saved—cows, pigs, chickens, people, all huddled together throughout the cold and kept from freezing by the fire from their tree.

The animals were back in the barn, now that power was on again, but the place still showed that they had been there—and smelled of it, too. I think Mama was more upset by the shambles of her immaculate living room than she was by the magnitude of the disaster. I don't think she realized that most of her neighbors were dead. It hadn't hit her yet.

Dad turned down Papa Schultz's offer to come with us to look over our farm. Then Papa said he would see us on the tractor truck, as he intended to go into town and find out what he could do. We had mugs of Mama's strong tea and some corn bread and left.

I was thinking about the Schultzes and how good it was to find them alive, as we trudged over to our place. I told Dad that it was a miracle.

He shook his head. "Not a miracle. They are survivor types."

"What type is a survivor type?" I asked.

He took a long time to answer that one. Finally he said, "Survivors survive. I guess that is the only way to tell the survivor type for certain."

I said. "We're survivor types, too, in that case."

"Could be," he admitted. "At least we've come through this one."

When I had left, the house was down. In the mean time I had seen dozens of houses down, yet it was a shock to me when we topped the rise and I saw that it really was down. I suppose I expected that after a while I would wake up safe and warm in bed and everything would be all right.

The fields were there, that was all that you could say for it. I scraped the snow off a stretch I knew was beginning to crop. The plants were dead of course and the ground was hard. I was fairly sure that even the earth worms were dead; they had had nothing to warn them to burrow below the frost line.

My little saplings were dead, of course.

We found two of the rabbits, huddled together and stiff, under a drift against what was left of the barn. We didn't find any of the chickens except one, the first old hen we ever had. She had been setting and her nest wasn't crushed and had been covered by a piece of the fallen roof of the barn. She was still on it, hadn't moved and the eggs under her were frozen. I think that was what got me.

I was just a chap who used to have a farm.

Dad had been poking around the house. He came back to the barn and spoke to me. "Well, Bill?"

I stood up. "George, I've had it."

"Then let's go back to town. The truck will be along shortly."

"I mean I've really had it!"

"Yes, I know."

I took a look in Peggy's room first, but Dad's salvage had been thorough. My accordion was in there, however, with snow from the broken door drifted over the case. I brushed it off and picked it up. "Leave it," Dad said. "It's safe here and you've no place to put it."

"I don't expect to be back," I said.

"Very well."

We made a bundle of what Dad had gotten together, added the

accordion, the two rabbits and the hen, and carried it all down to the road. The tractor showed up presently, we got aboard and Dad chucked the rabbits and chicken on the pile of such that they had salvaged. Papa Schultz was waiting at his turnoff.

Dad and I tried to spot Mabel by the road on the trip back, but we didn't find her. Probably she had been picked up by an earlier trip, seeing that she was close to town. I was just as well pleased. All right, she had to be salvaged—but I didn't want the job. I'm not a cannibal.

I managed to get some sleep and a bite to eat and was sent out on another disaster party. The colony began to settle down into some sort of routine. Those whose houses had stood up moved back into them and the rest of us were taken care of in the Receiving Station, much as we had been when our party landed. Food was short, of course, and Ganymede had rationing for the first time since the first colonials really got started.

Not that we were going to starve. In the first place there weren't too many of us to feed and there had been quite a lot of food on hand. The real pinch would come later. It was decided to set winter back by three months, that is, start all over again with spring—which messed up the calendar from then on. But it would give us a new crop as quickly as possible to make up for the one that we had lost.

Dad stayed on duty with the engineer's office. Plans called for setting up two more power plants, spaced around the equator, and each of them capable of holding the heat trap alone. The disaster wasn't going to be allowed to happen again. Of course the installations would have to come from Earth, but we had been lucky on one score; Mars was in a position to relay for us. The report had gone into Earth at once and, instead of another load of immigrants, we were to get what we needed on the next trip.

Not that I cared. I had stayed in town, too, although the Schultzes had invited me to stay with them. I was earning my keep helping to rebuild and quakeproof the houses of the survivors. It had been agreed that we would all go back, George, Molly, Peggy, and me, on the first trip, if we could get space. It had been unanimous except that Peggy hadn't been consulted; it just had to be.

We weren't the only ones who were going back. The Colonial Commission had put up a squawk of course, but under the circumstances they had to give in. After it had been made official and the lists were opened Dad and I went over to the Commission agent's office to put in our applications. We were about the last to apply; Dad had been out of town on duty and I had waited until he got back.

The office was closed with a "Back in a half hour" sign stuck on the door. We waited. There were bulletin boards outside the office; on them were posted the names of those who had applied for repatriation. I started reading them to kill time and so did Dad.

I found Saunders' name there and pointed it out to George. He grunted and said, "No loss." Noisy Edwards' name was there, too; maybe I *had* seen him in the Receiving Station, although I hadn't seen him since. It occurred to me that I could probably corner him in the ship and pay him back his lumps, but I wasn't really interested in the project. I read on down.

I expected to find Hank Jones' name there, but I couldn't find it. I started reading the list carefully, paying attention to every name I recognized. I began to see a pattern.

Presently the agent got back and opened the door. Dad touched my arm. "Come on, Bill."

I said, "Wait a minute, George. You read all the names?"

"Yes, I did."

"I've been thinking. You know, George, I don't *like* being classed with these lugs."

He chewed his lip. "I know exactly what you mean."

I took the plunge. "You can do as you like, George, but I'm not going home, if I ever do, until I've licked this joint."

Dad looked as unhappy as he could look. He was silent for a long time, then he said, "I've got to take Peggy back, Bill. She won't go unless Molly and I go along. And she's got to go."

"Yes, I know."

"You understand how it is, Bill?"

"Yes, Dad, I understand." He went on in to make out his application, whistling a little tune he used to whistle just after Anne died. I don't think he knew he was whistling it.

I waited for him and after a bit we went away together.

I moved back out to the farm the next day. Not to the Schultzes—to the farm. I slept in Peggy's room and got busy fixing the place up and getting ready to plant my emergency allowance of seed.

Then, about two weeks before they were to leave in the *Covered Wagon*, Peggy died, and there wasn't any reason for any of us to go back to Earth.

Yo Schultz had been in town and Dad sent word back by him. Yo came over and woke me up and told me about it. I thanked him.

He wanted to know if I wanted to come back to the house with him. I said, no, thanks, that I would rather be alone. He made me promise to come over the next day and went away.

I lay back down on Peggy's bed.

She was dead and there was nothing more I could do about it. She was dead and it was all my fault . . . if I hadn't encouraged her, they would have been able to get her to go back before it was too late. She would be back Earthside, going to school and growing up healthy and happy—right back in California, not here in this damned place where she couldn't live, where human beings were never *meant* to live.

I bit the pillow and blubbered. I said, "Oh, Anne, Anne! Take care of her, Anne—She's so little; she won't know what to do."

And then I stopped bawling and listened, half way expecting Anne to answer me and tell me she would. But I couldn't hear anything, not at first . . . and what I did hear was only, "Stand tall, Billy," . . . very faint and far away, "Stand tall, son."

After a while I got up and washed my face and started hoofing it back into town.

18.
PIONEER PARTY

We all lived in Peggy's room until Dad and I had the seeds in, then we built on to it, quake proof this time and with a big view window facing the lake and another facing the mountains. We knocked a window in Peggy's room, too; it made it seem like a different place.

We built on still another room presently, as it seemed as if we might be needing it. All the rooms had windows and the living room had a fireplace.

Dad and I were terribly busy the second season after the quake. Enough seed could be had by then and we farmed the empty farm across the road from us. Then some newcomers, the Ellises, moved in and paid us for the crop. It was just what they call a "book transaction," but it reduced our debt with the Commission.

Two G-years after the line up you would never have known that anything had happened. There wasn't a wrecked building in the community, there were better than forty-five thousand people, and the town was booming. New people were coming in so fast that you could even sell some produce to the Commission in lieu of land.

We weren't doing so badly, ourselves. We had a hive of bees. We had Mabel II, and Margie and Mamie, and I was sending the spare milk into town by the city transport truck that passed down our road once a day. I had broken Marge and Mamie to the yoke and used them for ploughing as well—we had crushed five more acres—and we were even talking about getting a horse.

Some people had horses already, the Schultzes for instance. The council had wrangled about it before okaying the "invasion," with conservatives holding out for tractors. But we weren't equipped to manufacture tractors yet and the policy was to make the planet self-sufficient—the hay burners won out. Horses can manufacture more horses and that is one trick that tractors have never learned.

Furthermore, though I would have turned my nose up at the idea when I was a ground hog back in Diego Borough, horse steak is very tasty.

It turned out we did need the extra room. Twins—both boys. New babies don't look as if they were worth keeping, but they get over it—slowly. I bought a crib as a present for them, made right here on Ganymede, out of glass fabric stuck together with synthetic resin. It was getting possible to buy quite a number of home products.

I told Molly I would initiate the brats into the Cubs when they were old enough. I was getting in to meetings oftener now, for I had a patrol again—the Daniel Boone patrol, mostly new kids. I still hadn't taken my own tests but you can't do everything at once. Once I was scheduled to take them and a litter of pigs picked that day to arrive. But I planned to take them; I wanted to be an Eagle Scout again, even if I was getting a little old to worry about badges in themselves.

It may sound as if the survivors didn't give a hoot about those who had died in the disaster. But that isn't the truth. It was just that you work from day to day and that keeps your mind busy. In any case, we weren't the first colony to be two-thirds wiped out—and we wouldn't be the last. You can grieve only so much; after that it's self pity. So George says.

George still wanted me to go back to Earth to finish my education and I had been toying with the idea myself. I was beginning to realize that there were a few things I hadn't learned. The idea was attractive; it would not be like going back right after the quake, tail between my legs. I'd be a property owner, paying my own way. The fare was considerable—five acres—and would about clean me out, my half, and put a load on George and Molly. But they were both for it.

Besides, Dad owned blocked assets back Earthside which would pay my way through school. They were no use to him otherwise; the only thing the Commission will accept as pay for imports is proved land. There was even a possibility, if the council won a suit pending back Earthside, that his blocked assets could be used for my fare as well and not cost us a square foot of improved soil. All in all, it was nothing to turn down idly.

We were talking about me leaving on the *New Ark* when another matter came up—the planetary survey.

Ganymede had to have settlements other than Leda; that was evident even when we landed. The Commission planned to set up two more ports-of-entry near the two new power stations and let the place grow from three centers. The present colonists were to build the new towns—receiving stations, hydroponics sheds, infirmaries, and so forth—and be paid for it in imports. Immigration would be stepped up accordingly, something that the Commission was very anxious to do, now that they had the ships to dump them in on us in quantity.

The old *Jitterbug* was about to take pioneer parties out to select sites and make plans—and both Hank and Sergei were going.

I wanted to go so bad I could taste it. In the whole time I had been here I had never gotten fifty miles from Leda. Suppose somebody asked me what it was like on Ganymede when I got back on Earth? Truthfully, I wouldn't be able to tell them; I hadn't been any place.

I had had a chance, once, to make a trip to Barnard's Moon, as a temporary employee of Project Jove—and that hadn't worked out either. The twins. I stayed back and took care of the farm.

I talked it over with Dad.

"I hate to see you delay it any longer," he said seriously. I pointed out that it would be only two months.

"Hmmm—" he said. "Have you taken your merit badge tests yet?"

He knew I hadn't; I changed the subject by pointing out that Sergei and Hank were going.

"But they are both older than you are," he answered.

"Not by very much!"

"But I think they are each over the age limit they were looking for—and you are just under."

"Look, George," I protested, "rules were made to be broken. I've heard you say that. There must be some spot I can fill—cook, maybe."

And that's just the job I got—cook.

I always have been a pretty fair cook—not in Mama Schultz's class, but good. The party had nothing to complain about on that score.

Captain Hattie put us down at a selected spot nine degrees north of the equator and longitude 113 west—that is to say, just out of sight of Jupiter on the far side and about thirty-one hundred miles from Leda. Mr. Hooker says that the average temperature of Ganymede will rise about nine degrees over the next century as more and more of the ancient ice melts—at which time Leda will be semi-tropical and the planet will be habitable half way to the poles. In the mean time colonies would be planted only at or near the equator.

I was sorry we had Captain Hattie as pilot; she is such an insufferable old scold. She thinks rocket pilots are a special race apart—supermen. At least she acts like it. Recently the Commission had forced her to take a relief pilot; there was just too much for one pilot to do. They had tried to force a check pilot on her, too—an indirect way to lead up to retiring her, but she was too tough for them. She threatened to take the *Jitterbug* up and crash it . . . and they didn't dare call her bluff. At that time they were absolutely dependent on the *Jitterbug*.

Originally the *Jitterbug's* only purpose was for supply and passengers between Leda and the Project Jove station on Barnard's Moon—but that was back in the days when ships from Earth actually landed at Leda. Then the *Mayflower* came along and the *Jitterbug* was pressed into service as a shuttle. There was talk of another shuttle rocket but we didn't have it yet, which is why Captain Hattie had them where it hurt. The Commission had visions of a loaded ship circling Ganymede, just going round and round and round again, with no way to get down, like a kitten stuck up in a tree.

I'll say this for Hattie; she could handle her ship. I think she had nerve ends out in the skin of it. In clear weather she could even make a glide landing, in spite of our thin air. But I think she preferred to shake up her passengers with a jet landing.

She put us down, the *Jitterbug* took on more water mass, and away it bounced. She had three more parties to land. All in all the *Jitterbug* was servicing eight other pioneer parties. It would be back to pick us up in about three weeks.

The leader of our party was Paul du Maurier, who was the new assistant Scoutmaster of the Auslander troop and the chap who had gotten me taken on as cookie. He was younger than some of those working for him; furthermore, he shaved, which made him stand out like a white leghorn in a hog pen and made him look even younger. That is, he did shave, but he started letting his beard grow on this trip. "Better trim that grass," I advised him.

He said, "Don't you like my beard, Doctor Slop?"—that was a nickname he had awarded me for "Omnibus stew," my own invention. He didn't mean any harm by it.

I said, "Well, it covers your face, which is some help—but you might be mistaken for one of us colonial roughnecks. That wouldn't do for one of you high-toned Commission boys."

He smiled mysteriously and said, "Maybe that's what I want."

I said, "Maybe. But they'll lock you up in a zoo if you wear it back to Earth." He was due to go back for Earthside duty by the same trip I expected to make, via the *Covered Wagon*, two weeks after the end of the survey.

He smiled again and said, "Ah, yes, so they would," and changed the subject. Paul was one of the most thoroughly good guys I have ever met and smart as a whip as well. He was a graduate of South Africa University with P. G. on top of that at the System Institute on Venus—an ecologist, specializing in planetary engineering.

He handled that gang of rugged individualists without raising his voice. There is something about a real leader that makes it unnecessary for him to get tough.

But back to the survey—I didn't see much of it as I was up to my elbows in pots and pans, but I knew what was going on. The valley we were in had been picked from photographs taken from the *Jitterbug*; it was now up to Paul to decide whether or not it was ideally suited to easy colonization. It had the advantage of being in direct line-of-sight with power station number two, but that was not essential. Line-of-sight power relays could be placed anywhere on the mountains (no name, as yet) just south of us. Most of the new villages would have to have power relayed anyhow. Aside from a safety factor for the heat trap there was no point in setting up extra power stations when the whole planet couldn't use the potential of *one* mass-conversion plant.

So they got busy—an engineering team working on drainage and probable annual water resources, topographers getting a contour, a chemistry-agronomy team checking on what the various rock formations would make as soil, and a community architect laying out a town and farm and rocket port plot. There were several other specialists, too, like the mineralogist, Mr. Villa, who was doodlebugging the place for ores.

Paul was the "general specialist" who balanced all the data in his mind, fiddled with his slip stick, stared off into the sky, and came up with the over all answer. The over all answer for that valley was "nix"—and we moved on to the next one on the list, packing the stuff on our backs.

That was one of the few chances I got to look around. You see, we had landed at sunrise—about five o'clock Wednesday morning sunrise was, in that longitude—and the object was to get as much done as possible during each light phase. Jupiter light is all right for working in your own fields, but no good for surveying strange territory—and here we didn't even have Jupiter light—just Callisto, every other dark phase, every twelve-and-half days, to be exact. Consequently we worked straight through light phase, on pep pills.

Now a man who is on the pills will eat more than twice as much as a man who is sleeping regularly. You know, the Eskimos have a saying, "Food is sleep." I had to produce hot meals every four hours, around the clock. I had no time for sightseeing.

We got to camp number two, pitched our tents, I served a scratch meal, and Paul passed out sleeping pills. By then the Sun was down and we really died for about twenty hours. We were comfortable enough—spun glass pads under us and resin sealed glass canvas over us.

I fed them again, Paul passed out more sleepy pills, and back we went to sleep. Paul woke me Monday afternoon. This time I fixed them a light breakfast, then really spread myself to turn them out a feast. Everybody was well rested by now, and not disposed to want to go right back to bed. So I stuffed them.

After that we sat around for a few hours and talked. I got out my squeeze box—brought along by popular demand, that is to say, Paul suggested it—and gave 'em a few tunes. Then we talked some more.

They got to arguing about where life started and somebody brought up the old theory that the Sun had once been much brighter—Jock Montague, it was, the chemist. "Mark my words," he said, "When we get around to exploring Pluto, you'll find that life was there before us. Life is persistent, like mass-energy."

"Nuts," answered Mr. Villa, very politely. "Pluto isn't even a proper planet; it used to be a satellite of Neptune."

"Well, Neptune, then," Jock persisted. "Life is all through the universe. Mark my words—when the Jove Project straightens out the bugs and gets going, they'll even find life on the surface of Jupiter."

"On Jupiter?" Mr. Villa exploded. "Please, Jock! Methane and ammonia and cold as a mother-in-law's kiss. Don't joke with us.

Why, there's not even light down under on the surface of Jupiter; it's pitch dark."

"I said it and I'll say it again," Montague answered. "Life is persistent. Wherever there is mass and energy with conditions that permit the formation of large and stable molecules, there you will find life. Look at Mars. Look at Venus. Look at Earth—the most dangerous planet of the lot. Look at the Ruined Planet."

I said, "What do you think about it, Paul?"

The boss smiled gently. "I don't. I haven't enough data."

"There!" said Mr. Villa. "There speaks a wise man. Tell me, Jock, how did you get to be an authority on this subject?"

"I have the advantage," Jock answered grandly, "of not knowing too much about the subject. Facts are always a handicap in philosophical debate."

That ended that phase of it, for Mr. Seymour, the boss agronomist, said, "I'm not so much worried about where life came from as where it is going—here."

"How?" I wanted to know. "In what way?"

"What are we going to make of this planet? We can make it anything we want. Mars and Venus—they had native cultures. We dare not change them much and we'll never populate them very heavily. These Jovian moons are another matter; it's up to us. They say man is endlessly adaptable. I say on the contrary that man doesn't adapt himself as much as he adapts his environment. Certainly we are doing so here. But how?"

"I thought that was pretty well worked out," I said. "We set up these new centers, more people come in and we spread out, same as at Leda."

"Ah, but where does it stop? We have three ships making regular trips now. Shortly there will be a ship in every three weeks, then it will be every week, then every day. Unless we are almighty careful there will be food rationing here, same as on Earth. Bill, do you know how fast the population is increasing, back Earthside?"

I admitted that I didn't.

"More than one hundred thousand more persons each day than there were the day before. Figure that up."

I did. "That would be, uh, maybe fifteen, twenty shiploads a day. Still, I imagine they could build ships to carry them."

"Yes, *but where would we put them?* Each day, more than twice as many people landing as there are now on this whole globe. And not just on Monday, but on Tuesday, and Wednesday, and Thursday—and the week and the month and the year after that, just to keep Earth's population stable. I tell you, it won't work. The day will come when we will have to *stop immigration entirely.*" He looked around aggressively, like a man who expects to be contradicted.

He wasn't disappointed. Somebody said, "Oh, Seymour, come off it! Do you think you own this place just because you got here first? You snuck in while the rules were lax."

"You can't argue with mathematics," Seymour insisted. "Ganymede has got to be made self-sufficient as soon as possible—and then we've got to slam the door!"

Paul was shaking his head. "It won't be necessary."

"Huh?" said Seymour. "Why not? Answer me that. You represent the Commission: what fancy answer has the Commission got?"

"None," Paul told him. "And your figures are right but your conclusions are wrong. Oh, Ganymede has to be made self-sufficient, true enough, but your bogeyman about a dozen or more shiploads of immigrants a day you can forget."

"Why, if I may be so bold?"

Paul looked around the tent and grinned apologetically. "Can you stand a short dissertation on population dynamics? I'm afraid I don't have Jock's advantage; this is a subject I am supposed to know something about."

Somebody said, "Stand back. Give him air."

"Okay," Paul went on, "you brought it on yourselves. A lot of people have had the idea that colonization is carried on with the end purpose of relieving the pressure of people and hunger back on Earth. Nothing could be further from the truth."

I said, "Huh?"

"Bear with me. Not only is it physically impossible for a little planet to absorb the increase of a big planet, as Seymour pointed out, but there is another reason why we'll never get any such flood of people as a hundred thousand people a day—a psychological reason. There are never as many people willing to emigrate (even if you didn't pick them over) as there are new people born. Most people simply will not leave home. Most of them won't even leave their native villages, much less go to a far planet."

Mr. Villa nodded. "I go along with you on that. The willing emigrant is an odd breed of cat. He's scarce."

"Right," Paul agreed. "But let's suppose for a moment that a hundred thousand people were willing to emigrate every day and Ganymede and the other colonies could take them. Would that relieve the situation back home—I mean 'back Earthside'? The answer is, 'No, it wouldn't'."

He appeared to have finished. I finally said, "Excuse my blank look, Paul, but why wouldn't it?"

"Studied any bionomics, Bill?"

"Some."

"Mathematical population bionomics?"

"Well—no."

"But you do know that in the greatest wars the Earth ever had there were always more people after the war than before, no matter how many were killed. Life is not merely persistent, as Jock puts it; life is explosive. The basic theorem of population mathematics *to which there has never been found an exception* is that population increases always, not merely up to extent of the food supply, but beyond it, to the minimum diet that will sustain life— the ragged edge of starvation. In other words, if we bled off a hundred thousand people a day, the Earth's population would then grow until the increase was around *two* hundred thousand a day, or the bionomical maximum for Earth's new ecological dynamic."

Nobody said anything for a moment; there wasn't anything to say. Presently Sergei spoke up with, "You paint a grim picture, boss. What's the answer?"

Paul said, "There isn't any!"

Sergei said, "I didn't mean it that way. I mean, what is the outcome?"

When Paul did answer it was just one word, one monosyllable, spoken so softly that it would not have been heard if there had not been dead silence. What he said was:

"War."

There was a shuffle and a stir; it was an unthinkable idea. Seymour said, "Come now, Mr. du Maurier—I may be a pessimist, but I'm not that much of one. Wars are no longer possible."

Paul said, "So?"

Seymour answered almost belligerently, "Are you trying to suggest that the Space Patrol would let us down? Because that is the only way a war could happen."

Paul shook his head. "The Patrol won't let us down. But they won't be able to stop it. A police force is all right for stopping individual disturbances; it's fine for nipping things in the bud. But when the disturbances are planet wide, no police force is big enough, or strong enough, or wise enough. They'll try—they'll try bravely. They won't succeed."

"You really believe that?"

"It's my considered opinion. And not only my opinion, but the opinion of the Commission. Oh, I don't mean the political board; I mean the career scientists."

"Then what in tarnation is the Commission up to?"

"Building colonies. We think that is worthwhile in itself. The colonies need not be affected by the War. In fact, I don't think they will be, not much. It will be like America was up to the end of the nineteenth century; European troubles passed her by. I rather expect that the War, when it comes, will be of such size and duration that interplanetary travel will cease to be for a considerable period. That is why I said this planet has got to be self-sufficient. It takes a high technical culture to maintain interplanetary travel and Earth may not have it—after a bit."

I think Paul's ideas were a surprise to everyone present; I know they were to me. Seymour jabbed a finger at him, "If you believe this, then why are you going back to Earth? Tell me that."

Again Paul spoke softly. "I'm not. I'm going to stay here and become a 'steader."

Suddenly I knew why he was letting his beard grow.

Seymour answered, "Then you expect it soon." It was not a question; it was a statement.

"Having gone this far," Paul said hesitantly, "I'll give you a direct answer. War is not less than forty Earth years away, not more than seventy."

You could feel a sigh of relief all around the place. Seymour continued to speak for us, "Forty to seventy, you say. But that's no reason to homestead; you probably wouldn't live to see it. Not but what you'd make a good neighbor."

"I see this War," Paul insisted. "I know it's coming. Should I leave it up to my hypothetical children and grandchildren to outguess it? No. Here I rest. If I marry, I'll marry here. I'm not raising any kids to be radioactive dust."

It must have been about here that Hank stuck his head in the tent, for I don't remember anyone answering Paul. Hank had been outside on business of his own; now he opened the flap and called out, "Hey gents! Europa is up!"

We all trooped out to see. We went partly through embarrassment, I think; Paul had been too nakedly honest. But we probably would have gone anyhow. Sure, we saw Europa every day of our lives at home, but not the way we were seeing it now.

Since Europa goes around Jupiter inside Ganymede's orbit, it never gets very far away from Jupiter, if you call 39 degrees "not very far." Since we were 113 west longitude, Jupiter was 23 degrees below our eastern horizon—which meant that Europa, when it was furthest west of Jupiter, would be a maximum of 16 degrees above the true horizon.

Excuse the arithmetic. Since we had a row of high hills practically sitting on us to the east, what all this means is that, once a week, Europa would rise above the hills, just peeking over, hang there for about a day—then turn around and set in the east, right where it had risen. Up and down like an elevator.

If you've never been off Earth, don't tell me it's impossible. That's how it is—Jupiter and its moons do some funny things.

It was the first time it had happened this trip, so we watched it—a little silver boat, riding the hills like waves, with its horns turned up. There was argument about whether or not it was still rising, or starting to set again, and much comparing of watches. Some claimed to be able to detect motion but they weren't agreed on which way. After a while I got cold and went back in.

But I was glad of the interruption. I had a feeling that Paul had said considerably more than he had intended to and more than he would be happy to recall, come light phase. I blamed it on the sleeping pills. Sleeping pills are all right when necessary, but they tend to make you babble and tell your right name—treacherous things.

19.
THE OTHER PEOPLE

By the end of the second light phase it was clear—to Paul, anyhow—that this second valley would do. It wasn't the perfect valley and maybe there was a better one just over the ridge—but life is too short. Paul assigned it a score of 92% by some complicated system thought up by the Commission, which was seven points higher than passing. The perfect valley could wait for the colonials to find it . . . which they would, some day.

We named the valley Happy Valley, just for luck, and named the mountains south of it the Pauline Peaks, over Paul's protests. He said it wasn't official anyway; we said we would see to it that it was made so—and the boss topographer, Abie Finkelstein, marked it so on the map and we all intialed it.

We spent the third light phase rounding up the details. We could have gone back then, if there had been any way to get back. There wasn't, so we had to dope through another dark phase. Some of them preferred to go back on a more normal schedule instead; there was a round-the-clock poker game, which I stayed out of, having nothing I could afford to lose and no talent for filling straights. There were more dark phase bull sessions but they never got as grave as the first one and nobody ever again asked Paul what he thought about the future prospects of things.

By the end of the third dark phase I was getting more than a little tired of seeing nothing but the inside of our portable range. I asked Paul for some time off.

Hank had been helping me since the start of the third dark phase. He had been working as a topographical assistant; flash contour pictures were on the program at the start of that dark phase. He was supposed to get an open-lens shot across the valley from an elevation on the south just as a sunburst flash was let off from an elevation to the west.

Hank had a camera of his own, just acquired, and he was shutter happy, always pointing it at things. This time he had tried to get a picture of his own as well as the official picture. He had goofed off, missed the official picture entirely, and to top it off had failed to protect his eyes when the sunburst went off. Which put him on the sick list and I got him as kitchen police.

He was all right shortly, but Finkelstein didn't want him back. So I asked for relief for both of us, so we could take a hike together and do a little exploring. Paul let us go.

There had been high excitement at the end of the second light phase when lichen had been discovered near the west end of the valley. For a while it looked as if native life had been found on Ganymede. It was a false alarm—careful examination showed that it was not only an Earth type, but a type authorized by the bionomics board.

But it did show one thing—life was spreading, taking hold, at a point thirty-one hundred miles from the original invasion. There was much argument as to whether the spores had been air borne, or had been brought in on the clothing of the crew who had set up the power plant. It didn't matter, really.

But Hank and I decided to explore off that way and see if we could find more of it. Besides it was away from the way we had come from camp number one. We didn't tell Paul we were going after lichen because we were afraid he would veto it; the stuff had been found quite some distance from camp. He had warned us not to go too far and to be back by six o'clock Thursday morning, in time to break camp and head back to our landing point, where the *Jitterbug* was to meet us.

I agreed as I didn't mean to go far in any case. I didn't much care whether we found lichen or not; I wasn't feeling well. But I kept that fact to myself; I wasn't going to be done out of my one and only chance to see some of the country.

We didn't find any more lichen. We did find the crystals.

We were trudging along, me as happy as a kid let out of school despite an ache in my side and Hank taking useless photographs of odd rocks and lava flows. Hank had been saying that he thought he would sell out his place and homestead here in Happy Valley. He said, "You know, Bill, they are going to need a few real

Ganymede farmers here to give the greenhorns the straight dope. And who knows more about Ganymede-style farming than I do?"

"Almost everybody," I assured him.

He ignored it. "This place has really got it," he went on, gazing around at a stretch of country that looked like Armageddon after a hard battle. "Much better than around Leda."

I admitted that it had possibilities. "But I don't think it's for me," I went on. "I don't think I'd care to settle anywhere where you can't see Jupiter."

"Nonsense!" he answered. "Did you come here to stare at the sights or to make a farm?"

"That's a moot point," I admitted. "Sometimes I think one thing, sometimes the other. Sometimes I don't have the foggiest idea."

He wasn't listening. "See that slot up there?"

"Sure. What about it?"

"If we crossed that little glacier, we could get up to it."

"Why?"

"I think it leads into another valley—which might be even better. Nobody has been up there. I know—I was in the topo gang."

"I've been trying to help you forget that," I told him. "But why look at all? There must be a hundred thousand valleys on Ganymede that nobody has looked at. Are you in the real estate business?" It didn't appeal to me. There is something that gets you about virgin soil on Ganymede; I wanted to stay in sight of camp. It was quiet as a library—quieter. On Earth there is always some sound, even in the desert. After a while the stillness and the bare rocks and the ice and the craters get on my nerves.

"Come on! Don't be a sissy!" he answered, and started climbing.

The slot did not lead to another valley; it led into a sort of corridor in the hills. One wall was curiously flat, as if it had been built that way on purpose. We went along it a way, and I was ready to turn back and had stopped to call to Hank, who had climbed the loose rock on the other side to get a picture. As I turned, my eye caught some color and I moved up to see what it was. It was the crystals.

I stared at them and they seemed to stare back. I called, "Hey! Hank! Come here on the bounce!"

"What's up?"

"Come here! Here's something worth taking a picture of."

He scrambled down and joined me. After a bit he let out his breath and whispered, "Well, I'll be fried on Friday!"

Hank got busy with his camera. I never saw such crystals, not even stalactites in caves. They were six-sided, except a few that were three-sided and some that were twelve-sided. They came anywhere from little squatty fellows no bigger than a button mushroom up to tall, slender stalks, knee high. Later on and further up we found some chest high.

They were not simple prisms; they branched and budded. But the thing that got you was the colors.

They were all colors and they changed color as you looked at them. We finally decided that they didn't have any color at all; it was just refraction of light. At least Hank thought so.

He shot a full cartridge of pictures then said, "Come on. Let's see where they come from."

I didn't want to. I was shaky from the climb and my right side was giving me fits every step I took. I guess I was dizzy, too; when I looked at the crystals they seemed to writhe around and I would have to blink my eyes to steady them.

But Hank had already started so I followed. The crystals seemed to keep to what would have been the water bed of the canyon, had it been spring. They seemed to need water. We came to a place where there was a drift of ice across the floor of the corridor—ancient ice, with a thin layer of last winter's snow on top of it. The crystals had carved a passage right through it, a natural bridge of ice, and had cleared a space of several feet on each side of where they were growing, as well.

Hank lost his footing as we scrambled through and snatched at one of the crystals. It broke off with a sharp, clear note, like a silver bell.

Hank straightened up and stood looking at his hand. There were parallel cuts across his palm and fingers. He stared at them stupidly.

"That'll teach you," I said, and then got out a first-aid kit and bandaged it for him. When I had finished I said, "Now let's go back."

"Shucks," he said. "What's a few little cuts? Come on."

I said, "Look, Hank, I want to go back. I don't feel good."

"What's the matter?"

"Stomach ache."

"You eat too much; that's your trouble. The exercise will do you good."

"No, Hank. I've got to go back."

He stared up the ravine and looked fretful. Finally he said,

"Bill, I think I see where the crystals come from, not very far up. You wait here and let me take a look. Then I'll come back and we'll head for camp. I won't be gone long; honest I won't."

"Okay," I agreed. He started up; shortly I followed him. I had had it pounded into my head as a Cub not to get separated in a strange country.

After a bit I heard him shout. I looked up and saw him standing, facing a great dark hole in the cliff. I called out, "What's the matter?"

He answered:

"GREAT JUMPING HOLY SMOKE!!!"—like that.

"What's the matter?" I repeated irritably and hurried along until I was standing beside him.

The crystals continued up the place where we were. They came right to the cave mouth, but did not go in; they formed a solid dense thicket across the threshold. Lying across the floor of the ravine, as if it had been tumbled there by an upheaval like the big quake, was a flat rock, a monolith, Stonehenge size. You could see where it had broken off the cliff, uncovering the hole. The plane of cleavage was as sharp and smooth as anything done by the ancient Egyptians.

But that wasn't what we were looking at; we were looking into the hole.

It was dark inside, but diffused light, reflected off the canyon floor and the far wall, filtered inside. My eyes began to adjust and I could see what Hank was staring at, what he had exploded about.

There were *things* in there and they weren't natural.

I couldn't have told you what sort of things because they were like nothing I had ever seen before in my life, or seen pictures of— or heard of. How can you describe what you've never seen before and have no words for? Shucks, you can't even *see* a thing properly the first time you see it; your eye doesn't take in the pattern.

But I could see this: they weren't rocks, they weren't plants, they weren't animals. They were *made* things, man made—well, maybe not "man" made, but not things that just happen, either.

I wanted very badly to get up close to them and see what they were. For the moment, I forgot I was sick.

So did Hank. As usual he said, "Come on! Let's go!"

But I said, "How?"

"Why, we just—" He stopped and took another look. "Well, let's see, we go around—No. Hmm . . . Bill, we will have to bust up some of those crystals and go right through the middle. There's no other way to get in."

I said, "Isn't one chopped up hand enough for you?"

"I'll bust 'em with a rock. It seems a shame; they are so pretty, but that's what I'll have to do."

"I don't think you can bust those big ones. Besides that, I'll give you two to one that they are sharp enough to cut through your boots."

"I'll chance it." He found a chunk of rock and made an experiment; I was right on both counts. Hank stopped and looked the situation over, whistling softly. "Bill——"

"Yeah?"

"See that little ledge over the opening?"

"What about it?"

"It comes out to the left further than the crystals do. I'm going to pile rock up high enough for us to reach it, then we can go along it and drop down right in front of the cave mouth. The crystals don't come that close."

I looked it over and decided it would work. "But how do we get back?"

"We can pile up some of that stuff we can see inside and shinny up again. At the very worst I can boost you up on my shoulders and then you can reach down your belt to me, or something."

If I had my wits about me, maybe I would have protested. But we tried it and it worked—worked right up to the point where I was hanging by my fingers from the ledge over the cave mouth.

I felt a stabbing pain in my side and let go.

I came to with Hank shaking me. "Let me alone!" I growled.

"You knocked yourself out," he said. "I didn't know you were so clumsy." I didn't answer. I just gathered my knees up to my stomach and closed my eyes.

Hank shook me again. "Don't you want to see what's in here?"

I kicked at him. "I don't want to see the Queen of Sheba! Can't you see I'm sick?" I closed my eyes again.

I must have passed out. When I woke up, Hank was sitting Turk fashion in front of me, with my torch in his hand. "You've been asleep a long time, fellow," he said gently. "Feel any better?"

"Not much."

"Try to pull yourself together and come along with me. You've got to see this, Bill. You won't believe it. This is the greatest discovery since—well, since—Never mind; Columbus was a piker. We're famous, Bill."

"You may be famous," I said. "I'm sick."

"Where does it hurt?"

"All over. My stomach is hard as a rock—a rock with a toothache."

"Bill," he said seriously, "have you ever had your appendix out?"

"No."

"Hmmm . . . maybe you should have had it out."

"Well, this is a fine time to tell me!"

"Take it easy."

"Take it easy, my foot!" I got up on one elbow, my head swimming. "Hank, listen to me. You've got to get back to camp and tell them. Have them send a tractor for me."

"Look, Bill," he said gently, "you know there isn't anything like a tractor at camp."

I tried to struggle with the problem but it was too much for me. My brain was fuzzy. "Well, have them bring a stretcher, at least," I said peevishly and lay down again.

Some time later I felt him fumbling around with my clothes. I tried to push him away, then I felt something very cold on me. I took a wild swing at him; it didn't connect.

"Steady," he said. "I have found some ice. Don't squirm around or you'll knock off the pack."

"I don't want it."

"You've got to have it. You keep that ice pack in place until we get out of here and you may live to be hanged, yet."

I was too feeble to resist. I lay back down and closed my eyes again. When I opened my eyes again, I was amazed to feel better. Instead of feeling ready to die, I merely felt awful. Hank wasn't around; I called to him. When he didn't answer at once I felt panicky.

Then he came trotting up, waving the torch. "I thought you had gone," I said.

"No. To tell the truth, I can't get out of here. I can't get back up to the ledge and I can't get over the crystals. I tried it." He held up one boot; it was in shreds and there was blood on it.

"Hurt yourself?"

"I'll live."

"I wonder," I answered. "Nobody knows we are here—and you say we can't get out. Looks like we starve. Not that I give a hoot."

'Speaking of that," he said. "I saved you some of our lunch. I'm afraid I didn't leave much; you were asleep a long, long time."

"Don't mention food!" I retched and grabbed at my side.

"Sorry. But look—I didn't say we couldn't get out."

"But you did."

"No, I said *I* couldn't get out."

"What's the difference?"

"Uh, never mind. But I think we'll get out. It was what you said about getting a tractor——"

"Tractor? Are you out of your head?"

"Skip it," Bill answered. "There is a sort of tractor thing back there—or more like a scaffolding, maybe."

"Make up your mind."

"Call it a wagon. I think I can get it out, at least across the crystals. We could use it as a bridge."

"Well, roll it out."

"It doesn't roll. It, uh—well, it walks."

I tried to get up. "This I got to see."

"Just move over out of the way of the door."

I managed to get to my feet, with Hank helping me. "I'm coming along."

"Want the ice pack changed?"

"Later, maybe." Hank took me back and showed me. I don't know how to describe the walker wagon—maybe you've seen pictures since. If a centipede were a dinosaur and made of metal to boot, it would be a walker wagon. The body of it was a sort of trough and it was supported by thirty-eight legs, nineteen on a side.

"That," I said, "is the craziest contraption I ever laid eyes on. You'll never shove it out the door."

"Wait until you see," he advised. "And if you think this is crazy, you should see the other things in here."

"Such as?"

"Bill, you know what I think this place is? I think it's a hangar for a space ship."

"Huh? Don't be silly; space ships don't have hangars."

"This one has."

"You mean you *saw* a space ship in here?"

"Well, I don't know. It's not like any I ever saw before, but if it's not a space ship, I don't know what it is good for."

I wanted to go see, but Hank objected. "Another time, Bill; we've got to get back to camp. We're late as it is."

I didn't put up any fight. My side was paining me again, from the walk. "Okay, what happens next?"

"Like this." He led me around to the end of the contraption; the trough came nearly down to the floor in back. Hank helped me get inside, told me to lie down, and went up to the other end. "The guy that built this," he said, "must have been a hump-backed midget with four arms. Hang on."

"Do you know what you're doing?" I asked.

"I moved it about six feet before; then I lost my nerve. Abracadabra! Hold onto your hat!" He poked a finger deep into a hole. The thing began to move, silently, gently, without any fuss. When we came out into the sunshine, Hank pulled his finger out of the hole. I sat up. The thing was two thirds out of the cave and the front end was beyond the crystals.

I sighed. "You made it, Hank, Let's get going. If I had some more ice on my side I think I could walk."

"Wait a second," he said. "I want to try something. There are holes here I haven't stuck a finger in yet."

"Leave well enough alone."

Instead of answering he tried another hole. The machine backed up suddenly. "Woops!" he said, jerked his finger out, and jabbed it back where it had been before. He left it there until he regained what we had lost.

He tried other holes more cautiously. At last he found one which caused the machine to rear up its front end slightly and swing it to the left, like a caterpillar. "Now we are in business," he said happily. "I can steer it." We started down the canyon.

Hank was not entirely correct in thinking he could guide it. It was more like guiding a horse than a machine—or perhaps more like guiding one of those new groundmobiles with the semi-automatic steering. The walker wagon came to the little natural bridge of ice through which the crystals passed and stopped of itself. Hank tried to get it to go through the opening, which was large enough; it would have none of it. The front end cast around like a dog sniffing, then eased gradually up hill and around the ice. It stayed level; apparently it could adjust its legs, like the fabulous hillside snee.

When Hank came to the ice flow we had crossed on the way up to the notch, he stopped it and gave me a fresh ice pack. Apparently it did not object to ice in itself, but simply refused to go through holes, for when we started up again, it crossed the little glacier, slowly and cautiously, but steadily.

We headed on toward camp. "This," Hank announced happily, "is the greatest cross-country, rough-terrain vehicle ever built. I wish I knew what makes it go. If I had the patent on this thing, I'd be rich."

"It's yours; you found it."

"It doesn't really belong to me."

"Hank," I answered, "you don't really think the owner is going to come back looking for it, do you?"

He got a very odd look. "No, I don't, Bill. Say, Bill, uh, how long ago do you think this thing was put in there?"

"I wouldn't even want to guess."

There was only one tent at the camp site. As we came up to it, somebody came out and waited for us. It was Sergei.

"Where have you guys been?" he asked. "And where in Kingdom Come did you steal *that?*

"And what *is* it?" he added.

We did our best to bring him up to date, and presently he did the same for us. They had searched for us as long as they could, then Paul had been forced to move back to camp number one to keep the date with the *Jitterbug*. He had left Sergei behind to fetch us when we showed up. "He left a note for you," Sergei added, digging it out.

It read:

"Dear Pen Pals,

"I am sorry to go off and leave you crazy galoots but you know the schedule as well as I do. I would stay behind myself to herd you home, but your pal Sergei insists that it is his privilege. Every time I try to reason with him he crawls further back into his hole, bares his teeth, and growls.

"As soon as you get this, get your chubby little legs to moving in the direction of camp number one. Run, do not walk. We'll hold the Jitterbug, but you know how dear old Aunt Hattie feels about keeping her schedule. She isn't going to like it if you are late.

"When I see you, I intend to beat your ears down around your shoulders.

"Good luck,
"P. du M.

"P.S. to Doctor Slop: I took care of your accordion."

When we had finished reading it Sergei said, "I want to hear more about what you found—about eight times more. But not now; we've got to tear over to camp number one. Hank, you think Bill can't walk it?"

I answered for myself, an emphatic "no." The excitement was wearing off and I was feeling worse again.

"Hmm—Hank, do you think that mobile junk yard will carry us over there?"

"I think it will carry us any place." Hank patted it.

"How fast? The *Jitterbug* has already grounded."

"Are you sure?" asked Hank.

"I saw its trail in the sky at least three hours ago."

"Let's get going!"

I don't remember much about the trip. They stopped once in the pass, and packed me with ice again. The next thing I knew I was awakened by hearing Sergei shout, "There's the *Jitterbug*! I can see it."

"*Jitterbug*, here we come," answered Hank. I sat up and looked, too.

We were coming down the slope, not five miles from it, when flame burst from its tail and it climbed for the sky.

Hank groaned. I lay back down and closed my eyes.

I woke up again when the contraption stopped. Paul was there, hands on his hips, staring at us. "About time you birds got home," he announced. "But where did you find *that?*"

"Paul," Hank said urgently, "Bill is very sick."

"Oh, oh!" Paul swung up and into the walker and made no more questions then. A moment later he had my belly bared and was shoving a thumb into that spot between the belly button and the hip bone. "Does that hurt?" he asked.

I was too weak to slug him. He gave me a pill.

I took no further part in events for a while, but what had happened was this: Captain Hattie had waited, at Paul's urgent insistence, for a couple of hours, and then had announced that she had to blast. She had a schedule to keep with the *Covered Wagon* and she had no intention, she said, of keeping eight thousand people waiting for the benefit of two. Hank and I could play Indian if we liked; we couldn't play hob with her schedule.

There was nothing Paul could do, so he sent the rest back and waited for us.

But I didn't hear this at the time. I was vaguely aware that we were in the walker wagon, travelling, and I woke up twice when I was repacked with ice, but the whole episode is foggy. They travelled east, with Hank driving and Paul navigating—by the seat of his pants. Some long dreamy time later they reached a pioneer camp surveying a site over a hundred miles away—and from there Paul radioed for help.

Whereupon the *Jitterbug* came and got us. I remember the landing back at Leda—that is, I remember somebody saying, "Hurry, there! We've got a boy with a burst appendix."

20.
HOME

There was considerable excitement over what we had found—and there still is—but I didn't see any of it. I was busy playing games with the Pearly Gates. I guess I have Dr. Archibald to thank for still being here. And Hank. And Sergei. And Paul. And Captain Hattie. And some nameless party, who lived somewhere, a long time ago, whose shape and race I still don't know, but who designed the perfect machine for traveling overland through rough country.

I thanked everybody but him. They all came to see me in the hospital, even Captain Hattie, who growled at me, then leaned over and kissed me on the cheek as she left. I was so surprised I almost bit her.

The Schultzes came, of course, and Mama cried over me and Papa gave me an apple and Gretchen could hardly talk, which isn't like her. And Molly brought the twins down to see me and vice versa.

The Leda daily *Planet* interviewed me. They wanted to know whether or not we thought the things we found were made by men?

Now that is a hard question to answer and smarter people than myself have worked on it since.

What is a man?

The things Hank and I—and the Project Jove scientists who went later—found in that cave couldn't have been made by men—not men like us. The walker wagon was the simplest thing they found. Most of the things they still haven't found out the use for. Nor have they figured out what the creatures looked like—no pictures.

That seems surprising, but the scientists concluded they didn't have eyes—not eyes like ours, anyhow. So they didn't use pictures.

The very notion of a "picture" seems pretty esoteric when you think it over. The Venerians don't use pictures, nor the Martians. Maybe we are the only race in the universe that thought up that way of recording things.

So they weren't "men"—not like us.

But they *were* men in the real sense of the word, even though I don't doubt that I would run screaming away if I met one in a dark alley. The important thing, as Mr. Seymour would say, they had—they controlled their environment. They weren't animals, pushed around and forced to accept what nature handed them; they took nature and bent it to their will.

I guess they were men.

The crystals were one of the oddest things about it and I didn't have any opinions on that. Somehow, those crystals were connected with that cave—or space ship hangar, or whatever it was. Yet they couldn't or wouldn't go inside the cave.

Here was another point that the follow-up party from Project Jove recorded: that big unwieldly walker wagon came all the way down that narrow canyon—yet it did not step on a single crystal. Hank must be a pretty good driver. He says he's not that good.

Don't ask me. I don't understand everything that goes on in the universe. It's a big place.

I had lots of time to think before they let me out of the hospital—and lots to think about. I thought about my coming trip to Earth, to go back to school. I had missed the *Covered Wagon*, of course, but that didn't mean anything; I could take the *Mayflower* three weeks later. But did I want to go? It was a close thing to decide.

One thing I was sure of: I was going to take those merit badge tests as soon as I was out of bed. I had put it off too long. A close brush with the hereafter reminds you that you don't have forever to get things done.

But going back to school? That was another matter. For one thing, as Dad told me, the council had lost its suit with the Commission; Dad couldn't use his Earthside assets.

And there was the matter that Paul had talked about the night he had to let his hair down—the coming war.

Did Paul know what he was talking about? If so, was I letting it scare me out? I honestly didn't think so; Paul had said that it was not less than forty years away. I wouldn't be Earthside more than four or five years—and, besides, how could you get scared of anything that far in the future?

I had been through the Quake and the reconstruction; I didn't really think I'd ever be scared of anything again.

I had a private suspicion that, supposing there was a war, I'd go join up; I wouldn't be running away from it. Silly, maybe.

No, I wasn't afraid of the War, but it was on my mind. Why? I finally doped it out. When Paul called I asked him about it. "See here, Paul—this war you were talking about: when Ganymede reaches the state that Earth has gotten into, does that mean war here, too? Not now—a few centuries from now."

He smiled rather sadly. "By then we may know enough to keep from getting into that shape. At least we can hope."

He got a far-away look and added, "A new colony is always a new hope."

I liked that way of putting it. "A new hope—" Once I heard somebody call a new baby that.

I still didn't have the answer about going back when Dad called on me one Sunday night. I put it up to him about the cost of the fare. "I know the land is technically mine, George—but it's too much of a drain on you two."

"Contrariwise," said George, "we'll get by and that's what savings are for. Molly is for it. We will be sending the twins back for school, you know."

"Even so, I don't feel right about it. And what real use is there in it, George? I don't need a fancy education. I've been thinking about Callisto: there's a brand new planet not touched yet with great opportunities for a man in on the ground floor. I could get a job with the atmosphere expedition—Paul would put in a word for me—and grow up with the project. I might be chief engineer of the whole planet some day."

"Not unless you learn more about thermodynamics than you do now, you won't be!"

"Huh?"

"Engineers don't just 'grow up'; they study. They go to school."

"Don't I study? Ain't I attending two of your classes right now? I can get to be an engineer here; I don't have to drag back half a billion miles for it."

"Fiddlesticks! It takes discipline to study. You haven't even taken your merit badge tests. You've let your Eagle Scoutship lapse."

I wanted to explain that taking tests and studying for tests were two different things—that I *had* studied. But I couldn't seem to phrase it right.

George stood up. "See here, Son, I'm going to put it to you straight. Never mind about being chief engineer of a planet; these days even a farmer needs the best education he can get. Without it he's just a country bumpkin, a stumbling peasant, poking seeds into the ground and hoping a miracle will make them grow. I want you to go back to Earth and get the best that Earth has to offer. I want you to have a degree with prestige behind it—M.I.T., Harvard, the Sorbonne. Some place noted for scholarship. Take the time to do that and then do anything you want to do. Believe me, it will pay."

I thought about it and answered, "I guess you are right, George."

Dad stood up. "Well, make up your mind. I'll have to hurry now for the bus, or I'll be hoofing it back to the farm. See you tomorrow."

"Good night, George."

I lay awake and thought about it. After a while, Mrs. Dinsmore, the wing nurse, came in, turned out my light, and said goodnight. But I didn't go to sleep.

Dad was right, I knew. I didn't want to be an ignoramus. Furthermore, I had seen the advantage held by men with fancy degrees—first crack at the jobs, fast promotion. Okay, I'd get me one of those sheepskins, then come back and—well, go to Callisto, maybe, or perhaps prove a new parcel of land. I'd go and I'd come back.

Nevertheless I couldn't get to sleep. After a while I glanced at my new watch and saw that it was nearly midnight—dawn in a few minutes. I decided that I wanted to see it. It might be the last time I'd be up and around at midnight Sunday for a long, long time.

I scouted the corridor; Old Lady Dinsmore wasn't in sight. I ducked outside.

The Sun was just barely below the horizon; north of me I could see its first rays touching the topmost antenna of the power station, miles away on Pride Peak. It was very still and very beautiful. Overhead old Jupiter was in half phase, bulging and orange and grand. To the west of it Io was just coming out of shadow; it passed from black to cherry red to orange as I watched.

I wondered how I would feel to be back on Earth? How would it feel to weigh three times as much as I did now? I didn't feel heavy; I felt just right.

How would it feel to swim in that thick dirty soup they use for air?

How would it feel to have nobody but ground hogs to talk to? How could I talk to a girl who wasn't a colonial, who had never been off Earth higher than a copter hop? Sissies. Take Gretchen, now—there was a girl who could kill a chicken and have it in the pot while an Earthside girl would still be squealing.

The top of the Sun broke above the horizon and caught the snow on the peaks of the Big Rock Candy Mountains, tinting it rosy against a pale green sky. I began to be able to see the country around me. It was a new, hard, clean place—not like California with its fifty, sixty million people falling over each other. It was my kind of a place—it was *my* place.

The deuce with Caltech and Cambridge and those fancy schools! I'd show Dad it didn't take ivied halls to get an education. Yes, and I'd pass those tests and be an Eagle again, first thing.

Hadn't Andrew Johnson, that American President, learned to read while he was working? Even after he was married? Give us time; we'd have as good scientists and scholars here as anywhere.

The long slow dawn went on and the light caught Kneiper's cut west of me, outlining it. I was reminded of the night we had struggled through it in the storm. As Hank put it, there was one good thing about colonial life—it sorted out the men from the boys.

"I have lived and worked with men." The phrase rang through my head. Rhysling? Kipling, maybe. I had lived and worked with men!

The Sun was beginning to reach the roof tops. It spread across Laguna Serenidad, turning it from black to purple to blue. This was my planet, this was my home and I knew that I would never leave it.

Mrs. Dinsmore came bustling out to the door and spotted me. "Why, the very idea!" she scolded. "You get back where you belong!"

I smiled at her. "I am where I belong. And I'm going to stay!"

ABOUT THE AUTHOR

Robert Anson Heinlein was born in Butler, Missouri, in 1907. A graduate of the U.S. Naval Academy, he was retired, disabled, in 1934. He studied mathematics and physics at the graduate school of the University of California and owned a silver mine before beginning to write science fiction, in 1939. In 1947 his first book of fiction, ROCKET SHIP GALILEO, was published. His novels include DOUBLE STAR (1956), STARSHIP TROOPERS (1959), STRANGER IN A STRANGE LAND (1961), and THE MOON IS A HARSH MISTRESS (1966), all winners of the Hugo Award. Heinlein was guest commentator for the Apollo II first lunar landing. In 1975 he received the Grand Master Nebula Award for lifetime achievement. Mr. Heinlein died in 1988.